To Cari & fami
Great to
T. R. Maxus

AENAMVS

Silent Blood

Book One

❖

by

T.R. Maxus

ISBN: 0988636506
ISBN-13: 9780988636507

Cover Concept: T. R. Maxus
Cover Photo Copyright © 2012 by Michelle Baade
Post Production Graphics: Meka Davis
Cover Model: Kristine Bredehoft
Cover Layout: D. Underwood

To Melany, the love of my life ~
For encouraging me to take this journey,
and supporting me when I did.

aen·a·mus ~ **{on-uh-muhs}**: *noun* 1. A feeling of frustration, anger, incredulity and helplessness brought on by injustices or offenses against mankind by one or more individuals. Often accompanied by a strong, often irresistible urge to take harsh, extreme and permanent action against said individuals. *verb* 2. Lethal and illegal action taken by members of society outside of law enforcement against individuals believed to be guilty of crimes against humanity.

Aen·a·maia ~ **{on-uh-mahy-uh}**

Find out just what any people will quietly submit to and you have the exact measure of the injustice and wrong which will be imposed on them.

~ **Frederick Douglass**

One who breaks an unjust law that conscience tells him is unjust, and who willingly accepts the penalty of imprisonment in order to arouse the conscience of the community over its injustice, is in reality expressing the highest respect for law.

~ **Martin Luther King, Jr.**

Prologue

Exordium

Nondescript. That was the word he would use to describe the large room. Unremarkable save for its size and the profound sullenness radiating from every dark and dingy corner. Though he'd never seen specs on the space, he estimated it was forty feet square with twelve-foot ceilings. It could be a room in any building, in any city, in any country. The interior revealed nothing about the room's location or function. There were no signs or decorations on the walls, which were entirely bare except for a light switch next to the sole entrance door and a few plain, cracked and yellowed electrical outlets. The light switch controlled the clear glass conical light fixture hanging in the center of the room, suspended by a thin, rusty chain with a single clear wire snaking between the disintegrating and corroded oval links. The walls and ceiling were a sickly yellowish gray, the color of anemic skin. Looking carefully at both in the dim light, he couldn't decide whether either had ever been painted or if it was simply the drab color of drywall. The surface of the walls looked smooth, but lacked any shine or patina. A doorway with no door attached led into an adjacent room, which was equally as dreary and unremarkable. Throughout the apartment the scuffed dark wood floors were now mostly covered with a hodgepodge of burnt orange and lime green carpet squares loosely fitted together. At a glance one could see by the upturned corners and overlapping edges that the carpet was not secured to the floor. It reminded him of the newspaper in the bottom of a birdcage – temporary flooring designed for fast and efficient cleanup. How appropriate, he thought. How very appropriate.

The large room's solitary window had been covered with innumerable layers of cheap plastic tinting, making him wonder what its previous occupants had been up to. Long thin-lined rectangles of fragmented artificial light from the bright halogen parking lot lights outside crept in around the peeling edges, speaking to the hastiness of the job. From his position opposite the window, the dark rectangle looked like one of Arthur C. Clark's mysterious black monoliths hanging above the floor like an omnipotent and sentient being, framed by thin lines of the bright, shimmering light radiating from an altogether different, more peaceful world. The thought pleased him – the idea of an advanced civilization where everyone worked towards common goals that served the whole as equally as the one – a society where the stronger beings tirelessly endeavored to lift up the weaker ones to ever higher levels. Real beings, perhaps male and female, who carried with them an insatiable thirst for a playing field that was simultaneously level and competitive, populated this society. It was a reality where *work,* as most humans defined it, would be something of a non sequitur. The world beyond the black window would represent the most civil, ingenious manner of existence. A new world. A new dream. A higher, more advanced consciousness. It could be our future, he thought. But in order for the Phoenix to rise from the ashes, the world of its predecessor must first be set aflame.

He clung to the belief that it was here that the genesis was in the making. This room represented the event horizon of something that had never been done before, at least not by people the likes of which were gathered here. It would be a silent and unexpected insurrection from an unlikely pillar of society. And if he proved to be right, if this was indeed the birthplace of a new mindset, then perhaps this gray den constituted a fitting womb. No stained glass windows, no ornate marble statues, no demonstrations of blind penitence and servitude, no rituals to memorize, no obscure books, no elaborately dressed and pampered figureheads, no sigils or symbols, and no inane deities. There was nothing here to worship except one's own existence, intelligence, love and conviction.

Beneath the stale incandescent light, nine chairs surrounded a large round wooden table – each seat occupied by someone whose face he knew better than his own. Behind the flesh he read the same emotions: restlessness, hope, eagerness, passion, and an intense concentration on the moment. He sensed these emotions as faint wisps of quiet conversations reached him. There was an air of open camaraderie and solemn concern. Postures were tense but friendly. Smiles were genuine and welcoming, bordering on conspiratorial. A stranger entering the room would immediately sense that the four women and five men seated at this table were family. But unlike most families, this one was not bound by blood and tradition – instead, it was united by ideas, ideologies and a shared sense of purpose. Through years of quiet, careful conversations off in the corners of forgotten parties and events, dimly-lit restaurants, boisterous coffee shops, hotel rooms, and unremarkable bars they had found each other and many like-minded others.

In the beginning, each person had been huddled, crouching in a tense, expectant repose, waiting to lunge with claws drawn, ready to sink their teeth into something. Anything. All senses alert for the hint of an answer, or the end to a perfect storm. When he'd provided them with that hint, the rest had melted into details and timetables. Now, after many years and so much intense planning and discussion, they all stood on the precipice of the unprecedented action and change that had germinated from that solitary hint.

"Ten knights at a round table," he thought, grinning easily at the analogy. How many were at King Arthur's table? Twelve? Or was that the number of codes governing the actions of the knights? He couldn't recall. Fleeting images from numerous movies about Arthur and his knights flickered through his mind, but no facts emerged. "I will look it up if I survive this *crusade*," he thought. The irony of the term normally reserved for religious endeavors was not lost on him. He allowed himself a final, thin smile before a serious mood and sharp focus returned and took over.

He stood up, grabbing the arms of his chair and setting it down behind him on a loose patch of green shag carpet. The sudden movement brought silence to the room and all eyes met his. One by one he made eye contact with the people seated before him. The quick inventory of the table revealed no surprises. There were a number of handguns, three rifles, two silver briefcases, a cluster of tear gas canisters at the far end, plus a pitcher of ice water, a bowl full of beef jerky in the middle, and several smaller bowls with individually wrapped candies. Behind the table, propped up against the far wall were additional weapons and munitions packed neatly inside large plastic bins like those used to keep household wares in storage. There were also two-dozen ordinary black suitcases and duffle bags.

"It has become painfully obvious to those of us who are awake and alert," he began, his voice steady but with a hint of regret, "that throughout the course of human history, abrupt change was often brought about by the use of force. Whether natural or man-made, blows are dealt swiftly, society shifts, and people adapt out of fear, necessity and self-preservation. By contrast, peaceful social change at the same scale requires simultaneous conscious behavioral changes in humans. They have to want it and be willing to work for it. This rarely happens. Why? Because people are, by and large mindless, self-serving cattle who spend the bulk of their lives avoiding their fears through shallow consumerism, materialism and a repulsive fascination with the dirty laundry and pain of others. They spare very little thought for anything outside of their daily lives. Complaints may arise when policies and procedures change, but ultimately people comply. That is because they must be told what to do. Ironically," he said, scratching the back of his head, "libraries are packed with volumes of popular literature explaining in detail how mankind is enslaved by authority, yet people still must be led and willingly choose to follow blindly, whether to their jobs or to a gas shower. The only difference is the speed of the demise. They will never rebel against the system that holds them in bondage. People are addicted to routine, to security, to appearances, and to material things. Those who lead by force know this well. It is their main weapon in the battle to maintain control. The simple cattle prod is no longer adequate. In its place, other more versatile tools have arisen: the sensationalist media, alcohol, tobacco, consumerism, the fear-based tenets of religion, and the omnipresent threat of force against those who dare to contest the use of such tools or those who wield them. Give a man his beer and football, a woman her sitcoms and physical insecurities, and you have control. Misdirection. Bring attention to *Survivor* and *American Idol* over here, and forget about the Patriot Act, a decaying educational system, abusive religions, counterfeit elections, and government scandals over there." He began pacing, feeling the familiar sensation of his mind driving his blood faster and faster through his veins. "Let's give the people all the violence, fear and paranoia they can handle. The more we give them, the more numb they become. The more political scandals that surface, the more people grow tired of them and simply change the channel in search of the latest scandal in Hollywood. Keep herding the cattle.

"The gullibility of the American public has reached unprecedented and nearly inconceivable levels. They accept information from any source, even Fox News, at face value. And the first smidgeon of tripe to reach them," he continued, "will sink in – and in their eyes, become fact, regardless of where it came from. The question now becomes what, if anything, would the public reject? What would they care enough about to refuse? Not much. If we just make sure that the average American knows that plants require carbon dioxide to grow, we can easily convince them that the threat of global warming is a farce created by scientists who hate seeing things grow. But why would the scientists do this? No need to explain that. People won't even think to ask. Forget the scientists with their academic accomplishments and degrees, years of studies and research, the scientific method and their "*theories*." Instead, let's talk about Atkins and the new slim you. Let's talk about gas guzzling SUV's and tax deductions. Cell phones, iPods, fashion, celebrity gossip, and so on down the twisted road.

"Let's test the nation's pulse from a dollar fifty for a gallon of gas to four dollars, then pull back and sit comfortably at three twenty-five and compare them. What are they going to do? Complain? Has that yielded any substantial results in the last hundred years? Does the will of the people really hold any weight? And let's not forget a healthy dose of religion and mysticism. The fear at the root of all religions has always proved to be a strong and reliable leash." He smiled and added, "No need to elaborate on religion with this group." A low rumble of laughs came from everyone at the table.

He continued, "Let's dumb up our young so they won't show up to vote. How do we do that? Easy. Violent video games, cigarettes, loose controls on alcohol, cheap cell phones, disposable technology, reality TV shows, and of course a plethora of websites and blogs where they can blast their whole lives into the electronic universe in hopes of some distant, abstract attention. And when they're bored with themselves, they can experience the unprecedented plague of celebrity worship. There are bound to be plenty of floozies in Hollywood and in the music business that we can rely on. Between their scandals and gossip and the rest of the garbage on television, who will have the time or the brain-power to vote or be concerned with anything else?

"It is through this rampant over-stimulation that the system perpetuates itself and drives humanity deeper into a blind, dumb darkness. People get used to their daily dose of garbage and devote little thought to anything else. Then, when the orders come down, they simply do what they are told. One can then conclude that in order to change the world, one must either manage to change each and every person and motivate them to action or otherwise change those who tell the people what to do, what to think and what to believe." Leaning over, he put his hands flat on the table and lowered his voice. "But make no mistake about it, these puppeteers are self-serving in the extreme. For hundreds of years, peaceful people of great intelligence have tried to persuade leaders to do what was best for everyone and to make the decisions they knew to be right. There have been marches, campaigns, protests, rallies, letters, petitions, debates, documentaries, cries and pleas, and yet the state of the world continues to decay.

"How is it that anyone of intelligence can rally behind the Tea Baggers without shutting off their minds? How can any American support the unintelligent monkeys on parade who feel they have the right to hold the United States government hostage until their extremist demands are met? It's a form of political terrorism. And our government shouldn't negotiate with terrorists – even when they're part of our political system. The Tea Baggers and all their extremist friends and allies are just another lump of foul-smelling solid waste in the shallow, festering cesspool in which many in this country willingly bathe."

"Those men," he said, stabbing a finger towards the world beyond the monolith, "cannot be reasoned with. They are held in check by means invisible to all but a select few. Whether it is money or drugs or power or fame or a clever cocktail containing a dose of each, they are beyond the reach of logic, humility and reason. There is nothing of greater importance to them, save one thing: their own mortality." His gestures became animated and his volume increased. "The one and only thing that takes precedence over their avid and voracious lust for power and control is the threat of their own death. Mortality. It is this threat that we...must... bring...," his fist pounding the table in sync with the words. "It is this threat that we must leverage. It is to this abominable level that we have been forced to stoop. But that alone isn't enough. We must break down the many rays of filth that pierce our skin, blacken our hearts, clog our veins and prevent the blood from getting to the brain. A message must be sent, not only to those with the cattle prods, but to the cattle themselves. We must use our enemy's tools and methods against them. There simply is no other way." A coy grin creased his lips. "With any luck... No, no I don't believe in luck. If we stay focused and resolute, this will work. If we see it through and come out alive, we can begin the process of recovery in the garden at Graycliff. And the first round is on me." Solemn eyes and warm smiles spread around the table.

Reaching back, he pulled the rolled up newspaper from his back pocket and placed it on the table. Staring at the photo of the disheveled man on the front cover, his stomach and jaw both tightened. Still staring down, he said, "As most of you know, the Justice Department is lobbing accusations of fraud, corruption, conspiracy, and outright deceit at former President Bush, Vice President Cheney, and several of his closest advisors." He looked up at the assembled group. "There isn't a person in this group who didn't want to put Bush and Cheney at the top of our list of offenders. But we also knew this wasn't an option. The Secret Service aside, the last thing we want to risk is any kind of sympathy for either man or his family. All we can hope is that they'll all get pinned to the wall and wind up disgraced and dishonored," adding with a wry grin, "even more so than they already are!" A hearty chorus of laugher and cheers rose.

A few moments passed before the noise died down and silence again reigned. "What's really important here," he said, pointing again at the newspaper, "is the thin smokescreen this will create. Those who do pay attention to what's going on will be focusing most of their attention on these proceedings. If things progress at even half the rate of the Clinton-Lewinsky scandal, many of our...*dealings* might go largely by the wayside, with the primary inquiries staying at the local level. The more local things stay, the less likely a connection will be made early on. So with any luck, Mr. Bush, Mr. Cheney, and their entourage might actually prove useful, for a change." There were grins and nods around the table. "However, we cannot afford to forget that time is always against us. This smokescreen will not be thick enough to shield us from everyone. So we must be ever diligent, alert and on guard at all times."

Standing up straight, he took a deep breath and sighed. Pensively he continued, "Time is running out. Mankind is at an absolutely crucial juncture. We are convinced of it. All the signs are before us, but the cattle choose not to believe. They would say such talk is caustic, extremist, reactionary, and melodramatic. This is the result of hundreds of years of oppression, conditioning and a view so myopic that the outside world exists only as a smudge of color on the periphery of their vision. They refuse to see the truth because it terrifies them and because any solution will require them to act. Reality, when looked at closely, illuminates each person's hypocrisy, irresponsibility, recklessness, lack of accountability, an unimaginably stubborn sense of entitlement to unearned spoils, and – most painfully – approval of a decaying system boiling over with inequity and injustice. In this country, murderous prison inmates on death row live better than the homeless and poor on our streets. Those same inmates have more legal rights than the men and women that serve in our military. In this country, more people are made wealthy through egregious and unjust lawsuits than through the lottery, hard work, ingenuity, and good old-fashioned luck combined. Right now in America, people who are addicted to drugs receive prison sentences instead of treatment. Out there," he said, again pointing towards the blackened window, "the men who run our country and whose decisions affect every man, woman and child, are allowed to vote on their own salary increases, allowed to send billions of dollars to their supporters in the defense industry who don't do the jobs they're paid for, and they have the audacity to pass legislation pardoning themselves from war crimes dating from September 11, 2001. And when they aren't doing that, they are coddled and enticed by special interest lobbyists who are adept at channeling funds, privileges, vacations, and lavish gifts in ways that won't attract attention. It hasn't been that long since we gratefully evicted a President with strong ties to oil money and a Vice President with a financial stake in the success of the defense industry. At one point, oil skyrocketed to two hundred dollars per barrel. Speculators were blamed, yet oil companies reported unprecedented earnings. During Bush's tenure, defense stocks soared, followed again by record earnings. Did the American public know? More importantly, did they even care? They don't seem to care now.

Is this the right answer?" he asked, pointing to the weapons strewn across the table. "Is deplorable violence and insurrection the best answer? Unfortunately, there is no way to know for sure. What we do know is that it is the best option we have. It is the *only* option we have at present. I wish there were a better way. I wish we could take all of the good, intelligent people somewhere far away from the licentious garbage and start anew. Unfortunately, that just isn't possible now.

Thankfully we still have a good President in office, though the 2012 elections were closer than I'd expected. He and his administration are doing a good job, but they continue to struggle with many of the same issues that brought all of us together. We hope the President will continue to guide our country and the rest of the world in a better direction than his predecessor. But in the face of Fox News Americans, a polarized and uncooperative Republican party, a world still leery of American politics – well, only so much can be accomplished by the President. He will need help. It is our responsibility to make sure those people who supported the corrupt, unconstitutional, illegal and avaricious policies of President Bush – and the next generation of their clones – will not interfere with progress. The corrupt must be held accountable. The message must be loud and clear: if they choose to stand in the way of progress, we'll be there to cut off their legs."

He took a moment and looked each person in the eye, then said resolutely, "We have debated and discussed many different options and approaches, bounced around all the possibilities, each and every time landing squarely in the same place. This place," he said, pointing down at the table. "For our plans to work, each person must be at peace with this. Every one of us must believe our actions will bring about positive change. Each one of us must be committed to every premise behind every action we take. None of us can go forward unless we fully understand the potential of what we're about to do. There are no…," he started, then said earnestly, "there *can be* no illusions. We must be ready to accept the consequences of our actions and the damage that these actions will inevitably do to our souls." He paused for a moment and then added, "There have already been casualties. It's likely there will be more."

There was a profound stillness in the air. It felt as though this moment might somehow echo throughout the rest of time. He took a deep breath and stood up straight. "The time has come to bring the war to them, to let them taste their own vile tactics, and to show the world there is a level of decency that we all must demand. Such is our conviction and our decision. This," he said pausing to glance around the table, "this is Aenamus."

He glanced down at the table, sighed and said, "We can force the world to listen, but we can only hope the message will be heard. Sometimes the only way to get their attention is through a demonstration of force and determination. Someone has to take out the trash." He turned and looked into the terrified bloodshot eyes of the man who sat bound and gagged against the wall to his left. "Wouldn't you agree, Congressman Delay?"

Chapter 1

Harare, Zimbabwe, Africa

On the morning of September 11th, 2004, Kina had ridden the blue line from O'Hare into downtown Chicago. Thinking back to that day, the scene and all its details were remarkably clear in her mind. The morning had been particularly humid – the air heavy, still and stale. Three years to the day since the terrorist attacks in New York, yet if there was any tension from the echo of that tragic day, it was only in her mind. Occasionally her eyes lifted from the newspaper bearing the famous fiery image of the second tower to quickly survey the other passengers in the train. Most of the morning commuters and business travelers were plugged into a portable music device, a laptop, or cell phone or a carefully balanced combination. Kina wondered how it was possible for so many people to be tuned in while simultaneously so oblivious. Since childhood she'd had a penchant for conjuring visual analogies based on the current moment, especially during situations that wouldn't allow for a quick escape.

Looking around at the jacked-in passengers, she concentrated on the picture forming in her mind. Within seconds the image of a gymnasium full of school children flashed into her mind's eye. Her mind surveyed the ethereal scene, slowly panning to and fro. Each of the basketball hoops had been retracted and hung precariously above the floor at odd angles. The room was bare and Spartan. All of the athletic equipment was crammed into the long rectangular room near the main entrance. The children, seated Indian style on the floor, sat facing a massive white screen that had been erected on the stage.

Projected onto the screen were random images depicting the quintessential storybook American lifestyle. Financial wealth, gross materialism and physical beauty were the underlying themes. Faint, random splashes of color flashed across the entranced faces of the children as images of slender runway models, sleek expensive cars and motorized watercraft, tropical beaches and credit cards came and went in rapid succession. Half-shaved men in sleek casual black suits and thick silver watches smiled confidently as they walked hand-in-hand with beautiful women endowed with long flowing, lustrous, commercial-ready hair. Then came the cocktail party aboard the mammoth gray and white yacht, the Cinderella ball and a champagne toast. A sleek black helicopter with dark-tinted windows circled the tallest building in the city. On the roof was a party populated by black and white tuxedos, elegant evening gowns, and sparkling crystal glasses filled with golden wine poured by obedient servants in pressed white coats. Ten-foot tall animal-shaped ice sculptures encircled the soiree. In every direction there were tables piled high with artistically carved fruits and vegetables, platters of exotic foods from around the globe, and shiny silver fountains filled with dark, liquid chocolate – all being casually consumed by voluptuous women adorned with gold and diamonds and men with the look and commanding presence of James Bond. This was the grand party to end all parties and was being held to celebrate a new world order. Somehow Kina was sure the mesmerized children understood that.

The image of the high-rise party melted away and was replaced with simpler scenes. Graduations with friends and family, smiling faces, birthdays with balloons and clowns, teenagers in a whimsical, light-hearted school play, a rough and tumble hockey game, the winning football team carrying the quarterback on their shoulders, the ROTC. Back to football and hockey. The focus now seemed to be on the hitting, the pushing, the jarring collisions, the lone player running into the end zone, the train wreck of players out of focus in the background. Boxing. Ultimate fighting. Self defense. Martial arts and hand-to-hand combat. American soldiers marching.

Mug shots of unsmiling Arab men in bright orange shirts with numbers stitched on the left breast. Grainy news footage of men with white turbans that covered everything but their eyes as they knelt on one knee and fired automatic weapons. Buildings exploding, the concrete turning to dust. The birthday party again. The clown with something deep and sinister in his eyes, staring earnestly into the camera. There was a menacing message behind those dark eyes that would frighten most adults. And still the children sat unmoving on the hard wood floor, reticent and absorbed, with their mouths hanging half open. Kina could see them clearly in her mind. But there was something she hadn't noticed until now. Every child had a single, white wire hanging from each ear. They were all plugged in. They were listening intently to something, but she could not hear what it was. The screen continued flashing between images of the life of privilege and wealth, to contact sports and war, as if to ask, "To control, or be controlled...that is the question."

Kina remembered taking another look at the other passengers. Something was different on second glance. Of course. Here they were. These were the children from the gymnasium. They'd all grown up. Mortgages, jobs, car payments, credit cards, student loans, doctor's bills, nights spent blindly consuming alcohol, days spent dealing with fear and envy. Yes, they'd grown up. But they were still plugged in. They were still quiet and obedient and striving to fill their lives with the spoils and promises the television had tempted them with their entire lives, only now it came via high-definition flat panel screens as far as the eye could see. Five days a week they made the exodus, consciously ignoring the nagging barrier of reality in hopes of taking just one more step up on the long, arduous climb to the middle. Just one more step.

Most of them sensed the gross inequities in the world. They knew a great many things were wrong, and yet the pursuit was all that mattered now. Every person bouncing around on this train was like a greyhound – forever damned to chase the fake rabbit around and around the track of life, never quite able to grab hold, but always striving to reach it. The greyhounds never gave up. They never *chose* to accept reality and let the shiny carrot go. Nor did they ever choose to go after real carrots, the kind that could be caught and consumed. The prize was always just one step away.

The screeching, metallic noise of the train's brakes engaging stirred her from the daydream. When she'd looked up again, Kina had made eye contact with a portly man standing thirty feet away at the other end of the train car. He wore a dark gray business suit and a white shirt, both of which needed to be ironed. Though she couldn't recall his face now, she did remember it had been pudgy, round, and unusually pale. One of several chins had been forced outside the tight collar and rested uneasily above the wide Windsor knot of a bright red tie. The skin on his cheeks and jaws bore scattered pockmarks she'd guessed were the remnants of a particularly bad acne problem. His slick, thinning hair had been combed back and looked as though he'd cemented it to his large scalp with a clear epoxy. The large man stood reading the morning paper. His right arm was curled around one of the vertical bars to help maintain balance. He had been staring down at his paper when his eyes shifted and met hers. Kina was used to having men stare at her, but this was different.

For a brief moment she thought the man had read her thoughts – that he'd caught a glimpse of the imagery flashing through her mind, that he understood the despair and pessimism that had consumed her thoughts for the past few years. The look in his eyes seemed to say, "I know where you're going, and I understand why." It was the reassuring and knowing expression a loving father might give his son before he said, "I was young once, too, and I know exactly how you feel."

Kina had held the man's stare for a few moments, her face remaining blank. The corners of her eyes wrinkled slightly as she tried to read his expression. Thinking back now, she realized she had been vaguely hoping for some epiphany, some sign the stranger truly understood. Perhaps he really did know where she was going. Could he know about *The Aenamaia*? She had desperately wanted to tell someone about her decision: the commitment, the oath, the training. Could he have known? Was he one of them, sent to make sure she went through with it?

Social norms had forced her to break the stare. She never knew whether there had been something there or whether he had just been admiring her. Looking back, she suspected it was the latter. Gray, who had been her first contact with *The Aenamaia*, had advised her to always present a public appearance that exploited her good looks, athletic body and long auburn hair. He'd said, "Beautiful women are suspicious on many levels, but none that would ever point to your real agenda or to us. They'll stare at you and imagine you're everything that you are not, and that's the way we want it. You never want your enemies to see beyond the flesh. This can be accomplished consistently with the right kind of armor."

The lesson had stuck with her for the last three-and-a-half years. Even today, sitting on a rickety antiquated bus heading away from Harare International Airport, she still dressed the part. Dark green slacks, matching pumps, and a white silk blouse had replaced her stylish business suit, along with a pair of rectangular glasses and a thin silver watch. Around her neck hung a circular gold locket engraved with the yin-yang symbol. Gray had given her the necklace on that first day of training in Chicago. He'd said it was the type of thing astronauts took into space and that she should never take it off. It was only after she'd finished her training that he'd shown her the secret to opening it and explained the lethal function of the two white tablets hidden inside.

A half hour after leaving the Harare city limits the outdated old bus passed through a small shanty village. The dirt and gravel road ahead was in a sad state of disrepair and the bus was forced to slow to a crawl. The driver did his best to avoid the large potholes that reminded Kina of miniature meteor craters filled with dirty brown water. Despite the driver's best efforts, the front right tire dipped into a deep hole causing the small bus to lurch from side to side. Instinctively Kina threw her hand up to the overhead rack to prevent the shiny metal briefcase from sliding off. The case was heavy and could injure someone. The last thing she needed was to spend the next day explaining why she was transporting a high-powered rifle, scope and rounds to the small town of Mutare. She pulled the case down and placed it squarely on her lap. "Better safe than imprisoned," she thought.

After a few minutes, the bus reached the end of the village and was back up to cruising speed. A small green sign indicated Mutare was thirty-four kilometers ahead. Kina guessed the driver was averaging around eighty kilometers per hour. Running the calculations in her mind, accounting for a few more small towns, she estimated it would take another thirty minutes or so to reach Mutare. She looked at her watch. It was almost noon. The drive from the airport in Harare had already taken up more of her morning than she'd expected. She had wanted to rent a car, but Gray had advised against it. Just getting her into the country and arranging to have someone meet her outside the airport with the weapon had been risky enough. Putting her assumed name and passport information into another computer was not worth the additional risk. *The Aenamaia* worked diligently to keep their people and activities off the grid as much as possible. They could never afford to forget: *Always watching, always listening, ready to bring violence, ready to forever silence.* It was therefore decided that Ms. Celeste Angela Tullah of Toronto, Canada and her silver rifle case would make use of the antiquated Zimbabwean public transit system.

The heavy, smooth metal case pressed down on Kina's thighs. The pressure was greater than could be attributed to the actual weight of the object and she knew it. The emotional sum of the last three years seemed to be contained within, sitting restlessly next to the dismantled weapon. It was waiting to get out, to accomplish its goal – to spend the currency that had accrued in the account she'd started that afternoon in Chicago. If the assignment went according to plan, if she returned safely to Harare on this same bus, the weight of the case would be reduced by only a few rounds, but Kina knew both she and the case would feel as light as a feather.

Kennebunkport, Maine

"What time was it in Mashhad?" he wondered, staring at the antique clock on the wall. It was just before seven a.m. here. "Eight hours ahead," he thought. "Three o'clock. The ambitious little prick will be done soon." TB, the abbreviated nickname his eldest son had given the man, never hung around to socialize after deal-making. Not anymore. The intel thus far showed he always left alone. The word he'd gotten over the last few days from his agents was TB had brokered a dozen lucrative deals while overseas. The further things progressed with these new business ventures, the more complicated the situation would become.

Despite the adroitness TB had demonstrated thus far in avoiding inquiries, both legal and media-driven, in the end, the little opportunist would undoubtedly be forced to testify. Federal prosecutors would offer up the usual little-fish deal: full immunity for all past transgressions and a hands-off attitude on the deals he was brokering right at this moment – or prison. Loyal or not, TB was no fool. The choice would be simple. After that, their world would be consumed by flames fanned by an ungrateful nation of whiners and rubberneckers and the media that never stopped whoring to them. The carnage would be everywhere, caught in high definition audio and video. Clips of interviews with turncoat friends and family would be on every news station. All of his son's greatest hits would be revived and polished. Internet video would see an unprecedented surge in downloads. His family name, already irrevocably charred over the last decade, would wind up in a dank and dark corner in the annals of history. "No!" he thought. He could not allow this to happen – not on his watch.

He glanced at the clock again. A decision would have to be made – several decisions. He'd been putting off action for over a week now, hoping a better option would emerge. Many sleepless nights had been spent trying to divine a solution. The aggravation was all too familiar, like chronic chest pains that come and go, but are mysteriously incurable. How many times over the years had he found himself in this position? How many messes had he cleaned up to protect the family? How much cumulative pain had wrenched at his being? Though he knew the number was high and the pain great, all of his eldest son's past transgressions paled in comparison to the current crisis. No one doubted that, except maybe his clueless first-born son.

Over the course of the last year, he'd earnestly hoped it wouldn't come to this – that the country would just let bygones be bygones and move forward. There were so many more pressing issues to be resolved. Unfortunately, sharks aren't the only creatures to salivate at the smell of blood in the water. When it had become clear that bad memories outweighed current problems and future hopes, he'd started quietly calling in favors and devising a plan.

He began by imagining himself as the lead prosecutor going after the big enchilada. Who would he need? Who would possess both the relevant knowledge and a flimsy sense of loyalty in the face of perjury and federal indictment? A short list of names quickly emerged. Originally he'd referred to the list as The Dirty Dozen, but then decided that was too obvious. Were details of what he was planning – even the reconnaissance phase – to ever become public, any title containing a number or quantity could prove damaging. He therefore referred to the potential squealers as The Rat Pack. The list represented a substantial portion of Washington's Who's-Who. Many on the list were linked in more ways than the most obvious.

Should it be necessary to eliminate members of The Rat Pack, each operation would need to be executed with exact timing, coordination and a little insightful creativity. The risks were monumental, no doubt about it. So much would hinge on small details and precise actions that he would have no direct control over. His family's reputation, power, wealth, and legacy would be in the hands of a select team of professional, well-trained and well-paid operatives.

He recalled what Italian President Francesco Cossiga had called such men "*Condotierri*," skilled and efficient thugs whose ironic code of honor made them both reliable and discreet. *Condotierri*. Just thinking of the word made him uneasy. But now was not the time for weakness.

"Sir?" the disembodied voice said over the staticky phone line. The leader of the team – his Condotierri – waited anxiously for the decision he could no longer avoid.

"Procrastination would get him nowhere," he thought, irritated with his own reluctance to act. Back when he was in control, he'd have already made a dozen such decisions before his breakfast had been served. Sitting here now, over two decades later, there was no staff to prepare and serve breakfast, no one to test the food for poison and no throng of people pressing for his time – just a very difficult decision to be made.

"How many teams do you have in place?" he asked, already aware of the answer.

"Eight, Sir," the man answered immediately. "Six domestic, two international. Targets are all in place and under constant surveillance."

"Full audio? You're listening and recording?"

"With the exception of The Angler, everyone is covered."

"Windows are open?"

"Yes Sir. Several per target. Extraction timetables are in place for each opportunity."

He thought for a moment then asked, "Has anyone broken the silence or been approached by the press?"

"No one has spoken of anything specific yet," again the answer was crisp and immediate. "Nacho Libre is set to appear for an appeal in two days. He'll be allowed to arrive via private transport. No foot or ankle cuffs, just an escort of prison guards keeping watch. Afterwards he'll be allowed to conduct interviews with the press, though specific case information will not be discussed. Conversations with his attorney indicate he'll again implicate the former President. He claims to have hard-copy proof of direct intervention and pressure, though he has yet to present it to his attorney or anyone else. When pressed he tells his attorney he'll not reveal this proof until the right moment. Intelligence believes the appeals court will uphold the ruling and send him back to prison. Should he possess evidence implicating the former President, he'll likely use it soon as a bartering tool to win his freedom."

He nodded, but did not reply. The mechanical briefing continued.

"The Spinner will be emerging soon. Our insider tells us he's brokered a lucrative energy deal here. Money will soon change hands. He'll most likely be heading stateside within the next few days."

"No doubt," he thought. "TB has calls to make and hands to shake. Favors to call in. Palms to grease." It was amazing how much easier such deals had become since 9/11 and the war in Iraq. "Never underestimate the power of misdirection in politics." Who had said that to him? His father? The source means nothing as long as the imbued wisdom remains virulent.

"Sir?"

He didn't answer, though he knew what was coming.

"Sir, when The Spinner returns to the states, the press will swarm. Slant and deflection are his specialties. He'll do anything to wash his hands clean of any personal involvement or liability, while also keeping curious eyes off of his current venture. Anything."

"True," he thought. He could see it in his mind. That arrogant, pudgy bastard would get off the plane, waving to the throng of reporters and cameras and posing for pictures like he was a movie star or decorated war hero. Under the right circumstances, attention was like a drug for TB. How badly he'd wanted to be at the top – probably an envy complex that began in childhood and continued today. The GOP had done its best to convince him it could be done. Unfortunately he'd been too much of a chicken shit to actually run. It was hard to imagine a better, more expendable mouthpiece. Even though the family would've had to forego the additional prestige, it would've turned out better all around. Bringing in his son had been a bad idea. The regret was palpable, but he shook it off. The past was untouchable and irrevocable. Reparation was all that mattered now. And TB, whom he'd nicknamed 'The Spinner,' was one of the obstacles that had to be dealt with.

"Has the Red Canary had any interested visitors?"

"A few rising stars hoping to uncover something new to make their name. Nothing new has turned up. He knows who holds the keys to his jail cell."

"He's still leaking like a sieve," he warned. "Is the CIA still squeezing him? Are you privy to what they're learning?"

"Yes, Sir. The Canary is refusing to sing a new tune. Until they can entice him with something more. Those deals are made deep inside the CIA and could emerge at any time. He's a loose cannon, Sir."

"Agreed," he admitted. A few moments passed before the silence was broken.

"Sir," the man hesitated, "what about The Angler, Sir? Do you want surveillance to re-engage?"

"No," he said too quickly, "No. Not yet. That one is tricky and dangerous. Besides, the way he's going, nature might take care of things for us."

"And the others?"

But he was still thinking of unlucky number seven. "Yes, tricky was right," he thought, "and too close to home." As it was, the commonality of those on the list was obvious. Accidents, misfortunes, dirt, and misinformation. In short, a smear campaign of a different flavor. That was the ticket to deflection. A few back doors into the media might have to be gently pried open in order to secure critical insertion points. He was going to need to place a few key people in the field to discredit any sources attempting to link the incidents together. The "conspiracy" label was the best deflection tool out there. "Old Faithful," it was often called in dark private rooms, amidst thick cigar smoke and the smell of brandy.

It was amazing how much weight and influence a single word could convey. Only within the last fifty years or so had Old Faithful been involuntarily and unconsciously morphed into a powerful weapon. The irony was fantastic, he often thought. Conspiracy was like a lead weight to any theory. Regardless of validity or initial buoyancy, a few strategically placed articles would relegate any connection to the overactive imaginations of idle and evil minds. With the possible exception of global warming, Old Faithful, when backed by the right people, had never failed. Human language was truly remarkable.

He glanced at the unfolded piece of yellow legal paper sitting on his desk. Twelve names. Twelve code names. Twelve minds full of shiny gold bargaining chips. Each one could be slid across a polished oak table in some obscure backroom, exchanged for a clean and quiet exit, the details of the transaction forever hidden from the public's eyes. Some would be loyal, but only to the point where they themselves would not be in jeopardy. Enough pressure and even the best seal will crack. This he simply could not allow.

"Sir?" the curt voice demanded.

This time he didn't hesitate. "Nacho Libre, Red Canary, The Spinner, and Speedy are authorized. Acquire, extract, and dispose."

"Yes, Sir."

"Remember, you are the sole link to this family. No one else is to know. Understood?"

"Yes, Sir."

"Make the remains public, but be careful not to leave any clues that could lead someone back to us. Random. Untraceable."

"Disposal sites have already been chosen, Sir. The subjects will be clean and interesting."

"No emotion," he thought. "None at all. Good survival tactic. Objectivity is always clouded by emotion. Always."

"What about the others? What is your current intel?"

"Thus far each bottle has remained corked," the operative said. "But the Justice Department has already started turning stones. It's only a matter of time."

"Response?" he asked.

"Teams are in position awaiting your authorization Sir."

He suddenly felt envious of this man's readiness and freedom to take action. No hesitation. No reluctance to engage. These men were cold, calculating and proficient. But what motivated them? It wasn't just the money, of that he was certain. Payment wasn't enough. There was better money to be made doing less dangerous work and they knew it. No. It was something else entirely. Sometimes, when pondering this conundrum, he could convince himself the drive was loyalty – to commander and country. That was enough to ward off thoughts of their being hired by someone else to target him. Loyalty was a noble ideal, though not usually convincing enough to allow a good night's sleep. Regardless, most of the time he wasn't so deluded. What else, then? Part of him liked to think it was good old-fashioned bloodlust, but that wasn't it either. No. There was something else driving these men. Perhaps they were extreme history enthusiasts who wanted a hand in shaping the course of the future. Admirable, though a bit too simplistic. Patriotism? A sense of honor and duty? Action with no care as to why? Robotic execution of orders? None of these felt right. The truth, he feared, was that they did it because they liked it and they didn't care who the target was – man, woman, child – good, bad and everything in between. Just so long as there was always another target in sight.

Suddenly, movement outside the window caught his attention. Pivoting in his chair, he saw his eldest son walking casually along the porch outside. He wore jeans, an old Harvard sweatshirt two sizes too big and tan hush puppies. In his hand was an oversized white coffee cup bearing the U.S. Presidential seal, wisps of steam escaping from the top.

"Sir," the voice demanded. "What are your orders?"

He heard the question, but was preoccupied with the figure outside his window. His son had stopped walking and was leaning on the railing. He watched as he casually turned his head from side to side to see if anyone else was near and then, satisfied that no one was around, pulled a small silver flask from his back pocket, unscrewed the cap, and poured some of the amber liquid into his coffee cup. Anger mixed with frustration welled up as he watched his son quickly slip the flask back into his pocket and cover the bulge with the large sweatshirt.

The younger man turned, sipped the coffee and flashed the grin of a child who thought no one had seen him steal a cookie. That stupid smirk. "He didn't get it from me," he thought. Human expressions, even blank ones, can be very telling. An unfortunate fact not lost on the country and media. "The Blank Face of Ineptitude" one headline had proclaimed. "Lost" had been the bold headline in an ultra-liberal paper. A third had gone so far as to print "Nobody Home." Not long after the now infamous "humans and fish" quote, one magazine had lamented, "When in history have the citizens of a superpower felt such shame? Years after this harbinger of ignominy vanishes from public office (and vanish he must), America, with head bowed, will have no choice but to beg forgiveness from all. Pride swallowed and tail tucked. We can only hope and pray the rest of the world bears forth the compassion, civility and understanding so noticeably absent in our leader." In each case, a photo of his eldest son appeared beneath the headline, ever bearing that empty, clueless gaze and the asinine grin. When this was all over...when he'd cleaned up the last of his son's disasters, he would personally erase that stupid smile.

"Are you there, Sir?"

Returning his focus to the task at hand he said, "Yes, I'm here."

"Sir?" the man said dryly.

He sensed the distant voice was growing impatient. Was there a question of his authority in that silence – in his ability to make difficult decisions? To decide the fate of people his son might have once called friends? An image of the crisp blue Presidential seal flashed into his mind. But this time it wasn't on a coffee mug. Instead it was surrounded by a pulsing red light, one that undoubtedly signaled an emergency. The image flashed again. Now the seal was melting. The eagle's wings were gone. Only the talons clutching the olive branch and the thirteen arrows could be seen. With the disturbing image came pressure, guilt, and acute regret. But there was something else. The eagle in the seal had faced the olive branch instead of the arrows to show a preference of peace over war. But now the eagle's head was gone.

The choice was now his. "A dozen decisions before breakfast," he thought again, and on impulse said firmly, "Hold surveillance on Powwow and continue recon. We still don't know how deep his honor and discretion run. Maintain twenty-four hour eyes and ears and let me know if there is a pattern change. Same goes for Sweetness, P-Nacle, Brother T, Sandscrat and The Leaker."

"That leaves Black Coffee."

"Affirmative. Black Coffee is also authorized. Extract all pertinent information. I need facts, not forced confessions. Use any and all means to achieve the mission objectives. Leave no witnesses. When the extraction is complete, finish the job. Clean, fast, and yes, *interesting* as well. As far as anyone knows these quarries are completely unrelated. I want a full report after each deletion. Transmit using standard encryption protocols. Code in with Murphy before sending anything confidential. No residuals and no fuck-ups. Are we clear, soldier?" The last question was thick with challenge and authority.

A full two seconds passed before the reply came. "Understood, Sir," the voice answered and the line went dead. Slowly he lowered the handset and replaced it in the cradle. Thoughtfully, he clasped his fingers together and considered what had just transpired. He felt certain this man, this *Condotierro*, upon hearing the order, had confirmed his understanding wearing an excited and sadistic smile. The man's eagerness to interrogate, torture and kill sent a strange tingling sensation through his whole body. The ramifications of what he'd just set into motion echoed and reverberated in his mind. Swift and decisive action was what the situation demanded, and he'd delivered. Anticipation coursed through his body, filling him with energy and a restored sense of authority and purpose. He bolted upright from his chair, turned and saw his reflection in the large antique civil war mirror. Staring back at him was a man of wealth and power bearing a devilish, malevolent smile. The same smile, he felt certain, was, at this very moment, on the face of the eager mercenary. And nothing, save for the hand of God himself, could stop either of them now.

Mutare, Zimbabwe, Africa

"Damn it!" Kina growled as the bullet shredded the bark on the left side of the tree.

"Nothing to be afraid of here, Little Girl," the shooter taunted. "I won't hurt you."

She wiped the sweat from her brow with the sleeve of her sweatshirt. Another shot rang out, this time tearing at the bark on the right side.

"This guy is obviously hitting what he's aiming at," she thought. Her briefing had failed to mention that the farm's owner was a fucking expert marksman! "That would've been useful information," she grumbled as she spun to take another shot. She squeezed the trigger and channeled the recoil to help quickly spin her back around. The bullet blew off the corner of the stone wall the farmer was crouched behind.

"You can do better than that can't ya, Sugar?" the man yelled playfully.

She crouched to take a low shot. An instant before she pivoted to fire, another shot rang out, this time ripping through the loose bark only inches from where her head would've been. "Fuck!" she hissed. "What? Is this redneck reading my mind?"

The shooter was Merle A. Shephard. Kina recalled the file she'd read on the flight from New York to London. Shephard had moved to Africa in late 2000 after fleeing federal prosecution for trespassing and poaching on federal lands, resisting arrest, possession of a sizeable cache of illegal firearms and other assorted weaponry, failure to appear on his appointed court date, skipping out on his bond, and firing shots at pursuing police officers and federal agents. It was around this time that he popped up on *The Aenamaia's* radar. During the standard file review, he had initially been placed towards the bottom of their list. That was until Gray learned that while the charges were never dropped, the entire investigation and search for Shephard was called off suddenly and without explanation on January 25, 2001, only five days after President Bush was sworn into office. Gray used his D.C. contacts to discover the order had come from on high, though he'd not been able to secure any solid proof. That same day, Shephard's name was moved up and *The Aenamaia's* deep investigation into his background began. In the end, even though *The Aenamaia* was never able to find concrete proof that President Bush himself had ordered the manhunt stopped, the research on Shephard continued.

Then in late 2004, amidst the unusually high volume of heightened terrorist alerts preceding the onslaught of Bush's campaign activities, they got a break. One of their deepest and most secret contacts in the Bush administration managed to get a photocopy of a handwritten thank-you note sent to Bush from one M. Shephard for the "aid" Bush had provided him. The main text of the note was ambiguous. It was the last line that had caught the contact's attention: "P.S. Tell your father to take good care of my old '73 Sharps. She's a beaut." After hours of painstaking research via several of the Presidential libraries, Gray learned that during his first term in office, George H.W. Bush had been given a rare 1873 Sharps Meacham rifle by an anonymous donor. No record of the donor was ever located, but the gun was rumored to be kept at the former President's summer home in Kennebunkport, Maine. Despite the lack of direct evidence of the connection between Shephard and Bush Jr., *The Aenamaia* was pleased to learn that Mr. Shephard had been kind enough to include a return address...in Africa.

Now, hiding behind a tree in Shephard's dusty front yard, Kina sincerely wished George W. was here at this very moment. "A thick, mindless human shield would come in handy right about now," she thought. Cautiously, she peered around the other side of the tree. Twenty feet from the front porch of the large house a man's body lay motionless facing the sky. Despite the dust in the air she could see the dark puddle of blood surrounding what remained of his head. Her first shot had been right on target. Devin Blanche, a wealthy D.C. lawyer famous for his defense of the tobacco companies and the associated lobby, had dropped like a stone. Fifteen feet away from his body was the cage holding the King Cheetah he had paid a hundred grand to personally shoot and kill. The cheetah paced the cage restlessly, always keeping an eager eye on the dead body. He was probably hungry. The scumbags who ran these places were known to keep the animals hungry and agitated so they would appear vicious and dangerous – therefore heightening the thrill of the kill for the weasel pulling the trigger.

Lying only a few feet from Blanche was the body of Mitt Holgren, the primary political lobbyist for the Safari Club International, an organization that advocated for hunter's rights to hunt and kill rare and endangered species. Holgren had helped scuttle an impressive list of legislation designed to limit hunting, add a number of species to the illegal and endangered list, increase gun registration controls, and so on. Holgren who, thanks to a family friend in the White House, had managed to be appointed as Director of the U.S. Fish and Wildlife Service under suspicious circumstances, had also been instrumental in helping establish secretive farms like this one where the wealthy could kill just about anything they desired – for a price. There were purported to be hundreds of such places all over the world, but only a select few knew them all. The arrangements were simple. Once funds were transferred, the farm owner would track, capture and cage the desired animal. Next they would tranquilize the animal so it could be safely cleaned and groomed. They would then put the animal back in the cage and keep it healthy until a few days before the paying client arrived. Then the feeding would stop and the taunting would begin.

In many of these cases interested parties would contact Holgren directly. Terms would be negotiated and he would coordinate the details of the trip. Having helped establish most of the farms, he knew which ones could capture and contain which animals. He and his clients also agreed that the fee paid to the farmer would only be around ten percent of the total. Holgren pocketed the rest for his services and his discretion.

Yet despite all the power and wealth he had accumulated over the years, all the profit he'd made helping to kill the world's endangered species, and all the powerful friends in high places, he was now lying dead in the dirt on the plains of Africa. And if Kina succeeded here today, no one would ever see how he'd died. Neither the left ear that had been blown off when he'd turned at the last second nor the second bullet lodged in his left lung would ever be found. Through all the commotion that ensued after the man fell, Kina wasn't a hundred percent sure Holgren was dead. But given where the second shot hit, she was confident he'd choked to death on his own blood.

It was only at the eleventh hour that Gray had somehow managed to learn that Holgren would be accompanying Blanche on this trip – hence the urgency in getting Kina in place quickly for the liquidation. It was only after she arrived in Mutare that their local contact informed her that the president of the Safari Den, Dearden Sanderson, had also come on the trip. At the time, her excitement had been palpable. Two of the people on her future jobs list showing up unexpectedly. "Three birds with one rifle," she'd thought then. She'd managed to take out two of the birds, but Sanderson, after having been shot square in the back of his leg, managed to escape through the front gate. Kina had sent two rounds in his direction amidst a barrage of shots from Shephard, one of which pierced the fleeing man's shoulder. Even though the man somehow managed to keep running, it really didn't matter. The closest human was at least ten long miles away, with nothing but wild country in between. With any luck Sanderson would meet his end in the teeth and claws of the purest, most poetic natural magistrate of justice imaginable.

Another shot rang out, clipping the side of the tree an instant after Kina whipped back around.

"You're not giving up already are ya, Darlin'?" Shephard yelled from behind the wall. "It wouldn't be as much fun if you just surrendered."

"This guy is nuts," she muttered. He's clearly not playing with a full deck. If she managed to kill him she could claim it as a mercy killing. No one this stupid should be allowed to roam free, let alone kill other living things."

Two more shots clipped the edge of the tree even though she hadn't moved an inch – which meant he was either trying to anticipate her next move or he was trying to make her panic. "Next time, if there ever is a next time, we shoot the owner first," she hissed quietly, nodding to herself.

As her mind raced about what to do next, she noticed how much of the tree bark lay scattered in two distinct piles to her left and right. She looked up and noticed for the first time that it was a canopy tree, and she recalled reading something on the plane about a family of canopies called acacias. One in particular called the "Paperbark Acacia" had caught her attention. The name had stuck in her mind because she'd mistakenly thought she'd read "paperback" and had been curious about why it would have such an odd name. The tree had received its name from the thin, paper-like bark that peeled easily from the main trunk. She couldn't be sure whether or not the tall tree keeping her from being shot was in fact a Paperbark, but she promised herself that if she made it through this ordeal alive she would make it a point to find out.

With thoughts of the tree came an odd, sharp pang of remorse. There was so much beauty in this country. So much to see and admire here in the cradle of life. Would she ever get to see more of it – to tell anyone of its wonders? Or would this be the last place she ever saw? Though the dangers of her mission had been carefully explained and covered, she realized she'd never really considered the possibility she might die today. And *here*, no less – fighting for her life, on this redneck egomaniac's property. Ironic that such a man would choose to live in the midst of such amazing abundance and splendor. Normally such a place would be a good place to die. But not like this. Not by the hand of Joe Bob, the inbred poacher.

Before the fear of death had a chance to take hold of her, she realized that her life wasn't the only one at stake here. There was purpose and utility in living through this ordeal that went beyond her own survival. If this man beat her, countless other animals would be mercilessly paraded and killed by wealthy, insecure heterosexuals who thrived on dispensing death. Spineless bastards. The rage she'd first felt when given this assignment resurfaced and she remembered why she'd fought and argued her way past Gray's doubts. Someone had to protect the endangered creatures of the world from the real predators.

Her thoughts shifted back to the caged cheetah as a new rush of determination engulfed her mind. Her eyes narrowed slightly and a cunning grin spread across her lips. "If I get out of this alive, Big Kitty, you're gonna get one hell of a feast!" Chambering another round, she reversed her grip on the gun and prepared to take a shot from her right side. *The Aenamaia* required all members handling liquidations to demonstrate proficiency firing a weapon from either hand and from multiple angles. During her struggle to overcome the oddness of aiming and shooting with her opposite hand, she had tried to convince Gray that such training would rarely be of any use to her. Why spend so much time and effort perfecting it? "Oh he's gonna have a field day when he hears about this," she growled in a low voice. "Kitty eats the bad men, sniper eats her own words," she added. Returning to the last spot on the tree the farmer had fired at, she pointed the rifle and waited until she saw the barrel of his gun appear – then she fired. The farmer hadn't been expecting her to fire from the opposite side. She caught a glimpse of the surprise on his face when the bullet grazed his right shoulder. She spun back around, holding the rifle upright and pulling it close to her body.

The moment of glowing satisfaction and triumph was short-lived, though, as reality muscled its way into her mind. Time to face facts. Despite the lucky shot, she knew he was a better marksman and had much better cover. To make matters worse, she was also running out of ammo for the rifle and her sidearm had only two rounds left. Even if she could somehow maintain the standoff, it was an unusually hot day for Mutare and her water bottle and food were in her backpack – thirty meters away. If Merle didn't manage to kill her on his own, dehydration would lay down a red carpet for him.

"Not too bad for a cute little princess," Shephard said, his clenched voice awash with sarcasm and petulant anger. "Hell, you must'a taken a little time off from cooking and making babies to learn how to shoot like a south paw. You must be the pride of your knittin' club."

"What kind of parents still raised these knuckle-dragging rednecks," she thought. IQ screening and mandatory birth control suddenly sounded like sound practices. Perhaps a little cleansing of the gene pool once in a while could be a healthy thing. She would have to write to her Congressmen – assuming he wasn't on *The Aenamaia's* hit list.

Kina had been silent up until this point, but now she thought perhaps a derisive comment might agitate him enough to create an opportunity. "You know Mr. Sheep-humper," she started, grinning at her own cleverness, "until I met you, I could never understand why some animal mothers ate their young."

She started to chamber a round when another shot was fired. She felt a sudden rush of heat on her left calf and then a sharp bolt of pain. Instinctively her left hand cupped her mouth, preventing her scream from escaping her lips. Gritting her teeth and tightly gripping the rifle, she looked down at her pants leg. There was already a slowly spreading red stain seeping through her jeans. Quickly she reached down and carefully touched the wound. The shot had nicked her pretty good. So much for creating an opportunity. Her calf hurt like hell, but she knew it could've been a lot worse. "Idiot, idiot, idiot!" she cursed in a hushed voice. "Why not stick your whole ass out there for him to shoot at!"

"Come on, Sweet Thing. Is this really necessary? Maybe we should just put down our guns and talk about this. After all, I've got a whole bunch of high-falutin' customers lined up for some sport. And once they make a kill, they git' kinda...well...anxious if you know what I mean. Sweet little drink of water like yourself could make a handsome living putting out those kinds of fires. Whattaya say?"

"As a rule I do know it is wrong to enjoy killing someone," she said to herself, "but like most rules, there are always exceptions."

Three more shots rang out, each one hitting the same spot on the ground. "This fucker is toying with me," she thought. I have to think of something and fast. How was she going to get out of this? Her mind was working on maximum overdrive – making it hard to hang on to any single thought for more than a second. "Take it easy, Kina," she said to herself, "There must be a way." Breathing deeply she tried to calm her thoughts and think rationally. "Okay. This guy runs an elitist farm for the illegal hunting and killing of endangered species. We know at some point he was a skilled hunter himself. And he's lived here, in the middle of fucking nowhere, for seven years. So he knows the lay of the land and that there won't be anyone coming by because they heard shots fired. So I'm on my own. "Ahhh!" she exclaimed as another bolt of pain shot up her leg. "Okay, so…this guy was bailed out by the President of the United States. He deals with wealthy, powerful clients. He captures dangerous animals for a living. He probably *is* an egomaniac and obviously a dedicated sexist. Right? Right. And, ouch! Despite being hit himself, he will not believe a woman could best him, right? Right. So, he's expecting to win," she paused and added with a nod, "he's sure he'll win. Yeah. Okay."

She surveyed the scene before her. Between her tree and the next one was at least twenty feet of open ground. Even without an injured leg, she'd never make it to cover. Her Land Rover was a half-mile up the dirt road. There was nowhere to run. Risking a quick glance around the tree, she could see Shephard was still hiding behind the wall. He's patient. Controlled. "That's a bad thing," she thought. "And on top of that, his cover is excellent."

"He's waiting for me to make a mistake. I'm sure he's earnestly hoping to have time to gloat over my bleeding corpse before he finishes me," she thought grimly. More than anything he probably wants to know who I am and how I came to be here. Then it hit her. He's been toying with me. Thinking back, she realized he probably could've gotten her in the head a few times, especially when she'd first fled from her hiding place on the side of his house. Given the sparse cover around the house, it had been the best place to take out Blanche and Holgren. Sanderson had started running as soon as she fired the first shot. She'd only managed to hit him while running for the cover of the tree. Shephard had gotten two rounds off, but had missed. The shots had hit only a foot or so behind her. He must have been going for her legs. Now he was waiting for her to either give up, or give him a chance at a center mass wound. If she wanted to get out of this alive, she would have to pit her brains against his skill.

She let a minute pass. Her mind was circling around the possibilities, but she had already made her decision. Careful to remain concealed behind the tree, she removed her dirty tan sweatshirt. Next, she pulled off her right shoe and stuffed it down into the empty sleeve. Taking a deep breath and clenching her teeth, she carefully pulled the shoe from her left foot. The pain from her calf was acute, but she managed to keep quiet. Lifting the dark brown shoe she noticed the dark-soaked patch behind the heel. Taking another deep breath, she quickly stuffed the second shoe into the sleeve. Holding the sleeve in one hand and the rifle in the other, she moved.

Shephard saw the woman's faint shadow shift an instant before the barrel of her rifle and her arm came into the view of his crosshairs. "Come to papa, you Wily Bitch," he muttered and fired. The woman's scream was louder than he'd expected. The moment the bullet had gone through her arm, the rifle had fallen onto the ground next to the tree.

He'd expected she would get anxious and try something stupid. "Sure, women like this could be taught to shoot, but no training could ever make them into true soldiers. They didn't have the nerves or the patience. That's why the front lines still consisted mainly of men. Women just couldn't hack it. Dumb broad oughta known better than to try a stunt like this with him," he thought. "Sure, she'd taken down Holgren and that pompous idiot Blanche, but who cares. He'd already been paid. It was unlikely these men had told many people where they were heading and what they were going to do. Out here, getting rid of their corpses would be easy."

Shephard took another look in his scope. He hadn't seen any movement yet and her rifle was still lying on the ground. "Fancy piece of equipment," he thought. "She must be some kind of ex-military." The sophistication of the weapon and her tactics thus far drove a thin wedge of doubt in his mind. Perhaps it was best to wait this out. See if she goes for the rifle or tries to run. Just then he heard a noise. He cocked his head slightly and listened. Crying. She was crying! A sly smile spread across his face. "Women need to learn their place in this world," he thought with satisfaction. "Oh, I'm gonna enjoy this," he said to himself.

Leveling his gun on the edge of the wall, Shephard took aim and fired. The bullet hit the butt of the woman's gun and sent the weapon sliding a few feet further from the tree. Then he squeezed off a few more rounds, hitting both sides of the tree and the ground next to where the woman was probably slumped. Then he listened. The crying had gotten louder and now had a panicky edge to it. Shephard laughed and got to his feet, all the while keeping his gun aimed and his eyes on the tree and the rifle. He doubted she would go for it, but he needed to be ready just in case.

Keeping his rifle leveled and aimed, he walked slowly towards the tree. He found himself thinking of all the fun in store for him over the next few hours. The shot wouldn't kill her for quite some time. If he was lucky, he would have time to apply a tourniquet, which could give him an extra day or two before she bled to death. That would be more than enough time to explore her body from head to toe. Just the thought of her strapped naked to the mattress in the attic, begging to be killed was enough to almost send him over the edge. A quick shake of his head brought him back to the moment. "Get a grip, Merle," he whispered to himself, "plenty a time for all that."

As he got closer he could hear the woman crying and babbling to herself. Shephard fired another shot next to the tree and heard the woman shriek in startled terror. "You know I'm coming for you, Sweetheart, don't ya?" he whispered. The crying got louder as he approached. He could hear her voice clearly now. What was she saying? He paused to listen, his gun still leveled. Her crying and talking at the same time made it difficult for him to make out her words, which irritated him. Stupid women have no honor or dignity when it comes to dying. Then he heard her weak, whimpering voice repeating, "so much blood. So much blood. Oh God, so much blood!"

Shephard lowered his rifle and chuckled out loud. "Quit your cryin'," he said adding with a wry smile, "tears are for the weak. Besides, Uncle Shephard hasn't even begun to give you a good enough reason to cry." He began walking at a leisurely pace towards the tree and the pathetic sobbing. When will women learn that this is, and always has been, a man's world? He almost wished his hunting buddies in the Safari Club could be here to witness this. Most of them had hunted more than just animals on at least one occasion, but he felt certain none of the boys had taken down anything so savory as this. He could still see the image of the fit young woman dashing across the yard towards the tree. It would almost be a shame to waste something so tasty. Almost.

With the volume and pitch of a circus master he bellowed, "Welcome to Shephard's ranch, My Dear. Home of the cage kill. 'Course you wasn't caged, but I'm certainly willing to make an exception to the rules." The anticipation was incredible, but he didn't rush. Better to savor the moment. Slowly, he rounded the tree on the side where the rifle had fallen, saw the edge of the limp tan sleeve, and stopped to say, "I gotta tell you something, Sweet Thing, I've killed thousands of wild animals in my time, but I must say…" he paused. He was breathing heavy and sweating. He took one step closer. Just before he saw the sweatshirt was empty, he bragged, "I never enjoyed hunting this much!"

In one swift motion the barefooted woman stepped directly in front of Shephard, her sidearm pressed firmly against his forehead as she said with a coy smile, "Neither have I," and pulled the trigger. A split second before the bullet blew a large hole in his skull, a single thought bolted through Merle Shephard's incredulous mind, "There wasn't a single tear in her eyes."

Chapter 2

New York City, New York

"Lie flat on the floor!" the man shouted again. He aimed his weapon at the stunned group of people. This time everyone obeyed. "There are plenty of other jobs in the world. This one isn't worth dying for."

Daring one last glance at the figure in the dark mask who was grasping the large, solid black machine gun, the night security guard quickly obeyed the order and flattened his body out on the rough plank wood floor of the large truck.

"Hands flat out in front of you where I can see them," the man with the gun ordered, this time directing the command at him. Barely cognizant of his own actions, the security guard saw his shaking hands shoot out in front of him like a jolted Superman who forgot this position was necessary to fly.

Motion a few feet away caught the black-clad man's attention. Without a word from anyone, the security guard heard the sharp, quick chirp of a silenced gun go off just above his head. "My God," he thought shaking, "has someone been shot?"

In answer to his concern, another voice shouted, "That was your one and only warning shot. All of you stay still, stay quiet and don't move a fucking inch. Challenge us and you will lose."

A few seconds later the guard heard another, more calm voice say, "We're not here to harm you. Do as we say and you will all be released within the hour. Now, our thermograph scanners indicated there were thirty-three people in the building. Our research indicated this number was consistent for this night of the week. However, we need to make sure this is everyone. You all work the night shift here every night during the week. You all work together. You were all escorted out and loaded onto this truck together. Does anyone know of a co-worker who was in the building who is not on this truck now?"

The security guard looked around at the faces of the other people lying on the floor of the truck, but no one spoke.

"Anyone remaining in the building will not be alive tomorrow. So I'll ask one more time, is there anyone still inside?"

Still, none of the prisoners spoke.

"Very well," the man said.

The guard had worked in the building longer than anyone else and knew without a doubt that thirty-three was the correct count for this time of night. Third shift folks left at ten p.m., while the first shift didn't come in until midnight. This gave the security guards and cleaning people, who constituted the thirty-three people in the truck, time to clean and secure the building. During that time, the only things running in the building were the computers, faxes, and the large presses.

"Restraints!" one of the armed men ordered.

The guard watched as several men dressed head to toe in black quickly and expertly secured each person's wrists with a plastic tie, while a few others used foot-long bungee cords to bind their feet. Once each person was restrained, another figure clad in black ran a long, nylon cord through each person's arm, making one loop per person. After every person was threaded, the ends were tied to metal loops bolted into the wall of the truck.

The guard was scared, but despite his shakiness something told him these men were not there to harm the people. Trying not to be too obvious, he carefully counted eight figures total, all dressed from head to toe in black. Each wore a black ski mask and carried either a large handgun or a semiautomatic machine gun. They moved quickly and rarely spoke to each other.

"Seven minutes, thirty seconds," one of the men yelled.

"Incendiary devices in place near the presses. Charges are synced. The rest of the fireworks are in place and ready for the show."

"Check," another man confirmed.

The guard watched as their captors adroitly wove through the bodies. Each man seemed to know his role, as was evident in each precise, measured movement. They reminded him of seasoned assembly line workers. Efficient, fast and dispassionate. Taking them all in together, the guard thought they looked like a school of synchronized black fish. The motions of one unconsciously affected the movement of the others.

"What do the sensors for the adjoining buildings show?" The guard was surprised to find that this time the voice was that of a woman. Unfortunately, he could not see which black figure had spoken.

"No heat in either building."

"Rear exterior?" again it was the female's voice.

"Negative. The box is cold."

"Confirm minimum safe distance," the woman ordered.

From the front of the truck a man's voice said calmly, "Quarter mile for debris, two to avoid responders."

He was transfixed by the rapid and exact execution of each task. Watching the two men with automatic weapons, it was obvious they had experience doing this sort of thing. With his cheek pressed to the wood plank floor of the truck, the guard cautiously observed the swift, calculated movements of the two weapons as they shifted aim from person to person. The guard felt certain they would not hesitate to fire a few rounds into anyone who posed a threat to them – or whatever it was they had come to do.

Before the thought had left his mind, the guard saw a blur of motion as Buck, one of the other guards, managed to flip himself onto his back and throw his feet over his head in an attempt to reach a gun the guard could now see was tucked into an ankle holster. The guard saw the whole thing in slow motion. The man's fingers came within inches of the six-shooter's handle when a single, muffled shot hiccupped from the rear of the truck. The guard saw the struggling man's tied hands thrown backwards a split second after a hole appeared in his right palm. The guard couldn't be certain whether the spray of blood and cartilage hit the wall and several other prisoners before or after the powerful, muted growl of anguish escaped the man's throat through the gag covering his mouth. The guard froze, expecting further retribution for the man's actions, but nothing happened. He could hear the muffled sounds of panic from several of the other prisoners. The shot had jolted him as well, but he was still watching as much of the sideways scene as he could see. The odd angle of his head, combined with the tension that came from straining his eyes and neck, was giving him a throbbing headache. But despite the pain, he couldn't steal his eyes away from the odd spectacle before him.

"Triage," the woman's voice ordered evenly. The guard heard the motion of footsteps.

"You were all warned. Now one of you has chosen to validate this warning. Any further deviation from our instructions will be met with force. Let me say this again," she paused and made eye contact with those who had dared meet her masked gaze, "We are not here to harm any of you. You are victims of circumstance. Hard as it may be to believe at this moment, had we not rounded you all up, you would be living the last two minutes of your lives right now."

The woman raised a two-way radio to her mouth and said, "Move out. T minus two minutes."

The guard heard the truck's engine come to life. An instant later a gear was thrown and the truck began moving. He tried to catch a glimpse of Buck, but he could only see the two black figures kneeling down beside him amidst the shaking bodies of the other prisoners. There was a blur of motion in which he saw medical tape, gauze, and a syringe.

"Sensors?" the woman questioned again.

"The box is still cold," a man's voice responded.

"Distance?" she asked into the radio.

"Almost a half mile from the heat."

The guard heard faint beeps he thought sounded like a cell phone being dialed.

"Gray," the woman said. "The box is clear and cold."

After a few seconds she said in answer to the other party's questions, "Ringside."

There was a pause and some muted talk from the cell phone.

Again she answered, "All accounted for. What about the other teams? Are they green?"

She listened, never taking her eyes off the people tied up on the floor of the truck.

"All five sites?" she asked.

She nodded her head, apparently approving of the answer she received. Then, with what the guard guessed was a wry smile beneath her mask, the woman answered, "No, we forgot the marshmallows."

The guard heard another beep and a click as the woman closed the phone.

"Stop the truck," she yelled. The truck pulled over to the side of the road and rumbled to a stop. The guard could tell the engine was still running. The vibration shook the loose planks he and the other prisoners were lying on.

The woman in black turned suddenly and looked straight at the guard. The cell phone had disappeared, but it looked as if she were still holding something. Her gaze was firm and full of intensity, but as he would later remark, even through the mask and the concentration, there was also a hint of sadness. She spoke solemnly and said, "You're all witnesses to history. Let's hope it's all for the best." The woman backed up against the wall of the truck, all the while maintaining her stare at the people bound on the floor. She raised her right hand and the guard could see she did in fact have something gripped tightly in her gloved hand. Her hand obscured the object, but he could see that on the bottom of the object was what looked like a flat, red button that was flashing.

In a deep, strong voice the woman yelled, "Fire in the hole!!" The interior of the truck seemed to contract as everyone braced for what came next.

Virginia Beach, Virginia

Tzaria strolled casually down the wide boardwalk. Though she was a hair over six feet tall, she blended easily with the throng of grinning and pointing tourists, most of whom were taking pictures or throwing food to flocks of bold and aggressive sea birds. Few people even noticed the passing of the tall, quiet woman walking alone.

She wore comfortable white tennis shoes, loose black cotton pants, a white tank top, and a light gray shirt. Beneath the back rim of a tan tweed summer hat, rested a tight bun of dark brown hair. She wore dark, oversized sunglasses, a round silver necklace bearing a Macedonia Star, silver hoop earrings, a simple wedding ring, and a heavy double-headed lion torc bracelet. Completing the outfit was an oversized backpack purse and a small silver camera dangling from her wrist. Her gait was intentionally casual and unhurried, which was exactly the opposite of how she felt.

Tzaria stopped next to the weathered wood railing and took in her surroundings. To her left was a wide, white beach standing in stark contrast to the dark green Atlantic. The postcard sands were speckled with tall reedy grasses, lumbering white seagulls, two whitewashed lifeguard towers, and fresh tire tracks from the frequent beach patrol trucks. Over the ocean and eastern horizon she could see a solid line of low white clouds. Otherwise the skies were sunny and clear. There were no ships in sight. She thought she could just make out the faint outline of an oil platform, though she couldn't be certain.

Further up the beach she spotted a large green tractor slowly making its way north. The tractors kept the beaches combed and clear of manmade and natural litter and biota, but she preferred her beaches au naturale. Picture perfect beaches were for painters to portray. Nature had taken four and a half billion years to perfect its cleanup techniques, working around whatever life and the universe threw at it. And though many would disagree with her, Tzaria felt certain nature was perfectly capable of working around mankind, with plenty of time to keep the beaches clean. Despite years of meddling, alteration, and blind consumption, the planet was not the domain of man – man was a guest of the planet. Best not to push Mother Nature's patience, lest she decide to exterminate the relatively young and decidedly ruinous species.

Wandering down the uneven walkway, Tzaria pondered nature and the universe. It was a habit she indulged in when there was time to kill. Chaos. Entropy. Natural order. These characteristics were related – siblings of the same contained system of life, death, and reorganization. Such topics had fascinated Tzaria since she was a child. Her parents, Russian defectors, had lain low in a quiet village in southern Greece, opening a small grocery store. When she wasn't working in the store, going to school, or struggling with the local Greek dialect, Tzaria would walk through the hillsides and along the beach.

Sometimes her father would walk with her. He would explain to her how nature breathed in cycles. Seed, water and nutrients, plant and flower, pollination and baby seeds, and voila the process began again. He spoke of animal life in similar terms. Humans were the same, as was the planet. Everything moved and progressed in cycles. Managed by the most ancient and sophisticated landlord known to man. Little did her father know that of the millions of species on the planet, out of the billions that had existed, one single species would begin to undermine the landlord with mind-blowing speed and potency. If her father were walking with her now, he would be astounded at the damage mankind had wrought thus far and would loathe what seemed to be on the horizon. No doubt he would see a dark, ominous future where…

"Excuse me, Ma'am, what time do you have?"

The dark thoughts receded quickly as she turned to find a middle-aged man and woman looking expectantly at her. The voice and question had caught her off guard, but she recovered quickly and said, "Signomi? Ime apó Ellada." She donned a look of confusion. The man, realizing she didn't speak English, pointed at his wrist. She smiled and said, "Ne, ne. Ti ora ine," and nodded enthusiastically. She reached into her pocket and extracted her father's old Swiss pocket watch. She opened the engraved gold cover and turned the face of the watch towards the couple.

"Oh, how exquisite!" the woman said staring at the watch, "It's beautiful." Tzaria wanted to smile, but knew better than to show any comprehension. She saw the husband was also surprised to see an old pocket watch. No doubt he'd expected a wristwatch or cell phone.

"Signomi, ala then milao Iglezika." Tzaria feigned a look of apology and added clumsily, "Tourista. Not English."

"That's all right, Dear," the woman said patting her hand. "The time was all we wanted." The woman pointed at the watch, nodded and smiled.

Tzaria smiled sheepishly, returned the watch to her pocket and said, "Efharisto," and gave the couple a polite nod. She turned and kept walking. Though her cover didn't require her to be in character every moment, the more she was seen and heard as a foreigner, the better. Practice makes perfect.

The name of Leandra Nestor was the outcome of an Internet search of Greek names. Tzaria, having lived in Greece until she was nineteen, had thought it wise to create a personality from her home country. She had never worked under an assumed name or personality before and thought familiarity could only strengthen her performance. Additionally, she'd been pleased to learn that a number of women by the name of Leandra Nestor were scattered all over Greece and neighboring countries. After piecing together the name, she'd spent the next few weeks building a reasonable background. Date of birth, hometown, early schooling, orphanage years, an unremarkable adolescence and so on. The details she chose were compiled using real histories and demographics of Greek women with the same or similar names whom she'd located on various dating and personal websites, blogs, and one webcast. The latter had also been helpful in practicing her Greek, which she'd not spoken regularly in almost fifteen years. Once her committee had gone over the details and ironed out the oddities and inconsistencies, the information was sent over to *The Aenamaia's* technical team headed by Osiro who then set about impregnating the Internet and three-dozen government and civilian databases with the Grecian tourist whose name translated as "the traveling lion woman."

Looking down at her bracelet, Tzaria smiled. She'd been pleased with the name and personality. So much so that if all went well, she would consider replacing her current assumed name Tzaria with one that reminded her of better, simpler times. When her family had been forced to leave Greece, her father had whispered to her, "You can never go back again child." He'd forced a smile then added, "But your mind is your domain alone. And there, you can visit and live anywhere you want." During hard times, Tzaria had found enough comfort in that idea to get her through. And when she tired of contemplating existence, her mind would sweep her away over the ocean, back to the seaside towns of southern Greece. And she would again feel at peace, if only for a moment.

Unfortunately, Tzaria knew it unlikely she'd find much peace here. The tension building throughout her body confirmed that much. Once she'd accomplished her mission, Virginia Beach would be one place she'd be unlikely to visit again. Hence the reason for the early start today. She'd spent the last week shadowing her target, verifying his movements matched the recon she'd been provided. So far the man had been right on queue every hour of every day, though keeping up with him had been more difficult than she'd expected. The self-proclaimed New Millennia Voice of God, sent to earth to speak to the Lord's children and provide the righteous a proper path to eternal salvation, moved about like a hyperactive pinball, bouncing from office to office, TV studio to corporate board room – even to the racing track on occasion. For a man who convinced millions of people every Sunday that the days of Armageddon would soon begin, he spent an inordinate amount of time protecting and growing his billion dollar net worth.

Over the course of the last twenty years, Gordian Iman William Robinson, known to his friends and fans as "Gipper," had risen from a simple Baptist preacher to the wealthiest and most powerful Christian Televangelist in America. Through her research Tzaria had learned a great deal – not only about the numerous sources of his wealth, but also the jagged and shadowed path that had led to power. It had been a painful and mind-numbing experience that at times had threatened to overwhelm her. On one occasion she'd found herself standing at her front door, coat and gloves on, carrying a fully loaded rifle case in one hand and an explosive kit in the other.

Robinson's dossier was open on her desk, the address of his mansion highlighted. Slowly, she'd set down the two cases and looked out of the spy hole in her door. Half expecting to see Gray looking back at her, all she saw was the lights from the houses across the street. But in her mind she saw something else – the highways and byways that could take her to Virginia Beach by car in just under eight hours. All she had to do was get in her car, start it up, and drive. In less than a day she was certain she could take care of Robinson once and for all and be on her way home well before anyone knew what had happened. Only then could she purge her mind of all that she knew. The dirty money, the children, the adultery, extortion, countless bribes to businesses and government personnel, and worst of all – millions upon millions of hopeful, needy minds drinking the black poison spewed forth by the wretched man and his army of brainwashed disciples.

She'd stood there facing the front door for what seemed like an eternity, weighing her options. Was she ready to go it alone? Without the help and support of *The Aenamaia*? Did she really think she could pull it off on her own? She wondered if they would try and stop her. Of course they would. And what would she accomplish? Separation from the only real family she'd known since her mother and father had passed away. *The Aenamaia* might very well take her back, but what did that matter when she knew she'd never be able to face any of them again. Was it worth it? Even with *The Aenamaia's* full support, sticking to the plan as it was would cost her plenty. Could she risk everything she cared about just to expedite the demise of a man for whom she only held contempt? "What was the cost?" she'd thought. "What was the cost?"

Tzaria pondered that same question now as she stared across the street at the white and gray-haired man standing next to the pearl white stretch limousine. "Well, well, well," she said to herself, "The Gipper hath cometh."

Just then her cell phone rang. She touched the screen and put the phone to her ear. "Yia Sou Oculus. Ti kanis?"

"I'm fine," Osiro answered. "But alas, ala then milao Elinika."

"But you *are* speaking Greek, Dear Boy," she replied, still keeping her gaze fixed on Robinson.

"I only know how to say, 'I don't speak Greek.' Beyond that I'm limited to the menu items at the local Gyros café."

Despite the intense feelings of anticipation she felt, Tzaria smiled. "Well, we'll have to work on that. I assume you're calling because you see what I see."

"Almost," Osiro added in his dry manner, "I see you and the look on your face. So in a manner of speaking, yes, I see what you see."

"Apollyon stands next to his chariot. Praetorians have already gone inside. They'll wait in the lobby until the master is satisfied."

"As the story tells. At half past the apex the carnal appetites of Apollyon are satiated. Artemis the great female warrior must be in place and ready to hunt."

Tzaria's jaw tightened momentarily. She relaxed, took a deep breath, and then said, "Okay. Enough with the mythology talk. Is the line secure?"

"I never utter a word unless," Osiro said, a small trace of condescension in his voice.

Normally Tzaria thoroughly enjoyed a good vocal sword fight with Osiro, but she knew there was a schedule to keep. She hadn't gotten all dolled-up just to miss her chance.

Osiro must have sensed her mood and asked, "Are you sure you're ready to go in there?"

"Yes," she said firmly, "I've waited a long time for this. I'm not going to sit on my ass and stew for another week."

The line was silent for a moment. "Cold, methodical, and *im-personal*," Osiro said. "Hate, passion and anger cloud judgment. All the work you've done won't do you much good if you aren't alive to enjoy the result."

"Cold," she echoed.

"Sub-zero," he confirmed. "Contact's name is Reginald. He's a simple, devout and pious Christian follower...with gambling, drug and drinking problems. Loading dock, money, smile, name, stairwell. The recording for the radio spot will only take an hour. When you're in the reverend's private suite, dial me up and keep the phone nearby. I'll be your ears."

"My own guardian angel?" she said nervously.

"Something like that. Above all else, remember the panic alert hanging around his neck. If he senses trouble and activates the alert, the odds of your getting out safely are not favorable. Grab it, give the Gipper his due, and kick-start the chase."

"I understand. The alert is the rabbit. The Praetorians, the dogs. Dogs chase rabbit while Caesar's ultimate beliefs are proved right or wrong in the span of a moment."

"You're ready. Get moving, Leandra," Osiro said, "and be careful."

Tzaria hung up the phone and sighed. "Osiro doesn't know," she thought. They were all deceivers to some degree, but never between each other. She hated the feeling the deception brought. She felt dirty, like she hadn't bathed in weeks. But it was necessary. *The Aenamaia* wouldn't condone her decision. Perhaps that was as it should be. She would bear the burden alone. And should her gambit prove successful, she'd gladly accept all the credit. Assuming they ever spoke to her again. Reward never came without risk. And one could never live life to the fullest by denying the possibility that death was around every corner.

Movement across the street caught her eye. She watched as a well-dressed man burst through the front door of the Hilton Virginia Beach Oceanfront hotel and made a beeline for Robinson. The man wore a formal three-piece black suit with gold embroidery that made Tzaria think of a turn-of-the-century banker or oil tycoon. Even from across the street, Tzaria could tell that the tall, lanky man was either flamingly gay or an unusually flamboyant heterosexual – her file had a question mark on that point. She'd guess the former. Though Reverend Robinson publicly scorned homosexuality and damned all gays, it was well known that many of the people he did business with and employed had to be quietly tolerated by Grande Nuevo Messiah. One of a host of hypocritical notches on the Second Comings' flaming sword.

The man in question was Preston Morton, one of Robinson's most trusted marketing and PR advisors. Morton's primary role was to ensure everything Robinson did or said to the public or his constituency was custom-crafted to deliver the appropriate message. Regulating what comes out of another man's mouth is a tough job – even when it wasn't a radical, racist, sexist evangelical preacher. Morton's job was made all the more difficult by the demonstrated fact that Robinson's mouth, like so many other televangelists, had a tendency to say whatever it damn well pleased. The Internet was full of ridiculous claims, quotes and predictions that Tzaria was certain never appeared on any of Morton's queue cards. Nevertheless, Morton was always on hand to ensure that at least the pre-recorded messages were both accurate and poignant.

As soon as the two men had disappeared into the hotel lobby, the stretch limousine pulled away from the curb and exited onto Atlantic Avenue to find a parking space in a nearby lot, where she knew it would stay until summoned. This weekly event was one of the few times the Gipper did not keep a precise schedule. Surveillance notes had shown he could be in his expensive hotel suite anywhere from a half hour to three hours. Tzaria recalled feeling sick when she'd learned the variance often coincided with the number of young ladies who showed up for what one of them quoted the Reverend as having called "spiritual penetration." Today there would be only one other occupant in the Gipper's suite, one in desperate need of enlightenment and freedom from mental bondage.

Tzaria took a deep breath, turned on her digital camera, and began walking towards the side of the hotel. Every so often she would stop and snap a picture or two. "Keep in character," she kept thinking. "Greek tourist. Signomi, ala then milao Iglezika," she whispered to herself. "Sorry, I don't speak English. 'Dumb Greek tourist,'" she thought with a grin. Keep it light. Focus on the plans...both of them.

"Reverend!" Preston shouted as he spotted Robinson getting into the elevator.

Robinson pressed the button for the top floor, then watched with amusement as the shiny elevator doors closed a moment before Preston Morton could reach them. The familiar look of frustration and veiled anger on Preston's face always made him chuckle. It seemed that man was always a few steps behind him. Every week that dimwitted fairy tried to control what he said during the recording session – to steer his words into the middle of the road and keep them there, an endeavor that usually failed.

True, he willingly employed Morton and paid him handsomely for his services. And when it came to enriching dialogue with delicately crafted half-truths that sounded honest and factual, Preston was first-rate. Around the office he was referred to as the Forked Silver Tongue, a title he'd more than earned. So much so that G.W. Bush's people had tried on several occasions to tempt Preston away from his ministry. But just like every follower and member of his constituency, Preston was even more interested in eternal salvation and forgiveness for his many trespasses than he was in money and material possessions.

Unfortunately, even after years of service, the man still failed to understand what was necessary in order to build an evangelical empire. People don't pony up money they can't afford to lose in order to pay for anything in *the middle*. They needed a regularly scheduled dosage of his special blend of fear, divine justice, deliverance from evil – and most importantly, a phone book-sized catalog of people to blame for all of their own inequities, doubts, and insecurities. Feed them that cocktail, build the addiction, and they'll gladly dig deeper than the well runs. He recalled what Reverend Falwell had told him one night over a decanter of twelve-year old Scotch: "Empower the masses with judgment and righteousness and there's no end to how much they'll bleed for you." Poor bastard, that Falwell. Jimmy brought the fire and brimstone, but despite his own advice, he never quite learned how to truly bleed the flock. Sure he had a huge following, but his business skills were for shit. Poor, dumb bastard.

The elevator chimed, indicating he'd reached the top floor. After a short pause the doors slid open. He stepped into the empty hall and headed for his corner suite. Thoughts of Falwell receded, replaced by warm recollections of the fiery performance he'd given during the recording session for this evening's broadcast. "This one was solid gold," he thought. He'd been in rare form. The content had been spicy, enough so to give Preston another ulcer, but it didn't matter. By the close of business tomorrow, the day's bankroll would break his all-time record, as would the outcry from the entire gay community. He smiled and laughed. "Thank the Lord for delivering unto my hands the homosexuals," he said to himself, and laughed again. The only way the world could get any better would be if gay men could have abortions. Until such a miracle was bestowed upon him, the controversies he and others like him stirred around homosexuality would fuel the fires of his success for years to come. "And a good thing too," he thought. 9/11 had proved profitable for a spell, but it was a touchy subject with a short lifespan. After 9/11 he'd publicly supported Bush and the war, but that had done little to fuel the fire of righteousness. Evolution had been a good target until those two Intelligent Design idiots Behe and Fuller stepped on their dicks in Dover. What a shambles that had been. He'd gotten one last hurrah in another ulcer-inducing statement condemning the entire town of Dover, but nothing ever came of it. Islam and Muslims had proved profitable for a time, but he'd backed off considerably after Van Gogh's murder in late 2004. "There'd be no glory in getting killed by an angry towel-head," he thought. Martyrdom just wasn't his thing. Best to stay out of the way and let them focus on killing each other. The Lord loves it when Muslims kill each other. It's God's modern-day version of Gladiator.

No, hammering the gays and feminists was his meal ticket. Those topics did well anytime – on the radio, on the 700 Club, at the university. The *where* made no fundamental difference, whereas the *when* was governed by distinct peaks and valleys. Over the years he'd discovered what he termed "fundraising seasonality." Raging against gays and feminists always produced good profits, but he'd notice many years ago that there were patterns in the giving relative to the time of year. At this very moment he had several bright students at the university crunching the numbers. What they had found so far was early spring and late autumn were the most profitable times, though they weren't quite sure why.

He'd shared this revelation on a visit to Jim Bakker while he served time in Rochester, Minnesota. Bakker had noticed a similar trend during his now infamous days of "prosperity theology." Jimmy wagered spring was good because people were piss-mad with cabin fever after the long winter. They were equally pissed in autumn knowing the confinement, cold and cabin fever were about to start again. The explanation coincided with studies he'd read about peak times of depression and anxiety, so maybe Jimmy had nailed it. Like Falwell, Bakker had failed miserably in the business, but Jimmy sure had a unique talent for simplifying complex problems, except of course, his own. Regardless, he and his student researchers would flush out the real answer, then put it to the test. "Gay prosperity," he thought with a chuckle. "Wrong. *My* prosperity."

Still grinning at the irony, Robinson fished out his electronic key and opened the door to his suite. Closing the door behind him, he walked absently past the security panel into the tile foyer, removed his jacket coat and hung it on the coat stand. The elation he'd felt after the recording session was starting to wear off. If he was to be ready for his weekly visitors, he'd better have a pick-me-up before popping his magic performance pills. Last week he'd almost lost his rigidity before wearing out that young Asian girl. He'd made a note to up his dosage slightly this week, as he'd been promised two new pristine Russian imports for tonight.

The appetites he satisfied once a week came at a high price. Absolute secrecy was paramount. If he were ever caught, the weakness of the flesh and the influence of Satan could always be tapped to help soften the blow, but time and history had proven this to be a one-time fallback only – one usually followed by sizeable damages and a lot of back-peddling and groveling. Best to keep that ace for a real calamity. That's where Haggard came in. Robinson had been extremely careful in selecting a single individual to handle procurement, delivery, and to manage the young girls and boys when he was finished with them. Most were foreign. The ones he was a little rough with were always sent back to their home countries. The others were never aware of who the man in the dark had been. And with rare exceptions, most never came back for a repeat visit. Haggard was thorough and methodical. He had a clever system for getting his prizes in and out of the suite and hotel with no unwanted witnesses, including the youngsters themselves.

Haggard had been resistant in the beginning, but he owed his freedom to Robinson, who could easily put him back in prison for life. Robinson had called in a huge favor, and Haggard knew it. After a few months of smooth sailing and even smoother cash payments, Haggard had relaxed into the role. Even commenting on how much he enjoyed the weekly challenges of finding quality stock, coordinating delivery and return, and covertly exporting those who couldn't be allowed to stay. The lingo was always business-like, never specific or personal. Names were never spoken. Anyone who managed to tap and record a call would think Robinson was paying for cigars, cognac, rugs, artwork, delicacies, etc. In one instance Haggard had referred to a young Roman boy who'd come all the way from Vatican City as a "sweet and tender ivory cherub statue sent with best wishes by the College of Cardinals." That had given him a good laugh. And oh, how sweet the boy had been.

Thoughts of the young boy made his mouth water and he realized how parched he was. He walked into the large living area and made his way towards the crystal glasses and carafe next to the large plasma screen. He was again thinking of his radio speech when he saw something out of the corner of his eye that caught his attention. Something was odd. He stared at the plasma, the bookshelf, the entertainment center...and then he saw it. The wall on the far side of the plasma was bare. It took him a moment to realize what was supposed to be hanging in the space. It was the large wooden crucifix, given to him by Oliver O'Grady as a thank-you before he fled to Ireland. Robinson had been instrumental in persuading the prison parole board to release the now infamous pedophile and had quietly helped finance his one-way trip to Ireland. The priest had returned the favor by sending him an authentic Irish crucifix that had once hung in the Cathedral of the Assumption in Thurles. O'Grady had never explained how he'd come by the three-foot tall cross, and Robinson had thought it best not to ask.

But now it was gone. Must've been those damn cleaning people. He could feel the blood rush to his face. Last month they'd forgotten to dust. Two weeks ago they'd failed to re-hang his painting of Mr. Rob, the half-million dollar thoroughbred colt he'd purchased a few years back. Now they'd removed his antique crucifix. "A hell-worthy trespass," he thought angrily. One he'd be sure to mention on his next show. In the meantime, he needed to be sure it wasn't here and that it had in fact been stolen. "Maybe those stupid spics put it in the bedroom," he thought wryly.

He was about to head for the bedroom when something occurred to him. The alarm tone hadn't sounded when he'd walked in. Normally the security panel beeped until he entered his eight-digit pin to silence it. Rage welled in him as he realized the cleaning people had also failed to re-arm the alarm when they left. He would have someone's head on a platter before the day was done. First he would locate his crucifix, then he would bury it in some illegal's useless, empty skull.

Before Robinson could turn towards the bedroom he felt a sharp blow to the back of his neck. The pain spread through his body with explosive, debilitating speed. It was like a controlled demolition blast tearing through his structure, weakening bones and muscles. Unable to support his own weight, he fell to his knees, barely noticing the unyielding granite tile. He tried to yell but the electric pain shooting out from the top of his spine prevented him from making a sound. The muscles in his body constricted, followed by a wave of nausea and dizziness. In that moment a thought formed amidst the pain, "He'd just been assaulted in his own suite." At the same instant the realization hit him, something struck him hard on the side of his head. The force of the impact sent his already stunned body crashing into the wall. Having lost control of his faculties, Robinson collapsed onto the hard tile floor and rolled onto his back. Slowly, and with considerable effort, he opened his eyes. Though his vision was blurry from the tears, he could just make out the image of a figure standing over him holding a large cross. His cross. The person carelessly tossed the large crucifix onto the black leather sofa and stared down at him. "It's a woman," he thought. "But why? Who is she?" Before he could utter the question, the woman's foot came down hard on his face and blackness engulfed him.

"Atheism leaves a man to sense, to philosophy, to natural piety, to laws, to reputation, all which may be guides to an outward moral virtue, though religion were not; but superstition dismounts all these, and erects an absolute monarchy in the minds of men...the master of superstition is the people; and arguments are fitted to practice, in a reverse order."

Gordian Iman William Robinson was frozen in an abstract and indescribable darkness. The quote, one he'd used many times in his sermons hammering on atheists and secular humanists, seemed to hang before him in a kind of vague, watery limbo. The words, uttered by one of the earliest known godless heathens, Sir Francis Bacon, now seemed to embody a consciousness. There was form here. Intent. Purpose. Though what it might all mean was lost on Robinson, whose own consciousness struggled to discern basic reality. Half of his mind was convinced this was simply a dream taking place in a dark, solitary room somewhere. The other half suspected the situation was much worse. The darkness was terrifying, though he wasn't sure why. The pitch-black space offered no warmth, light, orientation, and most importantly, no options. The place that time and space had forgotten. He felt cramped and immobile, almost claustrophobic. No dreams or calming images would come to him. His normal sense of God and his own divinity was gone. It was as if existence itself had vanished – or had been permanently supplanted, leaving only nothingness in its place. And still, the conscious quote was there – living, breathing, waiting, and looking down on him with disdain. It was alive. Judgmental. Unforgiving. But could it be real? What was happening to him? How had he come to be trapped in a void, alone with only these blasphemous words like a heavy weight burdening his blind self? "No," he thought. He was not alone. He was certain of it. There was someone or something there. He could taste its acridity. Close. Yes, very close now.

And then everything changed in a flash. Sensation overwhelmed his thoughts. The dark room receded and vanished into oblivion, replaced by an awareness of tightness, a feeling of constriction. Numbness. Before the haze faded completely, another wave broke over him. This time the darkness vanished, replaced by bright light. It was sunlight. Robinson gasped desperately, clawing towards consciousness. Through sheer will and concentration he slowly forced his heavy eyes to open. The brightness was acute, and his eyelids clamped down tightly. Spots bounced animatedly around his vision. He was shivering. It was then that he realized he was cold and wet. His breaths came in short fits as his body worked to deliver heat to the gelid and wet areas. After a few seconds he slowly opened his eyes and tried to focus. White and blue filled his vision. Clouds above an endless expanse of deep blue water. It was the ocean. Recognition dawned and his heartbeat quickened. He knew that horizon. It was his panorama. One he'd paid a lot of money to have at his disposal. Relief at the familiar sight quickly faded as he recalled what he'd sensed before the cold and shivers. He couldn't move…and someone was near.

"Good afternoon, Reverend," said a mild voice. "Or should I call you Bill?"

It was a woman. He tried to turn towards the voice, but found he was unable to move. What was happening? Anger welled up inside him. He shouted, "What in the hell is going on here!" but the words were muffled. Several things occurred to him at once: he was sitting down, something was across his mouth preventing him from speaking, and he was unable to move his arms and legs. In an instant his anger vanished, replaced by a gripping panic.

The woman seemed to sense what he was thinking. "I figured a mouthpiece like you would start screaming like a little girl as soon as you woke up. Thank God for duct tape." The woman's voice was serious and yet also sarcastic and playful. Robinson tried to shout again, but all that came out was a low, indiscernible string of gibberish.

"Must be strange for the 'Right Hand of God' to find himself bound and gagged, as helpless as say…a confused twelve year old Vietnamese girl?" An unmistakable razor's edge laced the woman's voice. "Or maybe two eleven year old boys from Vatican City sent here to 'study' under your expert tutelage?" Robinson could tell the woman was pacing behind him as she spoke.

"And what did they learn, Reverend? Did they feel the touch of God? Or were those simply your perverted, eager hands? Did they find anything different here than all the other children? Or the prostitutes? What about the few who left without bruises and cuts? Did they leave with their faith intact? Well? You sick, seditious fucker!"

Robinson was about to protest when a heavy object struck the back of his neck. He groaned in pain, though the tape over his mouth muted the sound. The next moment he caught sight of something dark out of the corner of his eye a split second before it struck his side. The Reverend heard a dull crack as the object impacted his ribs. Moisture welled in his eyes an instant before the terrible pain hit. He let out another involuntary series of low, muffled howls. The tears streamed down his face. He half expected to taste the saltiness, but the duct tape prevented the liquid from reaching his lips. Instinctively he tried to buckle forward only to find his torso was locked in an upright position. He groaned again as a new onslaught of pain and nausea swept over him.

The flow of time governing Robinson's life seemed to stand still. In the span of a few moments, his whole world had contracted. Every minute of his existence now was committed exclusively to breathing through the thick streams of pain flowing from his neck and ribs. Bouncing around his mind was a potent mixture of mortal terror and the most profound feelings of regret he had ever experienced. Though ironically, the focus of the regret was having been caught off guard.

As the country's most popular televangelist and spokesman for God, he had many enemies. Over the years he'd dedicated significant funds and resources to keeping him safe from those who would silence the country's most beloved spiritual voice. Security and surveillance systems, a team of bodyguards, thin next-generation Kevlar vests for public appearances, even a Walther PPK he kept in a custom-made lower back holster. Through the fog of pain, Robinson suddenly wondered if he still had the pistol with him. Carefully he shuffled around in his chair trying to see if he could feel the weight of the gun and holster, but he couldn't be sure. Just then something caught his eye. Through the blurry tears he noticed several items sitting on the windowsill a few feet from where he sat. For a brief moment the pain ebbed, partially replaced by confused curiosity. Blinking rapidly to clear away the tears, Robinson tried to focus his eyes. Like a camera coming into focus, his blurred vision resolved.

Sunlight pouring in through the window illuminated the three evenly placed objects sitting on the windowsill. The reverend's brow knotted as he tried to figure out what he was seeing. On the far left sat a glass vial that resembled a clear CO2 cartridge. The thin container was roughly four inches tall and was filled with a deep blue liquid that reminded him of a rare sapphire he'd once purchased and given to a senator's wife – a luxurious velvet blue that could only impart sophistication and wealth. He'd told the woman the stone was the exact color of God's eyes. The line had been a means to an end, but staring at the vial now, he wondered if it could be true. He wondered how soon he might see for himself.

With some difficulty Robinson stole his gaze from the beautiful translucent liquid and noticed another small glass container to the far right of his field of vision. This vial was shorter than the other. It was about the size of a D battery, with a similar cylindrical shape, and it was filled with an opaque, milky white liquid. A label stuck to the glass ampule displayed an ominous black biohazard symbol, which Robinson had always thought looked like a symbol for the devil. At this moment, something told him he just might be right about that.

Sitting between the two glass vials with the barrel pointed in his direction was his silver and black double-action Walther PPK. Robinson had no way of knowing for sure, but he felt certain the gun's magazine was full. He always kept it loaded, something he immediately regretted doing.

A second wave of pain fired through his body. Reverend Robinson winced, then coughed awkwardly. The duct tape kept the expelled fluid from escaping which caused him to gag and cough again. This time saliva and mucus shot out of his nose. The feeling disgusted him but he fought back the impulse to cough again.

"Kind of pathetic for a man who once called himself 'Christ Incarnate'." The woman was close, speaking quietly into his ear. "Ironic that God's Right Hand can't use his own right hand to wipe snot and spit from his face."

Robinson tried again to yell through the tape, but nothing discernible came out. He heard the woman's quiet footsteps as she walked out of the room. Concentrating all of his strength, the reverend struggled against his bonds. The chair rocked back and forth as he growled and fought, but he could not get free. The effort reinvigorated the pain in his neck and ribs, forcing him to stop. Breathing hard through his nose, he tried to think of what to do next, but no practical ideas materialized.

Soft footsteps sounded behind him, announcing the woman's return. Without a word, a towel was thrust roughly into his face, shimmying back and forth. The reverend resisted the temptation to pull his head back and in a moment his now-raw face was relatively clean and dry.

"Uggh. Disgusting," he heard the woman grumble. She threw the towel on the windowsill next to the vial containing the blue liquid. Alarm rang out in Robinson's mind as he noted several dark red spots on the white towel. It was then that he noticed a bitter, acrid taste in his mouth. The woman also noticed the spots. "Funny, I was sure your blood would be black. Or even coward yellow. Perhaps you are human after all. Try not to stress about it, Reverend. Coughing up a little blood should be the least of your concerns. Your life is about to take a very drastic and wholly poetic turn." Her tone was dark, cold and derisive. And Robinson believed every word.

"Whether you like it or not," she said, her voice now businesslike, "we both know the full extent of your...trespasses. Oh yes, I'm quite familiar with the life you've tried so hard to keep in the shadows. It would be impressive if it weren't so revolting. One could be forgiven for thinking you must be some perverted, amoral atheist – an aberration as atheists go, but a non-believer, nonetheless."

Robinson growled a response but she shushed him dismissively.

"How else to explain your behavior? How could a man like you believe in a judgmental God along with the fiery biblical hell of the Old Testament, and still do the terrible things you do? When I first started researching you, I chalked it up to the same delusional, narcissistic, holier-than-thou perspective religious leaders have historically used to justify the atrocities they committed. Somewhere in the world, way back in the day, the first of these scourges convinced himself that he had been ordained, and more importantly *empowered* by God to do His will. The next step in the thought process was obvious and, in many ways... inevitable. He determined that if God had a plan, and God worked His will through him, then he could do no wrong – for any actions he took, no matter how wicked or atrocious, must constitute the precise Will of God. Why else would God not stay his hand? Prevent the heinous event from happening? And suddenly, the world was his for the raping. That was until the next self-ordained idiot came along and challenged him."

Robinson could tell the woman was again pacing back and forth behind him while she spoke.

"I thought for sure you had acquired that same delusion, but I was wrong. The more I learned, the more I realized you were too smart for that. Your business sense, financial savvy, even the strategic nature of your weekly attacks, all pointed towards someone rooted in the reality of the world. The majority of your predecessors were different. They shot the delusion directly into their veins, all the while ignoring reality. And in most cases, reality eventually tore them down. Most of your contemporaries have either fallen or are on their way down. But you are different. Not only is your head above the water, but no part of you even gets wet." The woman snickered then added, "Until now." He glanced down and noticed the water stains on his shirt and slacks.

"You'll have to forgive the ice water, but I was getting tired of waiting for you to wake up. I must say though, Father O'Grady's generous gift made one hell of a good bludgeon. Really a remarkable piece of sculpture, though I'm normally not a fan of crosses. After I broke in and silenced the alarm with your personal pin code," the woman paused to let that little tidbit sink in, "I took a look around. As soon as I saw it hanging on the wall, I instantly knew what I wanted to do. Call it an epiphany," she said with amusement in her voice. "Of course, I could've just used my handy metal pipe, but I just couldn't resist the delicious irony of hitting a crooked televangelist preacher with a perfectly proportioned, stolen sixteenth-century wood crucifix. Yes, stolen. O'Grady filched that cross from a basement storage room in the Cathedral of the Assumption. I swear there was no limit to that man's psychosis. It's amazing the things you can learn from a shaking, pedantic pedophile with a shotgun shoved under his chin. The confessions we got were twice as disturbing as those in John Manly's deposition. Of course, a man getting ready to chew on the barrel of a shotgun will probably say anything to stay alive. That's why we made him do it three times. Over the course of a week we got the same sick confession over and over again, the details never changed. Neither did his incontinence."

He felt her breath on the back of his neck as she whispered, "I wonder what tales you could tell us. I'm almost sorry I didn't bring the shotgun." She stood and took a few steps. Robinson heard a chair being dragged across the tile.

"O'Grady was a confessed pedophile and rapist, and yet the church continued to ignore what he had done. Even after he managed to leave California unscathed, the church still would not get involved. Disgusting, don't you think?"

The reverend could see O'Grady's gaunt face in his mind. It had been some time since he'd heard from the unfortunate fool. And though he was curious to know what they'd done to him, right now his sole concern was his own hide.

"I know almost everything about you, Reverend," the woman said casually. "And there's a lot. I studied everything available online and in print. I spoke to family members, friends, colleagues, even a few other religious men who feel you're just too big and popular for your own good. Of course, that's merely their way of showing disdain while trying to mask their envy. *Envy*," she repeated, as if tasting the word. "Sin number six, if I remember correctly. *Invidia* in Latin. Do you recall what Dante said about Envy, Monsignor Robinson? He said envy was 'love of one's own good perverted to a desire to deprive other men of theirs.' Sounds like a winning premise for televangelism to me. But then how can I know for sure that's your recipe for success when you've got several deadly sins under your belt? In fact, aside from Sloth, I'd say you're batting a thousand on the sins. But," the woman said, her voice now enthusiastic, "what all this really comes down to is priorities and choice, right?" She slapped him hard on the back causing him to cough. "Well, here's your chance."

Robinson's chair was pushed forward until his knees pressed against the low wall beneath the window sill. Before him sat the two vials and his gun.

"My job, Mr. Robinson, was to sneak in here and end your life. No pain, no punishment, no choice. Deliver your judgment with no remorse, no absolution, nor call for shrift. I was to simply open the door to the great unknown and shove your fat ass through it. But the more I read about you, the more I realized that there was a more...poetic option. One designed to offer a choice in lieu of death. And isn't it always better to choose for yourself rather than have someone do it for you? My thinking exactly!"

"Now, the vial on the left contains a fast-acting, painless, and thoroughly untraceable poison. The vial on the right contains a particularly virulent strain of the Human Immunodeficiency Virus or HIV. You remember HIV don't you? Back in the early 90s a number of televangelists, including yourself, praised the arrival of HIV, saying it was a clear sign that God was punishing the evil sodomists. You tried to scare the religious right out of their minds and their wallets with predictions that God would spread HIV to supporters of gays and gay rights. 'The Lord will strike down even the most pious men for lending support to the Godless homosexuals.' I believe that's how you worded it," she said derisively. "A few years later you maggots realized HIV had infected all manner of persons – men, women, and children alike. So you backed off for a while. That was until the angle changed. One of your many epiphanies. You told your flock that God himself had revealed to you and you alone the secret behind HIV. It had started out as his weapon to slay the Godless homosexuals, but the Devil himself had gotten hold of this weapon and was using it against everyone. Then you managed to turn all the wrong-doing back on the homosexuals. Suddenly it was they who were responsible for everyone else's misery. They had incurred the wrath of God and had wound up bringing pain and suffering to the innocents. You'd come full circle, through a delicate issue, and still managed to blame it all on the gays. Both clever and utterly disgusting." The woman's voice dropped to a low, menacing growl. "The lowest act from the lowest life form."

The reverend felt his pulse rising again. Anger fought through the strong currents of pain and queasiness, landing squarely behind his eyes. This little whore had assaulted and insulted him and had now graduated to outright judgment of his actions. No woman on earth was allowed to judge him. The inferior sex had always been too imperfect and impure to hear the true voice of the Lord God. To know His will. That's why men continued to lead the church to this day. How dare she! With renewed determination he began struggling again, this time trying to overturn his chair. Perhaps if he fell over, the chair would break and he could get loose. But the woman was no fool. She sat patiently behind him, her foot on the rear support bar. After thrashing about for almost a minute, he gave up. Sweat beaded on his brow and he breathed hard through his nostrils.

"You really are a slow learner, aren't you?" the woman said mockingly. "As I was saying, life is all about choice. And now it's your turn to make one." For a few thoughtful moments she was silent. "Before I leave here," she said with a sigh, a tiny hint of resignation in her voice, "you will receive an injection of fluid. *Which* injection is entirely up to you."

The woman stood, took hold of his chair and slowly pulled him away from the window. The huge expanse of ocean that had filled his view was reduced to a thin horizon of blue resting on the silver window frame. The reverend heard soft footfalls and watched as his captor made her way to the window sill. She was turned away from him and appeared to be examining the vials and his gun. Robinson suddenly realized he still had not seen this foul woman's face. Now all he could see was a slender body dressed in casual, every-day clothing. He felt something akin to disappointment. He'd imagined a tight black leather suit. Or something reminiscent of a Bond girl – long flowing hair, mildly European features, light skin, and holding some kind of oversized weapon – maybe even a motorcycle helmet. Instead, what he saw was a secretary out for a casual day of shopping. How had this woman managed to assault and bind him?

The woman turned to face him. Robinson was shocked to see the plainly dressed woman was stunningly beautiful. Smooth alabaster skin with a hint of tan, claret red lips, strong cheekbones with no blush, cinnamon hair pulled back and intense brown eyes that now seemed to be studying him from beneath an unwrinkled brow. Despite all of his suffering, he felt instantly aroused.

The reverend's eyes narrowed as he tried to memorize the details of her face, her clothing, everything. If he managed to get out of this situation alive, any information he could provide the authorities would help in her capture. His eyes slowly scanned his captor from the face down. It was then that he noticed the rubber gloves. The sight confused him. What did it mean? No fingerprints. Was that it, or had this evil woman been even more meticulous in her assault? What if she didn't leave any evidence of her presence? Would the authorities or the press even believe him? Without proof, his story would sound crazy. They may decide to search the whole place looking for proof and wind up finding things he'd kept safely hidden.

Robinson tried to think logically, but his mind was bogged down with the pain signals his body was still sending. "Gloves," he thought with a mental nod, "Certainly a lot of calculation and patience." She obviously knew a great deal about him, which meant time and research. His eyes widened slightly as one word appeared in his brain: premeditated. Preparations, timing, planning. Up until this point, he'd assumed this was just another angry woman intent on extorting money, as several others had. But as he continued to stare wide-eyed at the rubber gloves, the dark and dire reality of the situation hit him almost as hard as the wooden cross had.

The woman noticed his gaze and with a sly grin slowly flexed the fingers of her gloved left hand. Their eyes met briefly. In that moment, in those intense brown eyes, the reverend saw confirmation of his worst suspicions. For the first time since he'd regained consciousness, he realized he might never leave this place alive. His body tensed with fear and anxiety as a single question loomed over him: Am I going to die today?

The woman watched him for another few seconds, then apparently making up her mind, held up the two vials. "If you choose the blue vial, you will be dead within minutes, but you have my word that your ministry will remain intact with no hint of scandal. All your transgressions and evils will die with you. You may even achieve instant martyrdom. Perhaps the so-called Christian Nation's faith will be galvanized by your passing. But make no mistake, you'll be as dead as a door nail. Of course if you truly believe that which you preach, then who better to arrange for the world's second great resurrection than the Right Hand of God himself?"

She lowered the blue vial and shifted her attention to the other one. She held the vial aloft and studied it for a moment, tipping it from side to side, as if something of its power could be seen at just the right angle. When she finally spoke, her attention was still focused on the small vial.

"If you choose option B, you have a chance to live on. You may be lucky enough to be a carrier of HIV, but to live for years and years without ever developing AIDS. Even if you do get AIDS, perhaps all your wealth and power might be channeled towards research and development of medicines – or even a cure. However," the woman leaned closer to him, "when your followers and board members learn you've contracted HIV, they'll abandon you with the utmost haste. All your years of preaching of the divine plan for HIV and AIDS will come back to bury you.

Additionally, I will personally unleash a deluge of damning and condemning virulent emails, blog posts, and Tweets, spewing forth in every social medium I can find. It will be a shit storm the likes of which the internet has never seen, seemingly confirming the Lord's punishment that has been bestowed upon you.

Lastly, I will publish every bit of research I have on you. Articles, photographs, private interviews, hour upon hour of incriminating recorded conversations, tax returns, O'Grady's full confession, and of course, a documentary-style release starring twenty of the children and young teens to whom you've provided 'sexual enlightenment'. *Everything* will be fair game, Reverend. Once all the shit hits the fan, it's doubtful anyone will even consider the possibility that someone broke into your private, guarded suite and injected you with HIV. When the waters are that chummed up, the sharks don't spare a moment to consider anything inconsequential. They have no desire to see through the delicious crimson cloud. They want only to feed."

Just then the woman's expression changed and a faint smirk creased her lips. Her eyes locked onto him. She appeared to be considering something. After a moment she gave a resolute shrug and said, "Poor little Billy. There must be so much conflict and turmoil festering in that conniving, demented little brain of yours right now. What to do? What to do? Well, I'm going to help you out. I'm going to tell you something that only a few other people know. The group that sanctioned your execution is called *The Aenamaia*. Before I joined *The Aenamaia*, I made it a point to – how shall we say, *freelance* – in a similar line of work.

"I investigated vermin like you on my own time. I watched, I listened, I researched, I questioned. It's really quite amazing how much information you can obtain if you have the guts and confidence to ask. I learned a great deal. I tell you this because your good friend Ted Haggard was my first serious project. I'm the one who discovered his homosexual infidelity, though I never took any credit for it." She watched with satisfaction as surprise and incredulity swept across his face. "The answer to your unspoken question is also the reason behind my telling you this. I confronted him with the proof of his disastrous and blatantly hypocritical transgressions. I gave him a choice, as well. He could choose a quick and painless death and all would be forgotten, or he and his wife and his followers could live with the disgrace his duplicitous and nefarious deeds would reap. At the time, I was a tad more compassionate than I am now and therefore did not infect him with HIV. Instead, I told him that should he choose the path of humiliation, he would have to agree to never again be involved with organized religion. No preaching or teaching of anything related to religion. That was the deal. The whole world now knows what his decision was, though no one knew he was given a choice. He consciously chose to put his family, friends and followers through public shame and ignominy – to flush any credibility and dignity he once had. 'How does such a man stand erect, when within his body the spine is absent?'"

The woman exhaled deeply and began pacing. "Cowardly though it was, I upheld my end of the bargain and let him live. I set events in motion and took a back seat while the flames of indignity raged. And though he was forced to endure it, he was nevertheless alive, as we'd agreed. However," she said, her voice growing darker, "I recently learned that he is not keeping to our agreement. He's building a new church and attracting a new congregation. Perhaps he thought because he'd not seen or heard from me in years that he was in the clear, that I forgot about him. Well he's wrong. He's dead wrong. This time there will be no negotiations or deals. They'll find his body in a dumpster, his blood chock full of strychnine or tetrodotoxin – and a note in his hand that reads, 'Teddy has been a bad boy.' But I digress." The woman stared out the expansive window for a few long moments, then returned her attention to her bound and gagged subject.

"And so with you, Robby, I decided there would be no outs – no room to renege on our deal. If you choose to live, you'll do so with much greater disgrace and loss than Haggard, but with one of the world's deadliest viruses coursing through your thick, black veins. Or you can simply go to sleep. Forever. Now all that's left is for you to decide is which path to choose. The path of the righteous man or the path of the red-handed thief?"

The woman slowly returned the vials to the windowsill and picked up the handgun. "I suppose the other option would be for me to empty all seven rounds of this gun into strategically-chosen areas of your body.

Then, just as you're about to pass out from the copious loss of blood and the unbearable pain, I'll choose the vial for you."

Robinson watched as the woman expertly handled the gun. First she slid back the hammer and peered into the ejection port. Seeing nothing inside, she released the magazine. Satisfied with what she saw, the woman adroitly shoved the magazine back into the gun and, in one quick motion, pulled back on the slide and chambered a round. Robinson saw her click off the safety. As the woman held up the handgun and aimed towards the far wall, he could see her arm was completely still. She squinted as she took aim, sitting perfectly still.

He recalled that the man who'd sold him the gun had mentioned the unusual calmness and focus common for many female shooters. The man had warned him, "Never enter a shooting match with a woman unless you're a damn good shot." At the time he thought the man was probably just sore over having lost to a female shooter. Now, he wasn't so sure.

Fear spread across the reverend's face as he realized in an instant that this woman was capable of killing him – that was indeed what she had come to do. This was not a joke or an extortion attempt. She'd made no demands. There was no use in trying to talk her out of it, and no chance whatsoever that she was bluffing. There was pure malevolence in those brown eyes, mixed with a calculating and terrifying sense of patience. She would either inject him with one of her poisons or she would happily shoot him seven times, waiting for a few moments between each shot, drinking in the pleasure of watching him bleed and writhe in pain.

Grotesque imagery burst into his mind. He saw himself bleeding, crying, terror filling his eyes as his body gave up the fight. Then death. Unseen flashes burst on all sides as his lifeless, chalk-outlined corpse is photographed over and over again. He could hear the pop of old-fashioned flash bulbs firing in quick succession. He could see his dead body reflect the bright white light for a split second, as if it were pulsing, releasing. Headlines rolled by like a funeral procession professing the end of the Robinson legacy, the 700 Club, his university – all of it gone in an instant. The IRS would investigate his bank accounts and most likely seize his assets. He watched as the scavengers swooped in and pecked at his life's flesh as his body was slowly rolled into the crematorium. Faces of people he knew, people he had used, people whom he openly mocked, all with wide, greedy, thirsty eyes, waiting for their chance to drink of his blood. The images kept coming, each one more terrible than the last. Eager faces, gnashing teeth, his bruised and lifeless body again, the headlines, disillusioned followers committing suicide, and those who feared and hated him dancing merrily in the streets. It was all too much. Heat and sweat engulfed his body. He began to shake, his breaths coming in fits. There was a gripping tightness in his chest.

In a blur of movement the woman reached a gloved hand back and brought it full force across his face. The shock at being slapped so hard momentarily replaced the terror he'd felt only a moment ago. Before the sting in his cheek registered she brought the backside of the same hand across the other side. A torrent of emotions jockeyed for control of his mind, but before one took the lead the woman brought the loaded gun up under his chin. He tried to gasp, but the tape prevented it. He coughed awkwardly, air and more snot shooting out of his nose and onto his sodden silk shirt and tie. As soon as he recovered he felt the gun shoved harder upward and he found himself eye to eye with the woman, her face only inches from his. He felt the heat of her skin and smelled the anxiousness in her scent. And then the terror returned.

"You have one chance to decide for yourself," she said through clenched teeth. "I'll give you sixty seconds to think about it. Then, I'm going to remove the tape from your mouth. All you get to say is 'blue' or 'white'. If you scream, I'll put a bullet through your corrupt little brain. The police will find you lying on the floor with this gun in your hand. After scraping small bits of brain and skull off the ceiling they'll rule it a suicide. Incriminating photographs and audio recordings found stashed in your bedroom will seal the deal. News of your cowardly death and all the other dirt I have on you will have circled the globe twice before they have time to tag your toe and zip up the body bag. You'll be another pudgy, pathetic little religious hypocrite who couldn't bear the scandal he knew was coming and therefore took his own life and would be eternally damned to hell for it. Or," she said with a deliberate pause, "you can tell me which vial has your name on it. Painless death, intact legacy and eternal martyrdom on the left – or life, shame and a crumbled empire on the right? You have sixty seconds to decide, Reverend Robinson. The choice is yours."

New York City, New York

The masked woman's arm swung down and smashed the red button into the side of the truck. An instant later there was a thunderous boom followed immediately by a loud, sustained cracking sound, like lightening tearing through the center of a giant redwood tree. Instinctively, the guard curled into a protective fetal position. The noise was deafening. It sounded like an enormous rocket was lifting off right next to the truck, which was now shaking twice as much as it had when they'd been in motion. Loud, sharp jolts sounded randomly as heavy objects landed on top of the truck or crashed into its side. Thoughts of 9/11 unwittingly coursed through the guard's mind and he felt the tinge of a familiar fear. "Maybe these people are actually terrorists," he thought. Domestic terrorists. Why then go to the trouble of rounding up all these people? Unless they were to be hostages, though for reasons that eluded him, that scenario seemed unlikely.

The rumble continued for what seemed to the guard like several minutes, then finally tapered off. Quietly, he exhaled the breath he was holding and cautiously inhaled. He had expected something to be in the air – the smell of smoke and fire or of chemicals, but there was nothing. Only the heavy, musty smell of a well-used truck that had carried a host of odorous cargos.

There were scared sobs and whimpers from the people on the floor who were starting to shuffle about, but otherwise all was calm. "Status?" the guard heard the woman ask, a hint of apprehension in her voice. He could not see her face, but her voice betrayed the fact that even she had been startled by the violence of the explosion she had initiated.

"Good Neighbor," one of the other men called into a radio, "Do you have a visual? Over."

"Hold," a faint voice said with a heavy Scottish accent, "all we see is smoke."

"Is everyone okay?" the woman asked the passengers.

Before anyone could answer, the radio crackled again, "Boy is my grandma goin' ta be fumin' angry! Bealin as hell, I tell ya."

There was an eruption of hurrahs as each of the black-clad men and the woman embraced each other and exchanged congratulations. This sudden outbreak of joy and emotion stunned the guard and confused the rest of the prisoners. He would later describe the atmosphere as being warm, jovial and friendly.

In a few moments, the woman hushed the celebrants and again spoke into the radio, "Corgi...your grandmother doesn't read *The Star*. Can I assume the other missions were successful?"

"I'd say that's an understatement lassie. *The National Inquirer*, *The Globe*, *The National Examiner*, *The Star*, and *The Sun* will all spend the next six months digging out what's left of their printing presses and delivery trucks. And they'll have to do it without the help of their fearless and soulless leaders."

"What do you mean?" she asked, her voice suddenly serious again.

"We just learned that the CEO and second in command of American Media who owns all these abominations of free speech have gone missing."

"What?" the woman asked, frantically waving a hand to hush the others who were still celebrating. She was obviously taken aback by this news. "One of ours?"

"Gray isn't sure," Corgi said uncertainly, "All of our principals are accounted for, but I hear told there are rumors of a few mavericks in our den. I think we'd best be getting back to the cave to sort this out."

"Roger that. Rendezvous as planned. We'll drop our parcels and head back."

"Aye, we're on our way."

The guard had managed to squirm onto his side and was now looking up at the beautiful, concerned blue eyes behind the black mask. Even with the mask obscuring most of her face, the guard could tell she was scowling. The woman was staring at the floor of the truck, her eyes darting back and forth as if she was trying to catch sight of something important that was eluding her.

One of the men put his hand on her shoulder and whispered something. It took a moment for her to react. When she did, she snapped immediately back into business mode. "I'm okay," she said firmly. "Everyone move out and scatter. This truck is no longer our shelter. Let's move!"

The rest of the men in black moved quickly to the rear of the door and waited. In a few seconds the guard heard a few clinks and clanks as the door was opened from the outside. He could feel a rush of cool air on his face – and this time the air smelled of dust and smoke.

The men jumped down quickly and disappeared from sight. Once they were gone, the guard turned his head again and was surprised to see the woman was now standing only a few feet away. More startling was the fact that she was staring right at him. When their eyes met, she took a few careful steps then knelt down in front of him. The guard could see her eyes were intent and full of purpose, but not unfriendly. He would say later that hers were the eyes of a teacher looking down on a new student.

"You've been watching all of this very carefully, haven't you?" she asked casually, almost playfully.

The guard was still lying on his side, but managed to nod nervously a few times.

She reached behind his head and untied his gag. "What's your name?" she said tilting her head slightly.

He hesitated, and then said quietly, "Venustiano. But everyone calls me Vinnie."

The frightened man saw small wrinkles appear at the corners of her eyes. Even with the mask obscuring most of the woman's face, he was sure she was smiling. The effect was strangely disarming and he relaxed a degree. Her eyes narrowed. She seemed to be studying him. The sensation was not altogether unpleasant, though he still did not trust her intentions. After a few moments she said, "I'm gonna go out on a limb here and guess you were named after Venustiano Carranza Garza, the Mexican revolutionary. Yes?"

Vinnie couldn't suppress his surprise. Despite the fear instilled by the events of the last hour, and in spite of his loathing of violence, he couldn't help but return the smile and nod graciously.

"My parents liked history," he offered.

"So did I – in my former life. I was fascinated by all that history could teach us, should we be open to learning. To me, the relevance and application of history stood out in sharp contrast relative to other disciplines. The study of history almost seemed like a prerequisite for carving out a proper existence. Not so much a blueprint for the future, but certainly a guide to drawing one. But up until that point, the endeavor had been largely academic. Until one day, sitting in the garden of an old estate in Nassau, a good friend convinced me that history was absolutely useless if we didn't learn from it. Useless..." she repeated. "Wouldn't you agree?"

"Yes," Vinnie said with a nod.

"Would you also agree that when it comes to learning from the mistakes of old, that we're very slow learners?"

He nodded and said, "Very slow indeed."

She cocked her head and asked, "Do you think Venustiano Garza was hoping to change history?"

"Yes. And for a time, I believe he succeeded."

"So do I," she said. "Well, Venustiano, it is indeed fortuitous that you were here to witness these events today, for another revolution is at hand. And this one is quite different from anything history can speak of. Since the dawn of written time men like the one you were named after have fought injustice through open violence in the streets. Common men were sent to blindly defend the spineless men who were the real source of all the problems. Innocents killing innocents – men killing men who could have just as easily been lifelong friends. Rarely did the real murderers and rapists ever see justice. Corrupt rulers can keep their power because they manipulate and control other men who are willing to bear arms and die for a paycheck, hollow promises of better times, or an afterlife brimming with mythical and eternal rewards. Only when they lie dying in the streets, terrified almost to the point of insanity and staring up at an ordinary sky do they realize that, were they to do it again, they would immediately lay down their arms and assume a life dedicated to peace and humility. But the message always comes too late. Always too late." Her voice trailed off as she looked around at the other people who were now looking at her, their fear replaced by a rapt curiosity.

"Venustiano," she said, her voice regaining its strength, "It will be your job to report what you have seen here today. You will corroborate what the press and authorities are just now learning – that the buildings housing the printing operations for the major U.S. tabloid newspapers have been leveled, the machinery rendered useless. We did everything in our power to ensure there was no loss of human life in these operations. Only time will tell whether we were successful. This is but one of many steps to come that will eliminate some of the filth that engulfs our country. It is neither our policy nor our wish to be in a position to make demands. Such actions have always proved useless in the face of men with guns defending their ill-gotten wealth and power. In order to convey our message, we have to speak their language. Bring the fight right to their doorsteps."

She leaned in closer to Vinnie's face and said quietly, "Tell them what you have seen and heard. Do not leave anything out. Tell them about the Revolution."

Without pausing the woman stood and walked to the end of the truck. She turned and addressed the people tied to the floor of the truck, "Do not be afraid. This revolution is for the people, not against them. Hopefully someday we'll all think for ourselves and control our own fates, and such rash actions won't be necessary." She paused and added, "Help is on the way. Best of luck to you all."

With that, the woman in black was gone and the truck was sealed back up. Fifteen minutes later police, firemen and EMTs were on-site tending to the hostages and asking questions.

The following morning, Venustiano Ramirez gave a detailed account of the incident to the police and the FBI. The other people in the truck would be questioned as well, but would refer to Vinnie when their memories became vague. The authorities quickly realized only one witness had a consistent and detailed story to tell. Before he'd been allowed to leave, news of the incident had spread beyond the hallowed halls of the FBI offices in New York – along with the name of the storyteller. By the time Vinnie crossed the lobby to exit the building, he'd already received seven offers to appear on TV. Out of nowhere, strange men and women with cameras and microphones were suddenly very interested in him, his life, and the ordeal he'd just survived. Less than twelve hours after he'd watched the strange woman in black hurry away, Vinnie was being asked to appear on a variety of shows and news programs. But for reasons he could not explain at the time, even to himself, Vinnie chose only two programs, one which aired exclusively on PBS, the other on NPR. During one of these interviews the long-time host of the show asked Vinnie why he had declined the offers from the major media, a few of which had offered him a substantial amount of cash.

Vinnie paused, took a deep breath and said, "Although this group... *The Aenamaia*, chose to contact *USA Today* to disclose their intent, I chose PBS because I do not trust the regular media. I believe that these people are on a mission to do something that has never been done before. To take the war directly to the generals and presidents and dictators who see their soldiers as nothing more than numbers on a game board. They want to strike at the black heart of those things which serve to poison and enslave mankind. The tabloid newspapers and the mainstream media make up a large percentage of that poison. They are messengers, if you will, bringing bad things. The mainstream media feed the public with whatever it is the puppeteers want us to believe or what the people are thirsty to consume. They push the agenda of whoever happens to hold their reins. And they've become very good at their work. How else do you think President Bush got re-elected? How is it we saw none of the gruesome imagery after the 'Shock and Awe' bombing of Iraq? How is it most Americans don't realize that anywhere between 85,000 and 1 million Iraqis have died since the start of the war? Did the media not sensationalize the Iraq War – fill our citizens with awe and magical wonder towards our marvelous weapons? Idealize our role in an unprovoked war?"

Vinnie shook his head, "How did we miss it? How could we, as thoughtful, caring human beings, for one moment think there was anything at all good about war? I should've known we'd gone terribly astray when I saw Dan Rather's teary-eyed apology to the American people. The failure was obvious, if you opened your eyes to what was happening."

"I myself was employed by one of the responsible companies until the day after the building I'd spent twelve years guarding was brought to the ground in a massive explosion. Once I learned the truth, I knew I could never go back to work there. Unfortunately, it had never occurred to me prior to that day to question the company I worked for." Vinnie shook his head wearily. "I'm glad someone else did what I should've – and took action. On that same day, all across the country, other such companies saw their production facilities permanently destroyed. In a few cases the entire building was brought down to its foundation. It wasn't until two days later that Americans realized the newsstands looked and felt different. Clean and condensed. Without the usual garish distractions, people found there were other things they could be doing with their time, other things to read to engage their minds. It was only when I put all this together that I realized that the woman in black had been telling the truth that night. This is a revolution – one that has been sorely needed for a very long time, one the American public should've demanded all along. Now that it has arrived, Americans need to stay on the sidelines and simply cheer."

A curious, eager grin spread across his lips as a newfound energy seemed to pulse through his body. He leaned forward and said, "So you see, had I gone to the popular media, little or none of what I've said would've been heard. Because the *truth* is the last thing they want to hear or see in print. Fortunately, the truth cannot be stopped!"

Chapter 3

Washington D.C.

Gray sat looking out the window at the expanse of the nation's capitol. The tall, bright white sliver of the Washington Monument was visible to the northwest. To the northeast he could see the towering rotunda and dome of the U.S. Capitol building, though the Statue of Freedom perched nearly three hundred feet above the ground was too dark to see clearly. Gray still remembered seeing her for the first time after she'd been brought down for restoration in 1993. He'd stared at her smooth face for almost an hour, trying to define her expression – or lack thereof. At first he'd thought she looked mildly incredulous. Appropriate, given what went on in the halls beneath her feet. But the longer he stared, the more her eyes betrayed a simple sadness, which was also entirely appropriate, given her station. More than once that day he'd silently wished she would throw down the laurel, unsheathe her sword, and sound the battle cry for true freedom. He would've gladly fought and died by her side. Instead, she sat frozen in time, her lifeless eyes betraying nothing.

"Freedom is out there," a friend had once said regarding the statue, "even if you can't see her."

"Seeing isn't always believing," he'd replied.

"You don't trust your own eyes?"

"Just because I see Freedom doesn't mean it actually exists. Or is attainable, for that matter."

"To see requires vision," his friend had countered.

"What's the benefit in seeing or believing in Freedom if Justice is blind?" he'd replied. "One means little without the other."

For most of his life Gray had considered freedom to be an abstract construct, more an intangible point of philosophy than a definable civil right. Every person divines a personal level of freedom for themselves and lives accordingly. But when true freedom becomes unattainable due to the selfish and parasitic actions of others, then Freedom becomes as blind as her sister Justice. Gray had gone to see Freedom that day in hopes of seeing something else in her face – some glimmer of hope. Instead he'd left feeling more certain than ever that Freedom and Justice sometimes needed a helping hand.

Gray shifted his gaze. Separating the Capitol Building and the Monument was the National Mall, L'Enfante's two-mile long park surrounded by botanic and sculpture gardens, museums, art galleries, memorials and government offices. Most of the buildings bordering L'Enfante's Grand Avenue looked as if they had been carved from massive horizontal monoliths of granite, marble, sandstone and limestone – like skyscrapers of ancient Greek and Roman gods that had been tipped onto their sides and lined up, one right after the other.

Less than a mile from the mall, at 1600 Pennsylvania Avenue, was the White House. Built at the end of the 18th century, the iconic mansion had been burned down, rebuilt, gutted and reinforced, and expanded numerous times. It has housed every United States President and his family with the exception of the President who selected the building's original design. Though many designs had been submitted for consideration, including an anonymous design by Thomas Jefferson, George Washington chose the design of an Irish immigrant living in South Carolina. Gray recalled seeing pictures comparing the north and south porticos of the White House laid side by side with those of the Leinster House in Ireland and the Château de Rastignac in France. Most historians agreed the similarities were far from coincidental. "We started out as a nation of borrowed ideas and principles," he thought. We brought with us a long history of progress, culture and knowledge – a new nation with such high hopes and dreams, yet somewhere we went astray. He shook his head. "Better not to dwell on that right now," he thought.

Clearing his head, he focused again on the White House. Although it was the center of power for the American government, the complex was modest in size compared to most of the buildings nearby. Even the surrounding clusters of trees dwarfed the two hundred year-old mansion. "Strange," he thought, "that anything so tall and thick would be allowed to grow around a building whose protection was paramount to national security." It was said that over a million dollars a year was spent guarding and protecting the White House. Maybe when this was all over he would send a letter suggesting the addition of a few arborists to keep the treetops lower and more manageable. Save the White House and the American taxpayer a few bucks. The thought of writing the President such a letter made him grin.

Between the lines of trees was a wide expanse of perfectly manicured light green grass. Gray couldn't be sure, but he thought he saw one of the President's Sikorsky VH-3D helicopters parked on the south lawn near the edge of the trees. The President was in residence, this much he knew. Gray wondered if the President and First Lady had had the entire building fumigated before they moved in with hopes of eliminating all the foulness that had transpired over the previous eight years. Even now Gray still liked to imagine the First Family and a host of Secret Service men, all brandishing two cans of air freshener, traipsing through the hallowed halls of the White House on a mission to clear the air once and for all. The thought was refreshing, in a manner of speaking.

It was a little after ten o'clock in the morning and the summer sun was already hard at work heating the landscape. On the horizon, loomed a thin tawny haze that seemed to surround the city, as if some unknown force was preparing a siege. Gray smiled at the symbolism. He wondered if the other cities bouncing around in the back of his mind also had rings around them. "Physical rings," he silently corrected the thought, "physical and dangerous rings threatening to bring change that was long overdue."

The chain reaction had already been triggered. Things had gone according to plan in New York, though there was the matter of the missing execs from American Media, Inc. He wondered if someone within *The Aenamaia* had opted for a side gig. "No," he thought shaking his head, "that wouldn't make sense." The missing men had been on their lists in the beginning, that was true, but both had been removed early on. Gray didn't recall any arguments or any suggestion that they be reviewed again. No, something else was at play here. He made a mental note to have someone look into it.

The media was sweeping it up and making an array of wild accusations and conjectures. But after eight years of media under the Bush administration, the American people were more likely to return to watching the latest reality TV show. It was a sad state for America, but right now it actually made *The Aenamaia's* work a lot easier. Who needed clever misdirection and deflection when the audience wasn't even watching?

Late last night Kina had phoned in from a pay phone in Harare. Altra took the call. Knowing the call could not be secured, Kina kept to the cryptic and banal format they'd agreed to ahead of time. The two had spoken as sisters. Kina said her football game had not been as easy as they had hoped. In fact, it had been a brutal match. Four players on the other team got kicked off the field, never to return. Kina had fought hard to win and had made it through with only minor injuries. After the game was over, she'd managed to safely free the other team's feline mascot and provide it a fresh and generous treat. The final score was four to zero. Kina told Altra she was exhausted and was going back to her hotel to clean up. She would fly back to the U.S. tomorrow as planned. Before hanging up, Kina asked if Altra would pass along a message to their father, "Tell him I was glad he made me practice kicking with my left foot. He'll understand."

He'd gone to bed before the call, but had asked Altra to call and wake him if Kina checked in. She'd phoned around one o'clock and passed along a quick summary of the call. Then she read off Kina's message to him. "Left foot," he'd said aloud and laughed. "Left foot, indeed." He'd thanked Altra for the call then hung up and lay back in bed. He knew sleep would be reluctant to return so he closed his eyes and thought about the message. Kina's comment had amused him, but more than anything he was relieved she was safe. The assignment had been a difficult one and he'd originally slotted two people for the job. But after much debate and argument on Kina's part, Gray had reluctantly agreed the job would be better served by a single operative, or "Augur," as *The Aenamaia* referred to those handling liquidations. So he let her go solo, a decision that had troubled him up until the moment he'd gotten the message that she was safe and had gotten the job done. Unlike many of their other jobs, he doubted if the quadruple homicide would make national news. Considering the remote and wild location of the farm, the parties involved, and Kina's comment regarding a "generous treat," it might be some time before anyone came across the scene...or what was left of it. For *The Aenamaia's* part, they would decide whether or not to reveal the names of the recently deceased at a later date and time.

The Robinson liquidation was set for yesterday, as well. Osiro spoke with Tzaria before she went in and briefly when she was done, but since then she hadn't checked in. Osiro had noted the tension and agitation in her voice, but that was normal after a liquidation. No matter how prepared a person was, the act of taking another person's life, even in as peaceful a manner as possible, was enough to rattle anyone's chain.

Sending Tzaria on this assignment had never sat well with him, given her history with religious fundamentalists, but the rest of *The Aenamaia*, Tzaria included, had argued that she was by far the most knowledgeable when it came to evangelicals and other religious extremists. He'd had to agree. Knowledge was power, but in this game it was also a necessary prerequisite to survival. Even the best hunters were no match for a dangerous prey they didn't understand. But an effective Augur should also be as cold, methodical and detached as possible. Emotion clouded judgment, which could lead to unnecessary risks and dangers. He'd had no illusions: Tzaria toted an ample store of demons wherever she went. In the end, he'd simply had to trust that she would place self-preservation above vengeance. At least she had made it out safely.

Feeling his lower back start to ache, Gray slid back on the bench beneath the window. There was a slight tingling in his left leg. He felt the warmth of the blood circulating as he crossed his legs and stretched them out on the bench. Altra had once told him that repeatedly crossing the legs for an extended period of time could result in damage to the muscles. Many moons ago, in her former life, she had cared for patients with circulatory and musculature problems. Although none of her patients' conditions were the result of extended sitting, she frequently assured him the results could be the same and urged him to listen to the thousands of tiny pinpricks warning of poor circulation. "Listen to your body," she still said on occasion. "That fantastic machine comes standard with built-in firewalls, virus software, nightly rebooting and defrag, automatic system diagnostics and reporting – the works. It even comes with an exterior calendar," she had said, gently pushing a finger into the patch of gray hair on his chin, "that records the passing of time." His retort was to say that the female machine came with a CPU whose encryption and logic system was unbreakable and inaccessible, even to the owner. "And men come with an indiscriminate joystick that overrides logic and reason and only works half the time," she'd said smugly. "Ouch! I should've seen that one coming," he thought, recalling the exchange. He always had to be on his toes when engaging in a verbal jousting match with Altra. She was one of the king's finest.

From the corner of his eye, he caught a glimpse of a flock of white and gray sea birds approaching from the southwest. They flew low over the Anacostia River, which flowed slowly a hundred yards from his window. The birds appeared to be heading northeast towards Chesapeake Bay. There were a number of bird sanctuaries and natural habitats sprinkled around the bay, attracting hundreds of thousands of birds every year. He watched the birds until they flew out of sight. Gray felt a small pang of envy, which manifested as a slight constriction in his chest. How he wished he, and those who followed him, could find such a sanctuary. A place of warmth, comfort, enjoyment and safety. A place where people could live, work and play, without care or fear of those things that continue to poison the people of the world. So much strife, so much hypocrisy, so much needless waste and suffering. He shook his head and glanced back down at the Anacostia. The wide river seemed almost frozen in time. The waterway's movement was detectible only in the slow progress of ships and barges silently cutting across its surface. Like the world, the river was as dirty, toxic and polluted as it had ever been. Native fish and plants had a difficult time just surviving from day to day, and many species of birds now chose to build their nests and find food elsewhere. Unfortunately, there was no "elsewhere" for mankind. Someone would have to clean up the waters if the species were to survive.

Gray knew where this line of thinking was taking him. He would begin to draw parallels between the river and the state of the world. Next he would compare those most responsible for the pollution in the river to politicians, the media, fanatic religious leaders, etc. After that the good people in the world would become the fish that were struggling just to stay alive from day to day, although neither the fish nor the people knew how bad things had gotten. And in the end, if nothing was done to clean it up, the river itself would eventually catch fire. And not a single person would lift a finger to put it out. Yes, this was an ever-darkening road he'd been going down for many years. But now was not the time to get lost in murky thoughts. Clarity was needed for the task at hand. In fifteen minutes he was to place the first in a series of strategic calls to the media. The first call would be to the chief editor of *USA Today*, the most widely circulated magazine in the U.S.

One week ago, Osiro had tailed the editor, one Jack Kelley, from the *USA Today* headquarters in McLean, Virginia to a nearby Chinese bistro. Osiro had tipped the hostess twenty dollars to seat him near the front window, two seats away from the editor. Using an expensive cell phone scanner purchased anonymously through eBay, Osiro was able to capture the editor's cell phone number, as well as the numbers of his incoming and outgoing calls. During the course of his solitary lunch, Kelley placed and received a number of calls, including several that sounded like they were to family. Thus Gray and Osiro had surmised that the editor only carried one phone and that it was likely to be with him at all times.

Gray picked up his cell phone and carefully connected the scrambler Osiro had sent him. The small black device had cost them almost three thousand dollars, but was well worth the investment. The scrambler masked the voice of the user, protected the call from nearby scanners, sent a false caller ID name and number, and hindered the receiver should they attempt to trace the call. Gray felt certain the *USA Today* editor would not try any of these things, but in this game, it was better to be safe than sorry – or dead.

His cell chirped twice, indicating a text message had been received. Gray scrolled to the new message. It read: *This river stinks. Eve is ready & waiting*. The message was from Osiro, *The Aenamaia's* computer genius and technology wizard. He was sitting in a surveillance van outside of Gray's building and parked next to the river. "Eve" was the code for *eavesdrop*, which meant that the cell phone scanner was ready. Osiro had returned from Virginia a few days ago, but Gray had not heard from him until now. Prior to his reconnaissance visit with the editor, they had agreed to use the cell scanner to test the scrambler, assuming all went well in Virginia. The day and time for the call had been agreed upon in advance, and Osiro had said he would send a message when he was in place and ready to go.

Gray typed in a quick text message. It read: *Pollution. Locals think it will catch fire someday. Any reading?*

After a few moments his screen lit up again and he read: *fire sounds plausible to me. no detection or scanning. rotide is clean and in the pocket.*

"Rotide" was *editor* spelled backwards. Even though Osiro had confirmed that the scrambler was working for Gray, there was no telling who could be monitoring *his* calls. The more nondescript and banal the content of their dialogue or text, the better. Although the FBI claimed to have abandoned the Carnivore project, a system used to read America's emails, *The Aenamaia* had solid intel from watchdog groups and privacy advocates showing that the government was not only still reading emails, but their search algorithms which monitor phone calls had been continuously upgraded and remained on the cutting edge of telecommunications science. To further protect their communications, Osiro had tried to obtain a satellite phone with a built-in encryption algorithm but had yet to find a safe, anonymous way to do so. Just the act of purchasing a satellite phone could throw up a red flag and attract negative attention. Additionally, Osiro was skeptical of the safety of such phones from a government that relies heavily on the very same technology to protect its own communications. In the end, Gray decided that keeping the verbiage soft and anonymous was the best way to avoid drawing attention.

There was one last point to check. He thought for a moment then typed: *Any word from Raven? Is he ready on his end?*

The reply came almost instantly. More than once Gray had suggested Osiro allow himself to be tested by people studying precognition and telepathy. Osiro had dismissed the idea with a wave of his hand declaring, "I'd just blow the bell curve." The response read: *got a message a few minutes ago. he's ready. will make fed contact soon. said "good luck."*

Gray took a deep breath. It was time. He opened the black notebook computer on his lap and made one final check of the text. He had written down what he wanted to say two weeks ago and had since reread it a dozen times. "It's good," he whispered to himself. "It's good." Gray opened a second window and used the small imbedded mouse to position it next to the text box. A small image of an hourglass flashed in and out of existence for a few seconds before two video windows appeared. The images were clearer than he'd expected. Moving the cursor slowly while holding down the left mouse button, he slid a virtual bar slowly back and forth, causing the top image to zoom in and out. Moving the mouse down, he did the same with the bar beneath the second window. Both zooms worked perfectly. Satisfied with the video, Gray fitted his ear with a small white earpiece and plugged the opposite end into the headphone port on his computer. Although he couldn't quite hear anything, Gray knew the audio was working. "Eyes and ears," he whispered to himself and added, "Time to interview the messenger."

With one last deep breath, Gray rechecked the scrambler, then dialed the phone. One ring. Two rings. Three rings. Then a man's voice answered with a question in his voice, "Jack here."

La Sierra, Colorado

Pou Lai was in a deep, restless sleep. He snored loudly, as he usually did following a night of heavy drinking. And last night had been a doozy, Lai's favorite term to describe a decadent party. Mrs. Lai was out of town visiting family. Lai usually experienced a deep sense of relief when she left. Kayla Lai had never liked Colorado. "It's too open here. There aren't enough people." That had been the point of buying such a large ranch – to escape the throngs of people and the press. But Kayla missed her role as a socialite. Lai's quiet and expertly orchestrated exit from his corporation left them financially set for the rest of their lives, but Kayla found no joy in getting dressed up and donning twenty pounds of jewelry and makeup at a quiet ranch far away from city life. What was a work of art if there was no one around to admire it?

Despite her seemingly endless complaining, Kayla was still beautiful and, fortunately for Pou, usually in the right mood when he needed her to be. The void her absence created had taken its toll much sooner than usual. She had been gone over a week and Lai had grown restless. After a boring afternoon driving his four-wheeler around the ranch, he had decided to extend an invitation to some of the friendly company employed by a men's club he frequented. He knew Thursday nights were usually slow and that the girls would be hungry to make some good money. Besides, he played golf regularly with the owner, who was also quite fond of making money, however he did it. Lai had ordered two stretch limousines from a company he held partial ownership in to pick up the girls and truck them out to his ranch. This time he had remembered to instruct the drivers to stock the vehicles with a few bottles of champagne and nothing else. It was a good forty-five minute drive and he didn't want any of the women to get too drunk too early. With any luck, a few glasses of bubbly would encourage them to get friendly with each other during the ride. And there was nothing better than having your delivery show up hot, bothered and ready to please.

The night went as expected: wine, tequila, women, song, skinny dipping in the indoor pool, a series of erotic and lesbian displays, two spent bottles of his wife's imported massage oil, and enough sex to satisfy his lust until his wife returned. The last thing Lai recalled was instructing the two drivers, who had been offered two thousand dollars each to keep an eye on things during the party, to remove any obvious evidence of the women from the house and to return them to the club. The specialty cleaning company he brought in on just such occasions would handle the rest of the mess. In addition to general cleaning, they were especially proficient when it came to disposing of evidence – and even better at maintaining a strict privacy policy when it came to clientele. They were due to arrive before lunch the following day.

The night's debauchery had cost him over fifteen grand, but it had been well worth a little extra pocket change. A few years back he had been the CEO of a major energy concern in Texas. Lai had known for many months that the company was perched precariously on the edge of a dark, frigid financial abyss. He had also known that once word of the company's actual financial position got out, the stock would crash. After the stock hit a three-year high, Lai, with the help of his attorney Joe Marquista, liquidated all of his shares and resigned his position under the vague pretense of "personal" reasons. Five weeks later the company and the accounting firm handling the books were locked dead center in the middle of what would later be cited as one of the biggest scandals in U.S. history. Thousands of employees and retirees, along with tens of thousands of stockholders, suddenly found themselves with a stock valued at forty cents a share, down from over seventy dollars a share when Lai had sold. As far as he knew, the lawsuits and trials were still going on. Luckily for him, he had seen the end coming and had worked diligently to cover his tracks.

Although the other executives had eagerly handed over both Marquista and himself to the authorities, there was no trail for them to follow. Lai had expertly run his side of the company through various assistants and managers, always careful to issue any and all "questionable" orders and mandates verbally. Lai had read the newspapers religiously since he was twenty and therefore was wise enough to avoid writing the types of damaging memos and emails which all-too-often ensnared overconfident politicians and businessmen. If matters got cloudy, Lai would rely on Marquista to guide him to higher ground.

When the smoke cleared around his former employer, Lai and Marquista were nowhere near the fire – they hadn't even been singed. Through an ingenious combination of political contacts, legal loopholes, a few charitable donations to key GOP players and a few long-held favors called in, Pou Lai's name stayed out of the trials and, even more miraculously, out of most of the newspapers. Marquista, through the bundle of money he made keeping Lai out of prison, had planned to start his own law firm. Strangely, less than a year and a half after their success, Marquista disappeared, taking all of his money with him. The news had shocked Lai, who had never imagined such an exit for his partner in crime. "Joe had always been a little strange," he had told his new attorney, "but who am I to judge?" Marquista had done well and deserved whatever course he had chosen. Lai could be nothing but grateful. Thanks to Joe, he would not have to work another day for the rest of his life. He couldn't hold a grudge – even though Joe hadn't been around when the SEC decided they wanted a small piece of the pie. Most millionaires would've been upset, but Lai had a different view on things. Rather than fight a losing battle, he'd simply cut a deal – a thirty-one million dollar payoff to keep the remaining three hundred million. Not the most ideal situation, but one he could live with. Before he'd signed the check, his new accountant had assured him he would find a way to take the payout as a loss for the next five years. Joe would've been proud.

Other than the one hiccup, Lai had escaped his company's colossal train wreck with little more than a scratch. Years of careful planning had certainly paid off. He owned an enormous ranch outside of Denver and his numerous bank accounts totaled more than four hundred million dollars. He was married to a gorgeous young woman who was respectful and did what she was told. Life was good for Pou Lai – and all the better that the world neither knew nor cared.

A few minutes before sunrise, Lai was in a deep sleep. He dreamt of climbing a small mountain covered in lush vegetation. In his subconscious mind, the sight reminded him of the Iao Needle on Maui. He had seen it a number of years back during an all-expense-paid, two-week vacation he and his then-fiancé had taken, courtesy of the governor of Texas. They had spent the first half of the day snorkeling off the bow of a large, luxurious catamaran. Shortly after lunch the owner of the boat, a lobbyist for a large U.S. manufacturing contractor, took them on a jeep ride to the Iao Needle. Now, as he approached the base of the mountain to begin his ascent, he thought he felt someone approaching him from behind. There was no need to turn his head to look – this was a dream. He simply told his mind to look back the way he had come. There was no one there. But across the river he noticed an enormous animal cage sitting beneath the lush green canopy. The large enclosure looked as if it had been built to hold an elephant or a family of polar bears. Even in the midst of the wild jungle, the cage looked strangely out of place. Instead of silver or gray metal, the barred, rectangular structure appeared to be made of shiny gold. Lai experienced an odd sensation of panic. As he continued staring at the unusual sight, he realized his panic stemmed from the fact that he was outside of the cage. But that made no sense. He was no animal. He was meant to be free. "This is ridiculous," he thought indignantly. "I came here to scale a mountain." Yet his mind would not pull his sight away from the gold anomaly across the blue river. His fear intensified. Something else was out there – he felt certain of it.

With some effort, he managed to pull his eyes from the cage, but something was still amiss. His gaze darted frantically from side to side, trying to pinpoint the source of danger. Sweat broke out on his brow, the beads running down his chubby, round face in streams. In the time it took five pudgy fingers to wipe the perspiration from his eyes, two lines of shabbily dressed people appeared from the trees and approached the cage from opposite sides. There were men, women and children. All of them looked extremely skinny and malnourished, but their expressions were strangely calm, as if this was part of their normal daily routine. Lai's body whirled to face them, his mind never breaking sight. It was clear they intended to enter the cage. *His* cage. This was not right and he knew it. He tried to protest, but no sound escaped his lips. He opened his mouth again, his lips slipping back, bearing his teeth like a wild animal. There was a sensation of straining deep within his chest, as if the scream needed to be birthed like a newborn. Still there was no sound. Wide-eyed, he watched, frozen in undefined desperation as the last person entered the golden cage and two gates slammed close. The people were crammed tightly in the cage, but appeared not to notice. In fact, he thought he saw a look of relief on their faces, as if they had been in the path of some terrible danger and were now safe. In that moment, Lai realized the people were looking directly at him. Somehow, he could see each person's eyes, even those in the back of the cage. There was something disconcerting in the way they looked at him. It wasn't sadness. It wasn't fear. It wasn't even curiosity. Standing in the open air, Lai suddenly felt exposed and unprotected.

The urge to escape was overwhelming. He looked around wildly, trying to remember how he'd gotten here. Was there a trail? Was it his helicopter that had brought him to this spot? He simply couldn't recall where he'd come from or where he'd been heading. In the back of his mind, he suddenly wondered where his wife and the lobbyist had gone. Had they been there before? Could they be in the cage? He hadn't looked closely at any of the people's faces.

Backing towards the mountain, Lai fought desperately to steady himself and figure this out. He was the brains behind the numbers. Surely this should be a simple matter to understand. Just as his mind seemed to be on the verge of the answer, there came a faint, familiar beeping sound. The sound came and went, like a metronome, then stopped. Before he could move, a series of softer beeps came. Then nothing. The sequence of the noises was familiar to him, but he could not make the connection.

He looked again at the faces in the cages, wondering if they had heard it, but there was no change in their expressions. Their calmness made him uneasy. It was their eyes: intense, knowing, and unforgiving. Something was wrong, terribly wrong, and unlike him, they seemed to know what it was.

Lai ran to the edge of the river and looked in. The river was shallow, its waters clear. The bottom appeared to be comprised of nothing but sand. There were no signs of life in the slow, ebbing waters. In a panic of motion, Lai waded in and headed for the opposite shore. The sun was high in the sky and beat down on him. He could feel the heat on his arms and shoulders. The sweat was still running in little streams around his eyes, down his nose, behind his ears and down his neck. Kicking his way across the river, he realized that the water had no discernible temperature. Or perhaps he was going numb. In his legs he could feel the resistance of the water as he made his way across, but there was no other sensation to speak of.

Just as he reached the other side, movement in the cage caught his eye and he stopped a few feet short of the shore. At the end of the cage closest to him, a young boy stood behind the bars. The boy appeared to be of African descent. The clothes that covered his small frame were in tatters and looked as if gravity would forcefully jerk them to the ground at any moment. His head was shaved and one ear carried a small ring made of the same lustrous gold as the cage. Lai felt the boy's two big brown eyes looking directly at him. Slowly, the boy raised his hands to his face and covered his eyes. In the next instant his small hands moved to cover his ears, then his mouth. A few seconds passed. Finally, the boy's hands dropped limply to his sides. Lai expected him to speak, but he said nothing. Instead, a look of genuine regret and sadness crept into the boy's eyes. *What?* Lai wanted to say, but the words would not come out. He stood on the river's edge, unable to take his eyes off the young boy. In the next moment the boy turned towards the closed gate of the cage, placed two hands on the bars, and with a wild animal shriek, flung the gate open. The sound it made was not that of a metal cage, but of a regular door being hurled open and crashing into something.

Suddenly Lai awoke with a start. Before he could sit up all the way, a large gloved hand clamped over his mouth and shoved his head forcefully back down into the pillow. He flailed wildly trying to gain purchase on something. Finding only sheets, he gripped them tightly and tried to roll over, only to find two strong hands had grabbed hold of his ankles. A surge of panicked energy hit him and he managed to kick one leg free, but the small victory was short-lived. The strong, gloved hand latched onto the free leg. In an instant, the man's grip tightened on both ankles and with great force slammed them together. Lai heard the dull crack of bone against bone, followed immediately by a surge of pain unlike anything he had ever experienced. Intense bolts of pain shot up his legs, coursed through his chest and bore into his brain, which was still half saturated with alcohol. Tears welled in his eyes and all the fight in him drained immediately. It felt like the strong man at the carnival had brought the sledgehammer down on the high striker, sending a weighted piston crashing into his skull. The agony manifested in a deep, terrified scream, but all that came through the leather glove covering his mouth was a muffled bellow. His breaths were coming in short snorts in and out of his nostrils. The pain in his feet and his head were almost unbearable, but his inability to breathe through his mouth sent a new wave of panic through his body.

"Be still, Mr. Lai," a man said harshly, an air of contempt in his sandy voice. "Struggling will only bring more pain."

Scared and desperate, Lai let go of the sheets he'd been gripping and swung a clawed hand in the direction of the voice. Another gloved hand caught the underside of his wrist in mid-air and, in the same motion, slammed the backside of his hand against the oak headboard. In the same instant, the gloved hand came off his mouth and locked onto his right wrist, which was still tightly gripping the sheets. Immediately, more tears broke through his clamped eyelids and he unleashed another scream heavy with pain and fear.

The sound of his own shriek brought back the image of the young boy opening the cage door. He could still see the look of pity in the boy's eyes, as if he had known this attack was about to take place.

"Let me go, you bastards! Let me go!" he cried, but there was no answer.

Lai was sobbing and his breathing was uneven. The pain seemed to be everywhere. Pulsing waves of agony from his crushed ankles and wrist made their way to his stomach and heart, the former sending out its own message of nauseous misery. Somewhere in his mind he was certain that if the pain retreated and his muscles relaxed even a millimeter, all the contents of his voluminous stomach would immediately evacuate his body.

Lai's attention was arrested when he heard a distinct ripping noise nearby. He tried to focus his concentration through the pain signals still flooding his brain. He was vaguely aware of leather hands touching him again and he winced. Someone was wrapping duct tape around his wrists and ankles – both of which were still throbbing. He turned his head to get a glimpse of his assailant, but it was too dark and his eyes were too wet to make out any details. Looking down towards his crushed ankles, he realized for the first time that he was naked. Even in the midst of the pain and unbridled terror coursing wildly through his mind, Lai also felt a stab of regret, even embarrassment at having gotten undressed before crawling into bed. Why, he wondered absently, had he gone to bed naked? He never slept naked. What had happened? Who were these people? How had they gotten in?

"Who are you?" he cried weakly, trying to keep the fear out of his voice. "What are you doing to me?" There was no answer. Lai could hear at least two men breathing, but realized there could be several more in the room. He tried to concentrate on what had happened last night. After the party everyone had left. Although he had been pretty drunk, he distinctly remembered watching the girls stumble uncertainly towards the limousines, followed by the two drivers hastily stuffing the night's pay into their pockets. Feeling a dire need for sleep, he had closed the door, set the alarm and staggered back to his room. "Why the hell did I…"

Before he could finish his thought, he felt himself being hoisted from the bed. He was being carried out of his own room by his throbbing wrists and ankles like a captured pig. Like the pig, he was naked, helpless and swimming in a thick sludge of pain accompanied by an indistinct, hollow regret. For the first time in years he *experienced* the weight of his rotund body. Hanging limply, the pull on his extremities was substantial, and painful. A vague hint of regret at being overweight and out of shape flashed somewhere in the back of his mind. It passed quickly, barely noticed through the confused haze cluttering his mind.

Lai heard repeated heavy footfalls as the two men carried him down the wide granite stairs. Though the air felt warm, he seemed to sense the chilliness emanating from the stone steps and a shiver ran through his body. How could this be happening? To him of all people? How was it that he was being carried like a felled pig through his own house? Who were these people? Thieves? Looters? Or had someone sent them? What in the hell was happening? Helplessness and frustration temporarily overrode pain and caution.

"Goddammit! What in the fuck is going on!" he yelled. "Do you know who I am?" There was no reply. "Goddammit, answer me!" he demanded. He tried again to struggle, but the bonds were too strong.

Looking around, Lai realized they were at the base of the stairs and crossing into the living room. Suddenly the two men released their hold on him and he dropped, landing with a hard thud on the cold tile floor. The violent impact knocked the wind from his lungs. He struggled to regain his breath, barely cognizant of the chill on his back and legs. After several agonizingly long seconds, his lungs obeyed his wishes and he gasped for air.

Why was this happening to him? Something occurred to him and he suddenly wondered how in the hell had they gotten past his security system. He had set the alarm...hadn't he? At that moment the dream began replaying behind his eyes. It was fuzzy at first, but slowly the images resolved. There was something important there, he was sure of it. He'd definitely heard something. Before he had crossed the river there had been two series of beeps – familiar tones. "Concentrate," he thought. Yes. The first set came rapidly, followed quickly by eight distinct, evenly spaced tones. Sequential. The memory caused the middle and index fingers on his right hand to twitch reflexively. "What the...?" but the thought was cut short when the answer burst through the darkness. With a force almost as brutal as being dropped on the tile floor, blinding incredulity hit him as he realized those sounds had come from the keypad of his home security system. He had heard them in his sleep. Why hadn't he awoken? It must have been the liquor that had kept him drowned in sleep. Then the second shockwave hit him. The first beeps had sounded because a door or window had been opened. The second set of beeps had been someone punching in the code to disarm the alarm!

But that was impossible. He was the only one who knew the alarm code. Even his wife didn't know it. She had a remote control to disarm the alarm. During the installation of the new system, it had been his idea to separate the means by which he and his wife deactivated the alarm. To accomplish this he had opted to purchase a top-of-the-line security system, which was hard-wired to his computer. In addition to monitoring each of the hundred and twenty-five sensors around the property and inside the house, the system could distinguish between his wife's remote control and his PIN code. Each day the system sent him an entry log showing times and entry points for both. Additionally, the system had been integrated with the GPS tracking system in his wife's Escalade. He could pinpoint and track her location at any given time. With this system at his disposal, he could easily keep an eye on his wife's comings and goings and not get them mixed up with his own, all the while protecting his home.

But that still left a nagging question: How had these men gotten past the security system and alarm?

One of the men moved to a nearby couch, picked up a heavy cashmere blanket and threw it hastily over the lower half of Lai's body. The hefty Asian watched the dark silhouette of the man move to the far end of the room and sit down. Though he wasn't able to make out his face, he couldn't help but notice the man's substantial frame and unusual height. Lai guessed his assailant stood well over six-and-a-half feet tall. That explained the long fall to the unforgiving tile floor and the control they'd had over him. From the man's posture, he appeared to be calm and at ease – even relaxed. He looked like a man preparing to read a book or listen to soft music. But Lai sensed something ominous in the motionless shadowy figure that caused the terror to return, stronger and more penetrating than ever.

Breckus sat down on a plush leather armchair and stared down at his watch. Ten minutes. Not bad. Talon had assured him it would be an easy in and out. The lump lying still on the floor ten feet away had struggled and squirmed, but he had been easy enough to control. "The richer they were, the easier they fell," he thought. Still, being half drunk and out of shape the man didn't have much to fight with. Despite his weakness, binding him had been a good idea. Fortunately duct tape stuck to even the slimiest men.

They had gotten the call earlier that evening from their contact at the nightclub telling them Pou Lai had "placed an order." Talon had been assigned to Lai over a year ago. Even though he already had several other maladies he tracked, this one was his top priority. He'd kept a close eye on the squeaky-clean former energy executive and was intimately familiar with every aspect of his life, including his licentious habits and appetites. Lai had been under continuous surveillance ever since his wife had left town. As usual, Talon's prediction had been right on the mark. He had said it would only be a matter of time before the sod would need to quench his thirst and satiate his libidinous cravings.

The crisp click of Talon's boots on the marble floors of Lai's kitchen resonated throughout the otherwise silent house. The steps grew louder as he crossed onto the tile. Breckus watched as his friend's silhouette approached the moaning figure lying near the front door. Talon stopped in front of the large windowpane next to the door. A thin sliver of light from the full moon shone through the window and cut across his angular face, giving the impression of a disembodied head that had materialized out of thin air. Breckus noticed his friend's face was calm, almost serene, as he stood staring down at their capture.

"Please," Talon said with genuine sincerity, "do not start screaming again. You know very well no one will hear you. The nearest neighbor is five miles away and even then, he's not very fond of you." He walked slowly around Lai's feet still talking, his tone matter-of-fact. "Your ancillary clean-up crew from Weedler Janitorial won't arrive until later this afternoon. And none of your other hired help are set to come in today – we made sure of that." Talon stopped. He was staring at something large on the wall. The only light in the room came from random beams of moonlight, but from where Breckus sat the object appeared to be a bear's head mounted prominently on the wall. Talon shook his head in disgust and turned back towards a frozen Pou Lai.

"Right at this moment," Talon said, his voice calm and casual, "your wife Kayla is sitting in her mother's living room in International Falls, Minnesota. Strange coincidence, that's the same little town that spawned Tammy Faye Baker. Not something you'd want to advertise in tourism brochures, wouldn't you agree?" There was no reply from Lai so he continued. "Kayla and her mother Maudna are drinking cheap wine from a box and watching back-to-back reruns of American Idol on an antique console television. On her way to the airport last week she phoned her friend Marci Dobbs, a stripper living and working in Cleveland, and bet her a thousand dollars the fake blonde with the implants would win. Marci has her hard earned money on the gay Puerto Rican guy."

Talon sat down on the arm of a couch, his hands folded in his lap. Lai had been following his movements as best he could. Now with the help of the moonlight, he could see Talon's face clearly. The expression on Lai's face was equal parts terror and stern concentration, as if he was still trying to solve some elusive problem.

After a few moments Talon said politely, "You may speak."

Lai's mouth opened and moved as if he were trying to speak, but there was no sound. After collecting himself, he managed to ask, "How do you…?"

Before he could get it all out Talon intervened. "You want to know who we are, why we're here, how I know so much about you and your wife, what's going to happen to you…and," he leaned closer to Lai and whispered, "how I got past your high-tech security system."

Lai's puffy eyes and small mouth opened wide in astonishment and he nodded slowly.

"Well Mr. Lai, while I fear my answers may not allay your concerns, I do believe you have a right to know. My name is Talon. The forbidding gentleman in the chair is Breckus. We're here for the same reason your janitors will be coming by later – to clean up a mess. As to my knowledge, well, we've been watching you for some time now. We know more about your life and affairs than anyone, save yourself. They say the devil is in the details. Well, in this case, I've made it my job to know the devil's own details."

Talon rose and took a few steps towards Lai. He knelt down beside the stunned man. From his jacket pocket he extracted a shiny silver case that resembled a miniature briefcase, like the ones seen handcuffed to important people in movies. Talon spoke softly, his expression suddenly serious. "As for your fate, you're about to take the ride of your life. And even though it will be the last ride you ever take, I can assure you it will be the best. You see, even though most of your fortune came at the cost of twenty-two thousand hard working people's pensions and retirement funds, the loss of thousands of jobs, a significant blow to the stock market, a national embarrassment, a crippled economy in the town where your company had its headquarters, stockholder losses and millions of taxpayer dollars spent on ongoing trials...well, Mr. Lai, you'll be relieved to know we're not here to repay you in torture. We're here to perform an excision. A biopsy of sorts." Talon stood and looked down at Lai. "We're here to remove people like you from society – to set an example. We're tired of sitting idle while police, investigators, and the courts fight a losing battle against throngs of clever, over-paid lawyers in a futile attempt to eek out a modicum of justice. In the end, the lawyers get rich, criminals like you remain rich, and the people you swindled have to struggle even more to survive. But this is an old story isn't it? For thousands of years kings, tyrants, dictators, warlords, and even popes centered their lives around war, murder, rape, plunder and unearned wealth and power, never paying notice to the river of blood flowing through the streets. And the people that survived were powerless to stop it, just as the American people are today. But today it's worse. Why? Because those who would devote half their lives to looting and pillaging will dedicate the other half to preaching the existence of freedom and justice to those whose pockets they're picking. We're led to believe that true and swift justice will prevail, that good judgment will be rendered." Talon's head dropped. He took a deep breath then said, "Men like you have gotten away with murder because good, decent people clung to a system of justice they believed was true, right and water-tight. Well, when the system itself allows the slime of humanity to slip through, then it's up to people like us to plug the leaks. Permanently."

Lai began whimpering and babbling. "It wasn't me. It wasn't my fault. I was just doing my job. I did what I was told to do. I didn't do anything wrong."

"Mr. Lai!" Talon barked harshly. Lai stopped talking. He stared wildly at Talon, as if expecting to be struck. "Mr. Lai," Talon continued more calmly. "I think you underestimate me. As I've already told you," he said confidently, "I know quite a bit about your life. Much of the information I gained was obtained...how should we say...by means outside the normal legal processes. And you would be amazed at what you can learn when you choose to play by your enemy's rules."

Lai stared up at him, his eyes full of fear and strangely enough, curiosity.

"I don't know what you're talking about. I didn't do anything wrong. No one can prove a thing."

Talon smiled earnestly, looking as though he regretted having to say his next words. "Joseph Marquista proved it. He had quite a lot to say about you." A tiny grin appeared at the corner of his mouth and he said to no one in particular, "A cocktail of Amytal Sodium on top of four shots of cheap scotch works wonders, especially when you have a...*captive* audience."

Lai gasped.

"Yes, Mr. Lai," he said nodding, "I'm afraid so. Mr. Marquista was a guest of ours for some time. He proved to be remarkably cooperative and useful. With his impressive list of political and business clients, and enough illegal transgressions to impress Capone, we just couldn't pass up the opportunity to liberate him."

Lai tried to speak, but again nothing came out.

"The accounts in the Caymans, the trips you sponsored for the Speaker of the House, the fifteen million dollars you accepted from a competitor to derail a government bid your company had all but secured, the underage prostitutes you purchased while on vacation in Thailand – and later left as gifts to various members of the Japanese government – the wiretapping of residences of various DOD officials... And those are just the greatest hits."

Infuriated, Lai began squirming and growling his words, "You can't do this to me. Someone will find out and come after you. Men like me don't just disappear!"

"I'm sure Marquista would beg to differ, if he could beg at all," Talon retorted, not attempting to hide the grim seriousness in his voice. The two men made eye contact. Lai saw something icy and dark behind those eyes that he couldn't face. The once powerful CEO turned away and tried to shrink into the background.

"Intense," Breckus thought. "Damn intense." Shaking his head and grinning slightly, he stood up and walked into the small dining room adjacent to the foyer. After a few seconds of searching, he found a round dial on the wall. He turned the dial all the way to the left then pressed it. Slowly, he turned the dial back to the right. As the lights of the crystal chandelier came up, he could just see Lai's bound legs on the floor. Talon was kneeling next to him. Breckus turned the dial further until he saw his friend's hand go up, indicating that was enough light for him to work by. As Breckus rounded the corner, he saw the shiny object in his friend's hand. He watched as Talon expertly inserted the needle into the clear, upturned vial. As he retracted the plunger, the glass tube of the syringe filled with a deep blue liquid. The deep ocean blue of the poison reminded Breckus of the Hope Diamond. It was the most beautiful, mesmerizing shade of blue he'd ever seen. But his eyes weren't the only ones locked onto the vial. The more liquid Talon extracted, the more Lai's eyes widened.

"Don't worry Mr. Lai," Talon said conversationally, "As I stated before, though the rift caused by your crimes against humanity runs deep, we're not here to punish or make you suffer. Our organization's purpose is to circumvent the blind ineffectiveness of modern courts, trials, investigations, committees, and hearings – to not only cut through the crap, but to cut *out* the crap."

Carefully, Talon replaced the ampule containing the velvet blue liquid in the silver case. Leaving the case open on the floor by his feet, he retrieved the syringe and stared at the vial. "In addition to sending you and your kind on your way, you'll also be happy to know that we're already in the process of distributing the money in your various bank accounts to the people from whom you stole it. But even that charitable donation doesn't come close to repairing the damage you and the other executives caused." Talon turned towards Lai with a look that said *you shouldn't have*. In answer to the confused look on Lai's face, Talon said, "Mr. Marquista was quite a resourceful man whose memory, with a little succor, proved remarkably resilient to the diluting effects of time. He kept very detailed records of your transactions, accounts, investments, passwords, etc. I'm embarrassed to admit he knew things that even I hadn't been able to discover. You know," Talon said, "I do believe he was planning to blackmail you at some point. Or rob you outright. The ammunition was certainly in his hands. Well, we put a stop to that. Instead, every dime we can extract from each of your caches will be spent buying salvation for your eternal soul."

Talon held the syringe pointed up and gave a few perfunctory flicks to the glass tube. The surgical steel glimmered in the light coming from the chandelier. Lai's wide Asian eyes were glued to the instrument. An expression of terror reshaped the bound man's pudgy face. Beads of sweat erupted from every pore, as if his whole head was being slowly squeezed. His heart began to beat wildly as his body flooded with adrenaline. Shallow, unconscious breaths came in rapid, short bursts. A new and powerful wave of panic hit and his body bucked and convulsed.

Talon looked up at Breckus and nodded. The large man knelt down next to Lai. He grabbed hold of Lai's wriggling right elbow and right leg and in one swift motion flipped the stout man onto his stomach. The shock of hitting the hard floor, coupled with the impact sustained by his groin, drained the fight out of Pou Lai in an instant.

Without hesitating, Talon jabbed the needle into Lai's ample right cheek and pressed down on the plunger. Lai inhaled sharply, then relaxed. Talon removed the needle and carefully cleaned it with a small white cloth from the silver case. As he was replacing the syringe in the case, he heard Lai's weak voice ask, "How did you get past my security system?"

Talon leaned down, and put his lips next to the man's ear and whispered apologetically, "It was really very easy. You see...I'm the one who came out to the house and installed it."

Chapter 4

Gainesville, Florida

On the morning of May 7, 1937 the township of Manchester in New Jersey appeared out of nowhere on maps all over the world, where it had been conspicuously absent only a day prior. Many people vaguely recalled hearing the name Manchester prior to May 7th, but only when preceded by Lakehurst Naval Air Station. And sometimes, Manchester was omitted completely, as anchormen and reporters referred instead to Ocean County, New Jersey. Regardless of which was named, most people never gave much thought to either until the large German zeppelin christened the Hindenburg burst into flames three hundred feet above the landing field. On the night of May 6, 1937, in a dramatic explosion of fire, the Hindenburg fell to the ground and collapsed, killing thirty-six people. Because of the ship's fame, much of its journey in America had been carefully filmed and documented. The last and most famous film was shot by Charlie Nehlsen with a horrified Herbert Morrison providing commentary. The film shows how quickly the mammoth airship was consumed by flames and brought down. In the background was the hysterical voice of Morrison frantically narrating the tragedy. It was during those moments that he uttered the now famous phrase, "Oh, the humanity!"

Almost as fast as the flames consumed the millions of cubic meters of hydrogen gas, speculation over the cause of the accident spread rapidly throughout the world. Since that fateful night, numerous theories have been put forth to explain why, after twenty successful trans-Atlantic trips, the famed Hindenburg should spontaneously explode. Theories of what caused the hydrogen gas to ignite range from sabotage to lightning to static sparks. There were implications of Nazi involvement, Zionist agents rebelling against Hitler's anti-Semitism – even a German acrobat that had been onboard and survived was accused. One author writing in 1962 even accused one of the riggers who died in the fire of being the saboteur. There is also controversy over whether it was the hydrogen gas or the paint used on the skin of the craft that caused the flames to spread so quickly. Even today, historians and aviators continue to debate exactly what happened that terrible night.

Many modern day conspiracy theorists consider the destruction of the Hindenburg to be the first true conspiracy theory in America to be captured on film. Some conspiracy enthusiasts refer to the small, nondescript field behind the current hangars as the first Ground Zero. Prior to the attacks on 9/11, the base received a healthy number of visitors each year, many of whom were there to see the spot where the great zeppelin had fallen. Most were disappointed to find nothing more than a small white flag marking the location of the crash. Others, trying not to be too conspicuous, treated the site with reverence and stood staring in wonder, as if they were witnessing the devastating crash replayed right before their eyes. They knew that this was not the birthing ground of lies and conspiracies. They knew disasters on far grander scales had been committed since time immemorial. But what marked this ground as sacred was the fact that the event itself, the burning blaze of the flames and the speed at which they spread, was all captured on film. That was when conspiracy theories really gained momentum. And tomorrow was the anniversary.

"Should be some kind of national conspiracy holiday," he thought smiling. Toman checked his watch. They wouldn't be out for another twenty minutes or so. He sat patiently concealed by the dark shadows shed by the cluster of trees under which he stood, the famous images of the slowly falling Hindenburg engulfed in flames still lingering in his mind. Toman loved history. To him, history was like a hundred trillion thin threads wound about the planet like an enormous ball of yarn. Many of the threads crossed and intersected hundreds of thousands of times. Each color of thread represented a different type of history: individuals, like-minded groups, nations and kingdoms, tribes, pure ideas, wars, the spectrum of human emotions, technical innovations, etc. And that was to say nothing of the histories of pre-humans, animals, plants, insects, bacteria and viruses. Those threads crossed ours as well, but with greatly reduced frequency. Throughout time the blind ambitions of Homo sapiens have increasingly resulted in larger and larger knots in the threads. Toman believed that over half of those knots only appeared within the last hundred years, and what was truly ironic was the astounding number of them tied by a relatively small number of individuals. One need only study history for an hour or so to get a taste for the extent of the damage.

Often times when he was stuck doing surveillance, Toman mused about the future. When all of this was over he would go back to school and get his second Master's degree, this time in history. With a little luck and the new view of the world he sincerely hoped would soon be prevalent, he would create a new kind of history course – one that combined history, philosophy, and cutting edge technology with a consciousness aimed squarely at the future. The class would focus on learning *from* history, rather than just *about* it. After all, what good was knowledge of history without practical application? But then how could you have practical application without first understanding the philosophies and, to some extent, the psychologies of the men and nations who relentlessly drove history? Students of the future must understand the *What, How* and *Why* of history as well as the *What Now*. It would be a difficult course and one where students would most likely have to sign a waiver absolving the professor of all politically correct requirements. Toman smiled broadly at the idea of teaching such a course.

After a few moments, reality swept back over him and his smile faded to a smirk. "History indeed," he thought. He was in the middle of history right now – playing a role in something that would soon spread through the real and virtual worlds like a virus on steroids. "Will it make the news right away?" he wondered. With the media still cautious from its escapades after 9/11, it was hard to predict what would and would not be on the news and in the papers. Fortunately, history was not dependent on the media. And before the humid Florida night surrendered to the morning light, he would play a small supporting role in changing the course of history. Tonight, the manipulative fringe on the extreme right wing would lose one of its media mouthpieces, and the balance of power and justice would receive a small nudge in the opposite direction.

Washington D.C.

Gray knew that the editor of *USA Today* would not stay on the phone long without good reason to do so. In fact he was likely to deliver a swift reproach to the stranger who had gotten a hold of his private cell phone. But Gray also knew that at his core, Jack Kelley was a newspaperman. Regardless of the invasion of his privacy, he would not let go of a good story.

"Mr. Kelley, listen carefully. Historic and unprecedented events have been put into play and you are the first person in the media to be contacted. As you can tell from my voice, this line is scrambled and any attempt to trace the call would be futile. You are a smart man, Mr. Kelley. You know that someone calling to sell you a timeshare or mortgage insurance would not go to such lengths. Additionally," Gray added watching the video on the screen of his laptop, "a salesman would be hard pressed to guess that you were sitting in the Starbucks in McLean Virginia at the corner of Greensboro and International, wearing a formal collarless black shirt and dark gray trousers. Sure is taking an awful long time to make the double espresso you ordered. Now, do I have your attention?"

There was a long pause. Gray watched the figure of Jack Kelley slowly lower his cell phone, attempting to casually look around the coffee shop. His mouth hung half open in surprise, but his eyes were full of suspicion. Gray waited patiently, having anticipated this reaction. Though Osiro's planted camera was one of the best, it was also one of the smallest. And while the clarity of the image was undeniable, the stationary nature of the device meant there was a small chance Kelley would move out of the camera's field of view. Fortunately, if Kelley panicked and went mobile, Osiro was standing by with four nearby security cameras he'd been able to gain access to. If Kelley went for his Mercedes, the tracking device Osiro had installed, which had pinpointed his location today, would allow them to follow him. However, once he left his car, Kelley would have to remain on his phone in order to get a rough calculation of his position. Luckily, the man hadn't left his seat.

After a few moments and a fruitless search, Kelley slowly raised the phone back to his ear and tried to look casual. His eyes still darted to and fro, but his posture was as stiff as a board.

"Yes," he answered trying to mask the slight shake in his voice, "you have my attention."

"Good," Gray said simply, his response laced with more warmth than he'd intended.

"Who are you?" Kelley asked cautiously.

"My name is Gray. I represent an organization referred to simply as *The Aenamaia*. Now listen carefully, and," he said playfully, "by all means feel free to pick up that Monte Blanc you were just writing with and take notes."

As expected, Kelley's head again jerked from side to side, still trying to spot the camera. Unable to locate the device, Kelley grimaced in frustration, but picked up the pen and flipped his notepad to a clean sheet. He sat silently, pen poised to begin writing. Gray watched the small screen of his computer, momentarily forgetting the phone pressed to his ear. After a few seconds Kelley looked up in the general vicinity of the hidden camera and raised his arms with the cell phone in one hand and his Monte Blanc in the other, as if to question "What are we waiting for?"

Gray shook his head and silently berated himself for forgetting he was a player in this game.

"My apologies, Mr. Kelley," he said pretending to clear his throat. "Let's begin."

"Today is May 5. As you may have read in your own paper this morning, the date has quite a history. On this day in 1260 Kublai Khan, son of Genghis Khan becomes the Mongol Emperor. In 1769 Napoleon dies at age fifty-one as an exile on the island of Saint Helena. In 1494 Columbus discovers the island of Jamaica and, as was customary for explorers, claimed it in the name of Spain. In 1925 a warrant is issued for a biology teacher who chose to teach evolution in Tennessee in spite of the presumptuous law that prohibited it. On May 5, 1961 astronaut Alan Shepard becomes the first American in space, only twenty-three days behind Yuri Gagarin. And in 1862 Mexican troops halt a French invasion in the Battle of Puebla. In each one of these instances, history was irrevocably changed, and as a result of each, a great many lives were either saved or lost or both. This conversation is taking place because a new revolution is about to occur and we wanted to give you, Mr. Kelley, the opportunity to tell the world *What* is happening, and more specifically, *Why*. We chose you because we thought you might actually have the courage and journalistic integrity to report these events accurately, a practice the mainstream media has all but forgotten. Are you game?"

Gray paused and moved in closer to the screen of his computer and the image of the editor. The image of Kelley was clear, but not up close. Upon hearing the word "game," Kelley had ceased writing and looked up. His pen was still poised on the white sheet of paper and his body sat rigid. Gray couldn't be sure, but he felt confident Kelley was staring at the floor.

"Mr. Kelley?" Gray said lightly.

"Yes, I'm here," the voice replied, an air of impartiality in his voice.

The response was quick and conscientious. Gray imagined the man was busy calculating whether or not this was real, how great the threat was, and if it proved to be very, very good, how best to use the information.

"Good boy," Gray thought with amusement, "Ever the hungry and diligent paperboy."

"*The Aenamaia*," Gray explained, "is not connected to any government, corporation, religious, or military group, and holds no political affiliation. We are a collection of men and women, representing various backgrounds and nationalities who have come together to bring about change that is long overdue. We expect some will label us terrorists or anarchists, especially given the dismal fear the media and government will undoubtedly, and with unbridled greed, seek to exploit to further their own ends. But this is to be expected. This is where you will begin to choose your course. The accuracy with which you pass on the initial information you receive will determine whether or not you receive future communications from us. Do you understand?"

"Sure," Kelley said, "You're throwing me a bone so I'll beg for more, is that it?"

"If you like, yes. We expect you will sensationalize the events that are to come. We probably wouldn't be here in the first place were that not the level to which the modern media has unfortunately sunk. Someday, with a little luck, you may come to understand the acute irony of this situation. In the meantime, you'll be relieved to know that you yourself have not been targeted by our group." Gray paused, then added, "Not yet, anyway."

"Targeted?" Kelley asked skeptically.

"For liberation," Gray said simply.

"Do you always speak in code?" the editor asked, sounding a little annoyed.

Gray exhaled and clarified, "You are not currently on our list as someone we will be summarily executing in the very near future," he said, his voice tight. "Is that plain enough for you?"

There was a short silence then Kelley asked whimsically, "How do I know any of this is for real? I sure hope you aren't wasting my time with these history lessons and cryptic promises because I'm warning you – I have the resources to track you down and make your life a living hell!"

"Mr. Kelley, I assure you…"

But Kelley was suddenly on a roll, "Your assurance isn't good enough. Why the hell did you call me first? Why not send proof, *then* make the call? You must be amateurs. And if this is all a farce, I promise you'll regret ever dialing this number."

Silence.

Kelley was about to hang up when Gray said calmly, "You're in no position to make threats, Mr. Kelley. We're ready and willing to provide you with adequate proof that this is no joke and that we're dead serious. If you would simply…"

But Kelley again cut him off, "Listen, Mr. Gray. I've heard a lot of stories and empty promises around *the next big story*. They never come true. Besides, I'm already pissed off that you've called on my personal cell phone." Kelley was practically shouting now as he settled into his well-rehearsed bossy tirade. "I'll have you know I can reach through this phone and track you and your rabble down with the snap of my fingers. So if you've got some proof you'd better damn well deliver right now!"

Gray took a deep breath, then quickly punched up two separate screens on his laptop. On one was a view of the parking lot just outside the Starbucks where Kelley sat. It was being photographed from a security camera on a roof across the street. The other was a thermal imaging camera perched atop a nearby building within the Tysons Galleria complex. The security system transmitted the thermal images to a centralized security outfit twenty miles away. The firewall protecting the transmissions had been relatively easy for Osiro to crack. So now Gray sat looking at the same parking area as the first camera, only from a different angle. It was a little after ten thirty a.m. in McLean, Virginia.

"Mr. Kelley," Gray began, now quickly punching keys on his laptop, "Do you have any idea what the crash test rating is on that Mercedes G500 you drive?"

"Look, you asshole, I've had just about enough of this shit. If you've got something to say then just...!"

Even on his best day, with the wind full in his sails, Jack Kelley could never have been prepared for what came next.

Washington D.C.

Roger Tarte sat staring at his computer screen. The small readout in the corner of the screen read 10:25 a.m. Normally he'd prefer to stare out the window, but all he could see was the façade of another bland, white building. All the impressive sights in D.C., and this was what he'd been stuck with. "Figures," he thought. Tarte sighed heavily and rubbed his red eyes. He'd been there less than two hours, yet it felt like he'd never left. Last night's meeting had run longer than expected due to an overdose of longwinded showboating courtesy of the Deputy Secretary. An arcane and pedantic relic left over from the Bush administration, the D.S. was suddenly facing a restructuring of several Department of Homeland Security offices, as well as heavy proposed cuts in funding. And with Bush, Cheney and half of the former President's advisors under federal investigation, old friends of influence were becoming more and more difficult to coax out of their hiding places. The D.S. was now scrambling to do everything in his power to make himself and the agency look strong, busy and absolutely critical to the safety of the country. Since its creation in November of 2002, the DHS had absorbed or merged with over twenty government agencies, becoming the third largest Cabinet Department in the U.S. In less than ten years DHS had grown into an enormous, fifty-two billion dollar a year hydra. With its many heads and arms, no place within the U.S. had been outside its sight or reach.

But a slow economy and a new President with a different view of diplomacy and a desire for positive international relations had spelled change for the DHS. Under the guise of an aisle-crossing initiative, the Democratic President proposed cuts in the DHS as a step towards appeasing the Republican ideal of a smaller government. Republicans, many of whom had vested interests in the DHS, found themselves wedged into a corner. The idea of "small government" had been a staple in their dogma from the beginning. Despite the unprecedented expansion of the U.S. government by former President Bush, along with record-breaking spending, republicans had continued the seemingly hypocritical war cry for smaller government. The ideal had been pushed so hard, that when the Democratic President publicly agreed to reduce the size of the government via cuts in the DHS, republicans were unable to mount an effective fight.

And while Tarte agreed publicly that the full-blown DHS was a necessity, he knew better than most that this was a case where reality was, in fact, stranger than fiction. "There is fat aplenty to be trimmed from this hog," he'd told his wife on more than one occasion. And each time she would retort by reminding him that he too was saddled to that obese swine. "You can't complain about fat and calories when you've got a first class seat on the gravy train," she'd said. How true.

Maybe he was just bored. Bored by always pushing the pretense of threats that simply didn't exist. It felt too much like a twenty-four-seven acting job without the multi-million dollar salary. The majority of real threats to the United States were handled by the FBI or the CIA, neither of which had many concerns over funding. Maybe he should see if they were hiring. He could get back into the field and...

His thought was interrupted when the phone on his desk sprang to life. The sudden noise startled him. The ring pulse was one notch louder than it needed to be. He made a mental note to adjust it after the call. Suppressing a yawn, he picked up the receiver.

"This is Tarte."

"Good morning, Tarte. Steven Floyd here," Floyd said, his Midwestern accent unmistakable.

Tarte bolted upright. Coincidence and karma were not concepts he put much stock in, but he had to admit how odd it was that the head of the FBI's Counter-Terrorism Division should call at the same moment he'd been contemplating changing teams. Stranger still that he'd first met Floyd only a week ago at Jimmy Marlow's house party. Jessica had snatched his phone to go out front where it was quiet to call their babysitter, leaving him standing alone admiring Marlow's pool. A few seconds later Steven Floyd quietly strode up beside him and commented on the warm night and the tempting azure waters. He'd agreed on both counts. Soon after, they were discussing deep-sea fishing in the Bahamas, Floyd's favorite haunts on Nassau and the best time of year to visit. Floyd had even suggested a cozy, old-world getaway on the island that had been built by a notorious pirate. Tarte had never been to the Bahamas, but he and his wife had it on their list to go so he tucked the hotel's name in his mind for later research. At the time Tarte had thought it odd that the man had made it a point to start a discussion with a perfect stranger. But then he'd realized it was a party after all. He also realized his own antisocial reluctance to do such a thing didn't automatically mean it was unusual or suspect. In fact, it was probably the exact opposite.

From what he could gather, Floyd spent much of his spare time traveling to sunny destinations. He came to the conclusion that Nassau was Floyd's home away from home, though he hadn't said as much. The career FBI man was intimately familiar with the city of Nassau, as well as the island of New Providence. Tarte had meant to ask if Floyd intended to retire there, but the conversation shifted to visiting Vermont in the fall and all thoughts of islands and beaches fell away.

Before Floyd took leave of him, the two exchanged cards and made mention of having lunch someday – professional courtesy, and all. He never really thought Floyd would have reason to contact him. Then a few seconds after Floyd disappeared into the house, Jessica reappeared and told him Alex, their nine-year-old, had put Nicholas, the six-year-old in the dryer with the towels. She'd been smiling, so he knew the boys were okay. Having done the same exact thing when he was younger, he could only smile back and shake his head. Some things were just inevitable.

"How long was Nick in there?" he'd asked as they walked back towards the house.

"Halfway into the permanent press cycle," she laughed and added, "At least we won't have to iron him for tomorrow's brunch."

Tarte smiled at the memory. Though it was only at this moment that he realized he hadn't seen Floyd again for the rest of the night.

"Floyd," he said jovially, "This is a bit unexpected. Planning a trip to Nassau?"

"As a matter of fact I am," Floyd said, "But that's not why I'm calling."

Tarte was intrigued and asked, "What can I do for you?"

"When we spoke the other night I got the sense that you were a bit... how shall we say? Under-utilized in your current capacity?"

"It's all right Floyd, you can say it. I'm bored. It's okay, though. An optimist would probably say it's really a good thing – means all is calm and well in the country."

There was a long pause and Tarte suddenly wondered if something bad had happened that he wasn't aware of.

"And what would a pessimist say?" Floyd asked, a hint of seriousness in his voice.

"A pessimist?" he echoed. "Probably that trouble is always lurking around the next corner."

"You a betting man, Tarte?" Floyd asked.

"I'm known to make a friendly wager once in a while. Why?"

"Because in this game, the smart gambler always puts his money on the pessimist."

McLean, Virginia

Before Jack Kelley could finish his sentence, a noise caught his attention. He turned and looked towards the parking lot just in time to see a massive fireball erupt beneath his Mercedes, propelling the heavy silver SUV straight up into the air, followed immediately by the deafening roar of the explosion. The forceful blast burst through the front window of the Starbucks, sending glass, tables, chairs, and Kelley's body hurtling inward. A few seconds later he found himself lying on the floor five feet from where he'd just been sitting. The wind had been knocked out of him when he hit the hard floor, and it took his body a few painful seconds to remember how to signal the muscles required to inhale a deep breath. The anxiety and effort made him cough, but he was relieved to be breathing again.

Slowly he opened his eyes. Fortunately, instinct had kicked in and he'd managed to shield his eyes and face with his right arm. A brief wave of relief washed over him as he realized all at once that he could see. He took a moment to examine his body. A blanket of broken glass covered him from head to toe, but he did not appear to be seriously hurt. Without thinking, Kelley rolled to his left and put his hand down as a brace to help him stand. The combination of pressure and jagged glass shards caused him to quickly snatch his hand back.

"Ouch!" he exclaimed, raising his hand for inspection. Irritated with himself, he flicked off the loose chunks of glass from his hand and scowled at the sight of a few small dots of blood. Still shaking his head, he wiped the sore hand carefully on his pants, then blew on it for good measure. "Stupid," he thought.

For the first time since hitting the floor, Kelley became acutely aware of his surroundings. Unconsciously his mouth lowered in stunned awe and his eyes widened. The scene looked like something from a thirty year old Beirut newsreel. The front window had vanished except for a few shards of glass still clinging to the aluminum frame. Most of the small tables, including the one he'd been sitting at only moments ago, had been blown over. Littering the floor were shards of tinted glass, newspaper pages, small brown napkins, cardboard cup holders, and a smattering of small fake leaves that had been ripped from the two synthetic ficus plants near the front door. Looking around, a glimmer of light caught the corner of Kelley's eye. Turning to find the source, Kelley caught his breath and held it. Three feet from where he'd fallen lay the crumpled and scorched passenger door of his Mercedes. The tan leather inside sat face up and he could see it was littered with black marks and heat bubbles. It had come through the window and hit another of the small tables with enough force to split the three-inch thick table in half. Kelley stared at the door, unable to take his eyes off it. Though the thought never fully took shape, he knew that only a few feet had separated him from a potentially lethal collision.

His breath returned in quick, jerky bursts. Through all his years at the paper, he'd seen some bizarre and even disturbing things. The paper frequently ran stories of war-torn cities, hospitals filled with burned or dismembered children, egregious acts of domestic violence, polluted water, the re-emergence of a stronger tuberculosis bacterium, detailed accounts of post-Katrina events, and so on – and he absorbed and processed them all with the hardened dispassion of a professor grading essays. Pain and suffering became easier to handle the further away they were from the reader. Years and years of bad news had crossed his desk, yet nothing had ever hit this close to home. Or this close to him.

Still in a daze, Kelley absently brushed the glass from a spot on the floor, replanted his left hand, and stumbled to his feet. The front half of the coffee shop was in tatters while the back half seemed relatively undisturbed. Kelley looked around to see if anyone else had been injured. The shop was empty. Was he the only one there? He couldn't remember seeing anyone else in the shop, but then he knew he hadn't really been paying attention. Following his usual pattern, he'd strolled in with his nose buried in the morning edition, ordered his coffee without looking up, paid, pocketed whatever change they'd given him, and then sat down to wait for his drink. And as the man on the phone had observed, his drink had never come.

Careful not to run into anything, Kelley made his way towards the now open front window. Having made it to where the window once blocked the glaring reflections from the parking lot, he raised his eyes to the upside-down burning metal box that used to be his Mercedes. Black and gray smoke poured from the interior of the vehicle as the leather seats and carpet floors were being relentlessly devoured by the flames. At the front of the upturned SUV, twisting plumes of bright orange flames danced seductively in the light morning breeze. Three of the four tires were still attached, each with several small fires slowly melting away the vulcanized rubber. In the back of his mind, the sight of the vehicle lying on its roof reminded him of an upside-down beetle, its legs flailing wildly in a futile attempt to right itself. Or perhaps he was imagining himself at that moment.

Kelley could feel the intense heat from the fires as they slowly consumed what remained of his Mercedes. He raised his right hand to his forehead to wipe off the sweat. Only then did it occur to him that he was still carrying his cell phone. He realized that he'd been gripping the phone tightly ever since the explosion blew out the windows and threw him to the floor. He looked at the phone like it was a relic from an alien world. "How is it I'm still holding this?" he wondered. Still staring, he saw the small LCD screen was lit up and showed the seconds from the current call still ticking away.

Gradually, Kelley raised the phone to his ear, not sure what to expect. After a moment a voice said, "Don't talk, just listen. This demonstration should be all the proof you need to believe that we are serious, Mr. Kelley. Forty-eight hours from now, parts of this country will also be upside-down and smoking. Prominent figures will vanish. Things will begin to change. I'm sure you'll want your paper to be the first one to report on these events. The opportunity to do so will come soon enough. In the meantime, I suggest you clean yourself up and prepare to give your report to the seven police officers who are currently racing down International Drive and will be there soon. If you choose to tell them about our conversation, you can rest assured it will be our last and another paper will be first to break the story. So just show them your identification, explain to them who you are and why a great many people might want to threaten you. Tell them you are unharmed and do not want medical treatment. They will push you to go to the hospital, but they must obey your wish if you refuse. If all goes well, tell the officer you're going to find a restroom. Walk south to the end of the Galleria and take a left. A black sedan with dark-tinted windows will swing by to pick you up." Gray paused then said, "Remember, we'll be watching, Mr. Kelley. And we'll be listening."

Jack Kelley sat on a concrete bench just outside what remained of the coffee shop with a wadded-up white handkerchief pressed to his forehead. The police had arrived shortly after his cell had gone silent. The first officer out of his car had his hand on his sidearm, but never drew the weapon. As soon as he saw the blood running down the side of Kelley's face, he immediately sat him down on the concrete bench and gave him the handkerchief. The next hour was a blur of activity. Another squad car arrived at the same time as the ambulance and fire truck. Despite the fact that a massive car bomb explosion had just wrecked his vehicle and destroyed half of the Starbucks, the rubberneckers amassed quickly, like mindless shards of metal drawn to a strong magnet, oblivious to danger. Throngs of people crowded up against the yellow police tape. From where he sat it looked as though the thin plastic tape was actually holding firm against the mass of onlookers pressing for a better view. Kelley wanted to shout to them that this and much more would be in the morning edition, but decided against it. Ever the salesman.

The first officer stayed with him most of the hour, asking him a barrage of questions. Although he'd been tempted to come clean with the officer, Kelley decided it was best to do as he'd been told. Like millions of other people around the world, Starbucks was the first stop on his daily commute. The young officer's eyes widened when Kelley explained that he was the editor of *USA Today* and that the paper undoubtedly had domestic and international enemies. The officer scribbled frantically as if he'd just been told the secret formula for Coca-Cola. Kelley could see it in the young man's eyes: bored McLean cop. Joined the force for some television-style action. Had yet to go on a high-speed pursuit or shoot at a car and watch it explode when he hit the gas tank. Was already sick of the heaps of paperwork, fingerprinting days at the elementary school, talks to D.A.R.E. parents, youth outreach programs, fast food, overweight cops recycling the same twenty year-old stories, calls to 911 because someone's dog was shitting on their neighbor's prized lawn. And so on. The finest Virginia had to offer. The young officer was oozing boredom from every pore. But now the tide had changed. Information power broker, attempted murder (or so he thought), car bombing, international intrigue (or so he truly hoped), the mysterious disappearance of the three baristas who were supposed to have been working, collateral damages, even a trickle of blood.

"The rookie is in hog heaven," Kelley thought. Unfortunately, Kelley's mind was in a different place altogether. In the span of a few seconds his day and his life had been stripped bare of all trivialities and concerns. Now he was left feeling as though he'd been dropped into the middle of a war zone. And something told him there might be more truth to it than anyone around him would guess.

He spent the next fifteen minutes convincing the green officer, the firemen, and the paramedics that he was not injured and would not be taken to the hospital. He was the editor of the largest newspaper in the country and he needed to get back to the office and get the story to press. Ironically, this was the way he really felt, though he knew there was no story as of yet. He promised to put in a good word for the professionalism of each and every person on site, as long as they didn't try to stop him from leaving. Sensing the hidden threat of bad press in his words, the young officer, paramedics, and firemen all wished him good luck and quickly found somewhere else to be.

Fearing he'd spent too long lingering, Kelley picked up his pace and headed south down the sidewalk. Rounding the corner of the mall, Kelley was surprised to see a black sedan already parked only a dozen feet ahead. The outline of a man in the driver's seat was all he could make out. He looked around to make sure no one had decided to follow him. Satisfied that he was alone, he returned his attention to the car. Slowing his pace, Kelley tried to concentrate on all the relevant details and storing them in his memory. Then, walking casually towards the car, he noticed the license plates were from D.C. Before he could commit the number to memory, the car lurched forward and came to a halt so the back passenger side door was right in front of him. Kelley hesitated for a moment, then opened the door and slowly lowered himself inside. He was still sore from the explosion and let out a low groan as his muscles objected to being used. Thankfully, the plush leather seats were smooth and soft. Taking one last look at the spot on the sidewalk where he'd just been standing in the morning sun, Kelley reached over and closed the door.

A dark-tinted privacy window separated him from the driver, preventing him from discerning any useful details. He would later recall that he couldn't even be sure of the driver's gender, let alone any identifying features. Glancing around the interior, Kelley found it was devoid of any personal objects. No umbrellas, sun screens, road maps, blankets, or loose papers. In fact, there was no indication that anyone had ever sat in the back seat. It was this immaculateness that made Kelley realize he was probably a filthy wreck. Self-consciously he patted dirt and dust off his pants and shirt. The smell of new leather was mixed with a faint gas-like effluvia. He thought he also smelled a hint of jasmine, but quickly dismissed the idea.

The car lurched forward and exited the parking lot. Glancing out of the window, he managed to get his bearings. The car was heading south towards the highway, but he knew that speculating as to his final destination was useless at this point. He considered knocking on the privacy window to see if he could learn anything about the driver or where they were heading, but he decided against it.

Suddenly his cell phone sprang to life. The sharp noise startled him. Kelley retrieved the phone. He stared at the bright blue screen for a moment. No caller I.D. or number. Another ring. He reached up and touched the cut on his head. The wound was no longer bleeding. A third ring. Kelley bit down on the inside of his lip, nodded to himself, then hit the Send button.

"Okay," he said uncertainly, "I'm listening."

Washington D.C.

Roger Tarte examined the many photographs on Steven Floyd's office wall. It looked as though each had been framed, leveled and hung with no consideration of the others. Wood, glass, and metal frames displaying faded shots from the sixties up through crisp, high-definition shots that could've been printed in the last few days. One thing was certain – there could be no doubt of the lawman's affinity for deep-sea fishing. Practically every picture contained a boat, ocean, mildly sunburned grinning faces, tall fishing poles, and more than one impressively large catch. Tarte, who had always possessed a talent for pattern recognition, scanned each image carefully. First he noticed many of the same people appeared in the pictures, though none of the faces were familiar except Floyd's. Tarte also noticed that, with the exception of a married couple that appeared in seven of the images, there were no women in the shots.

"Might be a cigar and brandy crowd," he thought. The boys go and play while the wives stay at home, wondering what their husbands are doing. But then why the exception? His eyes returned to the woman's face. He examined her in each shot, but saw nothing that would indicate why she would be allowed to permeate this seemingly testosterone-dominated club. In one shot she proudly exhibited a two-foot catch. In the next, her head was thrown back and she appeared to be laughing exuberantly. In the third shot, one of the few bereft of boats or sea life, she was seated amidst a host of wine bottles and a half dozen partially filled wine glasses on the table in front of her. Thumb and index finger pinched the stem of a seventh glass held beneath her nose. This appeared to be some kind of tasting event, and she was blissfully savoring the aromatic bouquet amidst her normal entourage of suntanned sportsmen. Tarte studied the look of peace and tranquility on her face and felt a pang of envy. Such contentment and happiness were rarely seen these days. Now, staring at the blissful serenity exuded from the face of a woman he'd never met, Tarte felt sure these qualities should be the goal of every person's life, including his own.

Tucking away thoughts of bliss and elation for later, he resumed his examination of the photographs. Fishing, smiling faces, more fishing – the theme here was obvious. Then something caught his attention. Of the dozen pictures, the same boat appeared to be in nine of them. The other two boats were normal sport fishing boats – probably charters – whereas the recurring ship was a schooner. Only six of the nine photos displaying the beautiful vessel revealed the name: *Cinzento Lobo*. Tarte had no idea what the name meant, but seeing it brought back a rarely visited memory.

Towards the end of his senior year in high school, Tarte had his heart thoroughly trampled and mangled by a tall, olive-skinned brunette named Geneva Parnino. Among her other talents and accolades, Geneva had been president of the Latin club and spoke the language fluently. During the four months they had dated, Geneva often spoke Latin to him. When he would ask what she said, she would just laugh. Had he not been intoxicated by her looks and smile, he might have pursued the matter, but he never did. Though Latin had nothing to do with their failed courtship, the experience had left him sour on the dead language. Though it was embarrassing to admit now, Tarte had purposely chosen to study Russian and Japanese in college, astutely avoiding anything Latin-based. Like most college graduates, he'd never had cause to use either of the languages he'd studied. But he was fairly certain that had things been different between him and Geneva, perhaps he might know what "Cinzento Lobo" meant. But alas, he didn't have a clue. *Scheisse*!

Light footsteps came from the direction of the secretary and Tarte heard muffled conversation. He glanced back at the woman's serene, untroubled face. "If only life was that simple," he thought. Taking a step back, he examined the pictures again. He realized his first conclusion about the haphazard arrangement had been wrong. There was something specific about the order of the images, but he couldn't put his finger on what it was. Before he could nail it down, the office door opened and in walked the head of the FBI's Counter-Terrorism Division. Steven Floyd wore an expensive blue dress shirt with white collar and cuffs, shiny silver cufflinks, black slacks and polished black shoes. His salt-and-pepper hair and friendly smile reminded Tarte of Richard Gere in his prime. Floyd walked with an easy, comfortable stride, like a man walking through his own den. He apologized for keeping Tarte waiting and gestured towards a leather chair in front of a large oak desk. Floyd set down the folder he'd been carrying and took a seat in his beaded leather desk chair.

"Good to see you again, Tarte. I hope my call didn't come as too much of a surprise to you," Floyd said lightly.

"As a matter of fact, I was a little surprised," Tarte admitted.

"I hope I didn't interrupt anything important."

"Not really. To be perfectly honest, I was going to start researching our next warm vacation destination." Tarte gestured over his shoulder and said, "You wouldn't have any suggestions would you?"

Floyd laughed and said, "My tastes are very specific to, well...the catch." Floyd had hesitated for half a second, which Tarte knew from experience was usually a sign of a lie, or at least a forthcoming half-truth.

Then he thought, "This guy is high up in the FBI and a lifer – he could tell me his name was Julio Iglesias and I'd swallow it." Regardless, he decided to try again.

"I assume from our conversation the other night that most of those pictures were taken in Nassau," Tarte said.

"Well, yes, and around the Bahamas," Floyd said, shooting a quick glance at the array of pictures, "Most of them, anyway."

"The fishing is really that good in Nassau?" Tarte asked.

"It's more than adequate for a novice like me," Floyd said casually, then added, "But if it's modernity and comfort you seek, I would recommend Hawaii. Nassau is still a bit...shall we say, native."

"Wild country, eh?" Tarte suggested. "Rugged men only?"

"Something like that," Floyd said hesitantly.

"With one notable exception. The infiltrator."

Floyd cocked his head sideways, like a dog that had heard a strange noise.

"The woman in the first few pictures," Tarte clarified. "She's the only sheila in a school of male sharks."

"Yes," Floyd said heavily, "She...was a friend. She made the trip with us a few times."

There was pain and sadness in Floyd's voice and expression. Tarte was curious, but decided not to press the matter. Instead, he tried a new angle and asked in an envious voice, "Is that big boat with all the sails yours?"

Floyd smiled and shook his head. "On my salary? I'm afraid not. It belongs to a friend."

"Cinzento Lobo," Tarte said. "That sounds Italian."

Floyd gave him a curious look, then said, "It might be. I never thought to ask what it meant."

Tarte had once read that most fisherman, sport or other, made it a point to know the name of every boat they boarded, as well as what or who it was named after. At the time he'd thought it was either superstition or a matter of polite etiquette. Whether Floyd actually adhered to such customs was unclear. He made a mental note to find out, then decided to change the subject. "Well, we've exceeded the standard two minutes for cursory niceties. Should we delve into classified government gossip, talk orthogonal Latin squares, or just cut right to the chase?"

Floyd smiled. "This is a good sign," Tarte thought. Sometimes his dry humor was wasted on those with underdeveloped intellectual palettes, which he encountered more often than not. Despite that fact, he firmly believed that things such as dry humor, unusual gestures and even the occasional non-sequitur were effective litmus tests for personality, confidence and intelligence. A quick slap in the face, even a verbal one, could reveal a lot about a person in a short span of time.

Floyd seemed to consider something, then asked, "Assuming the answers to my questions aren't top secret or too personal, could I count on you to answer – and answer honestly?"

Tarte considered this for a moment and asked, "Is the question germane to the purpose of my visit?'

"Not in any way, shape, or form," Floyd said with a curious grin.

"Is this discussion being recorded?" Tarte asked, phrasing the question in a manner that suggested that he, too, was asking for an honest answer.

"Not to my knowledge," Floyd said. "My office is swept for listening devices every morning."

Tarte thought for a moment then answered, "Then sure, fire away."

Without hesitating Floyd said, "How many stars are on the FBI seal in the lobby downstairs?"

"Is this a trivia game?" Tarte asked. When Floyd didn't answer, Tarte answered, "Thirteen."

"How many steps are there leading up to the lobby?"

Tarte looked at Floyd, who bore a curious expression. Like a man who had just discovered a marvelous new device. He shrugged and answered, "Well if you don't count the pavement at the top as a step, there are fourteen."

"You memorized all the United States Presidents in school, correct?"

"I've only attended school in the U.S. So, yes."

"Could you name them all right now?"

Tarte had an idea of where this was going. He'd had a similar Q & A session at the first interview for the position he'd once held with the CIA, so he answered, "Yes. And in any order including alphabetical by first or last name." He expected that would slow Floyd down, but instead the questions started coming even faster.

"What is my secretary's name?"

"She introduced herself as Joan Anderson. I assume that is her real name."

"How many X-ray machines are in our lobby?"

"Nine."

"Eight," Floyd said.

"Nine," Tarte repeated. "Eight in the front and one at the rear near the loading dock entrance."

Floyd's fingertips were pressed together forming a steeple, which he held in front of his lips. The FBI veteran smiled and kept going.

"What were the shapes of the tiles in your last house?"

"Hexagonal. Freckled taupe. One inch. Six hundred and ninety-four complete."

"What were the last names of your first grade..." but Tarte cut him off. "Johnson. Stow-Marshall. Denton. Hester. Michaels. And Coolly. Far Rockaway, Queens, New York. Is this an interview?" A trace of irritation laced the question.

Floyd ignored the inquiry and asked, "Do you remember the face of every person in those photographs on my wall?"

"No," Tarte answered flatly, "not my specialty. But I am relatively certain they all had two eyes, two ears, a nose and a mouth."

Floyd nodded and said absently, "Indeed they did. Indeed they did." The FBI man seemed to snap out of his reverie and quickly apologized. "Forgive me, Agent Tarte. I have a profound interest in people with your abilities. When I encounter someone with such, gifts, I'm compelled to learn more. To see what skills they have. In all honesty," he said confidingly, "I'm quite jealous. I'd trade five years of my life to be able to have such recall."

Tarte shrugged and said, "My memory isn't eidetic if that's what you're wondering. It's loosely related to savantism, though outside of the CIA I was never thoroughly tested."

Floyd nodded again and said, "I apologize, Agent Tarte. But I'm glad to know more of your abilities. Something tells me you're going to need them."

Gainesville, Florida

Thirty yards from the rear entrance to the university lecture hall, Toman sat patiently waiting. It was nearly eight-thirty. The evenly spaced lights straddling the edges of the main walks had been on since just before seven o'clock. It seemed like only a few minutes ago when he had been admiring the beautiful Florida sunset that his reverie had been interrupted by the sudden pop of the bright white lights. A short pang of regret at the instantly dulled reds and oranges had set in immediately, only to be answered as quickly by a voice in his head brusquely reminding him of exactly why he was here. "Someday we'll all take time to admire the sunsets," he thought wearily. Absently, he had looked at his watch when the lights came on. His watch read five after seven. Then, as if on cue, two women and two chattering assistants appeared from around the corner of the building, most likely coming from the pay lot. Each woman carried a business attaché case and walked purposefully without appearing to rush, as if to acknowledge they were each late, but far too important to run. The students had been piling into the hall since before six-thirty, while the ever-vigilant protestors had been there since before six.

This was the twelfth lecture in five weeks that the two women had given. The title was "God Punished Us on 9/11." Toman had sat in on the first few lectures, taking notes. With each lecture it became more and more difficult to keep silent when it came time for questions. Fortunately, he wasn't the only one outraged and deeply disgusted. Attendees regularly pummeled the two women with direct questions about patriotism, specific religious tenets that seemed to go against their opinions, points of biblical history, etc. Atheists often stood and questioned the validity of fundamental Christianity and the literal interpretation of the Bible in the face of the multitude of other world religions. How could they, or any believer, be so certain their doctrine was the correct one? Like any ridiculous, unthinking fundamentalist extremists, the women answered by quoting passages from the Bible. Arguments normally broke out, heated words were exchanged, accusations and condemnations were hurled back and forth. The overall tone of each lecture was not one of acceptance, but one of anger – on both sides.

Toman couldn't understand why universities all over the country continued to pay the women substantial sums to present at their schools. Word must have gotten around that the students, and even some of the faculty, disagreed vehemently with what these women were saying. Even if administrators from different schools didn't communicate much, a quick web search would reveal a plethora of information sufficient to make them think twice about extending an invitation, and later remitting a check to these women. There were a number of websites devoted to a virtual protest of the very existence of such speakers. Toman was familiar with most of them. Prior to physical tracking and surveillance, he had spent a great deal of time compiling a mountain of research on both women, as well as the organizations that supported them. The dossier on each woman was now thick, well used, and rank with the pungent smell of hate and fear.

Shirli Felps was a radical church leader hailing from an obscure church in Kansas that had recently gained recognition for its protests at military funerals and for inflammatory remarks about Canada. Ms. Felps had made appearances on a number of radio and television programs, preaching her beliefs. Toman had seen every interview and listened to every broadcast he could find. He had received his assignment over a year ago, but had not been told why this particular fanatic was of interest to *The Aenamaia*. Only a few days of searching, reading and listening had answered that question. Felps's rhetoric was common enough, although more extreme than usual. What was disconcerting was the calmness she maintained while under attack. Most of the programs featuring Felps did not support her beliefs or those of her organization. Show after show, dismayed and incredulous newscasters and radio hosts would pummel their stoic guest with a barrage of questions designed to discredit and taunt. Less than flattering comments and accusations directed towards the extremism of Ms. Felps and her followers were commonplace.

Heated emotions, which any professional journalist or interviewer knew should be kept at bay, would surface like molten lava. One could see and hear the incredulity rise even further when hastily-chosen, harsh words failed to get a rise out of Felps, the seemingly unflappable guest. Instead, Felps would sit perfectly still, apparently absorbing the insult and turning them into a weapon she was preparing to unleash. But instead of a reply ripe with anger and hostility, she would calmly answer with quote after quote from the Bible, followed, or sometimes preceded by, her interpretation of such. No matter how much she was baited, Felps always had a bit of scripture ready for the next volley.

In the first few days of his research, Toman had started with replays of radio interviews. With every insinuation and every accusation he had imagined Felps's face contorted with anger and hate, but her voice was incongruent with that image. It was only when he watched her television interviews that he understood the real source of her composure under fire. He remembered thinking she wasn't much to look at. But there was something in her eyes. It took him a few minutes of scrutiny before he knew what it was. He noticed her eyes were always open just slightly wider than was normal. He also noticed that her intense gaze was fixed on the speaker. Not once did she sneak a glance at the camera, the crew, the side of the stage, or the backdrop. Normally such attention would be seen as professional and considerate. In this case, it looked as if she were trying to extract something from the other person's soul through their own eyes. Or perhaps she thought she could impregnate her extremist views into the other person's brain by sending an invisible beam through their eyes.

Another more likely possibility was that she was simply trying to disrupt their thinking. Whatever the case might be, Toman knew the look in her eyes – knew it all too well. He had seen it countless times while doing contract work in an asylum in upstate New York. At the time, he had been a structural engineer, but did side work on large ventilation systems. Walking through the labyrinth of corridors on his way to the physical plant, he had passed by what the staff called the "fish tanks," cells made of clear, thick Plexiglas. Patients under constant observation occupied these special cells. Toman still remembered looking into their eyes and seeing the same thing he saw in Felps's penetrating gaze: insanity. But unlike the poor souls locked in the cells, Ms. Felps was loose in the world, protesting at military funerals, breeding hate against gays, indoctrinating children into her cult, praising the deaths of soldiers, and the attacks of 9/11.

A little over a year ago Felps had found a like-minded ally to help carry the torch. She and her flock had been protesting outside a hospital where four male students had nearly killed a young gay man attending the local university. The protest signs read "God Will Finish the Job" and "Satan Welcomes Gays." A few of the signs even had the student's name referenced as "The Punished." The display had attracted the attention of people deeply offended at the insensitivity and absurdity of the signs and the demonstration itself. With this, came the usual throng of overzealous media to cover the controversy.

One of the more knowledgeable reporters present was familiar to *The Aenamaia*. Upon arriving, Anna Kulter, reporting for a right-wing neo-conservative magazine, picked Felps out of the crowd and was able to interview her. Strangely, Kulter's questions focused more on Felps's political views than on the demonstration. After two subsequent interviews, Kulter and Felps co-authored a short paper for a national religious lobbying group titled, "A Vote to Forestall the End." The paper implied that Armageddon would be unleashed upon the earth if the Republican President failed to win his second term. The piece received quite a lot of press, which was not surprising since it was in support of re-electing the President. Strangely enough, no major media sources reported on a series of generous and anonymous contributions to a newly founded organization run solely by Kulter, as well as the accounts of Felps's church. Several smaller newspapers tried to trace the money, but came up short. But what they were able to discover was that the two organizations received over one million dollars each.

It wasn't long before Toman learned that Anna Kulter also had an abundance of websites and commentaries directed towards her, as well – most of which were less than flattering or supportive. It seemed that Kulter had a problem with letting her mouth get away from her at times. She had made a number of offensive comments about certain members of Congress, organizations supporting gun control, anyone she thought was a liberal, and various celebrities and reporters. The litany of offenses was extensive. She even made startling comments about the families of the victims who had died in terrorist attacks all over the world. Her banter was quickly becoming legendary, as were the lies and false statements made in the several books she wrote.

Anna was often referred to as a "mouthpiece" for the Republican right, a job for which she was well paid. In addition to numerous errors, mistakes, and outright lies, Anna continued to let her forked tongue run rampant, intent on offending any and all who did not worship her as anything less than a demigoddess.

Sitting outside the lecture hall, Toman remembered how his heart had begun to beat painfully in his chest the night he heard that Felps and Kulter had joined forces. Tzaria had called and told him the news. The fanatic duo had announced they would be kicking off a nationwide lecture circuit, as well as beginning work on a new book. How many scores of people would they reach? How many could they entice and convince? Toman pictured thousands of outcast college students staring ravenously up at two powerful speakers, wondering what they had to do to sign up. With every grateful handshake, with every new subscriber to their newsletter and website, with every fresh new convert, their egos would swell and their putrid influence would spread uncontrollably.

Toman had paced his office only a few minutes before the phone rang. It was *The Aenamaia*. He had expected it. Felps and Kulter had been on their list for some time now, but had never been considered a top priority. Now, with the announcement of their union, the ante had just been irrevocably raised. Tzaria had lobbied for the assignment, but the case was made that she already had her hands full. Toman volunteered to take over their files and *The Aenamaia* had agreed. Thus began the long process of research, discovery, and due diligence.

Since then, he had meticulously tracked the movements and activities of Felps and Kulter. Additionally, a second team had been assigned surveillance of supporting groups and organizations. Among those being monitored were the primary financial supporters, contributors and followers of Felps's church, sister organizations, and the CPA who handled taxes for the church and Felps. All related landline and cell phone calls had been tapped and recorded. Osiro had managed a clever and permanent hack into the mainframe that supported each of the church's computers, which gave them access to donor and mailing lists, website visitor tracking (including a list of unique ISPs), member names (including children), other churches quietly sympathetic to their cause, even politicians and lobbyists who had shown an interest in quietly and anonymously helping.

For Kulter, *The Aenamaia* had even more phone and computer taps in place. After the two women had joined forces, additional taps had been placed on Kulter's publisher, close family members, publicist, PR firm, both attorneys, and her hairstylist and personal assistants. *The Aenamaia's* research team had also managed to acquire a wealth of personal information on both women, including five years of tax returns and bank statements, numerous property deeds, criminal records, health insurance history, credit histories, credit card statements, insurance policies, and court documents for the numerous lawsuits both had been involved in. The team was also able to obtain two FBI files and ten hours of archived surveillance footage taken by the FBI. The last was supplied by Raven, the deepest undercover member of *The Aenamaia*, who had extensive resources.

Toman was intimately familiar with every scrap of information available on the two women. It was his job to know everything there was to know about them. He was the Augur assigned to this case, and thus, would have a primary voice in planning the endgame.

He looked at his watch again: eight-forty. On the lecture circuit, he had kept strict time records of their movements and had found that they rarely kept an audience for more than one hour and fifteen minutes. They also never stayed more than thirty minutes past the end of the lecture. Toman's time table analysis indicated that when the two arrived late, which was more often than not, they would still not exceed the allotted one hour and forty-five minutes. Unless new precedence was set tonight, the two should be emerging from the building any minute now.

Toman fished the cell from his pocket. He had bought it today and purchased a prepaid phone card at the same time, paying cash for both. From his other pocket he extracted a small rolled up piece of paper wound tightly around a short, metal rod. A small strip of tape kept the roll together. As soon as he pulled the tape loose, the rod dropped, unrolling a thin sheet eight inches long. Running down the center of the paper were two columns, each containing thirty single digits in seemingly random order. Using the Fibonacci sequence he'd memorized in his early conspiracy theory days, counting in reverse from fifty-five, Toman picked out ten numbers and dialed them into his phone.

"Dominos Pizza," a woman's voice answered enthusiastically. "We like it hot."

"Cute, Dia," Toman said, shaking his head. "Come up with that one yourself or are you thinking of pursuing your dream career?"

"No, you insensitive newt," Dia said testily, "I'm hungry. Olga the Wise here only packed water and trail mix."

In the background Toman could hear Susha say defensively, "How was I supposed to know you're allergic to nuts! You lived with your ex-husband for three years and never broke out in a rash."

"That's what you think," Dia responded playfully.

"I don't mean to intrude on this stimulating intellectual discourse, ladies," Toman said trying to keep the irritation from his voice, "but we have an extraction to execute here. Are you ready?"

"Sorry, T. Yeah, we're ready."

"Have you heard from *The Cabelleros* yet?" he looked at his watch and added, "They should be on base by now."

"Roger that. Hilos checked in twenty minutes ago. They had just pulled into the hangar and were helping unload your presents. Thirteen total, all gift-wrapped and deliriously mellow."

"Thirteen?" he said sounding concerned, "I only had twelve listed."

"Keep your shirt on. There was a last minute addition. An import that wasn't expected to be present but was on the list for possible future liberation."

"Full doc?" he asked skeptically.

"Full doc," she assured. "Courtesy of Raven. Hilos transmitted the info and Gray authorized it. A real bottom feeder. Instrumental in financial backing, laundering and 'creative' accounting. Trust me, you'll like this one."

"I don't like any of them," he muttered. Toman thought for a moment. He wasn't fond of unanticipated changes to his plans, but if the catch was as good as Dia said, he understood Gray's decision to take advantage of the opportunity rather than precipitate early exposure. Additionally, if the extra person was tightly linked to either Kulter or Felps, they might have been in daily communication with them and may have become suspicious when neither could be located. This scenario always presented the possibility of alarms sounding prematurely. Alarms would undoubtedly go off, but not before he wanted them to.

"Okay. One more now is one less later. Anyone going to miss them?"

"Raven is confident we have some time. According to the thick dossier he sent over, this one is a loner and always has been. It's the best way to stay off the radar and keep your record clean. This octopus has its tentacles in many pies, but none that will notice its absence for awhile."

"Roger that."

"What's the status on your end?" Dia asked.

"Both parcels should be ready for pickup in ten minutes or so. Keep to the plan. Extract near parking entrance beneath the tree cover."

"We're in place," Dia said.

"Use the chloroform. No unnecessary damage to the primary packages."

Then, in the tone of a flight attendant Dia asked cheerfully, "And will you be checking any luggage tonight, Mr. T?"

"Two light pieces," Toman said, trying not to chuckle. Sometimes he gave Dia a hard time for deviating from communication protocols, but in truth, he thought it decreased the tension inherent in an extraction. "They're relatively new bags and won't give us any trouble."

Dia and Susha knew he was referring to the assistants that followed the two women everywhere. Toman had detailed background information on both. As far as he could tell, they were just younger versions of Kulter and Felps in training. Each time he saw them the term Mini Zealots came to mind. They were usually only two steps behind and, for reasons he couldn't exactly explain, always seemed to stand out – even in a serried crowd. Tonight was no exception. They were both wearing bright, neon green, long-sleeved shirts with black lettering that read: God Hates Gays. Not the wisest attire to wear at a liberal college, but the bright shirts would make them easy to follow.

"Quad extract. Two heavy, two light?" Dia confirmed.

"Affirmative."

"Any sharp objects, black powder or Asian defense skills?"

"Negative. Blunt and untrained," Toman said adding in a derisory tone, "as the detailed briefs from a certain well-informed individual has outlined many times before."

"Yeah, yeah. Just thought I would double check. No need to get your panties in a twist," Dia said dismissively.

Before he could point out exactly which of them was more likely to be wearing the panties, the doors to the lecture hall flew open.

"Hold," his voice was quiet but serious.

First out of the doors were Shirli Felps and Anna Kulter, followed immediately by the two neon-clad assistants. Kulter wore beige slacks, a black suede coat and black heels, the latter putting her over the six-foot mark. Her long, straight, dirty blonde hair was put up in a thick ponytail. Swinging out of sync with her long stride was a burgundy attaché clutched in her left hand. Her face was plain and unremarkable. From a distance her thin frame and neatly pressed suit gave the impression of a sanguine, successful businesswoman.

In stark contrast, a much shorter Felps wore a long, plain taupe dress with a Southwestern style denim jacket and dowdy brown flats. She had thin, straight shoulder-length brown hair, which looked as though it had never been styled. From his observations and notes, Toman knew Felps never wore makeup or any jewelry, other than a slender silver watch. Although the two women were only a few years apart in age, Felps was clearly the senior. The lines in her skin hinted at an aversion to lotion and related skin care products. This premature aging stood out even more when she stood next to Kulter, whom Toman knew from his research embraced any and all products designed to forestall the signs of time's passing.

Toman watched as the motley four hurried quickly down the steps of the lecture hall while two large campus security guards held back a throng of students determined to follow them. He had seen comparable reactions at several other lectures. The students never sought to harm the two women, but merely to drown them in a flood of acute accusations, insults, and a slew of colorful metaphors. Luckily for the women, their reputations preceded them and security guards were always present. This time, Toman had actually been counting on the students' heated reactions. He had even gone so far as to have Osiro hack into the college's administrative email system and send out a brief and carefully worded background on the two speakers. One day after the mass email was sent, he had received a text message on his private cell saying that all remaining tickets to the lecture had been snatched up the next morning as soon as the ticket window had opened. Fueled by the email, along with the standard hostility drummed up by the speakers during their presentation, security would be forced to hold the students in the building for a few extra minutes. No doubt there were also guards at the front entrance doing the same. Any protestors that might not have gained entrance would be chanting and circulating in front of the hall. Toman judged they had perhaps five minutes before the guards would step aside to let the lecture hall empty.

Toman spoke quietly into his phone. "Brains are contained. Parcel and luggage have emerged from the rear and are power-walking towards conveyance. Four pieces total. Floodgates will open in five minutes. I'm heading your way, bringing up the rear. Field is clear. We'll intercept in the end zone."

"Roger that. Cage is ready and waiting. Dia, out."

Chapter 5

Washington, D.C.

"When did this happen?" Tarte asked, frantically searching his attaché case for a pen and notepad.

Steven Floyd paused for a moment. "The local police report puts the explosion at approximately 9:20 a.m. They're still on-site investigating what's left of the vehicle. Forensics and the bomb squad agree the thing went straight up, flipped, and came straight down. No major damage to anything else. There was some debris, but most of it landed only a few feet away – with the exception of the passenger door, which nearly landed on top of the vehicle's owner."

"Damn," Tarte said, picturing a man getting drilled with a twirling, flaming car door. "Is this guy being questioned?"

"Already been done," Floyd paused. He lowered his voice a notch and added, "They let him leave the scene."

Tarte stopped writing and looked up. "Leave? Where? Was he taken to the hospital?"

"Nope. Left on foot."

He found it difficult to believe a car bomb had exploded in northern Virginia and an hour later the owner, who he'd been told had witnessed the explosion, was let go. "Where in the he…? Who was the owner?" Tarte asked.

"Jack Kelley," Floyd said slowly. "*USA Today* Jack Kelley."

Tarte's eyebrows shot up with renewed interest. "Really," he said slowly, his mind already on overdrive. Images of the well-known editor danced through his mind. He'd first heard of Kelley in '04 when it was discovered that one of *USA Today*'s leading foreign correspondents had been fabricating his stories. Soon after, Kelley's face had appeared in dozens of newspaper and magazine articles.

USA Today itself had kept tight coverage on the story – careful not to let other publications beat them to the press with facts about their own investigation. Kelley, who up until that point had been relatively unknown, was suddenly thrust into the media limelight he himself had helped to foster. Tarte recalled seeing the editor's tall lanky form saunter on stage to shake hands with Letterman, Leno, Oprah, Larry King and others. Kelley would sit in the guest chair and banter casually with the host.

But when they got down to business, the topic was always that elusive, endangered animal: journalistic integrity. Kelley never missed an opportunity to sink his teeth into his fallen employee, an effective ploy for subtly distancing himself and his newspaper from the bad seed. Though the media had a history of guarding its elite, they were quick to prey on the weak and injured. During one of Kelley's more scathing criticisms of his recently resigned correspondent, Tarte remembered seeing the parallel between Kelley's attack and that of a lion viciously mauling an injured impala.

"According to my contact on-site," Floyd continued, "Kelley was inside the Starbucks when his Mercedes exploded. Strangely, the Starbucks employees were not present at the time of the explosion and have yet to be located. The police were able to locate the work schedule in the back room. Both had been hired in the last thirty days. We're checking with their corporate offices now. Only two people were scheduled to work, though Kelley swears there were three behind the counter when he arrived."

"Interesting," Tarte said absently. His thoughts were racing at breakneck speed now.

"Strange, I know," Floyd said and leaned back in his chair. "But that's what his statement says."

"What about background checks on the two we know?"

"Running as we speak," Floyd said.

"Was anyone else hurt?" Tarte asked curiously.

"As far as we can tell, Kelley was alone in the shop."

"Alone?" Tarte repeated. "No other patrons?"

"No. He apparently had the place to himself."

"Were there any other witnesses? Anyone outside see anything?"

"No," Floyd said, a hint of suspicion in his voice, "At least none have been found."

Tarte was silent, so Floyd continued. "No one witnessed Kelley going in, and no one saw the explosion. Even the security cameras on the mall stopped recording almost a half hour before Kelley arrived. By the time the cameras began recording again the police were already on-site."

"What happened with the cameras? Were they doing maintenance? Power outage?"

"None of the above. No one's sure what happened. PD has a tech out there working on it."

Something occurred to Tarte. Opening the internet browser on his phone, he began typing frantically. Google Earth.

"Tarte?" Floyd asked looking over the edge of his desk.

"Hold on a second, Floyd. That was McLean, right? At the Galleria?"

"Yeah, why?"

"I'm getting a satellite shot of it right now." Tarte pulled up the image and increased the magnification. He then cross-checked the location of the Starbucks.

"Floyd, any idea how many cameras should've captured the event?"

"I asked that myself. Looks like at least two, but they're checking that as well. What are you thinking, Tarte?"

"One camera malfunctioning during that time could be written off as a random fluke. Multiple cameras failing only moments before the explosion is highly suspect. My thought is whoever planted the explosives must've had access to the security systems in order to avoid being caught on tape."

"The explosives could've been planted ahead of time. That would almost certainly necessitate using a remote detonator. Use a straight timer and there's no way to tell when Kelley is driving. Not a very solid way to blow someone up."

"Unless that wasn't the intent," Tarte said, astonishment in his voice.

"Come again?" Floyd said with renewed interest.

"Think about it, Floyd," Tarte stood and began pacing. "You said before that Kelley had been in the coffee shop for a good twenty minutes before the explosion. No video of the event. And no witnesses in a Starbucks? I've never been to a Starbucks that didn't have at least three laptop addicts and a few serious readers at any given hour of the day. And that one is near a large intersection." Tarte stopped and thought for a second then asked, "How far is it from Kelley's house to the Galleria?"

Floyd thought for a moment then answered, "Ten miles. At that time of day, I would guess the drive would take about twenty minutes. But the coffee shop isn't very far away from his office."

"Here's what I'm thinking. Anyone who wanted Kelley dead wouldn't have that much trouble pulling it off. No private security, probably no real safety precautions. Finding his residence would only require someone to follow him home one night. He drives himself to work, his looks and height make him easy to pick out of a crowd. Same goes for his high-priced vehicle. And I'm guessing on the days he goes to the office he routinely stops at this particular coffee shop, even though there are likely a handful of other Starbucks along the way."

"So far so good," Floyd said approvingly. And for a brief moment Tarte felt sure Floyd knew more than he was letting on. There was something in his casual posture and patient eyes. It almost felt like the FBI Director was guiding him towards the answer. "What's your point?" Floyd said encouragingly.

"Whoever did this wasn't trying to kill him. There are too many other, much simpler, less risky ways to accomplish that. Getting him at his residence would be a snap. Explosions involve too many things that can point investigators in a specific direction. The type of explosives used, the timer, how it was wired, placement, etc. No. This was meant to frighten or intimidate."

"Blackmail?" Floyd offered.

"It's possible. But it seems a bit too drastic."

"Unless they had already made the threat and Kelley refused to pay. This might have been a way to prove they were serious," Floyd speculated.

"Does your file say anything about any kinds of death threats made towards Kelley?"

"Nothing in my folder. Hang on…let me see what else we have on him." Floyd began punching keys on his computer.

Tarte nodded but said nothing. He stopped pacing. Something about this whole incident wasn't sitting right with him. No witnesses. No cameras. The coffee shop staff mysteriously vanished. Kelley walks away from the scene shortly after the authorities arrive. Enough explosives used to flip a three-ton SUV, yet no other cars were damaged and no one else was hurt. "No. They weren't trying to kill him," Tarte reasoned. Anyone who would go to such great lengths to kill by explosives so publicly would want video and witnesses. They'd want plenty of proof to blast over the Internet or sell to the TV stations. No. There's a different agenda here.

"Got it," Floyd said. "He's reported several death threats against himself and other newspaper staff, but nothing in the last six months."

Tarte was shaking his head. "That rules out blackmail. If there had been a threat, Kelley would've reported it. Or at least written an editorial about it," he laughed mirthlessly.

Just then something else occurred to him. "Floyd, how did Kelley leave the scene?"

Floyd's right eyebrow rose and he said, "Yeah, I asked that as well. The last they saw of Kelley, after he made it abundantly clear the officers really didn't want to see their pictures in tomorrow's paper, he walked towards the end of the mall and disappeared around the corner."

"He left on foot?" Tarte said incredulously.

"That's what they said. I thought it was kind of odd too. A multi-millionaire walking anywhere seems strange. Especially after having almost been blown to bits an hour before. Of course *USA Today* headquarters is only about a mile away. That must've been where he was heading." The phone on Floyd's desk rang and Tarte gestured that it was okay to answer. He turned to give Floyd some privacy and found himself again facing the wall of fishing photographs. His eyes went immediately to the schooner and the name written eloquently on the hull. *Cinzento Lobo. Cinzento Lobo.* He pronounced the words silently, but nothing familiar came to mind.

Tarte shook his head and returned his thoughts to Kelley. "Who would want to send such an explicit and public message to Jack Kelley?" he wondered. No doubt the list of suspects could be a thousand miles long. The CEO of the largest newspaper company in the country was bound to make enemies and offend easily. Few people cared who penned the articles or failed to check the facts. In the end, even Ronald McDonald could get blamed for a stale hamburger. The view is great from the top, but so is the fall.

"Tarte!" Floyd said, sounding excited.

Tarte spun around.

"Kelley isn't at his office."

"What?" Tarte said incredulously.

"No one there has seen or heard from him all day. He's gone."

Washington, D.C.

David Lesser really couldn't believe his luck. Two hours is all it had taken – that and an eight hundred dollar dinner at Signatures, a restaurant in the trendy Penn Quarter neighborhood of D.C. This small, tax-deductible investment had bought his company the largest U.S. military contract since the first Gulf War. And for Afghanistan no less! The return on his investment would be enormous. In two previous contracts for redevelopment in Iraq, Lesser's company had been able to retain over eighty percent of the total contract amount as pure profit. Of course, some of those funds made their way back to the Republican Party and various individual republicans in the form of discreet contributions, but it was a pittance compared to the overall gains.

Before commencing work on the Iraq contracts, Lesser had confided with the head of Appropriations about the allocation of the contract funds relative to the work to be done in Iraq. With a wink, the committee leader had whispered, "Fuck em," Dave. "It's Iraq, for Christ's sake. As long as we make sure we're all financially sound and ready for Afghanistan, who cares what happens in Iraq."

That was not to say a few peripheral steps weren't necessary. The books had taken a little finagling to ensure proper cooking. He'd also had to fashion a number of creative methods for ensuring the greedy and often overzealous stockholders would only benefit from a small portion of the gains. Fortunately, he had a penchant for numbers, a predilection supported by his considerable talents as an accountant. Extensive training and experience with one of the top corporate accounting firms in the country, prior to the company being found guilty on obstruction of justice charges, had afforded him a virtual degree in what he liked to call "Financial Cartography." His philosophy was as long as you knew the destination, the map could always be redrawn.

Tonight Lesser had promised a number of concessions and financial donations to the three GOP congressmen sitting across from him. Over champagne and strawberries, Lesser had committed to over one million dollars in contributions. To avoid scrutiny, the funds would first be funneled through several obscure organizations and then redirected back to the appropriate entities. The names of the intermediary organizations had been typed on a regular sheet of paper and handed to Lesser. Looking at the many names on the list, Lesser had to suppress the urge to laugh. Although the names sounded official and vaguely familiar, he didn't have a clue who ran these concerns, where they were located, or what their purpose was – besides acting as an invisible and efficient filter for political contributions. For that matter, he couldn't have cared less.

Thinking of it now brought out the laugh he'd skillfully suppressed earlier. He could still recall the first three nondescript names on the list: Global Alliance for Policy Advancement, American Organization for Civic Research, and New Millennium Frontiers. Right in plain sight while simultaneously slithering in the murky shadows. "It's an admirable and advantageous quality in a company," he thought.

Emerging from the restaurant, Lesser was still pondering the cryptic list when he absently handed his ticket to the valet. It was only when the man turned and headed towards the parking area that Lesser happened to notice his substantial size. Unconsciously, he adjusted his glasses, pushing them slightly higher up the bridge of his narrow nose. Refocusing, he could see the smooth, tight curves of bulging triceps peaking from beneath a tight-fitting black polo. Dropping his gaze he noticed the man also wore black pants and heavy black boots. Lesser tried to recall if the restaurant's parking attendants had a standard uniform. He looked around for another valet, but no one was in sight. "It's late," he thought. The Congressmen hadn't arrived until almost eight p.m. By the time they had finished their dessert it was ten o'clock. It must've been a quarter past ten or so when the donor list was finally handed to him.

Thoughts of the valet faded quickly as he tried to recall which of the congressmen had produced the list. He distinctly remembered transferring the list from his left hand to his right, necessitating that he replace his champagne flute on the linen tablecloth. But he also recalled thinking something had been passed between the men a few moments before. Was it the list? Was it grade school note passing? Lesser shook his head. It didn't matter anyway. It had been made clear that the congressmen held significant sway with each of the organizations on the list. They assured Lesser of complete cooperation and the utmost discretion where monetary transactions were involved. A few checks sent as donations to these organizations and presto! Success. All that would be left to do then would be to sit back and decide how to parcel out the money. "Life is good," he thought, his broad smile returning.

Approaching headlights off to the right arrested his attention. In a few seconds his shiny yellow Hummer pulled up to the curb. Lesser grudgingly pulled a few ones from his pocket and picked up his briefcase. Positioning himself next to the passenger door on the driver's side, Lesser waited for the valet to emerge. A moment later a young man dressed in black jumped energetically from the driver's seat. Leaving the door open he rushed past Lesser, saying over his shoulder, "Have a good evening, Sir," and disappeared inside the restaurant. Lesser stood puzzled for a moment. Then he remembered he still held the tip in his hand. He smiled guiltlessly, shrugged and replaced the bills back in his pocket. "Tonight just keeps getting better and better," he thought.

Tossing his briefcase into the passenger seat, Lesser climbed into his favorite toy and closed the door. He was adjusting his glasses again when movement out of the corner of his left eye caught his attention. He turned and looked out through the dark tinted windows into the foyer of the restaurant. The single flicker of light from the candle at the hostess stand was momentarily blocked as one of the attractive young hostesses passed by, escorting two individuals to their table. Although the darkness of his window prevented him from seeing the young lady's face, the outline of her magnificent figure was unmistakable. Earlier that evening he'd turned down her offer to seat him before his guests arrived in order to relax in the foyer and casually survey her voluptuous figure. Despite the elegant knee-length black dress, high heels and perfect make-up, Lesser knew from personal experience that she couldn't be more than eighteen or nineteen years old. Amazing the way young women were developing so much earlier than in his day. All the better since he wasn't getting any younger. Looking at her dark silhouette through his window, Lesser now thought he would recognize that girl's body a mile away, despite what his wife would undoubtedly say about his poor vision.

He was confident the girl would call him. During a brief conversation, he had suggested someone with her talent and personality would fit in nicely at his company. He had given her his card with his company cell number written beneath the gold foil letters "CEO." It was true they were not hiring any entry-level positions now, but that was irrelevant. All he needed was to bring her in for an informal interview in his plush corner office. Once her eyes were frozen wide with awe, the rest would be easy from there. He would show her around, offering details on the various paintings and sculptures, the cache of important items in the four locked and armed glass display cases, and the expensive eighteenth century furniture. Then he would guide her towards the windows, his hand pressed lightly on the small of her back, and point out the most notable landmarks in sight. By the time they actually sat down, she would say yes to almost anything. This had been his standard modus operandi for years. And one thing Lesser firmly believed was that if something had worked well for you in the past, why change the equation.

As he inserted the key into the ignition it suddenly dawned on Lesser that the young man who had dropped his car off and strangely avoided accepting the small tip was not the hulking beast that had originally taken his ticket. Confused, Lesser turned to look back at the empty valet podium. "What the..." he muttered. Before he could finish his sentence Lesser felt the Hummer shift slightly as if something large had gently bumped it. He was about to roll down the window to see if another car had rolled into him when his whole vehicle shook. Turning slightly, Lesser caught sight of a massive shadow in his rearview mirror. Someone was in his backseat! A sudden panic shot through him. He reached for the door handle. In an instant a thick, muscled arm appeared out of the shadows of the back seat and curled violently around his neck, cutting off his breath. Instinctively, both of his hands latched onto his attacker's arm in a vain effort to dislodge it. Lesser could feel the blood rush to his face at the same time fear and adrenaline pulsed through his whole body.

"Stay perfectly still," a deep voice said slowly. The man's hold loosened enough for Lesser to take a desperate breath.

"What in the hell do you..." Lesser started to say, but the arm tightened again, causing a small squeak to escape from his lips.

"It is impossible to remain perfectly still when your lips are moving," the man said evenly. Something about the calmness in the voice scared Lesser more than not being able to breath. Unable to speak, Lesser nodded his head as best he could to signal he would comply. Again the man's arm relaxed a degree so he could breathe.

"Start the Hummer, put it in drive and slowly turn right onto the street. Try to be a hero, and the last thing you will hear is the sound of your neck snapping." The man spoke slowly and deliberately, with no accent and virtually no inflection. Lesser sensed this was not a petty, desperate criminal. This man was calm, collected and serene, as if he were listening to classical music and sipping wine by candlelight.

Lesser did as he was told. His hand was shaking, but he managed to turn the key and start the Hummer. Fumbling with the gearshift, he put the vehicle in what he thought was drive. He realized that his right foot had been pressing hard on the brake pedal. Nervously he pulled off the brake, then slammed back down on it, causing the vehicle to lurch.

"S-s-sorry," he said, trying to catch a glimpse of the man's eyes in the rearview mirror. It was too dark to see anything but a bulky, two-dimensional black outline.

"I'm not going to tell you to relax," the man said simply. "That's unrealistic. You're scared – that's to be expected. Take a deep breath and concentrate on what you're doing, as if your life depended on this vehicle leaving the parking lot in the next five seconds."

A new and sharp bolt of fear shot through Lesser's body. Trying to concentrate, he took a quick breath and removed his foot from the brake and gently depressed the accelerator. In a few seconds, they reached the end of the parking lot. Bringing the vehicle to a halt he looked into the rearview mirror. As if reading his mind, the man slid his arm from beneath his chin, choosing instead to clamp a powerful hand on the right side of his neck. Lesser breathed deeply, but did not break his stare into the mirror. In response the man said quietly, "Right, then left on Ninth."

Lesser lifted the turn signal, which proved he was scared, as he normally felt signaling was unnecessary, especially when driving a Hummer. Looking back and forth, he could see the street was relatively quiet in both directions. Resigned to do what he was told, Lesser stepped on the gas. The vehicle lurched onto Pennsylvania, then made a quick left onto Ninth Street.

They were now heading south, cutting through the middle of the National Mall. The hour was late. Only a few pedestrians and tourists were out. During the daytime it was a different story. "Tourists are like locusts this time of year," Lesser thought irritably. "Filthy beggars." They come en masse hoping to feel a sense of awe in the nation's capital and to leave feeling like their government is as pure and resolute as the hundreds of statues scattered throughout the district. The city felt more like a slum during tourist season rather than the powerful Mecca of the world. Be that as it may, he felt certain he would be willing to take all of the tourists in the city out to an expensive dinner if it would get him out of this predicament.

Hoping for some clue as to when this ordeal might be over, he directed a puzzled and expectant look in the rearview mirror thinking the man might read his questioning expression again. After a few seconds of shifting his gaze from the rearview mirror to the road then back to the mirror again, the man said, "Get on I-395 going south and keep to the speed limit."

Lesser was about to risk asking a question when he realized the onramp was coming up fast and was on the opposite side of the street. Nervously, he crossed the three lanes of traffic, only remembering to signal as he hit the onramp. The rear tires squealed as Lesser completed the turn. He righted the Hummer and accelerated onto the freeway.

"Take it easy," the deep voice growled, "And turn your signal off."

Lesser pushed down on the turn signal to shut it off. No wonder he hated using the stupid thing.

"Attracting the attention of the authorities via reckless driving is not in your best interest at this juncture," the man added indifferently.

Within a few minutes the Hummer passed over the Washington Channel and swung west briefly. Just over a mile ahead the road curved southwest. Looking out the passenger side window, Lesser caught the outline of the Jefferson Memorial. In a flash it was gone and they were passing over the Potomac River. He recalled hearing somewhere that it was one of the dirtiest waterways in the country. At night it resembled a long, thick vein of undulating tar heading off to the organ it fed. Something about that thought troubled him, though he did not want to admit that it had something to do with his unwritten future.

The silence was unnerving. Again he looked in the rearview mirror. The man remained silent. Lesser decided to venture a question. He chose his words carefully and tried to emulate the evenness of his assailant's voice.

"Why are you here?" he questioned. "What exactly did I do?"

"Maybe you should ask them," the man said, releasing Lesser's neck to point to the north. He followed the man's thick finger and was surprised to see the brightly lit Pentagon looming less than a mile away. There were still lights on throughout the building, as well as a number of brightly lit halogen lights around the perimeter and throughout the parking lot. Lesser had visited the building many times. Hell, he had probably seen at least half of the brass offices in the complex. He had even been led through a number of restricted areas.

"I'd be happy to. Should I head that way," he said trying to joke with the man.

When there was no response he tried again. "What does the Pentagon have to do with this?" he asked, still careful to keep his tone light.

The man sat back in the seat and said, "You can waste as much time as you like playing dumb, Dave," adding the first hints of derisiveness to the pronunciation of his first name. "While we're en route I have nowhere else to be."

Hearing his first name openly mocked by a meat sack posing as a valet infuriated him. Who the hell did this thug think he was? Less than an hour ago he'd had three of the most powerful and influential congressmen in Washington eating out of his hand. He'd brokered a deal for more money than this cretin would see in two lifetimes. His cell phone carried the number of dozens of movers and shakers in Washington,

New York, Texas, California, and Colorado. He even had the personal cell number of the commanding officer at Norad. Now some high-school dropout Buddhist Neanderthal was playing word games with him and slurring his first name in a contemptuous manner. And Lesser suspected this ape was actually treating him like a lower form of life – looking down on him. Despite the fear he'd felt only minutes ago, David Lesser was pissed.

Making the decision to confront his passenger, Lesser signaled and pulled the Hummer onto the shoulder. As he slowed to a stop he expected some kind of protest from the back seat, but his assailant was silent. He figured this was a good sign that this man could be reasoned with. "Confident aggression," he thought, "that's what bullies respond to."

Unbuckling his seatbelt, Lesser started turning in his seat saying, "Listen, I don't know who you are or what the hell you..." but before he could finish a clipped, wispy sound and a short burst of blinding white light came from the backseat followed by a loud, cracking noise. Lesser spun back around and immediately noticed a quarter sized hole in his flat, rectangular windshield on the passenger side. Radiating out from the fresh bullet hole in all directions were cracks of varying lengths. One such fracture extended all the way to the top of the windshield.

Lesser stared forward in disbelief, his pulse racing in sync with the hard, painful pounding of his heart, which threatened to break through the breast plate and flesh holding it captive. He could hear and feel the loud drumming in his head. It felt as though rope-thick bundles of nerves and veins carried the throbbing to the very edges of his ears. His breaths came in quick, shallow succession as he tried to form a single thought. There was a faint, burnt smell floating up from the back seat. In the back of his consciousness, Lesser was aware the acrid odor was the only smell he could pick up at that moment.

The gunshot had been quiet – merely a chirp that sounded like a small volume of pressurized air being suddenly released. Otherwise, the cab of the vehicle was silent. Then suddenly another shot spit from behind him. Lesser reacted immediately by thrusting his body forward and covering the back of his head with two clamped, shaking hands. His forehead collided with the dashboard, but he didn't have time to notice. He barely felt the tops of his knees as they rocketed up into the bottom of the steering wheel. Lesser's eyes were clamped shut, but he could still detect the bright flash that had emitted from the silenced gun behind him through his thin eyelids. Two more shots rang out. "Jesus!" he exclaimed breathlessly. "Shit! Oh shit!" His whole body was clenched in an attempt to coil into a tiny ball; his hands gripped the steering wheel with all the force his adrenaline-saturated muscles could muster. Tiny drops of sweat appeared immediately from every pore on his body.

Half a minute passed, then another. No additional shots had been fired and there was no noise from the back seat. Not a sound. Lesser waited a few more seconds then slowly released his grip on the wheel. Unsure of what might happen next, he gradually raised his head and sat back in his seat, absently wiping the sweat from his brow onto his jacket sleeve. Little by little, the tension in his facial muscles relaxed and he turned his attention to his windshield. He was amazed to see that there was still only the one sunburst hole. But now the hole was not perfectly circular. It had changed shape, but was only slightly bigger than it had been after the initial shot. The significance of this observation began slowly coalescing in Lesser's mind. The coolness the man had maintained, the swiftness of his movements, the single hole in the windshield – the implications hit Lesser like a swift blow to the head. This hulking man had fired four shots from the back seat, three of which had passed right through the small hole made by the first, barely chipping the loose glass around the edges. This guy was a professional. That much was obvious.

It had, on occasion, been necessary for Lesser himself to employ similar such men to handle all manner of business difficulties where the attorneys and courts proved too expensive, ineffective, or less than sympathetic to his company's goals. While he'd never seen any of them at work, just being in their presence was adequate testimony to their clandestine nature, composure and confidence. All of them were quiet, calm, and calculating. They never said more than was necessary, never negotiated, and each seemed to watch everything going on around them – even when their eyes were fixed on one point.

A jolting shiver ran through his body. One fact was undeniable: David Lesser was in deep shit.

Gainesville, Florida

"Idiots," Anna Kulter muttered through clenched teeth. "Fucking liberal idiots. Every campus in this godforsaken country is filled to the brim with bleeding heart liberals and over-indulgent idealists. Their parents should be drawn and quartered. The college administrators and professors should be turned over to a firing squad."

"God will punish them," Felps said confidently. Kulter glanced at Felps and wondered why she'd ever agreed to team up with this nut case. Religion had taken possession of the plain, anorexic women next to her, but Anna was still not convinced this dyed-in-the-wool martyr was the best choice to help further her career. Sure, the media outlets made it a point to cover Felps and the protests staged by her following, but in the back of her mind, Anna suspected it might somehow come back to bite her on the proverbial butt. Besides that, the hellfire this slight woman carried and spouted everywhere she went was starting to get on her nerves. Anna often wondered if it wouldn't be a good idea to hire a large, hairy biker to tie Felps up and take a run at her. Most of the time men were useless for anything other than repairing machinery and hard labor. But in Felps's case, a night of aggressive, savage sex might be just the thing for Mother Theresa here.

Anna was walking quickly and Felps tried to keep up without appearing to hurry. Felps's five-and-a-half feet had a difficult time keeping up with the legs of a six-footer. "His vengeance is swift," Felps continued, "but sometimes not as swift as we would like." The woman's southern drawl always seemed to land hardest on the last word of every sentence. Kulter knew Felps tried to lose the accent when she spoke in public, but when her emotions swelled, the accent inevitably returned, as did Anna's irritation.

"Perhaps a fleet of fuel-heavy 757s falling from the sky would change their minds," Anna said angrily. "Abortions are a sin against God, but I think there were a few hundred in that hall I could've made exceptions for. Especially that...spear-chucker in the front row."

Anna had barely opened the night's presentation when a large, black male who looked like he could comprise half of the university's football team had raised his hand. She had tried to ignore the student, hoping he would get the message that questions came at the end. A few minutes passed and the hand was still raised. It began to distract her so she gave him a chance to speak.

"Ms. Kulter," the large man had said, rising to his feet, "You had quite a loud and strong voice in the Terry Schiavo case. Your vehement opposition to the family's decision to remove Mrs. Schiavo from life support was carried on every news program and in every right wing publication. Do you still hold the opinion that the decision was unjust?" The student remained standing, waiting for an answer.

"Yes," she said confidently, "I think it's clear the husband and family acted selfishly and that the federal government had every right to step in and try to block the decision. Without a living will, I do not believe anyone has the right to make that decision except competent doctors, government officials, or God himself. There is always a chance doctors will find a way to save people in Terry's condition or that her body could, with enough time and care, mend itself."

"Would you want to be kept alive in that condition?" the man asked skeptically.

"Yes, I would. And I would expect my family to do everything in its power to keep me alive. It's the corrupt liberals in this country that would sooner pull the plug than put any faith in divine intervention."

"Ms. Kulter," the young man began, the tone of his voice betraying the trap he was about to close. "Isn't it true that only nine years ago your own father became incapacitated after an accident involving some mechanical contraption he'd erected in his back yard? Wasn't he living on life support? And also without a living will?"

Anna's eyes narrowed. This part of her past had come up a few times in various interviews, but she had always managed to deflect it. "I think we're getting a little off the subject here. Tonight's lecture is on the corruption of liberals and their open support of gays, which goes directly against the commandments laid down by..." But before she could finish the young man's deep voice overpowered her own, echoing throughout the lecture hall.

"Ms. Kulter!" he said loudly, "Any lecture presented at a U.S. university should first be subject to the qualification of the speaker, if that speaker is to be taken seriously by the student body who paid to hear them speak." The man's arm swept across the restless assembly. "Especially when the discussion focuses around your unwavering and unfaltering morality. Part of that qualification lies in the honesty, integrity and forthrightness of the speaker. So what I want to know, Ms. Kulter, is how you can stand here and defend your stance in the Schiavo case when you and your family chose to take your own father off of life support? Don't you think it's just a little hypocritical to publicly denounce the actions of a family and a husband whose loved one was in a vegetative state for over fifteen years, when your own father had his plug pulled after less than a month? Don't you think the God that you said would, and I quote, 'punish the family for its crime,' bring the same wrath down upon you and your family?"

Anna fumed. Gripping the lectern tightly, she tried to maintain her composure. The large young man was staring intensely up at her. She knew she had to take care of this quickly if she had any hopes of proceeding with the planned lecture.

"I understand the attack methodology of liberals like yourself, young man. I've dealt with it time and time again on radio and television. You choose two unrelated events and set them side by side for comparison. The old "apples-and-oranges" trick. Well, I'm sorry if I won't take your bait. My father's situation was very different in many ways from the Schiavo case and clearly not the topic of this lecture. The topic of this lecture…"

But the young man cut her off again, saying "…should be 'Right Wing Deflection of the Truth.' Or perhaps it should be titled 'The Ethics of Making a lot of Money on the Suffering of Others.' Only I've already studied both of those topics in great detail." The student pulled his jacket from the chair, turned and began walking up the center aisle. After a few yards he turned back and added, "By the way, most of the people in this room believe God loves everyone, even psychotic egotrons like yourselves." The hall erupted in applause as the man did an abrupt about-face and strolled purposefully up the aisle.

Anna watched him exit the rear door, hoping her gaze would burn a large hole in the back of his head. A few seconds passed before she remembered that most of the eyes in the audience were returning their attention to her. She smiled, trying unsuccessfully to mask her anger and irritation. She had to wait several painfully annoying moments for the applause to fade. Then, after making a cynical comment directed at freedom of speech, she continued with the presentation. Even though the pungent stink of the interruption seemed to hang in the air, she managed to finish her speech and turn the hall over to Felps.

Thinking about the student again now, Anna suddenly wondered if he was, at this very moment, lurking in the shadows. The thought seemed ridiculous, but she couldn't help but feel like she was being watched. She glanced around cautiously, but saw nothing. The campus seemed deserted. This was not the first time she had regretted not hiring any security, especially for the night lectures. If someone were intent on harming them, Mary Magdalene and the twins here would be useless in preventing it. The image of a lion attacking them from behind flashed through her mind. "Yes," she mused with a wry smile, "she was undoubtedly the fastest runner in the lot. If anyone would get away it would be her."

The irritated voices of her assistants drew her attention. The two had their cell phones out and were trying unsuccessfully to make calls. The two assistants practically lived on cell time. The only time they weren't on their phones was during the lectures. That rule had been established early on. Any other time the two grew restless if they weren't talking or texting. On the rare occasions they were unable to pick up signals, as seemed to be the case now, they would grumble about the evil cell companies and the conspiracy to block their communications. They would fidget with the phones until a signal was found or they passed out from exhaustion.

She looked back. In the darkness the neon blue emitted by the phones seemed unusually bright, as did the obnoxious yellow shirts the two were wearing. Every time they wore those ridiculous kick-me garments she felt the impulse to backhand both of them. Felps's appearance also annoyed her most of the time. Here she was, a best-selling author, dressed in an eight hundred dollar tailored suit, in the company of the Topeka twins and their zealot mother. If they weren't so well funded, she would drop these extremists in a heartbeat.

"I had my fair share of attacks too," Felps complained. "I wish I had known beforehand that the entire campus was crammed full of sodomites and sinners. I wouldn't be surprised if the Lord God himself didn't send a rain of fire to cleanse this patch of filth like he did on 9/11. Purification is what we need. Every faggot, every politician, every atheist. All the soldiers, Canadians, Jews, blasphemers, Muslims, you name it. They will all burn and perish in agony at the hands of Lucifer. There is no word other than the Lord's word. There is no opinion, only the laws that He set forth and the teachings of Christ. And when you disobey the Almighty you pay the ultimate price. God's wrath is awesome!"

Anna turned to look at Felps. She was staring straight ahead with that spooky look of obsessive intent she assumed whenever she spoke about the anger of God. Anna usually found it amusing, but tonight things had gone more sour than usual and she was in no mood for fire and brimstone.

"Let's just get to the car," she said hoping to curtail the river of condemnation that was certain to ensue. "We'll send one of the twins here to pick up our check from the university tomorrow before we fly back to New York."

They rounded the corner and found themselves walking in the shadows cast by two buildings flanking the narrow passage. Anna thought it strange that there were no lights mounted on either of the walls. Surely even a liberal institution like this could muster the funds necessary to maintain ample lighting throughout the campus. "Probably spent it all on fruit fly research and free speech bumper stickers," she thought.

Regardless, dark passages like this were a bad idea. Even through the irritation and anger still pulsing through her body, Anna couldn't shake the feeling that they were being watched. But when she turned to look behind her, there was no one there but the two assistants who were busy mumbling about a large-breasted young girl that had been seated in the front row. Up ahead she could see the lights of the parking area about a hundred yards away. Another twenty yards or so and they would cross the lighted drive that bisected their path.

They'd taken a dozen more steps when Anna heard a faint, but distinct shuffling noise coming from somewhere up ahead. She was squinting, trying to locate the source of the noise when two figures leapt out of a rectangular recess in one of the brick walls. Before she could make a sound she felt a strong arm lock around her neck and a cloth being pressed over her nose and mouth. A wave of terror broke over her. She tried to break free, but the assailant's hold was firm. From the corner of her eye she could see that a figure clad in black had the same hold on Felps, whose wide eyes were already glazing over. Before making another escape attempt, she inhaled deeply, knowing when she did that it had been a colossal mistake. A strong odor filled her nostrils and she felt herself slowly losing control. Her attacker expertly swung her around in time for her to see a huge man standing over the limp bodies of the assistants. For an instant she thought it might be the black student from the lecture, but behind the ski mask she saw pinkish skin around two intense eyes that stared knowingly into her own. To her left she saw the other black-clad figure let Felps's thin, limp body drop to the ground. Darkness pushed in around her field of vision, as if she were staring through a camera aperture that was quickly closing. She felt the strength drain from her muscles. "At least I was the last to go," she thought wearily. In the next moment the blackness consumed her consciousness and for the first time since her childhood, Anna Kulter's mind was at peace.

Washington, D.C.

Still holding the silenced weapon, the man sitting casually in the back seat said, "I apologize for interrupting you, Dave. I believe you were about to make a demand…or perhaps a clever volley of weightless threats. By all means, continue." The hulking man's voice was patient, almost apologetic, with a nearly imperceptible tinge of sarcasm.

Lesser's body was still tense as he continued staring at the quarter-size hole in his windshield. The four crisp chirps of the gun still resonated in his ears. This man could end his life at any moment – probably in several different ways. And there was nothing he could do about it. He knew he was trapped and the sensation terrified him.

"No," he whispered, slowly shaking his head. He swallowed hard and added, "No, sir."

"Formalities are not necessary. However, if you will agree to put this beast back on the road and maintain your ostensible urbanity, I'll provide answers to your questions."

"Who are you?" Lesser asked, trying to keep the shakiness out of his voice.

The man took a deep breath, exhaled slowly and replied, "You can call me Renker. Now drive."

Lesser heard the stress and urgency in Renker's voice and quickly shifted into drive and pulled back on to I-395. They drove in silence. After a few minutes, Lesser saw the Landmark Mall pass by on his left. It seemed obvious they were heading out of town, but to where? Was this some kind of a shakedown? Maybe this Renker could be bought off. Lesser was certain he'd never encountered the man, which meant he was here at someone else's behest. Which also meant he had a price. His lower jaw pivoted back and forth as he tried to think of how to proceed.

"Watch your speed," Renker instructed. Lesser eased off the gas pedal. The idea of using the cruise control had occurred to him, but then he realized he'd never taken the time to learn how to set it.

"So," he began, the hesitation clear in his voice, "how long have you been… I mean, how long have you done this kind of work?"

"Five years," Renker answered simply.

"Are you ex-CIA, NSA, Interpol?"

Lesser was surprised to hear a short, deep laugh. "No. But I suppose it's normal for someone like you to assume so. You hear those names in a movie and think you'll appear sophisticated and worldly by using them. Do you even know what Interpol is, Dave?"

"You're obviously proficient with a gun," Lesser pointed out. "I just assumed you had been trained to do this."

"I have been trained," Renker admitted, "but it wasn't for this. Not for this," he repeated. His voice was distant, as if his thoughts were focused on a time or place far from the present.

"This conversation is going nowhere," Lesser thought. In the meantime, they were already ten miles into Virginia and he still had no idea who this guy was, where they were going, and whether or not a blank check could turn the tides. "Keep talking," he thought. "Keep talking."

"You must make a pretty handsome living. I mean a man of your talents must be able to write his own ticket in Washington. Am I right?"

Renker laughed again and said, "Well, that took longer than I thought it would. I figured you would've made me an offer before we were out of the restaurant parking lot. I should've expected a little delay. Sometimes the fight-or-flight instinct collides head on with an ego like yours. Something to do with your overriding sense of superiority. Comes from years of bending people over, I suppose." Renker laughed again. "You can keep your wallet tucked snuggly next to your shrunken nuts, Dave. In this car, at this moment, your money has no value. Save it for your barely-legal fetishes."

Lesser was caught off guard by the insults the large man recklessly hurled at him. But what really disturbed him was the way he said "fetishes," drawing out his pronunciation. How much did this man know about him? Had he seen him admiring the sumptuous hostess back at the restaurant? Lesser felt strange thinking about the girl now. An unbidden and unwelcome little voice in the back of his mind suggested she might be the last woman he would ever see. He shook his head and pushed the images into the back of his memory. "Stay focused," he thought. "Try again."

"Look, friend, what's it going to take to make this whole unfortunate situation just go away?"

"I'm working on that right now," Renker answered matter-of-factly.

Lesser didn't like the sound of that. Perhaps a different route.

"Who is your employer?" he asked casually.

"*The Aenamaia*," Renker said simply, as if Lesser should know exactly who he was referring to.

"Say again?"

There was a pause before Renker repeated, "*The Aenamaia*. Don't try and hurt yourself thinking about it. This isn't any group or organization you've dealt with directly."

"Directly?" Lesser questioned.

"You've had dealings in the past with several members of *The Aenamaia*, but you've never crossed the organization's path directly."

"Pardon me for saying so, but you're being awfully cryptic. Couldn't you just explain what's going on, why you're here and where we're going?" Despite his best efforts, Lesser heard a hint of desperation in his own voice.

"Dave," Renker began with a sigh, "I spent many years of my life trying to tell men like you exactly what was going on, precisely why

I was there to tell them about it, and specifically where things were going. It didn't surprise me that a few of them didn't listen or pretended not to understand; that much I expected. What surprised me was how many did listen and did understand, but who still conscientiously chose to ignore reality and, in some cases, remain integral parts of the problem.

For example, most of the people I spoke with agreed that our government, under the Bush Junior administration, was undoubtedly more corrupt, manipulative, deceitful and destructive than any of its predecessors, including that of Bush Senior. These same people agreed emphatically that the mainstream media was in bed with the Bush administration despite his limp and fabricated dick. They concurred when I said that billions of dollars in military contracts were handed out like expensive candy to rich children like you who had no intention of making good on them and that education, healthcare, the environment, cutting edge science, and governmental oversight all saw astounding declines in quality and support since 2000. While violent crimes, immigration, religious influence, illegal campaign contributions, oil prices, wars, voting debacles, slander campaigns, egregious lies and political scandals all have had record years and raked in record profits.

Despite all of these facts being well known and understood, things continued to deteriorate. Neo-millennium hippy-types believed that letters to congressmen, like the three you got on your knees for tonight, protests, activist websites and blogs, and email campaigns would make a significant difference. Unfortunately, they have been proven wrong time and time again. Nowadays, you could have every gay person in America march down the streets of Washington and camp in front of the White House and it would receive less media coverage than the Alabama state beauty pageant. If America doesn't know about it, they don't tend to make an effort to find out." Renker paused. Lesser wanted to chime in, but something in the man's grave manner told him it would best to wait until he finished.

"There was a void, Dave. A massive void. Those of us who were furious over the state of our government, our country, and especially the apathetic, numbed indifference of our citizens, decided something had to change. Someone had to fill the void; someone had to act." Lesser expected to hear something with the ring of "In the beginning...," but Renker was silent.

Lesser was unsure what to say. He had to admit that deep down, in places he rarely visited, he agreed with much of what he'd just heard. There was a lot wrong with America. But hell, it had always been like this. You can't fight the system. Those with money and power spend all their lives focused on two activities: protecting what they have and doing anything and everything they can to get more. But that's how it works: democracy and Social Darwinism copulate and produce an awkward and unruly offspring named Capitalism. The strong do what they must to survive and prosper. Without the strong, the weak would be lost. Where would his company be without him to lead the way? Where would the economy be without a strong war effort? How many jobs had been created to support the wars in Iraq and Afghanistan? Sure, American men and women fighting in those countries had died, but that's what soldiers were for. They fight while companies like mine employ hundreds of thousands of people to make their weapons, clothing, food, vehicles, computers, etc. Some die, but most will eventually return.

"You know," Lesser began with his best boardroom voice, "Nobody likes war, but you have to admit that our economy has always reaped the benefits of our numerous transgressions. Jobs, technological advances in weapons, communications, logistics, medical care, operations, planning, etc. As for the other problems you mentioned, well you may have a point. However, at a time of war, when our country is threatened by terrorists, the President must keep to the agenda established by President Bush. After all, we have to keep driving our cars, right?" Lesser said with a chuckle.

Lesser expected an immediate return, but was met with silence. He still could not see the man's face clearly. Occasionally quick flashes of light would dance across the bottom corner of his square jaw, but a clear picture never materialized. Finally Lesser ventured to nudge the man from his reverie. "Well?" he asked, trying to sound like an opponent in a friendly debate.

Another minute passed before Renker said, "Get off on the next exit and head west towards Lorton. And watch your speed."

Lesser saw a green road sign pass overhead indicating exit 163 to Lorton was one mile ahead. Lorton. Lorton. That name sounded vaguely familiar to him. He had traveled this way many times on business. Perhaps he'd stopped there for a drink. Before he could put his finger on it, the answer presented itself when another sign suspended above the road read "Fort Belvoir three miles ahead." Then it hit him. "Of course!" he thought. How could he forget? Fort Belvoir was home to the U.S. Army Material Command, the Defense Logistics Agency, the Defense Contract Audit Agency, the Defense Technical Information Center, the Defense Threat Reduction Agency and several other agencies under the Department of Defense. Several of his best military contacts had offices right on base. Most of his company's best salesmen had at least one of the procurement managers on speed dial.

Lesser felt a wave of relief spread through his body. They must be going to Belvoir. There was nothing else of interest in the area. What could possibly happen to him on a military base that employed almost eight thousand people? But why this guy? And what was with the hijacking, the gun, and his whiny political speech? And who in the hell would go through all this trouble rather than calling and asking for an appointment? And who would know he had been at the restaurant meeting with...and then it hit him. Those sons-a-bitches. And after an expensive and amiable dinner, no less. They had the gall to set one of their goons right outside the restaurant and put him through all this! But why? He'd never failed to deliver before. Well, his "donations" to the GOP were substantially higher than ever before. And he had stammered a bit when they'd asked him about measures towards the utmost discretion. But to kidnap him! That was ludicrous. The more he pondered this new scenario, the more upset he became. "Christ, all this!" he thought shaking his head in disbelief. Fucking politicians. Fucking chicken-shit politicians! How about a goddamn phone call instead? And they damn sure were going to pay for the bullet hole in his..."

"Exit here!" Renker said loudly, startling Dave. Seeing that the exit was about to pass them, he pumped the brakes and pulled the wheel hard to the right. The obstinate Hummer swerved into the exit lane, just barely missing the water barrels in bowling pin formation.

"Dave," Renker said carefully, "reduce your speed. Myself, the Glock 22, and the Evolution 40 silencer I'm holding would appreciate not having to say it again."

Lesser had no idea what the speed limit was, so he slowed the Hummer to thirty-five and scanned for a speed limit sign. At the end of the off-ramp, he turned west onto Lorton Road. Within a hundred yards, a sign indicated the speed limit was forty-five. Lesser pressed down on the gas pedal until the speedometer read exactly forty-five. He had no idea how to reach Fort Belvoir from this road. They were still at least three miles from the northern tip of the base. And who would be there this late? He looked at the digital readout on the car stereo: eleven twenty-three. Would the base even be accessible?

Whoever had perpetrated this little scare tactic would undoubtedly have made arrangements for their entry. What a waste of his time. And the sons of bitches had stuck him with a lunatic who thought nothing of firing a gun in his Hummer – at his windshield! Scaring the living shit out of him. Bastards. But he would even things out. As soon as the funds were transferred to his company accounts, he would have his secretary make arrangements for the two of them to take another research trip to the north Mariana Islands, courtesy of the United States Government. Lesser grinned, just thinking about it.

The U.S. House Majority Leader had introduced Lesser to the decadent spoils of the north Mariana Islands. The Majority Leader, thankful for the contributions expertly funneled by Lesser's company, had made arrangements for a complimentary stay in a five-star hotel in Saipan, where he had been entertained by some of the island's most beautiful new residents. None of the girls had known English, but communication had not been a problem. A round of golf every day, a visit to the pool and the spa, drinks at the hotel bar, and his secretary's capable and skilled touch were just what he would need to forget about this little ordeal. And because of the contract he'd scored tonight, his wife would be content with a long and solo shopping trip in Hilton Head.

Lesser was about to call Renker's game and ask how he intended to get to the base when the man said, "Take the next left onto Furnace Road."

"Will this take us right to Fort Belvoir or will we be taking another turn?" Lesser asked confidently. He glanced quickly into the rearview mirror, hoping to see a small hint of recognition on Renker's face. Lesser was surprised to see that the man's close-shaved head was partially lowered, blocking his eyes and facial expression. "Ha!" he thought. "Finally called his bluff. Dumb jock."

Lesser slowed the Hummer and made a left onto what he assumed was Furnace Road. "What a strange name for a road," he thought. The road was unusually dark. Switching to the Hummer's high-beams, Lesser saw they were traveling down a straight two-lane road. Fifty feet ahead, a bright white streetlight hung low on the side of the road. Light began filling the interior of the Hummer. Still hoping for an expression of shock, dismay, or even defeat, he returned his gaze to the rearview mirror. Lesser was again surprised. He could now see the large man's face clearly. A new pulse of fear shot down his spine and landed with a nervous shaking in his right foot. The two men's eyes locked. Despite his assumption that his kidnapper was just a thug, Lesser saw a torrent of emotion and distress barely contained behind the man's intelligent green eyes. The conflict this man was enduring manifested in a tightly clenched jaw, hard stare, and an occasional ripple tearing across his forehead, as if some microscopic demon lurking just beneath the skin was bolting back and forth looking for a way to escape.

Unconsciously, Lesser slowed the vehicle. The confidence he'd felt only moments ago had vanished. He found it difficult to steal his eyes away from the disturbing expression stretched tightly across Renker's face. Flashing a quick glance to the road, he saw they were about to merge with another road a hundred yards or so ahead. Looking back at the man's tortured expression, Lesser's eyes and head jerked to the left with a questioning glance. Renker nodded slightly and threw his own glance towards the east. Fearful of stopping the Hummer, Lesser turned the vehicle left onto the merging road and sped up. The nervous shake in his foot had made its way up to his wrists and elbows. A thin layer of perspiration sprang up on his forehead. Holding the wheel with his right hand, he again used the sleeve of his jacket to wipe away the sweat. Switching hands, he reached over to turn on the air conditioning.

"This is ridiculous," he thought. "Why in Christ's name am I so scared? I've got a muscled-up, constipated monkey in my backseat who probably needs all of his brain cells just to tie his shoes, and I'm the one that's sweating?" Lesser tried to shift his thoughts back to the beautiful and enticing young hostess, but he could no longer recall her face. Nor could he picture the silhouette of her body. Was her hair brown or blonde? He strained to dig up the image, but came up short. Suddenly, he realized that he couldn't remember any woman's face. Even thinking of his wife, whom he'd successfully kept at arm's length for most of their nineteen-year marriage, brought only vague, blurred images. His panic intensified.

"Stop the vehicle," Renker said, his voice strained but firm.

Lesser slowed the Hummer to a stop in the middle of the road and shifted into park. "Why did I put it in park?" he wondered. He could feel the precursors of tears begin pooling around his eyes. Blinking rapidly, he fought to keep the liquid fear in check.

Looking for something to focus his attention on, he glanced out his window and saw they had stopped in front of a chain link fence with perfectly coiled razor wire running across the top. Ten feet behind the fence was what looked like a small guard station sitting next to a gate made of the same chain link and razor wire. The small guard station was empty and half of the gate stood open.

"What are we…?" Lesser started to ask when he noticed a battered sign on the open section of gate. He turned to look back at Renker, but the man's face was in the shadows again. Returning his gaze out the window, he pushed the power button and lowered the window to get a better look. He leaned forward and squinted to make out the letters.

David Lesser's eyebrows pushed in towards each other forcefully, his throat constricted painfully, and he began shaking when he read the name on the sign: Fairfax County Landfill – Waste-to-Energy Incinerator.

"Incinerator!" he thought as a new wave of panic struck him.

But before he could react, Lesser felt the vehicle shift slightly from side to side, just like it had when that dumb ape had…

Lesser felt a thick, heavy object strike the back of his head with considerable force. Reflexively his eyes slammed shut and his shoulders bolted upward. As unconsciousness engulfed his body, Lesser could vaguely sense the two throbbing orbs pulsing in his eye sockets and a thick, warm trickle snaking down his neck and back, staining his three hundred dollar Italian silk shirt. His last few seconds of consciousness were marked by irritation and anger at the debasement of his shirt. A moment later darkness took him.

Chapter 6

Atlantic, North Carolina

Anna Kulter clawed through the darkness slowly, wearily. Time felt like a giant anvil pressing down on her foggy mind. The pixilated reality behind her eyes began slowly resolving, but uncertainty still dominated her fragile mental landscape. She knew instinctively that consciousness was near, but locating it proved difficult. It was as if she were pushing through a thick, heavy jelly. Each time she pushed it aside, it fell right back into place. Was the dream holding onto her? What had she been dreaming about? Mustering all the mental power available to her, she tried to recall the images that had filled her mind only a few moments ago. Random pictures flashed behind her eyes in rapid succession, but she could not hold on to a single one.

The inability to recall anything began to irritate her. Subconsciously she pushed her mind harder to remember, but nothing came. The effort, however, had succeeded in increasing the blood flow to her brain – enough so that she began clearing the way towards consciousness. She was becoming aware of her body and its orientation. Weak nerve impulses began arriving at the cerebellum and suggested that she was lying down. How had she gotten back to the hotel from the lecture? Surely she would remember the embarrassment of driving that crappy little foreign death-trap into the parking garage. The irritation she'd felt at the car rental clerk suddenly came back to her. The young woman had patronizingly explained to her in a stuffy nasal voice that it was the weekend of Cinco dė Mayo and that making a reservation ahead of time would've ensured a larger domestic vehicle. That memory, along with all of the rude remarks she'd been lining up to fire back at that moment, were still clear in her mind. But the details of last night were locked up behind a steel door she could not penetrate.

Before the opportunity arose to berate herself for the temporary amnesia, she realized that she felt a chill throughout her body. "It's Florida. How can I possibly be cold?" she wondered in a daze. Then, without warning or forethought, her mind snapped back into action, drawing several conclusions all at once. She was lying down on something hard. It smelled like...what was it? Rain. It smelled like the streets outside her penthouse after a rainstorm. She tried to move but found that she did not have full control of her faculties. A jolt of fear shot through her body. Was she in the street? Was she wet? With considerable effort, she willed her eyelids to open. Her vision was foggy at first, but she could tell she was in a large, brightly lit room with white corrugated walls. She could smell the rain and even feel a mild breeze on the back of her head. Was she outdoors? She closed her eyes and tried to concentrate. When she opened them again, the reality of her situation flooded through her eyes and into her mind. She was lying on the concrete floor of what appeared to be an airplane hangar. The breeze was coming from behind her, indicating the hangar door must be at least partially open.

Lying a few feet away was Felps, who appeared to be unconscious. And something else was odd. Felps was dressed from head to toe in military camouflage – the kind used in desert warfare. For a brief moment the sight amused her. How ironic that this small woman, who spends her spare time protesting with her clan of followers at military funerals, should be dressed in camo fatigues. The amusement faded as quickly as it had appeared. Without thinking, she tried to prop herself up for a better look at Felps, only to find that her hands were bound behind her. She tried to scramble with her legs, but they too were bound. When she looked again, she saw that Felps was also bound hand and foot. Desperately, she thrashed to and fro, trying to sit up, but found she simply didn't have the strength. After a few seconds the futility of her actions became obvious and she gave up. She closed her eyes and lost her hold on consciousness.

Anna had no idea how long she'd been out this time. When she managed to open her eyes again, her orientation had changed and she was now looking towards the rear of the hangar. What she saw sent her heart up into her throat. There were camouflaged figures littered across the floor like a makeshift, post-battle morgue. Each person was bound hand and foot with plastic strips and most of them appeared to be unconscious. There were men and women of varying ages lying perfectly still on the hard floor. Anna felt certain looking at them that, although they wore the costumes, these were not military personnel.

It suddenly occurred to her that she might also be dressed in camouflage. With considerable effort she bent her head down to look. She too was clad from head to toe in the military garb designed to hide a person from sight in a desert setting. "I must look ridiculous," she thought, "lying here like an overdressed sack of potatoes with a blond sprout. I hope no one has pictures of this. How in the hell did I wind up in a hangar wearing camouflage? And where are my clothes?"

It took only a moment before the obvious hit her – someone must have removed her clothes while she was unconscious! The idea both repulsed and, though she wouldn't admit it to herself, even excited her. What else had they done while she was unconscious? She moved slowly and carefully, trying to focus her attention on her body. Nothing felt odd or hurt, though there was some numbness in her arms. Tentatively she licked her lips and found that she still wore lipstick. Concentrating on other, more private areas, there was no sensation of pain or discomfort anywhere. Jostling around a little, she could feel the straps of her sports bra. Her chest heaved as she took a deep breath, and released it slowly. There was no ache or pain in her breasts, which she knew from reading about rapes, almost always sustained damage. "Take another deep breath," she told herself. She was tired and her muscles were stiff, but otherwise she was not hurt. After a moment's consideration, she felt confident she had not been violated or abused. Still though, someone had gone through the trouble of removing her clothes and redressing her to look like G.I. Jane. Why?

Mustering her strength, she managed to roll onto her side. Tilting her head back, she could just make out Felps's serene face. The small woman was still bound and lay motionless ten feet or so behind her. The two of them had been set apart from the others in the corner of the hangar. For reasons beyond her comprehension, this fact seemed significant. Why had they been separated? Why were they so special?

She rolled over again and looked closely at the other faces. Who were these people? Looking from face to face she couldn't begin to guess who... and then she froze. "I know that face," she thought, trying to concentrate. "Hank!" It was Hank Azar, her attorney. The man who had spearheaded countless lawsuits against liberal newspapers and writers who had sought to defame her character. Azar had contributed his legal expertise to her books and numerous papers. He had even written a legal treatise on the negative effects of liberal thought on America's young people. Azar was a major contributor to numerous Republican officials. He rubbed elbows with some of the most powerful and influential people in the country. He held sway with some of the circuit court judges, and even a few on the Supreme Court.

The sight of the mighty Hank Azar lying catatonic on the floor of a dank airplane hangar and dressed in camouflage was almost comical, but she was too afraid to laugh. "Who would dare...?" she wondered incredulously. "Hank!" she yelled out, her voice reverberating off the back wall. Immediately she regretted the outburst, though nothing happened. Hank did not stir. "What is he doing here?" she thought desperately. "What are any of us doing here?"

Anna moved her eyes to the man next to Hank and was shocked to realize she knew him, as well. Brady Siller lay motionless on his side, his right cheek pressed like a pancake on the smooth concrete floor. Siller was her agent, manager, and occasional lover. "He looks ridiculous lying there," she thought absently. She remembered seeing him like this the morning after a night of boozing and bar hopping in upper Manhattan. "But this," she thought again, "this is not right." Quickly she scanned the other faces. A few feet away from Siller she saw the chubby face of Bill Crystol, conservative author and co-founder of PNAC. Before shutting down in '06 The Project for a New American Century had provided her substantial support in the form of funding and public relations backing for her books, lectures and television appearances. Crystol himself had accompanied her on a "research" trip to the Bahamas and wound up putting most of the trip on the PNAC's tab. It had been a wonderful trip. He had spared no expense and had gone on and on about how much the organization appreciated her vigilance in spreading their holy message. He had been magnanimous and larger than life. He'd acquired some extra girth since she'd last seem him. Now he looked something like a fat, tranquilized seal ready for shipment to the desert.

None of this made any sense. Anna tried moving her hands again. This time she felt a stab of pain as the plastic tie cut into her wrists. Her shoulders and upper arms were tense and sore from being tied behind her. She was trapped and helpless and she knew it. The fear began to well up inside her again, accompanied by a growing wave of panic. She could feel the tears gathering at the corner of her eyes. Why was she here? She didn't do anything wrong. Why were her associates here? And who were all these other people? Hoping to delay the tears, she looked around again. Some of the bodies were beginning to stir. "There must be a dozen people here," she whispered to herself.

"Seventeen to be exact," said a crisp voice behind her. The sudden, piercing sound startled her. Instinctively she had rolled over and was now staring up at a beast of a man dressed in traditional green army fatigues complete with polished black boots and a solid black beret partially covering a closely shaved head. The man's cool blue eyes were looking down at her, his expression serious, but otherwise unreadable. There was something strange about him, though she was certain she had never seen him before. He had a strong, angular face, with prominent cheekbones and a straight nose. It was only then that she realized what was unusual about the man's face: he had a salt and pepper goatee. Every military man she had ever interviewed or openly berated on TV had been cleanly shaved. Wasn't it against military policy to have facial hair? She couldn't remember, but she felt sure this was well outside of normal military etiquette.

Anna searched the man's uniform for rank or name, but found nothing. The uniform was pressed and conspicuously clean. It looked like he had just come off an assembly line, except for the goatee. He stood perfectly still, his hands clasped behind his back. She became increasingly uncomfortable under the man's intense stare. Not knowing what else to say she repeated, "Seventeen?"

The man continued to look at her as if she hadn't spoken. Suddenly, without breaking his gaze he barked, "Sergeant!"

"Yes, General!" a man answered loudly from a few feet away. The voice startled her and she jerked her head to look at the speaker. She couldn't believe she hadn't noticed him before. How long had he been standing there? She watched him take a few measured steps forward and stop a respectable distance from his superior. The sergeant was a younger black man. Anna guessed he was in his mid-twenties. Like the other man, he too had a goatee and a uniform with no rank or name anywhere to be found. However, unlike the first man, the sergeant carried two holstered side arms.

A thought began to materialize in Anna's mind. She hadn't heard the man with the icy blue eyes come up behind her. Nor had she noticed the young sergeant standing only a few feet away. Come to think of it, she hadn't heard a single sound other than her own breathing and her voice blurting out Hank's name. These men were trained for stealth. Neither man had a shred of emotion in his eyes. They were not hobbyists or backwoods, gun-happy hillbillies like she had been idly hoping they were. These were skilled soldiers. She returned her eyes to those of the man still hovering above her.

His eyes were still fixed on hers. "Sergeant," he began, his voice precise and measured, "it seems as though our guests are starting to awaken. Tell Major Kale to have the plane ready in one hour. Then get your men in here. I want each of these individuals at attention and ready for their briefing in twenty minutes. Prior to departure take each person to the latrine."

"General," the sergeant affirmed with a quick nod.

"And send someone to get Toman. He's sleeping on the couch in the front office."

"Yes, General," the young man said, followed by a sharp salute, which the general returned. As quietly as he had come, the soldier departed. Anna wondered vaguely how the man had known his superior was done issuing orders.

"Who are you? Why are we here?" she asked, trying to omit the fear from her voice. The man did not answer.

"Why are we dressed like this? Where are we? What is this place?" This time she managed to inject more force into her voice, but the general paid no notice. He was surveying the scene before him. The look of intense concentration on his otherwise indifferent face suggested he was deep in thought. She watched him carefully, hoping for some hint of what he was thinking, but received none.

Without warning, the general's head jerked sharply and he was looking at her again. Anna had no idea what thoughts were stirring in this man's head, but this time she felt even more uncomfortable. There was no expression on his face, but something hinted at a ferocity lying in wait behind those icy, azure eyes. The general gave her one last inspecting look, then turned and walked away.

She watched the general's hulking, stiff form until he was out of sight. A strong feeling of relief washed over her. Though he'd barely acknowledged her presence, there was something behind those stone eyes that had pierced her normally impenetrable armor. What it was she couldn't begin to guess, and that scared her more than anything.

Anna realized she had been holding her breath and exhaled, irritated at her own cowardice. Slowly, her confidence began to return and her rationality kicked into overdrive. "Okay, think this through, Anna," she told herself. "If these people were going to harm us they probably would've already done it. This was most likely a scare tactic by some rogue band of military nuts that disagreed with what she and Felps stood for. They would probably parade around with their guns trying to scare and intimidate everyone. Then they would have to endure some long, drawn out diatribe about how people like her were ruining America. They might even have to endure whiny speeches from ex-Vietnam vets who claim to have been forsaken by the government. Or some overly patriotic, flag-lovers would babble on about the atrocities of 9/11 and how it was our own government and not Osama Bin Laden that was behind the whole thing. Undoubtedly she would get reamed for her ruthless comments directed at the attention-hungry families of the people who died on 9/11. Once the speeches were done, then there would be the inevitable list of demands for their safe return. Calls to police and newspapers would be made. News stations all over the country would be reporting on the big story in no time. Hostage experts would be called in to negotiate their release. Her face and bio would be plastered across every TV screen in America. Yes...every TV in America."

In the span of only a few short minutes she felt a thousand times better. This incident, although annoying and decidedly inconvenient, could be a blessing in disguise. This was the type of press she could never buy. It would bring renewed interest to her books and bring the sales figures back in the black. Hits on her website would no doubt triple in a matter of hours. The country would rally around the hostages, which would lead to more followers, and therefore, more lectures. Felps would get her share of the hype as well. The thought irritated her, but it was probably unavoidable now. Either way, the ticket price on the lecture circuit would easily double overnight, as would their payout. But she would have to play her part. Strong, but cooperative, brave but not heroic. After all, she still had to be careful with these yahoos. One wrong step and they might snap. Perhaps it would be best if she were the spokesperson for these lunatics. "Yes," she concluded. It would put her out in front for all to see – and also provide a certain degree of control over the other hostages.

The more she examined her situation, the better she felt. In addition to renewed interest in her and her ideas, book sales and website, lectures and luncheons, she would also have the opportunity to step up and take charge of this small, camera-ready group of poor, defenseless and innocent civilians. With a little luck she might be involved in negotiating their release. And all of this in front of Bill Crystol! Yes, he would see her rise to the challenge and deliver the hostages, including himself, to safety. No doubt his readers and fellow conservatives would find out their friend was among those being detained. Once the whole ordeal was over, she would be even higher in their graces, as well as those of the conservative party. Funding would come from every corner of the party. She might even be able to dump Felps altogether and hit the circuit alone on behalf of conservatives. That could translate into more books, more interviews, bigger and better lectures, and an annual compensation package in the seven-figure range. All she had to do was play along with these idiots, quietly praising PNAC-style ideals and visions, injecting her femininity wherever it proved beneficial to do so – and she'd be able to carefully position herself at the head of the table. With some ingenuity and a little luck, in twenty-four hours, hers would be a household name. God bless America.

Fairfax, Virginia

David Lesser dreamt of a plush penthouse suite in a luxurious high-rise overlooking the ends of the earth. Standing in front of a ten-foot tall window, he marveled at the surreal image before him. At first glance it would appear as though his suite had been built over Niagara Falls. But upon further scrutiny he realized the awesome truth: he was perched directly over the end of the world. A flat world whose main water artery pushed billions of gallons of water over the edge of eternity every second. "The enormous river must be moving very fast," he thought as he stared in awe. The water appeared to be thicker than normal, like dark blue taffy coursing over a hidden horizontal spool. Tall, undulating clouds of mist and spray blocked the view of black space and stars beyond the massive falls. Lesser knew the sight was too fantastic to be real, but here, in this place, he had no cause to care. Incredulity and skepticism yielded to sumptuous indulgence, overdue reward, and the liquid gold elixir of entitlement. Here, he was king.

Aware of other people moving around behind him, Lesser turned casually and strolled back towards the oversized king bed sitting in the center of the room. The shiny, silver satin sheets were pushed towards the foot of the bed, crowned by a pyramid of carefully stacked matching pillows resting against an unusually tall and ornate headboard. There was a sensuality there – an invisible, tempting aura. "Those smooth lustrous sheets are so inviting," he thought loosely. But he wasn't tired. Instead he felt like dining. Yes, a feast fit for an emperor. He would dispatch his beautiful and obedient servant girls to scour the earth for his favorite foods. A pig slowly cooked in a Hawaiian Imu pit. Jasmine and mint rice from that trendy new place in L.A. Emerald green edamame with sea salt. White Tang Yuan dumplings from China. A loaf of fresh Panettone bread. And a bottle of Spanish Grenache Tinta. For dessert that delicious Tres Leches cake from the Costa Rican family that used to clean his house. And to top it all off – a bottle of sweet French Sémillon wine.

But where were the servants? Where were his women? Looking around the room now, he was surprised to find that he was, in fact, alone. Curious, Lesser walked to the other side of the large room, all the while searching the floor and furniture for some sign of his beautiful companions. He did have companions didn't he? "Of course," he thought, "don't be ridiculous."

He stopped abruptly when he reached the far wall and was surprised to see that it too was made of a ten-foot tall wall of glass. Confused, he looked beyond the window, only to see the same powerful flow of water spilling over the edge of the world. Lesser spun to his left, then to his right, finding the same glass walls were on both sides. Look up! Swirls of ominous and foreboding dark gray and purple clouds. Look down! Water the color of the sky. The whole room was one large square glass box. Frantically Lesser tried to find a door, window or hatch, but there appeared to be no way in or out. He was trapped and alone. Near the far side of the room he spotted a curvy, futuristic looking metal chair. Without thinking, Lesser ran to the spot where the chair sat, gripped the back of it in his hands, and with every ounce of energy he could channel, slammed the chair into the nearest glass wall. Nothing happened. He swung again. The chair hit with a resounding thump, but nary a scratch appeared. With a blood curdling shriek, Lesser spun around and sent the chair flying into the wall. This time, the chair passed unobstructed right through the glass as if it weren't even there. Lesser could see the odd shiny object plummeting hundreds of feet towards the raging current below until he could no longer distinguish it.

Approaching the unnamed state between pure panic and utter terror, Lesser looked towards the sky for help. As if in divine answer, the clouds parted and a single, bright ray of sunshine pierced the glass enclosure. The sight brought David Lesser a brief sense of relief. Then he remembered he was in a sealed glass box. A split second after this realization, the temperate in the luxury room began to rise precipitously. In less than a minute he found it difficult to breath. Sweat poured from his head, armpits, hands, behind his knees and on the tops of his feet, staining the silk pajamas he only realized at that moment he was wearing. Desperate to expel the stifling heat, Lesser stripped off the pajamas, as well as his underwear, until he was stark naked. It took only a few seconds before the severity of his situation hit him. He was a middle-aged executive with thinning, gray hair, flabby love handles and buttocks, standing sweaty and naked in a hot glass box, exposed for the whole world to see. He felt as if all of his wrongdoings were somehow visible to anyone who would chance a look in his direction. Although there was nothing but water and sky to be seen, David Lesser was sure someone was close by.

The heat! My God, the heat! And it was still getting hotter. Thin beads of sweat coursed down his face and landed in his half-open mouth, though he could not taste the bitterness. The heat intensified slightly, accompanied by a loud rushing sound. It wasn't the rushing sound of the water. It didn't sound exactly like wind or rushing air. It sounded soft and feathery. A white noise – not entirely unpleasant.

The glass beneath his feet began to heat up. And in that moment, David Lesser identified the strange whooshing sound. It was the sound of blowtorches spitting forth blue and orange flames.

Atlantic, North Carolina

Toman sat on the edge of the plush leather couch sipping a lukewarm cup of black coffee. Sergeant Booker had awakened him from a shallow slumber and was now leaning casually against the wall next to the office door. Of all the military men Toman had met, Booker was the most adept at modifying his behavior to the situation at hand. When he was under the scrutiny of his superiors, he was all business and stiff as a plank. When he was interacting with civilians like Toman, he was loose and accommodating. The strong cup of joe in his hand had been placed there by Booker, who had astutely assured him a single cup would put hair on his ass.

"What if I've already got that covered?" he'd joked with the young man.

"If that's the case, chances are it will sprout on your back," Booker replied.

"Just what I always wanted," Toman had said wearily, sipping the strong beverage.

Booker had reached for the light switch, but Toman, not ready for the brightness, had said, "Do you mind? I'm not quite ready for the starkness of reality just yet. There's plenty of ambient light."

"Sure thing Batman," Booked said. "Probably best not to have to look at you under fluorescents anyways."

"No argument there," Toman said with a nod.

Before heading back to the hangar, Booker had told him his catches had already been skinned and redressed and were in the process of being prepped for their journey. Outfitting would only take ten minutes with another fifteen for latrine visits. Toman had twenty-five minutes to gain his wits before the general spoke to the "guests." That was something he would not permit himself to miss.

Setting the cup down on the coffee table, Toman yawned deeply and ran both of his hands through his thick black hair. Long, thin tentacles of exhaustion snaked this way and that through his body, from the very top of his brain to the tips of his toenails. The hour of sleep he'd managed to snatch on the couch hardly made up for the previous thirty-six hours he'd spent awake. It was true, the extraction had gone off without a hitch, but only because of his meticulous preparations and timing.

Even as the four limp bodies were being carried towards the van, calls were being made to the hotel, the car rental company, the airline, etc. letting them know the plans of Ms. Kulter and Mrs. Felps had been changed. Just prior to extraction, Osiro, who had already hacked into two cellular phone companies, had blocked incoming and outgoing calls to the phones of the two speakers and their lackeys. Campus security had been alerted to a break-in at the chemistry building on the southern end of campus, which happened to be the building furthest from the lecture hall. The security officers posted at the lecture hall had been notified by a female dispatcher that the students attending the lecture were to be secured in the building for a few minutes after the speakers left to ensure their safety. Only some time later would these men learn that no female dispatcher was on duty that night.

It had been Dia's idea to paint the surveillance van to look like an emergency medical vehicle. Toman had thought this unnecessary until he'd found out that a concert at the massive auditorium next to the campus might be letting out around the same time. Getting stuck in traffic was always extremely risky in these types of operations. He couldn't be sure how long the four would remain unconscious. With Dia driving, that would only leave him and Susha to deal with anyone who awoke. Additionally, Hilos would be delivering the other "guests." If they were late in delivering their catch, it could throw everyone's plans off. In the end, Dia's idea was a good one. After getting the lettering added to the vehicle, Toman had set Susha to work finding the most likely dispatch point for an ambulance near the north end of campus. If they found that traffic had already accumulated, they would call for an ambulance to be sent to an address conveniently located near the freeway and simply follow it out. The oldest tricks were usually the best.

Fortunately the concert was still going when their van exited the campus and headed towards the freeway. From there it had been an hour-long drive to the hangar. The drive was uneventful and none of the captives even stirred.

After the unceremonious unloading of the four, Toman and Susha had helped Hilos unload his lot. They'd emptied three separate vehicles and carried the unconscious people, some of whom were rather rotund, and laid them out in the hangar. At the time, seventeen hadn't sounded like much, but at the moment his shoulders and back begged otherwise. "Next time we use dollies," he thought, "or we only target short, skinny offenders."

Slowly, he rose to his feet and stretched his arms skyward, his finger tips barely grazing the corrugated ceiling tiles. Exhaling slowly he stood still and savored the warmth that flowed through his veins. The sensation brought his body's lingering exhaustion into sharp relief. With it came a barrage of tantalizing images and supporting memories into his mind: the large, soft bed sitting next to the open glass doors in Ambergris Key – the soft whooshing of the beach only twenty feet away. Eating that phenomenal breakfast in bed. Crepes filled with fresh fruit, cinnamon biscuits, spicy hash browns and that fabulous mimosa with fresh orange juice and pineapple juice. He'd slept until almost ten o'clock that day, awakening to the perfect temperature and the intermittent sounds of the miniature rain forest. That day was at least ten years past, but he still held it as the most restful and peaceful day he could remember. Looking around the drab office now, he realized how alien his little cabana in Belize was compared to this place. But this was not the time for such tortures. He forced himself to bury the memory and focus on simply getting through the next few hours.

It was still dark in the office. Only a faint light from the hallway came through the opaque office door. Carefully he searched the wall near the door until he located the light switch. His eyes would hate the harsh fluorescents, so he kept them closed as he flicked the switch. A pinkish white glow pierced through his eyelids. Gradually he opened his eyes and took in his surroundings. He knew from Booker that the general had set up a temporary operations center here, though there was very little to suggest anyone had used the office in quite some time. It was moderate in size and spare in furnishing, as was typical for hardworking military brass. A few feet from the door stood a plain, dark wood desk that had seen better days. From what was left of the finish, he guessed someone had once taken a lot of pride in sitting behind it. Now the top and sides bore innumerous scrapes, scratches, a few gouges, and a chipped corner or two. Behind the desk was a three-foot high wood file cabinet that stretched the length of the back wall. In front of the desk were two bare wood office chairs. Light wood-paneled walls and a thin wool carpet, combined with the furniture, suggested nothing had been changed or updated since the 1950s.

The Atlantic Marine Corps Outer Landing Field had been the perfect choice for this operation. It was run down, but still usable. The land for the base had been purchased by the Navy in 1942 and established as a secondary airfield and command center for Cherry Point. The base had been used regularly until the late 1950s. For the next fifty years it would see intermittent usage, which was always temporary. As late as 2007 the base had been used for repair and temporary storage of V-22 Osprey helicopters and A-4 Skyhawk fighter jets. Activity in 2008 had been scant and the general had managed to clear time for *The Aenamaia* simply by cutting a ten thousand dollar cashier's check to the Navy to stage a "private veteran's ceremony." The check cleared and no further questions had been asked – confirmation that even American military assets are for rent if you have the right name in your rolodex.

Toman took another sip, then put the coffee down on a metal file cabinet near the door and strolled casually towards the desk. The top of the desk was bare, save for an eight-by-ten picture of a young man in formal military dress. Despite tradition, the man had chosen to smile proudly. Seeing the smile made Toman grin. He hadn't seen a picture of the young man for several years. Despite the gleaming white smile, Toman felt his chest constrict. "I'm sorry, Tommy," he said quietly to the picture, "I'm so very sorry." The young man's intense blue eyes reminded him that he would be late if he didn't get going. He took one last look at the picture, not realizing he had stopped breathing. Images of a military funeral procession flashed through his mind, but he pushed them back out. Abruptly he turned and picked up his jacket, grabbed his warm cup of coffee, and shut the door behind him.

When he reached the hangar, Toman found that all of the guests were standing in three rows of six. Each person remained bound at the ankles and wrists, though the latter were no longer behind their backs. Instead they hung limply in front. Most of the faces looked either dazed or terrified, though no one spoke. Standing in the front row were Anna Kulter and Shirli Felps. Both women stared at the general, who faced them solemnly. Flanking the general were two soldiers in port-arms stance, each carrying the latest FN-Scar assault rifle.

Toman walked around to the front of the assembled group of abductees. The general saw him approach and turned to greet him. Although his face had been an icy façade, he smiled slightly upon seeing Toman and extended his hand. Toman shook his hand warmly.

"Well done, Toman. Well done."

"Thank you, General. So far, so good."

"You look like shit," the general said brusquely.

Toman stroked the stubbly two-day growth on his face and agreed, "Yes, sir, I know. Once the transport takes off, I've got a private suite with a hot tub waiting for me."

The general's grin widened into a smile and he laughed. "You've earned it. But don't get too comfortable. There's plenty more to be done."

Toman sighed deeply and returned the smile, "Yes, sir. I'm looking forward to it."

The general released his hand, nodded curtly and resumed his stern countenance. Toman walked casually towards a metal folding chair that had been placed near the hangar door and sat down. He noticed some of the eyes followed him, but most quickly shot back to the general. Booker's men had done a good job getting everyone into position and explaining that no questions or talking would be tolerated. Eighteen people dressed in desert fatigues stood helpless in an old airplane hangar, facing a man none of them had ever seen before. Toman expected someone to break out with cries of injustice or pleas of mercy, but no one uttered a word. Each person watched the general while trying not to attract his gaze. The seasoned soldier commanded attention and respect, regardless of the audience.

Toman saw Sergeant Booker enter from the rear of the hangar and approach the general. After a brief exchange, the general nodded and Booker stood at attention a few feet behind his stolid superior. Toman looked at his watch. It was nearly five a.m. The general took two steps forward and addressed the assembled party.

"Ladies and Gentlemen. My name is Brigadier General William Andrew Payte. Welcome to North Carolina." The general's voice was loud, clear and precise. As he spoke, his eyes roamed over the sea of faces before him like a piercing searchlight from a guard tower. The fear, intimidation and loathing that emanated from each person were palpable, but the general was impervious to it. Years of dealing with soldiers, both young and old, naïve and wise, had taught him to suppress preconceived notions and focus on the task at hand.

"You are undoubtedly confused as to why you are here, why you are bound, and why are you are dressed like United States soldiers preparing to go to war. Let me start by assuring you that you are not going to war. Far from it. In fact," he paused and his eyes narrowed slightly, "you are leaving the war. All of you are here because you have been deemed unworthy of U.S. Citizenship. Neither the courts, nor the police nor any branch of the U.S. Government has passed this judgment. Nor was it I alone who made this decision."

The general began to pace, his eyes continuing to survey the people before him. "You have been selected by a civilian organization we refer to simply as *The Aenamaia*, which is comprised of men and women who have grown tired of the current state of affairs and have chosen to take matters into their own hands. Unlike the spy novels and movies you are used to, I will not spend time here outlining the details of our plans and intentions, other than those related to your future. *The Aenamaia* does not believe in wasting time and neither do I.

Each of you has been under surveillance for a long time now. *The Aenamaia* has gone to great pains to ensure that everyone here has committed sufficient offenses against the people of this country so as to warrant your permanent expulsion. Every member of *The Aenamaia* believes in a level of common decency among Americans; you have betrayed that decency. *The Aenamaia* believes in the freedoms outlined by the United States Constitution and the Bill of Rights; you have blatantly defecated on both. *The Aenamaia* believes that in order to co-exist peacefully, we must all learn to understand and accept one another; you have been deemed incapable of this. *The Aenamaia* believes that each person on this planet can simultaneously direct every action to benefit themselves while not harming others; your actions spit in the face of such a concept. *The Aenamaia*," the general continued, his words carefully spaced and his volume noticeably higher, "believes mankind cannot evolve or advance until people like you cease to exist." When he spoke the last word, Toman saw a lightening flash of suppressed anger streak across the general's face as he bared his teeth in a facsimile of a smile.

Regaining his iron composure, the general continued. "All of you are closely associated with one of the two women standing in the front row," he said, pointing a thick, leather finger at Anna Kulter and Shirli Felps, both of whom looked confused and uncomfortable at suddenly being the center of the forbidding man's attention. Kulter's jaw was clenched, as were both fists, but she remained perfectly still. "Each of you has actively promulgated your anti-life, anti-peace, anti-tolerance ideas in one form or another. Each of you has played a part in spreading fear, anger, hatred, resentment, and corruption in a world already bursting at the seams with plenty of each. Those belonging to the Felps clan have openly criticized and condemned the military men and women who have given their lives fighting for your right to do so. Many of you have also protested at military funerals and damned gays in the name of some inane and merciless god whom you believe gave you the right to do so."

The general stopped before Shirli Felps, who unabashedly stared right back at him with wide, insane eyes, her expression bordering on the primal. Toman watched, half expecting some sharp-toothed alien creature to leap out of Felps's mouth and attack the general.

"People like you, Ms. Felps, who have the audacity to protest military funerals, have no business living in a country you clearly despise. People like you, who are allowed to teach children to hate their fellow man, who put signs in their hands praising the tragedies of 9/11 and condemning those who love someone of the same sex – people like you who defecate on this country at every possible turn – do not deserve to be Americans."

The general was about to continue when Shirli's top blew.

"The Lord our God made it clear in the Bible that homosexuals are an abomination. And God will continue to punish those impudent military brats in Iraq for the persecution of our followers in that country and elsewhere. God sent a clear message on 9/11 and his wishes resonate every day he takes another soul and sends them into the black hands of Lucifer. Every man and woman serving in the U.S. military deserves the pain and death that will come to each and every..."

In a blur of movement, Toman saw General Payte's hand close around Felps's neck, abruptly cutting off the rest of her rant. The large man effortlessly lifted the woman up and slammed her violently into the corrugated aluminum wall, leaving her feet dangling helplessly six inches above the concrete floor. A loud crash, followed by a strained and guttural shriek from Felps resounded through the hangar. Kulter shrank back from the scene, her jaw now open wide in awe. Booker took a step towards the general, but halted when he saw Toman's eyes and the slight shake of his head.

"Listen to me, you psychotic bitch," the general growled. "My son died in Iraq trying to defend a shelter housing unarmed civilian families from a barbaric attack of insurgents whose morals and ethics are as transparent and merciless as your own. He was shot twice in his right arm and once in his gut. As he sat bleeding to death under heavy enemy fire, his last moments on earth were spent helplessly watching twenty-seven unarmed men, women and children get slaughtered, their cries of unbridled terror echoing in his head. Shooting with his left arm, he managed to take out several of those soulless bastards before he ran out of ammunition, but he was too late to save the families. Before his unit could reach him, the steel toe belonging to one of the butchers smashed his nose, sending his nasal bones crashing into his brain and killing him instantly." The general looked as if he was deciding whether or not to snap the insane woman's thin neck – end it all in one instant. Toman could hardly blame General Payte for the anger that was undoubtedly coursing through his disciplined mind. But this was not the way to do it. "Stick to the plan," Toman thought earnestly. "Stick to the plan."

Toman knew the story of Payte's son. It was the kind of thing even the sensationalist media, still weary from their role as propaganda whores of the Bush administration, wouldn't dare touch. When it came to the horrors of battle that could be employed by the media to dupe the country into believing war was justified, there was an unspoken line that was never crossed; a line drawn in blood. The media maintained a vigilant, hyper-sensitive awareness of this line, which demarcates the boundary between usable, hi-definition carnage, and the zone where the tragedy is so deafening to the human soul, it transcends any politically injected malice and actually turns the tide of public opinion against the war-mongers and the campaign in general.

If the awfulness of the event rips the breath from the average American, the mob will turn on the politicians who placed America's children in harm's way. Additionally, were the tale told in full, someone might be tempted to interview the highly decorated general regarding his feelings. Once they heard what he had to say, they would undoubtedly try to bury it. However, given the general's spotless service record and high profile, it would be difficult to keep his strong opinions from the public's ears. In the end, the story was suppressed, though, and the men of his son's unit who witnessed what happened were silenced. But from that day forward, the unit's war cry became simply, "For Tommy!"

The whole affair behind Thomas Payte's death and cover-up was disgraceful, but at this moment Toman's full attention was focused on the general and Felps. As much as he despised the woman and everything she stood for, he did not want to see the general kill her. This wasn't the plan. Toman knew all too well what the general was capable of doing to the scrawny figure currently in his grasp. He was about to intervene when he noticed Felps's chin sat squarely on the general's thumb and that she was breathing in short spurts between clenched teeth. He took a step back, but remained close in case things got even uglier.

"I served in the armed forces for twenty-four years, on four continents. I watched most of my friends die defending the rights and liberties you and your cult abuse every day. I've stood by and watched while your own children were indoctrinated into your world of hate and scorn. You wipe your ass with the American flag and set up your red meat picnics on the graves of those whose blood was spilt to defend you. There is nothing I'd love more right now then to snap your scrawny neck like a twig, but I won't." The general pulled Felps's insane and terrified face closer to his own and said in a low, growling voice, "God or no God, you'd better start praying, because you have no fucking idea what I'm capable of." In one swift motion the general released his grip and Felps fell to the floor, collapsing like a gangly rag doll. None of the other prisoners even feigned an attempt to help her.

He turned and addressed the shocked and incredulous faces before him. The redness in the general's face faded slowly, but his expression had already reverted to its measured countenance. "Most of you here belong to Shirli Felps's organization and have actively supported views which breed hate, fear and resentment. You have spat on the military, gays, followers of religions different from your own, the poor and destitute, Canada and Sweden, and most especially, America. You have been outspoken in your abhorrence of these things time and time again. While *The Aenamaia* believes you all to be unworthy of any freedoms including life itself, they have decided you should not be harmed – if you cooperate. *The Aenamaia* does not believe in torture, punishment or retribution. The goal is not to ransom your lives for any kind of gain. Instead, we are here to grant you asylum from the country and the liberty you so vehemently despise."

The general's pacing stopped. He now stood perfectly still before Anna Kulter, still addressing the assembled party. His hands were again clamped behind his back. With a mixed look of disgust and mockery he continued, "The rest of you are here because of your association to Ms. Anna Kulter. You too have been hard at work selling out America and soiling morality, honesty and integrity – balancing precariously on the very tip of the featherless and colorless right wing. Your tireless efforts to support the corrupt and ignorant pillars of power are no less contemptible than the crimes of Ms. Felps and her followers. However, your crimes are far worse." Toman watched as two soldiers lifted a stunned and dazed Felps off the floor and carried her to a folding chair propped against the hangar wall.

"*The Aenamaia* believes Ms. Felps and her cult are truly abominations, social mutations of humanity whose ideas and actions border on the clinically insane. What sets you apart from them is the fact that you fully comprehend that what you are doing is innately wrong. With every negative action, with every ill-spoken word, with every nefarious deed, you sense the poison in your gut. Yet you choose to consciously ignore the warnings. Ms. Felps is a religious fundamentalist with neurotic and psychotic tendencies and clear signs of obsessive and compulsive behaviors. But, in her deranged mind, she believes what she is doing is the work of God. She believes it with the unwavering, myopic fervor of a true zealot.

But you people," he said, staring down into the terrified eyes of Anna Kulter, "you spit in the face of America then turn around to collect your paycheck. You call it payment for services rendered; we call it bribery. You say you're acting in the best interests of the country; we say your only interests are your personal wealth and the pursuit of power. How many special interest groups have funneled money into your bank accounts? How many congressmen have you bribed to lend their name to your fallacious books? Do you think the general public is aware of the funds you receive when you appear on Fox News? Doesn't it bother you to publish books containing no less than two hundred factual errors and misquotes each? How many people and businesses have you and your spineless attorney back there sued for telling the truth about your books, which in and of themselves lack any verisimilitude? I can personally name over ten small businesses forced to shut down because they couldn't afford to defend themselves against you. And just as soon as their bankruptcy papers were filed, you withdrew the suit. Need I go on? You incite hate, fear, mistrust, and false righteousness. You feed off of it like a parasite. The bittersweet taste of corruption obviously suits you, as your list of offenses and crimes against this country is longer than the IRS Tax Code."

General Payte took two steps back to address the whole party. The skin of his face was stretched tightly as he tried to maintain his composure. Toman had rarely seen the general display so much anger and frustration, but as always it was fleeting. Within a few short seconds, the cool unreadable façade was back. He stood motionless with his head bowed and eyes shut.

"Sergeant!" he yelled suddenly.

Booker came forward, "Yes, General."

"Tell Kale to start the plane and bring it to the loading zone. Get the rest of your men in here to keep an eye on these...people," the general said, making no attempt to mask his derision.

"Yes, General," Booker answered firmly followed by a crisp salute. The clean-pressed sergeant pivoted on one heel then walked quickly out of the hangar. Within moments soldiers began pouring in from the rear of the building. Toman's eyebrows arched up in amazement. He had known General Payte's recruits were here, but he couldn't imagine where they had been stashed. Each soldier was alert, well-armed and dressed in the same desert fatigues as the frightened abductees. The men filed in quietly and surrounded the nervous and confused detainees.

"Toman," the general said calmly, not looking at him, "Can you explain what will happen to their identities and possessions?"

Toman smiled guiltily and said confidently, "Yes, sir, I believe I can."

The general gave a sharp nod and walked quickly out of the hangar.

Fairfax, Virginia

A sharp smack across his right cheek tore David Lesser halfway out of the distressing dream of sweat, fire and panic in the glass prison. The images of that strange place and the unbridled terror he'd felt still burned in his mind, as did the memory of the heat that had nearly consumed him. He felt vaguely grateful it had just been a dream. "It was just a dream," he thought. What had happened next? Had someone hit him? As if in answer to his thought, an even harder smack rocked him from his reverie. The hot pain in his cheek pulsed to the same beat as the headache quickly forming in the front of his skull. "From the frying pan into the fire." The phrase had popped into his head without warning. "Where did that come from?" he wondered. Though his eyes were still closed, something told him he had more immediate things to worry about.

Lesser tried willing his eyes to open, but nothing happened. Slowly, it occurred to him that one side of his body felt thick and partially numb. He was lying down. But why? A nervous jolt shot through his body. Sensations and impulses that came unbidden made him uneasy and uncomfortable. Twitches, little muscle spasms, cold shudders, the dizzy spells he sometimes got when he stood up too quickly, even sudden sneezes bothered him deeply. These manifestations brought into sharp relief the undeniable and absolute loss of control over his physical self that he dreaded. Control was not something he was fond of relinquishing.

He pushed the thought from his mind and tried to focus on the moment. "Pragmatism is what I need," he thought. "Logic." Where was he? What was the last thing he could remember? A sumptuous young lady in a black dress with a magnificent unspoiled body. If only there had been a rush of air blowing up through a grate beneath her! Just the thought of her was enough to excite him. Yet he felt no arousal. Come to think of it, could he feel anything? It was then that he realized two things simultaneously: he felt intense heat emanating from somewhere behind where he lay and he now felt certain his arms and ankles were bound. An acute, pulsing pang erupted deep in his chest as the memory of his abduction at the beefy hands of the gorilla came rushing back. It felt as if a dam had burst and was emptying into his mind. What was the man's name? Brinker? Rancor? No, it was Renker.

"Lesser!" a deep voice barked. His eyes shot open. Lifting his head, he felt a sharp pain just above his neck, causing his whole body to contract. He grimaced. Gently laying his head back on the hard surface, Lesser breathed in and out slowly, waiting for the pain to lessen. After a few seconds his breathing calmed and, keeping his head still, he let his eyes wander. The scene was ninety degrees off. Even accounting for the odd angle, what he saw still didn't make any sense. Everywhere he looked Lesser saw pipes of various sizes running in every possible direction. The pipes all seemed to bear the most drab and dull colors, as did the concrete walls they were bolted to. At the bottom end of his vision he could make out what looked like a machine panel from a cheesy 1960s sci-fi movie. The panel was covered with a variety of colored lights, dials, switches, gauges, and a few white rectangles with needles inside that reminded him of an old stereo he'd once owned.

As he tried to make sense of it all, something immediately in front of his face caught his attention. It was dark and flat, but blurry. Concentrating, he willed his eyes to stare straight down and focus on the dark object only a few inches away. "What the hell...?" Unconsciously Lesser sniffled and swallowed. The wetness in his nose and the saltiness on his tongue provided the answer: it was a puddle of his own blood. But that was absurd. Unless he'd fallen and hit his head. "Was he injured?" It was difficult to think. His head was still cloudy.

"Calm down," he told himself, "and the answers will come." He breathed in slowly and concentrated. There was a strange combination of unpleasant odors in the air, but he couldn't quite place any of them. Something was burning, that much he was sure of. The smells were... what was the word? Earthy? Organic? Pungent. Lesser frowned, despite the dull ache in the back of his skull. Where in the hell could he be? A low rumble came from somewhere behind him. Something was undeniably wrong here. Just as the image of a chain link fence bearing a rusted, dirty white sign came into his mind, a voice boomed from his left.

"Are you awake?" It was Renker. The man's voice was solemn and echoed eerily off the concrete walls. "Would you like to sit up?"

Lesser nodded slowly.

Renker knelt down. Carefully, he slid a hand between Lesser's right shoulder and the floor and lifted. With his other hand he grabbed the short length of rope he'd tied between the ankles and straightened the man's legs out. Renker stood and took a few steps back. Still somewhat dazed Lesser smacked his lips and tongue, trying to get the stale taste from his mouth. He was glad to be in a sitting position, despite the hardness of the concrete floor.

"Where am I? What is this place?" he asked looking up at the formidable figure of his captor.

Renker stared at him for half a moment then said simply, "This is the Waste-to-Energy incinerator at the Fairfax County Landfill."

"Incinerator?" Lesser thought. That was what he'd read on the aging sign outside. He'd seen it before...just before this sonofabitch had knocked him out. The memory came rushing back with a flood of anger.

"You hit me. You bastard!" Lesser squirmed, struggling to free his hands from the plastic strip, wincing as the action seemed to cause the restraints to sink deeper into his wrists. He'd half expected a reaction from Renker, but the man only watched him, his expression detached, as if his thoughts were somewhere else.

After half a minute Lesser gave up trying to get free. His efforts had burned off a lot of precious energy and he suddenly felt more drained and tired then he could ever remember being.

"Why am I here?" his voice was weak, almost pleading.

The man took a deep breath and squatted down so as to be at eye level with Lesser. The close proximity made him nervous, but he couldn't force himself to turn away. Renker's face assumed a resigned look as he bowed his head. Clearly there was something the man needed to say, but loathed having to do so. A few seconds passed before the hulking man made eye contact again and spoke.

"Tell me something Dave," he started, with no hint of sarcasm or incredulity in his voice, "Would it surprise you if I said you were being punished because of your business practices? Forget who was doing the punishment. Would you honestly be surprised? Or have you long suspected deep in the recesses of your mind where a microscopic amount of pride and morality still exist, that someday something like this might happen? That someone like me might show up on your doorstep with a gun?"

Lesser swallowed hard. He stared at Renker, but could not manage to speak.

"Perhaps if you dug all the way down to the honest truth, you would say it should've happened a long time ago. Personally, I would agree."

"*The Aenamaia* refers to us as 'Augurs,'" Renker explained. "We are twenty-first century adaptations of the ancient Roman Augurs, minus the religion. A professional coterie with an ambitious agenda and an eye on shaping the future. You see Dave, I've spent the last two years watching you. I know almost everything there is to know about your life. That's the way it works with *The Aenamaia*. Each Augur is assigned a group or an individual to research. It then becomes our responsibility to use any means and resource available to us to learn as much as we can about our query. We watch, we listen, and we read about you. We talk casually with people close to you. Occasionally we might interrogate a friend or relative under the guise of one federal agency or another. The deeper we go and the closer we get, the better."

Lesser felt his chest constrict slightly as he asked, "How close?"

He watched his captor's expression carefully. Renker's brows rose and his eyes looked up and left, as if he were running through complex calculations in his head. Or perhaps he was just deciding how much to reveal. Good. The more information he received the more pleasure he would get when he managed to get out of this situation and saw to it that this man was tracked, captured, caged, beaten senseless – perhaps a few times – then consigned to a watery grave.

"Over the course of almost two years," Renker started, still thinking, "I've been in your house a dozen times – maybe more. I've recorded over a thousand telephone conversations, all of which have since been transcribed and cataloged. Both of your cell phones and the one your wife uses most often contain a high-sensitivity digital bug developed by the CIA with an imbedded GPS tracking device. Every time you or your wife placed or received a call it was recorded and your exact location fed into a program I designed to track your movements. A high-tech 'Big Brother' you might say."

As he spoke, Renker saw the look of anger and resentment on Lesser's face melt into one of pure shock and helpless incredulity.

Renker continued. "Two years ago a team posing as carpet cleaners was dispatched to your house. It was a few days before a large party you were throwing to celebrate a profitable government contract to build a dam in an isolated region of southern China. It was supposed to help provide irrigation for a new settlement of disenfranchised farmers. Do you remember?"

Lesser's head drooped slightly, but he didn't answer.

"Your company built the dam at a total cost of eleven million dollars. Fortunately for you and your stockholders, only a select few people knew when the dam failed six months later, killing three hundred people and wounding another thousand – that the actual contract had been for thirty-seven million. That figure had a built-in profit margin of fifteen percent, but that wasn't enough, was it?" Renker waited for a response. When none came, he continued. "It was also fortuitous that one of those congressmen you met with tonight was able to keep the story away from the major media. He even brought in a few of his general buddies to help him convince the Chinese government that guerrillas from Burma were responsible for the dam's destruction."

Renker tilted his head slightly and added curiously, "You remember...don't ya, Dave?"

Lesser refused to meet the man's accusatory eyes.

"Anyways," Renker continued, "our carpet cleaners came in and installed what we call an analog changeling on your home computer. The program runs on its own operating system so as to go undetected by the user, spam software, virus programs, etc. The program tracks every permanent keystroke, copies any new data saved on the drive, and makes copies of all incoming and outgoing emails. Audio and video conferencing as well as all instant messaging are recorded. This information is transmitted to our mainframe every night at around two-thirty a.m. – later if someone is logged in. They installed the same program on your computer at work." Renker chuckled then added, "Both times they came in as carpet cleaners. And both times they did a real half-assed job cleaning your carpets."

Renker stood up. He turned and walked towards the Star Trek-looking light panel. Studying the colorful display he continued, "Besides that, I have copies of your driver's license, passport, birth certificate, ten years of personal and corporate tax returns, life insurance policies, medical records on you and your wife, current 401k and stock option statements, statements on all five of your overseas bank accounts, and the seventeen offshore tax havens your company uses. I also have taps on your accountant, your lawyer, your personal physician, even your stock broker – boy, is he an asshole. And three months ago I started similar compilations and taps on the three degenerates you met with tonight."

Seeing the disbelief on Lesser's face, Renker shook his head and turned to face him. Their eyes locked. "Like I said, I know just about everything there is to know about you."

Lesser glared at Renker and growled contemptuously, "Why? What do you want from me? Money? Power? Weapons? What?"

Renker shook his head slightly, never breaking eye contact.

"Then what?" Lesser roared. With renewed energy he again struggled to free his hands from the plastic restraints. "Why?" he repeated desperately, "Why do you need all of this information? Who profits from it? Why spend so much time watching? And why you? Why not the FBI or the CIA?"

Renker was silent. He appeared to be enraptured by the flashing lights.

"Answer me you, Neolithic ape! Why the fuck do you care about what I do?"

Renker walked to where Lesser still sat. Without pausing he reached down, grabbed a hold of the CEO's blazer and yanked him brusquely to his feet. Their faces were only inches apart. Lesser held his breath. He felt the re-emergence of sweat on his scalp and forehead.

"I have to know," Renker said angrily from behind clenched teeth, "because I am the judge. Each of us who agrees to take on the job of monitoring someone is ultimately responsible for advising *The Aenamaia* whether or not that person lives or dies." Renker stared hard into Lesser's eyes. "Do you understand? We target an individual or group, then assign someone to handle research, surveillance and," he paused, "...and to pass final judgment. *The Aenamaia* has the right to refuse the judgment, but has never done so. That's what we do. We take the assignment and learn as much as we can until..." he let the words hang in the air. "Until we decide and implement."

He let go of the blazer and Lesser fell clumsily back onto the concrete floor. Renker took a few steps back, his hands pulling hard on his shoulder muscles. The seriousness of the situation flooded across Lesser's face and into his widening eyes. He appeared to be staring aimlessly at the floor in front of his feet, but Renker knew better. There was no doubt that images of the man's life were careening through his mind at lightning speed – all that he'd done and all that he'd never do again. "It won't be long now," Renker thought. The fight-or-flight impulse will hit first, only to be dissolved instantly by futility. Renker braced himself for what every Augur knew was the hardest part: abject deprecation.

Several moments passed before Lesser looked up suddenly and stared pleadingly at Renker. No tears had fallen, but the well was filling quickly. Before the desperate entreaty began, Renker said firmly, "The decision has been made, Dave. There will be no attempts at ransom or extortion, bribery or payoffs. *The Aenamaia* have simply decided that a man like you, in a position of inscrutable power and far-reaching influence, wreaks too much havoc. We have determined that your corrupt and immoral wiring is beyond repair or rehabilitation. You've had every chance in the world to be a good, decent man. You have consciously chosen to live a life of fraud, deceit, selfishness, and shame. You've betrayed the trust of your wife, your company, your fellow man, and your country. Men like you are a plague upon this planet, a destructive virus infecting everyone around you. The only way to protect the rest of us is to excise the malady. Permanently." Renker softened his tone and added, "There won't be any pain, Dave."

Lesser was shaking his head vigorously back and forth muttering, "No, no, no. Not me. This can't be happening to me. No." Renker could see the tears were falling freely now.

Renker reached back and pulled the Glock 22 from his belt. From his back pocket he extracted the silencer, turned it over in his palm a few times, then affixed it to the barrel of the gun. Extracting the small case from his front pocket, Renker gripped the small glass vile between his forefinger and middle finger and slowly pulled it out. The vile was filled to the top with a deep-blue fluid. He glanced towards Lesser who was still mumbling to himself.

Palming the vile, Renker took a few steps forward.

"Dave. Dave!" He shouted.

Startled, Lesser jerked his face up. Tears streaked down his cheeks. His eyes were puffy, red and heavy with moisture. He stared wildly at Renker, as though he had forgotten anyone else was in the room.

Holding up the vile Renker said, "Listen carefully, Dave. I'm giving you a choice. You can go out quietly, feeling relaxed and calm. Or," he said holding up the Glock, "you can pretend you're the bad guy in a spy thriller. Understand?" he paused looking around the room. "No one will ever know what happened at the end. It's doubtful they'll even find any remains." Renker shifted his eyes to the large cement structure Lesser had been sitting against, then back. In spite of the obvious shock and fear slowly creeping through his mind, Lesser's brow furrowed questioningly and he turned around slowly to look. While his prisoner's gaze was transfixed on the faint orange light dancing behind the venting slits in the cast iron doors, Renker glanced quickly at the small pool of blood on the concrete. "That's how they'll know," he thought. "Forensics will put the pieces together."

Renker put his hand on Lesser's shoulder and gently pulled him backwards. Lesser's ankles were still tied, but he managed to shuffle backwards. As they backed up, both men could see the enormous steel doors at the opposite end of the wall Lesser had been sitting against. The doors were flush with the concrete wall and closed tight, but around the edges they could see the flickering glow of the flames that raged within the incinerator. Both men stopped and stared at the massive concrete structure. Although he could not see how far back it went, Renker guessed the side facing them was easily sixty feet long. There was a muffled roar from deep within the incinerator. From the frightened expression on Lesser's face, there was no doubt he'd figured out what caused it. Cautiously, as if the incinerator were reaching out to him, Lesser began backing away from the sight, only to bump into Renker, who did not move. Lesser shuffled around to face him again.

"You have to decide, Dave. It's your time."

"Why?" Lesser asked helplessly.

"It just is," Ranker said firmly.

Renker slid the silenced Glock back into his belt. He unscrewed the black cap on the vile and held it up. Lesser stared at the vile.

Absently Lesser asked, "What is it?"

"It was developed by three chemists in *The Aenamaia* specifically for this purpose."

"For me?" Lesser questioned.

"No," Renker said, immediately regretting the sarcasm in his voice. Conscious of the weight of the moment he said calmly, "I'm afraid not Dave. You're only one person out of many *The Aenamaia* has target… uh, chosen. Our goal is not to torture or deal out revenge on anyone." He waited until Lesser made eye contact and added, "Just to clean up."

After a few tense moments, Lesser nodded.

Softly Renker said, "Tilt your head back and open your mouth."

For a moment he thought Lesser might refuse, but after a few seconds the CEO closed his eyes, tipped his head back and opened his mouth.

Clenching his teeth, Renker raised the vile to Lesser's lips and poured. He quickly palmed the empty vile, and with his other hand carefully lifted Lesser's lower jaw. Lesser held the liquid in his mouth. A few jolts of stifled sobs coursed through his body like those of a stubborn child refusing to cry out. His head was still tilted, but now Renker could see his eyes were open and staring up into the darkness of the building. Still cupping Lesser's jaw, Renker stared up too, half expecting to see the night sky speckled with millions of white dots. Instead all he could see were hundreds of pipes clinging tightly to the walls like thick metal vines of ivy disappearing into the shadows. "Perhaps it would've been best to do this outside," he thought. But no, if Lesser had decided to scream or lash out, things could've gotten out of hand. It was just as Gray had told them from the start: "'This cleansing will be more painful and costly to us than to those we remove. We are on this path because we are good and decent and tired of seeing the evil and cruel rule the world. But it is precisely because of who we are and what we believe in, that we shall suffer the most from our actions.'"

The truth of that statement burned inside Renker like nothing he'd ever experienced before. In the beginning, his enthusiasm and thirst for justice had led him to believe he would play judge, jury and executioner for every last man and woman on their list. But now, standing next to this weak and corrupt shell of a man, he felt the full weight of every decision he'd made in the last two years, as well as the directives of *The Aenamaia*, bear down on him like a million tons of water. Still, he believed what they were doing...what he was about to do, was justified.

Lesser was still stifling his sobs. In a hushed voice Renker said, "It's okay, Dave. It's okay." Lesser blinked rapidly a few times, causing a single tear to escape down his cheek. Renker felt certain this single tear contained every emotion this man was capable of producing at this moment. Then, with one long breath inhaled stiffly through narrow and quivering nostrils, the CEO of Blackriver, Inc. swallowed.

Chapter 7

Atlantic, North Carolina

Toman took a deep breath and exhaled. His eyes swept over the weary group. The assembled party represented the culmination of many long months of research, surveillance, phone calls, credit checks, hundreds of computer hacks and phone taps, email tracers, and even a few PIs to fill in the gaps. This had been his first real project with *The Aenamaia* since signing on. He could feel the tiny pull of his facial muscles wanting to form a smile, but the irony of the situation would not allow it. The accomplishment this pathetic group represented was substantial and important to him, but the reality of what was to come was something he could not hide from. Before he began to speak, he shot a quick glance to the soldiers to assure himself that they were prepared to handle whatever might happen next.

"At this moment, members of *The Aenamaia* are in the process of locating and deleting evidence of your existence," he began, consciously keeping his voice even. "Most of your homes have already been thoroughly searched and all documents bearing your name have been confiscated and destroyed. Beginning last night, teams of specialists posing as FBI agents have been visiting hospitals, dental offices, medical specialists, insurance offices, car repair shops, your children's schools, schools you attended, your churches, county assessor's offices, Social Security, etc. Telephone and public service records will be deleted as well. Every scrap of legal paper we can find bearing your name will find its way into a shredder. Those of you who are married will soon find that any direct proof of that marriage, other than your children, will be difficult to locate.

"Thanks to the residual effects of the paranoid government you helped perpetuate, throwing around Homeland Security badges can move mountains of legal papers and records. Additionally, most state and federal records have been computerized and are relatively easy to access when you have a good hacker on staff. Driver's licenses and driving records, passports, and criminal records have been deleted.

"The IRS," he continued as if lecturing to a group of eager college students, "is a little bit trickier, especially for those of you who are married. However," he said with an ironic smile, "the IRS has been known to lose documents before. It's difficult and expensive, but it can and will be done. I will not bore you with the rest of the steps being taken to purge evidence of your wasted lives but be assured, we'll leave no stone unturned and no file cabinet unrifled.

"Because Ms. Kulter's book sales continue to decline precipitously, we have managed to purchase all copyrights from the publishers, who were quite eager to sell. Two days ago, the last book authored by Ms. Kulter rolled off the presses. Never again shall another be printed. Unfortunately, hundreds of thousands of copies have been sold over the years, an embarrassing testimony to the wretched state of the American public. *The Aenamaia* will not go to extraordinary lengths to recover those books as we feel certain most will find their way to recycle bins, as the used book market has shown little to no interest in carrying them. Good taste, it seems, is not altogether dead." Toman noticed Anna Kulter's fuming face out of the corner of his eye and felt a tinge of guilty amusement, but rather than press the point further and waste precious time, he decided it was best to move on.

"All of you hold assets. Those in Ms. Kulter's clan have significant assets. If you have children and spouses being left behind, the bulk of your assets will be transferred to them. If you do not have immediate family, or if your assets are valued beyond the amount we decide to leave to your family, those assets will be reallocated as we see fit. While *The Aenamaia* opposes any kind of physical torture, you can be sure that after years of watching your sordid and often nefarious activities, we do have a penchant for irony. Therefore, do not be surprised if excess funds from Team Felps find their way to the International Lesbian and Gay Association or Atheist Alliance International. I'm sure the National Negro College

Fund would appreciate a charitable and anonymous donation, as would the American Buddhist Congress. *The Aenamaia* has compiled a list of other organizations that might benefit from your generosity as well."

Staring up thoughtfully, Toman began counting innocently on his fingers as he named the ones he could remember. "Planned Parenthood, the American Red Cross, the American Gulf War Veterans Association, the National Coalition for the Homeless, and of course the Democratic and Green parties. So far, we've managed to liberate over half a million dollars from Team Felps, and there is still more to come. I have not received an updated figure for Team Kulter," he said, the last two words spoken with marked sarcasm, "but I'm sure the amount will be significantly higher.

"For the next several weeks our teams will continue to seek out any and all reference to your names and do whatever is necessary to remove or alter the records. The objective is to do what we can to erase the lives you've led and, in our opinion, wasted."

Toman paused for a moment facing the speechless captives. In their eyes and faces he saw the entire span of negative human emotions: fear, anger, resentment, hatred, incredulity, and panic. What surprised him was that no one had said a word, except for the brief outbreak by Felps. Perhaps deep inside they had expected something like this might happen. Judgment isn't always swift, but universally most people do believe it finds those who have intentionally forsaken general goodness. Looking again, Toman now saw the undeniable presence of grim comprehension in the faces before him. He had seen similar expressions on countless faces in courtrooms just after the verdict had been rendered against them: guilty as charged, and they'd truly expected nothing less.

Surveys done throughout the world showed that most people believed that every human knows right from wrong, good from bad, up from down. And each time a person purposely acted contrary to that knowledge and their gut feelings, he or she would retain a malignant blackness in their soul. This blackness, like an infection, could eventually be cured, but only if the person consciously chose to become healthy. They first had to acknowledge the degeneracy of the act, then work to amend any negative effects from it, and then labor to ensure no repeat would ever be committed. Conversely, if the wrong-doing were never expunged, then subsequent violations would continue to wreak havoc on the soul, all the while accumulating in a sort of black sclerosis that would eventually manifest itself in the forms of disease, painful illness and finally death.

"These poor souls," Toman thought, "are on that path, or were until a few days ago." Deep down inside, in the rarely visited dark corners of their minds, they sensed something like this would happen. But the powerful elixir of reassuring denial combined with the unwavering encouragement and shallow camaraderie offered freely by their fellow offenders had kept them believing they could continue defying the ethical principals they knew to be true and just. The irony was stunning.

Toman nodded to one of the corporals standing next to the retracted hangar door. The young man returned a barely perceptible nod and moved swiftly out of sight. Returning his attention to the assembled party, Toman spoke loudly, his voice devoid of any emotion.

"No doubt you are wondering why our organization has gone to such lengths on your behalf. While I am not permitted to disclose many details about *The Aenamaia*, what I can tell you is that you should feel fortunate to be alive. Normally when our organization goes to so much trouble to monitor and research a group or individual for so long, they wind up disappearing – quietly and forever. However, given the number of offenders in this case, *The Aenamaia* has chosen a rather unique way of showing you the errors of your ways." Toman knew General Payte had come in and was standing a few paces behind him, though the veteran soldier had not made a sound.

"General Payte," Toman said offering the general the floor. The general strode forward.

"You want to know what is going to happen to you," General Payte began, his voice sounding like that of a drill sergeant preparing to give instructions to his men. "You are effectively being kicked out of the United States of America. Your U.S. Citizenship has been revoked. Your offenses are such that *The Aenamaia* has determined that your presence in this country constitutes a direct threat to the American way of life."

General Payte whispered instructions to a nearby soldier, then began pacing. "In a few minutes you will be escorted to a C-130J Hercules transport aircraft which you will board through the rear. The aircraft will depart in twenty minutes. There you will spend the next twenty-seven hours on your journey to Iraq."

A ripple of gasps ran through the crowd, followed by low, muted talking.

"Quiet!" the general barked, his expression remaining unchanged. "As I was saying, you will be taken to a remote location approximately thirty kilometers south of Baghdad. There you will be supplied with the same provisions given to a United States soldier, minus the weapons. Those supplies, if used properly, should be enough to get you to Baghdad, which is the nearest place to find someone who speaks English. Anyone who sees you will assume, based on your camouflage that you are, in fact, a U.S. soldier. You may choose to shed your fatigues, but I wouldn't recommend it. Without ample protection, the desert will suck out every ounce of moisture in your body and you will die quickly."

The general stopped pacing and faced the assembled party, his face hard and stoic. "You have all, in one way or another, dishonored the men and women who defend this country. Therefore, you will not be afforded one iota of training or instruction. You are on your own.

"Now, if you should make it to Baghdad alive and manage to secure help from someone sympathetic to your situation, there is only one thing you need to remember: You are not, under any circumstances, allowed to return to the United States. Ever." The general paused to let his words sink in. "I want to make this point crystal clear to everyone here. Your citizenship has been irreversibly revoked. Should you try to return to the U.S., you will be shot and killed within twenty-four hours of touching American soil. Toman told you that your treatment is outside of the normal operating procedures for *The Aenamaia*, but make no mistake, the courtesy of sparing your lives will not be extended twice. Additionally, should you manage to settle into another country, I recommend that the rest of your lives be lived in quiet self-appraisal and reflection. Should you choose to call out *The Aenamaia* or continue the activities you are now being punished for, we will not hesitate to liberate the charred and shrunken brain matter from the confines of your skull, regardless of where you live.

"For the next twenty-seven hours you will be in a military aircraft flying five miles above the surface. You will be guarded by well-trained and well-armed soldiers. You would be wise to follow their instructions to the letter. Any attempts at escape or resistance will be met with immediate deadly force. Make no mistake, we are not fucking around here." Despite the use of the expletive, there was no change in General Payte's voice or expression.

Toman watched as the general surveyed the trembling, forlorn people before him. Each time one of the prisoners turned to eyeball the guards who surrounded them, they found there was no way out. And when they turned back to the front, they found the general's knowing eyes piercing their own, as if to reinforce the futility of the thoughts that had barreled through their minds only moments before.

Time seemed to slow down, as was often the case when witnessing the unnerving spectacle of surfeit cowardice and fear pressed helplessly up against such steadfast strength and conviction. From where he stood, Toman could see the profile of the general's face, but could not imagine the maelstrom of thoughts racing through his mind. What he sensed was that something had changed in the man's demeanor in the course of only a few moments. The general shot him a quick look, then returned his attention to the captive audience. But in that one moment, in the brief exchange of glances, Toman felt his chest and stomach tighten. And for the first time since he'd known the man, Toman saw true, raw feeling partially liquefy the cast-iron face of Brigadier General William Andrew Payte.

He felt certain there was no outright anger or hostility present, though he thought he saw Felps quail slightly. If he didn't know any better, Toman would guess this is what it looked like when a man like General Payte experienced physical and emotional pain drill through him at the same time, while straining to conceal it. His brow looked as though gravity was pulling it towards the center of the earth, while he himself was simultaneously infiltrated by the slightest hint of uncertainty. The sight made Toman decidedly uncomfortable, but he knew that to turn away would be an admission of what no one was supposed to know.

"My son, and countless other innocent men and women have given their lives to defend the freedom of this nation while you have dedicated your lives to destroying it. Your crimes are egregious, but you are being given the second chance they never had. I hope this experience will bring the error of your ways into sharp relief and that you will not piss away the rest of your lives. That is all."

Even as the general was making his final remarks, Toman could hear the deep hum of the C-130J as it approached the hangar. Most people could not distinguish the faint buzzing of a cargo plane or transport aircraft from the purring of a nearby air conditioner or the even moan of a moving elevator, but he felt sure these people knew what that sound meant. Still pondering this, he turned and walked out of the hangar into the crisp morning breeze.

Within a few moments, a large clay-colored airplane rolled into view a hundred yards from the hangar. Toman had never seen the C-130J in person and was impressed by the sight. The mammoth plane stood over thirty-eight feet tall from the ground to the top of the vertical stabilizer. The wing span measured in at one hundred and thirty-two feet, fully twenty feet longer than the full length of the aircraft. Already he could feel the stiff wind generated by two of the four turboprops. "The wind of change carries the unmistakable scent of justice," he mused pensively, watching the hulking military plane approach. No doubt many of the detainees were mowing frantically through a field where similar thoughts sprouted and grew with amazing speed. Random images and emotions intertwined with tense denial and copious incredulity. These situations were always rife with a perceivable and dangerous tension that was simultaneously heightened and kept in check by the presence of trained men with guns.

Only moments after the thought entered his mind, movement out of the corner of his left eye caught Toman's attention. Returning to the hangar, he found one of the soldiers had drawn his weapon and was aiming it cautiously at one of the prisoners who was lying face down on the ground. A second soldier kept the man pressed to the hard floor with a knee to the back and the man's right wrist upturned in what he knew was an unnatural and painful angle. The man's face was contorted and remained tense, but he managed to lie perfectly still – proof this foolish man understood that his wrist was only millimeters away from snapping.

"There's always one who tries to jump ship," he thought shaking his head. When soldiers receive training to deal with situations like this, they are often told to expect and hope that someone early on will "volunteer" to be made an example of. If the individual is dealt with swiftly using precise, expert force, it sends a clear message to onlookers that they are not in charge and that compliance with their captors' wishes is advisable. If there are no volunteers, a soldier runs the risk of multiple individuals getting the panic bug at the same time. The captor then must gauge the situation and decide whether or not a demonstration of force is necessary to prevent a revolt. Toman had seen it happen before and now felt strangely relieved that such an exhibition would not be necessary.

In less than a minute the man was back on his feet with his hands tightly bound behind his back. Toman noticed a trickle of blood running behind one ear and the bright red precursor to a bruise on his left cheek. The man looked a bit dazed and a little rumpled, but otherwise he seemed to be okay. The rest of the detainees stood motionless, watching the spectacle with the same morbid curiosity that slows traffic after a car accident. Their eyes followed every move mechanically. From the stillness in the room, Toman guessed every last one of them was holding their breath.

Turning back to the tarmac where the plane now stood still, Toman studied the scene. The rear cargo door had already opened and a few soldiers were busy unloading a dozen small crates. Each soldier was clad in desert fatigues similar to those worn by their prisoners – but with a few additions, including side arms and ammunition, handcuffs, plastic ties, and pepper spray. Toman noticed several of the guards also carried stun guns. If any serious trouble arose during the flight, the soldiers would not risk firing a gun inside the plane.

He was about to turn away when something out of the ordinary caught his attention. Watching one of the soldiers carry a wooden crate up the ramp, Toman noticed the man appeared to be wearing a thin, square backpack of some kind. Although he was fifty feet from the plane, he could see the packs were flat and relatively smooth. "Extra supplies," he wondered? "No, it isn't large enough." As he studied the scene, he realized with some shock that in fact, each soldier was wearing an identical pack. How had he not noticed before? He tried to recall the soldiers he'd seen subduing one of the prisoners a few minutes earlier. Had they worn these packs? Could he have missed something so obvious? Turning to look back into the hangar, he noticed several of the soldiers donning the square packs they had just removed from beneath a stack that had been covered by a thick, green army tarp. Toman had noticed the lumpy stack when he'd first walked in, but had dismissed it immediately, assuming it was spare parts or tools. "What the hell...?" he wondered.

Toman was still deep in thought when Booker walked up beside him. The pensive man's gaze was fixed on the airplane. When he spoke, his voice was both solemn and business-like. "You'd better tell them about the others," he said.

The sudden sound startled Toman. He shot the man a quick glance, his face betraying the concentration he was now having a hard time letting go of. Toman stared at the soldier for a few moments, trying to process what he'd just said. Thoughts of the packs quickly faded as he remembered there was still one bit of information he would need to pass on to the prisoners. Toman pursed his lips as he considered what he would say to the people. It was possible they would feel somewhat consoled at having company, but he thought it unlikely. Knowing this crowd, they would see the other passengers as hindrances on the road to Baghdad.

"How many are in there?" he said nodding towards the aircraft.

"Three from Hilo and nine from the general, all for shipment. Plus six black berets for containment and deployment," Booker said evenly.

"How many of yours are going?"

"Ten men volunteered. The general thought that would be adequate."

"Cargo?"

"Two crates with supply packs for each newly liberated vermin and two vehicle drops we'll be making on the way."

Toman shot Booker a puzzled glance.

Still eyeing the cargo plane, Booker said, "The general needed an excuse for the trip. Clearance for flights into Iraq is not as easy to obtain as it used to be, so he had to give them something in return. Bush didn't like anyone flying into Iraq unless they were going to kill someone or provide escort for one of his family's oil buddies. The President is doing his best to clean things up, but so far he's not granting easy access either."

Adept at seeing through Booker's sarcasm, Toman knew there was much truth to what he had said. With the former President's approval ratings among the lowest in history and the war in Iraq still taking its toll, the new administration and the military were under increasing pressure to ensure all flights to Iraq served some measurable military or political end. But it was more than that. Whenever any of the military personnel involved with *The Aenamaia* spoke of former President Bush, there was always an edge, a nearly imperceptible contempt.

Toman knew that both Booker and the general had seen the darker side of Bush's war in Iraq – the side that was not covered by the media in America: The hospital wards full of maimed and dying Iraqi children, the bodies of prisoners who had been interrogated by U.S. intelligence officers eager to further their own careers by any means necessary. The three out of four targets missed by bombers early on in the war. The carnage wrought by insurgent rebel cells against American soldiers sent in to an abandoned section of town without prior reconnaissance by an overzealous general who believed superior firepower would be enough to win the war.

All the while, Americans were fed a constant diet of fear-based, high-resolution images interlaced regularly with patriotic and arrogant bravado as it was spewed forth from the White House. It amazed Toman to think of the overwhelming amount of lies and unfiltered bullshit the American people happily swallowed. Anyone familiar with history should understand why it was happening. Ever since the graphic and incriminating media coverage helped demoralize Americans and turn them against the Vietnam War, the U.S. Government kept a tight leash on the media and an even tighter leash on the rations dribbled to the American public. Nowadays people were infinitely more interested in *American Idol* and *Survivor* than what their own government was perpetrating. Ironically, these unprecedented levels of apathy and ignorance were just a few of the reasons why Toman was standing in an old hangar in Atlantic, North Carolina at five-thirty in the morning. One thing was damn sure, the President still had a hell of a lot of cleaning up to do.

"Where will the drop be?" Toman asked, going back to his train of thought.

"Don't worry," Booker said answering his unspoken question, "they'll be over a hundred miles away from the drop."

"Base or retrieval?"

"Retrieval. A temporary encampment will be set up near the drop zone. Both vehicles will be recovered and on their way back to base well before any of the new 'soldiers' here ever touch sand."

"Any chance another unit will detect the drop and come to investigate?" Toman asked, the concern in his voice apparent.

Booker shook his head and grinned sardonically, "Give the general a little more credit than that. Besides," he said absently, "The general knows the commander of the unit receiving the vehicles. They're old friends."

Toman nodded pensively, but said nothing. His mind was racing in a thousand directions all at once: Images of the two vehicles being dropped from five thousand feet from the rear of the plane and bound for pickup by the general's contact. The frozen looks of utter disbelief on the faces of these people as they are herded away from the plane towards a barren, unforgiving desert. There would be crying, screams promising repentance or swearing innocence, and outcries of righteous indignation. There would undoubtedly be threats, obscenities, desperate promises of vengeance and everlasting damnation, mostly from Shirley's group, bribery attempts, pleas for forgiveness, and promises of second chances. No doubt some of the prisoners would straddle the frayed edge of insanity, while a few might actually cross it.

A vibration in his pocket stirred Toman from his thoughts. Before his fingers touched the phone, he knew something was wrong. Aside from confirming acquisition and delivery of Felps and Kulter to the hangar via text message, the phone was to be used for emergencies only.

Toman pulled the cell from his pocket and checked caller ID. The number read: 0-911-411. It was Gray. 911-411 was *The Aenamaia*'s code for "Emergency, Information needed." Osiro had been able to hack into each of their cell phones and change the programming to allow them to manually enter the number that would show up on the caller ID of each of their phones. If they called someone outside of *The Aenamaia*, it would simply show up as a blocked number. But between the phones, they could send coded messages. The actual caller was identified by the first number in the sequence. Gray was zero. 911 indicated something bad had or was about to take place. 411 indicated the caller needed to exchange information immediately with the receiving party. Translation: answer the damn phone.

Walking quickly away from the prisoners and the airship, Toman accepted the call and pressed the phone to his ear.

"Secure?" Gray questioned curtly.

Toman looked at the color LCD screen on his phone. In the upper left-hand corner he saw a small, closed padlock.

"Secure," he confirmed.

"Are you still at the shed?" Gray asked, his voice tight and knotted. 'Shed' was Gray's codename for the airplane hangar.

"Affirmative," he answered quickly and added, "What's going on?"

There was a pause. Toman could hear whispers and ruffling, as if Gray had covered the phone with his hand. "Sorry," Gray said, "Information is still coming in."

The concern in Gray's normally composed voice worried Toman.

"We're set to airlift the packages in fifteen minutes and I still have a few things to say to them. Can you sum it up?"

Gray's voice was distant as he spoke to someone nearby. "We've got an Augur off the reservation," Gray said. "It's Joust. He reported successful tracking and location of each of his targets in and around DC at ten o'clock last night. There's a three-day DOD conference funded by the K Street Project. His six and sixty-four more will be in attendance. When Teala told him to sit tight and await further orders, he became agitated and aggressive, saying that he was tired of watching and waiting. He told her it was time to 'Send the message.' When Teala assured him teams would be sent to extract the targets, he ignored her and said, "'We need to send the message now!'"

Toman thought for a moment then asked, "One-night sniper boost? A revisit to his black ops days? He could take out a lot of people all at once if he wanted to."

Gray exhaled with a frustrated grumble. "I don't know. Since the first day he joined us, he's wanted to go straight for the jugular, but I thought he understood the necessity of precise timing. When I first met him, he was an irascible young man, always eager to engage in any kind of conflict. No surprise the military grabbed him. But over time he mastered control over his anger – used it to his advantage. It's what helped make him the best. But what he did back then," he said searching for the words, "was not blood lust or machismo. He thought he was doing then what we're doing now. Purely patriotic and idealistic. Altruistic sacrifices for the greater good. Only," he paused again, "...only it wasn't that either." The phone went silent for a moment. Toman waited, sensing there was more.

"Later, when he learned who he'd really had in his crosshairs..." Gray said regretfully, "there were so many innocents, people who had simply gotten in the way of the wrong people. And the wrong people had friends and connections. He couldn't have known. How would he know? Snipers are rarely given a full dossier on their targets. Just a current photograph, time tables, maps, and exactly how the mark is to be retired."

There was an uncertain stillness on the line then Gray added, "I don't think..." he paused and took a breath. "No," he said with confidence, "I know he won't have it in him to fire through the scope again. He'll want one decisive action to clear the playing field. A single decision that, once made, cannot be reversed."

"What munitions does he have access to?"

"Aside from guns?" Gray answered thoughtfully, "The same as everyone else. A few vials of the blue, basic explosives, hand-to-hand implements, etc. Nothing strong enough to take out the whole group at once."

"That doesn't matter," Toman said with a sigh, "When it comes to operations like this, Joust has more creativity than Jackie Chan. He'll find a way. There's little chance we'll be able to anticipate what he'll do, let alone stop it." Toman considered the problem for a moment then asked, "Any intel from Raven?"

"He's looking into it, but so far there's nothing. We figured this operation was a slam dunk, so it wasn't on Raven's list to monitor."

There was a long silence on the other end of the phone. Despite Gray's superior intelligence and problem-solving skills, Toman doubted he would divine a foolproof solution. The error and problem was human, emotional and irrational. The only hope was to somehow contact Joust before he executed his plans...and his marks.

"Gray," Toman said, "Susha and Dia are en route to DC. They left here after the drop last night and were hopping the red-eye." He looked at his watch. "They should be there by now."

"I already thought of that. We checked. Their plane took off an hour and half late. I've sent word for them to call when they land. They'll join up with Teala and coordinate a search. Until then I was hoping you might try contacting him. Osiro said his phone is on and receiving, but he's not picking up. Perhaps if he sees your number..."

"I'll try as soon as the transport takes off," he said looking at his watch.

There was a long pause on the line before Gray said thoughtfully, "If he goes hunting tonight...it stands that our operations may become much more complicated than they already are."

"No doubt about that," Toman agreed, trying to think quickly. "We should be thinking about damage control."

He knew a lot about Joust's targets since he'd been part of the research team that had selected them, but he wasn't quite sure how the rest of their plans might be affected. "What about a phantom changeling – an infection rumor blaming a rogue DOD ex-employee or defunct contractor seeking revenge on the lobbyists? Insertion would be simple enough. Kelley is already on a leash. It only has to work long enough for us to execute our remaining plans."

"I've considered that. Problem is, I don't know if the press would buy it – even if Kelley were peddling it. We may have him on a leash, but the extent of our control is another matter. Something tells me he has an agenda of his own. We're keeping a close eye on him. If it becomes necessary to push a diversion through him, it will be a last resort. But I'm hoping we can find Joust in time to avoid the whole damn thing."

"Understood. I need to get back. The general will order my parcels loaded shortly."

"Go. But before you call Joust, phone Osiro so he can set up a three-way and try to triangulate the location."

"Joust would never fall for that," Toman said shaking his head. He tried to think. Absently he added, "He's way too smart for that. In fact, he'll expect it."

"Perhaps," Gray agreed, sounding like he, too, was mulling over something. "But, he would be looking for one of our numbers. It might be worth having Osiro pull his personnel file and see if he can't locate the number of a trusted friend or family member to use. We only need thirty seconds or so for a trace."

"Can we access calls from his phone over the last month or so?" he asked hopefully.

Toman heard a hand cover the receiver. A few seconds of muffled talking passed before Gray replied, "I'm not sure if Osiro can break through the scuds he put in place to scramble the phone records. We worked very hard to ensure no one could access those records. But," he added in a conspiratorial tone, "if I know Osiro, there's bound to be a backup in place that only he can access. See what you can find out, and fast. Joust isn't kickin' it on a beach in Maui right now; he's on the move."

"Will do."

"Good luck with the send-off," Gray offered.

"Thanks," he said and hung up the phone. The news about Joust was troublesome. So much time and talk had been invested in the beginning to ensure each and every member of *The Aenamaia* understood the role their single cog played in keeping the machine running smoothly. Thinking back, Toman recalled wondering why Joust had been somewhat withdrawn at many of their meetings. He'd attributed the man's silence to the kind of pensive focus and concentration found in any sniper. No doubt the man had demons in the closet. Each member did. But now it looked as though one of the more potent wraiths the shooter had kept at bay all these years had escaped and was wreaking havoc on his mind. Whether retribution or revenge, penance or atonement for past mistakes, Joust felt he'd found the panacea he was sure would close the closet door and cure that which ailed him.

Toman shook his head. He needed to focus on the task at hand. No doubt the general would be looking for him. Joust would have to wait. He shoved the phone back in his pocket and headed towards the open hangar door. The sun hovered a few degrees above the storm front that sat like a wall on the horizon. Closer in, he saw the silhouetted line of tall loblolly pines. The sight reminded him of an approaching army of strong infantrymen straddling the edge of the battlefield, eagerly awaiting the king's war cry and call to glory. Part of him wished he felt that way. Instead, a complicated mixture of resignation, a hint of reluctant doubt, and stubborn dedication to their cause fueled each step towards a hangar full of bad seeds.

Once inside, Toman found the general patiently watching as several soldiers moved quickly among the weary group of captives. Each person's gear was being given a final inspection and thumbs-up.

"Trouble?" the general asked as Toman approached.

"We're not sure," he answered, "We might have an Augur on the loose."

"Joust?" the general asked casually.

Surprised, Toman turned to look at the general. The stoic man remained facing forward, but a barely perceptible grin permeated the iron façade.

"You know Joust?" he asked incredulously. For reasons Gray never fully explained, *The Aenamaia*'s utilization of the general and his men would be specific and limited, as was contact. Only the Augurs working on assignments that utilized the small military force were allowed to have direct communication. It was one of the many unusual tactics Gray employed. Toman expected a full explanation should they all live to talk about it.

"His goatee didn't give it away?" the general asked simply.

Toman's lips were frozen in a fixed "O", his brow furrowed, as he pictured Joust in his mind. He'd first met Joust four years ago in Denver. And yes, he'd had his goatee then. And as far as Toman knew he still did. Before he could say anything, the general turned to look at him.

"Unfortunately there is no time to piece it together, Toman," he said calmly. "These people need to leave soon and we need to make ourselves scarce. Joust was under my command for about six years. I helped supervise his training when Special Ops began recruiting for assignments in Uzbekistan, Chechnya, Turkmenistan, and North Korea. I'm the one who brought him to *The Aenamaia* by way of Gray."

"And the goatees – yours and his?" Toman asked.

The corners of the general's mouth and small wrinkles around his eyes betrayed a subtle smile. At that moment Toman could swear the general's normally tight-knit brow had melted a degree. "Call it a symbol of why we're here and a sign that we're no longer serving under the United States military."

Toman was about to ask another question when the general beat him to the punch.

"Go, Toman," he said nodding towards the group of nervous camouflaged civilians. "We can talk about this later."

Reluctantly, Toman nodded and headed towards the abductees. There were so many random thoughts bouncing around inside his head that he found it difficult to focus. Joust and General Payte? How had he not known that? Why hadn't Gray ever mentioned it? Why had Joust never told him? And if the general had once been Joust's superior, why wasn't the general going after him? Though the general and his men were not Augurs, they had sworn to help *The Aenamaia* achieve their goals. Instead, Gray was sending Dia and Susha who would team up with Teala and try to bring Joust in – assuming Osiro was able to locate him.

But what would they be able to do even if they found him? The man had more conviction and enthusiasm for *The Aenamaia* and the insurrection that was underway than any other member. Joust, more so than anyone else, felt he had so much to atone for. Although he was intelligent and logical and held reverent respect for the other *Aenamaia* members, Toman doubted the women would be able to make a dent. And now, here at a deserted airbase, he learns of the general's relationship to Joust and their past together. What did it all mean? As he approached the nervous civilians, it occurred to him that the general hadn't seemed surprised that Joust was AWOL. But more than that, Toman felt certain the general knew what Joust would do – and might even condone such rash actions.

He stopped abruptly and turned to look at the C-130J. The rising sun was now well above the horizon and he could see the aircraft clearly. The monstrous plane had seen better days. In addition to peeling paint and rust spots, he noticed several sizeable dents in the hull. Towards the middle and near the top of the aircraft he could just make out a thick dark line. Was it a shadow? A gash? "What a piece of shit," he thought shaking his head. "I'm sure the plane's sorry condition had probably made it easier to acquire. Hell, nobody would even miss this thing if it never…"

The hairs on his neck stood up and he caught his breath. Unsolicited thoughts and images pummeled his visual cortex. "How many would be onboard?" he wondered. Three or four in the cockpit, fifteen-plus soldiers to stand guard and keep the peace, and thirty civilians. Toman suddenly recalled the burst of anger the general had unleashed upon Felps. It had caught him off guard. Even Booker had been surprised. Was it significant?

He turned and looked back at the general who still stood in the same spot. Toman studied the general's profile, hoping to see something that might put his mind at ease. Strong and straight jaw, intense stare, slightly dished cheeks, hands clasped behind his back. There was nothing. The veteran general watched the preparations with intense interest. He stood at rigid attention: pressed green camouflage uniform, polished black boots, rolled up sleeves, faded tattoos along both forearms, field watch, and standard army fatigue cap. Looking at him now the term "regular army" came to Toman's mind. Other than the goatee and the conspicuous absence of any rank or insignia, the term fit perfectly.

The general turned and met his stare, but Toman could not read his expression. The general then gave a slight nod and returned his attention to the plane and the cargo being loaded.

Now he was worried. But there was nothing he could do about it. Resigned to finish what he'd started, he returned his attention to the civilians. From the looks of it, the inspection was done and the soldiers awaited orders. "Thirty," he thought. "Probably just a tiny fraction of those who should be going." Though he couldn't even imagine the amount of collateral damage these people had wrought throughout their lives, he felt comforted knowing that the pain and turmoil they peddled so freely was about to come to a permanent end. He stopped before the ragged group and raised his voice.

"In a few minutes your armed escorts will march you onto the transport for your final journey out of America. There are seventeen of you in this group. When you board the transport, you will notice another assembly of exiles similarly dressed and bound. They will share your fate." Gasps rippled through the group. Toman raised his hand to calm them. "Please, please," he said repeatedly until the whispers died down. "Please pay close attention. The people onboard are not related to you in any way, other than the comparable damage they too have wrought on society." He began pacing. "When you land you will be escorted out of the plane. Once everyone is off, your restraints will be removed and you will be free to decide what to do next. It is my suggestion that you quickly agree to cooperate with one another and head towards Baghdad. Use your compasses and head northeast. I would also recommend you agree to rotate as scouts who will lead your party by a few miles. There will be thirty of you. Even in camouflage you'll be quite conspicuous. But if you take my advice and work together, you just might get the chance to start over again."

"Sergeant," he called out.

Booker fell in next to him. "This is Sergeant Booker. Do what he says and no one will get hurt. Get out of line and expect swift retribution. As you have seen, these men take their work very seriously. Do not fuck with them.

"Your various crimes and trespasses have landed you here. The wake you've left will take years to smooth out. Now a new journey of cleansing begins. Do what you're told and you may all survive this ordeal and live out the rest of your lives. New lives. Never forget what the general said about never returning to the United States. Please heed the warning, as your lives really do depend on it."

Toman watched as the soldiers expertly herded the civilians up the rear cargo ramp. Despite his warning, a few men tried to run. They were quickly apprehended and thrown to the ground. The soldiers expertly utilized pressure points to maintain control over the would-be escapees. The cool, professional demeanor of each soldier was almost as impressive as the utility of such simple control techniques. One prisoner's face was contorted in pain as a solder used only two fingers to turn his wrist in an unnatural manner. The power of the technique was further highlighted by the fact that the bear of a man being subdued was easily twice the size of the small man who was clearly in control.

The futile escape attempt had been brief. To prevent further incidents, each prisoner's feet were bound by metal fetters, the type used on dangerous prison inmates during transport. Once back on their feet, they were sprayed with a highly diluted pepper spray solution designed to temporarily impair vision. Having witnessed the whole debacle and the swiftness of the response, the remaining prisoners fell in line and did exactly as they were told.

Watching the last of the soldiers scramble up the cargo ramp as it closed, Toman again noticed the square bulge on the soldiers' backs. He also glanced quickly at the two large crates which held the vehicles Booker had mentioned. Within seconds the cargo door closed with a deep, metallic rumble. Still staring at the rear of the plane, the image of the general's face appeared unbidden in his mind once again as he recalled the speed and fury with which he'd attacked Felps. It had been over quickly, but the uncharacteristic nature of the attack still made him feel uneasy. Toman felt certain the general would've gladly taken out all the pain his son's death had caused him on Felps at that very moment, had he not felt certain that justice would soon be dispensed. The question was: Was exile good enough for Brigadier General William Andrew Payte? "The marionette of justice bears a different face for us all," he thought grimly.

Ten minutes later, with a tight, anxious feeling in his gut, Toman still pondered that question as he stood by and watched the colossal C-130J charge the runway and lift off. Four distinct curved brown contrails marked the passing of the transport plane as it banked east, the wings tilted at a forty-five degree angle, and headed directly into the bright rising sun. The night before, sitting in the shadows on the college campus, Toman had been confident he knew every detail of this operation – from the extractions to a carefully planned dishonorable desert discharge. Now, he reluctantly admitted to himself that he wasn't even certain the worn-down aircraft would make it to Iraq. And if his suspicions were correct, the implications would reverberate through *The Aenamaia*. Nothing would be the same again.

Washington, D.C.

"Well, who the hell cleared it?" Roger Tarte said incredulously into his phone. The email on his screen was marked "Confidential" and "Eyes Only." It had come from one of Steven Floyd's contacts in Atlantic Command. Floyd had been CC'd on it as well.

"Was a flight plan logged?" he asked. "Yeah, you could say I need to know!" he said sarcastically. "Yes, I'll hold."

Tarte let out a deep sigh and rubbed his forehead. Only a day had passed since Floyd had called and already he was sorry he'd taken the bait. He was even more sorry his boss had gotten wind of it. Clarke Banes, the Homeland Security Director, had been thrilled at the prospect of an interagency investigation in a matter he'd been told, "Had some meat." Banes never passed up an opportunity to make it look like he and his people were constantly working on critical issues of National Security, although the truth was much softer. Work at the DHS had been on the steady-to-slow pace for quite some time.

After Bush had left the White House, the new President had focused most of his efforts on what one journalist termed "Visible and mutually beneficial diplomacy." So far the effort seemed to be working. But for the DHS, things had really slowed down. So it was no surprise that Banes leapt at the possibility, however small, for a brief return to the limelight. It was inevitable, really. Despite the laws of inertia and motion, Tarte couldn't expect to coast forever. Approval for the operation was expedited and his email address and phone number sent to a dozen people already working on the issue. So far the government was keeping the matter as quiet as possible, mostly because they were unsure what was actually going on. There was no need to get the American people all riled up until they knew what they were dealing with. A strategy vastly different from that of the previous administration, which preferred to scare first, scare again, hold an election, and then tell the people they were safe.

Tarte shook the thought from his head. Now wasn't the time to be thinking of the past. Focus on the now. He was still on hold and growing more irritated every second. Billions of dollars in the most advanced communications technology available – and some desk jockey still had to go find the information on two numb legs.

While he waited, Tarte re-read the last email for the tenth time.

SAT Command confirmed takeoff of C130 from abandoned air base on the coast of North Carolina. Aircraft heading east towards coast of Africa. Flight plan authorization being investigated. Aircraft registration: Unknown. Aircraft origin: Unknown. Destination: Unknown.

Multiple vehicles seen exiting air base. Local PD dispatched to intercept vehicles. PD unable to locate. Investigative team from airbase found evidence of fresh blood in one hangar. Fingerprints: negative. Contraband: negative.

Anomalous Finding: Autographed copy of a new book by author Anna Kulter located in an office at the rear of the main hangar. Further investigation revealed the book has yet to go to press. Publisher confirmed only three copies were in existence: two being held by the publisher, one by the author. Note: book set to go to press one week ago, but was delayed due to an unexplained explosion that destroyed the printing press. No one was present in the room when the explosion went off. FBI is investigating. Confidential Findings: Initial reports suggest a compact incendiary device planted deep within the machinery resulted in an area of fused metal approximately five feet by ten feet.

"Mr. Tarte?"

"Yes, I'm here," Tarte replied eagerly.

"The flight plan lists CFB Suffield as the destination," the voice said dryly.

"CFB? As in 'Canadian Forces Base'?" he asked incredulously.

Silence.

"Lieutenant," Tarte said sternly, "are you trying to tell me that a C130 cargo plane currently heading east towards the continent of Africa logged a flight plan with a destination in Alberta Canada – a province north of Montana?!"

"Yes, sir," the man answered nervously, "that does appear to be the case."

"Well, I suggest you have your supervisor get his supervisor on the phone ASAP. An unregistered U.S. military airplane with a fake flight plan and questionable clearance is halfway across the Atlantic Ocean headed towards a host of unfriendly nations. We just might want to find out who is flying that plane, the nature of the cargo, what the final destination really is, and just exactly what the fuck is going on here!" he finished with a loud crescendo.

"Yes, sir!" the fear and panic obvious in the man's voice, "Right away, sir."

The line went dead. Squeezing the receiver with all his strength, Tarte was tempted to slam it down, but resisted. Deliberately and with considerable control, he gently replaced the receiver and reluctantly peeling away his reddened hand. "Deep breath," he thought, "slow and deep." It was another white rabbit to chase, but that had been the story all day. Five cars left that airbase, then up and vanished. Local PD was still scratching their heads on that one. Blood stains without a name and a book without an author – both were en route to the nearest forensics lab.

Four hundred miles to the north someone nukes the paperboy's hundred thousand dollar Benz. Immediately afterwards the paperboy vanishes. Houdini's two, PD's zero. Then there were the disappearances Floyd had sent him. The Blackriver CEO, a former energy exec and the soon to be indicted former Congressman Tom Delay. Now Anna Kulter, her bizarre sidekick and their entourage. Five high-profile figures evaporate into thin air – all in the last two days. And so far very little press coverage, which surprised him. People vanishing was one thing, but so many explosions across the country shutting down the major tabloid newspapers was big news. Yet most front pages were still focusing on the war efforts in Afghanistan. Old habits die hard, even for the media machine. And for once he was grateful for it.

While he wasn't as convinced as Floyd that these events were all related, his gut told him something big was unfolding here. If he didn't get his game face on and get moving, he would be reading about it on the unemployment line. Thanks a lot, Floyd.

He reached for the mouse to refresh his email when his phone sprang to life. Before the first ring went silent, the receiver was at his ear. "Tarte here," he said eagerly. As he listened, his fingers combed absently through his thick, wavy brown hair, a habit he'd picked up during the many tedious hours of his tenure at the NSA's Cryptographic Center. For years Jessica had predicted it would lead to his eventual baldness. At the moment he thought sudden and extreme stress a more likely culprit. Only time would tell.

"Well, where the hell has he been since the explosion?" Pause. "No, that isn't good enough. Send an agent over to his hou… Well, then where is he? That's even better. We won't need a warrant if he decides to be uncooperative."

He listened for a few more seconds. Exhaling slowly he tried to control his frustration. "What time does the story break?"

He made note of the time and website then added, "Better tell Floyd. We're going to need to be ready with some damage control here, or this is going to get out of hand."

Tarte's mind was racing. So much was happening all at once. He had to think. Many questions lined up in his mind in search of answers, but one in particular kept jumping to the front of the line: Why did Floyd send this to me? If the veteran FBI agent suspected a link between these incidents, surely he could make a case to keep the investigation in his department instead of sharing it with someone in a different agency, whom he'd only just met. If Floyd's instincts were correct, and these incidents were related, he would surely be the first one to have made the connection. Why forego the opportunity for recognition and yet be so helpful to a DHS agent at the same time? Nothing here added up.

His thoughts were interrupted by a loud noise next to his ear. He realized he was still holding the receiver. The fast-busy tone was urging him to hang it up. Still in deep thought, he leaned forward to return the receiver. Before he made it all the way the door, to his office burst open. In less than a second his long-time assistant Jasmine was at his desk talking excitedly about something. Tarte held up his hands.

"Slow down, Jasmine. I can't understand a single word."

"Okay, okay," she said, trying to catch her voice.

"Breathe, Jasmine. The last thing I need is a hyperventilating assistant passing out in my office. I know CPR, but my wife would never believe mouth-to-mouth was absolutely necessary. Take a deep breath and start again."

Jasmine closed her eyes and did as she was instructed. As he waited, Tarte realized this was the first time he'd seen Jasmine this morning. He'd already been at his desk for over an hour when she'd buzzed in on the intercom to say good morning. The moment she'd barged in through the door, he'd noticed several distinct differences in her appearance. Her usual designer slacks, blouse and flats had been replaced by a short, smart black skirt that ended a few inches above her knees, a white silk blouse, classy short black jacket and black heels. He also noticed her long blond hair, which he'd rarely seen outside of a tightly wound bun, hung freely. She looked quite stunning. "What's the occasion?" he wondered. Was her new and improved appearance the reason for his mouth-to-mouth comment?

Jasmine exhaled then continued, "You know how you wanted me to keep my eyes peeled for anything odd or suspicious?"

"Go on," Tarte said expectantly.

"I just heard from a friend of mine who is a dispatcher for the New York State Police. They got a call from Fox News about an hour ago. Apparently the CEO, Roger Ailes, hasn't been heard from in a few days. His wife has been in Europe for the past month so he's spent every day at the office."

Tarte relaxed. "That doesn't mean anything. He's probably taking the day off or is out at the country club hitting golf balls with Rupert Murdoch."

Jasmine's coy smile indicated there was more.

"I doubt he'd miss this day, Rog. Don't you know what's going on today at Fox News?" she asked incredulously.

"No, I don't. And I'm extremely proud to say so. The more I stay away from the festering spawns of Satan the better I sleep at night," he joked. But Jasmine was not amused. She stepped closer to his desk, still hugging a stack of files to her chest.

"Donald Rumsfeld and the former Vice President are spending the whole day at Fox News to talk about the indictments. Fox's anchors have hinted at the possibility that Bush himself might show up to discuss the allegations being brought against him by the Justice Department."

Tarte made the connection instantly. He looked at his watch.

"What time did they get there?" he asked with renewed interest.

"Before lunch time. And they're still there. But no one has seen or heard from Ailes since yesterday afternoon."

Tarte was familiar with Ailes. In his former life, the CEO had served as a close political consultant to Nixon, Reagan, and Bush senior. Known to play ball in the extreme conservative right field, Ailes had been influential in reviving campaigns and delivering underdog Presidents the most powerful office in the world. Ailes was graduated from Ohio University, married three times, and brought into the Fox News group by billionaire owner Rupert Murdoch. He was known for his commitment to pushing the right wing agenda by any and all means at his disposal and generally well-liked by other media tycoons, but not so much so by the hired hands at Fox News. Tarte had heard whispers of death threats against Ailes and Murdoch, though no proof had ever surfaced.

"Has Fox said anything about his absence on the air?"

"No," she said shaking her head slowly, "Not a peep about it. And neither Rumsfeld nor Cheney have mentioned it either."

"Has anyone gone looking for him?" he asked.

"Yes. No one answers at his home and there are no cars visible. However, local PD in Garrison went by his summer estate on the outskirts of town," she paused for a second then said, "but they couldn't get past the security gate. No one was on duty."

"No guards," Tarte guessed.

"No guards," Jasmine confirmed, adding, "and no one answered the intercom. But the gray limousine that takes him into the city every day is parked in the circular drive."

"Any indication of forced entry?"

Jasmine shook her head. "The local PD saw nothing out of the ordinary. With no probable cause, they left. But someone didn't feel right about it so they called the NYSP."

"And?" Tarte urged impatiently.

"So far they're jockeying desk-side. No one has been sent out. But, they did confirm that no one from Fox has heard from Ailes today and that he isn't answering his cell. They've also tried calling the house, but if he's there, he's not picking up. At the very least, someone like that would have servants, housekeepers and whatnot who would answer the home phone."

"Garrison. That's Virginia, right?"

Jasmine nodded.

"I still don't know if this means anything," he said skeptically.

"Did you know that two weeks ago CNN reported that Ailes had personally authored that controversial rumor during the Presidential race about Obama being a Muslim terrorist supporter?"

Tarte's eyes went wide. "Really?"

She nodded. "That one pissed a lot of people off, including many on the right."

She looked at him expectantly. Tarte knew Jasmine had been almost as bored as he had for quite some time. No doubt the tantalizing thought of some kind of action was behind her enthusiasm. He'd only told her the bare minimum about the airplane explosion and missing persons, but it had been enough to get her heart rate up and web-surfing senses on full alert. Now the CEO of Fox News had gone missing on what could arguably be a landmark day for his news station – especially if the former President crawled out of Crawford, Texas to make a rare appearance.

Just then something occurred to him. "Jasmine, that friend of yours at NYSP... Do you think perhaps with the former President rumored to be visiting Fox News today...?" he let the incomplete question hang in the air.

Jasmine's eyes lit up. "Of course!" she said enthusiastically. "I'll call them right now. Surely they would know, as would NYPD. The Secret Service always calls ahead and arranges for sweeps."

"Okay, okay," he said trying to calm her down a notch, "first things first. Call Dalton and tell him to have the plane ready in twenty minutes. Have a car and one of our field agents meet me on the tarmac in Garrison."

"Stewart International Airport just outside New Windsor," she corrected. "Garrison is about thirty minutes away. Fifteen, the way you drive."

Tarte smiled at her thoroughness. "How did you know I would just leave all this," he said swinging his arm towards his desk, "to follow some crazy lead?"

"Boredom, tedium, lethargy," she said, ticking off each synonym on her fingers, "disinterest, lassitude, apathy...."

"Okay, okay," he said, "I get the picture."

Jasmine was pleased with herself. Tarte switched off his monitor and pocketed his car keys and cell. While he put on his shoulder holster he asked, "Has anyone checked with Mrs. Ailes?"

"No one has been able to reach her so far," Jasmine said.

Tarte nodded. He put on his coat and holstered his sidearm. With the file he'd compiled from Floyd's leads in hand, he headed for the door with Jasmine in tow.

"I'll call you when I land. In the meantime check with NYSP on Bush's visit. Also, tell them to keep trying the phone at the house. Let me know if anyone answers." Jasmine was scribbling frantically on her pad.

"Alert the local PD that I'm coming in, but don't tell them why. No need to have a flock of Joe Bob's storm the gates. Routine case follow-up...something like that. They just need to know an armed agent is in the area."

Tarte checked off items on his mental checklist. The excitement of suddenly having something interesting to do was palpable, but he didn't want to make any mistakes. He needed to be absolutely sure he wasn't missing anything – just in case this turned out to be something.

"I'll call Floyd en route and update him."

"Should I tell Banes?"

"Not just yet. I don't want him to get all worked up and turn this into a circus. If he calls, tell him I'm pursuing a lead and to call me on my cell. Otherwise, keep this on the QT. Got it?"

"Roger."

"What?" he asked quickly.

She smiled guiltily. Tarte shook his head. He hated it when she did that.

When he reached the elevator, the down button had already been pressed, though no one else was waiting. Someone must have gotten impatient and taken the stairs. "Impatience begets good health," he thought sardonically.

Jasmine stood next to him, apparently expecting some last minute instructions. But he had none. His mind was already wrapped tightly around the task at hand.

After an impossibly long thirty seconds, the door to the elevator opened and he stepped in. He nodded to Jasmine and the doors rolled shut. At the last second he heard Jasmine gasp, "Oh!" followed immediately by her thin white arm as it shot through the small gap between the closing doors. The doors shot open violently as if the elevator's safety spirit suspected a child's neck had been caught in the narrowing gap. Jasmine, wide-eyed and surprised, took one step towards the elevator with her arms posted against the doors to keep them from closing.

"I'm sorry," she said excitedly, "I completely forgot to tell you something."

"I have my cell, Jasmine," Tarte pointed out. He waited a split second then added, "What is it?"

"Ailes!" she blurted out, as if it was the winning answer to a game show question, "I forgot to tell you, two nights ago Ailes had dinner with Rupert Murdoch and that man you're looking for."

"Which man?" he asked.

"From the newspaper," she said handing him the files she'd been guarding. "Jack Kelley."

Chapter 8

Raleigh, North Carolina

What do the massacres of Rathlin Island and Smerwick, the Tower of London, the legend of El Dorado, Queen Elizabeth I, the Lost Colony of Roanoke, and the French Huguenots all have in common? The mysterious and enigmatic Sir Walter Raleigh. Despite accounts of being a hopeless romantic and a decent husband, much intrigue surrounds the extravagant life of Sir Walter Raleigh.

Was he the first gentleman to throw down his mantle to allow the Queen to walk dry-shod across a puddle? Did he know the true fate of the lost colonists of Roanoke? Is it true he never spelled his last name with an "i"? How could a poet, husband, explorer, and historian of conscience partake in multiple massacres, advocate open assassination of Irish leaders, and even dabble in piracy? How many mysteries can surround one man?

Ten U.S. cities bear his name, along with countless statues, parks, clubs, airports, schools, seafaring vessels, government buildings, museums, and consumer products. But are they all really named for the same man? Raleigh is mentioned in songs, stories, poems, television shows, plays and movies. What was it about a man who was beheaded on charges of piracy that makes him worthy of such recognition?

Sir Walter Raleigh once said: "It is observed in the course of worldly things, that men's fortunes are oftener made by their tongues than by their virtues; and more men's fortunes..."

"Paging Mr. Kaparich. Mr. J.D. Kaparich. Please come to the United Airlines ticketing counter. Paging Mr. Kaparich..."

He was so engrossed in the tantalizing summary on the back of the history book, he nearly missed the page. Kaparich. Right. Replacing the book in the paper bag, he caught sight of the name printed in bold on the front of it and smiled: Raleigh-Durham International Airport Bookstore.

As he hurried along the main concourse, he wondered how many times they had paged him. And why? His flight wasn't for another hour and he'd already checked in.

"Mr. Kaparich," he declared to the tired-looking ticket agent. This time he remembered to inflect his voice with a proper British accent, "I believe you just paged me."

Without looking up, the agent typed noisily on her keyboard until she found what she was looking for. She read the screen. He watched as recognition and caution spread across her face. "Well," she said energetically, "it appears as though your seat has been upgraded to first class, Mr. Kaparich, courtesy of United Airlines corporate offices. Are you an employee or contractor for United?"

"No, madam, but I do log quite a few miles with this concern," he said, trying to sound both humble and important. "Perhaps such loyalty has finally garnered some recognition."

"Well, Mr. Kaparich, someone on high knows exactly who you are and where you're traveling to," she said with a smile as she handed him his new ticket.

He reached for it and said, "It never hurts to have a higher power watching over you." She smiled awkwardly and returned her attention to her monitor. He turned on his heel and began walking. Before he reached the end of the counter, his cell phone vibrated. After stuffing the ticket into his breast pocket, he retrieved his phone and looked at the caller ID, which displayed a single word: *God*. Despite all that was on his mind and everything that was at stake, Toman had to laugh. Using his right thumb he flipped the phone open and pressed the send button.

"Osiro...have you nothing better to do with your time and skill than to hack my phone?"

"You look like shit," Osiro said simply, "and you can drop the accent, Mr. Knottingham."

Toman stopped and slowly looked around. How the hell did he...and then he saw it. An off-white video camera mounted above the last ticket window. Staring directly into the lens he shook his head and said, "If we both live through this, I swear I'm going to get you laid."

"You of all people should know that most such Holy Crusades end badly for all involved."

"True. But not all crusades are holy," he corrected.

"Regardless, most do still end in disaster," Osiro said. Then he added, "Look, Mr. Kaparich...the wait at security is twenty minutes. There is a shift change in eight minutes that usually slows the line by another ten minutes. Best to put your bags through while the TSA folks with the tired eyes are still on duty. I recommend Barbara Milsner – she's working the last line and has almost nodded off twice this morning."

"Correction. Drunk and laid," Toman said, eyeing the camera. Still shaking his head, he started walking towards security. "You really need to get out more."

"Your tone is less than obsequious. I would at least expect a thank-you for the first class upgrade and window seat." Osiro said, feigning offense. "Though you look like you should be stowed with the animals and the luggage."

"Thank you, your eminence," Toman said sarcastically ignoring the second poke at his appearance. "Speaking of omnipotence, your lordship, have you had any luck locating Joust?"

"I have something for you," Osiro said. "Hold on one second."

Earlier that morning he'd received a coded text from Osiro telling him to place a call to a toll-free number in hopes of reaching Joust. The call would be forwarded and would carry one of the numbers Joust had called from his cell within the last twenty-four hours. The number belonged, oddly enough, to one of the environmental watch-dog and advocacy groups that had popped up after Bush had replaced many of the long-standing EPA directors and managers with his own people. Soon after the replacements took over, environmentalists saw a precipitous decline in the number of investigations, suits and fines being pursued by the EPA. Very quickly the word was out that the sexy but nearly inaccessible environment once again lay prostrate and helpless.

Joust had been instrumental in helping *The Aenamaia* gather recon on the continuing problems the environmental advocates were experiencing. Walls disguised as simple bureaucracy had sprung up all over the place. Calls and emails to contacts were suddenly being ignored. Politicians, even those who were normally cooperative, deftly side-stepped involvement, choosing instead to take their cues from Bush's new lackeys at the EPA. But a few days ago they'd had a breakthrough when Joust managed to convince an EPA official to meet with one of their people. So why was he calling the advocacy group now?

Posing as an FBI agent and delivering the caller ID of the FBI's main number, Osiro had learned that Joust had asked one of their directors questions about the funding they'd recently lost. The information the director gave Osiro didn't ring any bells until the woman casually added, "'Good ol' K Street strikes again.'" It was then he learned that several high-profile K Street lobbyists had deftly managed to reallocate a substantial science grant that had been promised to several universities, research firms, climate scientists, and the advocacy group.

In a decision that pushed the limits of incredulity and irony, the funds were quietly handed to the American Enterprise Institute (AEI), the Exxon-Mobil-funded think tank with close links to the Bush administration. It was the AEI that had offered the generous payments for articles over-emphasizing the shortcomings of a report from the UN's Intergovernmental Panel on Climate Change (IPCC). Travel expenses and additional payments had also been offered. Despite the inequity and paradoxical nature of the decision, the intended recipients of the grant had only put up a cursory fight due to concerns over losing their current funding. The news media never ran a single article or story.

Osiro guessed Joust, who was a passionate environmentalist and conservationist, had heard about the injustice and called the advocacy group to verify if it was true. After checking Joust's call log, Osiro found that the call had been placed only an hour before the conversation with Teala. It was no great leap to conclude that the outrageous news had pushed the Augur over the edge. Gray had suspected the lobbyists responsible for the switch were either on Joust's list, or had been unilaterally and very recently added to it, though they had no way of knowing for sure.

Toman had tried the number, but the ruse was unsuccessful. The call rang four times before the calm voice of his comrade announced that Alexander Florey, Joust's primary alias, was unavailable. It had been a while since he'd heard that name – the one he'd helped Joust choose. The name was derived by combining the first name of the discoverer of penicillin and the last name of the Nobel Laureate who first developed the antibiotic for use in medical treatment. Like many of the Augurs in *The Aenamaia*, Joust had wanted his alias to reflect an intrinsic personal connection to his own life. Such meaning made it easier to remember the name and to develop a personality behind it. In Joust's case, penicillin had saved his father's life in World War II and his own life when he was a boy. During the creation of Joust's alter ego, Toman had recalled a conversation they'd had shortly after meeting when Joust told him how he regretted knowing so little about the antibiotic that had played such an important role in his life. The two men agreed to research the matter further.

Soon after, "Alexander Florey" had materialized. "Where are you now Mr. Florey?" Toman wondered.

A few quiet seconds had passed before Toman heard soft static on the line, followed by a voice. Someone was talking. It was Joust! "What in the...?" he mumbled to himself. Joust was talking to someone. "A man," he thought. But the other voice was too faint to make out. The two were having what sounded like a philosophical discussion, albeit a tense one. Joust was saying something about honor and courage when the conversation abruptly stopped.

"Joust? Are you there?" Toman said loudly, stopping in the middle of the terminal. Several people who had been keeping pace close behind nearly collided with him.

"Keep your voice down, genius!" Osiro barked, "I don't control the surveillance devices in that terminal and I only know two or three of the undercover officers by sight."

Toman silently scolded himself for the outburst. Being reprimanded by Osiro had made the mistake even worse, though he knew he would've done the same. Significant deviations from the status quo was one of the quickest ways to attract unwanted attention and scrutiny. One of the first things all recruits to *The Aenamaia* studied was the intricate and ever-growing network of cameras, sensors, audio surveillance, and sophisticated tracking software that combined to make up what George Orwell had, in 1949, named "Big Brother."

Though the decadence of society and the ubiquitous and invasive technology Orwell had predicted had not yet come to pass, *The Aenamaia*'s training revealed how each day brought mankind one step closer to the nightmare world of Orwell's *1984*. The famous book was required reading prior to the training, as was a newer, more current book titled *The Traveler*. Both painted a frightening picture of the near future, but one every member of *The Aenamaia* needed to be aware of. The reading and the training constituted the first substantial reality check all *Aenamaia* members had to come to terms with. More than one recruit came out of the training with the same specific expression on their faces that said "playtime is over." Augurs and supporting field agents were taught that their lives and the success of *The Aenamaia* rested largely in remembering one short phrase: "Always watching, always listening, ready to bring violence, ready to forever silence."

Remembering the phrase now, he resumed walking, making sure to don a fake smile to throw off any curious onlookers. In a hushed voice he said, "Was that feed live?"

"No. I managed to intercept a call Joust placed about an hour ago."

"How in the hell did you manage to do that without his knowing?" Toman asked incredulously.

"Relax. I'm good, but I'm not that good. This was all Gray's genius."

"Okay, I'll bite. What did he…"

"Hey, Magellan," Osiro interrupted, "you just missed the turn to the security area."

Toman stopped to get his bearings. Turning around, he spotted the hallway he'd missed and headed for it. A fiery retort had already materialized in his mind, but he resisted the urge.

Without being prompted, Osiro continued. "You may recall, Gray has a master's degree in criminal psychology with an emphasis on violent behavior. Five years after graduating he landed a job working with black dot personnel whose morally impermeable skull casing had been cracked."

"Black dot?" Toman repeated. He was still smiling.

"Refers to black ops soldiers whose mental health has necessitated pulling them out of the military – permanently. Due to the classified information in their heads and the dissociative angst of leaving operations, they have to go through a rigid psychological therapy regiment before they're even allowed to interact with non-military personnel. The process is intense and requires someone with an enormous amount of focus, personal control, and a lightning-quick mind."

"Gray," Toman said, nodding to himself.

"Gray." Osiro agreed.

"By the way," he said, "You still haven't explained how you managed to 'intercept' the call without Joust knowing."

"It's too difficult to explain the details. Let's just say I detected the call, saw the recipient's number, and was able to quickly tap the call from the other end."

"Wow," was all Toman could manage.

"If we could return to the matter at hand," Osiro said matter-of-factly. "To make a long story shorter, Gray had worked with enough of these black dots to notice a number of behavioral consistencies, one of which was the tendency to request a meeting or conversation with a mentor or immediate supervisor prior to a particularly dangerous or morally questionable mission. Military psychologists sometimes call it a "support hill." They have to get over the hill before their objective becomes clear. Gray thought there was a good chance Joust would follow this same pattern. Not only had he been in black ops for many years, he had just disobeyed *The Aenamaia*'s orders and severed contact from his leader and mentor. The pattern was familiar, which made his next step predicta...."

The light went on in Toman's mind before Osiro could finish. "Of course! Gray figured if Joust was really serious about liquidating his query, against the orders of his superior, he would first have to contend with his doubts and therefore would seek some kind of conciliatory council."

"Bingo," Osiro said.

Toman reached the end of the security line. "Too many people with open ears," he thought. He turned and headed away from the line until no one else was around.

"General Payte? Was that who he was talking to?" Toman asked earnestly. He recalled how the general had guessed Joust was the one Gray had called him about. It had only been four hours since he and the general had left the deserted base in Atlantic. Surely the general would have called if he'd been in contact with...

"No," Osiro said, interrupting his thought process. "We thought of that right away. The general is en route to his next assignment in Atlanta and has been in frequent contact with Gray."

"Who then?" Toman pressed.

"Admiral Joseph Rosenthal. He was Joust's CO and mentor before he went into black ops. Gray found the admiral's information in Joust's file. The two kept in touch over the years. Each time a new assignment rolled his way, Joust would find a way to contact Rosenthal for help surmounting the next hill. He'd do it before he left. On several occasions he was reprimanded for delaying a mission due to 'personal' reasons – that's how it was cited in his personnel files. Odd thing was," Osiro sounded like he was still pondering this point, "the admiral always took his calls – no matter where he was or what he was doing. We're still checking to see if the connection between them goes beyond CO and subordinate. Gray figured this would be the best place to start so I ran Rosenthal down and tapped his lines. We got lucky."

"Were you able to triangulate?" Toman asked eagerly.

"Not at first. Linear triangulation only works if I am in direct contact with both parties. However, I had the idea of forcing a call through to the admiral while he was on the phone with Joust. Posing as an operator from Langley placing an emergency call for the Director of the CIA, I was able to hack the local carrier switch and initiate a three-way call."

"Jesus Christ, Osiro!" Toman said in amazement. "Where in the hell did you learn all this stuff?"

"Bell Laboratories," Osiro replied evenly.

There was a brief silence. "So?" Toman asked impatiently, "Do you know where Joust is?"

"Uhh...yeah. Yeah, I do," Osiro said, his voice uncharacteristically hesitant and uncertain, "But you're never gonna believe me."

Washington, D.C.

"Folks, we'd like to thank you for visiting the White House today," the tour guide said in what sounded like a pre-recorded voice. "Please feel free to wander around the entrance hall. When you're ready to leave, please follow the signs and exit through the north entrance. Thank you again for coming."

The woman's parting remarks registered, but he never turned to look. For the last ten minutes he'd stood perfectly still, his gaze fixed on the oil painting of John F. Kennedy. The muted colors, blank background and Kennedy's downcast eyes imparted a mystical seriousness to the onlooker. Unlike most portraits, in which the subject appears bored and lacks any expression, this work begged the beholder to ask "what was this person thinking about?" Anyone familiar with the events that took place in Kennedy's two short years in office could easily suggest a number of viable possibilities. There was little doubt the artist was suggesting Kennedy had had a great deal on his mind during those two years. But what was he pondering at this single moment frozen in time? A thought crept into Joust's mind that was as foolish as it was irrelevant, but at this moment in his life, even the non sequitur materializing in his head must be afforded unprecedented consideration. The desperation that he felt for answers outweighed any critical scrutiny of their origin or validity.

Slowly, Joust cocked his head and focused his eyes on the President's face. Silently he asked himself: Could he know? If the President were alive at this very moment, standing before him bearing that same solemn expression, Joust might swear the man knew precisely why he was here and what terrible actions he was contemplating. But if that were the case, what would he say? Would he condone such a drastic and violent act on American soil? Or anywhere in the world, for that matter? Would he designate the future dead as casualties of the most critical war facing mankind? Hundreds of millions had died throughout history as casualties of war. How much had their deaths influenced the corrupt and wicked? What if less than a hundred deaths might sway the powerbrokers and sewage-merchants? How many lives might be saved? How many improved? "What," he wondered again, "would Kennedy say?"

"You've disobeyed a direct order from your commander, son. You've gone AWOL." It was a young voice, full of confidence, knowledge and authority. One he'd heard many times throughout his life. Joust had heard or read every public speech that had ever been recorded – from Kennedy's time as a senator up until days before his assassination. Sometimes, when listening to the old recordings, he'd felt like Kennedy had been speaking directly to him – that the speech had been written with him in mind. Perhaps even with this future crossroad in mind.

Joust closed his eyes. Somewhere in the back of his mind he knew this illusion came courtesy of sleep deprivation and a hunger he'd been ignoring since yesterday, but that didn't matter. Whether from a dead President or a latent cluster of fresh synapses and neurons waiting in his mind like an emergency backup, he felt compelled to listen, even if he was a distant third party. What he desperately needed was guidance. So much so that he wasn't prepared to quibble over where it came from.

"You've deviated from the plan that you yourself helped devise and that everyone agreed upon," the President said calmly, almost empathetically. "A team must stick to the plan. Other people have put their necks on the line. They're relying on you to do your part, to do what you promised to do."

"Sir," his phantom self said, "after careful consideration I have determined that the original plan will fail to achieve the intended results. I tried consulting with *The Aenamaia*, but there wasn't time to convince them that a change was necessary. Therefore I chose to augment my own assignment in a way I believe will tip the scales back in our favor. There's no need for anyone else to place themselves at risk for my decision."

In his mind, Kennedy's image was now fully resolved and was looking at him. The ethereal President's gaze seemed to pierce through the part of him that stood rigid at attention.

"You think eliminating twenty lobbyists in a massive explosion will help your cause? What about the ones you haven't researched? Your original extraction only included six people. Men and women who, after careful research and consideration by *The Aenamaia*, had been deemed beyond help." The President's voice was becoming more intense as he said aloud what Joust had refused to fully consider. "You know what the implications are here. You know, better than most, what it means to take even a single life. What had you planned to do with what would remain of your soul, after having killed dozens upon dozens of people? Did you imagine yourself wading through the smoking, body-strewn rubble of the destruction you had wrought? You would, you know. There'd be no choice. You would have to face it. That was your pledge. To never hide from the results of your actions. You would walk through what was left of that warehouse. Taking it all in. Cataloging the destruction for future continuous consumption. Each time a new body appeared, wondering helplessly whether or not they were on your short list? Whether they had lain awake many nights wondering if what they had spent their day doing was noble or not? Just like you have done so many times in the past."

"Sir," his ghost self protested, "These people channel their morality through a myopic hole bored through time by self-interest alone. They bribe, cajole, and compete for a seat at the lemonade stand made of solid gold just for a chance to exploit our natural resources, the environment, free markets and open competition. The health and welfare of our nation are determined by the politicians with the most flexible morality. It's no longer about getting time with our nation's leaders to make your case, it's about whose bribe is the best. Who can get the biggest campaign contributions. Who can guarantee re-election. Don't you see that we must take a stand, sir?"

"Forgive me Joust, but it sounds to me like you're the one lobbying at the moment."

The statement caught him off guard. The President continued, "You are here trying to garner support for this new mission you've devised, are you not?"

"I," the ghost stammered uncertainly, "I offer no bribe, sir. And I ask for nothing in return but your approval."

"Ah," Kennedy said, indicating that something had just become clear to him. The President walked around behind Joust and, from behind him, said, "So, you're asking me to help shoulder this burden. To justify your actions so as to help lessen the paralyzing angst that would most likely tear through your being the instant you detonated the explosives in that warehouse. The people you love and respect most in this world will not side with you and your impatience, but you think perhaps I might.

Hmm..." the President paused. He leaned in closer and said in a whisper, "Sounds like self-interest to me."

Joust winced. He hadn't expected this. The illusion was supposed to see the necessity of his actions. To see the big picture. A clear and resounding message had to be sent. Fear must be instilled in those left alive who were as guilty as those chosen to die. Fear was their currency. It was the only thing they could understand. Surely the President would see this.

"Sir," he started trying to keep his voice calm and even, "I would indeed like your support. And yes, part of my motivation is self-serving. However, the end is all that matters here. If the people tied up in that warehouse achieved a positive end despite selfish intentions, I...we could forgive such things. I wouldn't liquidate a woman who managed to protect a thousand acres of wetland even though her sole motivation was a promotion or a raise. We can work with priorities that have gone askew. I'm talking about the powerful tobacco lobby that not only keeps cigarettes legal and easily accessible to people of all ages, but that also manages to garner millions of taxpayer dollars in subsidies for the tobacco farmers. We subsidize farmers to grow tobacco while people in this country starve to death. Their power and influence has kept the legalization of marijuana and the ubiquitous use of hemp stuck in a half-assed grassroots movement because they don't want the competition. This lobby works closely to limit restrictions on the consumption and distribution of alcohol because of the strong correlation with the usage of their product.

"I'm talking about the automobile lobby that keeps tariffs, taxes and prices high on foreign cars. These vehicles are safer and higher in quality than many American-made vehicles, but in order to make American products more price-competitive, our government happily complies. And why not? It's just one more source of capital sapped from the American consumer to go fight ridiculous wars and provide tax cuts for the wealthy, while discouraging efficiency and innovation in the American auto industry." Even as a removed observer, Joust could see his other self was settling into a smooth, rhythmic cadence. It was a familiar rant, but one he hoped would influence his listener. The President stood perfectly still, absorbing every word.

"And when money isn't enough to influence the vote, they hit with the heavy artillery – the votes of their constituencies. The harmonious mooing of the mindless cattle that are content to keep pace and direction with the fly-swatting tail and square ass directly in front of them. That's all they can see. They follow so closely that by the time they realize the cow in front of them just plummeted over a cliff, there's no time to yell 'Stop!' before the next in line pushes them over. The Christian Coalition, the National Right to Life Committee, the Teamsters and the AFL-CIO – and right at the top, the NRA. There's a pattern here of pushing beliefs on the country and using people's votes and money to do so. Can't you see that?"

The President looked up, but there was no shock or disdain on his face, just a cool and focused façade.

"Joust," the President said, "I agree that lobbying in this country has gotten out of control. I agree that special interests are using money and votes to get their way. But what you have to understand is that *The Aenamaia* and yourself did not set out to send a message to these organizations. You set out to remove the people whose own personal corruption was causing collateral damage and pain to others. The few people on your original list have demonstrated, for the better part of their adult lives, that they will do whatever it takes to further their own personal agendas – regardless of who or what it harms. They use money, votes and sometimes even brute force and threats of violence to get their way. Those are the ones who need to be removed.

"It isn't yours or *The Aenamaia's* place to play judge and jury on the lobbying efforts – even when you so vehemently disagree with what they're doing. The United States is still a democracy, albeit a bit more diluted than our forefathers had intended. If you want to change the hearts and minds of the people who own guns, believe in a literal interpretation of the Bible, and don't believe in a woman's right to choose, you'll have to do it the old fashioned way. Violence will not work here. It will only serve to strengthen their convictions through the same vehicle of fear employed by those you seek to remove. That won't work. You must appeal to them as one human to another. Through public forums, discussions, talk groups, email, the media and so on. You walk a fine line here. Do not become that which you despise."

The President put his hand on the ghost's shoulder and waited until the two made eye contact. When the ghost looked up, the President said, "Your task, as it was assigned, is difficult enough. You understand better than any of the other Augurs what killing another human really means. You've suffered because of the lives you took without knowing anything about them. I understand how that feels, I truly do. But things are different now. You've dedicated yourself to ensuring the people on your list are beyond help and will, in any job or capacity, continue to wreak havoc as long as they have a breath left to breathe. There is only one solution. So please," the President said softly, "Stay true to the plan. Leave the bigger, more complex problems for another day. One step at a time, Joust. One step at a time."

Joust felt a sadness descend upon him. No. Not sadness. The feeling was all too familiar. It was helplessness. Only a few moments ago he'd been so sure of himself – so confident that a grand and public statement needed to be made in order to get all eyes on Washington so the world could see what was really going on. But no. The President, or whatever it was, had been right. His plan was no solution. In fact, it would most likely bring about the opposite effect. No. If he wanted to get the world to put the lobbying underworld under a microscope he would have to find another way. But not today. Definitely not today.

Refocusing his attention, Joust again looked at the somber image of Kennedy.

"It's a magnificent piece isn't it?" a woman's voice commented brightly.

The voice startled him. He turned and was surprised to see the tour guide standing next to him. He's been so deep in thought he hadn't heard her approach. She was looking up at the portrait.

"What?" he said, still trying to resolve himself back into the present.

"The painting," she said pointing at the gold-framed image. "So much depth and emotion conveyed so subtly. It's really quite extraordinary."

"It certainly is," he said earnestly.

A few silent moments passed before he added, "I've always wondered what he was thinking about when he posed for the artist."

"Oh, that's an easy one," she said knowingly. "Nothing at all."

Joust looked at her askance.

Still staring at the portrait, she explained. "The painting was rendered nearly seven years after the President was assassinated...in 1970, I believe. The artist, Aaron Shikler, wanted the painting to convey that this had been a serious, deep-thinking President. I'm not certain, but I would guess the artist also wanted this painting to be noticeably different than those preceding his. So often portraits fail to really say anything about who the person was." The woman smiled sheepishly and lowering her voice said, "Most portray the Presidents as pompous and elitist." She grinned and added, "But that's just between you and me."

Even with a head full of chaos and no idea of what the next day of his life would bring, Joust smiled sincerely at the woman's conspiratorial admission. Recalling some of the other portraits he'd seen today, he was inclined to agree.

"Personally," she continued, her tour-guide voice back in control, "I like to believe the man in the painting spends his time in two-dimensional space considering what the world would have been like had he cancelled his trip to Dallas. What could he have accomplished? What if he'd lived long enough to sign the agreement with Khrushchev to enter into a joint space venture? Been alive to continue pushing for civil rights? Would Johnson have still been the thirty-sixth President? Would we have gotten out of Vietnam sooner? Who knows. But the world, indeed, might've been a very different place." Her voice trailed off.

From the corner of his eye, Joust studied the tour guide. He'd barely taken notice of her during the tour. Aside from a cursory assessment of the tour group as a whole, something he'd been trained to do years ago, he hadn't spared an extra moment on the woman. He now saw she was around five-eight, slender, early to mid-forties, fair skinned, green eyes with a few flecks of gold. She had shiny shoulder-length burgundy hair with a touch of red highlighting, no wedding band or jewelry he could see, a straight aristocratic nose and jawline, and pronounced cheeks that hinted at a strong European heritage. She wore a navy blue skirt and jacket, white blouse and shoes, and no pantyhose. She stood perfectly still, hands clasped in a noticeably proper manner. Still looking up at the painting, Joust watched as a suspicious smile spread across her lips. If he didn't know better, he would guess she knew he was inspecting her. And not only did she not mind, she knew before he did that he liked what he saw. There was amusement in her smile, and for a moment he felt unusually off balance.

"I have wondered," Joust said uncertainly, "especially lately, what Kennedy would think of the world today. If he would see how desperate things have become and how little is being done about it."

She turned slightly and looked at Joust out of the corner of her eye. He felt her gaze, but continued looking up at the bowed head of a man deep in thought. It was his turn to be sized up.

"I've wondered that myself," she said, still watching him. "What's strange is that I never consider the same question for any of the other Presidents. I think many were truly great men who did a lot of good for our country, but I don't feel as though I understand them well enough to value their opinion. It's different with Kennedy, though I'm not quite sure why."

"So much has gone wrong," he whispered, more to himself than to her. "So many at the mercy of so few."

"But that has always been the case," she said empathetically. "Throughout time a small number of people, usually men, have kept control over the masses. How the really terrible kings and dictators managed to stay alive as long as they did – and at the same time convince hundreds and thousands of guards and soldiers to do their bidding – that one is a mystery to me. History certainly has its fair share of rebellions – some noble, some not – but still, not as many as one would think."

"Were he alive today, what do you think Kennedy would do about the state of the world? Look at his expression," Joust said pointing at the canvas, "and imagine he's pondering the world as it is today. What would he do if he were President today?"

The woman took a step closer to the painting.

"Well," she said thoughtfully, "after he was caught up on the last five decades of history, I suppose he would analyze the biggest problems first. No doubt he would have many questions – especially about the technological progress we've made. The Internet alone would take a few months to wrap his head around. It would probably take the Pentagon another month to get him up to speed on advances in weaponry and the massive expansion of our military across the world – to say nothing of the multitudes of conflicts in the last fifty years. Then there are the medical advances, genetics, new pharmaceuticals and therapies...all coming onto the scene alongside new diseases like AIDS. Then there is the leviathan we know as the 'modern media.' That alone might send him over the edge." She shook her head and took a deep breath. "If he were still alive and hadn't suffered any brain damage, then I think he would begin taking small steps towards tackling all of the major issues."

"How small?" Joust asked.

She seemed to consider the question for a moment, her eyes squinting as if she were chasing down a solution or focusing in on one. "Small enough so as not to drastically upset the balance, but meaningful enough to lead him inexorably to the next step. Planned, incremental actions, but swift. I mean the world didn't form in a day. Change takes time. It's like Secretary of State Dean Acheson once said, 'Always remember that the future comes one day at a time.'"

Joust considered what the woman said. He had to admit, it fit well with what the shadow President had said. "One step at a time, Joust."

"Sounds like a wise man," he commented casually. "What else did he say?"

The woman smiled again and said, "He had a lot of insightful things to say. One of my favorites is 'The great corrupter of public man is the ego. Looking at the mirror distracts one's attention from the problem.' I always liked that one. Too bad no one ever mentioned that quote to the last family that occupied this house." The woman looked around cautiously, as if unsure whether someone might have heard her words – and read between the lines.

Joust smiled, and nodding, said honestly, "I couldn't agree more."

The woman was about to add something else when his cell phone rang. The chirping sound surprised him. Strange. He had shut the ringer off at the beginning of the tour and didn't recall turning it back on. No time to wonder about it.

The caller ID read Toman. Joust grinned. All at once he imagined what Gray and *The Aenamaia* must have been doing since he stopped communicating with them. Scrambling. Changing plans. He felt a small pang of regret at his rash actions, but in the end he was confident they would understand. Theirs was not an easy task, no matter the ideology or the best possible outcome. No excuses. He'd freely joined *The Aenamaia* and accepted this assignment. Now he needed to do everything in his power to get things back on track.

Feigning embarrassment, he excused himself from the tour guide, but stayed within earshot so she could hear his conversation. He flipped open the phone, pressed Send and said quickly, "Hi Mom. Sorry I haven't called. I needed to get away for a while. Don't worry though, everything is back on track. I'm on my way back to work now. I've got half a dozen people to take care of and a bunch more to free up. Why don't I meet you at Ebb's place around seven. It's probably best if you don't bring Dad as I'm sure he's in quite a gray mood. See you then." He hung up and grinned guiltily. He hadn't let Toman get a single word in. He had too much to do and didn't want to waste time explaining. Besides, he had no way of knowing who else might be listening in. Toman was a smart guy and a good friend. He would come alone and together they would work to turn his mistakes to their advantage. But first things first.

Pocketing the phone, he shook the tour guide's hand and graciously thanked her for the enlightening tour and conversation, assuring her he would come back to finish the latter. Looking up, he took one last respectful glance at the portrait of John F. Kennedy, nodded, then headed quickly out of the north entrance of the White House.

Garrison, New York

Tarte stared out the window at the trees rushing by. Every few seconds the forest thinned enough for him to catch a glimpse of bright sunlight reflecting off the waters of the Hudson River. Signs of spring were everywhere, but he barely noticed. Jasmine's news about Jack Kelley had remained at the forefront of his mind since he'd left his office. Coincidence was something Tarte had trained himself to examine carefully. More often than not, there was important information to be found in every seemingly innocuous chance occurrence.

"We'll be there in about eight minutes, sir," the field agent informed him.

"Are you always so precise?" The man glanced his way but didn't answer. "In Washington words like 'almost, approximately, roughly, about,' and 'nearly' are part of the gray-speak federal agents are expected to integrate into their daily speech. Rounding quantities and measurements is perfectly normal, as well. Time, dollars, age, the number of inbound missiles, and so on."

The agent looked slightly annoyed but only said, "I'll try and keep that in mind, sir." Tarte nodded and dropped the subject. White was an interesting breed of agent. Even before his feet had touched the pavement, Tarte had felt like something was amiss. He'd been surprised when only one agent had been parked on the tarmac. He knew for a fact they had well over fifty agents in each state. New York State must have twice that number. Though budgets had been slashed, the government was always reluctant to cut law enforcement staff. With so many agents available and most of them relatively idle, he'd expected three or four to tag along just to have something interesting to do. Perhaps they were all working the undercover terrorist watch at the local golf club.

The sturdy man behind the wheel had introduced himself as Department of Homeland Security Agent White, followed by a firm handshake from a large, flat hand. There had been something behind Agent White's eyes that said it was unnecessary to point out the irony of his name in relation to his dark ebony skin. Agent White was tall and thin, with close-cropped black hair, light brown eyes, and bright white teeth that made for a stark contrast behind a perfectly trimmed jet-black goatee. He wore black trousers, polished black Oxfords, pressed white shirt, steel blue tie, and a long tan raincoat. His movements were clipped and efficient, almost robotic. When walking, he had a slight forward lean, as if to counter the effects of a stiff breeze. When he wasn't speaking, White's face bespoke nothing but a quiet and serious alertness. Casting a casual sideways glance, Tarte thought his chaperone looked like a nondescript, unremarkable, standard-issue agent straight from a cheesy action flick. A rent-by-the-hour one-liner, the first to get shot and killed in a gunfight, or just a background prop. In the real world, White would probably go unnoticed most of the time – blend in with any crowd. While the thought of White as an extra in a movie amused him, Tarte appreciated the utility and practicality of such simple urban camouflage. Besides, who was he to make fun? It was doubtful anyone would ever mistake him for Brad Pitt or George Clooney.

Agent White's demeanor was precise, courteous and professional, but never crept close to friendly. After briefly outlining their course and the duration of the drive, White hadn't said a word until just now. Tarte had made an offhand comment about their both being federal blocks on such an unusual assignment, and still nothing. Tarte, who was normally inquisitive and chatty with other agents, resigned himself to silence. The adrenaline he'd felt on the way to the airfield had all but disappeared the moment he'd climbed aboard the jet – replaced by uncertainty and doubt. Were the apparent connections real or simply the manifestation of his deep and longstanding desire to get out of the office and play the would-be hero? What if they were real and something serious was playing out a few miles up the road? Should he have brought reinforcements? How much field training did White have? Forethought and planning skills could be greatly enhanced after hindsight kicked you square in the teeth. That is, assuming you survived the kick.

Tarte glanced casually at White. The expressionless agent remained maddeningly stoic and intensely focused on the task of driving, though Tarte thought he'd seen the man's eyes dart to the dashboard clock a few times. He mused that the man was part autistic savant and was obsessively watching the time, speedometer, mile markers, and angle of the sun in relation to the wind resistance and drag coefficient of the vehicle, the air pressure of all four tires, and the total weight of the vehicle – all variables in complex calculations designed to ensure they arrived precisely when he'd said they would. A dark, silent and armed Rain Man. Scary thought. Or perhaps White had another appointment today and was hoping this wouldn't take very long. Deep down inside, Tarte harbored the same hope.

Staring down at the folders in his lap, Tarte recalled what he'd learned so far. He'd read through the files Jasmine had prepared on Ailes, Murdoch, and Kelley on the plane ride, then skimmed through them again ten minutes ago. Though most of the relevant details had burned into his memory on the first reading, no obvious patterns had emerged. The reach of these three men, combined with their wealth and influence was impressive, yet there was little in the files that surprised him or pointed to any startling conclusions. Worse yet, he was five minutes from Ailes's summer house and he had yet to figure out how Kelley fit into this picture. Why would these three be meeting? Was *USA Today* looking to be sold by its parent company? Was Murdoch looking to expand his enormous media empire? Was Kelley interviewing for a job at Fox? Maybe Ailes was retiring and Kelley was the top candidate to take over. The current number two would be pissed as hell, which, if this switch in accession were found to be true, could point to a suspect and a motive – assuming something had indeed happened to Murdoch or Ailes. Whatever the reasons for Kelley's involvement, Tarte felt uneasy about this. Something just didn't feel right.

White signaled, slowed and rounded the corner. Tarte couldn't read the whole street name, but he was sure he saw the word "snake" on the sign. "A private road named for Ailes," he mused. But a few seconds later the name made perfect sense as the road presented a series of sharp turns and banks. He could imagine what this winding lane might look like from the air. Probably looked very picturesque with all the lush foliage. He made a mental note to pull it up on Google Earth the next time he was bored and sitting at his computer.

Glancing out his window, he noticed the houses were getting larger, set further back from the road, and most had wrought-iron gates blocking the driveways. He wondered what it was these people did for a living that paid for such auspicious properties. How many lived here full time and how many used these places only a few months out of the year? As he watched larger and larger estates roll by, one thing was painfully certain – he had definitely chosen the wrong line of work.

After a few more twists and turns in the tree-lined road, White took another left onto what appeared to be a private lane. Thick brown branches bearing small spring leaves arched over the drive, reaching out to touch their cousins from the opposite side of the road. Tarte noticed some of the trees and bushes were already sporting pink and purple flowers. For a few moments the scene put his mind at ease. There was a sense of peace and an admiration for the unbiased beauty of nature on display here. The trees and flowers stood oblivious to the often nefarious and devious acts perpetrated by mankind. Nature simply didn't understand or care. "Ignorance is bliss," he thought, "and such effortless bliss can be both admired and envied."

The car rolled to a stop in front of a tall and imposing black iron gate. A smooth concrete driveway led up the hill to a circular drive. Parked in the drive Tarte saw three expensive Sedans beside an obscenely large stone water fountain. Just beyond the fountain, perhaps eighty yards or so from the main gate was a large Victorian style two-story mansion built almost entirely of red brick. Rectangular curtained windows stretched across the front of the house on both floors. The white Roman columns and portico stood out in stark contrast against the dark red hue of the brick. Lining the front of the house were manicured bushes and a large front lawn of short, neatly trimmed grass. Tarte thought the place looked like something from Knot's Landing.

Tarte got out of the car and walked over to the keypad and console next to the gate. White was behind him, but as usual said nothing. He pressed the dirty white call button and waited. A faint beeping noise sounded behind him. From the corner of his eye he saw White holding his cell. The Agent punched a few buttons then returned the phone to the pocket of his jacket. Tarte punched the call button again. He was about to suggest they call the house phone when a shaky voice came though the speaker.

"Police?" The voice was male, and nervous. Tarte noticed the camera above the monitor move, as if to focus, but no image appeared on the screen.

"I'm Agent Roger Tarte of the Homeland Security Agency," he said holding up his badge to the camera. "Who am I speaking with?"

There was a pause. "Roger Ailes," came the reply.

"Mr. Ailes, I apologize for the interruption, but we had reason to believe you might be in some kind of danger."

"Agent...?"

"Tarte," he said again.

"What is your cell number?" Ailes asked.

"Sir? I'm not sure I..." Tarte started.

"Your cell phone number, your mobile phone," Ailes pleaded. Even through the speaker static, Tarte could sense the panic in Ailes's voice. "Surely you have one. You're a federal agent. Don't tell me you..."

"Mr. Ailes," Tarte interrupted, trying to calm the CEO, "Perhaps we could come up and talk with you. I'm sure..."

Now it was his turn to be interrupted. "No!" the man shrieked. "Don't come anywhere near the house. Don't even...don't even touch the gate. I'm not sure if they...I mean, they didn't say anything about the gate. But don't touch it. Keep your distance."

"Mr. Ailes," Tarte tried again, "I really don't understand."

"Your cell phone number!" Ailes insisted.

Tarte took a deep breath and after a moment's hesitation carefully read off his cell number. There was a click and the speaker went dead. He turned to look at White who, surprisingly, maintained a calm demeanor, as if this were nothing more than a routine domestic disturbance call. Tarte was about to deal out a sarcastic comment when his cell rang. The caller ID read "unknown."

He pressed Send.

"Just listen, Agent Tarte. Don't speak," Ailes's voice was urgent. "I've...we've been allowed to make this call, but we don't have much time. I'm here with Rupert Murdoch." Ailes had calmed down a tad, but his voice was still tense. He now sounded as though he was reading a prepared statement. Tarte scrambled to pull the pad and pen from his coat pocket.

"We're being held hostage in this house. We're not allowed to leave and no one is allowed to enter. Please make no attempt to do so. So far we have not been harmed. We've been allowed to move freely throughout the house as long as we stay away from windows and doors."

Tarte scribbled frantically, then asked, "Mr. Ailes, are you able to tell me how many people are in the house?"

"Mr. Murdoch and myself," Ailes said carefully.

Tarte stopped writing. "What about the people holding you hostage? Can you say how many are in there?"

He could hear muted talk on the other end, but couldn't make out what was being said.

"Okay." Ailes said, "I've been allowed to explain. We're being watched and listened to by the people who are holding us here. They call themselves *The Aenamaia*." At the sound of the name, Tarte felt a shiver run through his body. In an instant he knew this was no longer a routine visit. "Murdoch and myself are the only people in the house or on the grounds. These people have wired the house with cameras, listening devices and sensors. There are also speakers. We can ask questions out loud and a strange voice will answer through the speakers."

"Is it a man's voice or a woman's?"

"I'm not sure. It's something in between."

"Androgynous?"

"If by that you mean something in between, then yes," Ailes affirmed, sounding irritated.

"If you're free to move around, how exactly are you being held captive?"

He heard Ailes take a deep breath. "The house has been wired with explosives." The shakiness had returned. "And with some kind of aerosol poison. If we try to leave or someone tries to come in, one or the other will go off."

"How long have you been held captive?" Tarte asked.

"Since last night. We walked in the front door around eleven p.m. When the front door closed we heard a loud, rapid beeping. That's when the voice first came through the speakers and told us the bombs had just been armed. That's when he told us we would not be permitted to leave."

"Mr. Ailes," Tarte said slowly, "I must ask. How do you know this threat is real?"

"There are wired devices at every door and window. We've checked them all. Wires stuck into a small square of what looks like orange putty. Gold casings on both ends of the wires. And electronics."

"Thirty dollars at Radio Shack and a pound of silly putty," Tarte thought. He grinned.

Ailes added, "They said to tell you the explosive is called Semtex."

"Oh shit," Tarte thought as his grin vanished. He was familiar with Semtex. Last year he'd read a study conducted by the CIA about the explosive, which was manufactured by a company aptly named Explosia. After reading the study, Tarte had done a cursory internet search on Semtex. It didn't take long to realize the CIA had compiled a substantial amount of detailed information not readily available on the Internet. There were a number of chemical diagrams showing the reaction sequence, a breakdown of explosive yields relative to standard benchmarks such as dynamite and Nobel 808, yearly production statistics, sales tables, packing and shipping procedures, government regulation and reporting, the blacklist of countries Explosia was forbidden to sell to, a complete history of both company and product, and most disturbingly, a complete list of all known terrorist attacks involving the explosive.

While most experts agreed the bulk of the explosive remained in the Czech Republic where it was produced, enough of the substance had gotten through the security nets to have wrought considerable damages and loss of life. Getting the material out of the country legally was not easy. The study had also outlined the rigorous processes for purchasing and exporting the explosive. If the study was accurate, acquiring the volatile substance from Explosia and bringing it into the U.S. without anyone knowing about it would be quite a trick. In theory it was possible to purchase the explosive via one of several black markets specializing in weapons, but doing so was expensive and very risky. Tarte had heard stories of deviant men who'd tried to purchase Semtex with cash only to wind up being robbed and murdered by the sellers. Most of the time when bad guys tried trusting other bad guys, someone wound up getting arrested or killed.

Nevertheless, illegal exports of Semtex had been seized by authorities in most countries. Every administration over the past forty years had made it a point to keep every federal law enforcement agency on the alert for the dangerous explosive. Demolition companies wanting to use Semtex had to jump through a number of tightly controlled hoops to purchase, import, and detonate the explosive. Strict regulations required that every ounce of Semtex be kept safe and secure until it was time to detonate. Those who chose to circumvent the legal importation process faced a number of challenges. In many countries, including the U.S., specially trained dogs were used to check shipments coming from the Czech Republic as well as a host of unfriendly countries. New sophisticated sniffing devices which could detect trace elements of illegal explosives and chemicals were also used, but as far as Tarte knew none had ever been found in the U.S. Until now.

"I know what Semtex is, Mr. Ailes. But I must ask again, how can we be sure it is real?"

For the first time, Ailes sounded more irritated than afraid, "They said you would ask that. There is something...hold on, I wrote it down. There is an 'airborne detection taggant' that you'll be able to confirm."

"Aerosol," Tarte corrected. "Aerosol taggants require special equipment or dogs and close inspection. How am I supposed to accomplish that if I can't come into the house?" Tarte asked skeptically.

"There's a block of it affixed to the rear of the unit you're speaking into."

Tarte froze. An image of a fireball engulfing his crouched form blew through his mind like a scene from an action movie. In his mind he could see his body hurtling through the air while at the same time being consumed by the expanding cloud of fire. Should he run? What was the minimum safe distance? At the moment it was difficult to recall the explosive power of the substance. Concentrating, he remembered a reference in the study that said a mere two pounds of Semtex was enough to raze a two-story building. Which meant a small brick of Semtex the size of a candy bar would be enough to make his dental records useless in identifying what little remained of his body. And that was assuming the explosive hadn't been converted into a homemade Claymore mine – a simple and popular weapon for terrorists and rogue military cells wanting to create a homemade shrapnel storm.

"Relax, officer, it isn't armed. They don't want you dead," Ailes said sounding annoyed.

"It's agent," Tarte corrected him with a sigh of relief, "Agent Tarte."

"Agent Tarte," a voice said. This was someone new – a man. Calm, but urgent.

"Who is this?" Tarte asked.

"My name is Gray. I speak for *The Aenamaia* – the group responsible for confining Mr. Ailes and Mr. Murdoch to this house."

"Aena-what?"

"*Aenamaia*. I know who you are Agent Tarte and why you're here. I knew you were coming. The Semtex affixed to the back of this unit is our way of proving to you that this is not a joke. This property is loaded with it. We used enough Semtex to knock you and Mr. White on your asses and create a fifty-foot crater where this house now stands."

How did he know White's name? "Not now," he thought.

"And the aerosol?" Tarte asked.

"It's an alkaline-based chemical with a highly reactive agent. Airborne dispersal is quick. Once inhaled and absorbed into the blood stream, the agent reacts with hemoglobin to increase the body's natural conductivity threefold. Another chemical in the mix is stimulated by the newly created compound and sheds electrons. The electricity travels through the blood to the heart and causes immediate cardiac arrest. Electricity conduction is also increased in the brain, causing seizure and paralysis. Either the heart stops or the brain dies from shock or hypoxia."

"Jesus. Where in the hell did you..?" Tarte started.

"One of our members stumbled onto the formula while going through classified biowarfare research documents from the Korean military," Gray said curtly. As if anticipating another question, he added, "Agent Tarte we don't have time for this. Take the sample back to the nearest lab – I believe you'll find one less than half an hour's drive away – they'll confirm the Semtex is real. You'll be allowed to set up a police presence outside the gate if you like. However, do not attempt to approach or enter the house or these two men will die. I trust you've already been privy to some of our other accomplishments of late. Please do not test us. These two soulless men are a means to an important end. If they cooperate, they'll live to talk about it. If not, they'll have about fifteen seconds to wonder why the air suddenly smells like sea water."

"Mr. Gray. I'm sure you know perfectly well that our government does not negotiate with terrorists – foreign or domestic."

"That is convenient for both of us, Agent Tarte, since our position is not open to negotiation. We have no demands, no ransom, no political hostages to be released from captivity. Our business is with these two men, and it will be over very shortly as long as you don't interfere. The equation is simple – remain outside the fence and everyone lives; attempt to be heroes, and the body count will be your responsibility, not ours. Remember, Ailes and Murdoch are very wealthy, connected, and well-known public figures. Even though such situations are not distinct in your crisis manuals, you know very well this changes the rules of engagement. Preventable celebrity deaths are a burden your agency can ill afford at this point in time. I'm sure Director Banes would concur. If all goes according to plan, I will contact you when it's safe for your men to secure the property. Get moving now, Agent Tarte – there is much to be done."

Before Tarte could squeeze in another question the line went dead.

Replacing the phone in his pocket, Tarte walked carefully around to the backside of the console. Careful not to touch anything, he knelt down and looked up under the tin lip that protected the power cables from the elements. Tucked into the corner was a cellophane bag held in place by a strip of duct tape; the color of burnt orange peeking from behind the clear bag. He leaned in for a closer look. There didn't appear to be any wires or electronics attached.

"Sir?" The voice startled him.

"Jesus, White! Of all the moments to speak up. What is it?" Tarte looked up and saw White was pointing towards the house. "Upper floor, NE corner," White added. In the corner window Tarte saw a portly, balding man looking down at them. From the pictures he'd seen in the file, he was certain it was Ailes. He appeared to be wearing jeans and a tight-fitting dress shirt. Murdoch was nowhere to be seen.

"Do you have a First Aid kit in the car?" Tarte asked, still staring at the house.

"Yes, sir," White said, a hint of puzzlement in his voice.

"Bring it to me. Along with a pair of rubber gloves."

"Sir, can I safely assume you are about to remove explosives from the back of that thing?"

"Yes, White," Tarte said impatiently, "There is a small pack of Semtex here that I need to get to a lab ASAP."

"But sir that violates..." White started.

"We don't have time for the bomb squad to get here just so they can take an hour to tell me the sample isn't hot. I know enough about explosives to determine that for myself. We need to get this back to the lab quickly so they can analyze it. I need verification. Now go get me the gloves and kit."

White returned a few moments later with a small white First Aid kit and a pair of standard latex gloves which were routinely used in all manner of crime scene investigations. After putting on the gloves, Tarte hastily emptied the contents of the First Aid kit onto the ground. Carefully, he peeled away both ends of the duct tape until the small package came loose. He gave it a quick cursory examination, then carefully placed the bundle in the plastic First Aid kit and closed the lid. With the kit in hand, he stood and headed towards the car. Though he'd expected a protest from White, the man only darted around the vehicle and opened the passenger-side door for him.

A few seconds later they were back on the winding road, each with his cell phone in hand. White called the nearest lab and bomb squad and told them to be ready, then alerted the local authorities. Tarte called Floyd and gave him a quick rundown. Floyd said he would alert the field office and have their people coordinate on-site with the local PD.

"Make sure they hold to the perimeter," he reminded Floyd. "The last thing we need is some sheriff wanting to see his name in the headlines. That goes for air surveillance as well. Let's keep the choppers off it for now."

"Air support might be useful in confirming the prisoners are really inside the house," Floyd offered.

"I can't vouch for Murdoch, but I saw Ailes from a distance in a second floor window. I'm guessing they told him to stand there until I spotted him. Otherwise, he said they were prohibited from approaching any doors or windows."

"Could you see him clearly? How did he look?" Floyd asked eagerly.

Tarte thought about it for a moment. "Honestly? My first impression was, well, he looked pissed off. But I was too far away to be sure."

"That sounds about right," Floyd commented.

"What do you mean? If I was trapped in my own house by people who obviously had no problem with me exploding or inhaling heart attack vapor, I think I'd be scared shitless."

"Sometimes even the wealthiest and most powerful ignore the reality of their own mortality. They don't believe any man or group of men controls their fate. Every person that doesn't make them money or grant them power is just an impediment to such. I guarantee you, Ailes and Murdoch are quietly discussing how they'll go about searching out and destroying whomever is responsible for this."

"Gray," Tarte said absently.

"Excuse me?" Floyd asked.

"Oh, sorry. I forgot to tell you, the guy I spoke to identified himself as Gray."

There was a long pause before Floyd commented, "Well that's not much to go on, but I can at least start asking around."

There was another pause and Tarte sneaked a glance over at White, who was busy negotiating the road while giving instructions to his people. Tarte turned casually towards the window and lowered his voice to a whisper. "Floyd. Do me a favor and run a quick check on Agent White here."

There was silence on the other end. Tarte thought Floyd might have hung up when the FBI Director finally said, "Is something wrong, Roger?" There was a curious tone in Floyd's voice – almost like a challenge, but Tarte dismissed it.

"No," he said carefully, listening to make sure White was still doling out orders to someone. "It's just that, well, this Gray character knew White's name when I'd never said it. On top of that, Agent White hasn't seemed particularly surprised by any of this. He acts like this whole thing was scripted. Could just be a cold, seasoned professional, but I want to know for sure. Can you check it, Floyd?"

"Sure," Floyd said, "I'll see what I can find out. In the meantime, the perimeter should be set up within an hour or two. We're bringing in state troopers. The nearest station is in a town called Croton on the Hudson, about ten miles away. They'll at least make sure no one goes in or out, good guys or bad guys."

"Sounds good," Tarte said returning to his normal volume. "We should be at the lab in about..." he turned and looked at White who opened and closed his fist twice. "In about ten minutes. I'll call you when we have a positive on the substance."

"I'll send you a text when the perimeter is secure."

"Thanks, Floyd."

He hung up the phone and tried to think this through. What could the perpetrators hope to gain by holding these men hostage? Money was the most obvious answer, though no demands had yet been made – at least not to law enforcement. He thought about ordering wire taps on the lines, but decided against it. The last thing he wanted to do was underestimate or provoke his opponent. Still, more information was needed. Knowing what was being said inside the house – both by the captives and the captors – could prove very useful. Parabolics might work, but they would need to be kept out of sight. He made a mental note to ask the bomb squad what, if anything, could accidentally set off the firing switches on the explosives. It was doubtful that a listening device could affect such a bomb trigger, but best to check first. Something else occurred to him.

"White," he said, "make sure they get the dogs out there to sniff around the perimeter for any explosives. And send a sweeper team with them to check for electronics. Oh, and see what you can find out about Ailes's own security system – motion detectors and whatnot."

White nodded and relayed the instructions. "Calm," Tarte thought again, "very calm." He wondered if he'd been out of the field too long. Perhaps the latest generation of agents was selected for their even-keeled nature. Maybe the field offices were employing meditation techniques to help maintain clarity under fire. He hadn't heard of such things, but then he'd been far removed from the field for some time now. Still, a feeling in his gut told him to keep a sharp eye on White. What harm was there in that?

Just then his cell rang. The caller ID read Jasmine.

"Hi, Jasmine. What have you got?"

"Two things," she said excitedly, "New York PD and SP both confirmed that Bush landed this morning, but so far no one is sure about his agenda. Secret Service did a sweep at Fox, but that could just be for Cheney. Right now he's visiting a college upstate. Hard to believe, given the trouble he's in. Justice Department aside, why is it that colleges pay good money to have a C student speak to students who are all smarter than he is? I've known defective light bulbs that were brighter than…"

"Jasmine!" Tarte interrupted her. "I enjoy prodding Bush as much as anyone, but right now we have more pressing matters."

"Sorry, Roger," Jasmine said, "So yes, it is possible Bush could make it to Fox today, but I haven't been able to confirm any plans to do so. Did you find Ailes?"

"Yes," he said reluctantly, "Long story. I'll fill you in later. Any word on Kelley?"

"Two agents have tried reaching him by phone, but he hasn't returned any calls yet."

"By phone!" Tarte exclaimed incredulously, "You tell them to get their asses over there and bring him in ASAP. Try his house, then his office. I don't care if he's bound and gagged. If I'm not back in time, have someone question him about the explosion. I want a detailed timeline from when he woke up this morning to the moment the agents knock down his office door! Get voice and video on all of it. A twenty-four hour detainment should be easy enough." Tarte thought about it for a moment, then added, "but check with legal just to make sure."

"Got it. And Roger," Jasmine lowered her voice, "Banes has been asking for an update. What do you want me to tell him?"

"Tell him you haven't heard from me. I'll call him after I get a report back from the bomb squad." As soon as he said it he wished he hadn't.

"Bomb squad!" Jasmine exclaimed, "What's going on, Rog? You aren't in any danger are you?"

Tarte looked down at the First Aid kit wedged between his patent leather shoes. "Danger? Not at the moment," he said uncertainly. "I'm sorry Jasmine, I really can't talk about it right now. I'll tell you about it later." He wasn't sure, but he thought he heard grinding teeth on the other end of the phone and added, "It's nothing juicy, Jasmine."

He sensed her disappointment. No doubt she'd been in the office waiting for something to bring back the rush of this morning's activities. "What was the second thing you had?" he asked.

"What?"

"You said you had two things for me. What was the other?"

"Oh Jesus, Roger, I'm sorry. You said 'bomb squad' and I blew a microchip. Hold on." Tarte heard the shuffling of papers and waited.

"We got a report in about an hour ago. A whole group of K-Street lobbyists went missing earlier today. DCPD received a call-in tip a few hours later. All but six of those reported missing were found in an abandoned warehouse down by the waterfront. Everyone was okay. A few had minor concussions from being knocked unconscious, but otherwise they were unharmed. They think some kind of chemical was used to knock out the rest."

"What happened to them?"

"Hard to say at this point. For some reason, the CIA yanked them from DCPD before they could get any concrete details. However, a friend of mine who works there heard the officers on scene say they were all unconscious and bound when they were found. He also heard a few of them say the last thing they remembered was a strange smell in the air."

"Were they all together when they were taken?" Tarte asked.

"DCPD seems to think so. They had attended a mixer before heading to some kind of convention. Rather than take taxis, someone had arranged for a shuttle to transport the whole gaggle. Everyone remembers getting on, no one remembers getting off."

"Any leads on the shuttle?"

"They found tracks going into and coming out of the warehouse, but nothing they could follow. DCPD is checking on charters in the area."

"How many were there?" Tarte asked.

"Fourteen, I believe."

"Do we know how many are still missing?"

"Best guess? Six or seven based on what I heard."

"Any info on the missing ones?"

"Nothing that has been released yet. CIA has been unusually puckered on this one. The media knows something went on at that warehouse, but they don't have a clue what so they're not running with it."

He stopped to think for a minute when White spoke up. "We're almost there." Tarte nodded.

"Jasmine," he said slowly, "You said these were all lobbyists, right?"

"That's right. Different industries, different concerns. All set to go to some government shindig for a little bloodletting."

"Do we have any names?"

"PD might, but the CIA probably has them in a chokehold. I'll check."

"Okay. Keep me posted. We're almost there so I should get back to it."

"Bomb squad?" Jasmine asked expectantly.

"Later, Jasmine. I promise," he said still staring at the small plastic case on the floor.

"Don't detonate yourself before then, Rog. If I don't get the details on this, I'll chase you right into the afterlife!"

"Bush. NYPD. Kelley. Stay focused, Jasmine. Got it?"

"Roger."

"What?" He heard her laugh then the line went dead. He really hated it when she did that.

Chapter 9

Otivar, Andalusia, Spain

The Silver Mercedes taxi passed through the small village of Otivar on the road the locals called Calle de la Carretera. It was almost ten p.m. and the townspeople were filing towards one of the few local restaurants for dinner. Rush stared with contempt at the simply dressed people, the small white stucco buildings with the ubiquitous red tile roofs, and the occasional parked car, circa 1970. "How in God's name did I allow Black to talk me into this?" he wondered for the hundredth time. "That dumb shit gets talked into flying halfway across creation for a fucking pagan wedding, and suddenly I have a first class ticket to the same shit hole. What the hell had I taken that morning?" He wondered absently. "I must not've been right in the head."

The last of Otivar's buildings disappeared, replaced by darkness. In the distance he could just make out the shadowed curves and slanted edges of the low Andalusian mountains. The taxi took a sharp turn. "Oh boy," Rush groaned aloud, "my favorite part." The drive from Otivar to the rustic villa Black had rented for him was something he'd come to dread. Since his arrival five days prior, he'd only made the trip two other times. At the end of the second trip, returning in the middle of an unusually hot day, he'd managed to pay the driver and wait for the car to disappear before emptying the contents of his stomach behind one of the clay planters. That was three days ago. Since then he'd resigned himself to only going out at night, when it was cool and dark and car sickness wasn't as much of a problem. Sheer boredom had been the only thing that could extricate him from the large house tonight.

Clear skies and a full moon cast an eerie silver glow over the dark green landscape. Out of his peripheral vision, Rush detected the alternating of light and dark contrasts rushing by. This input, combined with the serpentine gravel road, induced small waves of carsickness which manifested in his stomach and directly behind his eyes. To avoid a messy and embarrassing incident, he bent forward and focused on his shoes, which he noticed with irritation were covered in a thin layer of dust. Frustrated, he used his hands to clear away the village grit, revealing the patent leather shine beneath. "Four hundred dollar shoes in a two dollar town," he thought with disgust.

"Twenty-five days," he muttered, still hunched forward, "twenty-five more days until I return to Florida. Lawyer or not, Black's gonna get his ass whooped for talking me into this. I'll put my dusty four hundred dollar moccasins here to good use." The thought of kicking Black square in the butt made him feel better.

Five minutes later the taxi turned off the main road and rolled to a stop. Rush sat up. The brightness of the headlights was lost through the tall wrought-iron gate. Above the gate, painted on the white-washed arch beneath the triangular Greek pediment was the name Cazulas. He had no idea what the word meant but it sounded like some kind of smelly Greek dish. Rush smelled diesel fuel and leather and thought, "If I don't get out of this damn car I'm going to hurl my *cazulas* all over the place." He quickly stepped from the car and shut the door. He handed thirty euros to the driver who accepted it with a nod. A moment later the taxi was gone and all was silent. He moved to the electronic keypad and punched in the code he'd been given. A moment later the gates creaked open and he stepped into the courtyard. He was almost to the main entrance by the time the gates closed.

Fishing the keys from his pocket, Rush shook his head. "Spain," he said derisively. "What the hell am I doing in Spain?" He found the main house key, unlocked the door and stepped inside.

"A month away from it all, Rush," Black had said, patting him on the back. "Let this little rehab thing blow over. Come back from romantic Andalusia and start afresh with the radio show. It'll be good for you. Trust me."

"Trust me," he thought, "humph. What's that saying about 'trust' being a four-letter word?"

Rush closed the heavy wood door and flipped on the light switch. He took a step and started as he noticed two men in the corner of the room.

"Jesus Christ!" he exclaimed. "Who are you? What are you doing here?"

The two men said nothing. One man sat calmly in the dark brown leather chair. Rush noted that he was black and thin. Even sitting down, he could see the man was unusually tall. He looked almost like a lanky youth sitting in a child's chair. The white man next to him was clean-shaven with a full head of jet-black hair and an expression that bespoke a tense and focused seriousness, as if he expected an attack at any moment. He looked to be about average height and weight, but something about his posture suggested he was strong and agile. Rush thought with some amusement that these two men must shop at the same store, as they were identically clad in all black: polished shoes, slacks, thin leather belts, shirts, and well-fitting leather jackets. The jackets gave Rush a moment of pause. Even this late it was still in the low sixties outside.

"I said, who the hell are you and what are you doing in my house?"

It was the black man who answered. "Good evening, Monsieur Limbaugh."

"Great," Rush thought, "a fucking black Frenchman. Double insult."

"Welcome home."

Rush waited.

"Please allow me to introduce myself. My name is Savante. As you have no doubt surmised, I am French. My companion," he said, gesturing towards his silent partner, "is Paien."

"He French, too?" Rush asked, taking a few casual steps towards the house telephone. He set the house keys next to the phone and stayed close.

"Oui, monsieur. He was born in Martigny in French Switzerland, but has been in France most of his life."

Rush wasn't sure who these men were or what was going on, but he knew for certain that he was way outside of his element. He was holed up in a villa twelve miles from any real civilization. It was then he realized that even if he had ample time to pick up the phone, he wouldn't even know how to place a call, let alone *who* to call. Best to keep this light and cautiously friendly.

"Savanty and Pie-Yen," he said, intentionally over-enunciating. Cute names."

"Merci. My name means 'learned or scholarly.' Paien is the name of a nobleman. It can also mean 'Pagan.'"

"Well, that just about sounds right," Rush said irreverently.

"And your name, sir? What does it mean?" Savante inquired.

"Just like Butch said, 'I'm an American. Our names don't mean shit.'"

"I'm afraid I do not understand the reference. But of course," the man said dismissively, "much of your culture is a mystery to me. However, does the dictionary not carry many meanings for your name? Surely one of them must suit you."

Rush stared at the man, but did not answer. There was something challenging and confident in the man's voice that made him nervous.

"Come now, monsieur Limbaugh, there must be meaning here, no? Are you 'rush' the action verb? A man who charges forward and attacks without warning? Are you the 'rush' of fraternity legend? Dragging the eager young to their knees through the thorny brush of humiliation, just so they can know your authority?"

Savante stood. He was indeed tall. "Six-six at least," Rush thought.

"Maybe it is...how do you say...an adrenaline 'rush'? Or are you simply the hollow, reedy grass found in smelly swamps?" The man said mockingly. "Forgive me. Such inquiries are fruitless. Perhaps it is just as you say," Savante took a few steps towards Rush. "Your name conveys no meaning whatsoever. I suppose then we must judge you by action alone, no?"

Rush experienced a tinge of uneasiness and indignity at the same time. Without thinking, he did what he did best. He opened his mouth and spoke.

"Listen, Savanty. I've had just about enough of this shit. You and your boyfriend here have worn out your welcome. Get out!"

"Boyfriend?" Savante questioned. "Ah, but of course. You believe we are lovers." He laughed, then said to Paien, "*Pédéraste. Les méchants.*" For the first time Rush saw the stoic man's countenance change. There was a trace of humor in his eyes and a smirk on his lips, but his tense posture held firm.

"Of course your reputation precedes you."

"Yeah? What reputation is that?"

"Come now, monsieur Limbaugh. Your disdain for homosexuals is not something you have taken pains to hide. It is a lucrative platform on which to stand in your country, is it not? There is more money to be made pointing out the sinners than in simply caring for your fellow man, no? The *Right*? The Conservative Right, yes? They have much money, no? You and they despise the méchants...er, the homosexuals, yes? And yet you pay a lot of money to come and spend your leisure time in Spain. A country very open and accepting of such things. It is the proverb, no? 'Keep your friends close – hold your enemies closer.' This is what you do?"

"This wasn't my idea. I don't give two shits about Spain, or Europe for that matter. Communism, Socialism, debauchery and laziness. That's what Europe traffics in. That and overpriced products. Of course the Americans and the rest of the world are dumb enough to buy the crap because the names sound posh and exotic. But a name doesn't mean shit when it comes to quality."

"How true," Savante mocked.

"It makes no difference where I decide to spend my time. The fact of the matter is homosexuality is an abomination of nature as clearly stated in the Bible. A third of the world believes in the Bible. Look it up. It's in Leviticus. You should read it sometime."

"Oh, oui, oui. I have. When I learned that much of the world's population judges one another and kills one another because of a seventeen hundred year-old document, written and compiled before the advent of modern science, I decided it was worth a look. You know," Savante stepped towards the window facing the courtyard, "when my father told me this, I thought he was pulling the wool over my eyes. I thought 'this cannot be true.' He told me what life was like back then, according to historians of the time. It was a terrible, barbaric existence. The true Dark Ages, if you will. An unlikely time and place for the creator of the universe to set up shop, don't you think?"

Savante stared out the window for almost a minute, then continued. "The people at that time knew nothing of how the world really works. Nothing of the expanse of the universe. Not even the basic forces of nature were understood. Life expectancy was only thirty years. Few expected to live longer. Such a short and difficult life. A wasted life. Is it such a mystery that they were such a superstitious people? When a man feels trapped and hopeless, he does not bother to question the man who shows him a tunnel, nor does he ask where it leads. He will crawl on bloodied hands and knees, pushed on by hope of salvation – of liberation from a dreadful existence. But it is not hope alone that drives him. Like any conscious being, he is terrified of death. Of an end to existence. An end to a life that never attained true happiness. And once again, he is ready and eager to believe and follow the first person to offer him a way out. A cheat on death. To attain the ultimate goal: eternal bliss."

The tall black man turned from the window and faced Rush.

"Is that what you believe, Monsieur Limbaugh?" he asked, his voice hushed and serious. "Can a tainted man like yourself hope to cheat death?"

"Listen, you pompous Frog," Rush started to say. In a flash of movement, Paien reached inside his jacket, pulled out a gun, aimed at Rush, and fired.

Rush's threat was cut off as he felt the sharp sting of a thick needle pierce the skin on his neck. Instinctively he reached up and pulled out the dart. The pain was excruciating and Rush screamed. His left hand shot up to cover the wound, which had begun to bleed. He looked down in shocked awe at the dart in his hand. It was thin and silver – about three inches long. There was blood on the needle, which he could see had four tiny, sharp barbs designed to hold the dart in place. In a daze he realized it was his blood. The dart slipped absently from his hand and hit the tile floor with a clink.

Rush's mind filled with rage. He flashed a fierce, burning grimace at his shooter and took a step towards him. Neither of the men flinched or moved an inch, but rather stared at him expectantly. Rush took another two steps when a wave of dizziness hit him. A prickly, tingling feeling was spreading through his body. He felt like he might fall over and threw both hands out in front of him for balance. It was then he noticed that his left hand and the white cuff of his shirtsleeve were soaked in blood.

In only a moment he'd forgotten about the wound to his neck. He could no longer feel the pain of the injury. In fact, he was losing sensation throughout his body.

"Il s'affaiblit. Asseoir," Savante said.

Paien nodded, returned the dart gun to its holster and stepped forward to help the weakened man. Rush saw the man move towards him, but was powerless to resist. He knew what he wanted to do, but somehow communication between his mind and body had been severed. He tried to scream in protest, but found that verbal communication had also been cut. He had no choice but to allow his shooter to shuffle him over to the chair across from Savante. Paien dropped Rush into the padded chair, and he watched as the man removed a small fold of gauze bandages and a roll of medical tape. Paien quickly placed the bandages over the wound in his neck to stop the bleeding, then taped the makeshift dressing in place. After replacing the items in his pocket, he turned to Savante and asked, *"Dois je l'attacher?"*

"No, Paien, restraints will not be necessary. Our host is quite captive."

Savante smiled and addressed Rush. "Monsieur Limbaugh, no doubt you have many questions, though you lack the ability to ask them. I will do my best to elucidate the nature of this situation." Rush still had a small degree of control over his facial muscles and eyes. With some effort, he glanced at Paien who appeared apprehensive. Savante saw this as well and said, *"Paien. S'il vous plaît se détendre. Nous devons expliquer à lui.* We must tell him. It is the honorable thing to do."

Paien looked at Rush, then to Savante, then down at his watch. After a moment he nodded and sat down on a nearby couch.

"Pardonnez-moi, Monsieur Limbaugh. Paien believes it a waste of time to tell you why we're here. Others in our organization believe the same." Savante studied Rush's face for a moment then asked, "Most of your body is numb. Can you move your head at all?"

After a few moments of concentration Rush was able to nod his head slightly.

"Bon. Very good. Let's begin, shall we? We have introduced a neurotoxin into your body, which you have no doubt surmised causes almost complete paralysis. Normally our organization does not resort to such measures unless we are dealing with someone very dangerous. We had no such concerns with you. So why, you may ask, did we go to the trouble of turning you into a temporary catatonic? What makes you so special? The answer is obvious, is it not? You have made a very prosperous career shouting whatever comes into your deranged little mind. Many in our organization referred to you as a 'mouthpiece.' This is a new term for me, but I believe I understand its meaning. Your mouth, or more specifically, the twisted and rank foulness that comes out of it, constitutes a threat to society. It is your greatest weapon. Your source of power, as it were. So, I persuaded those in my organization that there was a wonderful poetic license available here that could not be turned down. I convinced them that depriving you of the ability to speak was just too enticing an opportunity to pass up – if only for a few minutes. Once everyone was familiar with your, how do you say...greatest hits? They consented to my *unusual* request. And voila! Here we sit. You, deprived of your only weapon, and me with all the time in the world.

"Once the decision was made, the rest was really quite easy. A very talented German chemist sympathetic to our plight, created for us this powerful concoction. It is a derivative of the bacterium Clostridium botulinum, the same bacterium used to create Botox. Ageless skin, no? *Peau lisse, jeune.* The fountain of youth in a syringe. Ironically, most people do not know that the Botulinum toxin is the most toxic substance we know of. Amazing, the risks people will take to look younger than their years." Savante shook his head in wonder. "Unfortunately for you, monsieur, our derivative conveys no such aesthetic benefits. What it does is far more interesting. You are curious, no? It allows you to focus an unusually high percentage of your brain's computational capacity on what I am about to tell you."

Savante leaned closer. "You can feel it, yes? Right now your thoughts are crystal clear and precise? Your mind feels sharper than ever before. It is extraordinary, is it not? The human brain, like any computer, has only so much processing power. Much of its resources are spent processing sensory input – sight, sound, taste, and touch. It also expends a lot of energy conveying commands to all the muscles – coordinating balance, avoiding harm. But," Savante held up a finger, "cut the mind off from all tasks not immediately necessary to keep the body alive and voila! Your mind becomes a singularity within your consciousness. You know this to be true, yes? You feel it happening right now?"

Rush nodded slightly.

"You may find this difficult to believe, but I too have felt this. I was one of the first humans to be injected with the neurotoxin. When I first heard of this derivative, I volunteered for testing. I had theorized that while the body was restrained, the mind would be unleashed." Savante's eyes lit up as he recounted the experience. "And it 'twas so! I was able to think and contemplate like never before. To plan, to comprehend, and to refine my understanding of so many wonderful things. *Magnifique!* The paralysis normally wears off in about six hours, but our clever chemist was able to restore full function after only an hour. *Incroyable.* But," Savante said dismissively with a wave of his hand, "I digress. Let us return to the matter at hand."

Savante stood and walked casually around the room while he spoke. "Monsieur Limbaugh, you may have heard that some well-known people in the United States have recently, how do you say – 'Gone the way of the Dodo.' Although perhaps not. You came straight from rehabilitation to Spain. Perhaps you are unaware of what has happened. Well, Paien and I are part of an organization known as *The Aenamaia.* An uninventive name to be sure, but such was the design. Our objective is quite simple: to remove the worst of the influential people and elements from society. Perhaps you heard about the package we mailed to the White House? Of course, the package arrived very, very late. Monsieur Bush has been out of residence for some time now. C'est la vie," Savante smiled. "I'm sure he still got the message. We paid a visit to Monsieur Pou Lai, the infamous energy executive and Monsieur David Lesser, the defense contractor. We also bought a one-way ticket for one of your compatriots, Anna Kulter and company. They will be spending the rest of their lives as citizens of Iraq. Alas, the mademoiselle will finally have a chance to personally kill all of the men there and convert everyone else to Christianity – something she has desired for some time now." Savante shook his head again. "Tsk, tsk, tsk. These are very bad people, no? But, rest assured, Monsieur Limbaugh, the cleansing is not limited to individuals. We also stopped production of a great many ehh...Paien? *Quotidien populaire...?*"

"Tabloids," Paien answered.

"Oui, yes. Merci. We used explosives to shut down this pipeline of fallacious and useless dribble. Kabooom! The next morning the regular news stations were already labeling the event as 'The Tabloid Bombings.' Oh, your media is so fond of memorable phrases, all designed to scare the people and increase ratings. I have a list of over two hundred such titles. 'Tis a fascinating topic to me. I digress again."

Savante stopped at a nearby window and was silent for several moments. "I would guess that right at this moment, your mental faculties are on overdrive. You are wondering, 'Are these men here to spirit me away?'" Savante's lowered his voice and said with a reluctant nod, "Oui, monsieur. I'm afraid it is so."

The black Frenchman turned from the windows and made eye contact with Limbaugh. Rush could see the man's eyes were downcast and troubled.

"You are one of the Black Sheep that made our list. I myself added you to this list. You see, I have been watching you for some time now. Watching and listening. It is possible I know more about you than anyone else in the world. For that is how it works. We learn all that we can about a person. It is necessary to know as much as possible before we make a decision. You might find this difficult to believe, but I had sincerely hoped you would change your ways. When I heard that you were engaged to be married, I thought perhaps the fourth Madame Limbaugh would transform you as only a woman can. When I learned that you paid Sir Elton John one million dollars to entertain at your wedding, I felt sure your loathing of homosexuals was a thing of the past – that you had finally seen the error of your ways! How else could it be that the famous Elton John would agree to participate in such an event? I was certain you had changed," Savante ardently asserted.

Savante returned to his chair and sat down. "But, alas, I was mistaken. You have not changed a bit. You continue, with more vigor than ever, to push your agenda of fear, intolerance, hate, racism, and bigotry. Like Mademoiselle Kulter, the Internet is ripe with your foul diatribes and hateful quotes. *Scandaleux!* And all this under the red cloak of shameful hypocrisy. I'm sorry, monsieur, but people like yourself who are addicted to drugs should not get away with demonizing all the other drug addicts. The problem is equally yours, yet you do not pin yourself to the target you paint. You openly condemn homosexuality, then turn around and pay a million dollars to have a famous gay man play music for your conservative, anti-homosexual party guests. *Mon dieu!* Even when I'm not in a paralytic state, such things as this hurt my mind. I wonder," he said leaning in again, "How is yours doing right now? Do you harbor guilt? Are you feeling regret? Remorse?" Savante leaned in closer and whispered, "I would like to believe this. Truly I would." He leaned back and clasped his hands. "But alas, I cannot. *The Aenamaia* believes that corrupt people can cross a moral event horizon. Event horizon – this term is familiar to you?"

Rush shook his head ever so slightly.

"No? The event horizon is, for our purposes, the point of no return. Your immorality and your anger have driven you over the edge into an inescapable abyss. You peddle your filth, your fear, and your anger. For this terrible product, you earn much gold, and yet live to regret nothing. Money," Savante said to himself, "always it comes down to money. They never learn. They never listen. They never change."

Abruptly Savante stood, and looking straight at Rush, declared, "You, Monsieur Limbaugh, you are *les méchant*. You are a corrupt and wicked man and this world can no longer shoulder the burden of your continued existence. *Il est temps*." Paien got up and stood behind his friend. Savante reached into his leather jacked and pulled out what looked like a case for storing sunglasses. Without turning from Rush's stare, he passed the case over his shoulder and said, "Paien, *s'il vous plait.*"

Rush watched in horror as the fair-skinned Swissman opened the case and pulled out a syringe and an unlabeled ampule containing a clear liquid.

Savante saw the faint look of distress his captive was able to express. "Have no fear, monsieur. Paien is preparing your favorite treat. It is a special cocktail of oxycodone, hydrocodon, and a shot of morphine. In a few moments all your cares and concerns will float away like a leaf in a stream. You will be in a state of pure bliss and contentment. And because your brain is now hungry for stimulation, the experience will be more powerful and extraordinary than you could ever imagine. Oh…I'm sure you're concerned about being intruded upon during your euphoria. Fear not, we've made payment arrangements with the owner to ensure you will not be disturbed for the remaining twenty-five days of your lease."

Paien inserted the syringe into the ampule and retracted the plunger. Rush watched helplessly as the tube was filled with the clear liquid. The quiet man handed the syringe back to his friend, whose glance was still fixed on the paralyzed man.

"Relax, monsieur. You have my personal assurance that it will be the last and greatest ride of your life."

Paien rolled up Limbaugh's sleeve then grabbed hold of his wrist and squeezed. Rush was unable to feel the man's grip. He watched as the veins on his arm began to bulge.

Terrified, Limbaugh looked pleadingly into Savante's eyes.

"I am sorry monsieur, but this is how it must be."

Rush's eyes opened wide as he watched the black Frenchman insert the needle into his vein. The plunger was slowly depressed, emptying what he knew would be a guaranteed overdose into his blood stream. The needle was removed and his shirtsleeve re-buttoned. Savante handed the empty syringe and ampule to Paien who replaced them in the case and put it in his pocket. Savante continued to study his face, his expression a mix of curiosity and sadness.

It took only a moment for the drugs to begin taking effect. Rush's mind, as powerful as it had ever been, endeavored to hold on to the fear that had gripped it only moments ago. The irrational hope of survival depended on his being alert and aware. But his mind knew better. Even if someone walked in right at this moment, his paralysis would prevent him from telling them what was happening. By the time it wore off, if it ever did, it would be too late. At some point in the next hour, while his mind was swimming lazily in a drug-induced ecstasy, his body would slowly become starved of oxygen, triggering apnea followed by respiratory arrest. Then all would fade to black.

These thoughts flashed through his mind in a matter of seconds. Yet there was no panic. No concern. Only acceptance. Acceptance came despite the knowledge that he was going to die tonight. But where fear would normally overwhelm, instead he felt glad. He was thankful that he would pass into the next life without fear, remorse or regret.

Sensations of warmth and happiness were spreading through his body. Whatever they had given him was good – really good. Just then Rush felt a pang of guilt and embarrassment. The pleasure he was experiencing was similar to that which he'd been addicted to for well over a decade. He'd been sure this time, after two months of intense rehabilitation, that he'd beaten his addiction. And yet here he was, in the middle of a relapse – torn between psychological guilt and intense physical pleasure, each battling for control over his mind. Then, amidst the struggle, a calm rational voice inside his said, "It isn't your fault. It was the black Frenchman's needle that delivered the drugs into your system. You're not to blame." And with that, the guilt, anguish and regret faded away, replaced by a hazy, formless and familiar void. Rush had been here many, many times before. But unlike his previous visits, there was nothing in his head or heart urging him to leave. In fact, he had already made the decision to stay here – forever. Relief washed over him and in an instant all the negative emotions he'd been carrying disappeared. And while he could still see and hear Savante and Paien, his anger towards them had also vanished. And for the first time in many years, Rush felt at peace.

"Almost time to go," he thought wearily. "Goin' uptown."

Savante leaned forward and whispered into his ear, "I'm told it's quite a…rush. *Au revoir,* Monsieur Limbaugh. *Au revoir.*"

Chapter 10

Washington, D.C.

The taxi driver, a young Hispanic man, set the bags down gingerly on the sidewalk and closed the trunk. He repeated the fare, his words precise but courteous, ending with a respectful "sir." Toman smiled. The young man took his job seriously. There was a focus in his manner. He might go so far as to say the driver had an old soul. It was a rare quality these days. Toman had picked up on it the minute he'd been approached at the airport. Another, older man had asked for the fare at the same moment. Normally the choice would be purely arbitrary, but there was something in the young man's simple, unassuming gaze that had prompted him to hand over his bags without hesitation. The older man had scoffed and walked off, while the younger man only nodded and said thank you.

Toman had watched as the young driver, who had introduced himself as Hugo, quickly put his bags in the trunk and opened the door for him. "Old school," he'd thought. He'd thanked Hugo, who'd answered, "Yes, sir." Hugo hadn't tried to make conversation. He'd only asked for the destination, affirming with another "Yes, sir."

During the ride over Toman watched Hugo's every move. His driving etiquette, speed, route, attention, and every other choice he made along the way. Everything had been expertly executed. This man knew how to handle a vehicle and clearly knew his way around the city. This observation had set Toman's gears moving long before the cab pulled up to the curb.

Toman pulled out two fifty-dollar bills and handed them to Hugo who immediately reached into his pocket for change. "Keep it," he said, waiting for the young man's reaction.

"Sir," Hugo said surprised, "I cannot. It is almost as much as your fare."

Toman raised a hand. "I insist. I appreciate you getting me here quickly and in one piece."

"But that's my job, sir," Hugo declared, his face betraying confusion.

"Hugo," Toman said, "does your company allow you to take pick-up calls directly?"

"Yes, sir," Hugo replied and immediately handed him a business card. Toman hadn't seen him retrieve the card, nor had it been in his hand when he gave him the bills. Impressive. He took the card and examined it. Thick, off-white, and textured with a smooth glossy border. "Elegant and simple," he thought. It read Hugo F. Müller. The last name rang a bell, but he couldn't remember where he'd heard it.

"Your last name sounds familiar," he commented.

"It's German, sir, but my great grandfather spent much time in Santa Catarina. It's a state in the southern part of Brazil."

"Is he famous, your grandfather?"

Hugo looked somewhat timorous but answered, "Some people know him. He was a scientist."

Toman read the young man's body language and decided this was a conversation for another time. Waving the card he said, "Well, Hugo Müller, I just might be in need of your services again."

"Please, sir, call anytime, day or night," Hugo said with a slight nod.

"You don't sleep?"

"Of course, sir, where and when I can. But prosperity rarely lands on sleeping heads."

Toman nodded. "Well said."

Hugo nodded in return and said, "Thank you very much for your generosity, sir. I hope I am able to repay it someday."

As he watched the taxi pull away, Toman considered the statement and whispered, "You might at that, Hugo. You might at that."

McLean, Virginia

May in Virginia is extraordinary. All manner of life slowly rebound from the punishing cold and stillness of winter. Forest animals emerge from their shelters to feast on the emerging plant life and to warm their young in the sun. A sense of replenishment and abundance is ubiquitous. The dense forests around McLean, Virginia radiate with vivid, ebullient shades and colors. Dew on the grasses evaporates well before lunchtime, giving the air a comfortable dampness.

A light wind stirred the leaves of the maple trees and the long, uncut blades of emerald green grass just outside the *USA Today* headquarters. The placid waters of the lake behind the main building reflected the light amber of the morning sky. The dirt path circling the lake wove in and out of tall pines and short blue spruces. A few dedicated joggers were out early on the trail in hopes of avoiding the mid-morning power-walkers, mountain bikes and off-road baby strollers. Even from a distance, the thin, evenly spaced puffs of their breaths were visible in the chilled morning air, like small mobile factories. Staring out his corner office window towards the beautiful panorama, Jack Kelley saw nothing at all.

The headline story bearing his name sat atop his otherwise immaculate desk. Despite the resounding approval by the board of directors and his white-toothed acceptance of their praise, Kelley felt uneasy about the story. There was an indescribable tightness gripping his stomach accompanied by a bounding, nervous energy, both of which he couldn't seem to shake. It took a great deal of concentration and effort to sit still and direct the course of his thoughts. Every time he glanced at the photograph of the late Pou Lai on the cover of his newspaper his mind conjured up the memory of a massive ball of fire erupting beneath his SUV.

Even now, in the calm quiet and solitude of his plush office, he could recall the absolute stillness and silence hanging in the frozen, elongated moment immediately before the shock wave from the explosion sent his body, along with a million shards of tinted glass crashing to the floor of the empty coffee shop. How could such a moment last so long? If only he could return to that moment. Surely he would be able to wedge his mind into the opening in time and space and forestall the intrusion of the next moment – the next, terrifying moment.

Kelley's dark eyes darted again to the generic photograph of Pou Lai. He guessed his media people had swiped the portrait off the Internet. It had probably come from a site that routinely reported on slippery, white-collar criminals who managed to beat, or in this case, "buy" the system. Or perhaps they got it from one of their competitor's sites. "No matter," he thought. There was the chubby image of Pou Lai, alive and in color, grinning like he'd just won the lottery. The idea made Kelley chuckle harshly. "Some lottery," he muttered.

Still staring blankly out the window Kelley absently reached up and touched the cut on his forehead. The pain had subsided, but a thin, warm sting still lingered just beneath the surface like a sliver reminding him of a single unfortunate moment in time. Was the sting from the cut in his head or the damage to his ego? Did it really matter? Involuntarily his eyes closed and an image of the dark sedan's interior flashed into his mind. Why had he gotten into the car? Was he really just after the story? Or did he believe he would have the opportunity to meet the man who called himself Gray? The man behind the violence.

The vehicle had been empty except for the driver, whom he never did get a good look at. A thousand times in the last twenty-four hours Kelley imagined opening the car door and seeing a small, wizened, gray-haired man holding a cell phone and staring confidently back at him, as if to say, "Now you know not to mess with us, don't you." How he'd wished he'd really been there; that the little man had been Gray. In less than a minute the full force of his own anger and pulsing fear would explode upon the small man in a burst of savage violence. In an instant his hands would tear at the arrogant little man until nothing identifiable as human remained. He would walk calmly away from the sedan, leaving the back door wide open for some curious pedestrian to find the shredded remains of something that bled red.

In reality Kelley admitted to himself that this dream was merely a fantasy and that the only true aspect of it was the fear he still felt. The moment he'd closed the door, the sedan had pulled away from the curb and promptly exited the parking lot. He'd tried knocking on the thick, tinted glass between the front and back seat, but the driver had not responded.

They'd been heading south for a few minutes when Kelley heard a faint click. A moment later a panel imbedded in the ceiling slid open and a flat screen monitor slowly lowered. As he leaned forward to look for some kind of power switch, the screen came to life. Kelley sat back slowly and watched as an image of a man materialized. The man's face was familiar, but he couldn't recall a name.

The picture was replaced by that of another man. This one Kelley knew. It was Pou Lai smiling broadly and standing next to George and Barbara Bush. "Must have been before the scandal," Kelley had thought. After that the administration had distanced itself from the whole affair.

A few more pictures of Lai flashed by. Kelley was surprised to see Lai's picture replaced by the Fox News logo. Perhaps he was going to see a news clip. Instead, a portfolio shot of two popular anchors on Fox news appeared. Both men hosted a show on Fox that bore each of their last names. The show was popular and notorious for cleverly masking editorial and opinionated commentary under the guise of factual reporting. Once or twice in the past Kelley's own writers had made the mistake of running with a story aired by the two anchors, only to find out later it had been fabricated by Fox.

As the dark sedan continued south, Kelley watched the screen display pictures and videos of dozens of individuals. A few faces he knew; many more were familiar, and still more were completely unknown to him. After fifteen minutes or so, the pictures stopped and a voice spoke from the TV. The message had stunned Kelley. The voice, which he felt certain belonged to Gray, had said all the people he had seen had been deemed inhuman, irreparable, and unworthy of life in America. Some would be sent to other countries with instructions never to return. Others would be "removed". That had been the word: *removed*. Kelley could still remember the relief and the guilt at having not seen his picture flash by. The voice message ended by saying: "*More instructions will follow for you, Mr. Kelley. Please do not underestimate us again. In the meantime, welcome home.*"

When Kelley turned to look out the window, he was shocked to find the sedan was parked in the semi-circular driveway of his house.

"What in the hell is going on here?" he'd demanded of the driver, but there was no response.

Kelley heard the click of the door locks, then noticed only the passenger side lock had opened. Clever. He had planned on getting out on the driver's side to hopefully get a good look at the driver. Apparently this had been anticipated.

Opening the door, Kelley took care in climbing out of the car. The soreness of his back and legs were only slightly more acute than the pounding that radiated from the fresh cut on his head. He took a deep breath and moved a few feet from the car. An instant later the car lurched forward, the momentum from the acceleration slamming the rear door closed. He watched the nondescript sedan pull out of his driveway. No plates or other markings. "Of course," he'd thought.

He returned his attention to his house. Try as he might, he could not recall a time in the past when he'd been more pleased at seeing his home. Standing in the driveway, the stillness of the day and the oddness at being home on a weekday hit him. "When was the last time I was home during a weekday?" he wondered. Still pondering the question, he had taken a few steps when something ahead arrested his attention. His front door was wide open. Instinctively he looked around the driveway and courtyard, but saw nothing out of the ordinary. Surely his wife wasn't back from her trip to Greece. She'd only left two days ago and wasn't due back for almost a month.

Cautiously he moved forward, half expecting a burglar to rush out of the open door carrying silver candelabras and handfuls of jewelry. Had he forgotten to set the alarm when he'd left this morning? Even if he had, the security company he paid handsomely to monitor his house would notice the front door had been open for an extended period of time and would've called his cell phone. It had happened only a few weeks back during a dinner party. The imbecilic hired butler had failed to completely close the front door. Fortunately the security company had called his cell before they'd sat down for dinner. A swift and discreet reprimand had insured the hired help would not make the mistake again. "No," he'd thought looking into the dim interior of his house, "this is something different."

Crossing the threshold, Kelley immediately noticed the piece of white paper on the floor of the foyer. Wincing from the soreness in his back, he bent down and picked it up. It was a handwritten note. Thinking back now, he felt certain the handwriting was that of a woman.

A knock on his office door stirred him from his reflection.

"Yes," he answered somewhat irritated. He'd told Monique he did not want to be disturbed.

The heavy door opened and Monique poked her head in.

"I'm sorry to disturb you, sir, but I just took a second call from the Department of Homeland Security. They're sending agents over to pick you up."

Kelley sighed heavily and said, "Okay, Monique. Pull together whatever is ready for the next few runs and put them on a jump drive for me."

"Yes, sir," Monique said with a slight nod and closed the door.

"So," he thought looking back at the paper on his desk, "the boys at Homeland Security can read after all." He shouldn't be surprised. Legal had confirmed his suspicions about being contacted. In fact, he was surprised he hadn't heard from the CIA, FBI, or even the Secretary of Defense.

"Evidence," he whispered absently. "They want evidence."

Kelley reached into his jacket pocket and withdrew a cellophane bag with a folded piece of paper inside. He looked at the small white rectangle for a moment, then unsealed the bag and removed the paper. Careful to only touch the corners, he unfolded the paper and read it for the third time:

Welcome home, Mr. Kelley. Please be sure to close the front door, as we'll be remotely re-arming your alarm system in a few moments. Don't bother checking your closed circuit video. All images of our presence have been erased.

Please proceed to your private office upstairs. Instructions have been locked inside the safe you keep hidden in the office closet. The combination has not been changed. If you choose to contact the authorities immediately you will have to use your cell phone. We'll reactivate your landline in one hour.

It is likely that agents from a number of federal agencies will be by sometime this evening. It would normally be sooner, but at the moment, all of their databases show your residence as being on the other side of town. This was to allow you enough time to decide how you wish to proceed after reviewing the information we've left you. After they apologize profusely for breaking down the expensive oak door of a particularly nasty televangelist, they'll no doubt contact your newspaper and obtain the correct address. The next move is yours.

Staring at the paper, Kelley felt the panic and helplessness of paranoia creeping up on him. It felt as if invisible eyes were watching and listening in on his thoughts. The words on the page blurred as he tried to think. How could they have gained access to his house, circumvented his security system, and cracked into his electronic safe? How did they know so much about him? He shuddered to think what else they knew and what other areas of his life they had control over. Their capabilities spoke of government spooks, but which government he couldn't be sure.

He carefully refolded the paper and slid it back into the plastic bag. Decisively he returned the bag and paper to his pocket. The newsman inside him had already made his decision. It had been made the moment he'd opened the safe in his office closet. As soon as he saw the thick manila envelope lying on top of the untouched straps of hundred dollar bills, the feeling of invasion and vulnerability had almost overwhelmed him. "How in the hell did they...?" he'd asked aloud.

Slowly, as he'd gone through the contents of the envelope sprawled across his desk, a new sensation overtook him. It was an odd mixture of panic, excitement, uncertainty, and speculation. In one instant he was sure he could use the information to bring *The Aenamaia* down to its knees – and at the same time dramatically increase newspaper circulation. In the next moment he felt certain this was precisely what they wanted. Why else would they go to such lengths to make sure he was the first one to see it? The information could've been sent to any number of other newspapers or TV stations.

He was sure he was being used, but to what end he could not guess. And that was the most frustrating part. Even when he thought how clever it would be to suppress all the information and act as if nothing had happened, he quickly saw a number of ways that, too, could backfire on him. It would be easy for *The Aenamaia* to prove that he and his newspaper had been given critical information before anyone else. Withholding it would not only cause an uproar with readers, but might also land him in jail for obstruction. No, suppression wasn't an option.

In the end he'd decided he would release the information through his newspaper, but that it would be done his way. He might be a puppet, but he was one with his own voice. The only variable to deal with was the Feds. Fortunately, he'd played a similar game with them many times. Even if the few crumbs he tossed them wouldn't afford him much protection, the story he'd already published would. That and the First Amendment. Any legal action they cared to bring would be handled by the army of attorneys employed full time by his paper. Now he just had to figure out how to keep *USA Today* in the lead until the end. Until the very end.

Washington, D.C.

Toman stared up at the raised stone letters beneath the serrated Roman cornice: Old Ebbitt Grill. Washington's oldest restaurant, which had moved several times, now occupied the old B.F. Keats Theater. Simple, smooth Tuscan columns capped with scrolled volutes separated the three uniform gold and glass doorways, which appeared to have been carved out of the stone façade of the building. Each entrance was recessed a foot or so and was crowned by a simple beveled arch, reminiscent of elegant Roman architecture. In the center was a revolving door, while the flanking entrances were normal double doors with square panel windows. On both sides of the entrance hung matching poster marquees evocative of the building's theater years.

Almost a year had passed since he'd last been here, but the old place looked exactly the same. Taking in the sight he experienced a placid wave of nostalgia, which was unusual for him. So much of his adult life had been spent traveling and moving between cities, that he'd rarely frequented any one place long enough to form any kind of connection or bond. How many restaurants and cafés had he visited in the last twenty years? How many could he even begin to recall? The answer was awash in the same blur that shadowed much of his life, while so many other aspects were vivid and crystal clear in his mind. The sharp contrast was not lost on him.

A moment later a fitting analogy from his life overwhelmed his memory, preceded by one word: cenote. A relaxed grin formed unconsciously at the thought of the word. The memory was clear and wonderful. In the middle of the chilly D.C. concrete jungle, memories of happier, warmer days seemed to stop time. All at once he recalled the moisture in the air mixed with the pungent, earthy smell of the surrounding tropical forest, the enormous old trees, sinuous vines, sweet-smelling wild flowers, and the glowing azure blue water fifteen feet beneath the rim of the small cenote. He remembered taking a deep breath, then leaping off a narrow rock ledge. His fins hit the water with a loud "slap," his legs scissoring hard to cushion the landing and push him back to the surface. The water had been much cooler than he'd expected after having trekked sixty pounds of dive gear several miles through the hot jungle. It had momentarily taken his breath away. A few seconds later the Canadian man he'd met only a few days before jumped in, followed by their local guide.

They spent the first few minutes acclimating to the dim light, adjusting gear and making sure everyone was ready to go. After an exchange of nods they dropped a few feet below the surface for one final check. The dive master waited for the two men to give the "okay" hand signal then gestured for them to begin exploring the main cavern. Toman and the Canadian swam around the perimeter while their dive master anchored a guide line. By the time they'd swum the full circumference, the dive master pointed forward and they headed towards the main tunnel.

They'd been submerged less than twenty minutes when it had happened. One minute he had been admiring the crystal clearness of the water fifteen feet beneath the tunnel's limestone ceiling, the next his vision blurred. In a flash the world lost focus. Their guide had warned him of this, but nothing can prepare a diver for his first encounter with a halocline. Curiosity had stopped him short just inside the halocline. After studying the strange blurriness, he'd slowly back peddled until the water was clear again. Ahead only a few feet he thought he could discern the nearly imperceptible line demarcating the border between fresh water and seawater. Slowly he'd proceeded until again reality seemed to belie his senses.

Standing in front of Old Ebbitt, Toman understood why this particular memory had been accessed by his subconscious. The analogy fit perfectly. On one side were crystal clear memories readily available for recall, while on the other side everything was a blur, with only occasional bubbles of clarity. "'And all at once the road ahead and the future it leads to, which were crystal clear a moment ago, become blurred and fraught with uncertainty.' Was this a suitable description of *The Aenamaia's* current predicament?" he wondered. Hopefully not.

Images of azure waters, beams of light made visible by microscopic particulates and life in the water, curious yellow and orange fish, and fascinating blurry waters filled his mind. From the hot jungle to the cool water. From shorts, t-shirt and sandals to thin wetsuit and forty pounds of dive gear. From bright sunshine to pale blue water. Thinking back now, Toman wondered if the stark contrast and rapid transition between these two environments was a substantial part of the appeal for cenote and cave divers. Whatever it was, he hoped he would live long enough to go back.

Good memories are often the catalysts for longing and the involuntary contrasting with one's current situation. "How true," he thought, staring at Old Ebbitt's façade. "How true."

Toman heard heavy, familiar footsteps approaching from behind, but he did not turn.

"Even from down the block you look like you're a million miles away. Where were you just now?"

"Ojo del Dios," Toman said simply, "diving with a pale white Canadian and a pudgy Mexican with bleached blonde streaks in his jet black hair."

"Dorito," the man said with a chuckle. "That's what we called him. Papa Dorito. He liked it so much he probably put it in the brochure."

Hearing the name made Toman grin. He turned around. Joust's head was bowed slightly, but Toman could see his friend was smiling casually. Before he could say anything, Joust added, "And I was only a Canadian because my parents decided they just had to see Niagara Falls that particular weekend. Mom wasn't due to pop for another two weeks, so why not right? Little did they know then that I would always make it a point to be early to every appointment."

Toman glanced down at his watch: five 'til seven. "Indeed," Toman said nodding. "Indeed you do. But showing up on time is only half the battle," he said, an edge of seriousness in his voice. "Punctuality is irrelevant if you don't do the job."

"I agree," Joust said solemnly with a nod. "Good thing for me the job *is* done."

Toman studied his friend's face, but there was no hint of sarcasm or jest. "Good," he said, "I'm glad to hear it, though your unilateral action was well outside of protocol. You'll have to atone for that with Gray."

He was about to say something else when Joust put up his hands in surrender. "I know. Corner booth, grilled ribeye, Guinness Stout, and damage control." Joust flashed a disarming grin and with an inviting waive of his hand added, "After you, Mr. *Kaparich*."

Toman glowered at his friend and shook his head. Later he would ask how Joust had known the alias he'd used that day, but now he was too hungry and thirsty to worry about it. He bent to reach for his bags, but Joust beat him to it. The two men made eye contact and Joust said sheepishly, "It's the least I can do after what you've probably been through today on my account."

"The least is right," Toman quipped. He turned and stepped towards the door and mumbled, "I damn near *closed* your account today."

As the two men neared the entrance to Old Ebbitt, Joust asked, "And hey...Who are you calling 'pale white' anyway? Remember, it's your skinny butt Dorito nicknamed Palillo Blanco."

"I'll take 'white stick' over Mono Blanco any day, monkey boy."

Both men smirked and proceeded through the gold and glass revolving door into the foyer of the old restaurant. Though it was still light outside, the time of day was never betrayed inside Ebb's. The interior was dimly lit and subdued, providing an appealing air of privacy and anonymity. Very proper for a restaurant that was only a stone's throw away from the White House and a dozen other federal buildings. Toman himself had spent many a night tucked into a corner booth that afforded him a view of the main dining area and the front door. Though he'd never expected trouble, he and the other members of *The Aenamaia* were trained to always be ready for it. Ebb's was perfect because it offered a number of exits: the front door, kitchen, a side door through the avian bar, and several options via the attached arboretum. The trees in front also offered some cover from the security cameras mounted on top of the Treasury Building across the street.

Toman had mused more than once that, were the law to burst through the door, the routes to the exits could very well be clogged with other restaurant patrons who might readily assume it was their face the authorities were searching for. Ebb's sat at the epicenter of the good and bad of the U.S. government and all those who spent their lives courting, massaging, and occasionally circumventing it. And no place in D.C. was more saturated with the latter breed than K Street, which was only three blocks away. Locally it was known as Pork Belly Boulevard. Most of D.C.'s special interests and lobbyists had their offices on K Street. The K Street minions congregated there like leeches to a blood source – each one hoping for a warm drink before the coagulation began and they had to start looking for another wound. Toman recalled Joust visiting Ebb's on several occasions to casually observe potentials on his extraction list. No doubt several of the worst had spent time in here. The thought of such people in his favorite place made Toman's empty stomach churn. It was like finding maggots in your prime rib.

Before this visual could take full form, though, the hostess announced, "Kaparich, party of two?"

He looked at Joust whose too-innocent expression read "what did you expect?" Now he really wanted to know how Joust knew about his alias.

Pondering the question, he followed his friend and the hostess to their usual booth. He'd been too wrapped up in thoughts of K Street to notice Joust tipping the hostess in order to snare their coveted nook. Though the place was hopping, the booth had been unoccupied. "Coincidence?" he wondered. Given how many times and under how many different names they'd tipped the hostesses for the table, was it possible it was routinely the last table they seated? Did the hostesses collectively keep this table open hoping for some of their better tipping customers? It certainly seemed feasible. Even in the simplest business operation, there were always secret, collaborative procedures; practices carved over time by the strong and skilled hands of self-interest.

Whether a small government agency, the mob, a cop on the take, or a gaggle of hostesses, there was *always* more complexity than the unaided eye could see. And once a person understood the ubiquitous pervasion of that reality, *i.e.* the truth that it was everywhere, the world took on an entirely new and mysterious form. Only a few minutes of deep reflection were necessary to taste the awesome power of that truth. It changed everything: life, love, relationships, business, friendships… even morality.

"'*Despite what they tell you, there are simply no moral absolutes in a complex world.*'" The quote had stuck with him over the years, partially because it had come from a cartoonist. "Wisdom often comes from the most unusual places," he thought.

"What was that?" Joust asked.

Toman shook his head slightly and said, "What?"

"You muttered something about morality," Joust said.

"Oh," he said, a little embarrassed, "Sorry. I didn't realize my thoughts had gone on verbal leave." Toman took a sip of ice water.

"Well?" Joust pressed. "What was it?"

"Just a quote from Berkeley Breathed," he said dismissively.

"The *Bloom County* comic?" Joust asked.

Toman nodded absently. Joust eyed him, but did not press the matter.

After they had ordered drinks and food, Toman decided to cut straight to the chase. "Joust," he started earnestly, "I need to know what happened, and I need to know why."

Joust nodded but didn't answer immediately. Toman noticed his brow was furrowed and his jaw muscles appeared tense. Toman could almost see the images exploding in his friend's mind. No doubt he was running through the day's events at breakneck speed. His friend stared past him for a long moment, then jerked up to meet his gaze. Joust's expression was still serious, but a small measure of solace was in his eyes and his posture relaxed a degree. When he finally spoke, his voice was quiet and reflective, like that of an earnest narrator.

"I decided a few weeks back to deviate from the plan a little. I had already studied my designated targets. They were bad, Toman," he said with some difficulty. "Really bad. These guys made Jack Abramoff look like the tooth fairy. Anyway, the extraction was still a week away, the targets were under audio surveillance and each was being tracked by Osiro. So I really had nothing to do. I was restless. Bored. Eager. So," he started slowly, playing with his napkin, "I decided to break protocol and take a direct reading." Joust's head was still bowed, but he managed to make eye contact from beneath an uncertain brow.

Toman sat back slowly, never breaking eye contact. He sighed. "You engaged?" he asked quietly.

"Yep," his friend said nodding absently.

"How did you play it?"

"Freshman accomplice," Joust said simply. "Right down to the silk tie, fake business card and matching name badge."

Toman looked puzzled. Joust took a deep breath, then explained.

"They had arranged for a private function, sort of a pre-game warm up before the DOD convention. Standard glad-handing, competition recon, tag-teaming, the usual. I wanted to get in the game, okay? I was convinced my list was too short. I was just..." he trailed off, trying to find the right words. "I was tired of all the planning and waiting. All the tiptoeing around. There were going to be seventy-plus lobbyists at this thing plus a host of DOD officials, buyers, even a few members of the House Appropriations Committee. I wasn't convinced that six was enough. There wasn't time for the normal background research, so I decided to just go see for myself. I bought a new suit, shiny shoes, gold cufflinks, a new watch, and printed some fake business cards. Even went to a Capitol Hill hair stylist! Complete D.C. camouflage. I paid cash for everything and only went to small stores without surveillance."

Before Toman could interject a question, the waitress brought two tall glasses of Guinness. They both took a long drink. The dark beer tasted so good Toman lost track of time for a moment. He opened his eyes in time to see Joust wipe the light foam from his lips. One more gulp and his friend continued.

"You should've seen it, T," Joust said eagerly, his voice growing more animated, "Every handshake, every smile, every exchange of cards – and all of it caked in grease. It's no wonder the machinery of corruption rarely squeaks. I played along, but mostly I just listened. It was like America had been shattered into a thousand pieces and was now being sold and traded, piece by sharp piece. Tobacco, steel, the Teamsters, trial lawyers, the AMA," Joust was now ticking off each lobby on his fingers. "The Christian Coalition, the NRA, the Right to Lifers, the AFL-CIO, bankers, etc. They were all there. But here's the kicker: I learned that most of these guys weren't even attending the DOD Convention. They were in town specifically for this off-the-books pow-wow.

An hour or so into it I introduced myself to the most inebriated person I could find. He was an older man, late sixties, polyester special, who I found out represented AARP and was a regular at these functions. I put another scotch in his hand then said something like, 'These functions need a leader. Someone strong who makes it to every meeting.' Boom! I get a slap on the back and he tells me that it's a capital idea and that he makes it to every such meeting around the country. Says they have one almost every month. Sometimes in a bar, sometimes at a golf resort, once they even managed to hold one with full bar service in a Roman Catholic Church!"

Toman's eyebrows arched in surprise. This was not quite the conversation he'd expected, but he had to admit he was intrigued. So he remained silent and waited for his friend to continue.

"It's unbelievable, T. Grown men, and even a few women, coordinate schedules, rent out space, get dressed up, pay for cabs and parking...all to discuss America's money and the most effective strategies for securing more of it. They have hyper-accurate insight into every member of Congress and the senate. Each member knows every loose-stringed purse intimately and has the inside track on who controls access. This guy likes to golf, that guy hates his family so just send them all to Disney World for two weeks... It was unreal. And as the night progressed and the wine flowed, the lips in the room loosened. This woman's Swedish massage therapist is in the country illegally and she wants a favor from immigration. This guy has a thing for authentic Cuban cigars. This guy wants the Pope to forgive him for his pedophiliac transgressions! You wouldn't believe the shameless litany of corruption and immorality. It was like being a third ear in confession."

Toman watched his friend, who was still shaking his head in disbelief. "You felt disgusted?" he inquired.

"Hell yes!" Joust said enthusiastically.

"Couldn't believe what you were hearing, right?"

"I was stunned, T," Joust admitted, "Absolutely floored."

"And this went on for a while?"

Joust hesitated, eyeing his friend cautiously. "Yes," he said cautiously.

"You were immersed in scum, swimming in America's blood, beset on all sides by soulless merchants," Toman suggested.

This time Joust only nodded slowly, his brow furrowed skeptically.

"And yet you never reached for the ladder?"

"What do you mean?" Joust said, a hint of defensiveness in his voice.

Behind Toman's sardonic grin was a look that said "you know precisely what I mean."

"Relax, Joust," Toman said lightly, "You were mesmerized by it – like a scientist studying a deadly strain of polio. Part of you wants to throw acid on it and watch it dissolve, to make sure mankind is safe. While the other, stronger part of you can't help but watch it in rapt fascination. Occupational hazard I suppose." Toman sat back and took a drink of the dark beer, his eyes never leaving his friend's. No doubt the gears were turning.

After half a minute Joust's posture relaxed a degree. "I suppose that's true," he said reluctantly. "After the first few things I heard, I kept thinking of the guns and ammo in my car. I even started calculating a blitz. How many people, how many shots, the chaos after the first shot, exits, building security, even whether or not I would try to run. You know, go Godfather on them." Joust stopped and took a few swallows from his glass. Setting down the mug, he sighed deeply and, looking up at the ceiling added quietly, "I just couldn't leave."

To Toman it sounded like his friend was now talking to himself, reengaging his mindset during the lobbyist meeting. "Never even reached for the ladder," Toman offered.

Joust shook his head. "And then," Joust said, his expression puzzled, "in the middle of my incredulity, I started wondering about their parents."

"Their parents?" Toman echoed.

"Yeah," Joust said, lacing his fingers behind his head. His attention seemed focused on something distant, but he kept talking. "I wondered where they had gone so wrong. Excessive physical punishment, sexual abuse, impartial neglect, performance obsessions, residual psychological trauma transfer…" his voice trailed off, then he added, "or a cocktail containing multiple ingredients followed by a standard-issue anxiety chaser. It just…" he began, but stopped when the waitress returned with their orders.

After she'd gone, Joust shook his head and looked at Toman. "I just wondered how people could sink to such a point. Where the line between right and wrong gets so blurred and twisted."

"Where morality is abandoned altogether?" Toman offered.

"No," Joust said shaking his head, "Not exactly. Morality as you and I define it is almost completely gone. In its stead a new, contorted morality takes root. It's hard to define, but I could detect it when they spoke. There was a hidden sense of forced validation slithering just beneath the surface. Like they had somehow convinced themselves that what they were doing was in some warped way justified – perhaps even patriotic. Maybe even vital to their very survival. It was bizarre." Joust looked at Toman, then added with a guilty grin, "And yes, sickeningly fascinating."

Toman smiled. "I think you've stumbled onto something that *The Aenamaia* has never really defined," he said, putting a cut of tender meat into his mouth. Chewing, he clarified, "the source of attraction."

He finished chewing, allowing himself a few seconds to savor the taste. "Damn, this is really good," he thought. An odd image flashed into his mind. It was a classroom. His classroom. It was big. Three monstrous chalkboards behind him. Between him and the class of eager graduate history students was a large, square work table, like the kind used in science classes. Six by six, shiny black top, with cabinets all around its base. Stadium seating, but only a hundred seats. Best to keep it intimate. On top of the table was a full glass of Guinness and a plate heaped with tender, grilled ribeye – two of the best things he could imagine in one magnificent place, available at the same moment. The odd image made him smile.

"What?" Joust asked curiously.

Toman smiled sheepishly, embarrassed at being caught daydreaming at such a moment. "Sorry, just dreaming about my next life."

Joust smiled broadly and dug into his food.

"No," Toman continued hastily, "what I meant was the attraction. What is it about this type of corruption that attracts people and keeps them there? Have they lost all morality and decency when they start looking for it or does it fall away once the prize is found? Is it a kind of mental gluttony? An addiction? Certainly the money helps facilitate any rationalization necessary, but I think the hole goes deeper than that."

"Power?" Joust offered.

Toman nodded slowly, his mind trying to wrangle a better term.

"Yeah, but not in the traditional sense. It isn't the power over people or even resources." He took another drink of beer. His eyes narrowed as the elusive answer came into focus. After a long moment he took a thoughtful breath and exhaled. "I think," he started slowly, his fingers playing absently with his chin, "it has something to do with the fight, the challenge. Perhaps you're right and it is in response to some childhood trauma. Whatever the cause, I think they're attracted by the opportunity to talk and finagle their way into the vault instead of using dynamite. Instead of robbing the bank, they convince the bank president to just hand over the cash. But there's more to it than that," his voice grew more enthusiastic.

"I think you're right. There is a substituted morality lurking there, though it's grossly disfigured. That, and anything residual from childhood provides the justification. But ultimately, it's the game that entices them and becomes the addictive drug. These people thrive on beating each other to the punch and on using whatever tactics are necessary to secure the prize. They're meticulous and obsessive in their search for cracks, microscopic holes to be widened, and places where the membrane is too thin to prevent entry. Any weakness that can be exploited to further their cause."

"They're like children mapping their parents," Joust said simply, throwing a French fry into his mouth.

"What?" Toman asked, breaking his chain of thought.

"At a very young age, children have sufficient cognitive skills to understand that their parents are the primary providers for their needs, right? So, once this is understood, they immediately begin to analyze which parent provides which benefits, while at the same time cross-referencing the performance record of past actions. Cause and effect. In other words, what did the child do that resulted in a benefit, such as food or being held. And which parent provides which benefits and how often. Soon a picture begins to form and the child first grasps causality. What action must they take with each parent to get what they want? As time goes on, children and then teenagers, become extremely adept at this.

"Ask any siblings about their parents. Chances are they will both provide the same tactical approach for getting what they want. Which parent is the best bet for achieving a particular goal. Hell, when I was young I did it. My sister and I hated going to the grocery store with Mom, because she kept the purse strings pulled tight. However, on the rare occasion when Dad went to the store, we ran for the car because we knew Dad was much looser with the spending. But when it came to skipping out on violin lessons, Mom had more exits in her pocket. It's the same as the lobbyists. You map out your target, learn everything you can about the gatekeeper, gather your resources, and attack the weakest spot. Just like kids."

Toman nodded. "Makes sense. Could be where the corruption starts," he mused. "Increasing levels of success in gaining benefits, mixed in with any childhood resentments would make for a powerful combination. The sense of entitlement swells and fuels an ever-growing desire for more and more rewards. The process perpetually repeats."

"Until I show up," Joust said seriously.

Toman looked up. "That's what we're here to do, Joust," he said earnestly.

Joust sighed deeply. "I know," he breathed, "I know. I just…" his voice trailed off. "I lost focus. The more I listened, the more I convinced myself the world would be a better place if all these damaged people vanished."

"You might very well be right," Toman said simply. The comment arrested Joust's attention. "But," Toman warned, "in order to know for sure, we have to do our due diligence. That's where you strayed."

"I know," Joust said, his voice full of guilt and frustration.

"Joust," Toman said empathetically, "the only reason any of us agreed to take part in this was because we believed in the vetting process. Every single one of us has, many times, wanted to play judge, jury, and executioner all in a matter of seconds. And each time our hands were stayed by our sense of right and wrong and the premise of true and fair justice. Only when the reach of the law fails can we intervene and still sleep at night.

"The ones on your list had crossed the proverbial line in the sand and were never coming back. The damage they did was irreparable and had cost people their livelihoods, careers, reputations, and even some lives.

They would never quit. No one above them could be coerced into firing them because they were profitable. They were a cancer that, if left unchecked, would metastasize and eventually kill the body. But," he added pointedly, "until we identified them as an untreatable cancer, we could not operate."

Joust thought about what Toman said for a moment, then nodded solemnly.

"You're right, T. I know you're right. But what do we do with the rest of them?" he said pleadingly. "I mean, how long before they become inoperable? Should they be allowed to spread?"

"Remember, Joust, the goal is not only to remove the tumors, but to send a message to those who have yet to cross the line; the ones who still have a choice. The ultimate goal of every organism, regardless of the way it achieves it, is survival. If the message is loud enough, I think they'll back off. After that it's up to them what to do with their lives. And if they choose wrong, if they cross the line..." Toman spread his hands and left the statement hanging.

Curiosity and puzzlement spread across Joust's face as something seemed to occur to him for the first time. "Will we answer the call again?" he asked earnestly.

Toman stared back at his friend, but did not speak. The future was an abstract destination – one they all hoped to visit, but avoided considering in depth. The nature of their mission precluded any serious future planning efforts. Like a soldier who knows he or she is going to the front of the line. The life beyond the battle must remain blurry in order that the present remain in sharp focus.

"I don't know the answer to that," Toman said finally. "What we're doing is unprecedented in history. One group is fighting another on grounds that have never known this kind of battle. We're fighting people who send others to do the fighting for them, or who wage their war through words, money and the media. They fight for personal gains and influence. Our gains, if we are successful, will be shared by everyone. Many will publicly disagree with our course of action, but I suspect in their own minds many will experience a small measure of relief – even hope – for a world suddenly and unexpectedly rid of a few bad seeds. At least that's what I'm hoping for."

Toman looked at Joust. Seeing that the answer did not satisfy, he added, "My guess is no. If others rush in to supplant those we've extracted, that will mean our message was not widely received or understood and that our experiment has failed. While I can't speak for anyone but myself, if I live through this to actually have a life..." Toman paused, staring off into the distance towards his filmy, blurry future. "I won't be back, Joust. I don't think any of us should come back. We're already prepared to spend the rest of our lives trying to live with what we've done. Our philosophy and conviction is solid now, but that doesn't mean we won't all question both from time to time. No, when this is over, it should remain that way."

Joust raised his glass and said, "Then let's hope the message is loud and clear!"

Toman smiled broadly and raised his glass, "To the cause."

"To the cause," Joust echoed. Glasses clinked and both men drank. Each man noticed at that moment that the beer tasted a smidgeon better than it had a few minutes ago.

"Perhaps making peace with reality, staring it down, liberated more than the mind and soul," Toman thought. Another interesting concept he'd have to research someday. It was then that another thought unexpectedly entered his mind. "By the way," Toman asked with a grin, "what phone number did you list on your business card?"

"Mark Foley's personal cell phone," Joust said sheepishly.

"Congressman Foley? 'Capital Hill Male Pages Foley?"

Joust nodded, still grinning. "It was a toss-up between his cell and Larry Craig's. I flipped a coin."

Toman raised his hands and said with a laugh, "I know where this is going. Whether *heads* or *tails*, I don't want to hear your joke about what it was and why it pointed to Foley. I just ate."

"There's nothing written that says even the most difficult work can't have a few humorous moments," Joust said, feigning indignity.

"No, my friend, there isn't," Toman said smiling. "In fact, without our sense of humor bolstering us, I doubt any of this would be possible."

"'Let not the world perish lest we lose our sense of humor,'" Joust said.

"I'll be sure and tell Gray you quoted him," Toman said lightly, "Lest he not perish you himself."

"Anything to get back on his good side," Joust said wide-eyed. "Speaking of that," he added, "what's our next step?"

Toman considered the question. "Simple. I talk to Gray, you talk to Gray, and we both get ready for our next assignment. Tell him exactly what happened and that your doubts have been permanently allayed. You're back on the team, focused and ready to do what it takes to see this thing through. He's the smartest of all of us – he'll know you mean it."

"That's been the hardest part of this."

"What?"

"Knowing I'd let him down. And wondering why that didn't occur to me *before* I acted."

"Joust, we all do things we regret. Rash actions are part of human nature. If our brains always triumphed over our emotions, the world would be a peaceful place. Probably pretty boring too," Toman smiled. "Impulses and impatience are part of life. Everyone is prone to them. Even Gray."

Joust looked surprised and interested, as Toman knew he would be.

"You know the strange picture he has hanging in his office on that narrow wall behind his desk?"

"The square one?"

Toman nodded.

"The one of the guy being punched in slow motion? With his face all bunched up in front of a large fist?"

Toman nodded again.

"What about it?"

"There's quite a bit of art in Gray's office, right?"

"Yeah," Joust said, taking a bite of his neglected dinner. "Every wall is covered with art. Mostly nature photography and digital abstracts, if I recall. Place is like a museum."

"Right," Toman confirmed, "So didn't it ever strike you as odd that he would choose to put such an unusual picture behind his desk, on a narrow section of wall where it looks out of place?"

Joust shrugged. "I suppose."

"That picture went up in early November 2004 for two reasons. As a constant reminder that George Bush had been falsely re-elected – and to cover up the grapefruit-sized hole in the wall Gray's fist had made after the re-election was announced."

Joust gaped at him and nodded slowly.

"When you talk to him...*tonight*," Toman said, stressing the word, "and you're explaining what happened, just tell him you punched a hole in the wall. Then ask him to take down the picture. Hole's a beauty."

"Why'd he show you?" Joust asked. "...and when?"

Toman considered the question for a few seconds. "Because I made a mistake," Toman said reflectively, idly fingering his glass. Before Joust could reply, he held up his hand, "Another time, J. Another time."

"On a different note, I want to know about this," Toman said stroking his bare chin. When Joust looked puzzled, he added, "Goatees. General Payte. There's a history here I believe is relevant to *The Aenamaia* and what we're doing. That's my theory, and I need to know if I'm right."

Joust stared hard back at his friend, but did not speak. Toman could practically see the gears and sprockets in his friend's mind turning and grinding. "Mistake number one," Toman thought. Had he been thinking critically, Joust would've realized his delay in answering, coupled with the dour expression he now bore, combined to confirm Toman's suspicions. Otherwise known as a dead giveaway. Perhaps he was aware of his mistake. If so, the razor's edge he was straddling would've already come into sharp relief. Having answered in the affirmative with his silence, he now had to decide how to respond. Toman already alluded to a connection between the general and Joust. He would no doubt realize the general had provided that information, though he'd have no way of knowing how many details were proffered by the good general.

After several minutes, Joust looked him in the eyes and said, "You don't have to worry about me, Toman. There is a history here, and yes, the general continues to be an occasional mentor. But I'm not a good dog that obediently follows anyone when it doesn't make sense."

"Mistake two?" Toman wondered, then asked, "When what doesn't make sense?"

"I think these questions should be answered by the general personally," Joust suggested. "Anything I could offer would be speculation.

However, I can say with some confidence there are solid reasons why the general has never formally joined *The Aenamaia*."

"What do you mean by that?" Toman asked.

"Come on, Toman," Joust said. "You know Gray was reluctant to take the leadership role. He never wanted it because he wasn't sure he was the best fit. Wouldn't General Payte be a more appropriate choice?"

Toman mulled over the point. What Joust said about Gray was true – he'd been okay to organize early on, but when it came to running the game, he'd actively searched for someone else to call the shots. Toman had always thought it was because Gray wanted to be in the field instead of watching from the sidelines. Now he wasn't so sure.

Toman looked at his friend and asked, "Should we be concerned about Payte?"

Joust considered the question. "The general may agree on the final destination, but the course he charts to get there will likely be very different from ours."

"But will it conflict with ours? Are our people in any danger?"

"Not from the general," Joust said confidently. "No. He's a man of honor and integrity. Even if his agenda differs from ours, he would never knowingly put any of us in harm's way."

Toman nodded. This was something he would need to bring up with Gray – and soon.

Joust was about to say something else when the waitress arrived with a cordless phone in her hand. "Mr. Kaparich? There's a telephone call for you." There was nothing in the young woman's voice or expression that suggested this was anything out of the ordinary. Toman knew Ebb's had twenty-plus phone lines running throughout the restaurant. It was likely a necessity given the regular clientele. Some business was still best conducted on someone else's landline.

Regardless, the sight of phones in restaurants still seemed odd to him. Neither he nor Joust had ever received a call here. Mostly because no one in *The Aenamaia* would know what name to ask for. Toman saw Osiro's hand in this. He shook his head and accepted the phone. The waitress left hastily, probably the modus operandi when a patron received a call on the house phone.

"Yes," Toman said putting the phone to his ear.

"When you and your sidekick are finished, *Mr. Kaparich*," Gray said, "We have work to do here. I can expect to see you both soon?"

"Yes," Toman answered with a grin, "give us an hour."

"An hour it is. Now eat your ribeye – it's getting cold."

Toman fought the urge to look around for a camera. If there happened to be one, he wouldn't give Osiro the satisfaction of seeing him surprised twice in the same day.

"Yes, sir," he said.

"*Sir!*" Gray said with disdain and hung up. He hated being called "sir." Toman wasn't sure if his contempt for the word was military in origin or if it just made him feel old. What mattered was that even the collected and stoic Gray could be irked once in a while.

"Dad?" Joust asked casually.

Toman nodded.

"Well," Joust said optimistically, "with us both going, and you having just called him 'sir,' I just might live to see another day, after all."

Toman smiled. "You just might, Joust. You just might."

Chapter 11

Ashgabat, Turkmenistan

The afternoon sun was halfway down on the horizon when Karl Rove strolled casually out of the U.S. Embassy building. Something in the air suggested it had been an unusually hot day. A heavy, nameless scent hung in the air. A thin shimmer still clung to the asphalt – a strange musty dryness born on a light breeze. Somehow, perhaps subconsciously, Rove sensed what the day had been like while he'd been busy within the dry air-conditioned walls of the embassy. But the weather was irrelevant. There were far more pressing matters on his mind now.

The traffic on the 1984 Road, formerly known as Pushkin Street, moved steadily. Over half of the vehicles, mostly older models, ran with the headlights turned on, while the more stubborn drivers waited for the sun to disappear below the horizon. Rove's mind was a maelstrom of thoughts, ideas, plans, and checklists. He pushed it all aside for a moment – an invaluable skill he'd developed in the first year of Bush's presidency.

With the storm tucked away in a quiet corner, he stood for a moment and took in the scene. There was an odd irony in motion here, one that he himself had created, and he wanted to soak it all in. Cars, pedestrians, even a few men on bicycles were all vying for position on the road. Every person was headed somewhere – each driven by a specific purpose. Most were probably going through the motions required to carve out a living for themselves, probably a meager one by western standards. Many surely had families – hungry, demanding mouths to feed. Mouths that cared little how their sustenance had been obtained. "The providers," he thought as he watched pedestrians, drivers and men on bicycles moving about.

With the national unemployment still well above fifty percent, and a poverty level to match, there could be little doubt that desperate necessity bred a substantial amount of morally flexible ingenuity and creativity. Life feeds on life, feeds on life. Shady deals were common at every level of society – perpetuating an old and often ruthless cycle. Thousands and thousands of dollars worth of Manat bills flowing from one dirty hand to the next. "Economic stimulation," he thought with a wry smile, "desert style."

Rove stared across 1984 at the buildings, side streets, shadowed corners and narrow alleys. In his mind he could picture nervous handshakes exchanged between distrusting strangers huddled in dim corners and shaded alcoves, each man looking to and fro for curious onlookers or police. The former would usually scurry away in fear, while the latter could wind up costing both men what little profit was built into the transaction for themselves. Though Turkmen was the most widely spoken language in Ashgabat, a sharp and alert ear could also pick out deals being negotiated in Russian, Persian, Pashto, and Uzbek.

Despite being mostly covered by the Karakum Desert, this land was a crossroads. "A surrendered crossroads," Rove thought as he spotted the nation's flag. Five white stars above a white crescent moon rested top-center, surrounded by a sickly shade of green. To the left was a column of Soviet red containing five geometric designs – a few of which reminded Rove of southwestern art in the U.S. It was a lackluster flag to say the least, though that in and of itself was symbolic of this sad country. Sad for most, but a land of great opportunity for one with vision.

Opportunity, indeed. The irony was acute, and one he could barely keep contained. Here he stood, thousands of miles from his own country, in the only seat of power in this primitive and desolate wasteland. No press or media, no bleeding-heart liberals, and no watchdog groups vying for a split second in the limelight. Here he stood in the open air in front of a government building in a country run by a government that was less organized than FEMA, where practically every official's carefully concealed support was for sale. Where Americans were distrusted, foreign deals were difficult to negotiate, and where glad-handing only worked when your palm was solidly green. Business was tough here for most, nearly impossible for many, but quite lucrative for a visionary few. "Yes," he mused, "the irony was delicious." Standing tall in the capitol city, he was solid. Unnoticed. Anonymous. And on his way to becoming much wealthier than he'd been this morning. "'Third World Naiveté' should be in the thesaurus under 'opportunity,'" he thought with a chuckle.

With newfound excitement and anticipation tingling in his belly, Rove walked to the curb, pulled a wad of Manat bills from his pocket and hailed a taxi. Within moments, a pale green Russian Lada Riva came barreling up to the curb and stopped with a short chirp of the tires. Normally he would be irritated at such an open display of desperation, but today he didn't care. The driver stepped out, but Rove waved him back into the cab and opened the rear passenger door himself. Having gained an extra thirty pounds in the last few months, he'd grown accustomed to unbuttoning his blazer before lowering himself into the back seat of a car.

"Sheraton Grand," he said, adding, "*agyz beklemek*," which meant "fast" in Turkmen. He'd gotten into the habit of using this term almost everywhere he went. The result was usually a startled local jumping to attention and moving frantically to comply. The driver, no doubt realizing his tip may depend on his expediency, stepped hard on the gas and the car leapt into traffic.

A newspaper on the floor of the cab caught his attention. With some effort he leaned over and reached. The tips of his chubby fingers pinched the edge of the paper. A low groan escaped his lips as he righted himself and straightened out the paper. The irritation he felt at being mildly winded after such a simple task disappeared when he saw the incredulous, angry face of former President George W. Bush. The writing was in Turkmen, but Rove had a good idea of what it said. He was aware of the charges and imminent trial of his former employer.

Huddled behind the former President were two high-priced attorneys, two long-time aids, reporters reaching in with microphones, and three unusually idle Secret Service agents. The droll, disinterested faces of the agents contrasted sharply with the former President's, whose red face looked as frustrated and clueless as Rove could ever recall having seen it. Apparently the new guy's reigns were too loose. Rove sighed. How many times had he told the former President to always keep his emotions in check when the press was around, no matter the circumstances? Every day the missing evidence for WMDs hit the networks, he would have to coach Bush on how to react, what to say, how to say it, which reporters to call on during questioning, and fail-safe answers he could use if he got confused. It was like rehearsing for a play when the lead actor couldn't remember his lines and could not be trusted to improvise.

On and on it went. For almost seven years. And still Bush had been unable to contain the clueless redneck within. In the beginning, Rove had seen Bush as an outhouse turned Sistine Chapel. A lifetime under-achiever with a powerful and wealthy father intent on doing whatever was necessary to maintain the Bush legacy in U.S. politics. But despite daddy's best efforts, his eldest son not only didn't get first place at the races, he failed to show up altogether. And though Rove had worked miracles with the simple dolt, it hadn't been enough. The influence and personal agendas of the other players seeped through easily, clouding the former President's already questionable judgment and taking the country in all the wrong directions. True, an impressive number of Republican supporters had prospered during Bush's eight years in office, though none so much as those in the oil and defense industries. But now that Bush was out of office, those who owed him the most were the ones most adept at disappearing behind one of many convenient cloaks.

Rove shook his head and tossed the paper aside. He too had found a smart cloak to hide behind. One that, if properly played, might even garnish him a few patriotic points. Not to mention nine glorious figures in his Cayman account. He'd stashed some funds in offshore accounts just prior to the 2012 Presidential election as a backup should the election go awry – which it did. In fact, it had been something of a personal disaster for him. Newspaper and magazine articles, blogs, Twitter and Facebook had all painted him as a supreme and expensive failure for the Republican Party. Pirated videos of his incredulous reaction to the election results on Fox News had garnered over five million views on YouTube alone. The bullshit media he could handle. But it was his quiet and unofficial ban-ishment from the Republican power circles that had been the last straw. After years of hard work and history-altering political victories, he'd been brazenly thrown to the curb. And all because the rest of the spineless party hadn't carried its weight and followed his directions during the last leg of the campaign. Yet for some reason the decision had been made to label him as the fall guy for all of their failures. "Well," he thought, "we'll see who is mired in political quicksand and liberal sludge and who is crisscrossing the world with seven figures in their bank account. My recent past may be smeared with red, but my future will be awash in green."

Rove smiled broadly at the thought of his newfound retirement plan. And all of it thanks to an abundant odorless gas, the increasing world demand for it, and the pure naiveté of the people who relied on it. Russia, Europe, China and the rest of Central Asia were all buying more and more natural gas every month. Demand was greatest for the northern countries in the throes of an unusually cold winter. Turkmenistan relied heavily on the export of natural gas for its revenues, but had been unable to meet demand or maximize production due to a number of regulatory, political, and logistic roadblocks. Normally, high demand and low supply would result in higher prices and more control over margins. However, failing economies and tighter belts had resulted in some creative export strategies by the United States, Mexico, and South America. Saudi Arabia was also exporting its natural gas, though internal political strife had caused many countries in need to purchase from more reliable and stable nations at a slightly higher price. If these trends continued, Turkmenistan could be slowly nudged out of the game. That was where he came in.

Through a patchwork of contacts, favors called in, greased wheels and a little embellishment, he had managed to orchestrate a deal which could propel Turkmenistan to the top of the world's natural gas market. The elements of fast shipping across the Caspian by a Norwegian shipper, new pipelines built across Georgia by Japanese subcontractors to ports on the Black Sea, doubled production via the latest mining techniques pioneered by an American start-up, precisely timed currency exchanges via two discreet German banks, and – most importantly – strategically planted rumors of U.N. embargoes on Mexico and South America would make all the difference. Rove knew from past successes that rumors alone could move mountains. Perception across political boundaries was a complex and highly volatile tool. All he needed was to give Turkmenistan a small window of opportunity and a polished world image. From there, the task would be simple. And every step of the way, he would be there to supervise, coordinate, and collect his just rewards. "Yes," he thought, staring blankly out of the dirty taxi window, "money could indeed be cultivated from sand, if one knew where to plant the seeds."

But there were still a great many details to be worked out, calls to be made. The sooner he got back to his hotel room and got started, the better. The first task would be to contact his broker in New York. There were enormous gains to be had in several key markets and time was indeed money. Additionally, the more diversified his allocations, the less likely it would be that he would garner any unwanted attention – media or otherwise. With all that was happening around Bush, the last thing he wanted was to pop up again on anyone's radar. As far as the media knew he was simply out of the country pursuing the most mundane and un-newsworthy of political consulting work. To seal the deal he'd had one of his lackeys draw up a forty-page document exposing the challenges facing third world administrative organizations and discussing how Rove planned on lending a consultative hand. So basically, after brief mentions in the more obscure sections of a few newspapers, the press had all but forgotten about Karl Rove. And that was just fine with him.

Harrisburg, Pennsylvania

Joe listened as the man being interviewed concluded, "So you see, had I gone to the popular media, little or none of what I've said would've been heard. Because the truth is the last thing they want to hear or see in print. Fortunately, the truth cannot be stopped!"

"Driver, could you please turn that off," Joe requested from the back seat of the rented limousine. "The truth," he muttered derisively. "No one is interested in the truth."

"You wish," his wife said curtly. "If that were the case we'd be sipping Rum Runners back in Jupiter right now instead of heading to another damn courthouse."

A long succession of obscenities filed through his head, but he knew better than to get into this argument again. "Again," he thought sarcastically, "as if it had ever ended." Some women just never had enough. As he recalled, she was the one who had advised him to accept the CEO position in the first place. She'd said it would be good for them. Or rather good for her. He'd suspected she saw a substantial increase in their financial portfolio on top of an abundance of unencumbered free time to spend the money shopping and throwing extravagant pool parties at their home while he clawed his way through fourteen-hour days.

"I realize Pennsylvania is a far cry from Florida, but may I remind you that I'm the one serving time in prison, not you," he snapped. "As far as I can tell, your life has only improved. Lock up the man, keep the money. What more could you possibly ask for?" Were she to answer truthfully it would probably be something along the lines of, "A guarantee that the man will never get out of prison and the money will never run out."

His wife shot him a cold glance, but said nothing. Prison was the last thing he wanted to think about right now. Today he'd had a real breakfast, was back in a real suit and was being driven in a car that matched his social status. For the next few hours he would feel free again. His only immediate regret was agreeing with his attorney that having Karon with him would "play better for the press." He'd counter-argued that if she wasn't there people might suspect they weren't close, which could work in his favor when the matter of the transferred ninety million dollars was raised again. But in the end, his attorney had made a strong case that Karon should be in every photograph and attend every hearing. Joe decided the next time Karon came along she could ride with the attorney.

He pushed thoughts of prison, attorneys and his wife from his mind and focused on the interview he'd just heard concerning the recent bombings. The country's reaction to what the papers were now calling the "Tabloid Bombings" had surprised him, as well as the rest of the world. Bombs had gone off in a handful of cities, buildings had been leveled, media companies had been forced to lay off most of their workforces, and yet there was very little outcry from the public. After the attacks of 9/11 he'd thought any bombings would reset the fear alarms and drive the public into quiet complacency with whatever the sitting President suggested.

Instead, the incidents were being treated like everyday crimes. "Well, that isn't entirely true," he thought. The FBI and CIA were both involved, though by many accounts, their investigations were more perfunctory than anything else. Perhaps it was because there had been no human casualties. A few people had been hurt. Two men had even been shot, though the jury was still out as to how responsible each man was for his injury. Regardless of the details, many of the key facts surrounding the Tabloid Bombings were indisputable. Americans, or at least people who spoke perfect English, were responsible for the bombings. Every individual who had come in contact with the group responsible agreed they were Americans. And yet for reasons that were still unclear, most Americans didn't appear to be scared or even upset.

Though several media sources had compared the Tabloid Bombings to the Oklahoma bombings, the link wasn't strong enough to stick. What was even more odd was the speed with which the media shifted from its normal fear-based reporting, to an attitude analogous to a few isolated larceny or bank robbery incidents. After only two days of headlines shouting "Domestic Terrorism," "A New American Civil War?" and "American Communists," ratings showed that people weren't taking the bait. Was it numbness? Had too much stimulation finally put America in a permanent state of languid disinterest? Fortunately not, for his sake. He needed some public interest. And as of this morning, his appeals trial had garnered a lot more fanfare than the bombings.

He glanced out the window as they passed a newsstand on the corner of a busy intersection. He thought about the bombings and their affect on the culture. American's weren't outraged, but they also weren't cheering. All that had really changed was the selection at the newsstand. There were bound to be people whose insatiable greed for tabloid news would leave them feeling lost and insecure. Perhaps there would be strung out tabloid junkies begging people on the street for news of conspiracies, government cover-ups of alien abductions, four hundred pound human babies born from cows, and the spooky image of Christ that appeared to be hovering miraculously over a threesome in a cheap porno flick. "Hey mister, can you spare some dirty laundry? Celebrity gossip? Armageddon predictions? Anything will help!" The thought made him laugh aloud.

The sound caught his wife's attention. She'd been fidgeting with her perfectly manicured nails and the gold buttons of her expensive, strategically selected green business suit. Her dour expression was proof positive that nothing jovial would be permitted in this car – not if she had anything to say about it.

"Are you really going to focus our defense on Presidential conspiracy?" she said curtly. "You do understand that George is also on trial."

Even though Karon had been raised several rungs beneath those of society's upper echelons, she'd always fancied herself a true-blood member of the club. Years before, supplanting her family name of Fitzhugh with the patronymic Nacchio, she had mastered the art of advanced social interaction. She had always been confident that when money found her, magnificent doors of gold would open upon her command. And she'd be more than practiced playing her role. She'd once said, "There is no need to place history and tradition under a microscope," and she'd meant it. In her eyes, purchased class was just as good as an old-world pedigree. Once you are fluent in the language and the dance of etiquette, the rest is just detail. And in keeping with the traditions of her high society equals, everyone was referred to by their first names, even the former President of the United States.

"Joe! I asked you a question," Karon demanded.

Joe exhaled and said, "We've been over this before, Karon. Myself, my attorney, CenturyLink's attorney, and my judicial consultant have all been through this. Bush is on trial right now. His reputation is in the garbage sitting alongside his credibility. This is the best time for the stone to drop and muddy the waters. It's likely the Supreme Court will realize that the omitted testimony should've been allowed and that a retrial is in order. That will push things back another six years or so. Besides, the more Bush's name comes up, the more they'll see that there are bigger fish to fry."

"What makes you so sure he won't fire back in an attempt to muddy his own waters?" she shot back.

"So what if he does?" he said a little too defensively. "The more he spouts off about how I'm lying, the more public opinion will sway in my favor. After eight years of neglect that left the country broke, hated throughout the world, and...and just generally pissed off, anything that comes out of his mouth will sound like a lie or some kind of cover-up."

"But you were already convicted. The public thinks you're just another shit-stinking, irresponsible CEO who should have their balls handed to them," Karon sneered.

He turned and looked at his wife and shook his head. "You can take the girl out of the trailer park but you can't take the..."

"Joseph Paul Nacchio!" Karon interrupted angrily. "Don't you dare speak to me that way!"

Joe flashed a coy smile and said, "Like I said, *no one* is interested in the truth."

Karon scowled at him but said nothing. He'd seen that look hundreds of times before and knew nothing good would come from further argument so he decided to focus his attention elsewhere. At that moment it occurred to him that the armed escort from the prison was probably following close behind. The armed guards had driven him from the main compound to the front gates of the prison where they were to wait for the limousine. Nacchio remembered reading "FCI Schuylkill" printed in large black letters on three sides of the transport van. He'd been more than a little surprised his request for a limo had been authorized. Perhaps his name still carried a little weight in the outside world.

Whatever the case, he had been pleasantly surprised and grateful for the accommodation. Riding in the prison van would've been terrible. The last thing he needed to do was show up at the appeal looking guilty by association. In fact, that was precisely the argument his attorney had used to get authorization for the suit and transportation. At the time Nacchio had suggested it might be fun to have Karon ride in the prison van instead. His attorney, who had the unfortunate task of being the go-between for him and his petulant spouse, had thought the idea funny, but not practical. He'd even countered with the comment, "You just might have to ride back to Schuylkill with those same guards. No use pissing them off by sticking them with Karon." Joe chuckled and shot back with, "Who knows, might garner a little sympathy and special treatment." They'd both gotten a good laugh out of that one.

Ashgabat, Turkmenistan

The drive from the embassy to the Sheraton Grand was a short one – less than a mile, though the traffic was heavy this time of day. Occasionally

Rove finished his business early in the day and would walk the route. Today, however, was different. The sun had already set, leaving the streets dark and shadowed. Foreign countries, especially the underdeveloped ones, did not place public lighting high on the priority list. No doubt because the locals knew their way around and tourism was not yet an industry worthy of such government expenditures. Rove, though not prone to such concerns about personal safety, now felt inclined towards a higher degree of caution. Walking along the broken streets and sidewalks of Ashgabat could be a challenge when trying to see anything beyond a one with eight zeros in tow. No, millionaire power brokers did not take dark walks in primitive countries. They had far too much to lose.

Thoughts of his money sitting in other people's accounts only made him more eager to get moving on this project. Glancing through the dirty windshield, Rove noticed flashing orange lights a few hundred feet ahead. The driver slowed the vehicle and signaled to turn down a side street.

"What are you doing? The hotel is that way," Rove said, pointing down the way they had been heading.

"*Gurlush! Gurlush!*" the driver said emphatically, pointing towards the blinking orange lights. "*Garsylyk.*" The driver, seeing the confusion on Rove's face said, "Closed. No open. Fixing road."

Rove looked again. The orange lights did appear to be mounted on construction barriers, but he saw no other signs of construction – neither workers nor trucks. The driver was speaking quickly in Turkmen. Rove had no idea what the man was saying, but recognized his hand gestures. The man was signaling that they would go around the construction.

"*Biderek*," Rove muttered. It was one of the few words he'd learned from the Deputy Chief of Mission at the Embassy. "*Biderek*" meant "worthless." After several rounds of vodka and Diet Coke, the deputy chief shed his well-rehearsed PR face and confessed buried feelings of frustration and contempt towards the Turkmenistan people. The more the DC talked about the idiocy of the people, the more Turkmen adjectives he spat out. Rove, who made it a point to learn derisory language wherever he traveled, had paid attention even going so far as to write them down and review them at night before going to bed.

Knowledge of these words served multiple purposes. First and foremost, he was able to echo the DC's suppressed feelings whenever they were alone. This helped build trust and camaraderie with the man, who may come in handy in the near future. Second, he'd found utility in using such words during discussions with other embassy dignitaries. The subject matter of the discussion was irrelevant, though word selection and timing had to be precise. Use of these mildly derogatory words in carefully selected company expedited his acceptance with those who could prove vital to his success. Beyond that he simply enjoyed the variety of foreign words with which to label the people and culture – both of which were, and would forever be, beneath him.

Outside of embassy and business circles many of these words could be used to scare the local service people into action. Taxi drivers, wait staff, hotel staff, and so on. He'd even managed to drop in a "*kirli*" which meant "dirty" and a "*yabany*" which meant "wild" during his most recent encounter with a young Ashgabat prostitute. It was doubtful the native words conveyed the same meaning as they would in the West. Upon hearing "*kirli,*" the young girl might easily think he was commenting on the drab hotel room she'd taken him to. To a Turkmenistan woman "*yabany*" probably referred more to the jungle or animal kingdom rather than to a type of lustful behavior. Nevertheless, his use of the language in this context had served to intensify his excitement, to which the young girl immediately reacted. With poverty on the rise, the world's oldest profession was seeing record numbers of talented and open-minded young ladies enter the country's largest city markets – one of the few local enterprises he was more than happy to support.

Images of the attractive young girl lingered in his mind as he caught sight of a small pod of scantily clad prospects lingering next to what appeared to be a convenience store. Rove's eyes scanned and assessed each female quickly. "Sumptuous," he thought. "Dirty and decadent."

With his future earnings still resting comfortably in the back of his mind, it occurred to him that he hadn't even thought of how to celebrate the day's successes. What he had just seen would make for a nice start. Younger this time though. An open slate on which to carve his desires. What beautiful, young, female amateur wouldn't welcome a lesson in western-style debauchery? Rove's mind began sending a barrage of salacious imagery to his visual cortex. The reaction in his body was immediate. Salivation, a thin layer of sweat on his balding forehead, heavier and more deliberate breathing, and a tingling in his groin caused by the downward rush of blood. In his mind he could see her knocking nervously on his hotel room door. But wait? She had a friend with her. Of course! A threesome. Two young, inexperienced Turkmen girls, a lot of champagne, and his little box of ever-last pills. A celebration indeed.

The visual list of nefarious sexual escapades building in his mind was cut short when the cab bounced unexpectedly. Rove looked out the window and saw that they had left the paved road and were now driving on concrete. He took a quick look around, hoping to see the lights of the hotel, but only saw what looked like a few abandoned warehouses and factories.

"Where in the hell are we?" Rove barked through the small square window that had been hastily cut and removed from the thick plastic barrier. This time there was no reply from the driver.

"Did you hear me?" he tried again, this time banging his fist on the plastic. "Where in the hell are you taking me? If you think I'm going to pay you one Manat for this, you're..."

He was abruptly cut off when the driver slammed hard on the brakes. The rapid deceleration caused him to crash face first into the barrier. The cab came to a sudden halt, the violent last lurch of the vehicle throwing him back into the rear of the vehicle. Though dazed and barely conscious, he heard the opening of a door and what sounded like running footsteps that faded quickly.

Lying still, he tried desperately to think. What had just happened? Where was he? Clarity came slowly, accompanied by a throbbing pain that seemed to run throughout his body. "Help," he thought wearily. Half expecting to hear the normally annoying sound of sirens, he lay still. Surely someone would come for him. After a few moments devoid of sirens or any other sounds, he decided he'd better move. Carefully Rove stretched out his hands until they found purchase. With great effort, he gradually righted himself, exhaling a deep breath from the effort. Such a simple motion had taxed what little strength he had. And for the first time in months, he could actually feel the extra weight of his stomach and arms. Too many four-course dinners and an excess of desserts and scotches. A wave of loathing and self-contempt washed over him, but he chose to ignore it and instead focused on the current situation. He would first get his head clear, determine his next move, and then figure out a way to locate the driver and wring his skinny *biderek* neck.

Rove became aware of something warm running down his face and neck. The first word that entered his mind was gasoline, followed immediately by a surge of adrenaline flowing through his blood. Inhaling deeply and smelling nothing unusual, he sighed and relaxed a tad. It only took a few seconds before the second word hit his consciousness. Blood. Again the adrenaline hit and his eyes shot open. The driver's side door was ajar and the brightness of the dome light caught him off guard. The pain in his eyelids and temple was acute, but remained buried beneath the commanding power of pure panic. Holding his breath, he carefully reached up and pressed a palm to his plump cheek. A thick, warm liquid cascaded over his hand like water over a log. He pulled his hand away and slowly brought it into view. He stared in horror at the glistening red liquid covering his chubby hand. His mind searched for a point of pain that would indicate the source of his injury, but thus far the adrenaline and panic were keeping everything numb. But just as he reached his bloody hand to his head, bright lights from straight ahead arrested his attention. They were headlights. Someone was coming for him.

Fleeting hopes of rescue were supplanted by a new wave of fear as he realized the vehicle was speeding towards him. Keeping his eyes glued to the headlights, Rove moved frantically towards the door. Leaning over and reaching out, his hands searched anxiously for the door handle. The lights had nearly reached him. As his hands located the door handle, a Hollywood image of a man diving from a vehicle just before the fatal impact flashed in his mind. He felt a glimmer of hope and pulled the door handle, ready to leap from the cab, but nothing happened. Whipping his head around, he stared wild-eyed at the handle, willing it to open the door. He tried again and again. Nothing. The door was locked.

"Biderek!" he cried, realizing the driver must've locked the door. Rove reached up to pull the lock up when the roar of an engine forced him to turn and look. An instant later the vehicles collided. A deafening explosion burst through his ears. Metal being forcefully reshaped, headlights shattering, a radiator bursting, a windshield fracturing, cheap plastic in

the engine snapping. The cacophonous blast of sound reached his ears a split second before his body was again thrown violently forward against the seat and what remained of the plastic barrier. This time Rove managed to bring his arms up in time to protect his face. The extra surface area and the cushion afforded by his jacket sleeves were enough to keep him from shattering the plastic, though the force of the collision battered his already weak body. The second impact wave again threw him violently into the rear corner of the cab, his body finally landing sideways on the back seat.

What little consciousness was available to him was occupied with the loud ringing in his ears and the increasing number of pain signals rushing into his brain. Even before he'd come to rest on the seat, his body's natural shock response took control of his muscles, putting him in a temporary state of paralysis. Though his autonomic nervous system kept him breathing, little else seemed to work, save for the panic.

After what seemed like an eternity, muscle control was returned to him, along with intense, aching pain. Everything he could feel felt like it was on fire. Rove groaned aloud, and immediately regretted doing so. Through the rushing and ringing noises in his ears he heard footsteps on the concrete and men's voices. Before he could think of what to do, the rear passenger door was ripped open and a bright light shone in his eyes. He squinted and tried to raise a hand to block the light, but found his muscles wouldn't respond.

Two strong hands wearing black leather gloves reached in, grabbed onto his blazer and rolled him onto his back. Rove shrieked involuntarily as a hot pain radiated out from his left shoulder. Instinctively he tried to reach out and touch the injury with his other hand, but found he was having trouble moving his right arm. Concentrating, he tried to will his right arm to move, but immediately stopped when another surge of pain from his injured shoulder shot out. He winced and reluctantly relaxed his body. His breathing came in short spurts, and seemed to fall in between the crashing waves of pain.

A moment later the gloved hands took hold in his armpits like powerful hooks. The light was retracted and in one swift motion, his heavy body was pulled from the vehicle. Another scream of pain escaped his lips, but was cut short when he landed with a grunt on the hard concrete.

He moaned, then coughed. Tears of pain filled his eyes. But on top of the pain was something else: anger. "Someone will die for this," he thought darkly. "Nobody can do this to me and get away with it. Who would dare do this to me?" At that moment he realized these men must not realize who he was or where he was from. Perhaps this was some kind of ethnic hit and they'd been expecting a Turkmen government employee or wealthy businessman.

Taking a short breath he screamed, "I'm an American! I'm a goddamn American!"

Without warning a large fist came out of nowhere and slammed into his cheek, sending his head reeling. The pain came swiftly, followed immediately by more tears. There was a piercing sting around and behind his left eye, a throbbing on the left side of his face, and a bitter, salty taste in his mouth. He tried to throw up his hands, but they were being held. He opened his mouth to protest and managed to scream "Goddammit, I'm..." before he quickly closed it an instant before another blow landed on the same cheek. His head was pounding and it sounded like he was surrounded by rushing water or high winds – he couldn't be sure which. In fact, he was having trouble forming and holding onto a single thought. Words slowly pooled in his head, trying to aggregate like small islands of mercury. But before a full sentence could form, the pain returned, abruptly scattering every last letter into the oblivion beyond the crushing weight of agony.

"We know who you are, Mr. Rove," a man's voice said calmly. Through the fog, the words came slowly. Despite the pain, he experienced surprise at hearing English. Good English. He'd even detected a buried southern accent. A Texan? "In fact, you're just the gentleman we were looking for. How lucky for us that our paths should cross. Fortuitous, wouldn't you say?" Rove was having trouble focusing his eyes, so he wasn't sure which man was the speaker. But he was confident the accent was indeed Texan.

"Oh, not another Texan," he thought wearily as images of the grinning former President appeared in his mind. At least the last one he'd known had made it a point of going AWOL rather than serving in the military. The speaker on the other hand, had obviously chosen to go in the opposite direction. Straight to mercenary.

One man, the Texan he guessed, stood hovering over him. Rove noticed his face was painted with green and black in camouflage patterns reminiscent of puzzle pieces. He wore a black beret similar to that of the Special Forces men Bush Sr. and Bush Jr. had used in Afghanistan, Iraq, and Kuwait. On several occasions, Rove had eagerly accompanied G.W. Bush to several east coast bases. He'd even been allowed to accompany the President on a secret visit to Guantanamo. Tactical interrogation and information extraction fascinated him. He jumped at every opportunity to witness the various methods and processes employed. During the course of his observations, he'd seen plenty of men like this. Disconnected and robotic. And yet there was power and suppressed violence behind their eyes that had once excited and invigorated him. Looking up at those same ominous dark eyes now, though, he felt only fear and dread.

The Texan looked down at him and shaking his head said, "'To bottomless perdition, there to dwell. In adamantine chains and penal fire.'"

He knelt down and said casually, "John Milton said that. He too was a civil servant." The large man tilted his head slightly as if examining Rove and suggested, "A man could be forgiven for believing he wrote that just for men like you." The Texan flashed a menacing smile that sent a new jolt of dread through Rove's mind. The man's white teeth stood out starkly behind shadowed black and green lips.

"You finished stroking the mark's nuts, Max?" a disembodied voice asked contemptuously.

"Find a quiet and self-deprecating way to fuck off, Reggie," the Texan said calmly. Rove was sure he was the same brooding man hovering over him. A moment later the crouching man stood, thick arms folded tightly across his chest, still staring down at his helpless catch. Rove's lips parted, as if to utter a plea, but only quiet, shallow breaths came out.

"Let's get this soiree started," the Texan ordered.

"Pin him!" another strong male voice commanded.

In an instant several strong arms had taken hold of Rove's arms and legs. Before he could manage a weak protest, his shirt was ripped open, exposing his bare, pale white chest. Instinctively he tried to scream for help, but was cut short when a bright blue spark appeared out of nowhere and was pressed into his chest. The moment the small arc of lightning made contact with his skin, Rove felt five hundred Kv's of electricity explode through his body. It was as if the electricity frantically searched every square millimeter of his body in vain looking for a way to escape the wet, fleshy vessel, angrily punishing his flesh and nerves with white-hot razors at every dead end. An involuntary squeal escaped his lips and reverberated in his ears. A new torrent of tears escaped his tightly clenched eyes as the muscles throughout his body spasmed uncontrollably. Though his body continued to jerk and shake, he was no longer in control of it. He was absolutely helpless. Strangely, aside from the intense electric pain, Rove experienced the moment like a detached third party watching the incapacitation of a poor, dumb, defenseless animal.

After what seemed like an eternity of anguish, the blue spark with its loud, crackling voice ceased. His attackers released their hold and his battered and broken body dropped with a thud onto the ground where it lay twitching uncontrollably. Rove wasn't sure of anything at that moment. Thoughts still failed to form completely. Pain pulsed in every part of his body, every nerve sending distress signals to his overloaded brain. The passing of time was perceived weakly through a thick, dark fog. Every second, new bolts of agonizing pain pierced the fog like lightning.

One of the black-clad soldiers knelt down beside him. He removed his gloves, then proceeded to roll up the sleeve on Rove's left arm. With great effort, Rove opened his eyes and caught sight of the man's hands. "He's black," Rove thought wearily. For reasons he couldn't quite explain, this fact troubled him. The Texan had been white, as had the owner of the sledgehammer that had repeatedly plowed into his face. This much he remembered. So this wasn't some kind of racist assault.

"Racism?" he wondered. "In the middle of Turkmenistan?" The notion was incongruous with the facts. "Why then? Why me?" The answer eluded him, but one thing seemed certain: he'd been targeted. Someone was punishing him. Even through the haze, Karl Rove realized the list of suspects would be a hundred miles long and packed full of people who had made a career of doing bad things and not getting caught.

Only a few names had materialized in his mind when movement arrested his attention. Everything seemed to be moving in slow motion, but he was starting to see clearly again. Working quickly, the black man extracted a syringe containing a clear liquid. Without warning or pretext he jammed the needle into Rove's forearm. Rove experienced the pricking sensation from a distance, though he'd still winced when the needle went in – partially from the pain, but mostly from his lifelong fear of needles. A good bedside manner and a warm disposition had done little to assuage his distaste of needles over the years, and this thug possessed neither.

The large man studied him with detached interest, as if Rove were a doe the man had just felled and now watched patiently while the death throes ensued. Strangely, that was close to the way he felt. It was as if a tunnel had opened beneath his body and some higher power was simply waiting for him to let go of his life and let his thick, fleshy vessel fall into oblivion. He thought again of all the money and opportunity awaiting the skill of his hand and mind.

How long had it been since he'd walked out of the embassy and been convinced he was standing on top of a new world? For the first time in his life, real money and power had been within his grasp. And now? In an instant, a throbbing, stinging regret surged through him, permeating every cell in his body. His throat constricted and heavy tears again welled in his aching eyes. "So much lost," he thought in a haze, "I was so close!" Now, the tunnel below whispered for him to let go – to surrender. The mixture of despair, pain, pulsing aches and absolute exhaustion that managed to reach his brain tempted him to accept the offer. To accept death. To embrace darkness and nothingness.

The scene around him began to blur as the drug started taking effect. The pain began to subside, replaced by a welcome numbness. Everything was fading fast. Darkness was coming. Or maybe it wasn't the drug after all. Maybe he'd invited death to take him and the invitation had been eagerly accepted.

The large Texan knelt down, his face only inches from Rove's. As if he'd read Rove's thoughts, he said, "I'm afraid it's not over yet, Karl Christian Rove. We're just getting started."

Harrisburg, Pennsylvania

Karon's face was still frozen in a grimace suggesting she was conjuring another hostile diatribe to sling his way before they arrived at the courthouse. Joe thought about baiting her but decided instead to ignore his fuming wife and have a look out the rear window. The white van was still with them, though not following as closely as he'd guessed. "Good," he thought. Maybe they would do him the courtesy of hanging back even more when they arrived at the courthouse. With any luck, things would go so well at the appeals trial that he could walk out of the courthouse and personally tell the guards they'd be going back to prison without him. "Muddy the waters," he thought. "The murkier, the better."

Joe started to turn back around when he felt the limousine lurch forward. He was about to shout to the driver that he wasn't in a huge hurry to get to the courthouse when he noticed the white van had stopped at the last intersection. Joe looked up and saw the light above the opposite lane was red. The driver must've run the red light, forcing the guard van to stop. A number of thoughts hit him all at once.

For the moment, he was technically free. He could shout for the driver to stop, jump out the door and make a run for it. Escape jail, the media, and his wife. He had enough money stashed in offshore accounts to live out the rest of his life comfortably. He'd spent a considerable number of hours on the prison computers reading about countries with extradition laws favorable to those of considerable means who did not wish to be found. Unfortunately, getting there was another matter entirely. After the attacks on 9/11, getting out of the country under an assumed name was challenging and risky. Not to mention the escape of a high profile figure like himself. It would not go unnoticed for long. Police and the FBI would have airports, subways, train and bus stations for miles around on full alert. His face would be plastered on every news station in the country. Not to mention sixty thousand pissed off employees at his former company who would be keeping a sharp eye out for him. Deep down he knew he'd rather take on law enforcement authorities than his former employees any day. At least the authorities would think twice before shooting him.

He'd realized early on that escaping from the white-collar minimum security Schuylkill Correctional Prison would be simple. It would be almost as easy as hopping out of the limo right now. And if things went sour today, that's precisely what he'd do. He could get out of Schuylkill with a few hours lead time versus only a few minutes here. Escaping would be an easy matter – if that became his only option. However, he felt confident in his chances today at the appeals trial. The evidence he'd gathered against the former President should prove to be both influential to the court and newsworthy to the country. And that might just be the leverage he needed to cut a deal that would ensure his freedom. "No," he thought, "best to sit tight for right now."

Then it occurred to him that the guards might use this little embarrassing incident as an excuse to get rough with him. Of course shouting, "It wasn't my fault…I didn't do it," to a prison security guard was not likely to improve the situation. Perhaps it would be best if he asked the limo driver to pull over and wait for the van. If things didn't go as planned at the appeals hearing, the gesture might save him a little heartache later. The guards could hardly complain if they all arrived together, right?

The limo turned right onto North Seventh Street and accelerated. Joe looked back as they rounded the corner and just caught sight of the van a few blocks back before a cluster of office buildings obscured his view. "Driver," Joe called out, "our escort has fallen behind. Pull over and let them catch up."

There was no reply.

"Driver!" he said louder.

There was still no reply. He was about to demand that the driver stop when something odd happened. The driver's gloved right hand shot up in a gesture to stop him from speaking. Before Joe could protest, the driver splayed his five fingers. "What the…" Joe muttered, and Karon turned to see what he was staring at. The driver's thumb disappeared, then his pinky, then the ring finger. "A countdown?" Joe wondered. Now two fingers. Index finger. Another second passed before the driver pointed his index finger forward.

At that moment another limousine turned out from a side street about thirty yards ahead. The second limo was in the same lane as theirs, heading in the same direction. He couldn't be sure, but Joe thought the limo was the exact same make and model as the one they were riding in. Then it hit him. Their driver had known the other car would pull out. He'd known the precise moment when it would happen. Suddenly Joe felt a sinking feeling in his stomach and a tingling sensation on the back of his neck.

"What in the hell is going on here?" Karon demanded.

As if in response to Karon's haughty demand, the driver stepped on the gas, then jerked the wheel hard to the right. There was a loud squealing noise as the tires fought to maintain their grip against the strong centrifugal force. Joe had braced himself as soon as the car had accelerated, but Karon had been caught completely off guard. He'd watched helplessly as his wife was thrown violently against the left side of the car. She'd managed to throw her arms in front of her face an instant before impact, but had still hit hard. Her limp body bounced off the side door panel and rolled clumsily onto the floor. Joe stared down at her but remained frozen. There was no movement or sound.

"She must've been knocked unconscious," he thought. He was about to relax his brace and check on Karon when the limo made another fast hairpin turn. In an instant the daylight vanished, replaced by darkness. A moment later the car went over some kind of large hump, causing the rear of the vehicle to bolt upwards. This time Joe lost his grip and was slammed into the ceiling. He landed sideways on the seat and bounced off onto the floor, landing partially on Karon's motionless legs. Just as he tried to right himself, the car took one final turn, then screeched to a stop. The sudden deceleration threw Joe's body back up onto the seat. Even though the car had stopped moving, he instinctively latched onto the seat back. He held his breath for a few moments, waiting for something to happen. When nothing did, he cautiously released his grip on the seat and breathed a small sigh of relief. Lying flat on his back, Joe made a quick mental check of his body. There was a painful aching in his back and left shoulder, but otherwise nothing appeared to be damaged or broken.

All was silent inside the cab, save for his own heavy breathing. Slowly, he turned his head. It was dim inside the limo, but he could see Karon was still crumpled up on the floor and that she was breathing. He considered trying to rouse her, but then thought better of it. He didn't know what was happening, but he thought it best that she and her temper remain unconscious until he had a better understanding of their situation.

Alertness returned quickly and his mind began to reconstruct the events of the last few minutes. The driver had managed to ditch the prison van at a light. A block or two later they'd turned onto North Seventh heading towards the courthouse. "So far so good," he thought. Then their driver had silently demonstrated knowledge of an impending event, the second limo, which Joe now felt confident was identical to their own. Then they'd quickly turned right down a side street and right again into some kind of warehouse or garage. Replaying the chain of events again, Joe realized the prison van would've lost sight of them a moment after they'd turned onto Seventh. They wouldn't have seen the second limo pull out. Nor was it likely they'd seen his limo turn.

Then it hit him. This was all being coordinated. A third party had intervened. Part of him hoped a good friend with connections and resources had done all this to free him, just like in the movies. A diversion. Then the escape. The fake passport, the briefcase full of money, and the new identity. Unfortunately, reality wasn't as forgiving or inventive as a Hollywood script. He no longer had any good friends.

CEO 101 rules state clearly that once the guilty verdict is passed down and one is convicted, all communication and association ceases immediately. You receive various condolences and gifts the first week in prison, but nothing is signed. No one outside of immediate family calls or visits. Your universe contracts and your world consists of only one person you like or trust: yourself. Outside that universe the people with the power, money and balls to pull off something like this were either friend or foe – there was no other category. So which one was it? Which hand was controlling the marionettes this time? At that moment Joe heard a single metallic click from the front seat. He turned to look in the direction of the sound. Directly ahead, aimed straight at his chest, was the black, silenced barrel of the answer.

Derweze, Turkmenistan

Josh hugged himself tighter as he slowly made his way towards the glowing hole in the ground. He was cold. Cold in the goddamn desert. He'd heard stories of how temperatures in the desert can drop precipitously after the sun set, but he'd thought they were exaggerated. These were told by the type of wimpy people who were always cold – or at the very least these stories did not apply to spring or summer. That attitude had changed drastically about ten minutes ago when two things happened: the sun set over the perfectly flat horizon and a particularly chilly wind had come out of nowhere and had yet to diminish. Reality and experience are the best teachers of truth – and humility.

The ruffling of his windbreaker and the howling of the wind were the only sounds Josh could hear. "Windbreaker," he grumbled. It sure didn't feel like the wind was being broken. In fact, it felt like he wasn't even wearing a coat. "But it's a dry cold Josh," he said aloud. "Yeah, all the better to preserve my body until the sand swallows it," he thought. What the hell were they doing out here?

"Come on Andy!" he shouted.

He turned and saw his friend was still putting on his jacket next to the battered Jeep they'd rented in Ashgabat. Andy waived and began running towards him. He caught up and said, "Does 'a well-digger's wallet' mean anything to you?"

Josh grinned. "Yeah, fuckin' cold isn't it?"

"My nipples feel like they're made of stone, my nose is frozen solid, and my dick has receded so far into my body it's poking my stomach," Andy said jokingly.

Josh laughed. "Nice visual. Thanks for that."

"I can't believe a desert could be this cold."

"I was just thinking the same thing," Josh admitted. "We should've called in your dad's helicopter for this one."

Andy scowled and said, "Hell no. This trip has nothing to do with him. I paid for this all by myself. With money I earned. And I resent..." but Josh cut him off.

"Relax, Bogart, I'm just giving you a little shit. Being rich is perfectly okay from time to time. I mean, a helicopter would be a great way to see this...whatever it is. Not to mention a helluva lot warmer."

"Forget it," Andy said assertively. "We're real men. Hardy men. We don't need any of Daddy's toys."

Josh turned and met his friend's eyes, then cast his glance down towards the bulge in Andy's coat pocket. Their eyes met again and he raised a challenging eyebrow. Andy huffed and said, "I promised him I would take it everywhere I went. It was the only way he'd agree to let me enter an 'industrially challenged' nation."

"I never thought *your* dad would go extreme PC on us," Josh joked.

Andy ignored the comment and added, "Besides, Professor Morgan was thrilled to know at least one of us would never be completely out of contact range. Lost students always hinder a professor's chances at tenure."

"And if the right satellite doesn't happen to be overhead when you want to make a call?" Josh questioned.

"There's *always* a satellite above to pick up the signal," Andy said confidently. "That much is guaranteed by the service provider."

"Fat lot of good their guarantee would do us out here," Josh said rubbing his hands together.

Andy changed the subject and asked, "Whose bright idea was this, anyways?"

"That would be yours, boy genius."

"Mine!?" Andy said incredulously.

"Jesus, Andy," Josh said through clenched lips, "How much of that vodka did you drink last night? Don't you remember your conversation with that Russian girl? What was her name? Zaneida? Zelda? Zena?"

"Warrior Princess," Andy mumbled.

"Whatever. She's the one that convinced you to come out here and find this...*thing*. Said it would look very manly on your Facebook page."

There was a long pause before Andy sheepishly asked, "Did she actually use the term 'manly'?"

"Yeah, Tarzan. And it obviously worked. Again! How is it that every woman you meet knows exactly which words to use on you when they want something? Do you have an instructional website or something?"

"Oh, and what exactly did she want?" Andy said defensively.

"Control, dummy! To send our dumb asses into the barren, freezing desert while she stays behind sipping Hot Toddies. That's precisely what she wanted. And she got it, thanks to your gullibility. Raggedy Josh and Andy are always good for a laugh. And they say Russians have no sense of humor!"

Andy remained silent for a few moments then confessed, "I don't know how they know. Women just have a strong sick sense."

"That's 'sixth' sense, Freud," Josh corrected.

Andy blew past the comment and explained, "There's just something so persuasive and powerful about words like 'manly' and 'burly' and 'brute' delivered eagerly and enthusiastically by a woman. The hotter the woman, the stronger the effect. Especially when I'm slightly intoxicated."

"Slightly?" Josh said skeptically.

"Three sheets to the wind?" Andy countered.

"How about the whole ream of paper in a raging tornado!" Josh said playfully. "You were far beyond 'slightly,' Andy. And I've got the video to prove it."

"Can I see it?" Andy asked politely.

"Now? Here?"

"Sure. Why not?"

"Because getting the camera would mean opening my coat, which is not going to happen until we got closer to the heat. *My* nipples are still lukewarm and I'd just as soon keep them that way. Besides, I wouldn't want you to accidentally erase your soon-to-be-famous lamp shade dance."

Andy stared down at the dark sand and muttered, "Shit, I forgot about that."

"I doubt Professor Morgan will ever forget it. He had to keep a straight face while trying to explain to the party host what 'alcohol intolerant' meant."

Before Josh could continue his jibing, Andy stopped. "Damn!" he exclaimed.

Josh followed his friend's gaze. A hundred yards ahead, he saw a long, oval shape on the ground. No, not on the ground, but *in* the ground. Missing ground. And it was glowing. Red, orange and yellow light poured from the slit. When they'd first arrived, they couldn't see it at all. Even when the sun had set, it was just a tiny pink dot on the horizon. Now it was an enormous, radiant hole in the ground.

"Wow," was all he could say.

The two friends doubled their pace. With every step toward the light, the warmth teased, and in less than a minute the heat engulfed their chilled bodies.

"Oh, hell yeah!" Andy exclaimed as he eagerly stretched his cold fingers towards the warm light. "That's what I'm talking about!"

But as they approached the light, they both slowed cautiously. On the far side of the hole, about ten feet below the rim, they saw dark rock and dirt – both of which were surrounded by fire. Thin red and amber flames spewing forth from nowhere. "What's the fuel source?" Josh wondered. As they got closer, it looked as though the flames were coming from the ground itself. And yet there was no smoke. It was a bizarre sight. "Heat or no heat, caution is a good policy," Josh thought. After all, they were in the middle of Desert Nowhere in a foreign country and it was nighttime. If something bad happened here, they would be royally screwed.

The same moment the thought of disaster entered his head, something caught Josh's attention. He'd seen a dark shape out of the corner of his eye. Still rubbing life back into his hands, he shifted his gaze to the left. Then he saw it. A quarter of the way around the rim he spotted a black square sitting upright on the ground. Squinting, he thought he saw something lying next to the square.

"Andy," he said, absently tapping his friend's arm, "What do you make of that?"

Andy turned and followed the invisible line from his friend's finger until he saw the object.

"Beats me," he said, "The lines are too smooth to be a rock. Looks like maybe a box of some kind."

"Is it moving?" Josh asked, though he was fairly certain of the answer.

"Doesn't look like it to me," Andy answered.

"Might be something that belongs to the people in that little village we passed," Josh suggested. "Or it could be a sign of some kind. Like 'No jumping or diving into the fire pit.'"

Andy flashed a sardonic smile and said, "Only one way to find out." Before Josh could protest, Andy began walking quickly around the rim towards the object.

"Andy!" Josh called out. "Haste makes waste."

"Beats wasting time standing here like two dumb rocks just staring at it," Andy yelled back over his shoulder.

"He has a point," Josh thought.

"Wait up!" he called out.

As they made their way around the pit they occasionally glanced inside. "No wonder the locals called this the 'Door to Hell,'" Josh muttered. He noticed all the rocks were various shades of gray. He knew from his Chem 101 class that Brimstone was the ancient name for sulfur. When they'd burned sulfur in the lab it had melted and turned into a dark red blob. It also gave off a pungent, noxious gas. There was no foul smell in the air and the rocks in the pit weren't melting, though, so the biblical reference wouldn't hold here. Regardless, if ever a place had been given a fitting name, this was certainly it.

Andy had stopped ahead a few feet and appeared to be examining the square object. Josh caught up and was surprised at what he saw. A briefcase. An average, everyday, ordinary briefcase just lying next to a flaming pit in the middle of the desert. Sitting next to the case was what appeared to be a neatly folded men's blazer. The two objects would look perfectly normal sitting on a desk or at a bus stop, but here they looked almost surreal. No doubt Andy was equally puzzled, and at the same moment, they both looked around to see if they could see anybody. Surely someone had set this here and would be back.

Josh was still scanning the darkness when he heard Andy take a step and exclaim, "Ohhh shit!"

Josh stepped next to his friend, who stood looking over the edge of the pit. The sight of the burning hole was impressive, as was the heat, which Josh could feel on his face. The words "winds of hell" came to mind. Cautiously Josh leaned over and followed his friend's gaze. There was nothing but fire, dirt and rock. What was the big....and then he saw it. Or what was left of it.

"Is that what I think it is?" Andy asked uncertainly.

"Looks like someone fell in," Josh said, looking down again at the briefcase and coat. "Or jumped in."

"Hell of a way to go," Andy said uneasily.

"Interesting choice of words," Josh commented.

"Sorry."

"Came an awful long way to wind up down there," Josh said, still trying to make out details of the remains. "I'm surprised there's even anything left. Must be really damn hot down inside."

"Helluva way to go," Andy repeated.

"Who's gonna believe this?" Josh wondered aloud.

The two turned slowly, faced each other and at the same time exclaimed, "Video camera!"

Josh pulled the compact minicam from his pocket and switched it on. He flipped open the side LCD panel. "Come on," he said impatiently. When the LCD flicked to life, he leveled the camera, acquired the object and hit Record. He zoomed in slowly, trying to keep both the image and his breathing steady. The closer he got, the harder it was to look at the remains. "It's not like the movies," he thought absently. While he filmed the grim image of burnt flesh, bones, and an odd steam coming from what he imagined could be boiling blood, Josh began a simple narration – citing the day, time, and location. He began describing what he was seeing, then realized the hi-def video footage would be more than adequate for the viewer.

While Josh filmed the scene, Andy knelt down and examined the briefcase. After a few seconds of inner debate, he nodded resolutely and took hold of the leather case. Laying it flat, he positioned his thumbs on the lock releases and was surprised when the latches popped up in unison. Biting down on his bottom lip, Andy slowly opened the case.

"Oh fuck!" Andy exclaimed.

Still staring at the image, Josh said, "What is it?"

When Andy didn't answer Josh turned and looked down. Andy had turned the open case and tilted it so he could see inside. Andy was looking up at him, confusion reflected on his face. Sticking out of one of the file pockets was what appeared to be a passport. No, several passports. Josh could distinguish several different hues, though in the dim light he wasn't sure exactly what colors or countries they represented. On the front book, the word "Passport" was printed in shiny gold lettering above what looked like a strange round design and wings.

Sticking out of another pocket and resting at an angle was what looked like a white rose. "That's odd," he thought. Lowering his gaze, Josh saw a short stack of eight-by-ten black and white photographs of a pudgy, mostly bald white male. The man wore thin wire-framed glasses, a suit and tie. The chubby face bore something between a smile and a sly grin. It looked like the type of picture celebrities used for autographs. The man looked vaguely familiar. Josh studied the man's face, but still could not think of his name. He nodded towards the picture and wondered aloud, "You think he's the one in there?" He jerked a thumb over his shoulder towards the pit. "Kind of weird to be carrying around a stack of portraits like that. Maybe he's famous and expected to run into fans at the Door to Hell. Maybe he's a soap opera star or something. And what's up with the flower? Maybe he had a date here that went sour. Guy pissed off the wrong girl and she pushed him in," Josh joked, forcing a laugh.

"Josh!" Andy exclaimed, "What in the hell are you talking about!?"

Josh looked questioningly at his friend and replied defensively, "What?"

Andy pointed to what was beneath the photographs. Josh took a second look. His eyes grew wide as he realized what he was looking at. Turning slowly, he leveled the camera and re-acquired the image of the burning body. The minicam was still recording. He wasn't sure what he'd expected to see, but the image was the same. Returning his gaze to the briefcase, he took a second glance at the contents. Josh zoomed the camera in, focusing on the clear bags of white powder and the shiny silver handgun. Still filming he said slowly, "Andy, I think now would be a good time to break out the satellite phone and call your father."

Chapter 12

Newburgh, New York

It was well after one o'clock by the time Tarte and White dropped off the First Aid kit containing the purported explosive sample at the lab. Jacob, the head of the lab, had said they would have the results back in about an hour. Normally Tarte would've waited with his nose pressed to the glass, urging the techs to work faster, but there was a more urgent matter he had to deal with. He was starving.

Most days Tarte traded breakfast time for an extra twenty minutes of sleep. He liked breakfast, but not as much as he liked sleep. This was made all the more ironic given his fondness for both hot and cold cereals. Since he'd been in college, breakfast foods had always worked better for lunch, dinner, or both. On the nights when Jessica had plans, he fixed cereal and toast for dinner, which suited his boys just fine. Later Jessica would make a stink about it until he brought up all of the vitamins and nutrition in cereal. If that didn't work he would casually remind her of his lack of culinary skill. In the end, cereal was preferable to processed nuke-meals, pizza delivery, or Chinese takeout. "Besides, breakfast is always a good idea," he would say, knowing she would roll her eyes and give up.

Today had been a sleep-for-breakfast day. Had he known he would be jetting off to New York, things might have been different. As it was, he hadn't even had time to dig into the sizeable stash of junk food hidden in a cabinet behind his desk. Just the thought of the oatmeal chocolate chip cookies, peanut butter, pita chips, and pop tarts had been enough to make him feel light-headed. "I need food, White," was all he'd said. Ten minutes later he found himself devouring a pastrami and mayo on rye, barely pausing to breathe and swallow. The cold Diet Coke tasted as if it had come down from food and beverage heaven. He couldn't remember the last time he'd been so famished. There was something spiteful about the type of hunger that creeps up and attacks without warning. It was almost as if the body was mad at the mind and decided not to send warning of the impending barrage of urgent and demanding hunger signals. Then, when the onslaught came, the brain fired back with a vengeance of its own. Why oh why did he have to be caught in the middle? He was about to raise the question with White, who was himself devouring a sandwich, when the cell in his pocket sprang to life. "Those lab guys are really fast," he thought.

Extracting the phone, he expected to see an unlisted number. Instead it showed a familiar name: Jimmy Marlow. He hadn't talked to Jimmy since the party. Staring down at the second half of his sandwich, Tarte was torn. His ravenous hunger was only partially satisfied. But Jimmy was a good friend and never usually stayed on the phone for very long. Tarte gave a low growl. He stood up, muttered a quick apology to White, then took the call.

"Good King James. So very proper of you to call. How are you?"

"G'day, Tartsy," Jimmy said gaily. "I'm bueno. Hey, sorry to disturb your noble, world-saving endeavors, but I need a favor."

"What can I do you for?" Tarte asked.

"Do me for? A hundred bucks, an immense amount of alcohol, and a promise you'll never tell either of our wives." Jimmy joked.

"You're a sick man, Jimbo," Tarte said matter-of-factly. "Remind me to have you added to our Most Wanted list."

"Thanks, but no thanks. Already have to beat the women away with a large stick."

"You wish, Don Juan. So what's the favor?"

"We're going to throw another shindig in a few weeks and I wanted to see if I could borrow your new monster grill?"

"I suppose I could part with it for an evening. Is there an invitation out there with my name on it?"

"Naturally, provided the grill comes too. Just kidding."

"No worries, it's yours. Say," Tarte said wiping his mouth with the napkin in his hand, "I have to call Floyd here in a bit. Do you want me to invite him again or did you already do it?"

"Floyd?" Jimmy sounded puzzled. "He a friend of yours?"

"No, Steven Floyd. From the FBI. I met him at your last party."

"You met or were met by?" Jimmy joked. "I don't remember seeing you the second half of the night."

"That's because you were already schnockered and we had to go relieve the babysitter. So no, he wasn't there to arrest me. Seriously though, you don't know Steven Floyd?"

"Can't say that I do, Rog," Jimmy said honestly.

Tarte thought for a second. "Were there a lot of people there you didn't know? Did Trish invite friends from work or something?"

"No. This was an Evite-only party. It was small...there were only a few dozen people there."

Tarte tried to think back. Had Jimmy been too lit to remember how many people showed up? Though he hadn't taken a head count, he thought the number sounded about right.

"Rog," Jimmy said, "Are you yanking my chain or did you really run into an FBI agent at my party?"

Tarte was still thinking but answered, "No Jimmy, no joke. But he's not an agent. He's a director for one of the FBI divisions."

"No shit?" Jimmy said sounding impressed.

"No shit," Tarte confirmed. "In fact he's the one that brought me onto the case I'm working right now. An opportunity that wouldn't have come my way otherwise."

"What, you guys just struck up a conversation about international terrorism or something?" Jimmy asked skeptically.

"Yeah, that was it," Tarte said. "No, he just came up beside me and we started chit-chatting. Nothing official. You know, I thought it was strange, too, but then I'm normally so antisocial I figured that was the normal MO for a Jimbo party."

Jimmy was silent for a moment then asked, "Did Jessica meet him?"

"No. She was off somewhere on the cell checking on the boys. He left just before she got back. I doubt she even saw him."

"Could we possibly be talking about imaginary friends conjured up with the help of alcohol?" Jimmy poked.

"I made all of my imaginary friends stay home with the boys that night. No," Tarte said, his voice serious again, "He was definitely there. We spoke for a good fifteen minutes."

"Weird," Jimmy said.

"I agree. What about Trish – think she might know him?"

Without answering, Jimmy called out to Trish. A few seconds later he came back on.

"Neither of us has ever heard of the guy, Rog. How old was he?"

"Mid-fifties I would guess, maybe a little older. Tan white guy, normal build, gray hair and goatee."

"Well there's your answer right there. Aside from our parents we don't associate with anyone that age. Most of our friends are young and childless – the types who can still come to a party and stay past *eight*." Tarte knew the comment was directed at him, but suddenly he had more important things on his mind.

"Do me a favor, Jimmy. Double check your Evite list – just for giggles. Let me know if something turns up."

"No problem, Rog."

"Thanks, Jimbo. I've gotta run. Drop by the house any time for the grill. I'll give you a shout in a few days."

"Roger," Jimmy inquired, sounding concerned, "do you think this guy came looking for you?"

"I'm not sure. Could just be a coincidence."

"I don't believe in that kind of coincidence," Jimmy said seriously.

"Neither do I, Jimbo. Neither do I."

Denver, Colorado

Breckus ran his long fingers through thick, curly black, unkempt hair and yawned. The deep inhalation felt good. Unconsciously he arched his back and stretched out his arms, the left one hanging out of the driver's side window. He barely noticed the cool, dry morning air. Clenching his fists, he held the moment, reveling in the warmth of blood rushing to stretched muscles. The taut corners of his mouth felt as though they were a millimeter away from tearing. The strain made his eyes water and he imagined at that moment the contorted expression on his face must be rather comical. A long, slow exhale left his body feeling slack and relaxed.

Despite two decades of sunrise meetings in his former corporate life and innumerous assignments from *The Aenamaia* requiring a great deal of clandestine antemeridian activity, he still preferred sleeping in. Strangely, the actual time when he fell asleep had little to do with the quality of his mood or his available energy when he had to get up early. Five a.m. was five a.m., regardless of whether he'd gone to bed at nine o'clock or midnight. Doing surveillance for *The Aenamaia* had given him ample time to contemplate this conundrum.

In the end, he determined that it must be a glitch in his own psychological programming left over from his youth. Back in those days, getting up early usually meant going to school. And the appeal of school, even on a good day, could never compete with the warm and sublime blanket of deep sleep. Supporting evidence of this conclusion came when he realized that there were certain days in his past when he couldn't wait to get up. Christmas mornings were the most common for kids, but there had been other times – other adventures which could not commence until daylight broke. On those days, the bundled energy and enthusiasm that would catapult him out of bed lay eagerly waiting just this side of the thin membrane straining to suppress consciousness until it was time to awaken.

Unfortunately, the insistent buzzing of the generic hotel alarm clock had not heralded such a morning. Before his hand could hit the snooze button, regret at having agreed to meet at seven a.m. had penetrated the fog of his consciousness, followed closely by the first snippets of rationality. A little voice had whispered through the fog, "This is important." The man he was meeting was a high-level manager at the Environmental Protection Agency who worked beneath the Deputy Administrator. He was in Denver visiting the regional office that had been built next to the historic Union Station depot. His packed schedule for the day was already laid out and firm. With the first meeting of the day at eight thirty and the last taking place in a government vehicle on the way back to the airport, seven a.m. was all he had available. The man had managed to reach Joust through a shared contact who happened to be an active environmentalist. They had spoken for some time, though the man had refused to give his name. Through a carefully worded conversation, Joust had learned that the man was sympathetic to their cause and wanted to help. Unfortunately, he was hesitant and reluctant to reveal anything more over the phone.

Back at the main office, Osiro had managed to track down the phone number and run a trace on it. After a few hours of research, he was able to confirm that the call had been placed from a cell phone registered to the EPA's technology division. But despite his best efforts, Osiro was unable to determine who the phone had been issued to. The man must have suspected *The Aenamaia* would trace the number. "Smart," Breckus had thought. Keep your name anonymous, which conveyed to *The Aenamaia* that you were probably legitimate. Probably. Unfortunately, the gray void separating probability from absolute certainty is often filled with the bodies of those who failed to understand or recognize the difference.

After much discussion, Gray had decided to grant the meeting. Breckus and Talon had wrapped things up at Pou Lai's place late in the afternoon and were only a few hours drive from Denver. Gray already had a new assignment for Talon in D.C. while Breckus was set to head home to Oregon and remain on call as backup. The call from the EPA man, who was calling himself "Mr. Poe," had been tantalizing enough to warrant modifying the game plan – something Gray didn't make a habit of doing. Breckus felt wary about the meeting, but agreed the potential reward outweighed the risk. If Mr. Poe was on the level, he could provide sufficient information to justify augmenting their plans.

The drive into Denver had been delayed due to what seemed like an endless series of nighttime construction projects. Faceless figures in orange and neon yellow vests busily went about their work. Each worker wore a white construction hat, thick boots and a dirty sweatshirt. They moved around soundlessly while drivers navigated the narrow makeshift lanes, endeavoring to get back to the open road. Thinking back, Breckus could still see the flashing caution lights, barriers covered in diagonal white, black and orange stripes, and the eerie steam clouds, the sources of which remained a mystery. It was a surreal scene repeated over and over again, as if a traveling band of construction gypsies were intent on delaying the late night drivers. They set up the cones and signs, donned reflective clothing and got into position. They rejoiced at the sight of the weary, slow-moving drivers. Then, once the cars had passed, they would pack it all up and somehow race ahead of the traffic just to do it all over again. Over and over again, like a bad Vaudeville play.

The drive had been awkward and silent. Breckus and Talon had worked together before on research and surveillance projects, but this was their first joint termination. On the way out to Lai's place, the conversation bounded back and forth with a metronomic cadence as the two men hashed over every detail of the plan. Contingency plans, escape routes and exits, what-ifs, and how-tos. They tested each other on rendezvous locations, each of their fake identities and backgrounds, details about their work as security consultants to the wealthy, false permits for the handguns, ticket stubs and stats from the most recent Colorado Rockies baseball game they had never really attended, and details about the food at the steakhouse they had never visited.

They avoided small talk or discussions about *The Aenamaia,* philosophy, or the state of the world. Stick to the task at hand. Concentrate on the details. Review each step – pre and post termination. Keep the mind clear of useless clutter. This was how each man helped the other remain focused and objective before the job. During the ride to Denver the weight of what they had just done hung in the air and suppressed conversation. Each man's thoughts and questions remained unspoken.

Breckus had never asked Talon if he'd killed before, but felt certain he had. Despite their current areas of expertise, many of *The Aenamaia's* members had at one time led very ordinary lives. When he'd first joined, Breckus had been amazed at the variety of backgrounds and professions represented. Accountants, restaurateurs, chemists, civil engineers, seventeen college professors and nine high school teachers, a dog groomer with a master's degree in French literature, twin brothers who had both worked for Greenpeace, and a woman who had been the executive secretary to one of the wealthiest oil families in Saudi Arabia.

The two men currently working on a termination in Japan had worked as explosive technicians for one of the largest family-owned demolition companies in the U.S. Six of the seven people responsible for weapons procurement had all worked for Lockheed Martin or Boeing, buying and trading top secret technologies. The seventh was a twenty-four year veteran of the United States Customs Office. Representing the more unusual occupations, was a six-foot-two former runway model currently running a ghost company that handled international relations, a marine biologist who'd been threatened by the CIA after abruptly abandoning a project involving porpoises and underwater explosives, and twelve professional athletes, including a former NFL linebacker, two rugby players, a gymnast, three cyclists, four skydivers, and one long distance runner.

There was a sword maker from New Zealand, a German pharmacologist with a PhD in biochemistry, two airline pilots, and an Indian materials engineer who had invented a super strong magnesium-aluminum-tungsten alloy, the patent for which had been appropriated by the United States Government and immediately handed over to DARPA for advanced weapons research. Twenty-eight nationalities were represented in *The Aenamaia*. Member ages ranged from a seventeen year-old French computer programmer to an eighty-one year-old Australian dive master.

During the drive back, it had occurred to Breckus that Talon was one of the few members whose former life had never been openly discussed. As far as he could tell, Talon was a jack of many trades. He was one of those people who seemed to be skilled in whatever the situation called for. Because of his skills and versatility, he'd had more assignments than anyone else in *The Aenamaia*. If Gray was unavailable, Talon was second in command, though no such protocols had ever been formally established within the organization. It was just understood and logical. He was proficient with a variety of guns and weapons, had the field skills of a seasoned sniper, and had taught himself a unique form of drunken boxing. He had also amassed an impressive knowledge of political history, which often constituted the bulk of what he spoke about outside of their work.

During the planning of Pou Lai's deletion, Breckus discovered Talon also knew a great deal about anatomy and physical fitness. When he wasn't working, he could often be found exercising or meditating. The man's personal discipline was something people sensed immediately – usually describing it as a quiet but formidable confidence.

So much about Talon was interesting. But what had impressed Breckus the most was Talon's philosophy and controlled restraint towards food.

Over the years, Talon had trained himself to only consume the calories he determined were necessary to sustain him until his next meal. During an unusually casual conversation at Gray's house, he'd once explained how he'd managed to eliminate cravings and similar food-centric desires, though he'd openly admitted it was the single most difficult undertaking of his life.

He felt that food had become too much of a distraction to most people. This was partly due to the social nature of meals. People had gotten into the habit of eating when they weren't hungry simply because it was that time of day or because it was considered rude to abstain when the company you kept was indulging. Consumption became habitual and excessive, resulting in a grossly overweight population. Many of those who managed to keep corpulence at bay did so only through a substantial investment of time and energy in the form of diets and exercise. Talon saw all of this as a vicious and ridiculous circle. People consumed food when they didn't need the energy simply because they lacked the discipline or courage to refrain. It then became necessary to waste more resources to burn off the excess calories or risk bodily deformation, social stigmatization and poor health.

In essence, people sacrificed a great deal in order to satiate their cravings or to keep to a regular eating schedule – regardless of whether or not they were hungry. In the beginning, Talon had started by simply refusing to eat when he was not hungry. If it made the other people uncomfortable to eat while he did not, that was their problem. When his body felt hungry, he took great care in selecting healthy foods and in consuming much smaller portions than was normal. Through careful study, Talon had learned what foods were the most psychologically addictive to people and took care to avoid them. But it was the final step that had arrested Breckus's attention.

Talon said that whenever possible, he would eat while flooding his other senses as much as possible. This could mean listening to loud music, rubbing strong, aromatic oils beneath his nose to dull the taste of the food, or eating while walking on a treadmill. He'd even created a series of complex computer animations accompanied by powerful classical music to actively engage his mind. And while Breckus initially thought it all very strange, he knew for certain Talon was in peak physical condition and that the upkeep of this required only moderate exercise. When he thought of the time, money and energy the average person could save and what they could do with this savings…such possibilities.

Breckus had never been exceedingly overweight, but like most people, he had carried excess baggage and was eager to be rid of it. After the conversation that night, his consciousness had been irreversibly raised. Food *looked* different to him. He found that he now resented the time spent preparing meals, eating, and the chore of cleaning up. Or the time invested in sitting in restaurants waiting to pay for calories he didn't really need. Grocery shopping, fast food, even waiting in line for the expensive morning caffeine fix. Then there was the money spent on food, the egregious amount of garbage produced, the energy necessary to dispose of it, and the extra time in the restroom to get rid of what the body couldn't retain. So much unnecessary waste. It boggled his mind when he thought of the implications on a global scale. Extraordinary and disturbing.

Talon's philosophy and results had fascinated Breckus so much that he'd begun limiting his own eating. It only took a few times of saying "no" during a social dinner, or refusing some decadent dessert for him to realize how monumental and unique Talon's accomplishment was. "Slow and gradual change is what's needed," Talon had said, "because old habits don't die without a fight. Discipline and a steadfast dedication to the ideology and benefits are essential." Sitting now in his rental car, his mind was already racing forward to the meeting in the coffee shop. Almost unconsciously, his brain scanned his body and determined that the early morning toast and orange juice he'd eaten at the hotel was more than adequate to sustain him until the early afternoon.

Small Earl Grey tea, please. Thank you.

Thinking back, Breckus wished he'd felt comfortable broaching the subject during the long drive, but clearly Talon had a lot on his mind. During situations of stress brought on by pensive reflection, Breckus preferred to delay deep thought on the subject until a little time had passed. With time and rest, came perspective. He'd coined it the "HIP Method: Healthy Internal Procrastination," and so far it had not failed him. Talon on the other hand, most likely believed in confronting strong emotions immediately and head on. That would certainly account for his somber disposition during the drive to the airport.

Once they'd reached the outskirts of Denver, it had taken another forty-five minutes to circumnavigate the city and reach Denver International Airport. A quick handshake and Talon was off. After he'd disappeared through the sliding doors, Breckus drove around to where the hotel shuttles were picking up the last of the day's weary travelers. He spotted one marked Hyatt Regency Downtown. Pulling up to the curb, Breckus watched nine adults and three children step aboard the hotel shuttle. The air was chilly and he could see the evanescent breath of each person as they hurriedly boarded the shuttle in search of warmth. As soon as the folding double doors closed, he pulled the rental car in behind the vehicle and followed it all the way into Denver. It was a good trick to use when you were unfamiliar with the geography.

He'd driven around the immediate outskirts of downtown for a few minutes until he found a Holiday Inn. Burning the last remnants of energy afforded by the four hours of sleep he'd had in the last two days, he walked resignedly to the front desk. The young female behind the counter was noticeably excited at having something to do at the late hour and quickly processed his information. After one final signature and a polite nod to the desk clerk, a man by the name of Angelos Sikelianos picked up his credit card and Grecian passport and headed for his room. By the time his head hit the mushy white pillow, it was well after midnight.

Breckus checked his watch again: 6:40 a.m. Feeling restless and ready to be done with the meeting, he decided it was time to leave. The sun was already up and he could see pedestrians and cars at the nearby intersection scurrying along, barely cognizant of one another. Reaching beneath the black sports jacket, he checked his shoulder holster to make sure his .357 Magnum P345 was strapped in tightly. Satisfied, he jingled the keys in his left hand and closed the door with his right.

Pocketing the keys, he made his way through the right-angle maze of parked cars and trucks and headed towards the coffee shop. Part of him felt like he could be on his way to meet another member of *The Aenamaia* to talk about life, dreams, and ambitions. Curiosities, possibilities and ideologies. Members of *The Aenamaia* spent a lot of time talking about these subjects. They shared their ideas openly and defended their validity and value with enthusiasm and passion. The common dream was that one day people would spend more time talking, sharing, and doing.

The familiar image of a pristine, vibrant and peaceful earth had just appeared in his mind when a loud yell arrested his attention. Instinctively he knew someone was angry. Calmly, he stepped next to a passenger van and slowly peered around the front. It took only a moment to locate the source of the ruckus. A hundred feet away, he spotted a chubby young man in dark shorts, backpack and a bright green sweatshirt rolling through the parking lot on an older model ten-speed bicycle. Even from a distance, Breckus saw puffy, pale white calves, un-muscled arms, round face and pug nose framed by short, dirt-brown dreadlocks. "He must not have ridden too far," Breckus thought, "or he'd be too out of breath for such forceful bellowing." He watched as the stout figure coasted slowly through the parking lot while shouting profanities at someone. The crudity of the language and the hostility with which it was delivered pricked at Breckus's spine and immediately ignited a fire in his belly.

Following the slow moving bike, Breckus quickly assessed the man and concluded that he was neither armed nor particularly dangerous. Just an overweight and out of shape Chihuahua who liked to hear his own high-pitched bark.

Breckus walked quickly between the cars in a zigzag course to intercept the man, all the while watching for curious spectators. He wasn't sure why he felt compelled towards confrontation, but he could not ignore the urge. It was almost as if he were a character in a video game, and some modern day Robin Hood was teasing the game controller.

The shouting continued and he could see now that the man was yelling at a black-haired woman who had just gotten out of her car. The woman remained faced away from the man, undoubtedly trying to pretend he was talking to someone else. This repudiation only fueled the man's rage.

"Hey!" the man shouted angrily, trying to get the woman's attention. "Hey, stupid! You almost fucking killed me, you asshole. What the fuck? You crazy bitch! Don't you look where you're going? Bicycles and pedestrians have the right of way, you moron. You need to fucking pay attention, you stupid bitch. You almost fucking killed me!!"

The last sentence came out with particular force and volume. Breckus gritted his teeth as he made his way towards the brash cyclist. Glancing to his left, he could now see the focal point of the cyclist's tirade was a short, middle-aged Asian woman wearing a silky white blouse, black pants and black pumps. Hanging from her wrist was a small red purse with a cell phone clipped to one of the handles. Her thin frame moved quickly towards the crowded intersection, her head partially bowed as if an invisible helmet would deflect the insults. Breckus could see enough of her face to know she looked confused and frightened.

"Are you listening to me?" the man was still shouting, "You almost fucking killed me, you cunt! You're lucky I don't come over there and punch you in your fucking face, you..."

"Hey!" Breckus barked, interrupting the torrent of obscenities. "Knock it off."

The man steered the bike towards the voice and stopped.

"Fuck you!" he yelled back to no one, "This is none of your goddamn business." Conscious of his own size and the intimidation most people felt around him, Breckus was sure the man hadn't seen him yet.

He emerged from behind a large pickup truck and moved swiftly towards the lime green sweatshirt. The man's head jerked slightly and he made eye contact with Breckus. But instead of backing off as he'd expected, the young man's top lip curled up into a sneer, like an angry Rottweiler sensing danger. The cyclist threw down his bike and backpack and took a step towards Breckus.

"I said this isn't any of your fucking business, you asshole. This is between me," the young man paused, turned and taking a deep, purposeful breath raised his voice and shouted, "and that dumb fucking bitch whose car I'm going to thrash and who I'm going to personally...." The rest of the threat was lost when Breckus's large hand reached out like a claw and clamped tightly around the cyclist's fleshy neck. The young man made a sharp, gurgling noise as his oxygen was suddenly cut off. Breckus guessed he was in his mid-twenties, probably a student, and would weigh in around two-twenty. Breckus lifted the young man off his feet and slammed him violently into a nearby minivan, pinning him against the bright red paint job.

A brief look of fear and confusion flashed across the man's reddening face and landed squarely in his eyes as they locked on Breckus's face. Expecting an apology and the normal blubbering that usually spilled out at this point, Breckus loosened his grip enough to allow the foul-mouthed young man to take a shallow breath. The inhalation sounded like a sharp, cold gust of wind tearing through a narrow stone passage.

In an instant the man's expression changed and his face lit up with as much rage and hate as Breckus could ever remember seeing in one moment. The snarl was back and now included a bent bottom lip revealing the dull, yellow teeth of a chain smoker. The corners of his mouth looked as though invisible hooks of gravity were pulling them towards the asphalt. Fight or flight mode had been activated. Breckus could feel the muscles in the man's neck tighten. Two flailing hands were searching for purchase on the side of the van. "Unbelievable," Breckus thought, "This idiot is preparing to attack me." Obviously fight had been chosen over flight.

"I swear I'll kill you!" the man growled.

In one fluid motion Breckus punched the man square in the stomach. The thick, distended belly did little to soften the powerful blow. What little breath remained in the cyclist's lungs was instantly expelled. The stale smell of cigarette smoke almost made Breckus gag. The wide-eyed man coughed and was about to speak. Taking one step back and tightening his grip, Breckus threw the man's thick body down forcefully, slamming him back-first onto the wet, black asphalt. The force of the impact again knocked the breath out of the rider, bringing with it a forced groan.

This time the look of terror remained intact. Breckus released the man's neck and with both hands, grabbed hold of his left arm and leg, and with one heave, flipped him onto his stomach. The cyclist landed with a thud, followed immediately by a desperate, almost violent inhalation. Having done something similar to Lai the morning before, Breckus knew to expect an erratic, panicked escape attempt. Quickly, he pressed his left hand down onto the man's neck and laid his right knee firmly in the middle of his back. He could feel the expansion of the neck muscles and veins indicating panic, followed by spasmodic jerking, like a fish out of water flopping madly, attempting to escape capture. The man's arms and legs thrashed wildly, trying to gain purchase, but found only hard ground and a heavy knee pinning him down and digging into his spine.

Breckus looked around to see if the commotion had attracted any onlookers, but saw no one. No doubt the Asian woman had heard him shout and had taken the opportunity to make a hasty exit. He quickly scanned the tops of the lights and poles in the parking lot, but there were no security cameras. They were alone and out of sight.

The man's breaths were coming in fits now, and he was trying to talk. Breckus was confident no one was within earshot. And even if they heard the man scream, they would probably assume he was still ranting and raving and would tune it out for fear of attracting his attention. Regardless, a terrified scream for help would only complicate the situation.

Breckus reached into his jacket, tore the .357 Magnum from its holster and pressed it firmly into the man's right temple. In an instant all of the fire and struggle evacuated the man's body. It was as if the body unconsciously knew it was in grave danger and that immediate surrender was the only option for survival.

"This is a semi-automatic Desert Eagle .357 Magnum," he said sounding like a proud collector giving a lecture to an eager young student, "one of the most notoriously powerful handguns in the world. It is cocked and loaded. Now, at this moment it might surprise you to learn that I actually hate guns and deplore violence. But when dealing with someone like yourself, whose pent-up sexual aggressions and unresolved childhood dramas make him overly eager to resort to malevolent hostility, perhaps the only thing you can understand is the barrel of a very large gun. Sad, really," he added shaking his head, his voice incredulous. "It always seems to come down to a dumb...fucking...gun."

"You know," he started in a contemplative voice, "if we were in a philosophical and theological mood, we could theorize that God only let you escape being run over accidentally by that woman just so that someone like me could plaster your brains all over the ground and the surrounding vehicles. That would mean the Almighty not only wanted you kicked off the planet, but he wanted you to be roughed up and scared shitless immediately before your messy departure. If that were true, it would mean that I had been ordained by God and could therefore maintain a clear conscience after pulling the trigger. Hmm?" he paused then added thoughtfully, "You can see how popes and kings in the past justified so many heinous acts of violence and unjust persecution."

Breckus looked around again. They were still alone.

"Now here's an interesting angle," he said, casually tapping the barrel of the gun against the man's head. "What if natural selection is at work at this very moment? The ongoing and epic intra-species struggle for dominance? Now, based on our current positions, me being on top with strength and gunpowder on my side, you being pressed forcefully into the wet asphalt – that would mean I'm the strong here to purge one of the weak and corrupt from humanity's ranks. I kind of like that. Remove any kind of deity from the picture, and still there is intent, purpose and utility at work. And that is important here. Because," he paused, his voice becoming quieter and more serious, "while that little woman may not have been paying attention, I seriously doubt she was purposely trying to run you over. Were it otherwise, I'm confident you would be lying dead in the middle of Speer Boulevard with a crowd of fascinated and disgusted gawkers hovering over your lifeless, pungent and thoroughly soiled corpse. Not a pleasant thought is it? Instead you're alive, for the moment, wondering whether or not you'll ever stand in the warm sunshine again. I, on the other hand, am carefully ruminating over whether or not me and Monsignor Magnum here can liberate your imbalanced and disturbed mind while not getting any brain matter and blood on my shoes."

"But...she...almost killed me!" the squashed face managed to say, a mixture of righteous indignation and scared desperation in his raspy voice.

Breckus grabbed the man's left wrist and twisted it violently behind his back. The cyclist let out a sharp shriek, his face clenched in agony.

"Now this is just too interesting!" Breckus said excitedly. "I'm so glad you brought that up. Consider this. At this very moment you're attempting to justify threatening violence and bodily harm against another human being whose only crime was a harmless error in judgment. Even though she could've mistakenly injured or even killed you, you survived unscathed. Yet your response at being spared is to threaten to do that which was almost done to you. You do see the irony, don't you? Now, you've gone and made the mistake of lobbing obscenities and threats in the presence of someone carrying a holstered hand cannon. Someone who abhors unnecessary violence. And now, you're again being threatened with violence, only this time it is intentional and, I can assure you, quite a bit more serious. So, based on your own actions and the aforementioned convictions, I can surmise that you must certainly condone my actions, and thereby won't mind in the least if I break both your arms, then you're legs, and then blow your brains out." Breckus raised the man's arm slightly higher to emphasize his point.

"No!" the man pleaded, his breathy voice ripe with panic, "please don't. I wasn't going to hurt her. I was just mad that she almost hit me. You can understand that, can't you?"

At that moment it occurred to Breckus that Mr. Poe would be walking into the bakery across the street any minute now. "Damn," he thought. This was a great opportunity to explain to one U.S. citizen the foundation behind what *The Aenamaia* stood for and the basis for the chain of events they'd put into play. This man, young Joe Average, exhibited a tendency towards rash acts of thoughtless violence. He walked around ready to roar and pound on his chest to elicit a fearful response from anyone nearby. This mentality, this attitude of contempt for the lives and happiness of others, is exactly the same putrid poison that has allowed men of power to rape the world for thousands of years. Empty, unsubstantiated and unfulfilled entitlement – that was the recipe for pain and plunder.

"What's your name?" Breckus asked the man quietly.

"Danny," the young man said reluctantly.

"You're full name, please," Breckus said politely.

"Danny Seamus Schade, " the man replied in a raspy voice.

"And where do you live, *Danny boy?*" Breckus asked.

Silence. Breckus jerked the man's arm.

"Ahh!" the biker shrieked, his face knotted in pain. "Boulder! On Pearl Street, near the Old Chicago."

"Now there, you see? That wasn't so difficult, was it?"

Breckus removed his knee from Danny's back, but kept the gun to his temple.

"I have to go now Danny. But I will be watching you from now on. And if I find out that you're involved in any acts of egregious and unnecessary violence, I will find you and remove you from the world in the aforementioned manner. Do you understand?"

"Yes....yes," he stammered.

"Someday people like you will learn to appreciate and accommodate your fellow man....and woman. In the meantime, you're on the government plan: you're being allowed to live at the point of a gun and under the scrutiny of someone who won't permit any unconstructive deviation. Are we clear?" he asked, lowering the man's arm.

"Yes," the man said, nodding.

Breckus stood up, putting his foot on Danny's back.

"You'll need to stay here, on the ground, for five minutes. Find a curious pebble or ant and consume yourself with it. Contemplate the universe and whether or not you care to remain in it. Do not watch me leave. If I turn and find your eyes following me, I'll send your neglected brains hurtling into your feet. You just count out three hundred Mississippis and keep your eyes to the ground. Then get up, find your way home, and do some serious thinking. Do we have an accord?"

"Yes," Danny said obediently, his voice shaking.

Breckus knelt down. "There is hope for us all, Danny Seamus Schade, but the decision to change has to start here," he said, tapping the barrel of the gun lightly against the man's temple. "It must start here," he added solemnly.

Slowly Breckus withdrew the gun from the young biker's shaking head and returned it to its holster. With one last glance at the soiled green sweatshirt, he stepped past the young man. Danny remained face-planted and shaking on the asphalt between two parked vehicles. Walking slowly, Breckus looked around casually. They were still alone. Pulling his jacket straight and stretching his neck, Breckus headed for the small bakery and never looked back.

Newburgh, New York

"I'm okay," Roger Tarte assured his nervous wife. Jessica had called only a few minutes after he'd hung up with Jimmy Marlow. He'd just managed to swallow the last bite of his sandwich when the phone rang with a familiar urgency. He'd programmed his cell phone to deliver the first nine notes of the Dragnet march when his wife called. The ring tone and theme were well known, but somehow it always sounded different on occasions when he would realize after the call that he'd been hesitant to answer.

Tarte sometimes wondered how much control he himself had versus his untethered subconscious mind. There was probably a simple equation at work behind the scenes. In this instance, the subconscious had known all along that he should call his wife before he left D.C., but had chosen not to share that little nugget of wisdom with the conscious mind. The instant Jessica's ring tone sounded, the subconscious put the two together and raised the alarm. The conscious mind recognized the alarm and immediately notified the "oh shit" nerves in the body – most of which were connected to the stomach. Thus a mixed sense of foreboding, regret and butterflies had erupted before the first ring went silent. Hell hath no fury like a woman scorned...or a wife forsaken – and every husband knows it.

Jessica bypassed the normal, "Hello honey, how is your day going?" for the classic, "Where in the hell are you and what in the hell is going on?" opening. Now that the conscious and subconscious minds were on the same page, he could begin the reactive and apologetic self-preservation initiative – otherwise known as groveling. Tarte launched immediately into his standard-issue assuage and damage control mode.

"I had a lead to follow, that's all. Besides, I needed to get out of the office for a while."

"Out of the office is the Czech bakery two blocks away. Or a stroll down the National Mall." Jessica's sarcastic cadence began picking up speed...and steam. "Maybe even a doughnut and coffee at the White House. A simple breather isn't a jaunt to a town in southeast New York three hundred miles away! Give me some IQ credit here, Roger. What's going on?"

"Jessica," he said firmly, "you know I can't discuss the specifics of a case – especially over a cell connection. I'm following a routine lead. Besides, you know I hate doughnuts."

"Roger," Jessica said in a low growl.

"Shield yourself behind the badge," whispered a little voice in his head. "Probably sound advice," he thought.

"I'm sorry, hon. You know the rules. If there is going to be any break in my sworn code of classified silence to protect National Security, it *will* be to you, but it will have to be in person."

"And when will that happen?"

"I don't know yet. However, I didn't bring my toothbrush and bunny slippers, so I'll do my best to be back in DC this evening."

There was a long silence and Tarte braced for the worst.

Jessica let out a low growl of frustration. "I guess this is what I get for marrying James Bond. But I liked it better when you were bored and safely chained to your desk."

Tarte quietly exhaled his relief and said, "James Bond was British and he was a player. Such a shallow man could never know anything of the deep, warm love of a perfect, devoted and eternally understanding wife."

"Nice try, silver tongue, but you've still got a leg in the doghouse for not calling me before you hopped a jet out of DC. Protocols, Special Agent Tarte, protocols. Hell, Money Penny always knew where Bond was."

"So does my secretary." Whoops, dumb thing to say.

"I know!" Jessica exclaimed, "How do you think I found out? You know, if I didn't really like Jasmine and know she was hot-to-trot for an interpreter at the state department, I might wonder where your loyalties lie."

"The state department? Really? No wonder she was all gussied up today. 'Bout time that girl had a date. Wouldn't you agree?"

"Don't try and change the subject, *Agent Tarte*," she said derisively. "Your government issue butt is still on the hot seat. The loop, Roger. My cell phone and I need to be permanent fixtures in the loop."

"Okay, Jessica, okay. But I'm only going to keep you posted on my schedule and whereabouts, that's it. Jumping out of airplanes with gorgeous foreign women, disarming nuclear weapons, shooting people while on skis, rides into outer space…all that stuff has to remain classified."

"Keep it up, Double-O, and I'll handcuff you to the lawnmower!"

"The velvet-lined cuffs or the real ones? You know what happened the last time we tried…"

"Roger!" Tarte could picture Jessica's red face as embarrassed laughter overwhelmed her irritation. "Besides, that was your idea, warden."

"No, no. I was the prisoner and you were the warden. And boy, were you a hard-ass."

Tarte heard a beep in his ear and checked the LCD – it was the lab calling.

"Damn. Jess, I have to take this, it's the guy from the testing lab."

"Okay, Double-O. But remember, I'm in the loop, okay?"

"Okay. Call you later, Penny."

Tarte hit the Send button before Jessica could get the last word in. "Tarte here." He listened carefully as the lab tech confirmed his suspicions.

"That's what I thought. Taggants, just like they said. Okay. Hang onto it for now and keep it quiet. Thanks, Jacob."

Replacing the cell in his pocket, he signaled White who had just finished his lunch. The agent quickly dumped his garbage in the trash can and walked over to where Tarte was standing.

"Positive?" White asked.

Tarte nodded. "High grade and pure. Could be military or homemade, they're not sure."

"Where did it come from? How did they get it?"

"They don't know," Tarte reluctantly admitted.

"What now?"

Tarte headed towards the car and White followed. "Have you heard from the local PD?"

White nodded. "They're on-site. Officers, pups, and bomb squad. A SWAT team is standing by a few miles away. They've got a perimeter set up and eyes on, but they know not to breach without express orders from you or me. CO is on-site and is a career man – he won't move until ordered to. Pups didn't find anything outside, other than a residual scent where our little present was attached."

"Ears?"

"No parabolics available nearby. They tried a laser microphone, but couldn't pick up anything. All the curtains and window shades have been drawn. Whoever set this all up knows what they're doing."

"And what we're doing," Tarte said quietly.

"There are eyes and ears everywhere," White commented.

Tarte stared curiously at Agent White for half a second.

"Is something wrong, sir?" White asked.

"No. No. Nothing. Look, I have one more call to make. Then I need to get back to the airport. Do me a favor, check in again with the team on-site and see if there have been any developments. Make sure the CO's boss is also onboard. Find out how long they're prepared to remain on-site. If the press show up, keep them off the site – including airspace. No comments and no pictures. In fact, have them block the road in and out – local traffic only with ID checks. I'll be ready to go in a second…just have one more call to make."

A flicker of suspicion flashed across White's face – a tiny narrowing of his eyes, a slight tilt of the head – then it was gone. The stoic agent nodded and within two seconds was pacing about with his cell glued to his ear.

Tarte put twenty feet between himself and White and pulled out his phone. He held down the three button and waited for the speed dial to start. The line clicked after only half a ring. "Hi, it's me. Look, there's something else I need you to check on." Tarte relayed the instructions, always keeping a close eye on White. "Got it? Good. Now, protocols: use a secure line for any related calls. Call Chadwick in security, he'll set it up for you. Also, ask him to have one of his techs scan your computer before you use it again. Don't tell anyone what you're doing. Send any curious rubberneckers my way. I don't have time to explain. And one more thing, this needs to be kept quiet." Tarte glanced back at Agent White and lowered his voice. "Very quiet."

Chapter 13

Baltimore, Maryland

"Tell me again – why did Gray insist we drive to Maine rather than fly?" Joust asked, stuffing a hunk of beef jerky in his mouth.

Toman frowned and glanced at his passenger. He, along with every other member of *The Aenamaia*, knew Joust had a particularly strong dislike for long drives. Claustrophobia, sciatica, irritable bowel syndrome, even a strange condition called thaasophobia – or fear of idleness or boredom, had all been suggested as the source of Joust's peculiar disdain. Joust had dismissed each possibility, saying simply that he didn't like being cooped up in a car for very long.

When Toman didn't answer Joust suggested, "He's still pissed. I know he is. He said he wasn't – said he understood my...well, momentary lapse of reason."

"Momentary?" Toman said, making no attempt to hide his doubt and sarcasm.

Joust glowered at him, but didn't reply. Toman smiled and shook his head.

"Ten hours trapped in a metal box with a history buff," Joust mumbled. "It has to be some kind of punishment."

"Thirteen hours," Toman said. "More than likely it'll be thirteen hours."

A look of stunned disbelief crossed Joust's face and he bellowed, "What? Whatta ya mean thirteen?"

"Well it took us over an hour just to get out of D.C. And look at this?" Toman said pointing straight ahead. "We're slowing down."

Joust turned and stared out the windshield, his mouth agape. "Well what the hell is this?" he exclaimed, gesturing towards the other vehicles.

"Baltimore," Toman said simply. "It's the tail end of rush hour."

Joust slumped in his seat and stared at the glove box mumbling, "Thirteen hours. Oy vey. What did I do to deserve this?"

Toman remembered something he'd read recently and suggested, "Maybe you suffer from triskaidekaphobia? At least I think that's what it's called."

"There's nothing wrong with my legs or my ass Toman," Joust retorted sarcastically.

Toman smiled. "I'm so happy to hear that. I'll sleep better tonight – really." He chuckled. "Triskaidekaphobia is a fear of the number thirteen."

Joust stayed silent for several moments and Toman thought he was still fretting over his unfortunate predicament. Toman was about to suggest he lighten up when Joust said, "Humans are funny about that number."

"Thirteen?" Toman asked.

Joust nodded. "Have you ever noticed how some airplanes don't have a thirteenth row?"

"I have," Toman said, happy to have a subject to talk about other than Joust's discomfort with the duration of their journey.

"I've been in buildings – old and new – that didn't have a thirteenth floor," Joust said.

"Me too. In fact, I was once in a building in Richmond, Virginia where the builders had put all the mechanical equipment on the thirteenth floor. I learned this after asking the woman at the information desk in the lobby why there was no thirteenth floor. She said there was, but that it was only accessible via the freight elevator or the stairs."

Joust nodded then asked, "Did the freight elevator have a button for the thirteenth floor?"

Toman smiled. "I asked the same question. The lady said the button for that floor was marked 'M' for 'Mechanical.'"

"Crazy superstition," Joust said shaking his head.

"Now that I think about it," Toman said, "I believe there are airports that don't have a thirteenth gate."

Joust pulled his cell phone from the backpack on the floor and began poking at the screen.

"What are you doing?" Toman asked.

"I'm curious what Google has to say about the number thirteen," Joust said as he tapped, then slid his fingers across the screen, and then tapped again.

His passenger appeared to be engrossed in his web search so Toman shrugged and focused his attention on the road. He glanced at the clock and noted the time. A few minutes before six o'clock he exclaimed, "Time's up!"

The sudden noise had startled Joust who nearly dropped his phone.

"Jesus, Toman!" Joust exclaimed. "Inside voice brother. Inside voice."

Toman laughed. "Come on time's up. What did you find out?"

"Time's up. What are you talking about?"

Toman frowned. "Aren't you supposed to have a really high I.Q.?"

Joust was still rattled, but stated, "Higher than yours anyways. What's your point?"

Toman pointed at the blue numerals on the dash and said, "It's been thirteen minutes. Time to report what you've learned so far."

"Well, 'irritating' is only ten letters," Joust muttered.

Toman ignored the jab and said, "Fascinating. What else?"

Joust exhaled. Still staring at his cell he said, "There's a ton of things. We've already covered airports, airplanes, and buildings. There's a lot on thirteen as both bad luck and good. There are books, songs, video games, movies, and plays all named 'thirteen'. Of course there's Friday the thirteenth. Let's see." Joust moved his finger up and down the screen then said, "Oh yeah. According to Wikipedia there are thirteen turns in a hangman's noose – any less causes the rope to snap before the neck does."

"Well there's some practical and useful information," Toman said mockingly.

Joust ignored the comment and continued. "There's a whole bunch of stuff about thirteen and the cycles of the moon."

"Did you find any conspiracy theory sites that mention thirteen?" Toman asked.

"Yep. Skipped 'em. Thirteen hours in a car *and* conspiracy theories? No thanks. I value what little sanity I have left."

Toman was about to comment on Joust's recent break from sanity when Joust held up a hand and added, "Don't go there my friend." Joust gave a forced, crazy-man's laugh and said, "You know a thing or two about my past and what I've been trained to do. Sarcasm and open criticism might result in my concluding that I really don't have to actually remain captive in this metal coffin for thirteen hours."

Toman grinned. Using his best effeminate voice said, "Sensitive. Very sensitive. Such a bitch to everyone."

Joust laughed and Toman followed suit. After a few moments Joust regained his composure and remarked, "It's frightening how good your 'flaming gay guy' voice is. Scary shit."

"My ex-wife used to say the same thing," Toman said.

"Speaking of that," Joust said, "I did find a legend about a mullah who had twelve wives, but of course wanted more. But, the guy was superstitious – which, by the way, also has thirteen letters in it. Anyways, the guy was so nervous about having a thirteenth wife that he decided he would marry two women at the same time – reasoning that you can't have two thirteenth wives. As if polygamy alone isn't crazy enough."

Toman blew out a breath. "Whew! Fourteen wives. I had a hard enough time trying to understand one woman, let alone fourteen. Forget thirteen – anything over one would be terrifying."

"There are guys in other countries with hundreds of wives," Joust noted. "But I doubt they know much about any of them. Probably don't even know most of their names."

"Ignorance really can be bliss," Toman observed.

Joust was about to return his cell to the bag at his feet when Toman asked, "Say...did you see anything in there about books missing a thirteenth chapter?"

Joust shook his head. "Nope. There are books with thirteen in the title, books about the number thirteen and all the superstition around it, and so on, but none that omitted the thirteenth chapter. Why?"

"Well, someday I hope to write a book about history and I thought, perhaps, it might be kind of interesting to exclude the thirteenth chapter. You know, as a jab to all the weirdness we've been talking about. Think my readers would get it?

Joust shook his head again. "No. What would happen is they'd think the publisher screwed up and accidentally omitted an entire chapter."

"But if the continuity of the text from chapter twelve to chapter fourteen is smooth and concise then it shouldn't be an issue right?"

"Doesn't matter," Joust insisted. "Your readers would assume there was something there they had missed. And they'd be hassling you and the editor to find out what it was and why they didn't get it."

"So you're saying I should plan on having a thirteenth chapter?" Toman asked.

Joust nodded. "The idea is funny. And if you told your readers that you had planned on leaving chapter thirteen out they'd probably appreciate the humor in it. But in the end, it's probably best to just put it in there. Even if you have just one page that explains how you think all the superstition around the number thirteen is ridiculous."

"Just a single page in chapter thirteen?" Toman asked. "A one page chapter?"

Joust shrugged. "Why not?"

"I could spend a few pages making fun of the number thirteen, the superstition around it, and some of the unusual places it does and does not show up?"

Joust thought about that for a moment then shook his head and said, "No. I'm pretty sure some cocky new fiction author has already done that."

Chapter 14

Denver, Colorado

He closed his eyes and tried to concentrate, his brow furrowing with the effort. Slowly, the accumulated mass of dark and troubled thoughts began evaporating – fading into the ether like a morning mist burned off by silent, invisible rays of sunlight. An image emerged from the shadows, the resolution blurred and vague at first. "Patience," he told himself. "Focus." Faint, rigid outlines appeared. A dark, jagged silhouette. Mountains. Familiar mountains.

In the opposite direction was the impressive semicircular granite rock wall towering over the landscape, demarcating the end of the narrow valley. In the foreground tall mature evergreens swayed so slightly in the breeze that he would swear it was, in fact, the earth that was swinging beneath them, held in its pendulous arc by their thick, strong roots. The sky above the serene landscape was a deep blue marked by thin, feathery white clouds all seeming to point to some fantastic far-away destination.

The cabin was close, though he could not see it. A warm, bright sun stood attentive at high noon. He could practically feel the rays warming his face and shoulders. Now his eyes closed in his mind and he imagined the slowly pulsing pink light behind his eyelids. Or perhaps it was an illusion – his mind suggesting that sunlight striking a thin shield of skin would result in a dark pink glow on the other side.

Something else was at odds here, though. There was a persistent and steady purring. "No," he thought, tilting his head, "Not purring. Humming." The word popped into his mind and was made solid by the faint smile it brought to his lips. Yes, humming. A white noise. His head turned again, as if he'd heard a new sound. "Concentrate," he thought. "Hold the moment and make it last, like the dream one cannot bear to forget or release. Augment your reality through focused visualization – if only for a short spell. The cabin is close. A gentle breeze is blowing. The river is near. Can you hear it?" Inhaling slowly, he was barely conscious of his chest and shoulders lifting. Certitude. Projection. Recognition. Time slowed. Exhale.

His eyes were still closed and his body remained perfectly still. Stillness of mind, voice, and being. An unnatural sound was unconsciously transformed into a familiar natural analog. The picture was becoming clearer. Through careful concentration mixed with a profound longing, he transformed the deep humming of the airplane's dual jet engines into the tranquil, undulating roll of the river near his cabin. The inimitable sensation usually reserved for a true physical presence seemed within his grasp. He was almost there. Wasn't he?

The familiar vision came in two flavors. The first was the simple, blissful natural scene devoid of context, purpose or human history. A two-dimensional microcosm of fecund abundance. A still shot – vibrant and beautiful, but flat and unreachable. A high-definition, two-dimensional photograph of perfection – or rather the perception of perfection. The second flavor added a complex and powerful third dimension comprised of equal parts past and future. As with any reality, one extra dimension resulted in a fantastic and mathematically disproportionate inflation of all things contained within it. The flat image of a tree is transformed into a long, measured history of changing seasons, fires, winds, rains, insect invasions, bird nests, electrical storms, high and low growth years, and the slow, penetrating advance of ever-stronger roots.

The rings hidden within the trees told the story with exquisite accuracy and clarity. Every plant, animal, insect, and rock was afforded a unique history, with each story infrequently intersecting others, each meeting forever altering both paths. One could spend a lifetime studying these interactions and the millions of small resulting changes and still never have a solid grasp on it all. But it would be a fantastic and worthwhile voyage.

Sitting with his back to the bulkhead, his eyes still closed, Talon knew his vision contained multiple dimensions. He knew because he imagined himself in the middle of this dream, a significant fact he could not ignore. For he, too, was a benefactor of the third dimension. He, too, now possessed a history – both past and future. The latter was a history he was now in the process of carving. Developing. Earning. The vision could only become reality if he succeeded – if *they* succeeded. So much was at stake. So much needed to be accomplished before he and the other members of *The Aenamaia* would allow themselves to go to their respective forests and cabins and smile unabashedly at the guiltless pleasure they took in being there – in just *being*. Existing happily in a tangible Nirvana.

The psychological and emotional price would be high. But every man and woman had been open and forthright with themselves and with each other on this point. They'd had to be. A strong group ideology was crucial, but not sufficient in and of itself. There must also be solidarity. Theirs was a monumental and distinctly unprecedented undertaking, levying a heavy and lingering tax on mind, body and soul. It was imperative that everyone stay connected and never hesitate to lean on each other for support, comfort and council. The prescient irony of this necessity was never lost on any of them. It was the severing of this connection thousands of years ago that had set mankind on its destructive course. To effectively heal such a massive wound, one must be careful to avoid self-infliction of that very same malady.

"Mr. Svenson?"

Talon's eyes bolted open. Images of his beautiful forest were gone in an instant replaced by that of the flight attendant who was staring down at him questioningly.

"I'm sorry, Mr. Svenson, you'll need to fasten your seatbelt before we depart."

"Yes," he said, grinning sheepishly and feigning embarrassment, "Yes, of course."

He fastened the seat belt, never taking his eyes off the woman. She was tall, almost to the point of precluding a career in air travel. Talon made a quick assessment of her. Mid-thirties, lightly tanned, auburn hair wound tightly in a perfect arrangement he guessed she could fashion blindfolded, natural unpolished nails, single (no ring or tan band), strong and athletic. A mild accent and subtle mannerisms betrayed a

Midwestern upbringing. Her dark blue uniform conformed perfectly to the subtle curves of her body, obviated by the lack of wrinkles or bunching of the fabric. Talon wondered if her workouts were designed around ensuring this fit remained exact – each exercise conscientiously targeting specific vectors and working them until the tangential curvature was perfect. Despite his best efforts, his discomfited smile melted into one of sanguine amusement.

The woman's smile followed suit and changed from one of perfunctory necessity to something more understanding – bordering on conspiratorial. If he didn't know any better, Talon would think she read in his smile everything there was to know about him. For the briefest of moments, he felt transparent.

"I'm sorry," he said simply, "Believe it or not, my mother really did teach me that it was discourteous to stare."

Her smile broadened revealing immaculate white teeth. After a short chortle, she nodded and said, "So did mine." She held his gaze adding, "A parental imperative, I'd wager. Straight from the handbook."

"Undoubtedly," he agreed. "Only during adolescence do we learn that forward progress in life often requires that some rules simply must be broken."

"If we learn it at all," she said coyly.

"Indeed," he said nodding approvingly.

"I'm afraid transcendental philosophy isn't served until later in the flight. To be continued?" she asked playfully.

"If the gods will it?" he said with a wry smile.

She looked at him with interest, as if studying a new species then said, "I'm confident they will."

Casually the flight attendant returned to the front of the cabin, her slender fingers lightly grazing the backs of the gray leather seats. After a well-rehearsed greeting to a late arrival, she disappeared into the small alcove between the front bulkhead and the lavatory. He thought again about his wonderful utopia in the forest; then pictured the woman's beautiful face. He closed his eyes and watched as the two images orbited each other in his mind – like two curious, sentient beings evaluating one another – attracted by a force neither could comprehend. Talon recalled a quote from a soliloquy a friend had written: "Deliver unto me sweet attraction and in return I shall take the first step towards discovery." Talon smiled. "Oh, sweet attraction," he whispered, "the strength you've sapped was stored to resist you. Silly me for thinking resistance could be anything other than futile."

USA Today
Evening Edition
"Domestic Terrorism: The War Against Americans"

by Jordes Grossler and Jack Kelley

Wake up America – this is another terrorism alert. Only this time it isn't orange. The alert is red, white and blue. America is under siege again – only this time from its own citizens. A deadly cancer has infected our beloved country. A plague upon our freedoms and a direct threat to our way of life, our families, and our right to live in a civilized, ordered society. Don't kid yourselves. This is not Oklahoma or Waco. The attack is not being directed at our government, but at us. Is anyone safe? The blood is already running in the streets and the fires are just now beginning to burn.

Recently our own chief editor, Jack Kelley, was given exclusive access to a dangerous new domestic terrorist party, which refers to itself simply as "The Aenamaia." The leader of this organization contacted our editor using sophisticated encryption communications, combined with a voice scrambler so as to avoid tracing and subsequent identification. The leader, who calls himself Gray, immediately claimed responsibility for several terrible affronts to this country. Our sources say this group has been operating underground for many years and can be linked to dozens of assassinations and acts of egregious violence in the United States and abroad. One former Bush official who wished to remain anonymous even suggested that this group provided technical support and financing to Al Qaeda and the terrorists directly responsible for the attacks of 9/11. During his conversation with the terrorist leader, Kelley was told that The Aenamaia was not a faction of any one terrorist organization, but instead are for hire to the highest bidder. Now it seems there must be some very high bidders, indeed.

Yesterday, Pou Lai, formerly of the Energy Corporation, was found murdered at his Colorado ranch. Colorado State Troopers and the local sheriff hurried to Lai's ranch after receiving an anonymous phone tip. Officials are unsure at this time whether the mysterious caller was a man or a woman. However, they did say the caller knew enough details about the homicide to warrant a trip out to the ranch. Upon arriving, officers found the front door wide open and the expensive alarm system disabled. A few feet inside the door lay the cold, naked body of Pou Lai. The former financial magnate was found lying face down, his wrists and ankles bound tightly with duct tape.

The coroner's report revealed Lai had been drugged. But despite a thorough autopsy, the substance used to kill Lai has yet to be identified. Sources which chose to remain anonymous told USA Today *that the body showed signs of sexual violation. Although the coroner denied having found such evidence, investigators say they are not prepared to rule anything out at this point.*

"This is unlike anything we've seen before," said Colorado State Trooper Chief George Delloner. "Two examiners spent almost ten hours thoroughly examining the body, analyzing fluid samples, and running multiple UV exams, but could not determine what killed Mr. Lai. Additionally, no other evidence was found at the scene. We really just don't know what we're dealing with here," Chief Delloner said, "and that troubles me. We have a new lethal substance out there that no one knows about, in the hands of professional killers who appear to have both patience and an agenda. And for all we know, someone could unleash this toxic harbinger into the water supply." Chief Delloner's comments raised immediate concern regarding the public welfare.

"The fact that the toxicology report came back clean indicates this new substance is designed to work quickly and then disappear. But at this time, we have no reason to believe there is a threat to our water system," said Walter Camber of the U.S. Centers for Disease Control. "An investigation will be conducted. Our best toxicologists will work around the clock to ferret out this new threat."

According to The Aenamaia's leader, Gray, this was payback for the Energy Corp scandal – revenge for the damages caused by Energy Corp's leaders. Though Lai was never implicated in the scandal, The Aenamaia chose to ignore the law and the United States Constitution and render judgment and punishment without jury or trial.

During their initial phone call, USA Today *editor Jack Kelley received word that police were conducting a search of the incinerator at Fairfax County landfill in search of the remains of Blackriver CEO David Lesser. Another anonymous tip was received by local police early yesterday morning. The caller again provided specific details of the crime. Within an hour, investigators arrived on the scene and ordered the incinerator to be shut down. While the interior of the incinerator is still too hot to be examined, police have said charred human remains could be seen. Additionally, Lesser's wallet and personal possessions were found near the incinerator door. A few hours later, Lesser's Hummer was found at the bottom of a nearby mining pit. The exterior of the vehicle was intact, but the inside had been completely destroyed. Officials believe a high-tech incendiary device was detonated from within the vehicle in an attempt to erase any evidence of the perpetrator.*

David Lesser was last seen alive the previous afternoon at an upscale hair salon in Washington, D.C. According to the statement taken from the stylist, Lesser was preparing for a big business meeting with some "heavy hitters." The story was corroborated by Lesser's personal secretary. Strangely, police have not been able to locate Deborah Lesser. A close friend of Mrs. Lesser's told police the executive's wife had mentioned taking a long-overdue vacation only a few days ago. Although Mrs. Lesser has not been named as a suspect in the investigation of her husband's disappearance, officials are eager to question her. APBs have been issued in Washington and the surrounding states for her immediate return.

While murder is commonplace in our society, domestic terrorism is not. Is there a connection between Lesser and Lai? Why did this organization target these two wealthy businessmen? And does the story end here?

Yesterday, residents of New York City were once again awakened by a thunderous boom. Hundreds of phone calls flooded police stations as panic-stricken residents experienced painful flashbacks to the horrific attacks of 9/11. Sifting through the deluge of calls, one call in particular stood out: "My name is Venustiano Ramirez, "I'm a...I was a security guard at the National Inquirer *building. This morning my building and others like it around the country were razed to the ground, completely destroyed. A single group is responsible for the demolition. No one was hurt. Please send help."*

Within minutes, police and FBI agents confirmed the destruction of nine other buildings across the country – each one housing tabloid newspapers. The devastating explosions appear to have been timed and coordinated to go off simultaneously, eliminating any possibility of coincidence. Based on the relatively small area containing the debris, officials have concluded that each of the buildings came down in a controlled demolition. Due to the complexity of such demolitions and the limited number of people with the requisite knowledge and access to the necessary explosives, officials are confident it is only a matter of time before the terrorists responsible for this act are captured.

Although everyone scheduled to be in each of the nine buildings destroyed has been accounted for, police and rescue workers are still sifting through the rubble, looking for bodies. Buried beneath thousands of tons of stone and steel are the offices and production equipment that were the lifeblood of the top ten tabloid newspapers in the country. With the production of millions of papers a day stopped cold, many Americans will now be forced to turn elsewhere for their entertainment.

Who are the terrorists? How do we know they are Americans? How do we know they are responsible for these horrific acts? Because they told us.

During his exclusive interview with the terrorist leader, Gray, USA Today *editor Jack Kelley was given the planning details of each of the above acts, including time tables, geographic coordinates, descriptions of weapons and methodologies, and comprehensive descriptions of the acts themselves. But how do we know this information wasn't quickly compiled and researched? After all, each of these events had already taken place when Kelley received the phone call. The horrific proof came several hours after the call had ended.*

Before ending the call to Kelley, the cell leader Gray told him of the next horrendous news America would be waking up to, as well as the names of the victims. Their next targets: Anna Kulter, the well-known political writer and Shirley Felps, the leader of the controversial religious group out of Kansas. For over a year now, Kulter and Felps have been lecturing to college students, churches, and even high school students on a variety of topics ranging from politics to religion – to more controversial subjects such as abortion, euthanasia, and capital punishment. Although many people have publicly condemned these lectures, most would agree on the absolute protection afforded by the First Amendment. Most...except Gray and his followers, apparently.

In the cold, lifeless tone of a computer voice, Gray told Kelley that Anna Kulter, Shirley Felps, and at least fifty people associated with the two women have been kidnapped. Police and FBI, working in conjunction with USA Today, *have confirmed that both Kulter and Felps disappeared shortly after a lecture at the University of Florida in Gainesville. The two women and two of their associates were last seen by campus security exiting the auditorium building. The next morning, campus security found the women's rental car still parked in a campus parking lot. So far, police have not been able to find a single person on campus who saw the women after the lecture. Additionally, police have been unable to locate anyone who has since spoken to either of them.*

During his conversation with Gray, Kelley asked what The Aenamaia had done with the women. The cell's leader refused to comment. Despite his best efforts to negotiate the safe release of the hostages, Kelley was unable to obtain any details as to their whereabouts. When asked what the terrorists would demand for the safe release of the hostages, Gray told Kelley no demands would be made and there would be no negotiations.

Then, less than an hour before this article was to go to press, USA Today *learned that approximately thirty of Washington's top lobbyists had gone missing. More than half the missing men and women were due to meet for a strategy conference to develop a cohesive defense against the proposed mandates restricting lobbyist activities. While there is no direct evidence linking their disappearance to the domestic terrorists, unnamed sources have linked this band of criminal anti-American killers to the act. So far authorities have not disclosed the names of the missing persons.*

America is under attack from the most terrifying enemy, its own citizens. For many years now, this group of anti-American terrorists have been sabotaging our way of life, taking away our freedoms, and threatening the lives of every man, woman, and child in this country. This group of mercenaries has admittedly forged alliances with hundreds of terrorist groups and factions, rogue nations, and other hostile enemies of the United States. They're driven by money, power and a lustful desire for chaos, destruction and anarchy. How they've avoided detection all these years is a mystery, but one thing is certain – no American is safe.

Our fundamental freedoms are at stake. These people have sold out America. They are vultures that do not wait to stumble upon their food, but rather bring about the carnage and violence that creates opportunities. Through fear and intimidation, they will try to divide America, to pit Americans against each other. To sever the strong, united front America has maintained since the attacks of 9/11 and through the war of liberation in Iraq. We must not let this happen. We must stand together and demand the fight that our government will wage upon these foul and wretched betrayers.

It will be imperative that we, as citizens of the greatest free nation on earth, demand that protective measures like the Patriot Act and intelligence agencies like the Department of Homeland Security, which were created by President Bush, are not overturned or softened by the current liberal President. We must ensure that we provide ample funding and flexibility to law enforcement agencies to do whatever is necessary to hunt down The Aenamaia – along with anyone aiding and abetting them.

Wake up America – a new war is upon us!

Tarte stared again at the story White had just handed to him. The story had been posted on the *USA Today* website about an hour ago. A comment beneath the article had made clear that Kelley was not available for quotes or comment. "His ass won't be available for much of anything when I get my hands on him," Tarte thought. White had told him DHS brass had already put the word out to the other agencies that due to the nature of the car bombing and the now clear link between Kelley and *The Aenamaia* responsible, this was clearly within the DHS's jurisdiction.

They would bring him in for questioning. DHS would cooperate with the other agencies, but they would have to wait their turn. Normally, such brashness might cause blowback from the other agencies, but given the volume of investigations caused by this group, everyone had their hands full. Despite the rhetoric and PR each agency constantly passed to the media, interagency cooperation was still a tense and sporadic venture.

Federal and state law enforcement agencies were a lot like professional sports teams. They all played the same games, abided by the same laws, and were all after the bad guys. But while the game might be televised, only the winner of the game got the spotlight in the end. Good spotlights meant more federal funding which ultimately lead to more promotions, higher salaries, and more autonomy. Every law enforcement officer's three favorite things. And Tarte knew that if this "domestic terrorism" story caught on, the race for the coveted spotlight could be even uglier than usual.

The plunging of the knife, then the grin, then the pain and bleeding. *Et tu*, CIA? *Et tu*, FBI? Tarte looked down at the article in his hand and muttered, "*Et tu*, Kelley. Now you're in it too."

Chapter 15

En Route to Washington, D.C.

Even with a host of pressing matters demanding his attention, Talon found himself unable to dismiss thoughts of the unusual woman and the strange, subtly intimate encounter. A wealth of information had been exchanged – far more than could be credited to a sixty-second conversation. There *had* been something there. An exciting hint of possibility in his impossible world. There was a connection, he felt sure of it. But he also knew that emotional surety could be wickedly illusory, especially in matters of the heart. It was prudent to be suspicious of any charged premonitions generated by a muscle so unaccustomed to such activities. How long had it been? When had he last felt that extraordinary, invisible grip around his heart?

This single questioning thought, in the few nanoseconds it took to register, brought the whole of his life into painfully sharp relief. The vital importance and incontrovertible danger inherent in his work – in *their work* – seemed so paramount and simultaneously so tangential to the concerns of a normal, oblivious life. Sitting here now, in this airplane, on the way to what would be his third liquidation in two days, the inimitable nature of his existence made him feel as though he were an impossibility in this reality. He felt invisible, paradoxical, and thoroughly unavailable.

While thoughts such as these were unproductive and feeble, he knew they must not be ignored, but dealt with swiftly and decisively. There was another, more powerful layer of emotion flowing just beneath the surface that must also be acknowledged, analyzed and processed. He turned his palms face up and stared down at his hands. They were unusually flushed.

The sight was unsettling and called forth detailed, graphic images of the job he'd completed only a few hours before. A random, slightly blurred, jerky replay rushed unbidden into his mind. Absently rubbing his left palm, he watched and evaluated the disturbing images. They seemed to carry a hint of judgment and a subtle suggestion of doubt, both of which he discredited immediately.

He tried to mediate the unpleasant mental activity he was about to engage in by conjuring images of the flight attendant's face. An image came quickly, softening the hard lines of his face ever so slightly – and ever so briefly. Then it was gone and again images of violence and struggle rushed back inside the ever-shrinking chasm in his head. But despite the vicious maelstrom twisting incessantly through his mind, it was the redness in his hands that kept arresting his attention. How long had he been rubbing them? Was he flush from the encounter with the woman? Was it the image of the dead body looming at the fringes of his consciousness? Or was it simply...? No, it couldn't be. He'd taken great care to scrub his hands – to make sure it all came off. Even if it really was blood, it was most likely his own, though there was no comfort in that thought. Absently, he reached up and gently rubbed the bandage covering the multiple lacerations that blanketed his left shoulder. He winced slightly and his jaw tightened.

Despite months of careful planning and calculation, his last target had not gone gently into that good night – much to his surprise and dismay. Bernard Luke Arville was the president of the Discovery Institute, the neo-conservative organization whose primary and most public goal was to inject creationism into school curriculums. The "enemies of science and reason," as one scientist labeled them. Another was quoted as lamenting, "They're the people screaming that evolution is false while they sit at the hospital and receive treatments for fast-evolving diseases like tuberculosis and HIV. The hypocrisy is astounding!" Even after the shattering Dover Trials and outright rejection of creationist claims by the scientific community, the Discovery Institute, funded largely by conservative religious organizations, continued to push its agenda, warp or ignore the scientific facts, and find new ways to wedge creationism into schools and public debate. Arville and his organization were on *The Aenamaia's* list from the beginning.

The dossier Skalle had compiled on Arville said nothing of a quick temper, violent tendencies, or any predilection towards fighting. Yet the man had proved to be more resourceful and cunning than Talon would've believed him capable. The well-dressed man had pretended to submit immediately, preparing to grovel for his life. He'd immediately collapsed into a penitent posture as Talon pulled out the syringe and the blue poison. In the middle of a despondent entreaty espousing the virtues of a humble servant to the almighty, Arville had suddenly let out a blood-curdling roar and lunged at Talon.

The move was so unexpected Talon had been forced to drop the vile and syringe in order to defend against the attack. The vile shattered on the tile floor at almost the same moment both men went careening into a large glass trophy case. An instant before impact Talon had managed to plant his foot and pivot, resulting in his attacker's bald head making first contact with the thick glass door and the mirrored rear panel of the case. The impact and sudden stop had caused both men to lose their footing, and Talon wound up lying sideways on the broken glass with the large man on top of him. An instant later the upper glass shelves fractured and came crashing down on Bernard Arville.

The pain in his shoulder had been agonizing, but the adrenaline still pulsing through his veins gave him sufficient strength to carefully roll the dead man off him. The blood was everywhere. Looking back now, it seemed likely the glass had severed an artery or two in Arville's neck. Talon had managed to get back to his feet despite a little vertigo. He'd felt the warm blood running down his arm, but the scene before him held him fast. So much blood. It had been everywhere – on the floor, the wall, around the man's collar, on the thousands of glass shards – everywhere. Talon's hands and clothes were also saturated. Had he been knocked out for a few seconds? How else could he explain the saturation? *Blood everywhere.* The words kept resounding through his mind. *Blood everywhere.* The scene was familiar, as he had witnessed similar events in his old life.

The difference was that he had not been prepared for it this time. Not at all prepared. Slowly, he had realized someone in the building might have heard the loud crashing. Certainly the man's obedient assistant would be back soon. Without losing sight of the dead man, he'd backed away and managed to find the expensive attaché case he'd laid on the edge of a leather couch at the beginning of their meeting. Backing slowly away, he had found it difficult to break his gaze, but he'd opened one of the side pouches and managed to find the spool of bungee cord he always carried. Carefully, he wound the cord around his bicep, a few inches above the group of erratic dark red lacerations gaping from beneath his shredded shirt. He hooked the ends of the makeshift tourniquet, wincing again at the sharp, throbbing pain. Tears escaped from the corners of his eyes while he waited for the burning pain to subside. Fortunately, the cuts had all been separate and relatively superficial. The blood had quickly coagulated, sealing up the wounds. Slowly and with great care, he'd collected the broken remains of the vile and syringe and replaced them in his bag.

He'd been tempted to dress the scene to make it look like an accident, but after evaluating the situation, he'd decided against it. There was no point to it other than as a temporary distraction from the harsh truth of the situation. The grave truth. Each member of *The Aenamaia* knew there was no luxury of denial or disillusionment in this game. If you could not be harshly honest with yourself every step of the way you were a danger to yourself and the organization. This was the nature of the beast – of the self.

The plan had been simple. He'd walk through the lobby doors of the corrupt think tank's corporate offices in Seattle with the intention of killing its leader. Posing as a wealthy and sympathetic supporter referred by former President George W. Bush, he would be granted an immediate audience. After convincing the eager Arville to send his assistant in search of food and drink, he would be told what was to happen and why. A silenced nine-millimeter would be flashed to keep him from running or screaming. The syringe would come out and the blue liquid would be injected into his neck or arm. Arville would get a one-way, first class martyr's ticket to his creator. All of his earthly problems would be behind him. The god-fearing man would offer no more resistance than Pou Lai. Easy.

Unfortunately, Talon had allowed himself to believe it would be simple. "'Give them an inch and they will gladly take your life with more than a modicum of pure, unfiltered satisfaction and justification,'" Gray had once said during training. "'Never ever forget who you're dealing with. Just because these people don't have a branded swastika on their foreheads doesn't mean they're any less dangerous than a psychopathic killer. However, unlike most psychopaths, these people are clever enough to be dangerous while standing front and center in the public limelight. Do not be fooled. Most of them are far more dangerous, patient, calculating and cunning than a psychopath. And most have done a great deal more damage. Never,'" he'd repeated, "'never underestimate your opponent.'" Despite Gray's earnest oft-repeated warning, Talon had indeed grossly underestimated Bernard Arville. He'd paid for his mistake in pain, blood, and graphic memories.

No, disguising the scene had not been an option. Although all had not gone according to his plan, the end result was the same and the objective ultimately achieved. Besides, once the papers received word from Gray, any suggestion of an accident would disappear. Masking the scene would only confuse things and cloud the intentions they hoped the public might someday understand.

The plane shook as the baggage loaders secured the cargo doors beneath the plane. It was a welcome distraction. Talon took a deep breath, exhaling slowly through pursed lips.

"Don't like flying?" Talon looked up. It was the attractive flight attendant's voice. She was looking down at him, her expression mirroring the doubt in her voice.

"What makes you say that?" he replied, trying to sound like a man downplaying her observation.

"You're breathing like someone who is either nervous or is trying to avoid vomiting, you're alternating rubbing your palms, your face is flush and," she paused and tilted her head slightly to change her perspective, "I would guess you're trying in vain to seek thoughts of a better time or place." She smiled sardonically, her expression begging him to prove her wrong.

"Anything else giving me away?" he asked.

She hesitated, then said, "Well, if the muscles in your face get any tighter, your skull is likely to implode. Otherwise, you just look like you'd rather be somewhere else."

"You're very perceptive," he complimented.

"Occupational hazard, I'm afraid," she agreed with a nod.

He smiled despite himself and said, "I was recalling a favorite quote from my childhood reading. 'Always remember Bilbo, when your heart wants lifting, think of pleasant things.'"

The attractive woman returned his smile. "That was your childhood reading? Tolkien?"

"Yes," he said simply with a tiny hint of pride.

Her eyes looked up and left as she considered something, then said, "'When things are bad, we take comfort in the thought that they could always get worse. And when they are rock bottom, we find hope in the thought they can only get better.' I think that's right."

"Tony Robbins?" he guessed playfully.

"My mother," she said still smiling.

Talon knew this game. "'Do not believe that he who seeks to comfort you lives untroubled amidst the simple and quiet words he offers to lift your spirit. His life has known much difficulty. Were it otherwise, he would never have been able to find those words.' A derivation on a Rainer Rilke quote."

"'In the sweetness of friendship let there be laughter, and sharing of pleasures. For in the dew of little things the heart finds its morning and is refreshed.' Kahlil Gibran," she offered.

"'So many of our dreams at first seem impossible, then they seem improbable, and then, when we summon the will, they soon become inevitable.' Christopher Reeve," he said with a solemn smile.

"Were it that neither of us had pressing demands being placed upon us at this moment, it is likely this tennis match could run for a while," she said playfully.

"A high probability, to be sure," he agreed with a considerate nod.

A male flight attendant slipped by and whispered something in her ear. She grinned slightly and nodded, momentarily watching the thin young man expertly dodge and weave down the narrow aisle towards the rear of the plane. She returned her gaze to Talon. She was looking at him with a thoughtful expression, as if studying him. Talon was surprised to find her scrutiny made him feel strangely nervous – as if the solution to her calculations might be of great interest to him. A minor change in the woman's expression suggested she'd finished her calculations and had made a decision. Without a word she turned abruptly and hurried back towards the front of the plane, disappearing around the corner into the food and beverage preparation area.

Talon remained in his seat, puzzled by the woman's sudden retreat. This hadn't been what he'd expected. Come to think of it, he wasn't sure what he'd expected. Why was he expecting anything? Despite the dark memories waiting impatiently at the edge of his consciousness, he found that his mind was now amusingly distracted by the mysterious actions of a perfect stranger. It was a break he welcomed with open arms.

Talon understood that the shift away from dark thoughts had not been a conscious one. This was a line of thought he was very familiar with. Many times in his life he'd had cause to contemplate the innate nature of the mind and the self. Even though neuroscientists and psychologists had been able to prove there was a distinction between the two, experience seemed to suggest otherwise. The important demarcation was more obvious during times of stress or tension. Unfortunately, the very nature of such situations usually precludes any possibility of immediate analysis, or quite often, even reflection afterwards. But there was a boundary – of that Talon felt certain. On many occasions it had seemed as if his mind were on cruise control, and he was a helpless passenger watching from the back seat.

Many things could trigger this feeling. Thoughts of all kinds often came unbidden into his mind – good, bad, ugly, sad, tragic, bizarre, and sometimes a witches' brew with a little of everything. When this happened, he would attempt to trace the source of the thoughts. If they were particularly bad, like the image of someone suffering or of gratuitous violence, he would examine his own situation and mood in search of similarities. In addition to his mood, he would examine events of late, things he'd encountered in his environment, conversations he'd had, even the foods he'd eaten. Once he went so far as to seek out particularly spicy Cuban food one night in Havana to see what thoughts resulted. Besides a flop sweat or two and breath that could stop a grizzly bear in its tracks, nothing unusual had come of it.

The mind's nocturnal activities often helped elucidate the matter. The randomness and inconsistency of dreams lent credence to his theory that the human brain had evolved two levels of consciousness, which he referred to as awake and alert, subconscious and unconscious. The barriers between the two were membrane-thin which resulted in a fair amount of crossover. Thoughts flooded in randomly and at will. Or, as Talon preferred to put it, against his own will. Which suggested the mind indeed operated two wills simultaneously – one that he could manipulate and one that seemed to be well outside of his control. The latter, he guessed was usually the subconscious.

Recalling his past operations now, however, he suddenly realized that during periods of intense concentration, the second level was largely suppressed, giving extra power and focus to his primary state. Perhaps when the mind relaxed and wandered, the barriers weakened. From an evolutionary standpoint, it could very well be that the subconscious and the unconscious mind evolved to protect the body when the conscious mind was occupied with things not related to survival. "That," he thought, "would explain a lot." Even cooped up in a stuffy airplane, this made perfect sense.

Talon smiled broadly. He imagined two young, ancient human ancestors – perhaps Australopithecus – hunched down on the planes of Africa, both enthralled with a brightly colored patch of spring wild flowers. The two were engrossed in examination, throwing all normal alertness and caution to the wind. But when a stampede of African Buffalo approached, the one fortunate enough to have been born with the two extra levels of consciousness managed to get out of the way. This one would go on to have many children, all with the same gift – the same "other minds" watching out for the safety of the fragile, fleshy shell. No doubt such automatic protection helped the species survive and prosper. He wondered how long it had taken those without this gift to eventually fade from time. Our clumsy, not-too-bright ancestors. Images again flashed through his mind – cactuses, hungry lions, cliffs, and many other hazards for the prehistoric dimwitted.

Before he could broaden this line of thinking, the flight attendant reappeared and headed straight for him. Thoughts of reckless cavemen and barren landscapes receded as more primal instincts emerged. He felt his heartbeat quicken and thought with some irony, "Some habits definitely have not evolved much."

Looking around cautiously, she knelt down beside him. She seemed to have made a decision, but her expression suggested she wasn't quite sure it was the right one. Her mouth opened but no sound escaped. It was as if she were trying to remember how to form and pronounce words. Her eyes darted to the right and in a split second, her face had returned to its airline-issued, bright and cheery façade.

"Beer and wine are seven dollars. What can I get you?" she asked him innocently.

It took Talon an extra moment to realize another flight attendant must be coming up the aisle. Something interesting was about to happen, that much seemed certain.

"Do you have anything from Domaine de la Romanée-Conti? Perhaps a "78 Montrachet?"

The attractive woman watched from the corner of her eye as the male flight attendant passed behind her. "What?" she said absently. She returned her gaze to Talon and repeated, "I'm sorry. What did you say?"

"Just a bit of trivia," he said apologetically. "I read somewhere that a bottle of 1978 Montrachet recently sold for around twenty-four grand. I figured a glass at seven dollars would be a steal."

The woman smiled, but he could see the uncertainty behind the jovial façade. Talon decided to act on his hunch. "Actually," he said casually, "I was hoping you could recommend a good hotel near the Dulles airport. One with a nice restaurant."

She studied him for a quick moment, a hint of relief spreading across her face. She steadied herself and said, "Of course, Mr. Svenson. The Hyatt Dulles is a very nice hotel. It isn't far from the main terminal and does have a five-star restaurant."

"That sounds great," he chimed in cheerily. "Since you folks decided to stop serving real food on these tubs I usually land at Dulles with a ravenous appetite." His smile was friendly, but otherwise his expression was unreadable. He looked down and pulled an invisible speck of lint off of his slacks. "In fact," he added, "the restaurant is the first place I go when I get to the hotel." He looked directly at her, a hint of question in his eyes.

She looked casually from side to side to see if anyone appeared to be eavesdropping. Apparently satisfied, she said, "I can certainly understand that."

Although he was unsure why, Talon felt strangely amused and even somewhat reassured by the woman's uncertainty. It was obvious this type of play was not a normal part of her job – or her life, for that matter. Throughout his travels Talon had encountered many women happy to straddle the extreme other end of the flirting spectrum. They would banter, play, feign, and flash innocent smiles after every innuendo. Fortunately, he had become adept at detecting these types early and casually avoiding any extended interaction with them. Let the players play and let everyone else keep their distance. By his early twenties, his core definition of quality and the hierarchy of priorities continuously strayed away from the more carnal and hormonal pursuits of youth. And for this he was eternally thankful.

The woman was about to walk away when he added, "You're a lifesaver. Thank you so much for your help, Catherine."

Talon watched as the beginning of the sentence "How did you...?" formed on the woman's lips. He nodded knowingly towards the small name tag on her lapel.

The woman smiled coyly. She laughed silently and said, "Glad to be of assistance – Mr. *Svenson*," pronouncing his assumed last name as if she doubted it was really his. Turning quickly on her heel, Catherine walked a few rows forward and began engaging the other passengers in polite conversation.

Talon smiled, pulled the classified FEMA manual from his attaché case and muttered, "Dinner it is, then."

McLean, Virginia

The buzzer on Jack Kelley's desk rang three times in quick succession. That was his secretary's way of informing him that Harrison Beckingham was on his way down. The president and publisher of *USA Today* usually only made personal calls when something particularly controversial was published without his blessing. Shortly after Kelley had submitted the article on domestic terrorism to the online publishing department, he'd sent Beckingham a short blurb via email about the article, but had intentionally left out any specific details. "Why was I so vague?" he wondered. "Was I preserving a bit of plausible deniability for Beckingham? An invisible shield of ignorance and incredulity the boss could honestly employ should the proverbial shit hit the proverbial fan?"

Unfortunately, that excuse rarely afforded the top dogs much cover these days. "Besides," he thought, "if the pompous ass were to be burned at the stake, I'd be the first one fireside with a bratwurst on a stick and a broad, unmistakably satisfied smile." Truth be told, Beckingham's name hadn't floated down his stream of consciousness until after the story had gone to press. This story was just as much personal as it was professional. For the first time in his career, Kelley had become a character in one of his own stories. His life had been threatened, his car detonated, his home broken into, and his privacy violated. But where there was suffering – even his own – there was a story and opportunity. With a little luck, this story might even turn out to be his swan song. Damned if he'd let anyone take it away from him. Therefore, the less Beckingham knew about it, the better. Or so he'd thought.

A few minutes passed before there was a quiet rapping on the door. Kelley suddenly wished he were somewhere else. In fact, almost anyplace else would do. But he'd known this was inevitable and decided it was best to get it out of the way now.

"Come in," he called out.

Kelley watched as his secretary opened the door and quickly stepped aside. Harrison Beckingham strode confidently through the door, walking headlong and full of purpose, as if into his own private corner office. This was Beckingham's signature entrance. He would enter a room with such fervor and speed that one got the impression the *USA Today* president would charge right through a closed door if no one was there to open it. Kelley's secretary nodded nervously and quietly closed the door on her way out.

Kelley had known for years that Beckingham avoided opening or closing doors wherever he went. It was an odd habit everyone in the company knew about, but no one discussed openly. It was almost as if the mere act of opening or closing a door was somehow degrading and therefore beneath him. Beckingham had been born into old money, but nowhere near enough to justify a Rockefeller or du Pont snobbery. It was also a well known fact that Beckingham washed his hands a dozen times a day – sometimes more. Kelley wasn't sure whether his boss was a germaphobe, had a bad case of OCD, was a pompous snob who felt superior to everyone around him, or a bizarre combination of all three. All Kelley knew for sure was the oddball had taken time out of his day to visit him – and that was never a good sign.

The publisher was slender and fit, but not muscular. He had short-cropped cinnamon brown hair with thin lines of gray near his temples. Beckingham boasted an impressive six-and-a-half feet, his ample height providing a perspective Kelley imagined reinforced feelings of superiority and dominance. He had faded blue eyes, a narrow nose, pale lips and fair skin. The man's face was so cleanly shaven one could be forgiven for thinking a short-lived puberty had left the executive incapable of growing facial hair. Hard lines, narrow face and pronounced cheek bones hinted at a Scandinavian lineage, minus the blonde hair. More than once Kelley had pondered his superior's odd looks. The man was handsome enough, but at the same time there were subtle nuances in his appearance that caught one's attention. His was the type of face people often found themselves staring at – though most never understood why. "Strange nut, this one," Kelley thought.

No one knew Harrison Beckingham's true age, but Kelley guessed he was in his late fifties. He wore an expensive tailored suit, tan coat on pressed white shirt, dark brown Berluti dress shoes with a high shine and a faint underlying pattern that resembled polished mahogany. In the breast pocket of his blazer was a neatly folded white handkerchief embroidered with the initials HDB. A bright silver and blue tie with an indiscernible abstract print stood in stark contrast to the otherwise picture perfect ensemble. Kelley imagined Beckingham walking into an overpriced tailor, seeing a model's picture on the wall, and saying, "Make me look like that Tommy."

"Jack!" Beckingham said, extending a pale, freckled hand. "Jack, how are you?" There was a mild hint of distress in the man's droll voice – false concern over the morning's violent events. Kelley reached across his desk and took the man's hand. "Soft and clean," he thought. Kelley wondered with amusement how long the towering executive could hold out until his next hand washing.

"I'm fine, Harrison. Thank you."

Beckingham stood before his desk, hands on his hips, and surveyed him. "You certainly don't present the appearance of a man attacked by domestic terrorists."

"Please," Kelley said gesturing to one of the leather chairs. Beckingham unbuttoned his blazer and sat down. He crossed his legs casually and staring down at his shoe repeated skeptically, "'Domestic terrorists,' Jack?"

Kelley felt his face flush, but replied calmly, "That's what they are, Harrison, not the local Rotary Club or ROTC out for a little fun detonating SUVs. High grade explosives. Enough to lift a two-ton vehicle ten feet off the ground and flip it in mid-air."

Beckingham looked at him with reluctant eyes and said apologetically, "I didn't mean to diminish what happened this morning, Jack. It's horrific and I'm grateful you're safe. I only mention it because – well, I'm concerned about the content of our editorials relative to the verifiable facts."

Kelley remained silent. He had an idea where this ship was heading, but he thought it best to let Beckingham be the one to steer them into the choppy waters. After a prolonged silence, the publisher continued.

"Frankly Jack..."

"Frankly," Jack urged.

Beckingham took a deep breath, sighed, then said, "All right then. Sources, Jack. Your 'sources' seem to know an awful lot about this *Aenamaia* group."

"That's what sources are for, Harrison," Jack answered, unable to hide the defensiveness in his voice.

"Jack," Beckingham said pleadingly, "every law enforcement agency in the country is gnashing its teeth on this one. High profile murders and bombings tend to rile them up. Congressmen, senators, the joint chiefs, and a number of influential committee members are all shouting for answers. Every law enforcement agent who carries a gun is on the prowl. Now, I have contacts in high places in many of these agencies and they're asking me how you got your information."

"Freedom of the press," Kelley declared. "We don't have to tell them anything."

"Unless they subpoena you," Beckingham fired back.

Kelley considered this, but said nothing.

"Jack," Beckingham tried again, "Al Qaeda and 9/11? And from an undisclosed Bush official, no less." Beckingham threw up his hands. "A Bush official, Jack? Now? I thought we all agreed that while Bush was under investigation, all published facts and comments would be disclosed and on the record. What are we going to say when the FBI, CIA, and the Department of Homeland Security throw the Patriot Act in our faces and demand that we disclose *everything* in the name of national security? If there is nothing there, the world will hear about it – whether we like it or not. That's a death warrant for a news agency."

When Kelley didn't answer, Beckingham stood up and began pacing.

"Look, Jack," he said somewhat apologetically, "don't get me wrong. This is one fantastic story. But you have to understand how it might be received right now. Our circulation is down fifteen percent, something our competitors have made note of more than once. They're trying to paint us as an antiquated old ship only moments away from sinking. So when the editor prints an earth-shaking editorial, with himself as the only source cited by name – let's just say the vultures have begun circling."

"I was there," Kelley said pointing out the window. "I was on the phone with this sonofabitch when my car exploded. The coffee shop was blown all to hell. I was almost killed by a projectile that only a split second before had been one of my car doors!" Kelley stood and leaned over his desk, his voice low and serious. "He told me all of this, Harrison," he said pointing down at the article still lying on his desk. "Everything I put in here."

"Everything?" Beckingham said skeptically.

Kelley's hesitation was not lost on Beckingham.

"These guys abducted fifty people in the Kulter camp, but we only have two names? Who are the other people?" Beckingham asked.

Kelley kept his eyes fixed on his boss, but chose not to comment.

"Jack," Beckingham placated, "I know that on a few occasions we've found it necessary to make – well, assumptions and calculated conjectures. But with a story like this, the United States government isn't really going to care about the freedom of the press." Beckingham saw Kelley's expression change and added, "And with a fifteen percent decline in circulation, now isn't the time to try and fight them. Our competition is ready and willing to tear us apart at the seams. We just can't afford to step on our goddamn dicks here."

Kelley was momentarily taken back by Beckingham's use of profanity. The career newspaper man rarely resorted to such blue-collar language. Kelley weighed his words carefully.

"Are you suggesting a retraction?"

Beckingham stood staring out the window.

"No," he said, "No. That would be more damaging than just letting it go." He turned and faced Kelley.

"What we need is *more*, Jack," Beckingham said excitedly.

"Here comes the pep rally," Kelley thought.

"We need a recording of this guy's admission to these crimes and offenses. We need to show we're in the know by printing something just before it happens. If that isn't possible, then we need to be the first to press with the details. Then we need to throw the authorities a bone – something to show we're playing ball. We need to be on top of this one."

Beckingham approached the desk again and the two men made eye contact.

"Jack," he said earnestly, "this could be the story that gets us back to the summit and puts you there on top holding the *USA Today* flag. But it has to be done correctly. The climb is steep. One false move and we're all toast."

Beckingham leaned on the desk, his eyes almost wild. Kelley sank into his chair and stared at the editorial. He'd been so certain when he'd written it – so confident. The world had been his for the overturning. Now he wasn't sure about anything. After a few moments he asked, "What do you suggest?"

"First things, first," Beckingham said, lowering his large frame into a chair. "You've already mentioned Bush and that's playing with fire. Since you don't actually have a source, go out and find one – someone from Bush's clan who will go on record and confirm what you've published. Preferably someone who is likely to be involved in the trials. There's bound to be some yahoo out there looking for attention – or even a job offer. Second, have some of your top people get in touch with the FBI, CIA, and DHS. See what they know. Let them know we're willing to cooperate. Run a follow-up story outlining what those agencies are doing to catch this group. Put out a call to all Americans to keep their eyes open and to report any suspicious activity or useful information to us or the authorities. A call to patriotism and all that. Steer the story towards the pursuit – the chase – the action. See if we can rekindle the flame of pride and anger that burned after 9/11. Stay away from conspiracies and unnamed sources. Most Americans don't know the difference between a factual story and an editorial anyway. And those that do, don't care which is which. They want to be entertained – and afraid. With a little focus and some clever writing, we can keep this story going and at the same time bury your editorial."

Kelley looked up anxiously, his face flushed with anger, but Beckingham put up a hand and said, "Now take it easy, Jack. This is still your baby. Your story started the ball rolling and is the jumping off point for this campaign. But you stuck us out on a limb at a bad time. Now we need to pull things in and keep our hand close to the chest."

Beckingham stood abruptly and walked towards the door. After a few steps he turned and said, "Above all else Jack, you need to find a way to get back in touch with this Gray. Get him talking and get it on tape. Until you do, we're paralyzed and bleeding in the water – and the sharks are on their way."

The two men stared at each other for a moment. Beckingham's expression changed from solemn to something resembling expectation. Without breaking eye contact, Kelley reached over and pressed the intercom button on his phone. "Mr. Beckingham is ready to leave now, Ms. Cutter."

Derision and satisfaction crept into the towering executive's expression. The instant the door opened Beckingham spun around and bolted for the lobby. Ms. Cutter leapt out of his way, barely avoiding what would've been an awkward and messy collision.

"Addlepated peacock," Kelley muttered, watching his shaken secretary quickly pull the door shut. He could feel the heat and blood rush to his face. Beckingham was more of an effete politician than a dyed-in-the-wool newspaperman, but that didn't mean he was completely wrong. Maybe he had been too hasty in publishing the editorial. Of course he knew about the decline in circulation, though he'd heard the true number was closer to twenty percent. Somehow he'd convinced himself his article could help bring those numbers back to normal. And it still could.

Beckingham had been right about one thing – the story wasn't finished. If he wanted to champion the newspaper's recovery, he would have to find a good shovel and start the digging. "First things, first. Now," he thought, "how does one reach out and touch a domestic terrorist?"

Chapter 16

Washington, D.C.

"I should've just lied," Talon thought, "but what choice did I really have?" The truth here is the key to Pandora's Box. His vague and elusive reference to an "unfortunate altercation" wouldn't hold up – not with someone like her. She'll eventually want to know what actually lies beneath the bandages and what *really* caused the "accident." Women are curious and remarkably intuitive. Millions of years spent caring for their young and their males had hard-wired a desire to heal wounds – regardless of what had caused them. Even with years of experience using false identities and accents, selling strangers on false backgrounds and invented lives and projecting personalities opposite that of his own, he hadn't been able to avoid the split second of hesitation when she'd asked what had happened to his shoulder. The implications of his reluctance to lie to this woman were both profound and inescapable.

Talon turned onto his side, careful not to make any noise. The ghostly silver glow of moonlight coming in through the hotel window silhouetted a slender back, smooth shoulders and long wavy hair. "Remarkable," he thought. Women have such magnificent power in so many areas – mind, body and soul. There is so much strength there. How was it that men still had a stranglehold on the world's power? Give the women of the world a hive-mind for one week and the next week they would control everything. Talon smiled. He'd been saying that for years. But at this moment, barely able to stay afloat in a torrent of his own feelings, staring hungrily at this remarkable creature, it felt truer than ever.

The evening had started with a glass of chardonnay and a table for two. He'd spent the first twenty minutes trying to veil his eagerness and anticipation. More than once he'd laughed quietly at himself for his trepidation. Images flashed through his mind of days past when his personality, appearance, voice, accent, mannerisms, even eye color had been altered and amalgamated into one of countless fictional persona. How many different characters had he portrayed, in how many countries and for how many years? And in all those cases, he had never experienced an overriding sense of anticipation to match the tumultuous storm that had raged in his stomach and his mind during last night's dinner. The details from last night were crystal clear in his mind.

Staring blankly through the supple gold liquid in his oversized wine glass, he felt a small wedge of doubt creep into his mind. Had he miscalculated? Would she show? A moment later, movement at the hostess stand caught his attention. Their eyes locked instantly. Unconsciously, he rose slowly from his chair, the cloth napkin in his lap falling unnoticed to the floor. He couldn't believe his eyes. "Was this really the same woman?" he'd wondered.

Time seemed to slow to a crawl. The hostess and Catherine exchanged a few words, then made their way across the restaurant. Talon would bet his life that every set of eyes in the place had locked onto this magnificent creature, though he couldn't be sure since he himself couldn't take his eyes off her.

Her gait was confident, measured and purposeful, yet simple and graceful. "Has this been orchestrated?" he wondered. "Is it some kind of dance?"

An image from their first encounter on the airplane came back to him, as if his mind anticipated his need for a comparison. Still staring at the radiant creature moving slowly towards him, he realized the transformation was no less than astounding. The bland, standard issue airline uniform was gone. The clipped, professional hairdo had been replaced by long, wavy, flowing strands of shiny reddish-brown hair.

She wore a sleeveless black evening dress that hung to an inch below her knees. The neckline ran parallel to her shoulders, barely concealing her collarbones. Two inch-wide straps ran over her shoulders and joined halfway down her back – the "V" framing smooth, strong shoulders. Around her waist, folded black cloth radiated elegantly in all directions from a simple gold buckle hanging to one side. Despite the tendency for black to trick the eye, it was obvious this dress softly caressed every line, curve and contour of this stunning woman's body – and did so by design. When she moved, every inch of the fabric glided on a razor thin pocket of air just above the skin. Talon could not recall ever seeing another person look so natural in elegant clothing – or so beautiful.

As Catherine approached, Talon noticed two additional accoutrements. In her right hand she carried a small, black sequined clutch. On her left wrist was a shiny tennis bracelet. Out of habit he again scanned her fingers. He felt relieved and ridiculous at the same moment. Clearly her presence here tonight should be ample proof that she was bold, interested and unmarried.

"Well, good evening," he said with his best pleasantly-surprised smile.

"Good evening," she replied with a casual nod.

As he pulled out her chair he confessed, "I must admit I am surprised to see you here." He pushed in her chair and reseated himself.

As he bent to retrieve his napkin, she smiled and said, "I was wondering how we would start this off. I wasn't sure if the game was still in play or if you would just cut to the chase."

Talon bowed his head slightly and laughed warmly. He considered his words for a moment then said, "I believe the start of the game coincided with the start of the chase. Isn't that how all good games begin? The real question is, who is chasing whom?"

"Perhaps," she said thoughtfully, "the perspective is wrong. What if we're both chasing *something* and our paths happened to cross? Then suddenly, we find ourselves stopped dead in our tracks, sitting in a beautiful restaurant, wondering exactly what it was that we had been so fervently chasing."

Before he could respond, the waiter sauntered up to their table. He was a portly man in his early forties with short, neatly combed black hair. He was clean-shaven and walked with an odd, perky bounce in his step. Striding up to the table in his pressed white uniform, he reminded Talon a little of Oliver Hardy, minus the toothbrush mustache.

"Good evening, madam," he said pleasantly. Talon noticed that Catherine's beauty didn't appear to have any effect on this man. "Professional or gay?" he wondered.

The waiter raised his notepad as if to take an order, then did a double-take and asked Catherine, "Have you been a guest here before? You look very familiar."

Talon was surprised when Catherine blushed slightly and answered, "Yes. I've stayed here many times. I work for the airlines."

"Ah. That would explain it. Very good, madam." Redirecting his attention back to his notepad he asked, "What can I bring you to drink?"

"Whatever the gentleman is having," she said, her eyes fixed on Talon.

Without breaking eye contact, Talon replied casually, "Sonoma Cutrer."

"Very good, sir," the waiter said, turned and left.

"Cutrer?" she inquired.

"I'm not sure what it means," he said honestly spreading his hands. "A good friend of mine was a viticulturist in Sonoma Valley. Ordering it makes me think of her."

Catherine saw the brief flash of pain and remorse on his face and did not press further.

"So," she started, trying to sound pert, "should I call you Mr. Svenson all night or can I know your first name?"

Talon had been so wrapped up in his thoughts about tonight that he had almost forgotten which name he had told her. He silently berated himself for losing sight of his objectives so easily. Even when an opportunity arose on a mission, it was imperative that one always remain in profile. Fortunately, when he'd made the hotel reservation an hour ago, he'd remembered to use the correct name. He'd called the hotel from his cell while walking through the main terminal. After several wrong turns he'd finally managed to locate the exit door and hail a taxi. The fact that he'd been in this airport hundreds of times and never once made such mistakes hadn't made the situation any easier. Stepping into the cab, he'd silently mused that perhaps the esteemed Mr. Svenson was not only smitten, but also directionally challenged.

"I suppose since I've taken the liberty of using your first name it would only be proper to return the favor in kind. My first name is Göte, but my friends call me Talon." There was something about lacing a lie with a smidgeon of truth that seemed to take the edge off the foulness of the act. It made it seem as though it were a game and the solitary fact was inserted as a show of goodwill to legitimize it as such.

"Talon," she said, pronouncing the name carefully, as if she were testing it for validity. She looked at him askew with a playful grin. "There must certainly be an interesting story behind such an unusual nickname, yes?"

It was a question he'd been asked many times before, though he had only told a few close friends the truth. As always, the inquiry prompted the familiar image of a magnificent snowy mountain vista to flash into his head. Talon felt like his mind had taken a slow, deep breath. He remembered something his father used to say when confronted with something awe-inspiring. "'There are moments in one's life that gain such magnificent purchase on the soul that they never lose their hold on it,'" adding with a wink and a smirk, "'nor do we want them to.'"

Throughout his travels, Talon had cause to recall that quote many times. And of the many such moments in his life that qualified as awe-inspiring and memorable, that day in Switzerland still stood out the most. Even though it had been almost twenty years since his first climb in the Pennine Alps, he still remembered the awesome and humbling sensation he'd felt standing on a narrow ledge high on the Ober Gabelhorn mountain, more than halfway up the Arbengrat climbing route. He and his two guides had left the village of Schwarzsee at first light that summer morning, hiking first down into the Zmutt valley to reach the base of the Arbenbach. The climb to the south face of the Ober Gabelhorn had been relatively easy, but he hadn't taken much time to enjoy the view. It had been his first thirteener in Europe and he was determined to make it a textbook ascent.

Six hours into the climb they came upon a wide, flat ledge and decided to rest and have something to eat. The two guides moved to the end of the ledge, pulled off their packs and sat down. Talon dropped his pack and immediately began fussing with his harness and ropes, trying to make sure everything was ready for the more technical climbing ahead. Several minutes passed before one of the guides, Claus, tapped him on the shoulder. The man was grinning like a wise old man who knew a secret his young apprentice had yet to discover. Claus looked at him for a moment, shook his head, then pointed into the distance. It was then that it occurred to Talon he hadn't spared a moment to take in the view.

When he finally stood up, the landscape that met his gaze had been utterly spectacular. A panoramic view of the entire valley lay before his eyes. Everything looked frozen in time. There was no movement that he could discern. All worlds, including his own, had assumed a reverent silence. It was as if the earth's many geologic processes had rushed to create all that he could see and then stilled the moment to allow him to admire the results. Talon, too, had frozen – unable to take his eyes from the majestic beauty before him. He barely noticed when the grinning guide patted him on the shoulder and returned to where he'd been sitting. "Remarkable," he'd whispered. "Absolutely, undeniably remarkable."

While his guides busied themselves with food and conversation, he tried to get his bearings. When he'd decided on this region for the climb, he'd spent several weeks studying the details and challenges of each route on each mountain. Recalling the main geographic features of the area, he recognized the Dent d'Hérens and the Dent Blanche peaks, both of which were dwarfed by their famous neighbor the Matterhorn. The three mountains sat opposite the Ober Gabelhorn peak. Running between the two ranges a kilometer below his feet, stretched the thin, hourglass-shaped Zmutt glacier. By definition all glaciers were in constant motion – advancing only a few inches per year, mercilessly carving and shaping the dirt and rock beneath them. What made the Zmutt somewhat unusual was the rigid resistance of the valley it was slowly pushing through.

Although it was clear the thick body of ice was still advancing, its gradual brute force came at a high price. Instead of the typical smooth and flat surface one might expect, the pressure from the bottlenecking caused the ice to buckle, fracture and compress. Scattered along its length were innumerous fissures, crevasses, a sprinkling of circular and oblong melt water pools and supra-glacial lakes, and a variety of nested stratigraphy of concentric folia – the many layers of different ice types and entrained sediment. The geologic forces and stresses, combined with the annual melting-freezing cycle, resulted in a rough-textured surface comprised of pristine white patches intermixed randomly with light gray areas. It was the gray sections that had puzzled him the most.

Years later he would learn about band ogives – downward-pointing bands or undulations of the glacier that were the result of a nearby ice fall. Though he'd never taken the time to fully research what he'd seen while on top of Zmutt glacier, he had speculated that the gray radial sections he saw were in fact ogives – the discoloration being a different type of ice.

Lying peacefully beneath the Zmutt was the picturesque Lötschental Valley. The lush verdant area was nestled below the base of the towering Matterhorn. Even from his small ledge high up on the Ober Gabelhorn, he could clearly see the loose network of dirt and paved roads leading to quaint houses, farms, green pastures, and the small township. He had thought he could even see the inn where he'd spent the previous two nights.

Combining all the pieces – the contrast of pure white snow and ice, clear blue sky, emerald green valley, and every shade of gray slate imaginable still pushing toward the heavens – he beheld a fantastic testimony to nature's stunning grandeur. The humbling feeling imbued by nature was unlike any other, though one very familiar to him. Many times during his climbs Talon was compelled to ponder such vistas – to try and grasp the time, forces and innumerable natural processes that had contributed to the amazing sights before him. Though the exercise usually resulted in his becoming lost in thought, he thoroughly enjoyed letting his mind roam free while his legs propelled him upward.

While admiring the view from the Ober Gabelhorn, a sad emotion found its way into his psyche. It was a pang of melancholy from the realization that only a tiny handful of people on the planet got to experience such awe-inspiring splendor. He wondered how the world might change if every one of its occupants could experience a moment like that. To be unplugged from everything except nature in all its glory, to experience the serenity and joy of witnessing something so spectacular. He took comfort in the sincere hope that perhaps someday the world's values and ideals would shift enough to make the exploration, appreciation, respect, and protection of nature a high priority.

That day on the ledge he'd had to force himself to break his gaze from the stunning vista and concentrate on the tasks at hand. Food and water first, then a supply check: ropes, carabineers, descender, spikes, hammer, and harness. He'd need each piece of equipment for the difficult ascent ahead. The plan had been to climb the south face of the mountain then bivouac for a few hours after they had reached the summit.

After they had finished eating, the party continued their ascent. The two guides he'd hired were leading the way with Talon in tow a meter or so behind. The men were having an animated discussion in German, most of which Talon didn't understand at the time. They had rounded a sharp, jagged corner balancing on a thin ledge and found themselves facing a headwall, a section of the climb where the ascension path had steepened dramatically. Talon watched as the two men leaned into the angular rock face and prepared their ropes and pitons for the climb to the next ledge. The next traversable ledge was around thirty feet straight up. Despite the narrowness of the ledge and the five hundred-foot vertical drop beneath it, the two men continued their discussion, seemingly oblivious to the danger. The constant jabbering made Talon a little uncomfortable, but he refrained from saying anything – a decision he would soon regret.

"Excuse me, sir, but the plane has landed," Catherine said staring across the table at him.

"What?" he said, as thoughts of mountains and climbing gave way to embarrassment.

Catherine was looking at him with a puzzled grin. "Even though the plane has landed and you're now having dinner with your flight attendant, you're not really here."

He was about to explain when she added, "And you had the exact same distant look on your face again. So," she said pausing for effect, "maybe I could barter my willingness to have dinner with a complete stranger for an honest answer. Would that be a fair trade?"

Talon laughed. "Women's intuition," he thought to himself, "it's marvelous." He felt a little foolish, but decided not to make up an excuse. Instead, he allowed his desire to relay the story to take over. The next twenty minutes were spent detailing the events of that day climbing in the Swiss Alps. Though he had told the story a few times over the years, he suddenly found himself more animated than usual, and also strangely determined to add enough vibrant color and detail so as to paint a splendid three-dimensional image for his listener.

Looking now at the beautiful woman sleeping peacefully next to him he guessed it had worked. During his story Catherine had given him her undivided attention. At the time he'd been confident that each new piece of the narrative he revealed added another important piece of the landscape she was imagining. When he casually mentioned the headwall she had stopped him.

"What is a headwall?" she asked.

"Sorry. It usually refers to a section of the climb where the route you're taking suddenly ends at a steep or vertical section. In order to continue, someone, usually the most experienced climber, has to climb up to the next ledge. That someone was Claus."

"What about 'bivouac' – what does that mean?"

"It's a climber's term for sleeping or lying down out in the open. We had planned to get to the summit, have a quick look around, then nap before heading back. To make a bivouac you dig a shallow, narrow trench in the snow, lay down a thin liner, then curl up inside a special type of waterproof sleeping bag called a bivouac sack. The trench keeps you out of the wind and the sack keeps you dry and warm."

"Bivouac," Catherine repeated, stretching out each of the three syllables. "Bivouac. It's a strange word, but also kind of fun to say."

Talon smiled. "It can also refer to a shelter made of natural materials like branches, leaves, and plants. A well constructed natural bivouac is dry and insulated."

Catherine looked at him askance and commented, "You don't strike me as the outdoorsy woodsman type. Boy Scout?"

"Wandervogel," he replied with a wry grin.

"Gesundheit," Catherine said returning the smirk.

"Beautiful and witty – dangerous combination."

"Ah, but you knew that when you extended the invitation, did you not?"

"Ja, ich wusste, dass," Talon said smiling. "Yes, I did know that."

Catherine cocked an eyebrow while she considered what to say next. After a few moments she asked, "So are you fluent in German or do you just throw out a few phrases to try and impress a girl?"

Talon thought about it for a moment then answered, "Wir zogen nach Deutschland, als ich elf Jahre alt war. Wir lebten dort, bis ich neunzehn war." He leaned towards Catherine and added, "Sie haben sehr schöne Augen, Catherine."

"Why thank you," Catherine said. "My mother gave them to me."

Talon looked surprised.

Catherine laughed and said, "Don't worry – apart from your comment about pretty eyes I have no idea what you said."

"Then how did you…?"

"We fly regularly to Hamburg, Berlin and Munich. I hear 'schöne Augen' quite often."

"And how do you respond to such a compliment?"

"The same way I responded to you."

"In German?"

"Oui, monsieur," Catherine said confidently.

Talon looked skeptical. Catherine sighed, thought a moment, then said cheerily, "Danke. Meine mutter gab sie mir."

Talon nodded approvingly, but remained silent. He felt like he was back on the airplane – unable to stop staring at this exciting and intriguing woman. Catherine's transformation from attractive and conservative flight attendant to stunning and radiant beauty only made matters worse – and better.

A few moments passed before Catherine asked, "Are you going to stare at me all night or are you going to explain what all the rest of that *gehuginspoonin* meant?"

"If I thought I could get away with it, I would definitely stare at you all night," Talon admitted, adding, "me and every other person in this restaurant."

Catherine started to turn to see if anyone was indeed looking at her, but seemed to decide against it and instead leaned back in her chair and looked expectantly across the table.

"'Wandervogel' means 'youth group' in and around Germany," Talon explained. "Mostly nature-friendly activities – hiking, biking, camping and some basic survival training. What I said after that was that we moved to Germany when I was eleven and we lived there until I was nineteen. That's when I was involved with the Wandervogel and became interested in the great outdoors."

"And the German?" Catherine asked.

"I'm not as fluent as I used to be, but I still know enough to be dangerous."

"The 'dangerous' part I can buy," Catherine admitted, but before Talon could comment she said, "No need to explain. Let's go back to the high rock ledge on Oober Gabberdorn."

Talon smiled and said, "Ober Gabelhorn."

She nodded and motioned for him to continue.

"Well, as I said, Claus was the most skilled, so he volunteered to climb to the next ledge. He was about twenty feet up when he stopped to hammer in another piton. He was hugging the rock face and his stance was overstretched – that is to say, he wasn't properly braced. For reasons which I'll never understand, the other guide, Friedrich, had thought that moment was as good as any to continue their discussion. They were speaking Swiss German – which is very different than the German I learned – so I had no idea what they were saying.

"Apparently, whatever Friedrich said was decidedly contradictory to Claus's ideas on the subject. While yelling back his riposte, Claus leaned over slightly to try and make eye contact with Friedrich – I guess he decided it was more important to drive home his point than to hammer in the piton. Trying to turn his body and yell at the same time caused him to lose his foothold. The hammer dropped from his hands as he tried to catch himself, but he couldn't find a hold in time. He slid down the nearly vertical rock face and collided with Friedrich who had been belaying him. Right before my eyes both men went tumbling over the ledge!"

"Oh, my god!" Catherine exclaimed, her hand covering her mouth. "Did they fall?"

"Fortunately, Friedrich had remembered to tie off to a piton he'd hammered in a few feet above the ledge. However, he'd put it in hastily, not counting on it having to not only bear the weight of two men but also the force of the tug when the rope went taut. To make matters worse, Claus had somehow been knocked unconscious during the fall. When I rushed to the edge and looked down, both men were dangling five feet below the ledge. Claus, as I mentioned, was out cold and Friedrich was frantically searching for a place to grab hold of the rock wall. Unsure how long the rope and piton would hold both men, I pulled out my strongest piton and hammered it firmly in place a few feet from the Friedrich's. I then managed to thread one end of my rope through Friedrich's piton and tie a thick double knot at the end. Once I had the other end looped through my piton, I lowered the rope down to Friedrich and told him to grab hold. He tied the rope to himself and then to Claus, who was still unconscious.

Donning my leather repelling gloves, I coiled my right arm around the tight rope and slowly began pulling the men up. Though I'd like to say I was the reigning Mr. Universe at the time, the truth is I couldn't have hauled both men all the way up had Friedrich not managed to find a few holds along the way. Finally, after what seemed like an arduous eternity of pulling, I saw a hand grasp the ledge, then the other took hold. Just when I thought they were home free, Friedrich yelled out, 'I can't pull myself up – Claus is in the way!'"

Catherine's eyes grew wide and she leaned forward, hanging on his every word.

"Keeping a firm hold on the rope I shouted back, "Do you have a firm hold? Can you hold on if I let go?"

There was a moment's hesitation and then I heard, "Yes. But not for very long."

Tightening my grip with my right hand, I shouted back, "Then hold tight!" Then leaning down slightly, I used my left hand to wrap the rope around my leg three or four times. Were I to slip over the ledge, I wasn't sure it would hold all three of us, but I didn't see that there was any other option. Carefully I lowered myself down onto the ledge, all the while keeping my hold on the other rope. Then I said, "Okay, hold on. I'm going to release the rope and reach for Claus."

Before Friedrich could respond, I yanked my right arm from the rope and lunged for Claus. The rope went taut again, but Friedrich's hold was good and I managed to get my fingers around Claus's harness. Bracing myself with my left arm, I slowly pulled the unconscious guide up. His chest had just cleared the edge of the ledge when the most amazing thing happened. In one seemingly impossible instant, Friedrich's right hand slipped and was caught by Claus who had only a second before regained consciousness. In one swift motion Claus had managed to grab hold of the ledge with his right hand and catch Friedrich's wrist with his left. The sudden movement nearly caused me to lose my grip, but I managed to hang on. Still clutching Claus's harness, I began pulling again. Finally after a few very long and tense moments, both men managed to clamber up the last few feet and we all collapsed on the ledge."

He paused and took a drink of his untouched wine. Seeing Catherine stare blankly at an invisible spot on the table had made him grin. No doubt she was imagining the whole event with all the drama, tension, and precarious camera angles of a big-budget Hollywood action sequence.

In the dark and quiet of the hotel room, Talon could still see the look on Catherine's face as she imagined the three climbers fighting for survival on that rock ledge. After that she'd made him describe the rest of the day's events in as much detail as he could manage. Her eagerness and fascination had amused and invigorated him. In a short span of time, two dressed-up, grown adults sitting in a nice restaurant suddenly had the vibrant, carefree wonder of their youth restored. They'd chattered on like teenagers – barely aware of anything or anyone else. Thinking about it now, he couldn't help but chuckle. The sound caused Catherine to stir and slowly her eyes opened. She turned her head, rested her chin on his chest and looked up at him with a tired half smile.

"Why are you still awake?" she said sleepily. "And what are you smiling about?"

Still grinning he said, "Just thinking about our first date."

She sighed and said, "Oh? What about it?"

"I was so engrossed in telling my climbing story, I don't remember ordering and I barely remember eating."

"That's because I ordered while you were talking. The waiter came up quietly behind you and I nonchalantly pointed at a few things on the menu. You didn't seem to mind my selection," she said with a yawn.

He laughed, "I must admit, I'm a little embarrassed. Normally I don't let anyone sneak up behind me – let alone order my food."

"That's okay," she consoled, "you were immersed in your narrative. You're quite the storyteller when you get going." She bowed her head and lightly kissed his chest a few times, sending shivers down his leg.

She looked up again and asked, "After they gave you your nickname right there on the ledge, did they ever use your real name again?"

"No," he said shaking his head. "They called me Talon all the way to the peak and all the way back down."

"I can't believe you kept climbing after the fall and close-call rescue," Catherine said, shaking her head. "Weren't you just a little afraid to keep going?"

"At the time I thought we should go back down, as well. However, Claus and Friedrich were adamant that my reaching the peak for the first time should not be ruined due to their carelessness.

"'Besides,'" Claus had said, patting me on the back, 'it's easier to go up to the top and down the other side.' I wasn't convinced, but they had obviously made up their minds. So up we went."

Catherine rolled onto her back and stared at the ceiling.

"While I admire your spirit and theirs, I still think you were all a bit nuts to keep climbing. But I can see where they wouldn't want to deprive you of the goal you set out to achieve. And it does sound like the view from the summit was magnificent."

He was silent. Her words conjured images from those glorious moments on the peak of Ober Gabelhorn.

"It really is an amazing mountain," he said. "Every peak is different. Every view is different. Even the sense of accomplishment came in different flavors along the way."

"I guess I can understand the attraction – even if it is crazy," Catherine mused.

"Pure achievement is the most intoxicating elixir mankind will ever know," he said to no one in particular.

She turned and said with a pleading smile, "We're not starting that game again are we?

"Well," he said thoughtfully, "we never really finished it."

She sighed, her eyes innocently downcast. "Perhaps there are other things we should discuss."

"Such as?"

The look on her face told him exactly what she was alluding to, but he wanted to hear her say it – to see in her eyes that she cared enough to ask.

Her face became earnest. For a moment he thought perhaps he had misjudged what this conversation would be about. Then she held up her index finger and said, "I'm interested in only one thing: 'Neo, the future. And believe me, I know – the only way to get there is together.'"

He laughed and flashed a smiled broadly. It was a quote from the second *Matrix* movie. He'd enjoyed the series and knew the lines well.

"I suppose they showed that one on the red-eye from Zion, right?" he asked. "Should I call you Catherine or just 'the Oracle'?"

"Either is applicable," she quipped, adding seductively, "Of course, Trinity is the one with the tight leather cat suit."

He stroked her hair lightly and said, "Who needs leather when there's lace aplenty to go around?"

A quick flash of embarrassment dotted her cheeks, then vanished. "Amazing," he thought. "She really is a magnificent creature." There was another universe behind those bright eyes – another existence with its own path coursing freely through space-time. In this woman, there existed the possibility of a new formula for life – one where he was a key factor. Maybe this was what people felt like when they fell in love. It was like arriving suddenly and unexpectedly at a fork in the road. Straight ahead was the path you had been following and had been intent on keeping to. But to the right was an altogether different course – one you never knew existed. A path you didn't have to navigate on your own. Prior to that moment the possibility of another path would've seemed ludicrous – yet there it was. And it was beautiful, mysterious and green with potential. So seductive was this new path, that you had to concentrate intensely on what your original destination had been. Did you have one? Or were you just cruising through life with nothing more than a vague notion of where you would eventually call home? Looking again at the two roads, one could not help but ask: Could they wind up at the same place?

Though he lived his life according to a strict regiment of careful assessment and caution, this business had taught him that the ultimate rewards sometimes require the greatest risks. And though he intended to see *The Aenamaia's* plans through to the end, he did not want to jeopardize a future beyond that end – a future with Catherine. The calculations in his mind ran quickly and a map began to form. "Stick to the facts Talon," he thought. "What do you know so far?" First, he already knew he was not comfortable lying to this woman. Second, he knew he would have to ask her to trust that he could not safely reveal all she wanted to know about him. Not yet. Third, he desperately wanted to tell her everything, but that was impossible right now. Other people's lives relied on his ability to stick to the code of secrecy they had all agreed to. Fourth, he knew if he told her nothing she could reasonably suspect the worst and he may lose her forever. Finally, right now her eyes were yearning for him to say something that would assuage her concerns and doubts.

"Catherine," he said, gently stroking her soft cheek. "There is so much I want to tell you that I don't know where to start. I..." A short, abbreviated chirping stopped him. He knew what that noise meant, and he knew why he was suddenly holding his breath. It was an emergency message from Gray.

He looked at her uncertainly for a moment, but did not speak.

Retrieving his phone from the nightstand, he punched in his ten-digit access code and waited for the message to appear.

"What is it?" Catherine asked, the concern obvious in her voice.

The message scrolled slowly across the screen and he answered solemnly, "The future just got darker."

Talon stared at his phone's bright screen and silently read the message again:

Toman's bird just exploded over Iraq. 75 tons of debris fell on Wadi al Khirr airbase 240 km S of Baghdad. All aboard killed. Payte pulled from Atlanta assignment. Now en route to DC.

As he finished reading, the phone beeped again indicating a second message:

Payte's men not onboard and are unaccounted for. Meet eagle's nest 9:30 am.

Talon scrolled back to the first message and read it a third time. He was having a difficult time grasping what had happened. The plan had been for the plane to land in Iraq and dump its passengers. From there they would have to fend for themselves, but *The Aenamaia* had estimated that they all had a very good chance of surviving the ordeal. Something had gone terribly wrong. Or had it? He looked again at the second message:

Payte's men not onboard and are unaccounted for.

The implications hit him like a freight train. Someone had had a different agenda all along. There was no other reasonable explanation. And in his gut he felt that this might just turn his world upside down.

Catherine sat upright and waited silently behind him. Though she'd only known this man for a day, working for the airline had further sharpened her already exceptional gift of intuition. Such skill was very useful in proactively addressing the needs of her passengers. Now it was telling her to remain silent and be patient. He had already indicated that something bad had happened. And though she couldn't see his face clearly, something told her that this man, whom she guessed prided himself on always being prepared for everything, had been caught off guard and was struggling to understand how and why. What was odd was how she suddenly felt like she was intruding – that she shouldn't be there at that moment.

She also knew this feeling had something to do with the unusual circumstances that had brought her here. Over the years, many of her female co-workers had habitually extended their pledge of service to an attractive passenger's hotel room or house. For her, this was only the second time in fifteen years she had ever succumbed to a man's charms so quickly. It had been ten years since the first time and she'd labored ever since to purge the unpleasant memories from her mind. And while this time felt completely different, she was unsure what the outcome would be.

Talon keyed in his confirmation code and hit send. Absently he returned the phone to the nightstand. He felt like a raging tornado was tearing through his mind. There was so much that needed to be done – plans that would require augmenting – and a host of questions to be answered. No doubt General Payte would be *The Aenamaia's* first priority. The questions came at him like gunfire. How did Gray know Payte's men hadn't been onboard? Who else knew about the explosion? What did the press know? Had anyone linked it to *The Aenamaia* yet? Once the link was confirmed, should they admit it was an accident, deny it, or abstain from answering? Should they provide a list of names of those onboard? How would the world react when it was learned that a large portion of the public records of these people could not be located? Could they use that to their advantage?

So much unauthorized access to encrypted systems was sure to spook the government. If the authorities learned of their capabilities, they might invoke the Patriot Act to keep the media from reporting it. That may prove useful to them in the end, but would likely also entail a veritable witch hunt for those responsible. "One problem at a time," he thought. What to do now? No doubt his next extraction would have to be postponed. Based on the dossier he'd read he was confident that...

And then, just as abruptly as the whirlwind had started, it was gone and only a single train of thought remained. He turned and looked at Catherine. "She really is stunning," he thought. The moonlight that crept through the thin crack in the drawn curtains cast a soft, pale white light on half of her naked torso – the rest was lost in shadow. The faint moonlight reflected off level shoulders and long, shiny strands of hair. Her expression was both patient and concerned, with a hint of uncertainty. No doubt this was an awkward moment, given how little she knew about him.

He tried to smile, but his furrowed brow betrayed the apprehension he felt. The expression on her face changed ever so slightly, but enough that he saw she understood. Without knowing what he would say, he opened his mouth to speak, but she put a finger to his lips.

"Let me take a shot at this," she said quietly, never breaking eye contact. "I can tell something is troubling you and that you feel uncomfortable talking about it. It's okay. I understand. For now it's enough for me that you know I'm here for you. I'm guessing that's probably as strange for you to hear as it is for me to say, but it's the truth."

She reached up and gently caressed a face awash in concentration and concern. "So much emotion somehow kept in check," she thought. "So much self-control and restraint."

Bowing his head, Talon said, "I should....there are so many things I want to tell you right now – so much I want to say. So much that you deserve to know." He paused. He looked up at her with an empathetic half smile. "I know your coming here was anything but a matter of habit for you. I suppose you could call it a leap of faith for both of us. Now I have to ask you to take another leap." He took her hand in his and held it firmly. "I have to leave now. There is a lot of work to be done, fires to put out, and plans to be restructured. I don't know when it will all be over. But when it is, if you're still interested, I promise I'll find you and tell you everything. I don't expect you to wait, but I sincerely hope you do."

He stood up. The room was dark, but he managed to find his clothes and began dressing. Catherine stayed silent, unsure of what to say. A voice in her head said she should get up and get dressed, ask for answers to her questions, or at least cover herself with the sheets until he'd gone, but such cautionary sentiments went against what her heart told her. No, this was a time for strength and confidence. So she casually turned on the lamp on her side of the bed and lay down on her side to watch him. The sudden light caught his attention and he turned to look at her. She hoped he saw the face of a woman who was proud of what they had shared and was not embarrassed that he could see her this way. There was a statement of strength and assertiveness in her posture – in her relaxed, naked body – and in her eyes.

She was sure the half smile and expression on his face revealed much more than he'd intended – doubt, conflict, calculation, urgency, and a soul torn between duty and desire. The sight was both distressing and endearing. This man seemed grander than his size, stronger than the sum of his muscles and poised to rush into action.

She watched as he finished dressing. There was a swift economy to his motions. There seemed to be a rhythmic resolve in every movement. Suddenly she recalled a quote from her favorite author Ayn Rand: "Every man builds his world in his own image. He has the power to choose, but no power to escape the necessity of choice." It was then that she realized that this man reminded her of Rand's strongest male characters. Standing before her was a modern day Howard Roark or Hank Rearden. Perhaps even a twenty-first century John Galt. So much purpose worn openly and yet shielded from anyone who failed to recognize it. Hidden in plain sight. But despite this realization, she couldn't help but wonder who he really was. Where was he going? What was so urgent that could tear this man out of bed and away from someone he obviously didn't want to leave? That something could so drastically alter this man's mood in just a few seconds sent a shiver through her body.

Talon moved to the side of the bed, knelt, and kissed Catherine. She let out a soft sigh of pleasure as their mouths met. A tangled and complex dance of warm lips and desire began anew, and for the briefest of moments, all concerns, uncertainties, and apprehensions vanished.

When their lips finally parted, Talon waited for Catherine's eyes to open. He took her hands in his. They were soft and warm, but also strong.

"The last twelve hours have been like a delicious and unexpected dream. As odd as it may sound I didn't want to fall asleep for fear of waking up."

Catherine smiled and whispered, "I understand. And thank you."

Talon squeezed her hands. "I'm not one for speeches or poetic adieus. Suffice it to say, I will find you – if you still wish to be found."

Catherine leaned forward and kissed him tenderly. She held his face in her hands and looked into his eyes. "This type of thing doesn't happen every day," she said earnestly, "It's very rare." She smiled guiltily and added, "But there's no good reason it has to be. Everyday – every other day – every week. I'll take what I can get."

Talon stood, grabbed his bags and headed for the door. He thought for a moment, then turned and said, "My name really is Talon. I don't hate flying, though I prefer trains. My German improves with a few drinks, though my English suffers. I've been to every continent except Antarctica. I'm the polar opposite of a foodie, I refuse to talk about the weather for more than thirty seconds a day, and I always prefer playing sports over watching them. I've always preferred music over art – audio over visual." He took a step towards the bed and stared at Catherine for a moment, then said, "But now that the visual has a powerful new ally, I may have to switch teams."

"There's no reason you can't have both."

Talon smiled, turned, and headed for the door.

As he opened it, light from the brightly lit hallway flooded the room. Talon took one last look at the statuesque women lying on her side.

"Au revoir, mademoiselle Catherine."

"Au revoir, monsieur Talon," Catherine said in her best French voice. "Jusqu'à ce que nous nous reverrons."

"Oui, mademoiselle. Until we meet again," Talon said with a nod and a grin.

Chapter 17

Washington, D.C.

The cab from the hotel made quick progress east along interstate 66. A green highway sign read North Roosevelt St/Roosevelt Blvd exit one-half mile. Talon stared out of the rear passenger side window. The deep purple twilight heralded the coming sunrise, but it was still mostly dark out. Less than a mile away he could see cars coming and going on the Seven Corners interchange. Red and white dots moving in unison, outlining the direction and course of each road. Stretching into the distance in every direction were the headlights and taillights of early morning commuters moving steadily along one of seven distinct lines.

The two main thoroughfares were Arlington Boulevard, running east to west, and Leesburg Pike, running northwest to southeast. Wedged between the seven lines of asphalt was a spattering of office buildings, apartment buildings, fast food restaurants, gas stations and the Seven Corners mall – all fitted carefully into the triangular patches of land between the roads. The whole thing looked like an engineer's nightmare.

Seven roads. Every driver passing through had six different directions to choose from. "What chaos," he thought. Though from here, everything looked quite orderly. The sight of cars on the highway at night always reminded him of the arterial network around the heart. The analogy fit well with a day in the life of a city, albeit somewhat reversed. The blood cells (in this case the cars and their passengers) entered the heart (which represented the city) carrying knowledge and energy. Throughout the day, the passenger cells would release this knowledge, interact with other passenger cells, and create new ideas, processes and possibilities. At the end of the cycle, they left the heart feeling empty and exhausted, and most of their energy was spent as they headed to their homes to recharge. The concrete and asphalt arteries delivered the energetic cells to the heart in the morning and removed the depleted souls at night. Each day the system reset and the process was repeated without fail.

But, just as in any such system, there were bound to be irregularities, faults and problems in the form of damaged cells, harmful parasites and bacteria, viruses and cancer. Tiny, potent anomalies that, when left unchecked, did immeasurable and often irreparable damage to the other cells. The problem was systemic and constantly worsening. Though the malevolent cells were the same size as the healthy ones, they brought with them an uncanny and disproportionate capacity for manipulating and corrupting other cells. These black butchers were stealthy, fast and clever. Courtship was brief, the culprit never expending any extra energy on the task. Once the damage was done, the perpetrator wasted no time finding and wooing its next victim. Resistance came in the form of strong resilient cells, leukocytes and antibodies that managed to incarcerate individual destroyers or, on occasion, eliminate them altogether. Unfortunately, the protectors were outnumbered, outgunned, and fighting a losing battle. At any given moment in time, it looked as though the contaminative abnormalities threatened to destroy the entire body.

Talon stared out the window and pondered this last point, wondering whether or not it was related to the battles and competition that drove evolution and natural selection. The elegant beauty and simplicity behind Darwin's radical new idea had arrested his interest at a young age. The concept and the intrigue around it fascinated him. Such a simple solution to an age-old question – yet so powerful that its influence was far-reaching. Anthropology, archeology, biology, biochemistry, genetics, zoology, pharmacology, physiology, medicine, virology, and now cosmology, astronomy, and astrobiology. There were few sciences whose work did not reap the benefits of evolution and natural selection. Beyond the sciences, evolution could be found center stage mixed in with politics, education, legal battles, religion, sociology, psychology, and so on. The reach of evolution was astounding, and he'd spent most of his life studying it.

Yet there was one thing that had troubled him since the beginning of his studies. How did evolution favor any parasite, bacteria or virus that routinely killed the host on whom it relied for its own survival? What possible advantage towards survival could be gained by destroying one's only source of food, energy, warmth and shelter? Talon knew the simple answer was that these predators had become adept at jumping from organism to organism. They spent enough time in one location and multiplied to such an extent that the odds of at least one copy finding its way into a new host were high –all the while unknowingly, due to a lack of consciousness, destroying their environment.

The concept became even more bizarre when contrasted with other microscopic organisms that had succeeded in forming a symbiotic, mutually beneficial relationship with their host. The human body alone is home to thousands upon thousands of different species of bacteria, fungi, and archaea, known collectively as the human flora or microbiome. What most people didn't know was that many of these tiny organisms were critical to the body's survival. They perform all manner of vital tasks, assisting their host organism with digestion, respiration, reproduction and birth, fighting disease, and much more. This symbiotic pattern is practically ubiquitous throughout nature. And yet, despite the obvious benefits of such arrangements, evolution and natural selection have continued to also favor those relationships that poison and usually destroy the host. "Why?" Talon wondered. And what processes or circumstances represented the demarcation point between microorganisms surviving on carnage instead of choosing symbiosis? The answers continued to elude him.

The hidden meaning behind these thoughts was apparent and very familiar to him. The analogy was equally as obvious. The host could be the earth, the United States or simply the social consciousness of America. As was the case in nature, symbiosis was ubiquitous in America. Using the multitude of tools and skills they had developed, most humans worked together to achieve common goals and provide a better life for themselves, their offspring, and the rest of humanity. Then there was the small minority of people whose agendas were devoid of any form of altruism, cooperation, ethics, fair play, or common good. They were the microscopic predators plaguing, infecting and feeding off mankind. It was a simple analogy. And one he'd used many times over the years to help justify the cleansing he and *The Aenamaia* had engaged in.

Arguments against their course had been numerous in the beginning. Questions like, "Who are we to decide?" "If we do this, are we not as guilty as those we punish?" "Can these problems really be solved or even eased through violence?" There were always doubts. *The Aenamaia* consisted of highly intelligent members with a keen sense of fair play and a sharpened sense of right and wrong. Yet in the end, every member agreed on one simple premise: you cannot argue with disease. Just like viruses and bacteria, men and women who prey on others cannot be reasoned with. Their agendas are hard-wired and are not subject to debate or negotiation. This has been demonstrated throughout recorded history.

Wars, insurrections, assassinations, overthrows, dictatorships, eugenics, non-consensual human experimentation, mass genocide, biological warfare, the selling of arms, coercion, crime, physical and psychological torture are all examples – every act carried out by humans at the cost of human suffering and life. Sometimes the acts were hidden. Other times they were committed in plain sight. In the recent past the President of the United States was lobbying for the complete loss of human rights and an increase in the acceptable forms of torture and interrogation for political prisoners. Suspension of *habeas corpus*, indefinite detainment, imprisonment without trial or legal representation, and sentencing without presenting proof or even telling the condemned what they had been found guilty of. People hurting people. It was flesh and blood people that did these things. It was people at Abu Ghraib and Guantanamo Bay. People at Auschwitz and Mauthausen. People in Cambodia, Armenia, Kosovo, Bosnia, Afghanistan, Sierra Leone, Timor, Rwanda, Tibet, China, Russia, and Bangladesh. The list ran on and on.

Talon shook his head and pinched the bridge of his nose. More than once over the years he'd realized that there were several lines of thinking that always took him to the same dark, depressing destination. What was strange was that this fact rarely stopped his mind from repeating the journey, despite the predictable unpleasantness he always encountered at the final destination. Why did the mind do that? What purpose did it serve? To justify? To rationalize one's actions or emotions? When this was all over, he'd make it a point to find a good evolutionary psychologist. If he could learn where it came from and why it was favored by evolution, perhaps there was a chance he could figure out how to use it more effectively. Perhaps.

As the cab rounded a corner, the left rear wheel hit a deep, watery pothole and the whole cab lurched.

"Sorry," the cab driver said over his shoulder, "I thought it was just a little puddle."

Talon remained silent. Dark thoughts and images receded to the back of his mind, slowly supplanted by thoughts of General Payte and Gray and *The Aenamaia*. Ironically, the future seemed to be even cloudier than when they'd first embarked on this dangerous and unprecedented journey. Although no one knew quite what they would see along the way, the road had been chosen and the course charted. Unfortunately, no one had anticipated a smoldering, mile-wide crater appearing in the middle of that road. And having been detonated from someone on their side, no less. "What do you call the mysterious, elusive realm beyond contingency?" he wondered.

The cab turned into the circular drive and stopped under the white oval portico covering the building's entrance. Talon heard the trunk latch release. He got out of the cab and helped the driver unload his bags and set them neatly on the curb. Fumbling intentionally with the cash, he thanked the driver, making sure to speak with a heavy Swedish accent. When the yellow car had disappeared down the drive, he turned, picked up his bags, and walked inside the building. "Home," he thought wearily. Strange how little meaning that word held for him – its definition was more akin to a furnished storage unit than anything else.

When he reached the elevators, the door to the first car was open. He stepped inside and pressed the button for the eighth floor. How long had it been since he'd last stayed there? Four months? Six? He couldn't be sure. The thought of checking his calendar to determine when he'd last spent any real time at this condo was both amusing and a little disturbing.

The elevator door opened and he stepped out. It took a moment to remember which way to turn. When he got his bearings he turned left and walked casually down a long winding hall until he reached the last unit. Setting down his bags, he punched in the nine-digit code on the keypad. There was a faint click and the locks released. Grabbing his bags, he pushed open the door and flipped the light switch with his elbow.

For a few moments he stood rapt, slowly gazing around the room. "How strange," he thought again. This was a place to maintain the appearance of a life he didn't lead, filled with material things that he barely recognized, a place visited more frequently by the cleaning people than the owner. There were pictures on the wall of people he didn't know and places he'd never visited. Movies he'd never seen, a baby grand piano he didn't know how to play and books he hadn't read. Furniture someone else had selected, linens that had barely touched his skin, and a bed that had never held more than one body in its embrace. The only thing moderately familiar was the expansive view. Everything else seemed foreign and staged. Had he not stayed in similar such places on and off for the last few years, he would've felt like he was trespassing. Instead, this was nothing more than a very private and discreet hotel room.

"Hotel room," he thought dimly. Images of Catherine flooded into his mind, followed immediately by his pristine forest hideaway. The two tantalizing dreams interwove just behind his eyes. This wasn't what he needed or wanted right now. It wasn't the first time he'd realized that he was not always in control of his own mind. It was almost as if there was another part of him observing in the background, deciding when and where to introduce thoughts, dreams, ideas, concepts and constructs. A little gnome with an agenda of his own. A gnome with an uncanny knack for bad timing.

The cab stopped in front of Gray's home. The house's façade was an unassuming three-story combination of red brick and white trim that framed tall, rectangular windows. While no curtains or blinds could be seen blocking any of the windows, none of the windows revealed even the slightest hint as to what lay beyond them. No lights or decorations were visible behind the glass. Nor could anything of interest be gleaned from the front of the house. The style was vague but familiar enough to belong to the largest residential architecture category in the northeast: Victorian.

Even the true size of the building seemed somehow diminished. Part of this effect came from the large open terrace on the third floor. The rectangular area was as wide as the building and extended deep enough to hide most of the floor from onlookers at street level. The terrace was dotted with Italian cypress trees and surrounded by ivy vines that traversed back and forth horizontally along the brick stratum. A half dozen heat lamps formed a semi-circle near the tables and chairs and chaise lounges, a clear sign the area was not just a seasonal retreat.

The other aspect that skewed the perception of the structure's size was its unusual depth, which also could not be easily discerned from the street. The house, which was not large enough to be called a mansion, stretched over three quarters of the way to the next block. Abutting the back side of the property was a narrow, paved alley that always seemed to be wet. Telephone and electrical wires drooped lazily between dark wood posts and tall gray metal poles. The numerous wires, some of which criss-crossed above the shiny pavement in places, ran the length of the alley, giving it a sinister, dangerous look. Directly behind Gray's house, on the opposite side of the forbidding alley stood a wide but shallow four-story retail building – the front of which faced the next block. Seen from above, the house and the retail building would form a near perfect "T," minus the alley.

The sides of the house, which were much less ornate than the front, were also difficult to see from the street. Perfectly manicured hawthorn hedges ran the length of the structure on each side. Running parallel to the waist-high flat-topped, barbed shrub was a narrow, uneven stone path and an equally narrow stretch of yellow grass still dormant from the long winter. The outside edge of the petite patch of grass marked the beginning of a wide line of tall trees that formed a near perfect perimeter on three sides of the property. The miniature forest was perhaps twenty feet wide on the sides and ten at the rear, comprised of tall, slender birch and aspen trees. Though they retained only a few leaves now, Talon recalled how the trees seemed to illuminate the house with orange and gold light in the fall. Combined with the lush gardens lining the backyard, Gray's house was a particularly beautiful and tranquil place to visit in the fall.

Halfway down the home's length on both sides were identical twelve foot brick walls, each with a thick iron gate six feet tall and barely a shoulder's width across. The wall cut across the stone path, a small swatch of dormant grass and through the trees, ending at the property line. Here it connected with a thick rod-iron fence that delimited the entire property. The bars of the fence were simple black cylinders, two inches in diameter, eight feet tall, and ending in a sharp point. The lowest support bar was flush with the ground because Gray had required that the eight-inch spike on the other end of each rod be sunk into the ground. When asked about it, Gray had said he did it to increase the stability of the fence. Talon thought he'd done it because it told the potential trespasser, "This fence isn't here because it's pretty. Stay the hell out."

Looking at the house now, Talon really saw a lot of Gray in it, though he'd likely be at a loss to explain the connection. How would he describe it? Old but strong. Guarded but inviting. Elegant but simple. Austere on the outside, complex and secretive on the inside. An oasis from the things of man, yet a mecca for railing against such. Talon smiled at the thought.

Out of habit, Talon checked his watch. Nine twenty-eight. Arriving right on time usually gave him a measure of satisfaction, but not today. The unexpected ray of sunshine lying in a hotel bed twenty miles away had pierced the long-standing grayness of his life, only to be replaced a moment later by a billowing, ominous darkness.

Talon growled and shook his head. Focus Talon, focus. With renewed vigor, he handed the driver a hundred dollar bill, waived off the man's suggestion of change, and picked up his bag. He walked through the open gate and up the steps to the solid oak door. He rang the doorbell. It was at that moment that the reality of the situation hit him like a freight train. It was so simple. The only way to get back to Catherine and to the new life he'd been planning on leading since his first days with *The Aenamaia* was to concentrate all of his efforts towards finishing what they'd started. All he had to do was see it through to the end and he would be free to start anew. "Why hadn't this occurred to me before I left her?" he wondered. Perhaps if it had, he could've told her with genuine confidence that he had a plan – and she was part of it.

Energy surged through his body from all directions and his mind began to race. If the will was there, the way would be found – crater or no crater. Right now, his will and resolve were stronger than they had ever been and he intended to put both to good use.

Cumberland, Maryland

"The irony was far too manifest and felicitous to be hastily disregarded," he thought. "Besides, there is no reason to ignore the odd synchronicity of seemingly unrelated events that have led up to this moment and the contemplation of such." His internal monologue continued. "After all, was it not irony alone that colored mankind's otherwise black and white existence? Without irony, life would be mundane, linear, and monochromatic. For the path of each life is defined through the perception of each individual. Even the shape and direction of a single life's path was a matter of perspective. Therefore, to understand one's own purpose required first knowing of the existence of irony and simultaneously understanding how best to use it to one's advantage."

The voice in his mind continued the philosophical lecture. "Through understanding, mankind gladly sheds its imperfect color-blind lenses. Concurrently, any nominally sentient being needs to be perpetually conscious of any and all irony around them in order to recognize and react accordingly to the ultimate constant: causality. Realization at this level often compels one to wonder when it was that mankind first conceived of such things. Such speculation served as nourishment to his starved, voracious mind."

The framework was solid and deliciously tantalizing. A philosophical construct applicable to all men and women who chose to embrace it, then hold themselves up to it's light. "Arguably now isn't the best moment to dive so deep, but what the hell," he thought. "I've got a few spare minutes."

"Where was I going with this?" he wondered. "Ah yes, the elusive spark." Spader imagined a wise and seasoned university professor pacing before a large and eager crowd. He could hear the astute instructor's voice echoing in his mind. He was saying, "Hundreds of thousands of years ago, the evolutionary scale that pitted consciousness against animal instinct began to tip in favor of the former. As the scale shifted, so did the ratio of rational thought and problem solving to purely reactive responses governed solely by input from the senses. As human intelligence grew and developed, primal instinct proportionately withered and diminished. Fortunately, the newfound aptitude strengthened the existing survival tactics which had, after all, proven remarkably successful up to that point. This was extremely important for mankind considering the fact that when this mental shift came about, humans still routinely found themselves on the dinner menu of other animals. Survival, dominance and prosperity came as a result of more refined cunning and increasingly sophisticated planning abilities – courtesy of that simple, yet graceful, beauty – natural selection.

"Despite the lurking dangers and stiff competition for resources, our ancestors survived and multiplied. And with this strange new sense, which we would later call consciousness, the bipedal members of the genus homo understood the concept of self. From there, the leap to causality and beyond was simultaneously simple and monumental. The minutiae behind every decision, every step, and every gesture could now be contemplated and analyzed. Cause and effect. And thus the basic mathematics of life were born. Trial and error – trial and success. Avoiding one and remembering how to duplicate the other at will helping foster a new kind of natural selection. Consequently, with even this rudimentary knowledge, the individual could, and still can, understand precisely how they had arrived at each and every moment throughout their lives – and how they would decide what to do next. And more importantly," the professor concluded, pausing for effect, "we can also see that at any given moment, our lives, our personalities, and everything about us, are the sum of every moment, every thought, and every decision since the beginning. Think about it."

Spader pursed his lips. In his mind he saw the professor give him a nod of approval before exiting the lecture hall, as if to say, "Nice piece of work, Mr. Spader." The thought made Spader smile. The line of thinking was solid, albeit a little on the rhetorical side. No doubt it wouldn't be taken seriously in its current state, but he didn't care. In his line of work it was important to have a philosophical framework grounded in reality and with a strong historical component as the foundation. Besides, it was far and away more fresh and interesting than the standard-issue concept-execution and future-certain-victims garbage the government programs were still dishing out. Sniping was one occupation where a little philosophy, married happily to reality, could go a long way. And indeed it had. Brains, brawn, and bullets. His mum would be proud.

Slowly he moved the rifle a few degrees back to the right. He was now looking at a ten-by-ten square of empty cement nestled in a corner of the large courtyard. A small portion of the peeling gray steel door that led into the recreation room was visible in his scope. From his research he knew the yard would be empty for another ten minutes or so. What was even more interesting was the email he'd received from one of the guards a few days before. The guard had informed him that due to anonymous threats against certain white-collar criminals, the warden had decided to segregate the inmates during recreation time. Those who were deemed "low risk" would have their time in the yard first thing in the morning, while the rest would emerge just after lunch.

The new schedule would be on trial for one week, after which the warden would decide whether or not to make the change permanent. The guard had made sure to tell Spader, whom he knew as Randall Castor, that he thought it was a "real bad idea." Despite the guard's pessimism, Spader saw the change as an opportunity to both simplify his task, as well as complete it ahead of schedule.

The persona of Randall Castor had been Gray's brainchild. During the initial stages of planning, *The Aenamaia* had deliberated on how best to quietly research a high-profile prison inmate. With the help of one of Gray's loyal contacts inside the Maryland Department of Public Safety and Correctional Services, Spader had managed to pass himself off as a researcher conducting a dry academic study on U.S. prisons and the protection of inmates' rights.

Soon after, the administrator in charge of public relations had gladly passed him off to a green prison guard. Spader conducted a quick check on the guard and learned he was twenty-two, never married, had no prior security or military training, and had just barely managed to graduate from high school. At the end of their first meeting, Spader had promised to quote the guard in his paper and mention him in a footnote. As an additional gesture of his appreciation, he'd also casually offered the guard a new bottle of expensive tequila autographed by the rock star who had made it. Without further adieu, the guard eagerly offered to provide any information he could legally divulge. Some people will do anything to see their names in print – or possess a bottle of high-octane bragging rights. When Spader later commented that it would be a shame when neither the quote nor the footnote would ever be printed, Gray had remarked, "I'd wager he'll get far more pleasure from the contents of the bottle. If that isn't enough, all he has to do to get his name in the newspapers is tell the truth about what he did."

A faint movement from the upper left-hand corner of the scope caught his attention. Less than a second later, the crosshairs of his scope were trained on a chubby, black-haired man in dark blue overalls bending over to pick up trash at the base of the chain-link fence. When the man stood up, Spader could see a blue and white identification badge dangling from a breast pocket.

"A rubbish picker in a prison? Not all banged from the looks of it," he whispered to himself. The lower his volume, the more acute his English accent became. "I suppose that's right. Wouldn't make sense to have an unsupervised inmate picking things up. Just never know what the wind might carry into the yard. Although with such abundant free labor, one would think the lowliest jobs would be handled by the inmates."

"And if irony is the color of life," he whispered, continuing his train of thought aloud, "then causality must surely represent the brushes used to apply it. We therefore conclude," he paused to adjust the focus of the scope, "that in order to be a true artist, one must understand the tools of one's trade – i.e. irony, reality, and causality. Unfortunately, we can't all be artists, right? Bloody shame, that. But if you're not painting Mr. Rubbish Man, then you can't be an art critic. That also goes for those poor souls who linger glassy-eyed and mute on the sidelines watching the world go by without a care for their wants. They really have no cause to argue with their future. Because in the end, everyone else was obliged to hit reality head on and not delude themselves about what they were steppin' in. Or where the foul smell was coming from."

A stiff breeze blew through the trees, pushing the cool wet air through the fabric of his jacket. He bit down hard until the urge to shiver passed. The weather center had estimated the temperature would reach seventy by midday. But for now, he guessed it was forty degrees and humid. In one quick movement he transferred the Russian-made Dragunov SVD rifle to his left hand. Gripping a thick branch, he again checked to make sure both of his footholds were secure and that the dampness would not affect his stance. Although the rifle's magazine was loaded to capacity with ten

7.6mm rounds, he did not want to take more than one shot. After months of surveillance and research, and the inevitable rush of anticipation he now felt, he knew he'd have only one chance to get it right.

Again he spoke quietly to himself. "It's odd, really. The more serious the action, the more certain we are that it will always be a part of us. It's as if a red-hot branding iron is poised just above our flesh. The brander now...he's waiting for the serious eye contact and the barely perceptible nod that gives him leave to plunge the iron into your flesh, marking you forever. And even as the excruciating pain surges through your body, the true weight of the decision is still beyond your reach. Only in the last moments of one's life, after having lived with the puffy pink flesh, will that weight be fully understood. Be it an iron or a high-powered rifle."

He checked his watch. Still a few minutes to go. The guards here were nothing if not punctual. During yesterday's surveillance he'd been surprised at the clockwork precision of the routines he'd witnessed. By the end of the day he'd shaved two minutes off his own watch's time to be in sync with the schedule he'd observed.

Leveling the rifle, he took a quick survey of the grounds. By all accounts the Federal Correctional Institution – or FCI – in Cumberland was your average mid-security prison. Plain brick buildings dotted with small square windows. Long, triangular white aluminum roofs crowned most of the buildings, giving the complex a dull, industrial look. Outside of a few administrative offices which sat opposite the compound, the rest of the buildings were surrounded by double chain-link fences topped with evenly spaced coils of razor wire. Within the fence there wasn't much to see. From his perch Spader could see a few narrow fenced-in walkways used to move prisoners between buildings, a basketball court, a weight-lifting area, and the recreation yard – all under the watchful eyes in the inmate traffic control tower. The guard had given him a cursory outline of prisoner movements and schedules. Prior to the segregation of yard times, he had thought the walkways would be the best place to drop the mark, though the lack of detail on movement times would've made it a very tedious task.

"But what of the irony, Spader?" he began again in a low voice, trying hard to mute his accent. "Is it divine intervention? Are the planets aligned? Is simple coincidence sufficient or merely the most convenient smokescreen for something grander?" He thought about that for a moment.

One year ago to the day more than three hundred mature black locust trees graciously donated from the estate of one Max Borneo were being carefully uprooted only ten miles from here. Mr. Borneo – of the law firm Borneo, Graham and Schmidt – had been kind enough to offer the trees to FCI Cumberland. Strange that in the midst of their humanitarian rhetoric the local papers failed to mention the trees were dug up, loaded, and hauled away by the prisoners and the groundskeepers employed by the prison. How could they have missed the very relevant fact that this was done at no cost whatsoever to Mr. Borneo? And that the following week construction started on the pool, tennis court and greenhouse that were to go on the cleared plot?

Spader shook his head in disgust. A little glad-handing or elbow grease – or both – and you get the local prison to clear twenty acres of land to build your playground. Who did that ambulance chaser have on a leash that could quietly allocate state resources for something like that? During their research on Borneo they had been unable to determine conclusively who pushed the project through. Whoever it was knew how to stay off the radar. He'd made it a point to stress this mystery to *The Aenamaia* during Borneo's case review and subsequent addition to the liquidation list, though he wasn't sure if anything ever came of it.

"Three hundred mature trees," he thought. "Unbelievable." Despite his dislike for the attorney and whoever he was in bed with, Spader had to admit replanting the trees just outside of the prison fences on prison land had been a stroke of genius. How better to hide a political favor involving so much time, free labor, extra guard supervision, and equipment than to not hide it at all. The whole operation had been executed in plain view, as many of the best crimes were. And not only that, the scumbag actually came out looking like a humanitarian! One thing was certain – someone had put some serious time and thought into this little project.

But the real question here was whether or not the choice of FCI Cumberland had anything to do with the fact that one of Borneo's close personal friends was a guest there. During his research period, Spader had been surprised to see Borneo's name show up on the visitor's manifest provided by Gray's contact. Was it coincidence that he'd been assigned to research both men simultaneously? Thinking back, he was sure Gray had known there was a connection between the two. In public the wicked surround themselves with angels and saints. In private they find solace and comfort in the foul stench of their own kind. Birds of a feather to be sure.

He checked his watch again. Almost nine thirty. They should be coming out in a few minutes. Flexing the fingers of his left hand, he carefully gripped the underside of the flash-hider and leveled the weapon.

"So," he whispered, "Let's review. You're perched eight meters off the ground in the branches of one the black locust trees Mr. Borneo donated to this fine federal prison, and you're preparing to revoke the life permit of one of Mr. Borneo's good friends. The liquidation would've been infinitely more difficult had Mr. Borneo not provided such splendid cover, given that there was none before. Also interesting that the prison officials would allow such dense foliage to be planted so close to the fences. Seems a bit odd, don't you think, Mr. Sniper? And finally, without further adieu, is it coincidence that today is the first day the prisoners will be segregated? The day one year ago when the wonderful natural cover in which you now sit was dug up?"

Spader paused as movement in his scope arrested his attention. Ahhh yes, and let us not forget the proverbial icing on the cake. On this same day many years ago the man in white paper pants now walking out of the recreation room door was shaking hands with the soon-to-be-buggered former President George W. Bush. Spader's pulse jumped as his quarry stepped into the sunshine. To FCI Cumberland prison, he was inmate number 27593-112. To the Indian Casinos from whom he stole millions of dollars, he was known as Casino Jack. To the press, former President Bush, federal prosecutors, and almost everyone else in Washington, he was Jumpin' Jack Abramoff. To Spader, he was the man whose grinning, bearded face was centered in the crosshairs of his Russian-made sniper rifle.

Washington, D.C.

Talon heard two noises at once – the disengaging of multiple locks from the other side of Gray's door and the high-pitched shriek of rusty brakes on the street behind him. Less than a minute after his taxi had departed, the one with the worn-out brakes pulled up to the curb. He watched as the driver reached over his shoulder to accept his fare. A moment later Dia and Susha exited the beat up taxi and quickly headed for the steps. He glanced at his watch: nine thirty on the dot.

The front door opened and Gray appeared. He was dressed in jeans and a well-fitted black turtleneck sweater. Even through the tiredness and the twenty-four hour stubble on his face, Talon could still sense the energy and vigor driving the man. It always felt that way in Gray's presence. There was an air of greatness mixed with a staunch humility. A great man who did not want to be admired for his greatness – only respected.

Before anyone could speak, Gray held up a hand. Talon noticed the wireless earpiece and figured he must be in the middle of something important. Dia and Susha had reached the porch, but said nothing.

"Negative. I don't want anyone nearby when it happens. Especially the doctor." Gray said. A moment later he nodded then said sternly, "Make the call."

Gray was still concentrating on what he was hearing, but waived the three Augurs inside. Their host closed the heavy door behind them and quickly secured two of the four locks, then motioned for them to follow. They walked down a long narrow hallway that opened up into what was once a living room. For the last few years the room had served as one of numerous bases of operations for *The Aenamaia*. At the end of the hallway they took four steps down into a large rectangular room. On either side of the room sat two of the longest and most unusual desks Talon had ever seen. Each desk was fifteen feet long and almost four feet wide. What was odd was their shape. It looked as though they had started out as perfect rectangles, but then somehow the ends were turned inwards. The resulting shape reminded him of a symmetrical, two-dimensional telephone handset. The two odd pieces sat parallel – with the ends bent towards the center of the room. Ten computers and chairs lined each desk and were oriented such that every other was on the opposite side of the desk. Talon had spent many long hours in this room doing research, monitoring prospects, and maintaining the few remaining aspects of his real life.

Talon recalled now how the configuration was conducive to conversation with other users. This was especially useful when multiple people were working on the same project. At the moment, there was only one person sitting at the desk. It was Altra. She looked up when they walked in, but only nodded. Tension and concentration were manifest in her face and posture as she stared intently at the monitor. A wireless headset rested precariously on a thin cushion of long, platinum blonde hair pulled into a perfect, tight ponytail. Strong, skilled hands sat poised on the keyboard, ready to act. Talon had seen her like this before and knew better than to say anything.

Gray stepped beside him. "She's listening to a military channel out of Baghdad," he said quietly. "The Iraqis were the first to report the explosion. They're a little on edge, but that's to be expected. Right now they're more confused than anything else – as is the Pentagon. An envoy from a nearby U.S. military base arrived an hour ago and is examining the wreckage. The little intelligence we have tells us the plane exploded at low altitude. Best guess is somewhere around two thousand feet. The wreckage is spread out over a few square miles of desert."

Talon looked around and then asked, "Where are Toman and Joust? I thought they were supposed to be here."

Gray shook his head absently, "I sent them to Maine."

"Maine?" Talon replied, unable to hide his surprise.

"Eyes on," Gray said absently.

Talon was going to question him further when he saw Gray's expression change as he unconsciously put his hand to the earpiece and listened.

"Patch me in," Gray whispered with a nod then added, "I'll mute."

Dia came up beside Talon and whispered, "Any idea what's going on?"

"I believe Altra is monitoring military communications, both U.S. and Iraqi, for more information on the wreckage. He," he said pointing uncertainly towards Gray, "is apparently calling shots on a liquidation. Abramoff, I would guess."

Susha had also been listening and whispered something into Dia's ear. Both women nodded in agreement and headed for two of the open computers. Even with the palpable tension in the room and the lingering thoughts of Catherine, Talon couldn't help but smile as he watched the two women don headsets and begin typing wildly. This was why he had joined *The Aenamaia* – intelligence, ambition, drive, and an immutable sense of purpose and solidarity. Each member was wholly committed to their cause and, more importantly, to each other. Even in situations like this where chaos and uncertainty seemed to hang in the air like the precursor to an approaching and inevitable storm, everyone was focused and engaged. Being around sharp, motivated individuals always infused a sense of rightness in him. There was an infectious energy at work that never failed to imbue him with warm camaraderie and firm resolve.

Even as a young man Talon had been drawn towards certain types of people and personalities. Many nights in college had been spent burning the midnight oil discussing one topic or another. Sometimes it was related to an assignment, but mostly it was nothing more than curious people exchanging information, debating and test driving ideas, and mining each other for the same. Each was hungry for knowledge and eager to make a contribution. Through the years these types of discussions had been like a drug for him. Even when traveling he'd sought a variety of gatherings and groups: philosophers, humanists, atheists and agnostics, futurists, skeptics, science cafes, chess enthusiasts, chaos theorists, musicians, science fiction writers, and teachers. More often than not he'd been one of the last ones standing, his energy and enthusiasm seemingly inexhaustible. Early in his youth this process had hooked him with the enchanting power of a narcotic, and he was in no hurry to drop the habit.

The hardest part had been pursuing all of his curiosities to a comfortable stopping point. Each new encounter or meeting would either stir a new fascination or rekindle an old one. There was so much interesting information in the world. Just the thought of such unimaginable magnitude and abundance was mind-blowing. The problem with it all was absorption and retention. The knowledge was out there and relatively accessible. But when it came to consumption and processing, there was an obvious and inescapably frustrating bottlenecking. How to get it all in the brain, understand it, integrate it with existing knowledge, and be able to recall and apply it on demand?

Assimilation was spotty at best without frequent and persistent repetition and practice. Who had the time or bandwidth? Quite often, this line of thought brought back memories of seeing the film *The Matrix* for the first time. He'd been in Amsterdam at the end of a grueling research tour that had taken him all over Europe, the Middle East, and North

Africa. The movie had just come out and had been a big hit in the United States, though at the time he'd known very little about the story line. Even now he recalled the scene in the film where the lead character experienced his first "download." Vast knowledge of innumerous martial art disciplines had been electronically loaded into his mind in a matter of hours.

Sitting in the small theater only a few kilometers from the famed Red Light district, he had experienced an overwhelming envy and desire for such a capability. To be able to connect the human mind to the billions of petabytes of information already available in electronic storage was almost beyond comprehension. Each time the mere possibility entered his mind, his yearning manifested physically as an uncomfortable tightening of his chest. There was so much possibility in the world – so much potential for mankind. Unfortunately, such progress was buried beneath miles of mundane emotional detritus – fear, hate, anxiety, envy, inadequacy, suspicion, and greed.

For now all Talon could hope was that the bold and unprecedented events they'd set in motion would send a resounding message to the rest of mankind that there was still hope for a better tomorrow. That there were still people who cared about more than just themselves – who valued knowledge and understanding over personal wealth and power over others. He just hoped it would all be enough to jump-start some kind of progress. And that he would live to see the outcome.

But first things first.

Cumberland, Maryland

Spader watched through his scope as "Casino Jack" Abramoff strolled casually across the dirt courtyard. A few feet behind him, four more prisoners lumbered through the door and headed towards the opposite end of the long rectangular yard. The little information he'd been able to gather about Abramoff's prison life suggested he kept mostly to himself. The consensus among the other prisoners was that the man was something of a snob. Seeing him now, he wondered how he could still have enough self-esteem to even pose as a pretentious elitist, especially in a federal prison.

Staring through the scope, it was obvious Abramoff had gained weight since the trial, in spite of the common assumption that prison cuisine was barely palatable. The fact that this man had once owned an upscale restaurant in DC made the sight all the more ironic. From what he could see, Spader guessed the man lumbering across the yard weighed around two-fifty. The stiffness of his gait suggested the daily walks around the yard represented the bulk of his exercise. The increase in girth was further emphasized by the tightness of the shirt around his distended stomach. Apparently FCI Cumberland's clothing budget, based on consumption observations from the kitchen staff, did not anticipate a steep rise in prisoner weight gain. Nor did it appear that anyone had given the former lobbyist access to a razor and shaving gel.

Though there were no guards visible, Spader could see half a dozen shoebox size cameras tracking the movements of the prisoners. Early in the planning stages, *The Aenamaia's* advisory committee had discussed whether or not they could make use of the prison's surveillance system. It had been Dia who'd suggested tapping into the system and using it to film the liquidation. The idea had ignited considerable debate from the other members of the planning group. Once all the arguments had simmered down, she calmly explained that having documentary evidence from the prison's own security system might prove useful if the government decided to try and cover up what had happened.

Gray had suggested it was more likely that the government would choose to spin the story around an escape attempt by Abramoff. Either way, it was unlikely they would openly admit a sniper had gunned down one of their high profile inmates. Not only would it be embarrassing, it would also rekindle debates on inmates' rights – a subject most in the government wanted to avoid because it usually resulted in significant increases in prison spending.

Gray had also suggested it might renew interest in the heinous injustices being carried out by the military and Bush administration at Guantanamo Bay. In 2007 the Bush administration had quietly supported the making of a comedy movie with the infamous base's name in the title. Two of the President's PR advisors had made numerous visits to the writers and the film set to ensure the detention camp's purpose was left out entirely and that the seriousness of actual events taking place there was played down. If the issue of inmate rights and safety were to make headlines, Guantanamo Bay opponents would have a field day. Though the film had the desired effect at the time, it did nothing to dissuade investigators from bringing forth a slew of human rights charges – most centered on events at Guantanamo.

Regardless of the outcome, they had decided it could prove useful to them to have evidence of the shooting, especially if it came from FCI Cumberland's own monitoring system. As the technical advisor on the Abramoff committee, Osiro would be in charge of gaining access to the system. After several weeks of research, the techno wizard had informed the committee that he could indeed get into the system and record the shooting. However, he saw no easy way to override the individual camera controls. It would therefore be necessary for Osiro to coordinate directly with the shooter on-site. Once the camera had Abramoff in sight, Osiro would give the order to retire the mark.

Spader heard a low beeping in his ear. "Right on time," he thought. He pressed the answer button on the earpiece and waited. The line picked up, but he heard only silence. Putting his eye back to the scope he quickly reacquired Abramoff. Casino Jack had moved to the south end of the enclosure and was smoking a cigarette. "Maybe we should wait for him to die of lung cancer," he muttered jokingly.

"Panning," a faint voice said in his ear, ignoring the comment. It was probably Osiro, but he couldn't be sure. The technical wizard had a reputation for being extra cautious. Often when communicating via cell phone he employed a voice synthesizer or some other kind of mask and insisted upon using an alias. Most of *The Aenamaia* thought it was a techie's way of refreshing his inner child. Spader figured it was just a guy amusing himself. "Ever the cautious techno-spy," he thought.

Spader made two distinct clicking sounds to indicate he had heard and was also tracking the mark.

"Coming into frame..." the voice said.

Spader tightened his grip on the rifle and centered the thin red lines of his crosshairs on the left temple of inmate 27593-112. Gently, he flexed his right index finger in front of the trigger and waited for the command to fire. This was the part he hated – pulling the trigger. The front-end activities were more to his liking. He thrived on the various aspects of the planning process as well as the preparations before deployment. The late night reconnaissance trips to the land around the prison, pulling recent satellite photographs of the prison from the Geologic Society, the cash rental of his transportation, assembling and memorizing his fake identity and background, etc. Even the late nights of research into the subject's background and the long hours of committee discussions over the final verdict. He'd worked tirelessly on putting the project together and tying down all the details. But this part, having to be the one to pull the trigger and watch the man fall, this was what he dreaded. Early on he'd considered suggesting someone else could handle this part. Sensing his doubts, *The Aenamaia* had decided someone should talk to him about it.

So out of the blue, Gray had phoned and asked him to come to his house late one night in December. They'd had an unseasonably cold winter that year and the temperature at night was still well below freezing. As he pulled up in front of the old Victorian house, Spader noticed the four feet of snow piled along the streets and sidewalks. The path up the concrete stairs had been cleared and sprinkled with salt crystals. He still remembered the crunching sound beneath his boots as he ascended the concrete steps. Though it hadn't been his first visit to Gray's house, something in the still air suggested he might be in a very different state of mind when he again stepped out into the cold.

After dispensing with formalities, Gray led Spader up to the second floor study. The room had an air of severity mixed with a quaint old world style. Ten-foot bookshelves lined the walls and ran two thirds of the way down the length of the room, which he estimated to be around sixty feet long. A few feet inside the double doors stood two more bookshelves like two great sentries guarding the entrance. Immediately to the right of the shelves was what appeared to be a restored antique grand piano. Spader couldn't be certain of the color, as the only light came from the mammoth hearth at the opposite end of the room, but he suspected it was dark brown or black.

They walked through a maze of couches, chairs, coffee tables, and end tables. The room's furniture was laid out so as to accommodate many people and facilitate separate discussions. Spader noticed two of the coffee tables held four laptops, each with screensavers running, and wondered what Gray had been working on. Perhaps there had been another meeting that night. He looked around but saw nothing else out of the ordinary.

He did, however, notice something interesting about the room. There were very few objects in the room that were not designed to provide some kind of utility. Practically everything he saw could be put to use in some constructive way, or had been at some point in the past. Chairs for sitting, shelves for holding books, two rolling ladders to retrieve books high up, a fireplace to provide heat, laptops for working, a large modern globe on a pedestal, a piano for playing music, and a small bar at the end from which to serve drinks. In addition to items currently in use, the room housed an array of odd antiques, each one designed for a specific purpose. Many of the objects were old scientific devices – gauges, monitors, scales, even an old 19th century refractor telescope rumored to have been used by Johann Galle prior to his discovery of Neptune. Other items had a more international flare and included weapons, clothing, hand-drawn maps, various navigational devices, and many other interesting objects. The place was like a small museum.

Slowly he swept his eyes three hundred and sixty degrees around the room, imagining a distinct purpose behind its design and furnishings. There was a mood here. An ambiance. To Spader it felt like the room had history, though he'd never asked Gray about it. A reverent somberness hung in the air. It was the type of room that could've once accommodated the founding fathers as they debated the Constitution and the very definition of freedom and civil liberty. Where supporters of the Underground Railroad mulled over maps and timetables. Perhaps attorneys had met privately with CEO Arthur Vining Davis in 1912 to discuss the antitrust lawsuit being brought by the U.S. Justice Department. The room could've played host to Bobby Fischer and Misha Tal who might have met in secret to wage a fierce fireside round of chess off the official books. Spader imagined important men and women sitting in plush leather chairs around the large, smoothly finished table in front of the fire, drinking cognac and making decisions that would shape and influence the history of the world.

As he moved around one of the tall bookshelves, Spader noticed that there was, in fact, another light on in the room. It was a small wall-mounted lamp illuminating a framed piece of art hanging on a wall near Gray's desk. On one side was an old ink drawing of what appeared to be the super-continent Pangaea. On the other, were two faded, handwritten pages that looked as though they'd been taken from an old diary or journal. Spader wandered over to have a look at it and was surprised to see all the writing appeared to be in German. Africa and South America were easy enough to make out. He thought he knew which shape represented North America and what would later become South America and Africa, but the rest was unfamiliar. In the bottom right hand corner was what appeared to be a man's signature in shiny gold ink with a date written beneath. He moved in closer and tried to read it.

"Alfred L. Wegener," Gray said, the sudden sound startling Spader. He had been so consumed with the drawing, that he'd forgotten Gray was there. "He was the one to postulate the Theory of Continental Drift. Engraved on the plaque beneath is a quote from his only book on the subject. I had Talon translate the original, which was written in German."

Spader read the quote aloud:

"Scientists still do not appear to understand sufficiently that all earth sciences must contribute evidence toward unveiling the state of our planet in earlier times, and that the truth of the matter can only be reached by combing all this evidence. . . It is only by combing the information furnished by all the earth sciences that we can hope to determine 'truth' here, that is to say, to find the picture that sets out all the known facts in the best arrangement and that therefore has the highest degree of probability. Further, we have to be prepared always for the possibility that each new discovery, no matter what science furnishes it, may modify the conclusions we draw."

"He wrote that in 1915. Even though the focus is on earth science, the message alludes to the all-inclusive and self-governing necessity inherent in solid science. If the rest of the world employed such rigorous logic and rationality..." he paused and smiled at Spader, "Well, we probably wouldn't be here tonight."

Spader nodded, then asked, "When did he draw this?"

"He didn't," Gray said returning his gaze to the drawing. "I'm not sure who did. Probably someone at the University of Graz in Austria. That was where he worked right before he died."

"How did he die?" he asked, still examining the aged signature.

"On a rescue operation in Greenland – October, 1930. He had brought supplies to colleagues at a remote site who he knew to be in desperate need – a life or death situation. He reached the camp, but knew the supplies weren't enough to sustain everyone so he insisted on heading back the very next day. What happened next is a matter of debate, but he is believed to have died of hypothermia, heart failure, or a combination of the two. He was buried by the man traveling with him – Villumsen was his name. Sadly, Wegener died somewhere around his fiftieth birthday."

"Around? No one is sure when he died?" he asked incredulously.

Gray shook his head. "No. His body wasn't actually discovered until May 12, 1931 – almost six months after he left the encampment and headed back. After his body was found, it was concluded that Villumsen must have buried him and then moved on. But Villumsen never made it. His body and Wegener's journal, which were believed to have been with him, have never been found."

Spader pictured a cold, icy rivulet barely wide enough for a simple schooner to pass. The darkness of the water contrasted sharply with the pristine white of the ubiquitous snow and ice. He thought about the chill he still carried from the winter outside and wondered what it would be like to die from hypothermia. The body goes numb, time slows, and confusion sets in. By the time you realize you're too cold to survive, the mind has slowed, leaving ample time to think while the body starts to shut down. Time to reflect – and to regret. But if the departing soul had spent his life well and endeavored to remain true to his heart, dying might bring a flood of peace. In the last minutes of life, surrounded by cold and ice, with the torrent of one's last thoughts being the only reality, only a clear conscience could bring true peace.

Deep in thought, Spader suddenly wondered how he would die. It was something every human had pondered at one time or another, yet few dared to linger on such contemplations. There was a proscribed stigma behind thoughts of one's own death, which bordered on a kind of fearful superstition. Most avoided pondering their own end for fear of hastening its arrival. It was as if people were sure death waited patiently at the intersection of reality and denial. Spader himself sometimes wondered if there was a subconscious link to the inevitability of one's passing. Something like a psychological hypochondria – whereby too much time spent thinking about dying inadvertently sped up one's demise.

Then something from the back of his mind halted his train of thought and he turned again to look at Wegener's signature and the date beneath it. Coincidence? Could Gray have planned this? "I'm at my crossroads," he whispered to himself, still staring at the gold lettering. Beneath the scientist's signature was the date of the signing: Dec 7, 1928. "Today is Dec 7th," he thought.

He whirled to look at Gray, who was as calm as ever. This man saw right through him, and that realization brought a new chill to his spine.

"Is this a coincidence?" he said pointing at the date on the drawing, raising his voice. "Or was I supposed to come in here and see this? Is this one of your damn psychological games – some whimsical shred from your former career?" He suddenly felt anxious and angry, though he couldn't say exactly why.

Gray's piercing blue and silver eyes studied him for a moment, as if trying to see through the flesh and into his soul. Despite the minor outbreak, the stoic man seemed unaffected, as though he were studying an experiment. Gray remained silent for a few moments, though it felt like a year to Spader.

"You're right, Spader," Gray said simply. "You are at a crossroads. And you're not the first. Many great men and women have come before us and faced decisions just as difficult as those that keep us awake at night." Gray gestured towards the map. "Over eighty years ago Wegener also had some difficult decisions to make. Like so many scientists, he'd struggled for years for the respect of his academic contemporaries." Gray turned and walked slowly towards the long polished table. "He was a visionary. His ideas were born of passion, knowledge and careful calculation. And yet the recognition he deserved came posthumously. But in the face of harsh criticism he chose to push on with his work, revising his seminal theory of continental drift and planning his trip to Greenland to continue his research. To continue to fight for what he believed was right."

Standing next to the table, Gray gestured for him to take a seat. Spader hesitated a moment, then sat. Gray was a great orator and his words commanded attention. After seating himself, Gray leaned forward, his eyes intent.

"Spader," he said in a low voice, "we came together because we had a vision – a dream of a world where knowledge, intelligence, morality, passion, boldness, and discovery triumphed over ignorance, fear, predation, deceitfulness, and bandwagon pessimism. This world has never existed because the latter has always defeated the former. Why? Because the people with the guns know the shortest path to wealth and control is through intimidation and fear, which usually leads to submission – total obedience and compliance from the worker bees. History books are chock full of such examples. Presidents, tsars, kings, queens, religious leaders, military commanders – you name it. Since our first prehistoric ancestors learned how to gain power through force, mankind has been a slave to its own. Enslave the worker bees and gorge yourself on sweet power and control."

Gray leaned back and stared into the hearth. The blaze in his eyes was as bright as the fire raging in the hearth. "This planet has seen so much unnecessary death and suffering," he said solemnly. "So much pain dealt by so few. At least the bees and ants don't torture and kill their own. They're smarter than that."

He seemed to snap out of his reverie, and the sudden intensity in his eyes pierced through Spader. "There are only a few, Spader! Only a few. How can so few bring so much misery to so many? It boggles the mind to think how it could happen! Of course, there were some cases where submission was a simple matter. The millions of African slaves shipped to the Americas between the sixteenth and nineteenth century were primitive. They had no faculty for comprehending the world they were forcibly brought to. What they saw in the Americas must have been something akin to our visiting an alien world. There was no way they could effectively retaliate.

"The same is true for child slavery, which still persists to this day in places like China, Africa, Asia, and Malaysia. They can't defend themselves. But the rest of our species' history is a lengthy study in the most stunning contrast mankind is capable of creating. It involves people being manipulated, exploited, hurt and often times killed by individuals of comparable or lesser intelligence and capacity whose obsession with wealth, control and subjugation overwhelmed any tiny vestiges of decency they might have once possessed. And this still exists today!" For a brief moment Gray's eyes were wild with incredulity and frustration. Quickly he reigned in his emotions, took a deep breath and sat back resignedly in the leather chair. Spader waited, unable to translate his thoughts into the right words.

"Spader," Gray said calmly, "you've heard all this before. You know why we've chosen to take such an unorthodox, unprecedented, and seemingly..." he groped for the right word, "*hypocritical* path. We, who vehemently oppose war, violence, and unilateral judgment are bringing the fight to the – well not to the fighters. We're certainly clear on that point. We're bringing the battle to those who would send others to fight and die to achieve their hidden agendas.

"We're fighting the men in suits and polished shoes who spend their time whittling complex and convincing lies out of the smallest bits of half-truths. Men like former President Bush and Vice-President Cheney – both of whom have heavy financial ties to oil and arms companies – yet they managed to convince the American people that the war in Iraq has nothing to do with oil and guns. They're just like the lobbyists who casually discuss over a five hundred dollar round of golf how best to pollute the environment without getting caught. We, who value peace, reason and enjoyment, have chosen to take up the arms we despise and assign ourselves as judge, jury, and executioner. We do this in the hope that those who hide behind their henchmen and bodyguards will finally see that their own vile tactics can and will be used against them. Not for power or control, but simply to rid the world of the most vulgar members of our species. We," he said pointing his finger at Spader and then at himself, "we have made this choice. And with this choice, we consciously accept the terrible responsibility and the incalculable damage it will do to us. But," he said moving closer, "we can neither waiver in our resolve nor shy away from the full obligation we've accepted."

Spader was looking at Gray with a mixture of intense realization and resolve. He knew where Gray was going with this. In his mind he saw the face of his, yes, *his* mark. The man he'd spent the last six months researching. Countless hours had been spent going through emails, recorded phone calls, boxes of trial documents and all manner of public record. With the help of his assistant, they'd managed to break into the man's home without being detected. They'd copied and replaced his mail, even followed him to numerous public meetings, and eavesdropped using sophisticated miniature microphones. Locked in his office were stacks of files, including personal and business tax returns, ten years of personal credit reports, expense records, medical and dental records, college transcripts, family photographs, a genealogy compilation, and much more. Even after he'd reported to a federal prison in Virginia to begin serving his sentence, the due diligence had continued. Since the beginning of the project, the study of this man's life had consumed most of Spader's time. In essence, he'd traded his own life for that of another. Now the responsibility for that man's life was also his.

Gray was looking at him as if he'd read his thoughts. He said, "Every member of *The Aenamaia* must bear the burden of their assignment. *Every* aspect of it. To the end."

It had been over a year and a half since that cold December night, yet the earnest expression on Gray's face still hung clear in his mind as he tracked the sluggish, shuffle-like movements of Jack Abramoff across the dirt yard. "Every aspect," he thought, "to the end." The rest of the conversation that night was somewhat of a blur now. He remembered sitting quietly in the plush leather chair imagining the climactic moment of his assignment. This moment. Watching a man through a sniper's scope. A man who had no idea he was about to die. It seemed wrong that no sentence would be read to him – no conviction – no warning of what was to come. No last words. Maybe it was better that way.

Planning for death was probably much less important to someone in prison. But that wasn't entirely true. Those on death row might agree, but a man like Abramoff, who still had friends in Washington and money in the bank, and a release date less than a decade away would definitely want to plan for his death. More than that, he'd fight tooth and nail to prevent it. But a scholarly voice in his mind pondered, what if such a man had mended his ways? Was it possible, by the standards of the soon-to-be executioner and *The Aenamaia*, for such a man to repay his debt to society? Was it really necessary for him to pay for his transgressions with his life? Though this man clearly possessed a morality with the firmness of a wet noodle, no one had died as a result of his actions. No one they were aware of, anyway.

This was a matter he'd struggled with throughout this assignment. The question was always the same: could a person be toxic enough to society, without being lethal, to warrant an execution? The more he'd researched this man, the more he'd seen how far-reaching his treachery went and how much collateral damage had been done. Additionally, as Gray had said in one form or another over the years, the message these men sent to the rest of the world did incalculable damage. They demonstrated time and time again that the wicked were rewarded by the honest blood of the good. For thousands of years their predecessors were required to be outwardly bold, fearless, strong, fierce, and skilled as leaders. Though their actions were atrocious, they were often on the front lines charging into harm's way and conquering by skill alone.

Abramoff and his kind were a different breed altogether. They schemed, deceived, conned and cheated people – and as evidenced by the stream of emails the prosecutors had acquired, seemed to truly enjoy each ill-conceived victory. They prided themselves on the cleverness with which they designed each scam. Delighted in adeptly hiding and lavishly spending the proceeds. Gray had once said these men should be afraid to own mirrors for fear of what they would see. Unfortunately, an acute darkness had long since clouded any morality or decency they possessed. What was really frightening was how much they'd done that still had not been uncovered.

These thoughts swirled around in Spader's head as he continued to follow his mark in the scope. "No," he thought, "I made my decision a long time ago." Gray was right. Not only must the damage cease forever, but the message must be sent. He had accepted this responsibility and was prepared, as best as one could be, to live with what he was about to do.

"I need an update here!" he hissed. He took a short breath, then calmly asked, "Am I clear?"

"Negative," the quiet voice returned. "Review target."

Spader had pulled away from the scope to ask for clearance. When he reacquired his mark, he immediately saw the problem. Walking next to Abramoff was FCI Cumberland's second most famous and controversial inmate, convicted murderer of his pregnant wife and two children, Dr. Jeffrey MacDonald. And he was dead center in Spader's scope.

Chapter 18

Washington, D.C.

Talon eagerly scoured the web for information on the explosion of the plane carrying Anna Kulter and company – all of whom were supposed to have been dropped safely in the middle of Iraq. So far information was scant and fragmented. The few pages that came up were in Arabic. A Japanese conspiracy blog mentioned a mysterious explosion over Iraq, suggesting that a UFO might have been involved.

Strangely, British and American media had failed to make mention of the event. Since the onset of the war in Iraq, the Pentagon, via direction from the White House, had kept a tight leash on media reporting from the Middle East in situations where they were just as clueless as everyone else. Apparently someone high up in the U.S. government had decided they'd had enough embarrassment during the Bush administration. It was best to gather the facts and make it look like they were well informed, versus the deer-in-the-headlights scenario caught on camera so many times during the Iraq war.

Gray paced the room, still listening intently to whatever was happening with Spader's operation. For his part, Talon had only been consulted during the initial planning stages of the Abramoff liquidation. He recalled that the options for eliminating Abramoff were limited given his current location. A number of possibilities had been discussed – everything from a poisoned care package to actually sending in an Augur posing as an inmate. Both had been ruled out due to obvious complications in planning and probable secondary obstacles. In the end they had decided on keeping as much distance as possible between themselves and

Abramoff. Though sniping was a hairy business and would result in a more public and graphic hit than they preferred, the planning committee had concluded it was the safest option. No doubt Gray was intent on making sure it went off as smoothly as possible and that Spader made it out safely.

"Negative," Gray said, "hold until the shot is clear. Osiro, is the call through yet?" He nodded, then said, "Good. Patch his feed through, as well. The doctor is a smart man. He'll make the connection and pass it on to the media – and do it before prison officials realize the true implications to them and their compromised security systems. The doctor's high profile case – along with being an eyewitness to the shooting – should ensure the media will pick up the story. With any luck the warden won't figure it out before he reads about it in the newspaper."

"O, what a tangled web we weave when first we practice to deceive!" Talon recalled the famous quote. "How true," he thought. "How very true."

Cumberland, Maryland

Spader remembered the doctor well. Early in the planning stages with the Abramoff advisory committee, he had learned that Dr. MacDonald had previously been suggested as a candidate for the liquidation list. Susha had been the one to submit the nomination and had immediately volunteered to handle the case and the hit. Initial due diligence had revealed enough plausible doubt about the doctor's guilt to cause his name to be dropped as a candidate, however. When the name came up again, the long dormant coals flared back to life and Susha, who was originally on the Abramoff committee, again lobbied for his termination. Despite the obvious appeal of a convenient double liquidation, the committee reminded Susha that the evidence against the doctor was still too controversial. They tactfully reiterated the importance *The Aenamaia* placed on a consensus verdict based on hard evidence, but she wouldn't let it go. The discussions went on for days. Finally, after a long and heated debate,

Susha reluctantly agreed to surrender her seat on the committee to Dia so that the Abramoff project could move forward.

Thinking the matter settled, Spader had been surprised when Susha showed up at his house late one night. She'd phoned and said it was urgent that she speak with him. That night she again laid out her case against MacDonald: forensics, psych analysis, chronology of events, apparent holes in his testimony, statistical analyses, blood samples, etc. Spader, seeing the obvious passion behind her conviction, had listened patiently, only speaking to interject questions. Remaining impartial and objective had been difficult, as it usually was when someone he knew and respected was thoroughly convinced their position was the correct one. It had been especially difficult when she'd pointed out that the doctor claimed four people had entered his house and started killing his family while he was asleep on the couch.

Susha stressed that Jeffrey MacDonald survived with only minor injuries, while his wife and three children had been brutally murdered, and not one of the four alleged attackers was ever caught. "Why did they let him live?" she'd asked over and over again – sometimes directing the question to him, other times to no one in particular. "If they were acid-tripping why leave anyone alive? They wouldn't even have the mental faculties to leave him alive so the blame might fall on him. It's ludicrous!" she'd exclaimed. On and on it went that night, until finally he'd told her to give him some time to think about it.

Over the course of the following week, he'd immersed himself in the MacDonald case. Nearly four decades worth of information spread out over various websites, blogs, articles, books, documentaries, interviews, TV programs, transcripts, trial notes, and character testimonies. There were just as many people convinced of MacDonald's innocence as there were of his guilt. The split went right down the middle. For his part, Spader's gut told him the man was guilty, which he felt was well supported by evidence that seemed to point to a high probability MacDonald's story was too fantastic and improbable to be true. Yet there was also persuasive evidence pointing in the other direction. It was the photographs and graphic descriptions of the crime that pushed him over the edge. He knew there wasn't sufficient evidence that the doctor had committed the crime, but because there were no other faces available to blame, MacDonald lost by default. He'd known such judgment was emotional and unfair, but it was too late – the impression had already solidified in his mind.

Despite his commitment as a member of *The Aenamaia* to remain objective and impartial, he felt compelled to take up the fight with Susha. But before they could gain any ground, other more urgent matters arose and the issue was tabled. Susha had been sent on assignment to profile a U.S. senator accused of having sex with underage boys in Taiwan during a visit paid for by the American taxpayers. Allegations of physical abuse of the boys had also been raised. The senator, a top fundraiser for the Republican Party, popped up on *The Aenamaia's* radar when he was quietly acquitted of all charges on the same day as one of the Bush administration's mysterious and unjustified heightened terrorist alerts was sounded. When the major media failed to cover the story, Gray decided to put Susha on the trail while the evidence was still fresh.

Shortly after she left for Taiwan, Gray confided in Spader that Susha had lost her only child ten years ago. Though he wouldn't reveal any other details, he did say her work since then made her the best candidate for this type of assignment. And while her tragic loss infused her with an acute protective fervor and a desperate desire for justice, she was also a professional who wanted to get the job done right.

Spader hadn't known about Susha's child, but he immediately realized why she was so adamant about Jeffrey MacDonald – though it begged the question, how thorough a professional was she? Gray seemed to think her top priority was a fair decision based on incontrovertible evidence. But from what he'd seen from the MacDonald case, he saw no way she could've reached a solid, logical conclusion.

Staring through the scope, Spader watched as Jeffrey MacDonald walked casually next to Abramoff. Spader had seen pictures of the doctor, but in the flesh he looked much older and more frail. It had been almost thirty years since MacDonald had been convicted and began serving four consecutive life sentences. He'd been thirty-six years old at the time of sentencing. His hair had begun going gray in his early thirties, but with age and the stresses of prison life, came a receding hairline and half a scalp of fine snow-white hair.

From his vantage point Spader could only see MacDonald's profile, but the sight was enough to bring back his initial conviction of guilt. He swallowed hard and took a deep breath. "Concentrate," he thought, "This is important. Don't lose focus." Then he had an idea.

"Oculus, do you copy?" he whispered.

"Affirmative," came the calm reply. Masked voice or not, it was Osiro all right.

"Do you have audio on the mark?" he asked, trying to mask the anxiousness in his voice.

"Affirmative. It's low but audible."

"Patch me through. I want to hear this."

There was a momentary delay then came, "Authorized. Audio patched."

Within a few seconds he heard two faint voices. Keeping his left hand locked on the barrel, he pressed down on the earpiece in his right ear. It took him a few moments to realize which voice belonged to which man. MacDonald was saying something about everyone feeling gray and isolated in this place. His voice was soft and conciliatory, as if he was trying to calm Abramoff.

"I guess I should be thankful they've separated us," Abramoff was saying. "I mean it isn't as though we have to contend with rapists and murde....oh, sorry Jeff. But you know what I mean. The joint isn't brimming with a bunch of crazy mad-dog killer types. I suppose I'm just feeling sorry for myself. They put me in, let me out again, then one little interview – and wham! I'm right back in. Sons'a'bitches. They let me taste freedom for just a moment then tore it away from me. Again! Not that I miss having that lojack up my ass all the time. Still, there's just nothing worse than being incarcerated in this shit hole with money in the bank and capable friends in Washington."

Abramoff's hands were in his pockets and he made a habit of kicking up dirt and rocks while he talked.

"Jack," Jeff said, trying to get Abramoff's attention.

"I mean you're about the only person in this zoo with any class or sophistication. This white-collar Loserville just isn't for me. I should be in my restaurant churning deals, making introductions, proffering my expert advice at five hundred dollars an hour." Abramoff laughed greedily. "Five hundred an hour minimum, Jeff. And both sides paying me! The world is just brimming with idiots with deep pockets. You wouldn't believe how many are out there. It's not my fault they're too clueless to know what's going on. I mean, come on. Wouldn't you even try and find out who your competition hired to shut your casino down? Might that not be useful information? They don't deserve to have money or power. They deserve exactly what they get. It's survival of the fittest and that means cunning – and balls of steel. God, I can't wait to get out of here. Those bastard Feds keep using that carrot on me. 'Yeah, Jack old boy, you keep cooperating and giving us what we want and we'll see about shortening that sentence.' Fuckin' idiots."

"Jack," Jeff repeated louder, "there's something I have to tell you!"

The sheepish, slumping, and humiliated Abramoff from the trial was gone. The old Abramoff – the original Casino Jack was doing the talking now – and he was on a roll. "Then they try and get tough with me. 'Well Jack, if you want to keep all that dough you've got stashed in offshore accounts, you're gonna have to do better than that. 'Cuz we can make it all vanish. And that includes all the money your wife has stashed, *Jack*.'" Abramoff snorted petulantly.

"But what I really love is when they get creative with my name like, 'You better tell us more than *Jack shit* or that's exactly what you'll have when you walk out of here. *If* you walk out of here.' Bastards. You know if I ever get out of here I'm going to systematically make every one of those fuckers vanish into thin air. Bubbye! Oh, and I'll be sure and give your love to that pretty wife of yours. You can *count on it*. I'll kill you.... and your pretty friends too!" Abramoff said angrily, kicking up more dirt. "And if that wasn't enough, I found out this morning that a different group of government assholes is going to pay me a visit. Hell, they're probably signing in right now. Except when I asked, no one seems to know who they are or what agency they're from. They just let in anyone who feels like threatening me or wasting my time."

Spader looked up from the scope and his eyes lost focus. Something wasn't quite right here. He knew Abramoff's visitor schedule better than Abramoff himself. He'd checked it one last time yesterday afternoon and it had not shown any visitors today.

"Oculus, did you catch that?" he said quietly.

"Yes," Osiro said sounding distracted, "Nothing has popped up on our radar, but we weren't monitoring his schedule. When did you last check in with the site contact?"

"Yesterday. All was clear for today – nothing out of the ordinary." Spader tried to think. Who the hell could be coming to visit Abramoff today? And on such short notice?

"Please advise," he requested.

"Stand by," Osiro said.

Spader reacquired the two men in his scope while he waited. Thirty seconds later the reply came.

"Continue as planned. If the mark gets dirty or takes cover, abort and return tomorrow."

"He's already dirty," Spader mumbled to himself. He couldn't take the shot while MacDonald was nearby – or anyone for that matter. That much had been determined ahead of time. It had to be clean. Abramoff needed to be alone.

"Damn sneaky bastards," he heard Abramoff say. "They're worse than most of the dirt bags in here."

MacDonald seemed irritated. There was obviously something he wanted to tell Abramoff, but he couldn't get a word in while the former lobbyist raved on and on.

"Delay'll help me do it. He's got the best connections of all my friends. If you want something done, Tom's the man you go to. We used to call him 'The Architect.' Seriously. That was his nickname in some circles. Tom could find a way to make anything happen. He's smart as they get. That's why they've never been able to pin anything big on him – he's always one step ahead. They tried to give him three years, but he's on parole and free to do what he wants. Hell, he was just on TV not too long ago dancing up a storm. They just can't keep up with him. And if he happens to fall one step behind, he just dials one of the numbers in his little black book and the cage doors open wide."

Abramoff seemed to be enjoying himself now. "Yeah, Tom is the best. He does business based on the way the law should be, not the way it is. That may sound criminal to you, but what else can you do when the law is written by a bunch of whiny, sniveling weasels bent on fighting social evolution? I mean poor and uneducated people are that way by choice. No really, they are. Even with our people controlling Congress and the White House, there are still plenty of handouts and programs for people to start climbing the ladder. If they wanted to be better they would work for it – but they don't. So why should the rest of us have to suffer for it? Why should the laws protect those who don't want to do better for themselves? Tom and I used to talk about this sometimes. If the world would just let the poor and ignorant die off, then what would be left? The rich and strong. What's so wrong with that? Nothing, I tell you."

The two men had stopped near the far end of the yard. Abramoff was leaning against the wall lighting a cigarette while MacDonald stood next to him staring down at the ground. Spader had a clean shot of both men. But he still hadn't received the order to retire the mark.

"That's what Hitler was trying to do," Abramoff said exhaling a thick cloud of smoke. MacDonald's head bolted upright and he stared hard at Abramoff.

"Now don't get me wrong, Jeff," Abramoff said defensively, "Hitler was a crazy sonofabitch – I know, I'm Jewish. What he did was terrible, but the idea way in the background – the fundamental concept wasn't all bad. He just wanted the world to be populated with a certain kind of people. He just picked the wrong people to get rid of – that's all. He wanted a cleaner world. A brotherhood of like-minded men and women who all wanted the same things in life. That isn't half bad is it? You know they even tried it here in the U.S. Eugenics. Started back in the early 1900s with one of the Presidents – um, Wilson or Roosevelt. Wilson I think. Anyways they tried all sorts of things to weed out the weak. Prevented 'em from marrying, compulsory sterilization, putting more people in padded rooms – that sort of thing. Then the liberals and democrats butted in. Might have been a much different country right now if they hadn't interfered. I mean things are better now that the republicans are mostly in control, but just imagine if they weren't! That's why we need guys like myself and Tom Delay out there. Somebody has to shape this country and reap the rewards. Damn sure can't leave it to the dumb and poor veggie-masses out there."

"Jack, will you just shut up for one minute!" MacDonald barked.

"What the hell is your problem?" Abramoff said defensively.

"Congressman Delay is dead, Jack," MacDonald said with finality. "Dead," he repeated curtly.

"What?" Abramoff stuttered. Through the scope Spader could see his mark clearly. Abramoff was now breathing in short fits – as if he were having a panic attack. It looked as though powerful invisible hands were pressing down on his chest. The stress and confusion was obvious on his face.

"What happened?" Abramoff asked uncertainly.

MacDonald hesitated, his face serious. "Are you sure you want to hear the details, Jack?"

Abramoff threw down his cigarette, grabbed the older man by his shirt collar and growled, "Goddammit. You tell me what happened to Tom!"

MacDonald didn't move an inch. He was shorter and thinner than Abramoff, but that didn't matter. He stared menacingly at Abramoff until the man released him. MacDonald smoothed out his collar, never breaking eye contact.

"I've been in here for a long time, Jack," he said, his voice suddenly ice cold. "I've survived here because I choose my associations carefully. I too have friends who can make things happen. Bad things, Jack. Right here," he said firmly pointing to the ground between them.

Abramoff's face was twisted with nervous emotion, but he remained silent.

MacDonald continued slowly. "Whoever killed your friend Delay has a strange sense of humor. After they killed him with some kind of unknown poison, they wrapped the body in a vacuum-sealed body bag, packaged him in a crate and had him delivered to the White House, attention George Bush, Jr. Yes," he said nodding, "delivered. More uptight and on-edge than usual thanks to the unpopularity of the former President, you can imagine how the Secret Service and White House security reacted. They came out with guns blazing, cleared the block and diverted traffic on Pennsylvania Avenue. After the bomb dogs sniffed the thing, they opened it up and out fell the cadaver formally known as Congressman Delay. It was a damn mess. They confiscated the courier's electronic manifest, but when they tried to track the delivery, all they found were dead ends."

Abramoff looked stunned and confused. After a few seconds of silence, MacDonald continued.

"Then the Secret Service really stepped on their dicks by trying to deny any such incident had occurred. The story had been reported anonymously to the local police and the media. Shortly after the Secret Service issued a formal statement denying the story, a suspiciously clean video of the whole thing turned up on a hundred different websites and blogs. The *same* video. It hit the internet a few days ago. According to the story I read, the high quality of the video suggests the ones who filmed it knew what they were doing, and presumably, what was about to happen. It wasn't a tourist with a cell phone filming the White House. The article said it was likely they used a broadcast quality camera, but so far no one can figure out how they managed to film the incident without the Secret Service noticing. Anyways, once the video hit the internet, the news stations had no choice but to air the story. The Secret Service has since retracted its statement, but has yet to release another one. The White House has not commented on the incident other than to say it will be investigated and the group responsible will be brought to justice."

Abramoff seemed to come out of his stupor. "Group? What group?"

"Jesus, Jack, haven't you been reading the papers?" MacDonald said incredulously. "Where have you been? There's some crazy group who call themselves *The Aenamaia* going around killing people and blowing things up. Most of the media is labeling them domestic terrorists, but I think that's just a smokescreen. These people are pissed, no doubt about it, but they're not asking for anything. Nada. No demands. No public proclamations, blogs, or anything. And they're very specific. Celebrities, high-profile businessmen, lawyers, and...former members of Congress. Everyone is pretty sure they're the ones who snuffed Delay and filmed the incident at the front gates of the White House. Apparently they're going after everyone they don't seem to like or agree with. Mostly bad people as best as I can tell. They even killed one of those crazy televangelists. Cops found the fat bastard lying dead on his office floor next to an open safe. Inside they found a ton of cash and jewelry, obscene video tapes starring the deceased, bank ledgers, even a sort of confession the man had written years ago and never showed anyone.

Again they got the story aired on public access TV and the internet a few hours before the major news stations picked it up. They're smart, organized and determined."

The comment made Spader grin. But there was more. In the span of a few short minutes, his rationality and logical faculties had returned. He felt again that there was sufficient doubt about MacDonald's guilt. Something about the man's manner, tone, and control. Something. Whatever it was, he knew it was enough. Where the doctor was concerned, he would leave the pursuit of truth and justice to others. In the meantime the man would have to continue playing the hand fate had dealt him – for better or for worse. Now he just needed the good doctor to leave. Instead, he kept talking.

"...tabloids shut down, their buildings blown all to hell. But not one casualty in the explosions. Not one. They got everyone out first, then pressed the button. No, these guys are careful, calculating and patient."

"Come on," Spader whispered, "go back inside. Oculus, you there?"

"Affirmative."

Spader checked his watch, "Rec time is over in ten minutes. Any suggestions?"

"Already working on it. Stand by."

MacDonald was still talking when a loud metallic thud stopped him in mid-sentence. One of the doors leading back into the main building had opened. Someone was calling for the doctor. Spader again pressed down on the earpiece. It was definitely a man's voice, but he couldn't make out what he was saying. "What the...?" Spader whispered.

"The variable is being told he has an urgent phone call," Osiro responded quietly.

"Phone call," the voice yelled.

"From the DNA testing lab," Osiro added.

"Clever," he thought. Osiro must've remembered that MacDonald was awaiting word on some forensic testing he and his attorney had finally gotten authorized. He had to admire the man's persistence. Nearly three decades and the guy was still fighting.

"Okay," he heard MacDonald say eagerly, "I'll be right there." Spader saw the doctor start backing away from Abramoff. "You'll have to take a look at all this stuff, Jack. No telling who these guys are or what they're after."

"Confirmed," Gray said evenly, "Watch for blowback. Don't linger." He turned and made eye contact with Talon. His demeanor was still serious, but Talon could tell the end was in sight.

"Retirement authorized."

Jeffrey MacDonald ran across the yard and darted through the heavy door leading back into the recreation room. There was no running allowed anywhere inside of the prison so he slowed his pace to a fast walk. Several inmates sat at the various tables playing cards and checkers, but he barely noticed them. The excitement was almost too much to contain. He nodded to the guard who'd come and gotten him and took a left down the hall towards the small room where they allowed inmates to place and receive calls. Three other inmates were making calls, but the fourth phone near the window was available. Lifting the phone off the receiver, he pressed zero.

"Hi, Margaret. This is Jeffery MacDonald. I was told I had a call. Yes, I'll hold. Thank you."

He was too excited to sit so he took two steps over to the window. It surprised him to see Jack Abramoff still out in the yard. Though he couldn't see his face clearly, his posture suggested he was nervous and agitated. News of Delay's unusual and sudden death had obviously rattled that man. He'd heard Abramoff speak many times of his association with Tom Delay. At first Jack had been reluctant to be too forthcoming. But after a few months he spoke candidly about the various "deals" he and Delay had orchestrated. Pulling strings in Washington, shutting down casinos, filtering money to various places, doctoring paperwork, the visit to the Northern Mariana Islands, even working the books at his own restaurant. Together their collective transgressions would've made for an attractive resume for the mafia or the CIA. It wasn't the crimes that had bothered him. He'd spent enough time around white-collar criminals to be used to such things. It was just difficult to comprehend how the two men had done so many illegal things before being caught. Abramoff surely had some bad wiring. On the outside, MacDonald would have avoided consorting with such men. But on the inside, his options and expectations for friendship were, by necessity, considerably lower.

A voice came over the phone. "Dr. MacDonald?"

"Yes, I'm here," he answered excitedly.

"I'm afraid I have good news and I have bad news."

"What is it?" MacDonald asked eagerly.

"The good news is your DNA results are in."

"That's great! What are the results?"

"But the bad news is, I'm afraid Mr. Abramoff won't be around to share the news with you," the man said, his tone genuinely sympathetic.

Still looking out the window, MacDonald said, "What? What does Jack have to do with…" Just then he heard a short, abrupt chirp come through the phone. Confused, he looked down at the phone, then absently scanned the yard. Abramoff was leaning awkwardly against the wall, a forgotten cigarette dangling loosely from his hand. Another chirp sounded and he saw a faint circular shockwave emanate from Abramoff's chest. MacDonald's mouth dropped open as he watched in horror as Abramoff slid sideways along the wall, revealing two jagged, blood-spattered holes in the brick. Just before the plump man hit the ground, MacDonald spotted two dark circles on the front of Abramoff's shirt.

"Oh, my God," MacDonald said slowly, his voice shaky. He couldn't believe what he was seeing. The man he'd been talking to only minutes ago lay dead or dying twenty feet inside the razor wire fencing of a federal correctional facility.

In his ear he heard a faint new voice say, "Mark retired."

MacDonald was about to shout for help when something occurred to him. He had *heard* the two silenced gunshots through the telephone. Whoever had pulled the trigger had been listening and was also transmitting. Now he'd apparently heard the gunman confirm that Abramoff was dead. Pulling the receiver away from his ear, he stared at it as if it were an alien object that he'd never seen before. His mind was moving in slow motion – his thoughts sluggish and muddled. How could this be? What was happening? Slowly he replaced the receiver to his ear and whispered, "Hello?"

"Congratulations, Dr. MacDonald," it was the first calm, confident voice again.

"What? Congratulations? Why?" he asked, still staring at the lifeless body of Jack Abramoff.

"Based on the DNA findings, I think it's safe to say that you and your case are back in the game."

Chapter 19

Denver, Colorado

The man was edgy and it rubbed off on Breckus. There was something in the EPA investigator's posture that had kept him on guard throughout the discussion. Initially, Breckus had written it off to the same nervousness a devoted husband feels when he finds himself flirting with another woman. Now he was sure the man who called himself Mr. Poe hadn't completely made peace with the decision to pass along confidential government information to a source he didn't fully understand or trust, which was understandable. But the more Breckus heard, the more he assumed the same anxious and tense posture as his informant. What he was hearing was remarkable. So much so, that more than once during the conversation, thinking of the sensitive recording device hidden beneath the sleeve of his jacket, brought him a fleeting moment of comfort. Years of this kind of work had taught him many things – one of which was that shocking, disconcerting information, and the resulting fascination and incredulity often merged in the mind, leaving holes in even the best photographic or eidetic memories. Osiro's homemade device ensured those holes wouldn't sink the ship, which was comforting, given that this ship had plenty of holes already.

The conversation had started slowly. Breckus could tell from Poe's actions and mannerisms that he was not a professional spy, spook or intelligence agent. He was nervous, cautious, perhaps even a little scared. Breckus had been somewhat surprised to find the man sitting with his back to the door. "Definitely not a professional operative," he'd concluded. Every thirty seconds Poe looked expectantly at his cell, though the device never made a sound.

It had taken a few minutes of small talk, pastries and a cappuccino before the tension waned. Breckus learned that this was Poe's first time in Denver and that he had hoped to extend his trip in order to see the mountains, but with new allegations against Bush coming out every few days, it was only a matter of time before the eyes of the Justice Department turned to the EPA. Preparations for the imminent investigation were now in full swing, albeit quietly. It was unfortunate, but the mountains would have to wait. Breckus assured him they would be here whenever he returned. Poe muttered something and smiled politely.

Gradually the subject matter changed. Hints, rumors and roundabout suggestions began emerging. Breckus offered some subtle encouragement and expressed empathy for the precarious nature of Mr. Poe's position. But it was only when Breckus congratulated Poe for his great courage, fortitude and conviction, that the floodgates began to open. Shelved investigations, conveniently lost paperwork, payoffs, coercion, department downsizing, precisely timed announcements by the former Bush administration designed to bury EPA-related stories, legal roadblocks and dead-ends for environmental action and watchdog groups, reappointment of key officials, and even blatant threats to the job security of senior-level managers and directors.

The litany of subterfuge and the outright violation of so many kinds of laws was mind-boggling. And even though the sitting President promised a return to better and higher environmental and regulatory standards, investigations of the EPA's practices or interference by the previous administration had yet to be included in the charges brought against the former President and his staff. Breckus was stunned to learn that several EPA researchers, scientists and climate change specialists had pushed hard for precautions against a natural disaster along the Gulf of Mexico. Most of the paper trail of internal work had vanished, but Poe cited a spooky article that had appeared in *Scientific American* which had come to the same conclusions.

"The article had been written in 2001 – five years before Katrina, but reading it now you would never know it," Poe had said. "The effects of a massive storm surge were outlined in stunning detail. It read like an article written after the disaster to describe what had happened – not what was being anticipated five years prior. This and studies from at least three independent researchers and scientists within the EPA outlining the gaping holes in the country's natural disaster response plans had been thrown at anyone in the White House who would listen. No one did."

"History, as they say, is often the ultimate judge of both success and failure," Breckus had commented.

Poe stared off into the distance for several long moments, his face lost in time. Something told Breckus this man had seen a good bit of action during the Katrina aftermath. For a brief moment he likened the man, and others who had seen first-hand the devastation and the subsequent FEMA disaster, to a war veteran. Snatched from a normal, domestic lifestyle of daily commutes, overpriced coffee, clean sheets and a warm house, and thrown into a disorganized microcosm of destruction, confusion, and intense emotional outpouring and suffering. Breckus looked at the pained expression on the man's face and reminded himself that not all soldiers wore green and carried guns.

"Would you like another danish?" Breckus asked.

"No," Poe shook his head, "No, thank you."

"I'm still trying to wake up, so I'm going for another coffee," Breckus said, trying to keep the mood casual and friendly.

When he returned, Poe still appeared lost in thought. The nervous investigator looked over his shoulder for the umpteenth time, exhaled, and returned to his cappuccino. "Ironically," he continued, "many of Bush's people are still here. And many of the ones that left still hold considerable sway over EPA matters. Our caseload is still a long way from where it was in 2000," Mr. Poe said, the frustration obvious in his voice. "Every time I try to figure out what's holding things up I wind up chasing phantoms and shadows or I get stuck in a spider web of red tape." Poe looked forlorn and worried. "I'm making too many waves," he said absently. "Drawing too much attention to myself."

"Is there a uh...a trail of money that can be followed?" Breckus asked.

Mr. Poe considered the question for a moment then shook his head. "Not that I've ever found." He hesitated then admitted, "But there's always money involved. It's difficult and, well, dangerous to look for something that isn't supposed to exist. It's a bit like being a detective and interrogating a suspect you believe is guilty. The law protects and treats them as innocents pending proof of guilt. But you *know* they're guilty – you just need the evidence. So you have to tread lightly and only ask carefully chosen, non-intrusive questions, hoping someone slips up or gives you a hint – or a look. If you're a seasoned Sherlock Holmes the whole thing is second nature. But don't let my moniker fool you – I'm neither a clever writer nor a detective."

Poe seemed reluctant to continue, so Breckus echoed, "But there *is* always money involved."

The investigator looked up from his drink and nodded. "Yes. That's what I believe. Me and, well…others."

Breckus saw something in the man's demeanor that suggested there was something he wanted to say, but was reluctant – so he took a shot in the dark.

"You think there is money motivating action behind the scenes, but you've been unable to find anything concrete. But someone else in your agency believes they've sniffed a trail – and you think they're right."

"I don't know," Poe said with a doubtful shake of his head. He seemed lost in his thoughts, like he was trying to nail something down in his mind. "I mean there's certainly reason to believe there is something major going on in the background. Why else do it? Why suppress agency investigations? Why choose to not protect the environment? Political favors? Financial gain? Could be, but we're not sure. Carver thinks they have friends in the World Bank that have somehow facilitated the financial side of things." The investigator looked up and immediately realized he'd made a mistake. Breckus shot the man a questioning glance and waited.

Mr. Poe grimaced. "Damn," he hissed. "Carver is another investigator. We have both been looking into these matters," he said adding in a hushed and serious voice, "as quietly as possible."

"Is there anyone else investigating with you?"

"No," Poe said nervously, "It's bad enough that I brought Carver in."

"Could anyone be suspicious of your activities? Pick up on the trail?"

Poe took a half glance over his shoulder. "It's difficult to say. This Bush investigation has become much more intense than any of us would've guessed. Most people thought the only reason the media was digging around so much was because they were tired of all the positive news from the White House," Poe said with a grin. "They're not used to it. People don't normally buy papers and tune in for brightly-colored clean laundry." Breckus couldn't argue with that. Human nature had shown time and time again that the pen usually doesn't hit the paper to praise – only to complain. And to sell newspapers.

"Whatever the reason for it," Poe continued nervously, "They're scouring around looking for any dirt they can find. The problem is, most of the dirt has been out in the open since 9/11. But when none of the media felt they could afford to bet their White House press passes on a gritty story, the trail got buried. Now the bloodhounds are back on the case."

Poe took a drink of his cappuccino and glanced at his cell phone. After eyeing a stack of steaming, glazed cinnamon rolls the clerk had just placed on the counter, he continued.

"If you ask me, Bush senior is plenty pissed about junior finishing dead last in the race for greatness in the White House. The Bush name has been irrevocably tarnished. But that doesn't mean it can't get a whole lot worse. My bet is the old man will employ every resource he has to make sure that doesn't happen. I saw the old man in action first hand during his administration." Poe shook his head despairingly. "I wouldn't put anything past him."

"I'm inclined to agree," Breckus said, "but that's not what we're here to talk about." Poe nodded absently.

"How many players?" Breckus asked, looking around cautiously.

"Best guess?" Poe asked.

Breckus nodded.

Poe shrugged. "Half a dozen or so."

"Can you give me names?"

Mr. Poe didn't answer. Just then the front door to the bakery banged opened. Poe's head whipped around – too quickly to be inconspicuous. The young girl who walked in was busily tapping on her cell screen and didn't appear to notice. Poe turned back around slowly. He looked at Breckus.

"I'm sorry," he said, unable to mask the tiredness from his voice. "I'm not used to...this," he said gesturing to the space between them.

"Names," Breckus repeated.

Poe let out a sigh. "I'm not sure that I'm ready to..." but Breckus cut him off.

"Look Poe, or whatever your real name is, you came to us. The only way people find us is through someone who knows who we are and what we do. You came here to give me more than suppositions and blind alleys. Now rest assured – nothing happens until we've done our due diligence and we are sure the guilty parties cannot be brought to justice or convinced to voluntarily atone for their transgressions. Our resources are impressive and the investigations are fast. But without a place to start..." He left the point hanging.

Mr. Poe stared directly at him for over a minute, his face awash with conflict. Breckus watched him carefully, trying to read his expression and posture. A tightening of the jaw, a slight pursing of the lips, and a narrowing of the eyes. Breckus could practically see the calculations running feverishly behind Poe's eyes. The pros, the cons, probabilities, scenarios, perhaps even moral dilemmas. He'd seen this type of reaction before and knew it was best to wait. The EPA investigator was straddling a razor's edge. Pushing from behind wouldn't guarantee which side he might fall on.

After a few long, silent moments, Breckus saw the resolve alter Poe's expression.

"All right," he said finally. "Just speaking names out loud is neither a crime nor a death sentence right?"

"The investigation, judgment, final decision, and the burden of action rests solely with us," Breckus assured him. "This is no different than reporting suspicious activity to the police. You observe and report; we'll determine whether a crime has taken place." Breckus removed a pad of paper and a pen from his coat pocket. After checking over his shoulder again, Poe sighed and started reciting names. Breckus wrote them down diligently – both as a backup to the recorder and to keep up the appearance that these names were the only material proof of their meeting.

When Poe was finished, Breckus looked down at the names. Seven in all – two of which were significant. Front-page headliners to say the least.

"Is this it?" Breckus asked.

"Those are the ones I know enough about to be suspicious. The fellows on the other end of the line are more elusive. However," he continued thoughtfully, "I assume if you can pick up the scent of the money trail, it just might lead you to the hallowed halls rising high above this nation."

"It usually does," Breckus said simply. "Perhaps I should meet with Carver to corroborate this list."

Mr. Poe raised a hand to protest at the same moment Breckus heard a faint, sharp crack. Before the bloodstain appeared on Poe's shoulder, Breckus had his .357 in one hand and Poe's collar in the other. In the blink of an eye, he'd pulled the stunned man to the floor and tipped the table forward for cover. The sudden movement and crashing of porcelain cups and plates silenced the other people in the bakery. A moment passed before the red-faced young man behind the counter spotted the weapon in Breckus's hand and yelled "Gun!"

A second shot pierced the shop's window then glanced off the edge of the table and into the spot Breckus had been seated only moments before.

"I'm a police officer," Breckus barked, "Everybody get down!"

He and Poe had been seated closer to the front door than anyone else. Since he was holding the gun and appeared to be watching the door, no one tried to run. Keeping his gaze forward he spotted two small holes in the bakery's window. Doing the geometry in his head, he quickly realized that the shooter would have been perched on the roof of one of the buildings across the street. Out of habit Breckus had surveyed the immediate neighborhood before entering the bakery. Across the street were two single-level converted duplexes that now housed an art gallery, an attorney's office, and a real estate office – each with a framed plate glass window in front. Behind the buildings to the west was a long, narrow parking lot. No one had been out on the street when the shots had gone off and there were no other buildings that afforded a clear view into the bakery. The shooter must've been on top of one of the duplexes, which meant he would be too public and exposed for comfort. He wouldn't linger.

The thought had barely formed before Breckus was on his feet. A hand grabbed him before he could run. It was Poe. The man was wild-eyed, his breathing quick and shallow.

"Carver," Poe moaned.

"It's okay," Breckus said "We'll get you some help."

"Carver," Poe said emphatically, "You must protect her."

"Her?" Breckus was about to question the man when motion on the opposite side of the street caught his eye. Someone was running across the roof of the art gallery.

He spun and knelt, gently peeling Poe's clenched fist from his trousers. "I'll take care of her," he said quickly. "You just lie still – help will be here shortly."

Breckus pulled a handkerchief from his jacket pocket, laid it on top of the wound and placed Poe's bloody hand on top of it.

"You've seen the movies Poe. Put pressure on it."

Poe winced then nodded.

Breckus leapt to his feet. "Someone call 911!" he shouted as he made his way to the front door, "He's been shot – right shoulder. Have them send an ambulance!"

Breckus burst through the front door of the bakery. Cell phone in one hand and gun in the other, he bolted towards the alley across the street with no thought of what or who he might find waiting for him.

Washington, D.C.

Gray pulled the wireless unit from his ear and took a deep breath. Slowly he scanned the room, as if trying to determine where he was and what he was supposed to do next. His eyes met Talon's. He sat down heavily in the seat next to Talon and let out a deep sigh.

It had only been a few weeks since their last meeting, but to Talon it seemed like his friend had aged beyond his years. "A normal impression," he thought, "when seeing someone who probably hasn't slept more than a few hours in the last week."

"You remind me of a week-old roadkill my old retriever dragged in one day," Talon said jokingly.

Gray seemed to consider this for a moment, his eyes slightly glazed. "If I were roadkill, all of my problems would be behind me," he said heavily.

"So would the rest of your life," Talon reminded him.

"True," Gray said, his body rocking slightly in agreement. "I suppose there are always trade-offs."

Talon watched as his friend's face changed from weary to thoughtful. He knew from experience that Gray was accessing his visual cortex – picturing something in his mind. There was a distant look in his eyes, as if he were slowly letting himself become part of whatever it was he was seeing.

"You know," Gray said dreamily, "I will only allow myself to see the ideal end with my eyes open. I can see us all there, seated around a table full of colorful drinks and platters of fresh fruit, vegetables, bread, and the morning's catch. Everyone is content and at peace. No guns, no plans, no agendas, no false identities. Just real people living in the moment – happy to enjoy that moment and each other. And to contemplate and discuss their futures, which have only recently become visible through the thick fog of uncertainty. But," Gray paused, his expression changing to one of concern, "I won't let myself close my eyes. I won't allow that much concentration and focus on something so tantalizing and uncertain. Even if the image permeates my dreams, my subconscious mind keeps it at arm's length – where it belongs."

"A quiet and temperate morning at the Graycliff?" Talon asked with a smile.

Gray nodded thoughtfully and said, "The flower garden near the pool – the one with the small statues and the antique marble tables."

Talon let the image enter his mind, colored by Gray's description. Filed away in the recesses of his own consciousness, were a host of fond memories from the Graycliff. Toman, who had been fascinated with its colorful history, had introduced Talon and other members to the historic landmark. Soon after, it became their regular retreat. A place away from all places. He could still see Toman standing up and giving a toast on their final day in Nassau. He'd said, "To that which must be done. To the forging of a better world. And to our safe return here to the Graycliff to start anew. Salude!" Talon smiled at the memory, but he knew better than to dwell on thoughts of a day none of them may live to see.

He turned to Gray and said, "You don't want to dream about it because you know that it could be real – *now* – by tomorrow. We could all implement our exit strategies today, forego the rest of the plan, and be on flights by morning. It's too tempting to take the easy way out."

Gray nodded solemnly, his eyes still distant. "Easy," he whispered, "and safe. Everyone would be safe."

"No, Gray," Talon said firmly, "safety is an illusion. We're here precisely because the world isn't safe. And you know as well as I do that we couldn't enjoy the drinks or the cuisine or the company knowing that we'd abandoned what we've spent so long preparing for. When something eats at you for the better part of your adult life, you do something about it. In the end, it's harder to stop and turn around than to never take the first step."

"I know," Gray said wearily. "But what happens if you get lost along the way? Take a wrong turn?"

"It's not always easy to press on," Talon said, his voice strained. "Not for any of us."

Gray looked at Talon and nodded, but said nothing.

After a few moments Talon broke the silence. "Gray," he said softly, "you knew...*we* knew it wasn't going to be all smooth sailing. New trails are always the roughest. Forging ahead requires confidence, skill, knowledge, and the conviction that you're doing what's right. There are always – sacrifices. And difficult choices. But that's how it goes with new paths. We're just a small group in the wilderness trying to find the safest, most direct route to the end game. With no precedence, no historical roadmap, hey...we're doing well to still be walking."

A hint of a smile broke on Gray's lips.

"You're right," he said finally, "You're always right Talon. It's one of the things I loathe about you."

"Same here," Talon fired back with a sardonic smile. "That's why you and I are never allowed to disagree on anything. The arguments would never end."

"As I recall, we have disagreed on a few things," Gray pointed out.

"And we still do," Talon said matter-of-factly. "The tampering of voting machines in the '04 elections, genetics as the cause of aging, the big bang," Talon ticked off each topic on his right hand. "And of course, there's the matter of the tunnel system beneath the White House."

Gray held up his hands in surrender. A few odd moments of silence passed before Talon spoke. "I've...experienced this temptation, Gray," he confessed.

This caught Gray off guard and he turned and studied his friend's face. Talon's expression was serious, and he appeared to be deep in thought.

Several moments passed before Talon continued, "But for me, temptation just – well it doesn't feel like the right word. It's more like being seduced by a powerful idea that has its own consciousness – a kind of abstraction with an alluring and irresistible offer."

There was a sharp edge in Talon's voice that set off an alarm in Gray's mind. For a brief moment, his friend wore a strained expression – like a man grappling with a serious challenge, the answer to which he'd found, but still could not accept. Talon added, "This morning I realized that dropping everything now would require something none of us possess."

Gray was about to ask what it was when his phone sounded an emergency ring. In an instant the tired man who had been slumped in the chair bolted upright – awake and alert. Before Talon could react, Gray had the wireless back in his ear and the shrieking cell in his hand.

"Go ahead, Breckus," Gray said.

From the intense concentration on Gray's face, Talon knew something was very wrong. On a hunch he returned to his computer, donned a headset and dialed Osiro on a secure line. The line clicked before the first ring tone expired.

"Talon. So nice of you to call," Osiro answered smugly.

"Not now O," Talon said seriously. "Can you lock in on Breckus's phone? He's in Denver and it sounds like he's in trouble."

"Is he on it?" Osiro asked, his voice serious now.

"Yes. He's talking to Gray," Talon said quickly, adding, "Gray's cell."

"Triangulating. Hold on."

Talon could hear the rapid clicking of computer keys.

"Got him," Osiro said. "He's on the west end of downtown Denver."

"Do you have eyes on?" Talon asked.

"Working on it," Osiro answered somewhat impatiently.

"How many are there?" Talon heard Gray ask. The two men made eye contact and Gray headed to where Talon sat.

Gray covered the end of the wireless and said, "The EPA lead was marked. A sniper ticked off two rounds. Shot right through the front of the bakery in broad daylight."

"Breckus?"

"He's okay. Shooter probably didn't know who he was."

"Is the mark dead?" Talon asked quickly.

Gray shook his head. "He doesn't think so. The shot hit the guy in the shoulder. Breckus moved to cover, pulled his piece, and ordered everyone else to get down. The sniper was probably watching through his scope and realized he'd missed his chance. So he took off running. Breckus is..." Gray broke off.

"Where?" Gray asked. "How big?" He paused again. "Residential or commer...." Nodding his head he said, "Got it. Let me call Osiro and," but he stopped when he saw Talon point a finger towards the phone, then point his index and middle fingers at his own eyes.

Gray nodded. "Talon's got Osiro on the line. And he's got eyes on." Talon made another gesture with his hands and Gray added, "He's got thermals as well. Pick a corner and find cover. Keep your cell close by and your eyes peeled. Out."

"What've you got, O?" Talon asked.

"Resolving," Osiro said, "Hold on."

"Do we have anyone else in Denver right now?" Talon asked Gray.

Gray shook his head. "There are a few friendlies, but no one skilled enough to flush a pro – especially a pro we don't know anything about."

"I wouldn't say that," Talon said.

Gray looked at him expectantly.

"Let's look at what we know," Talon spoke quickly, "The shooter either tracked the mark or knew where the meeting would be. This wasn't an EPA convention. Clearly the shot would've been easier before entry or upon exit. A clean shot, with no glass to shoot through, no bystanders to get in the way. Instead, he chose a public display inside a business. And he did it during the day. I'm thinking they were desperate. That could mean the shooter or his employer suspected there would be an exchange of information at this meeting. I think it's also safe to say that this was a last-minute decision. Otherwise why not take him out at his hotel or on the drive in from the airport? If it was a last minute decision, the shooter probably got into position well after the meeting began." Talon was up walking around the office now and everyone was listening.

"Osiro, how big is the building directly across from the bakery?"

Another pause and more clicking sounds.

"One level…looks like a duplex."

"And what's behind it?"

"A large public parking lot," Osiro answered after a few seconds.

"Easy in and out?"

"Yes. Three exits leading to two different streets and an alley."

"Okay," Talon continued his pacing, "so the shooter was perched on a one-story building with a parking lot out back. Yet he didn't have a car waiting nearby – he took off on foot. Which means he would've parked a block or two away and walked the rest of the way – probably thinking no one would be crazy enough to follow him after the shot was fired. I'm guessing he's dressed in plain clothes and the rifle is in some kind of gym or duffle bag, something inconspicuous. Take the shot, pack up the Sunday special, hop down, and blend into the crowd. Park away from the scene in case the Denver PD was on the ball and blocked off the streets. There would be too many morning commuters out to stop everyone. Not a bad plan. Except he didn't factor in the possibility that the other party was an armed professional, hence the hasty foot retreat."

Gray nodded, a hint of respect in his eyes. "But why not head for the vehicle? Why run the other way?"

"I don't think he had a contingency plan in place for a fast getaway. My guess is he parked his conveyance to the east. After the shot was fired and he spotted an unanticipated armed man crouching next to the mark, he realized there was a gun between him and his getaway vehicle. So he panicked and went the other way, thinking he could lose his pursuer in the city. What he didn't realize was that he was on the western-most edge of downtown – the city was in the opposite direction. Pretty dumb mistake given that all you have to do is look up to see where the skyscrapers are. Maybe he got confused. Anyway, not knowing what to do, he headed for the nearest cover. Basically, amateur day. Or," he added thoughtfully, "he's a pro, but this really was a last minute decision and the guy didn't have time to prepare – to survey the lay of the land. Hard to say without more information."

"Talon," Osiro said, "thermals show only one person in the building. Appears to be an abandoned factory or warehouse. Shooter is climbing. Looks like he's making his way up to the roof."

"Patch three-way with Gray," Talon said. A second later, Gray was listening in.

"Can you tell if there is a chopper in the area?" Talon asked.

"You thinking spy-movie escape here?" Gray asked.

"Well I don't think he's going all the way up to the roof just to climb down a fire escape," Talon replied. "And I'm ready to rule out suicide. So unless he's got a pair of wings handy, he's got to get down somehow. Osiro?"

"There are a hundred thousand commuters heading into downtown on one of four major highways within a five mile radius. There will be plenty of news helicopters. I don't have a way of distinguishing or tracking them. There are also at least three airports controlling the air traffic nearby. I could try hacking one of them ..."

He was cut off by a new voice, "Don't waste your time." It was Breckus.

"How long have you been listening?" Gray asked incredulously.

"Osiro patched me as soon as I hung up with you."

"Three points for you, O," Talon thought.

Gray reached across the desk and pressed a button on his wireless console so everyone in the room could hear the conversation.

"I don't hear any choppers," Breckus's strained voice boomed through the box. "Besides, there are too many power lines running to or around the building for a safe extraction."

"Are you in pursuit?" Talon asked, flashing a worried look at Gray.

"Yeah. How did you think Osiro knew where to look? I caught sight of him around the back of the art gallery and ran after him. Now he's in the building and heading for the roof. He'll be exposed at the top." They heard a loud crashing sound followed immediately by a grunt. "I'm in," Breckus exclaimed. Before Gray could protest Breckus continued. "The shot was public, people in the bakery will tell police which way I ran. It's likely they'll be heading this way soon."

"Take a left," Osiro said, "follow that hall north to the back stairwell."

"Got it," Breckus grunted.

"I'm not sure this is a good plan, Breckus," Gray said carefully. "You're rushing towards an unknown variable."

"This wasn't a random hit," Breckus said, his breathing getting faster. "I agree with Talon, it was probably last minute, but he still knew where the mark would be and what he looked like. Except I don't think he followed the mark to the shop, otherwise why let us talk for almost an hour before taking the shot. And why not shoot me first to plug the leak?"

Talon considered this, then asked, "How then?"

"Poe is smart, but he's not an agent. He wouldn't have told anyone he didn't trust about the meeting." Talon heard Breckus's labored breathing and faint footsteps. He could imagine the scene and the adrenaline that must be driving the large man, who had never been much of a runner or sprinter.

"Tagging his clothes would be difficult," Breckus was saying. "A twenty-four-hour tail, impractical. I'm guessing his cell was low-jacked. It was issued by the EPA. For all we know all of their phones are carrying a GPS tracking device. A hack-and-track would be easy enough to arrange. Once the phone was being monitored – ahhh! – someone was assigned to track his physical location at all times. They probably had access to his calendar. So when he ducked out of the hotel around seven this morning with no appointment on his schedule, someone sounded the alarm."

"Seems a little rash," Gray commented, "How would they know he wasn't just going out for coffee?"

"Too far," Breckus answered, his voice strained. "The bakery is more than half a mile from his hotel. There are a dozen restaurants, cafes and coffee shops between. And he hoofed it – no cabs. They saw how far he went on foot and scrambled to get the contingency in place. Shooter arrives, sets up, sees him talking to me, and sees him looking nervously over his shoulder every thirty seconds. He reports what he's seeing and someone approves the contract. Poe was probably on a short-list anyway."

"Where is the shooter now, Osiro?" Talon asked.

"Just broke through the door to the roof. Heading towards the north-east corner."

"Where am I?" Breckus asked in an impatient and gasping voice.

"Two more flights and you're there."

"Take it easy Breckus," Gray cautioned. "This guy is a trained killer."

"Osiro, can you patch visuals to us here?" Talon asked.

"Gray's terminal," Osiro replied quickly.

In an instant they were all crowded in behind Gray who was seated in front of his flat screen. The image showed a green and black grid-like schematic of the building from a forty-five degree angle looking up. Two pulsing red and orange figures raced through the three-dimensional image. Talon could see the shooter had reached the roof and was almost to the edge. He really wanted to ask Osiro how in the hell he was managing to track the shooter, but now was not the time. Then something occurred to him and he asked, "Do you have eyes on the north side of the building?"

"I've only been able to get one," Osiro replied, "Grainy and no zoom. It's a building security cam across the way. Cheap bastards." Osiro was clearly irritated. "They pay five million dollars to build upscale condos then use an antiquated shoebox camera for security. Brilliant!"

"Patch it," Gray ordered.

A few seconds later another window opened on Gray's screen. The grainy, blue-tinted image showed a parking area in the foreground, a wide sunken street, and the first four floors of a dilapidated white building. Many of the windows were broken or gone altogether. Several windows still had old box swamp fans attached – each with a long, spiked rust stain running from both corners.

Talon was about to speak when Osiro said, "Panning."

A moment later the image tipped vertically. Talon leaned in and studied the image. Then he saw it. "There!" he said, pointing to a black shape near the edge of the building. The resolution wasn't high enough to make out a face, but the outline of a human figure was unmistakable.

"He's at the edge, Breck," Gray said quietly, as if the shooter might hear him. "Are you on wireless?"

They could hear Breckus's heavy breathing. "I am now," he whispered. "I'm on the southeast corner. Moving in for a better..."

"Cover!" Talon shouted as he saw the figure on the roof suddenly pivot. There was a rifle in his hands they'd not been able to see before. They heard two shots fired. The sounds came a split second after they saw two bright flashes erupt at the end of the rifle barrel.

Breckus dove towards the metal door he'd just come through, landing hard on his shoulder. He'd caught sight of the sniper an instant before the man had turned and fired. Talon's voice had boomed through his earpiece at the same instant the first shot rang out. He scrambled and took up cover behind a rusted commercial air conditioning unit, handgun ready.

Reaching carefully up to his ear, he made sure the wireless was still there, then whispered, "I'm okay. Pissed, but okay." From where he sat he could see two distinct gouges where the sniper rounds had hit. Both were inches from where he'd been hiding only moments ago. "Shots were close. Too close. Talk to me, eyes-on."

"He's crouched down. Still on the northeast corner. He's looking around but not moving," Osiro said.

Breckus took a deep breath, turned and fired two quick rounds left-handed. He spun back around just as a single shot ricocheted off the top of the AC unit.

"O," he said carefully, "I'd sure like to know when he turns around again."

"Hold," Talon heard Osiro say. "Be patient. He's looking around. He's…he's backing up towards the ledge. Hold. He probably thinks you can hear him moving. Rifle is level and aimed. He's baiting – waiting for you to try something. Be patient and stay hidden."

Talon watched the security cam as the shooter's head came into view. The two men appeared to be at an impasse when he heard the faint sound of blaring sirens. At that moment the shooter turned to look over the edge.

"Take the shot!" Osiro yelled.

Breckus stood straight up and fired. He managed to get off three rounds before he ducked back down, but knew none of the shots had hit the shooter. The sirens were growing louder.

Talon watched as the dark image of the sniper scrambled along the ledge. No doubt he heard the sirens and knew his time was running out. It was then he realized Gray had a second phone up to his ear and was nodding.

"How close are you?" Gray was asking. "Good. Put a few armed guys on foot – one to the west and one to the east – and keep the engine running to the north of 20th. PD is en route coming from the south – probably only three minutes away. Keep everyone casual, but avoid a witness tag. Thanks."

Talon's brow contracted in confusion. Gray saw the look, but said nothing. Returning his attention to the monitor, he spoke into the wireless.

"How are you on ammo?" Gray asked.

"Five rounds, best guess," Breckus said. "I'm pretty sure the rifle has a magazine. If it was full when this started, he's still got plenty of shots left."

"If we can just immobilize him, I've got a pick-up team en route. They can get you both out. Just have to get him before the cops do."

Talon looked questioningly at Gray, but didn't speak. "The man is as sharp as a shiny new razor," he thought, "and always one step ahead of the game."

Breckus reached over the AC unit and fired two more shots.

"It's only a matter of time before..." Gray started, but Talon's incredulous voice interrupted him.

"Oh, you can't be serious," Talon said speaking to the computer screen, his nose only inches away from it. Gray followed Talon's gaze to the video image from the security camera and couldn't believe what he was seeing. The sniper was standing on the ledge of the building jerking hard on some kind of cable connected to the roof. Before Gray could verbalize his own disbelief, the shadowed figure dropped the rifle, threw his right arm over the wire and jumped. Susha and Dia gasped as the figure fell fifteen feet before the wire went taut and he began sliding along its length.

Osiro was the first to break the stunned silence. "Breckus, he jumped!"

Without thinking, Breckus turned and darted for the north side of the roof. The rifle was lying flat on the gravel surface near the ledge. Sliding to a stop, he picked it up and said, "Where the hell is he?"

"James-fucking-Bond down the cable, " Talon answered incredulously. "North. To your right!"

Breckus looked and saw the sniper sliding along the line. It appeared as though the wire was tucked up under the crux of his arm between the forearm and the bicep. He was moving fast and was nearing the other side of the street. This guy was either a confident, seasoned professional or a desperate lunatic.

Returning his gaze to the screen, Talon saw the image from the security camera tilt down vertically. He leaned in closer to the image and squinted. Then he saw it. "There!" he said pointing at a thick black line on the screen. "That's the pole the cable ends at. Across the street. He's almost there."

"How in the hell does he plan on slowing down?" Gray asked staring intently at the screen. "Damn it. My team isn't in place yet. If he lands safely and takes off on foot we're screwed. We can't let this guy get away. We need to know who he works for and how he wound up across the street from..."

The sound of two shots stopped him in mid-sentence. They had all heard them. An instant later they saw the sniper's body fall from the cable ten feet away from the pole. Talon guessed the cable was a full twenty feet above the ground. The drop, combined with the momentum from the slide sent the sniper's body hurtling headlong towards the condo parking lot. The resolution of the image was good enough to cause everyone watching to wince as the sniper collided sideways with the hood and windshield of a parked pickup truck. The speed and force of the fall were sufficient enough to send the sniper's body over the top of the truck like a rag doll. He landed hard in the truck bed and lay motionless.

For the next few moments everything was silent. Only the sound of sirens could be heard. Everyone stared at the security camera image, though only the sniper's unmoving legs were visible.

"Is he," Altra started, "is he dead?"

No one spoke. A few seconds later Breckus's irritated voice said, "Of course he's not dead. You think I've never fired a rifle before?"

Gray and Talon breathed a sigh of relief and grinned.

"I hate being shot at! It pisses me off every time, but I'm not gonna kill the guy. Not until I have a chance to kick his ass! For the time being I'm pretty confident he won't be running any marathons any time soon."

Osiro was the first one to get his thoughts in order. "Breckus, you should get moving. PD will be there any minute. Better take the rifle since your prints are on it, but leave the shells."

"Way ahead of you," Breckus said. "I've got his duffle bag and the rifle. Shells are on the beach where they fell. I'll be out in sixty seconds."

"Go out the west entrance and head towards the town center two blocks up. Should be easy enough to get lost from there.

"Getting lost is something I'm exceedingly good at," Breckus said panting.

Gray reached for the other phone and punched the redial key. After a moment he said, "The target is lying in the back of an old red Ford pickup in the condo lot on the north side of 20th near Delgany St. Osiro is sending coordinates to your GPS. Look for the broken windshield. PD is near. Pick him up quickly and quietly and exit to the north. Subject dropped his rifle, but may have a handgun, so be careful. He has a gunshot wound in one leg, so get a tourniquet and field-dress ready. Do you have reliable and discreet medical support nearby? Good." Gray nodded and said, "Thanks Neil, I owe you one."

Talon stood up, closed his eyes and rubbed his temples. When he opened his eyes again he noticed the three women looking at him, amusement spread across their faces.

"What?"

"'James-fucking-Bond'?" Susha said with a wide smile. "That's not like you Talon."

He smiled abashedly and ran his fingers through his hair. "Well," he muttered, "the guy caught me off guard. I mean," he gestured to the computer screen, "that isn't the kind of thing you see in real life. That's Hollywood stuntman nonsense."

"Pretty ballsy, I have to admit," Altra said with a nod. "You know what else? I'm betting it wasn't the thought of being arrested that sent him over the edge of that building."

"What do you mean?" Dia asked.

Talon turned to look at her, as well.

"That was a crazy stunt. Desperate. Clearly he still had ammo left. A rifle with a magazine holds more shots and is more accurate than a handgun. He could've fought his way out. Why jump until you had no other option? Something tells me he was more concerned about what his employer would do if he were brought into custody. You know, 'plug the leak' as it were. Silence the sniper."

"Why do you say that?" Talon asked.

"Just a hunch," Altra said. "Just a hunch."

"Who do you think he's working for?" Dia asked.

Talon thought about that for a moment. "The mark was specific, but not high profile. Maybe we're not the first ones he's contacted. Either that or someone found out he'd been digging around. Question is, who would care enough to want him killed? And so publicly? Who would go through the trouble of tracking his movements and acting so rashly on any suspicious deviations? If you wanted him dead, I would think staging an accident would be the best option. A public execution by a professional hit man makes national headlines and forces a lot of people to ask 'Who?' and 'Why?'."

"And what could he possibly know that was worth so much risk?" Altra added.

"From what I've seen today, the sniper didn't seem to be that professional," Dia commented. "Made a lot of dumb mistakes."

"Ducking into that building was the biggest," Talon said. "Jumping was the second."

"Why do you suppose he went for the roof in the first place?" Susha asked.

Talon shook his head. "I'm not sure." Movement on the computer screen caught his attention. Osiro was still locked onto the image from the security camera, which now showed three men hastily exiting a white van. He watched as they quickly pulled the unconscious sniper from the bed of the red pickup truck. In less than thirty seconds, the men, the sniper, and the van were gone. Talon finished his thought and said, "I'm not sure, but I'm certainly looking forward to asking him."

Cumberland, Maryland

Spader pulled off the dark brown wool cap and scratched his head. When he reached back for the seatbelt, he caught his reflection in the rearview mirror and laughed. He ran a gloved hand along the sharp peak carved from his disheveled hair. A little hair spray was all he needed to look like a punk rocker for the rest of the day. After replacing the cap, he took a deep breath and sighed. "What a day," he thought wearily. "There will be time for reflection later, old chap," he said to himself. "The show has played and the curtain has fallen. Exit stage left."

Glancing at the long duffle bag in front of the passenger seat, he inserted the key into the ignition and started the rental car. One by one, he pulled the thin black gloves tight over each finger. There was a certain masculine confidence that came with tight-fitting gloves. They represented cover, protection, warmth, function, and fit. He shook his head. "Reflection later, Socrates," he thought. "Get a move on."

He shifted the rental into gear and pulled the car back onto the dirt road. The morning moisture and the humid air combined with the dirt to make a pliable, lumpy driving surface. "Feels a bit like driving on packed clay or putty," he thought. The rental probably wasn't the best vehicle for back roads, but it would get the job done.

The car was a new Dodge Charger, slate gray, with lightly tinted windows, automatic transmission, and less than a thousand miles on the odometer. On his way out to the prison grounds early that morning, the slick wet streets and a heavy foot served to warn him that this particular model had rear wheel drive. He'd thought it an odd feature for a car that would most likely spend its life in a state where snow could remain on the ground for more than half the year. Even today he'd seen small patches of snow in the forest, nestled up against thick trees where direct sunlight couldn't reach. Had his extraction been a month earlier, he would've requested a four-wheel drive vehicle to be on the safe side. As it was, paying in cash and using a dummy credit card for a deposit, he hadn't fussed about the choice of vehicle. One of hundreds of small habits an Augur employed every day in order to avoid unwanted attention. Members of *The Aenamaia* often joked that "Augur" was an acronym for "average, unremarkable, genial, unmemorable, and random."

"I am but a figment of your..." Spader's thought was interrupted when he noticed a vehicle in his rearview mirror. It looked like a boxy Ford – blue or black – though he couldn't tell for sure. It was coming up quickly. Spader felt a familiar tingling running down his spine and encouraging his body to take action. Casually, he reached over and yanked the duffle bag onto the seat. Quickly he unzipped the pouch at the end and pulled out two handguns.

The larger of the two was a hefty revolver he'd picked up in South America a few years back that would've humbled Dirty Harry. It was a Brazilian-made gun called the Raging Bull. Spader had just been recruited by *The Aenamaia* and had been sent to a private ranch in Brazil for firearm and self-defense training. Towards the end of the training, he'd asked the ranch's owner to suggest a suitable firearm for him to purchase. The rancher, known locally as Pico, took Spader to a nearby gun shop known for its selection – and discretion. After looking at several models, Pico suggested he purchase two guns. The first was a semiautomatic Beretta M9, which was the primary handgun of the U.S. armed forces – a widely known fact that might come in handy someday. The second was the Taurus Raging Bull, which packed enough punch to fell large game. The Raging Bull fired fifty caliber bullets that were so large, the cylinder had only five chambers. When he'd asked Pico why he would need such a powerful gun, the rancher had said simply, "If you knew the answer to that, you probably wouldn't need the gun in the first place." Looking into the rearview mirror Spader was inclined to agree.

He placed the Beretta under his right thigh and quickly checked to make sure the Taurus was fully loaded. Satisfied, he placed the heavy gun in his lap and checked the rearview mirror again. The late model sedan had pulled up close to his bumper. Spader caught sight of the front license plate – regular, non-government D.C. Though the vehicle looked like a standard-issue government POS, there was no CB antenna or searchlight. In fact Spader saw nothing to indicate it was a government or local PD vehicle. Movement in the rearview mirror caught his eye and Spader saw the passenger place a flashing red light on the dashboard.

"Something tells me this is about to get ugly," he said aloud. Placing the large handgun in his lap he tightened his seatbelt and tried to think. Could this be coincidence? Why were they following him? He'd carefully surveyed the roads that led to the back side of the prison and made sure to avoid any that were private or restricted. There was nothing nearby that would have a private security force. "No," he thought, "this is something else." Another mile and he would have to decide whether to head north towards town or south through the countryside. The former would be more public and, in theory, safer – assuming they really were some kind of law enforcement. But south would be better for finding country roads where gunshots might not attract as much attention. Which would be best?

The question had barely entered his mind when a man with a handgun leaned out of the passenger side of the sedan and fired. The shot hit his back window, leaving a quarter-size hole and a spider web of cracked glass.

"Bloody hell!" he barked. "South it is then!" he yelled and stepped on the gas. The vehicle's V6 growled and the car lurched forward. He could feel the back end start to swing and eased off the gas. "Rear wheel drive you stupid dolt!" he exclaimed as he fought to keep the car on the road. Spader felt the vehicle's traction system adjust to the loose dirt road. He spun the wheel to help compensate for the fishtailing, then pressed down on the gas pedal. "Bugger!" he growled. "Next time we get front wheel drive, Spader!" Having regained control of the car, he checked the rearview. The sedan's driver had anticipated his reaction and was still close behind. Just then another shot rang out. This one hit somewhere near the rear passenger side. They were going for the tire or the gas tank. "Definitely not law enforcement," he mumbled grimly. The only way he could get a good shot off would be to blow out the back window, which might deflect the bullet. Regardless, with the rear glass window gone, the shooter would have a clean shot at him. He only had five shots in the Taurus and would most likely not have the opportunity to reload. "How many in the Beretta," he wondered? "Three or four rounds at most." Why he hadn't remembered to load the clip was a mystery and an error he hoped he would live to ponder.

Fifty yards ahead Spader saw sprinklers watering the grass on the side of the road, as well as the road itself. There were no puddles, but the dirt road would still be slick. An idea popped into his head. "Crazy," he thought, "Absolutely nuts, Spader." But what choice did he have? He rolled down his window and grabbed the heavy Brazilian handgun. A third shot rang out and he heard the crackling sound of his rear taillight exploding.

"Enough of this shit!" he proclaimed aloud. As soon as his car passed by the first sprinkler, he tightened his grip on the steering wheel and pulled it slightly to the left. Bracing himself, he let off the gas and pulled the emergency brake. The rear wheels locked up and the car spun around. Spader straightened his left arm, aimed forward and waited a split second for the sedan to come into view. He saw the look of surprise on the driver's face, then braced and fired. The loud crack from the weapon's discharge caught him by surprise, but there was no time to react. Without waiting to see if the shot hit, he released the emergency brake and fought to keep the car on the road.

A second later the sedan crashed into the back of his car, causing the rear of the rental to fishtail again. Spader cranked the steering wheel in the direction of the slide and stepped on the gas. The car righted and he managed to steer it back onto the road. He flashed a quick glance in the mirror and saw that the sedan had also swerved, but was now back on the road and was gaining on him again. The boxy car's windshield was almost completely blown out. Risking another look, he saw the passenger's bloody right hand pressed to his shoulder.

"I can't believe that worked!" he exclaimed.

Recalling the exit route he'd planned, Spader remembered that the dirt road dead-ended at Old Town Road 51, which should be coming up fast. He came around a long bend in the road and saw the intersection a hundred yards ahead. Glancing left, he noticed a tractor-trailer was coming down the road perpendicular to his current course. At the last second he hit the brakes, turned hard right and slid across a patch of wild grass and bounced up onto the road. He stomped on the gas as soon as the rear tires hit the pavement directly in front of the tractor. The tractor driver threw on his brakes and laid on his horn. Throwing a glance over his shoulder, Spader saw the cloud of dust from the sedan's tires as his pursuer slammed on the brakes to avoid colliding with the rig. Spader grinned, but he knew it wasn't over yet.

"Well this is a pickle isn't it Mr. Spader," he said to himself. "You've got a maniac following you, intent on ending your life as soon as possible. And," he said thoughtfully, "he's doing this even while his wounded passenger continues to bleed. Hmm. Something tells me this guy won't be calling on the local PD for any kind of back-up. But it's likely someone will take notice of our little..." Just then the sound of another gunshot interrupted his monologue. Looking back again, he saw the sedan was back on the road and coming up fast. It looked as though the driver intended to pull up alongside him. "That's bad," he groaned. "They have two people, one of which may still be able to shoot. And their vehicle is probably heavier. Doubtful I would win a pushing match. And I can't get a clean shot behind me. Doesn't leave me a lot of options."

Spader saw the driver's arm appear outside the window. He jerked the car to the right a second before two more shots range out. The second shot hit its mark and the rear driver's side window exploded. He accelerated and quickly steered the car back to the left, preventing the sedan from pulling alongside. He braced as the driver rammed the heavy car into his rear bumper. The Charger lurched and started to shimmy from side to side, but he managed to keep it under control.

"Bollocks! You're running out of time here, genius," he screamed to himself. He made a quick decision. "If I'm going to die today, it bloody hell won't be with unused bullets in the chamber."

Still gripping the Raging Bull tightly in his left hand, Spader pulled the car to the right, leaned outside his window, aimed, and fired. The heavy kickback from the gun, combined with the odd angle of his arm, sent shockwaves of pain from his fingers up to his shoulder. "Fuck me!" he shouted, pulling his arm inside. "Bloody hell that hurt!" He was about to openly castigate himself when he noticed smoke pouring from the sedan's radiator. The shot had been right on target, but the screaming pain in his left arm precluded another shot.

Despite the damage and danger, the sedan kept coming. The smoke had lessened and Spader could now see both men clearly. Each was wearing a dark suit, white shirt, dark tie and black sunglasses. "Great, I'm being chased by the Men in Black," he mumbled sarcastically. "Do I look like a fucking alien to you!?" he yelled into the mirror. A second later the driver fired two more shots, the second of which succeeded in shattering the rear window. "Bad news," he thought, ducking down.

Spader was contemplating his next move when an old red pickup truck pulled onto the road a hundred feet in front of him. He made a split-second decision and swerved into the oncoming lane. A quarter of a mile ahead, another vehicle was coming straight towards him. He stepped on the gas and within a few seconds, jumped back into the right lane only a few feet ahead of the pickup. The truck's driver laid on the horn, but Spader ignored it. He looked back and saw the sedan had chosen to go around the truck on the shoulder. It was tempting to step on the brake and bring the sedan onto his right side. He would have a clean shot, but then so would they. He might be able to force them off the road, but he wasn't sure he could do it before they got a shot off. Then it occurred to him that any action at this moment could put the driver of the pickup truck at risk. So he opted for speed and distance and accelerated. The sedan followed suit.

His mind raced with choices and possibilities. Scanning the surroundings, he noticed there were no structures of any kind visible. No houses or gas stations. Recalling satellite photos he'd studied of the area, he was confident the next patch of civilization was another four or five miles ahead. Not only would a town present too many unpredictable variables, but it was likely one of the truck drivers had a cell phone and had called the police. Local law enforcement would further complicate an already thorny situation – innocent people could get hurt. No, whatever he was going to do needed to happen before the police arrived.

The sedan came up quickly and slammed into the rental car's rear bumper. "Damn!" he yelled, fighting to maintain control of the car. He pressed down on the gas pedal and put a dozen feet of space between the two cars and was about to turn and fire when movement caught his eye. In the rearview mirror he saw the passenger unbuckle his seatbelt, turn and reach into the back seat. Even from a distance he could see the shiny silver barrel of a twelve-gauge shotgun in the man's right hand. "Bugger!" he exclaimed. "Not good."

Thinking fast, he wedged his handgun under his thigh and shouted, "There's nothing for it, Spader!" He braced himself and with both feet slammed down on the brake pedal. There was no time for the other driver to react. The sedan plowed into the back of the Charger. The sudden deceleration sent the unbelted passenger hurtling forward through the hole in the windshield – shotgun in hand. The passenger came through rear first, the force violently folding his body, and spitting him out onto the hood of the sedan. Spader saw the silver and brown shotgun slide across the hood and fall off the side as the man rolled forward and landed with the upper half of his body resting on the Charger's spoiler. Doubt and hesitation paralyzed Spader for a full second before resolution sent a lightning bolt through his body and down his right leg. He let off the brake and jammed his foot down on the gas pedal.

In the rearview mirror, time slowed and Spader watched the look of shock and horror streak across the man's bloody, lacerated face before gravity and forward momentum pulled his body off the hood of the sedan. The injured man grabbed frantically for the spoiler, but his hands were slick with blood and he couldn't get a grip on the smooth fiberglass blade. Spader caught a last brief glimpse of the terrified face before it was gone. The sedan lurched as the passenger's body was pressed beneath the right front tire, then again as the rear tire finished the job. Looking back, he could see the limp and bloody body roll to a stop on the side of the road.

The gory, moving image was burned into Spader's mind, but there was no time to lament his decision. The relentless driver of the sedan was coming up fast and Spader was fresh out of ideas. There were only three shots left in his revolver. No sense pulling out the rifle – too difficult to load and get a clean shot. And the longer they stayed on this road, the more likely they were to encounter the police. That would only exacerbate an already complicated and dangerous situation.

Just then he remembered seeing a dirt road a few seconds before the passenger had made his fatal mistake. Spader steered the car over towards the shoulder, hoping the driver would take the bait. "Come on," he mumbled to himself, "you can't pass up this opportunity." Just as he'd hoped, the sedan accelerated and pulled alongside of the rental car. No doubt the driver had his sidearm aimed and ready to fire. As soon as it was clear, Spader hit the brakes and jerked the wheel to the right. He heard another shot ring out, but kept his concentration on controlling the vehicle. Amidst the white smoke and the high-pitched squealing of rubber, the Charger began sliding. Spader deftly held the wheel firm, released the brake, and hammered the gas pedal. The spinning back wheels helped complete the 180-degree turn and the car began accelerating in the opposite direction.

It took a moment for Spader to get his bearings. He shook his head to clear the fog and looked back. The sedan was executing a similar move and would be back on his tail in less than a minute. He had to think. He had no idea how long the dirt road was or where it lead to. For all he knew, it was someone's driveway. Had he seen a mailbox? He didn't think so, but he couldn't be certain. If law enforcement was on its way, it was likely they would be coming from both directions. Unless a better opportunity presented itself, he would have to take the dirt road and hope for the best.

Spader was contemplating how best to execute a high-speed turn onto the dirt road when he realized he would soon pass the passenger's dead body. What surprised him was how the remorse and emotion he'd felt seeing the man fall had all but vanished. The body on the side of the road was now just another small variable in the equation that governed his own survival. The lack of feeling troubled him, but he pushed it aside. There would be plenty of time for reflection and contemplation if he managed to get out of this alive. Even if he managed to evade or eliminate the bloodthirsty lunatic chasing him, he would still have to elude the authorities. He was in the middle of nowhere America. The rental car was no longer a safe means of transportation, which left taking off on foot. No doubt they would hunt him down with bloodhounds. Unless...

Washington, D.C.

"Shut it off," Talon said disgustedly as he turned away from the flat screen TV. "I can't take anymore."

Gray pressed the power button and the image of the obese, grinning man in the wheelchair vanished. Slowly, he lowered the remote to the desk, replacing the plastic rectangle in perfect alignment with the corner and side. He liked things to be orderly. It provided a measure of solace in a world that was anything but orderly.

"Unbelievable," Talon thought. The violence, tragedies, the fear, the hype – all that he could handle – he was used to it. But when the major news stations aired stories about everyday average people who had lost all sense of right and wrong, whose degraded sense of ethical and moral responsibility allowed them to prey on their fellow man...it was enough to churn his empty stomach. He pressed his hands to his face and winced at the pain in his shoulder. Gray noticed the grimace.

"That something you want to tell me about?" Gray said nodding towards his friend's shoulder.

"First round at Graycliff," Talon replied with a wry grin. It was an expression he'd used early on that had quickly been adopted by each *Aenamaia* member. When the final buzzer sounded and Gray announced their mission was over, those still standing would go their separate ways for ten days. If the coast was clear they would all reconvene at the discreet Graycliff Hotel and Restaurant in Nassau. It was there that all the gaps would be filled in, final assessments would be made, and plans for a return to a normal life would be finalized and implemented.

Gray nodded but said nothing. The two men stared at the blank screen for a minute. Talon was the first to break the silence. "What would you say to a last minute addition to the list?"

Gray was tempted to chuckle, but decided against it when he saw the earnest look on Talon's face.

Gray shook his head. "He's not worth the risk Talon. It was a short story aired in the middle of the day that will vanish into the media wastelands with the others of its kind. That's the natural order. But martyr the guy, and it will be front-page news everywhere. Infection can be immediate. Copycats and shallow opportunists don't care what happened to the inventor, they just want an idea laced with dollar signs and attention."

"What about a convenience mask?" Talon suggested still intently staring at the empty black screen.

"A domestic accident?" Gray asked.

Talon's eyes narrowed and he nodded slowly.

Gray shook his head. "Maybe sometime, but not now. Burn the house down or fill it with carbon monoxide – either way the death comes too soon after the story. Additionally, being handicapped will provide the perfect catalyst for extended coverage. It would attract national attention and in all probability resurrect the story. I'm talking network coverage, internet streams, outrage and political pressures from ADA and other such organizations. Someone will suggest foul play as retribution for the man's questionable practices. An investigation will ensue. It's possible something bigger might come along and bury it, but there's no guarantee."

Talon sat in deep contemplation, the bloodless white tips of his fingers pressed firmly together. The story had been about a disabled California man in a wheelchair making a handsome sum of money suing restaurants and other businesses for minor violations of the Americans with Disabilities Act. The unemployed man spent his days looking for the smallest oversights and violations. He chose to do this instead of seeking gainful employment. The chair-bound man would take digital pictures as proof of the violation, then immediately have his attorney draft a letter to the establishment citing the violation and threatening to sue. Each letter sent included an out-of-court settlement figure – usually thousands of dollars.

Most of the businesses simply paid the settlement because it was less expensive than defending against the suit. Ironically, the normally progressive state of California allowed the disabled to bring such suits against businesses even though the violator was given no opportunity to avoid the suit through corrective action. Even the news anchor agreed with another attorney who said the man was guilty of extortion. As of the program's airing date, the rotund man had brought over fifty suits over the course of a year, earning him well over a hundred thousand dollars – and that figure was on top of what he paid his attorney. Talon felt sick just thinking about it.

"How in the hell did we come to this?" he asked absently. "How… where did morality go? Fairness? Civility? Personal responsibility? Decency!"

"The story is complicated," Gray said with a sigh. "Normally, I would say the lion's share of responsibility lies with parents who don't know how to say no to their children. If a child never hears 'No,' or can always negotiate their way out of punishment, the ultimate answer is always 'Yes,' and that leads to a surfeit of other issues. There's no accountability or discipline. Then pile on the kindergarten graduation ceremonies, sports that don't keep score under the sickening guise of 'everyone is a winner,' schools where parents are allowed to chastise teachers for giving their kids the bad grades they clearly deserve, and all the technology that unplugs our youth from real human interaction. And that's just early adolescence! The instant a teenager has access to a credit card they, too, can feel the warm glow of instant gratification from shopping online. Everything they could want without ever leaving the house. It's too easy, too immediate. There's no work or skill involved – the reward is not earned. And nary a single firm 'No' to be found anywhere – not from parents, teachers or coaches. Raising a good child takes work. But most people nowadays are soft and lazy – or just plain afraid."

"But what about this slime ball?" Talon said, emphatically gesturing towards the blank screen. "How does this guy sleep at night? He's extorting money from honest, small business owners who are just trying to get by from day to day. The restaurant owner they interviewed paid that lazy, corpulent bastard two thousand dollars because the bottom of the mirror in his bathroom was three inches too high! How in the hell is that not extortion? How can he get away with it?!"

"Talon, it's more complicated than that."

"Goddammit," Talon said leaping to his feet, "it's not right! You know it's not right, Gray. He's not on our list, but it's people like him that brought us here in the first place! Aenamus, remember?"

"What would you like to do?" Gray said, trying to remain calm as alarm bells rang in his head.

"I'd like to explain to him why he doesn't actually qualify as a human being right before I put a large bullet through his empty fucking skull!" Talon shouted, adding, "It'd be a mercy killing!"

Gray watched his friend pace back and forth in a tight ellipse, staring at the floor. Talon was red with anger – the muscles in his face pulled tight, brow furrowed, teeth and fists clenched tight. The veins running vertically at his temples and along his arms were prominent. It was a sight Gray had never seen, and for a moment he felt a primal panic pierce the back of his mind. Talon had always been a model of discipline, self-control and restraint. If he lost control altogether, Gray wasn't sure he would ever fully regain it. And that was one storm he didn't want to be anywhere near – especially right now.

A few tense moments passed before Talon finally collapsed back into the chair. He sat staring blankly at the ceiling. Gray held his breath. It had been years since he'd been taken completely by surprise – and even longer since he'd been at a total loss for words.

"I'm sorry, Gray," Talon said quietly, his face blank. "I'm so sorry. That was uncalled for. I don't know what…I just…" he left the words hanging.

"I know," was all Gray could manage.

"I just don't understand how we've come to this. Here we are putting all of our lives, our futures, our very souls on the line to remove the far-reaching filth in the world – the loudest and most vile voices. To show the world the meaning of Aenamus. And yet right here," he gestured weakly towards the screen again, "we find a lone parasite aggressively poisoning the host, the source of whose offenses we can't even trace back to the slime we're eliminating. How can we be sure we'll even make a dent? How can we know it's worth the risk?"

Regaining his composure, Gray stood and walked over to the window and looked out. The sky was pale blue and streaked with jet trails – the telltale sign of people on the move. Mostly good people going somewhere to conduct business, meet with loved ones, or just to take a vacation and reflect on their lives. People doing what they believed was right and necessary to keep life moving forward.

"We're not here to fix everything, Talon. You know that. A small group like ours can only expect to have so much impact on the world. The best we can hope for is that people, and even those animals who choose to poorly impersonate people," he paused and heard Talon's reluctant chuckle, "will all see what happens to those who profit by spreading and encouraging the worst ideas and emotions available to humanity. We can't take on the whole world. In the end, all we can do is remove a handful of the worst and hope for the best."

Gray turned and faced Talon.

"I'm preaching to the choir here, my friend. You know all this as well as I do," he declared. "So, would you like to tell me what it is that's really bothering you?"

Talon shot a hard look at Gray but remained silent. The two men locked gazes, each one trying to read what the other was thinking.

"All the power in the world rests in the eyes, fella." Talon recalled the quote from the movie *The Crow*. In his mind he saw the beautiful, worried eyes of Catherine. "How true," he thought. "How very true." Of course, the quote had come from the bad guy. In both movies and literature, the villains often recite words of wisdom and insight. It helps generate ironic empathy from the audience. "But what happens when you find yourself in the middle of the narrative, and you don't know which side you're on?" he wondered.

"Are we the good guys or the bad guys?" Talon wondered aloud.

"Talon," Gray said quietly, "we all found each other and connected through the ideals and beliefs we share. One of those ideals was honest forthrightness. We agreed in the beginning that holding back pertinent thoughts, ideas, and even emotions could prove detrimental to the whole group. Imagine if you'd have exploded like this during an extraction alongside another Augur. Think of the damage that could have been done. You're not like that. We're not like that. We're the good guys." Gray sat on the edge of his desk and added, "Even when our emotions run beyond our control."

Talon shot him another look, but quickly his expression changed from defensive to one of acquiescence.

"You're right, Gray," Talon said reluctantly, "You're always right." A thin smile pierced his lips and he added, "It's one of the things I really hate about you."

Gray smiled. "Touché, my friend. Touché."

Both men laughed easily, each staring at the floor. After a few moments Talon broke the silence.

"Her name is Catherine," he said simply. "I met her yesterday on the flight to D.C. It was chance. Happenstance. There was no effort or intention. Neither of us was even on the lookout. It just happened. Like in the movies. It was almost instant. Playful bantering, innuendos, volumes of information lurking just behind the eyes." Talon recalled the movie quote again and grinned. He suddenly wondered where she was. What was she doing? Was she flying? If so, what was her destination? Was she thinking about him? Was she worried?

Talon stared at the ceiling for a moment, then moaned in frustration. "I left the most remarkable creature I've ever met lying worried and utterly confused in a hotel room," his voice was laced with incredulity. "She has no idea," he whispered.

Gray waited and watched as his friend worked through his thoughts. After a few moments Talon declared, "I've made a lot of difficult escapes and exits in my time, but this one was by far the most agonizing and difficult. Just standing up and walking to the door took an extraordinary amount of effort. It was like a powerful force had taken hold of me. Every step was a protest against its merciless grasp. After what felt like an eternity, I reached the door. But the moment my hand touched the door knob, I..."

Gray read his friend's mind and said, "You thought about quitting – about giving up the mission and *The Aenamaia*. Dropping it all and never looking back."

Talon looked up, his face a tangle of emotions, and nodded guiltily.

"Talon," Gray said softly, "do you really think you're the first one to have these thoughts? To contemplate walking away? Not just the act but how to do it, how to tell the rest of us, how to absolve yourself from the overwhelming weight of guilt? How to convince yourself that what we're doing really isn't necessary? On the contrary, my friend," Gray said putting his hand on Talon's shoulder, "I truly believe you are the very last one of us to have this thought – and the only one of us to have it only once."

"Thanks, Gray," Talon said, his voice still uncertain.

Gray lowered his voice, "If she's truly that extraordinary, she'll understand."

Talon looked skeptically at Gray who added, "She'll understand that, too. She might not condone what we're doing, but I'm confident ten minutes alone with your files would be more than enough."

Talon glanced uncertainly back at the flat screen.

"And don't worry about the lump of flesh in the wheelchair. Something tells me poetic justice will catch up with him sooner or later."

"We can only hope," Talon said.

"Subject change," Gray said. "General Payte doesn't know anything about Breckus or the sniper and I'd just as soon leave it that way. Agreed?"

"Agreed," Talon said nodding.

"Good. No use in muddying up those waters just yet."

Talon opened his mouth to speak when the phone on Gray's desk rang. Gray reached back and pressed the intercom button.

"Gray here."

"General Payte has just arrived," Susha said, a hint of nervous anticipation in her voice.

Gray and Talon both looked at the clock on the wall. Three o'clock on the dot.

"Thank you, Susha. Please have him come up." Gray depressed the intercom button and the line went dead.

"At least he's punctual. You've gotta give him that," Talon said.

"Oh, I plan on giving him a hell of a lot more than that," Gray said firmly.

Cumberland, Maryland

The blue sedan came speeding around the corner. The driver hadn't expected the other car's abrupt change of direction and it had taken a few minutes to catch up. The driver was clever, but clearly desperate and inexperienced. In the end, the field rats could never compete with seasoned, disciplined professionals. They were out of their league, as this particular varmint was about to learn the hard way. The sneaky rat had gotten lucky once with his partner, but that wouldn't happen again. One final lesson was all it would take.

A few seconds later the driver caught a glimpse of his passenger's limp body still lying by the side of the road. He would clean the mess up if he had time. If not, the lump wasn't wearing any identification. No one would ever figure out who he was or how he came to be a lifeless, bloody pile on the shoulder of the road. Only he would know the guy was an idiot who had died because of his own inexperience and stupidity. The field rat had bested him and he got what he deserved.

A hundred feet or so beyond the body was the shot-up Dodge Charger. The driver tapped lightly on the brakes and inserted a full clip into his gun. Anticipation of the kill pulsed through his body, the adrenaline in his blood eager to reach every extremity. "Patience and control," he thought. "Assess the situation, plan, and act accordingly." Looking again, he realized the target's car wasn't moving. It appeared to be parked on the shoulder. No brake lights. Squinting, he could see the driver's head, but there wasn't any movement. One of his shots must have made contact after all. The idea pleased him, but he knew better than to celebrate just yet. Field rats were cunning. This one could be playing possum, hoping for another careless mistake. Best to be cautious. No use in taking any unnecessary chances. The target was clever and knew how to shoot. He'd done the driver and his employer a huge favor back at the prison. Too bad he was playing for the wrong team. He'd never get to tell anyone about it.

As the driver passed the lifeless body on the shoulder, he hunched down low. Slowly, carefully, he pulled in behind the Charger. About fifteen feet separated the vehicles. "A good distance," he thought. Gun in hand he remained ducked down behind the dash, while still keeping an eye on the target. He'd expected a last ditch volley of shots, but nothing happened. In fact he had yet to see the man move an inch. Rising slowly, he kept his eyes trained on the figure's head. Something was odd here, but he couldn't quite figure out what it was. No time to contemplate. Time to finish this and get out of here before the cops arrived. Gripping the weapon with both hands, he reached forward and balanced the butt of the gun on the dashboard. Aiming squarely at the back of the man's head, he squeezed the trigger and unloaded four shots in quick succession. When he re-focused his eyes, all he saw was a spatter of blood on the windshield. No sign of the target.

Carefully, he opened his door and got out, his weapon still trained on the gray vehicle. Keeping low, the driver moved quickly. When he was within a few feet of the passenger door, he fired another three shots into the cab, then ducked down. Still no sound or movement. He looked up and down the road, but there were no cars or people in sight. Five seconds passed. In one deft movement he stepped in front of the driver's side door and fired one more round. Keeping his weapon trained, he looked inside the vehicle. The body was lying sideways on the front seat. Inside the car he saw thousands of glass shards and a blood-spattered windshield. Taking a step closer, he could now see the side of the man's head and the gaping hole that was still oozing blood and brain-matter. The driver smiled smugly as a second batch of adrenaline spilled into his veins. He loved this moment. No matter how many bodies he wracked up, no matter how many confirmed kills he had, this moment never failed to infuse him with a warm sense of satisfaction and energized gratification.

"Stupid field rat," he mumbled derisively. Looking in the car, he felt a mild sense of regret that no one he knew would get to see his handiwork. There was an added sense of pleasure, given that this amateur had managed to kill his partner. Regardless of that lucky move, this guy was simply outclassed. "What does this rat look like?" he wondered aloud. Leaning through the window, he used the barrel of his gun to roll the body over. The man's bloody face came into view. Stunned recognition quickly replaced the smug smile as a bolt of pure terror and panic froze the driver in his place. Slowly, he turned and looked out the rear window, past his sedan, to the side of the road. Empty.

"I told your partner he could drive," a voice said from behind.

The driver spun around in time to see a flash of light, followed by a loud crack. A patch of blue sky and upside down trees streaked past his eyes. Another crack rang out, only this one sounded far away. Then everything went dark.

Spader stared in shocked disbelief, his eyes transmitting every gory detail for permanent storage in his mind. Two bodies. Thousands of glass shards. Blood. Flesh. Smoke. A dark and ominous stillness. The nearby forest was completely still, as if the birds and insects were staring in stunned silence. Something in him said to look away – to act – to run. But he couldn't move – couldn't breathe – couldn't believe what he was seeing was real – that it was of his doing. Who were these men? Did they love? Were they loved? Did they have families of their own? Did they care for elderly parents? Children? Wives? Would they have slept soundly had they succeeded in killing him? Would they feel regret or remorse? Or were they men who were never public enough to catch *The Aenamaia's* attention, but would otherwise make the A-list? Callous, cruel men with no souls.

As he stood transfixed, Spader saw in his mind a large bullet fall in slow motion. It tumbled as it fell, end over end. There was a brief flash of light from the shiny silver tip each time the bullet made a full revolution. Then it struck. Into the smooth, glassy water it went. A surge of displaced fluid collapsed in on itself and consumed the bullet, followed by a smooth spike of water reaching skyward. The spike collapsed. Perfectly circular and smooth ripples appeared, one after another, as if they were the final desperate shouts coming from the drowning projectile. The ripples grew taller and taller, until they were waves. Repercussions manifesting in physical form. Destructive shockwaves heading to unknown destinations. Eventually crashing over unseen, nameless people, their lives forever changed. Spader saw himself in front of one of these massive waves, its awesome power moments away from crashing down on him.

The faint sound of approaching sirens tore him from the vision, leaving him planted firmly back in the real world. He jerked his head in the direction of the sound. Rationality returned with shocking speed and his mind shifted into automatic flight mode. He looked again at the scene, but this time it appeared as nothing more than a logic problem requiring a quick solution. Pulling his gloves tight, Spader reached down and grabbed hold of the driver's arms. The limp body was heavy, but he managed to lay it out perpendicular to the driver's side door of his rental car. Darting to the opposite side of the vehicle, he opened the passenger side door and extracted his duffle bag. He unzipped the bag and pulled out a small, clean hand towel. As he walked back towards the driver's body, he gave his Beretta a thorough cleaning. The sirens were growing louder. Reaching inside the driver's side window, he carefully lifted the occupant's left arm. He placed the Beretta in the dead man's hand and gently laid the arm and gun across the corpse's lap.

A second set of sirens rang out – these coming from the opposite direction. Spader guessed they would be within sight of the two cars in less than a minute. After stuffing the towel in a pocket, he quickly appraised the scene. No telling what the authorities would ultimately decide had happened here, but at first glance there would be nothing to indicate a third person had been involved. The initial conclusion would be that the two men had played road warrior then shot each other. Only later would the forensics team realize the body in the Charger had not died of multiple gunshot wounds. A thorough investigation would undoubtedly reveal a high likelihood that a third person had been present. Unless, of course, those who employed these men had the ability to quietly close down the investigation. Either way, *The Aenamaia* would need to keep a close eye on this one for a while.

Satisfied with the scene, Spader wasted no time. He bolted around the car, grabbed his duffle bag, shut the passenger door and darted into the nearby woods. He stopped a few feet in, crouched and took a last look in both directions. The sirens were getting close, but the police cars were not yet visible. Confident no one could've seen him fleeing the scene, he took off again. Weaving between trees, he recalled the aerial maps he'd studied of the area surrounding the prison. The satellite images of the area to the east and southeast of the prison had shown mostly dense forests for several miles, with only a few houses scattered here and there. He felt confident if he headed southeast four or five miles he should run into local highway 51.

Spader ran for another three minutes, then slowed to a fast walk. He pulled the cell from his pocket and hit the number nine speed dial.

"Operator," the familiar dry voice said.

"Osiro," Spader said trying to catch his breath, "Two unknown aggressives down cold. Local PD en route to scene. Transport abandoned and I'm on foot. I need a quiet extraction at local five-one. ETA forty minutes."

"Are you hurt?"

"Nothing serious, just a little banged up. Nothing overt that would attract attention."

"Pursuit?"

"Negative. Scene is dressed. Doubtful Augur presence will be detected immediately."

"Cover?"

"Dense forest. Unpopulated."

"Hold."

Dodging through the trees, Spader felt very odd. The situation seemed surreal and distant – almost imaginary. It felt as if the images from the morning's events came from something he'd seen on a late night TV show. So much had happened in the span of only a few short hours. He'd shot and killed a high-profile prison inmate. Less than half an hour later two unknown men who had no qualms about hastening the end of his life were in pursuit. Through a stroke of incredible luck he'd managed to eliminate both of those men without knowing who they were or why they'd come after him. Now he was trudging through a Maryland forest carrying a duffle bag containing a high-powered sniper rifle and the Raging Bull – and talking to someone sitting at a computer in DC on his cell phone. It was at that moment that the image of the incredulous face of the driver returned to his thoughts, followed by Abramoff's face in his scope just after the first shot was fired.

Retiring the second mark is usually the most difficult for a sniper. It's a test of sorts. The first shot rocks even the coldest of shooters. It's like an earthquake of the soul. All the arguments, the hollow justifications, the steadfast patriotism – they all work together to wrestle and subdue the mind. Moments after that first shot, a genuine mental melee ensues. Descriptions differ from man to man, but most first time shooters recall feeling like an outsider in their own heads, watching the shit-storm of thoughts and images crash through their skulls like debris in a hurricane. The maelstrom calms down after a few days. Soon after, the shooter either decides to continue on or quit cold turkey. In either case, the sense of resolution is usually very strong. If the choice is to continue, the shooter's superiors will get them back in the field as soon as possible. Often times the second mark will have been located, researched, and approved before the first mark is retired. The shooter is sent out immediately to take the second shot. If the shot is fired – if the sniper can pull the trigger a second time and retire the mark, then the deal is sealed and the shooter's resolve is solidified. If he can't do it right then and there, he's finished.

The single most important caveat involved in sniper sanity is distance. Distance is a luxury of sorts. It allows the sniper to avoid the label of assassin. Distance also enables continued objectivity. Similar sentiments are described by airmen charged with dropping bombs from airplanes. The equation is simple: weapon, target, timing, trigger. The precise and skilled execution of the task is all the mind focuses on. Emotions and thoughts of morality are all filed neatly in a folder to be opened at a later date – or never at all. This convenient omission is further bolstered by the distance to the target. The greater the distance, the easier it is to stow the file.

When the distance is reduced to a matter of feet and inches, the file is unable to hold its contents for very long. For Spader the file had exploded in his hands. The two men lying dead a mile behind him had not been marks. There had been no planning, no research, no time to make an informed decision. As it stood, the only thing keeping his mind from bursting was the concept of self-defense. Somewhere in the deep recesses of his mind, Spader knew it had been self-defense, and he would cling tightly to that notion until he was safe and had time to evaluate all that had happened.

"Cell signal acquired," Osiro said. Spader had been so lost in his thoughts he'd almost forgotten he was still holding the phone to his ear. "Maintain present course and heading. If you keep at your current pace, you'll be at the rendezvous point in just over an hour. Transport is en route and should arrive in about two hours. White minivan with West Virginia government plates. Maintain cover near the fifty-one. I'll send a message when transport is near." There was a pause and Spader wasn't sure if the line had gone dead. He was about to say something when Osiro asked, "You okay?" There was something peculiar in his voice – masked empathy perhaps. Certainly a degree of concern, which was out of character for Osiro. Spader grinned.

"Yeah, I'll be all right. But given the extra load today, perhaps I'll scurry on down to the Graycliff sooner rather than later and start brewing the tea."

"I doubt you'll be the only contestant competing for that privilege."

Spader ducked a low-hanging branch and said, "All I care about right now is living long enough to get into the race. Winning it is a distant second priority."

"Understood," Osiro said solemnly. "See you soon."

Chapter 20

Washington, D.C.

Brigadier General William Andrew Payte closed the door behind him and began walking through the study. It had been over a year since Payte had last been in this room. Little had changed. Crammed bookshelves, a hodgepodge of antique and modern furniture, and of course Gray's prized 1877 Steinway baby grand piano. The general recalled hearing the piano's voice the first time he'd taken a meeting in this room. He'd ascended the stairs and sat outside for a few minutes just listening. Though not a music buff, the general had surmised the piece was classical and guessed it required skill well beyond that of a hobbyist. The moment he'd knocked on the door, the music had stopped.

The general sensed Gray's piercing gaze from the other end of the study and thought, "And so the music has once again stopped abruptly before the song is over."

Swiftly stowing his service cap, General Payte walked purposefully past the bookshelves and furniture. Without turning his head, he noted Talon was seated on a leather couch a few feet from Gray, who stood perfectly still in front of his desk, arms crossed defensively. He'd expected no less. The instant he'd decided to break from Gray's plans he'd known this moment would come. It was the deception that had been most difficult for him. Gray was intelligent, trusting and dedicated, but most of all he was a friend. Despite years of military training and discipline, theory and mission-oriented prioritization, the general had always placed personal relationships, friendships, loyalty and trust ahead of any operation. Except this time.

The general approached the two men, stopped and nodded curtly to both. He spared a quick sidelong glance and noticed the souvenirs and memorabilia that spoke of a well-traveled, nostalgic, and thoughtful individual. He saw items from every continent on earth – spears, hats, a handmade bamboo box with no visible handles or openings, an authentic samurai sword crafted by a swordsmith living deep in the Akaishi Mountains, a Grecian amulet, and the cantaloupe-sized sphalerite crystal Gray had found in one of the abandoned Casandra mines in northern Greece. Nearly every trip abroad that Gray took produced some kind of new and intriguing memento – behind which was usually an equally interesting story. Payte, who had watched the collection grow over the years, knew the tales behind almost every object in the room. "Military men have their own tales," he'd once told Gray, "but they aren't usually ones we wish to remember." Now he thought, "How very true."

Returning his gaze, the general locked eyes with Gray, whose expression was both intense and unreadable. In the past he'd seen his friend stare down the most imposing opponent without any open display of emotion. In dangerous situations, such control and focus could mean the difference between victory and defeat – life and death. The general wondered whether this was one such situation, but quickly dismissed the thought. Gray's training and former life made him an exceedingly dangerous adversary, even for a veteran soldier. Were he to wish such a confrontation, it was doubtful even Talon could stop him. But he knew there would never be violence between them. They had both been forced to use their skills before. Every such situation had one thing in common – lethal violence had been a reaction to a threat, and the only means of survival. Aside from the history and friendship they'd shared, both men held to the creed that violence, especially of the lethal variety, should always be a last resort. The general hoped his old friend hadn't changed in this regard.

Silence hung heavy in the room. Over the last few days, Payte had given a great deal of thought to this moment. Knowing a situation is inevitable, and understanding most – if not all – of the dynamics governing it, gives one an almost omnipotent spherical perspective. Examine the facts, compare and contrast from multiple angles, understand the objectives of the person at the center, and do your best to chart a safe course. The only problem was the strong likelihood that Gray had also analyzed the situation. In the end, Payte had decided to just be honest and perhaps a tad more humble than he was used to. And, whenever possible, keep things light and cordial.

The general noticed a familiar item in a small, lighted glass curio case behind Gray.

"I've always liked that piece," he said casually, nodding towards the item. "A mobius strip carved from kauri wood. Am I correct?"

Gray looked at the military veteran for a few moments, then nodded and said, "It was a New Zealand kauri. Over a thousand years old. Cut down by an ignorant American industrialist turned rancher." There was a heavy sadness and regret in his voice.

"He probably didn't know what he was doing," the general suggested.

"No," Gray agreed, "he didn't. But you did."

General Payte ignored the comment and continued. "The artist was from New Zealand, as well, if memory serves. Didn't he also carve an infinity symbol from the same tree?"

"He did," Gray said, offering no additional details.

"They go together I think," the general commented thoughtfully, adding, "the mobius strip and the infinity symbol. I'm no mathematician, but it seems like there is something about the topology that links them. Some commonality." He made eye contact with Gray and said with a slight grin, "They differ in the details, but ultimately the design and purpose are comparable. Familial perhaps."

Gray eyed his old friend, but remained silent.

"'The only way to comprehend what mathematicians mean by infinity is to contemplate the extent of human stupidity.' Voltaire said that."

"'Falsehood has an infinity of combinations, but truth has only one mode of being,'" Gray countered, adding dryly, "Rousseau." Payte heard a hint of righteousness in Gray's voice, but ignored the jab.

"Ah, Rousseau," he said, respect and recognition in his voice, "Father of the French Revolution. Interred at the Pantheon in Paris. Around the same time that Jean Paul Marat was disinterred correct?"

"Same year," Gray replied, "Marat was interred in September of 1794 and disinterred the following February. Rousseau was interred in 1794, sixteen years after his death. You'd have to ask Toman for the exact date."

"Revolutionaries," the general said, respect and awe in his voice. Slowly he turned and gazed around the room. "Men with ideas about changing the world for the betterment of mankind instead of just their own. Noble wouldn't you say?"

"You compromised everything by detonating that airplane," Gray said evenly. General Payte seemed lost in his examination of the room's contents. After a few moments of silence Gray continued. "Over a year of meticulous planning and preparations. A thorough post-expulsion plan for the media. Counter-intelligence ingeniously implanted into the State Department to throw them off Kulter's trail. There was supposed to be video from the ground proving they were alive – running rampant on the internet." Gray raised his voice and added, "This was our one chance to show the world there was more here than just death! That our actions were not those of terrorists or lunatics, but humans bent on sending a message."

"The message has been delivered," General Payte said coldly.

"And just what right do you have to make that decision?"

"What right do you?" the general snapped, turning to face Gray. "Everyone in this group has played judge and jury with the lives of those who made the cut. Though blood does not always fall, our hands are all awash in it. We embrace Aenamus and the bad guys die. That's how it works."

Gray turned and faced the window.

"You're a fan of quotes," the general said mockingly, "'The messenger of death imposes his tax on those who are attached to duality.'"

Gray remained silent. Talon watched as the general's stare threatened to burn a hole in the back of Gray's head. Both of these men had prepared for this encounter. Staring at the tense scene, he thought it unlikely either would back down. Something in the pit of his stomach told him this had the potential to get out of hand. If these two fell to blows, the last place he wanted to be was in the middle of it.

Talon glanced at Gray and saw the tension building in his shoulders, as if heat from within was rising and on the verge of erupting. He was about to intercede when he saw Gray's posture relaxed slightly.

Gray took a deep breath, composed himself and said, "Then perhaps we should get right to the operative question." He turned and faced the general. "Why Bill? Why did you do it without telling us? Without even a warning?"

General Payte also relaxed a degree. Talon watched as the formidable man's expression went from one of indignant challenge to something closer to a rehearsed and thoughtful countenance – as if this is where he'd hoped the conversation would begin.

After plucking the service cap from beneath his arm and setting it on a nearby table, General Payte lowered himself into one of the large leather chairs facing the two men, crossed his legs and leaned back. A coy smile appeared on his lips and he said, "Yours were the correct questions to ask, my friend. Just asking 'Why?' would be a waste of time since our very presence here signifies that we all know the reasons why. With each mission, with every syringe or bullet or explosive, we drew a line in the sand. I simply chose to draw my own line – and cross it. For that I alone must bear the burden."

General Payte's expression became pensive. Almost a minute passed before he continued. "The mobius strip is really a fascinating construct. Do you know why? Because no matter where you choose to start, if you trace a course along it you will always wind up on the opposite side of where you started. Upside down, if you will. But," he said holding up a finger, "if you keep to that same course, you will eventually find yourself right back where you started."

"In other words, you never really get anywhere," Talon offered.

Payte looked at him skeptically and offered, "If a man sets sail in New York, circumnavigates the globe, then winds up back in New York harbor, would you say he never really got anywhere? Of course not. It doesn't matter where you start or where you finish, but rather what you accomplish along the way."

"And the mobius analogy?" Talon asked.

"The analogy fits on many levels," the general explained, "but for our immediate purpose the point is simple. Had I followed your plan, I would've completed the mission only to find myself on the other side of where I started – hanging upside down. That wasn't good enough for me. But, I knew that if I went beyond that point and followed my instincts I could take the journey, accomplish what I wanted, and still wind up..."

he patted the arm of the leather chair, "in the exact place I started. Same room, same chair, same hard ass."

Talon was tempted to laugh, but there was no hint of a smile on Gray's stone façade. Payte saw the same mask and, pursing his lips, rose from the chair. Placing his arms behind his back, he looked at Gray and said pointedly, "You wouldn't have agreed. You would've argued. Eventually you would've pulled Toman and everyone else from this mission. I couldn't allow that." Payte began pacing.

"Sure, I could've used my own personnel for the extraction – assuming you chose to stay out of it entirely. However, planning was already in the final stages when I made my decision. Starting over would've put us back a week or two. That wouldn't have been problematic were it not for the rest of your crew leaving a trail of bodies all over the world. Once news of the new threat hit, our two primary quarries and their minions may not have been so easy to capture. No, the timing was imperative. I couldn't risk it."

"But why not ask me? Why not tell me of your decision?" Gray pursued.

"Because I know you almost as well as you know yourself. I knew there was no way you would agree. You would've fired back that the matter had been carefully examined, the various end-games argued and debated, and that the decision had been made." Payte spread his arms wide. "Impasse."

"It wasn't good enough for you?" Gray asked incredulously, "It wasn't enough to drop them in the desert, to kick them out of the country and forbid them to return? That wasn't good enough? A violent death at twenty thousand feet was the only way you would feel whole?"

Payte stared at Gray but said nothing. After a long few moments he said quietly, "I don't expect you to understand. You couldn't. The concept is too abstruse, for either of you. Too personal." There was something in his voice that arrested Talon's attention. There was emotion there – raw emotion that had slipped through a small crack in the cast iron dam.

Gray had caught it as well. Talon watched his friend's reaction to this declaration and time seemed to slow to a crawl. The changes were subtle, but there were a lot of them. It was as if he were seeing the thought and intuition process unfold on Gray's face. One by one the small wrinkles around the eyes and the corners of the mouth melted away. The ridges on his forehead also seemed to melt, leaving behind only smooth skin. Slowly, Gray's body and head straightened, as if an invisible tube was replacing the air that had been lost the moment he'd heard the plane had exploded. A light went on inside Gray. Talon saw it in his widening eyes – the incredulity spreading across his face. And he wasn't the only one taking notice.

Conversely, General Payte's features hardened, as if in defense of what he sensed was coming. Nothing else had been said, but in these few moments Talon saw firsthand the volumes of information that can be conveyed via non-verbal communication. "Astounding," he thought.

"Oh, Bill," Gray said, his voice a thick mixture of disbelief and empathy, "You didn't?"

General Payte glared hard at Gray. "You don't know anything, Gray," he said in a low growl. "You can't!"

Gray nodded, confirming his suspicion, then bowed his head.

In that moment, staring at these two weathered warriors, Talon suddenly understood everything and the answer became clear. "Jared," a voice in his mind whispered. Jared Andrew Payte. He leaned back on the couch and rested his head on the back. He stared up at the ceiling and allowed a wave of emotion to wash over him. Fifteen minutes ago he'd expected an explosive verbal tug-of-war, a heated argument over ideologies, crime and punishment, the wise and the wicked. He'd even entertained the possibility that he would have to wedge himself between the two men yelling "Okay, break it up, you two. Break it up!" In a perverse way, he'd actually been curious to see which of the stone-cold professionals would crack first and be the catalyst for the verbal lashing that would ensue. Now things had changed. The naked truth had been exposed, though never spoken. It hung in the air like a dark specter – the ghost of the general's only son, looming above and affecting all three men in different ways.

For Gray, the full meaning of what he'd just figured out wouldn't hit him until later. He realized the speech he'd been formulating in his mind was now hollow and inapt. The origin of his old friend's aberrant and risky caprice came into sharp focus. The worst part was he had failed to see it. It hadn't occurred to him, though it should have. In tackling this conundrum, he'd failed to see the most obvious answer. Even now, knowing the truth, it was difficult to grasp. Or perhaps he simply lacked the strength or perspective to process the information. It wasn't even four o'clock and already he was emotionally and physically drained. On top of all that, this was the second time today he found himself at a loss for words.

Payte was the first to break the silence.

"I understand that I have betrayed your trust and that of *The Aenamaia*. I ask for neither understanding nor forgiveness. I did what I had to do – whether right or wrong – and it cannot be undone. I am not delusional. I know perfectly well that Kulter and her clan had nothing to do with, Jar...my son's death. But," he said, his voice regaining strength, "I do believe the people who were responsible were of the same corrupt seed. They were all siblings of the same treachery that killed my son and the people he was trying to protect." The general paused, then said with conviction, "No, Gray, it wasn't enough. And I was not about to risk the lives of my men or yours just to facilitate a desert family reunion. No," he said shaking his head, "Not on my watch."

"I understand," Gray said. "I do. You're not the only one who has lost a loved one and..." Gray hesitated, then sighed, "and used the pain as a fuel – and an excuse. We're not foolish enough to believe our actions will bring our loved ones back. All we can do is hope that what we do today might save the lives of good people tomorrow." Gray looked directly at General Payte and added, "I'm sorry, Bill. I'm sorry I didn't see this coming. Though," Gray said chuckling uneasily, "I don't honestly know what I would've done had I suspected you would...alter things the way you did. Part of me wishes I had known, while the rest of me thinks it's probably better that I didn't. I can only hope we were...right...about everyone on that plane. Everyone who died."

A heavy silence hung in the air. After a few moments passed Talon said, "It isn't a matter of hope. Those people, all of them, were there for plenty of good reasons. The only reason we spared them from liquidation was because we thought forced deportation to Iraq would have a greater impact – send a stronger message of what it is this organization is trying to accomplish. Besides," Talon said with a chuckle, "the Iraqi people have been through enough as it is. Dropping that kind of garbage in their backyard would've been, well...rude." Talon and the general laughed, but Gray was still deep in thought.

"You're probably right Talon," Gray finally said, his voice pensive and heavy, "but we're still left with the fallout – the angst and uncertainty – of rogue *Aenamaia* taking matters into their own hands. No matter the reason and regardless of the motivation or the benefits of the outcome, there is still the matter of deceit and duplicity. Dare I say, conspiracy?" Gray turned and looked at the general as if expecting an explanation.

General Payte stared back at Gray, his expression thoughtful, as if he were trying to sift and sort Gray's words in order to understand what his old friend wanted to hear – or needed to hear.

"I know that neither my honor or integrity is being called into question here, Gray. I also understand that your primary concern is the safety and, to some degree, the solidarity of your people. For what it's worth, from one old soldier to another, I admire your devotion and dedication. *The Aenamaia* couldn't exist without it. They're a sharp and strong group of people – firm in their conviction. This incident will not shake their foundations. You stick to your guns, and they'll stick to theirs."

"Your unilateral actions put us all at greater risk than we would have been had you kept to the plan," Gray admonished. "But as you said, it cannot be undone. You're correct in your assessment of *The Aenamaia* – they're motivated, intelligent and steadfast. I just hope for all of our sakes that this incident will not compromise our remaining operations."

Payte eyed Gray wearily, then picked up his service cap and tucked it beneath his arm. He turned and headed towards the door. He'd only gone a few steps when Gray called out, "Bill."

The general stopped and turned around. Before Gray could speak, Payte said, "My men and I will cease and desist all activities pending the judgment of *The Aenamaia*. I understand if you choose to exclude us from any future operations. However, every one of my men and myself are at your disposal and will gladly help in any way we can. That includes damage control in Iraq. Should you decide that we can be of further use, you have my word that your directives and instructions will be followed to the letter – by my men and myself. No deviations."

"I appreciate that," Gray said.

"You have some thoughts on damage control, yes?" Talon asked.

"I do," the general confirmed with a nod.

Gray took a deep breath, then said, "Talon and I need to go to Denver. Tonight. I'm going to leave Altra in charge here. She'll monitor operations with Osiro on remote. I'd like you and your men to work with Dia and Susha on cleanup. Thus far the media has little to go on. Korea, Afghanistan and the Bush trial are likely to stay on top of the news charts, but we'll monitor it closely." Gray stood and took a few steps towards General Payte and said, "I'm told you have a high-ranking and resourceful friend on the sand near the crash site?"

"Yes. He and his men have already begun cleaning things up. They've pitched a few bones to the media about a stray commuter plane crash, but left out the details. As you pointed out, the news networks have bigger fish to fry at the moment." Payte smirked and added, "The ones they know will sell best at the market."

"The public's rapt fascination with the inane, along with the media's eagerness to deliver it, is something we've counted on all along," Talon admitted.

"Indeed," the general said with a nod. "The crew on the ground will have the bulk of the wreckage hauled away and either stored or destroyed inside of twenty-four hours. After that, the media will have little more than scraps to photograph – assuming they can find them."

"What about Sat-Com? Is there any need to be worried there?" Gray asked.

"I'm monitoring all government satellite activity, as well. They have the technology to read my dog tags from space if they want to, but right now most of the surveillance is focused on Afghanistan, Pakistan, China, and Korea. This President may not have any military background, but he's sharp as a razor. Just because Bin Laden is dead, doesn't mean the game is over. He knows where the major threats are coming from. And it isn't Iraq."

Gray nodded approvingly. "I agree. And I appreciate your thinking ahead. You seem to have this matter under control."

General Payte grinned and said, "When I make a mess, I clean it up. That's just how I was raised."

"As was I," Gray said with a nod.

"Bill," Gray said, his voice thoughtful, "I still don't agree with what you did, but I'm glad we understand one another and are still on the same page. I don't know what we'd do without you on our side."

"We've been friends for a long time, Gray," the general said. "I knew how you would take the news and how this conversation would likely play out. And when I walked in that door and we made eye contact, I knew everything would be all right."

"And just what was it that supported your confidence?"

"It was obvious you were pissed. But," the general leaned forward and lowered his voice, "your poker face is crap, Gray. Always has been."

General Payte smiled coyly and both men laughed. Gray took a few steps and stopped in front of the general. Extending his hand he said, "Until Graycliff."

"Until Graycliff," the general repeated. The two men shook hands and smiled. General Payte turned and shook hands with Talon, nodded to both men, then turned to leave. Just as he reached the tall bookshelves he turned and said with a wry smile, "Were you boys planning on taking a commercial flight to Denver or would you like me to arrange for something a bit more expedient?"

Chapter 21

Kennebunkport, Maine

"There is a phone call on your private line, sir," Margaret whispered.

A moment passed before he remembered to acknowledge his assistant with a curt nod. She'd been with him long enough to know when it was time to make a hasty exit. He watched her go, then closed his book and checked his watch. A quick mental calculation told him something must be amiss. The next update was not due until tomorrow morning. Due to the delicate nature of these operations, direct contact had to be limited and discreet. From the corner of his eye he could see the insistent red light flashing, no doubt a portent of unwanted news and unforeseen developments. There were strict rules to this game and before lifting the receiver, he reminded himself of a few things. Don't use names, times, dates or numbers. Avoid specific action words. Make no allusion to remuneration. "Crypticality," was what they'd called it in the CIA. Nodding to himself, he lifted the receiver.

"Go ahead."

"Sir, there's been a slight change of plan regarding the Red Canary." As usual the operative's voice was as cold as ice and devoid of emotion. Such stark and even efficiency might lead one to believe they were speaking to an artificial computer voice. "No," he thought, "computer voices were designed to sound warm, human, and eerily androgynous. This is something very different."

"Explain," he ordered, making no attempt to hide his disdain.

"Our associates were on-site as planned. Half of the team was inside making arrangements for private access. The other half was off-site establishing a good place for..." the man hesitated, "bird watching. Before we could gain access to the Canary..." There was another pause and he sensed a trace of irritation, perhaps even embarrassment in the man's voice. "An unknown variable silenced the animal and retired our associates in the field."

The man's choice of words was careful and calculated. Even if someone had managed to bypass the security in place on both ends of the line, nothing in the conversation could translate into any sort of connection or culpability for either party. Still, the news was distressing and would require further inquiry. For now he needed to shift his thinking to damage control, something he'd become exceedingly adept at.

"Permanent silence? Confirmed?"

"Yes, sir."

"Associates, as well?"

"Yes, sir."

He nodded and tried to think. Several scenarios were possible here, but he needed more information to choose the next move. Fortunately, he and the operative had agreed to several key words and phrases to help convey specific details when necessary.

"Two shows. Was the curtain call before coffee or after?" 'Coffee' was code for eight a.m.

"Not long after. The show was played during lunch." 'Lunch' referred to the span of one hour. The operative was telling him someone killed Jack Abramoff before their people could. It also sounded like the same people had managed to eliminate the two trained operatives they'd sent to establish a suitable perch and quick exit strategy for one of their snipers to retire the loose-lipped lobbyist.

Normally killing a prison inmate was best done through internal channels. Abramoff's situation had been different. The prison population, though predominantly white-collar and stable, was prone to occasional bouts of violence and turf fights. Normally this would prove useful. However, due in part to the high profiles of a handful of inmates, measures had been instituted to segregate the stable from the unstable. Additionally, Abramoff himself had been assigned to the cell closest to the guard station. The closer the cell was to the guards, the safer the occupant. To make matters worse, Abramoff maintained daily contact with the federal officials and attorneys keeping him as safe and as cozy as possible in exchange for information.

Fortunately, a number of powerful individuals were less than pleased about this relationship. The Red Canary had burned an impressive number of bridges before he'd finished his first song. His death while in prison would generate a long list of suspects. The cover would've been perfect. But someone had beaten them to it.

"Was act two viewed by the public?"

"No sir. The show was private."

"Any residual?"

"Local PD were first to arrive, but we have them under control. The stage is clear and the air is clean."

"Will there be any reviews in the Sunday *Times?*"

"No, sir. The media were not privy to this performance."

"Is there any information on the visiting actor or actors?"

There was a moment of silence before the operative answered, "No, sir."

"What exactly do you know about this...*performance?*"

"Professional. Informed. Doubtful the actor knew another team was set to perform."

"Based on what?"

"The stage, sir. Our cleanup crew was able to reconstruct some of the second performance. The visiting actor walked away from the scene, but the performance took its toll. Additionally, before leaving, the actor rearranged the stage. The new arrangement allowed us to divert the local flat feet."

"Recommendations?"

"Make inquiries, but keep operations moving forward. There are other similar...performances going on around the country that may prove useful. There's a thick veil of smoke on the national stage."

He nodded to himself as newspaper images from the last few days filed by in his mind one by one: Tom Delay murdered, Anna Kulter and her entourage missing, the Bill Robinson incident, Blackriver CEO David Lesser, and that slippery energy executive Pou Lai. Eight prominent lobbyists found dead – cause of death still unknown. "A few members of Congress might go bankrupt," he thought with amusement, "without the lobbyists shoving cash into their wallets." He shook his head.

A very strange town, that Washington. They used to say the buildings were horizontal instead of vertical so the lobbyists and bribers didn't have to haul all that cash up so many stairs. "Padding," they'd called it. Unfortunately, that padding proved as hard as a rock when the politicians fell from on high. Frail bones shattered on the hard floor of public prosecution. Strange town, indeed. And deadly of late.

But death wasn't the only newsworthy item on the menu. There was the now infamous Tabloid Bombings, the Murdoch-Ailes hostage situation, and the attempt on Jack Kelley's life. The opportunistic media were having a field day with what some were labeling the "Fear Express," as demonstrated by a substantial increase in circulation, ratings, and web hits. And the media weren't the only ones catching the train.

Gun and ammunition dealers, home and personal security companies, even camping and survival outlets – all immediately retooled their marketing campaigns to prey on consumer fears. The overreaction and panic could be seen in other, less obvious places. Sick calls and sudden vacation requests were up thirty percent, while daycare enrollment was down almost the same. Yesterday morning a city newspaper published a column by an editorialist who posited that several military bases and chemical manufacturers were prime targets. Though the conclusions had no factual basis, by the afternoon, thousands of calls had been placed to police departments, politicians, the FBI and CIA, and the newspapers. Fallacious emails piggybacking on the editorial went viral. Within hours parents were showing up en masse at schools demanding their children be released immediately. An employee at one of the chemical companies panicked and started spreading doomsday rumors, and within an hour, a fight broke out resulting in four people being sent to the hospital. And these were just the headlines.

Then there were the less obvious effects. Bottled water, propane and butane gas, canned food, fishing and hunting supplies, matches and candles, firewood, batteries, flashlights, toothpaste, First Aid kits, and room-temperature alcoholic beverages had all vanished from store shelves. And all this despite the obvious fact that the general public was neither being targeted nor caught in any kind of crossfire. The public, it seemed to the rational observer, had nothing to fear. But logic rarely triumphed over bandwagon panic. This reaction was quite similar to that of the days following 9/11, with one interesting exception – American flag sales had practically flatlined. Unlike 9/11, this time Americans didn't have a clear and obvious enemy and thus had no direction in which to channel their fear and hate. Additionally, the government wasn't pandering fear and distrust. Patriotism, it seemed, swelled only when the infection came by way of the media and the White House.

"Maintain operations. Keep to the plan. And make damn sure that debacle of a play never opens again!"

"Yes, sir," came the tight-lipped reply.

He slammed down the phone to further emphasize his disappointment. But he knew it was more than that. Anxiety hung thick in the air around him. Anxiety or acute apprehension. Was there a difference? He'd felt the pulse of decisiveness, authority and power when he'd ordered the first round of executions. But that high, like any other, had vanished, leaving behind a systemic and hollow sense of loss and deprivation. His eyes darted from side to side, searching for something he could damage or destroy. Shaking his head, he cursed himself for such weakness. This was a process, pure and simple. Another mess to sweep up. By now he should be able to do it in his sleep. There was no need to over-dramatize the situation. So someone else wanted the Canary dead. No surprise there. He knew the uneasiness came from the knowledge that the person responsible for retiring one of his marks was more skilled than the two agents his Condotierro had sent. Another player was at this table. The unwelcome and uninvited Mr. X.

"This could be good, though," he mused. Examine all the angles. Think it through. How could this be beneficial? If this player kept in the game, he could be just the mask they needed. But there was another angle he'd failed to consider. Even without Mr. X the spin would be easy. Each of the targets on his list, facing possible involvement in federal trials, along with possible indictment and sentencing, took matters into their own hands to eliminate those who could implicate them. Each would expect the media and prosecutors to target his son, being the main person on trial. But a few carefully positioned ideas would serve to further confuse and complicate the situation. Possibly to the point where even junior would be lost in the upheaval.

Whether this change of events was a blessing or curse, he couldn't be sure. But the more suspects on the list, the more convoluted the issue became. History clearly demonstrates that those at the top of the power chain usually have the easiest time slipping away. If he was lucky, history would once again prove a resilient and effective accomplice.

New Windsor, NY

Roger Tarte leaned against the car and stared off into the distance. On any other day the white noise of the airport would have engulfed him and made thought impossible. Today was different. Oddly enough, it had been those same three words that had immediately plunged him into deep thought twenty minutes ago.

"Today is different," he thought again. The events of the day contrasted sharply with the mundane redundancy of the last nine months. But there was more to it than that. Today had been unusual on a number of levels. At first he'd attributed the tingling in his mind to the excitement of action that comes after long-term mental hibernation. When used to cutting with a spoon, even the dullest blade seems sharp. However, as the day had progressed, he'd became acutely aware of something entirely different lying just beneath the surface. Though there wasn't a single word to accurately describe it, he thought "instinct" was in the right ballpark.

The same intense concentration and focus he'd once employed to solve complex encryption problems had been awakened from a long dormant sleep. Ever since Jasmine had burst into his office this morning, his mind had been carefully absorbing, analyzing and meticulously cataloging every new bit of information. And though he was far from a solution, connections had already been established. Though he despised clichés, the thought of a fragmented puzzle kept coming to mind. There were numerous clusters of pieces he'd put together – or that had just fallen into place, but the picture was far from clear. And even though there was no guarantee all the pieces belonged to the same puzzle, he suspected that somehow all the little clusters were somehow linked.

The addictive rush of urgent purpose coursed like a raging river through his veins again. Parts of his mind long dormant were suddenly animated, aroused by the scent of numerous conundrums – the promise of stimulating challenge. He had left the CIA and joined the Department of Homeland Security believing every day would stretch, tear, and rebuild his mental faculties. And in the beginning it had. Terrorist cells, complex *hawala* networks and laundering schemes, communication intercepts, etc. There had been all-nighters working with a host of agencies from Interpol, MI5, the World Bank and IMF, all the way down to state and local police. The mountains of gathered intelligence, some from undisclosed and sometimes illegal sources, had kept him very busy in the beginning. Those days had flown by in a blur. Hours upon hours spent combing through the information, always seeking connections, patterns, and complex relationships.

In addition to the data from outside sources, he'd put Jasmine to work combing the internet and news banks for more. They'd both been so consumed in the work, Jasmine had been forced to set an alarm clock to remind them to stop for lunch, with a second timer set a half hour later – just in case her preoccupied mind subconsciously silenced the first alarm, which happened regularly. They'd both loved the work, which explained Jasmine's excitement that morning.

Agency life had calmed considerably over the last year. Budgets and personnel slowly dwindled, interagency cooperation increased, data crunching and analysis were quietly shipped overseas to Singapore and New Delhi, and the overall number of investigations tapered. In many departments, including his, the daily job had been reduced to something akin to report and data assembly and filing. On one occasion he'd asked Jasmine "Which papers are mine to push and which are yours?" The jab had earned him a sour scowl.

But this morning, all that had changed in the blink of an eye. The alluring potential for a return to the days of constant stimulation and action was obvious and tempting. No doubt Jasmine had sensed it as well. Now, after less than a day on the case, the puzzle was slowly taking shape. The million dollar question was where to go from here?

The vibration and soft chirping of his cell broke his concentration. He was sure it was his wife calling to see if he'd taken off yet. Still trying to make a mental note of where his train of thought had been stopped, he flipped open the phone and answered.

"Yeah, Tarte here."

"Hello again, Agent Tarte. This is Gray."

Tarte stood up straight, shifted the phone to his right ear, and dug frantically through his coat pocket for his pad of paper. "Mr. Gray," he stuttered, "so good of you to call." He'd managed to extract the pad of paper and was now trying to find a pen. The line was silent so he asked, "Are you still there?"

"Whenever you're ready, Agent Tarte," Gray said calmly.

Tarte wasn't sure what the man was talking about, but he welcomed the delay. Where the hell was his pen? Then from the corner of his eye he spotted a white object. He turned and saw a cheap white pen sitting on the dashboard. Spinning on his heel he reached through the passenger side window and grabbed it. After a quick scratch test he set the pad down on the hood and returned the phone to his left ear. He was about to say something when he heard, "Now that you're ready…." The man's voice wasn't annoyed. In fact, Tarte thought he detected a hint of amusement. How the hell had he known?

"First," the man continued calmly, "formality is not necessary. 'Gray' will do just fine. Second, I assume you've had ample time to verify the Semtex, yes?"

"Yes," Tarte replied. "It's genuine. And very illegal."

"So good of you to point that out. But let's try and keep to the facts, shall we?" The man's tone was patient – even playful. But Tarte knew better than to let down his guard.

"Better yet, perhaps we should get right to the point. To what do I owe the pleasure of your call, Gray?" he said dryly.

"Very well," Gray replied curtly. "I would like to offer you a deal."

"I'm listening."

"I'm going to hand over Ailes and Murdoch to you," Gray said cheerfully.

"Now why would you do something like that?" Tarte asked suspiciously.

"Because I want something in exchange, of course."

Tarte was already growing tired of this so he said seriously, "You want to choose how you'll be executed?"

The line was silent and for a moment Tarte second-guessed his harsh tactic.

"Let's get something straight right now, Agent Tarte. If this game ends and I've lost, then two things will happen. One, while I'm in custody the media circus will explode in a way unseen since the days following 9/11. Contingency arrangements for that possibility were set in motion long ago. Second, should I be condemned to the death penalty, I can personally guarantee that the only one taking my life will be me. Those arrangements were also made long ago. For the time being, you have two wealthy hostages who might think less of you for not cooperating to achieve their safe return. So can we dispense with the bullshit?"

Tarte remained silent for a moment. He looked around, but no one was within earshot. He was about to speak when Gray said impatiently, "No one will hear you and I give you my word that this conversation is not being monitored or recorded."

Tarte thought about looking around again, but decided against it. Gray was watching him – that much was certain. Best to play it cool.

"I'm still listening," Tarte assured him.

"I can see that, Agent Tarte," Gray said matter-of-factly.

"I know you can," Tarte replied coolly. To further make his point, he reached a hand back behind his head and waved awkwardly.

"So glad we understand each other," Gray said. And Tarte knew the man was smiling. Gray continued, "The terms are simple. I will release Ailes and Murdoch whenever you are ready. You can allow the local PD to handle the matter or you can fly back that way and handle it yourself. In return I ask only that you pull your men off of Jack Kelley."

Tarte stopped writing, but did not look up. Instead he looked at his watch. When had he made the call? He closed his eyes and worked out the timeline. If his calculations were correct, two agents should be en route to Kelley's office right now. Which meant there wasn't a whole lot of time to dally around. Once Kelley was in custody, matters would become far more complicated.

"What does Kelley have to do with this?" he asked, still trying to make the connection.

"Agent Tarte," Gray said impatiently, "you know perfectly well that we don't have time for this now. Four agents are en route to Kelley's office now. They'll be there in less than ten minutes. We are not in the habit of eliminating federal agents, even when they pose a threat to our plans. Please do not force me to augment that policy."

"Are you threatening…" Tarte started to say, but Gray cut him off.

"Time, Agent Tarte! We don't have time for this. Pull your men off Kelley or I'll do it for you. You have eight minutes. Comply and we'll talk. Try and be clever and you'll be picking up what remains of Ailes and Murdoch for the next year. You'll also answer for the deaths of four federal agents. You know what to do. And remember, Agent Tarte," Gray paused and then said quietly, "we're watching." And with that the line went dead.

Tarte remained frozen in place and tried to think. He was pissed at having been threatened and at having a criminal fill his plate with demands, but now was not the time to let emotion splinter logic and reason. "Consider the whole situation," he thought. "No doubt Gray is somehow watching me right now." Focusing on his procedures, he ran through several likely scenarios. It only took a moment to realize there was no easy way out of this. If he wasn't careful he'd wind up facing charges for negotiating with a terrorist. However, the fact that Gray wanted or needed Kelley alive and not in custody might just be cause enough to back off Kelley and just observe. He would set up surveillance and taps at Kelley's home and office. It would be enough to justify pulling the agents – not to mention possibly saving their lives. Use the little baitfish to find the Great White. Gray would expect the covert DHS spotlight to shine on Kelley, but perhaps that also could be an advantage.

Tarte nodded to himself. He dialed his office and began pacing in front of his car. Jasmine answered on the second ring.

"It's me," he said quickly, "Don't talk, just listen. I need you to pull our agents off Kelley right now. Call them directly. I want both cars back within the hour."

"Two cars?" Jasmine said, "I only requested two agents."

Gray had said there were four agents and Tarte believed him. He wasn't sure why two extra agents had tagged along, but he was certainly going to find out.

"There's no time for explanations right now, Jasmine. There are two cars heading towards Kelley's office. Make the call. I want both cars to return immediately. When they get there I want an explanation of the two extra agents. And tell them not to discuss this with anyone until they speak with me. Understood?"

"Got it," Jasmine said.

"Good. Send me a text when it's done."

Tarte hung up the phone before Jasmine could ask what was going on. She would get right on it. Barring any difficulty reaching the two units, they should be turning around in a few minutes. If Gray was good to his word, he would be calling back soon to discuss Ailes and Murdoch.

"White!" Tarte shouted. Agent White appeared just inside the hangar door. Tarte waved him over.

Agent White jogged to where Tarte stood and announced, "Your plane will be ready in ten minutes."

"Good. Listen, White. I need you to call the site commander at the Ailes estate. Tell him to be ready to pick up Ailes and Murdoch – they'll be coming out soon. Have the bomb squad ready to go in and defuse every wired device in the house. Tell them to wear gas masks. Have emergency medical services standing by. Once the wires are cut get two teams in to assess the hazmat situation. I want them all ready to go in thirty minutes."

"Yes, sir," White said. Tarte watched as the man turned, dialed his cell phone and waived at someone in the hangar – all in one motion. The guy may have a stick up his ass, but he was certainly efficient.

Tarte looked again at his cell, which rang an instant later. No caller I.D. or number.

"You're nothing if not punctual," Tarte commented.

"As are you," Gray said quickly. "Both cars have turned around."

"That means you owe me two hostages," Tarte said firmly.

"Right now? Don't you want to be there?"

"There are fifty officers and agents right outside the gates. I don't need to be there. Release them now!" Tarte demanded.

"I commend you, Agent Tarte," Gray said coolly. "Most men in your position would delay the release in order to be on hand for the front page photographs – start working their way up to middle management and mediocrity."

"Your opinion of our public servants is less than flattering, Gray. I like to believe any man in my shoes would grab the hostages the first moment the opportunity arose. And that moment is now."

"You're quite right, Agent Tarte," Gray agreed. There was a pause, and Tarte could hear muffled speaking. Then Gray returned and said, "They'll be out in fifteen minutes. Agent Tarte," Gray said hesitantly, "at the risk of questioning the integrity of your word I'm forced to ask what guarantee I have that once the trophies are safely in your hands, Kelley won't be immediately scooped up?"

"None whatsoever," Tarte commented dryly, "other than my word. Of course we never agreed to any terms regarding Kelley other than prolonging his being brought into custody. Protective custody, I'd wager."

"On the contrary," Gray countered, "I think we both know that if I wanted Kelley dead, I would've made sure he was still at the wheel when I gave his vehicle an overhaul."

This surprised Tarte and he said, "You're admitting responsibility for the explosion?"

"Call it a show of good faith," Gray offered. "More kindling for burning the witches."

"Interesting analogy," Tarte said. "Though I can assure you, we no longer burn witches at the stake."

There was a moment of silence then Gray said in a low and serious tone, "I wouldn't be so sure of that, Agent Tarte."

Something in Gray's voice sent a chill through Tarte's body.

"Would you care to explain that?" Tarte asked.

"I doubt you'd take me at my word," Gray said cautiously.

"Try me," Tarte challenged.

The line was silent. Tarte thought he sensed hesitation. This man doesn't mince words, nor does he waste time. Tarte suspected Gray was considering something very carefully. If he was right, then whatever the man had to say could be very interesting indeed.

Washington, D.C.

Dia leaned over the black leather armrest and whispered in Talon's ear. "Why do you suppose he opted for a limousine rather than a taxi?"

Talon thought about it for a moment then quietly replied, "Given the weapons in the trunk and the fact that he's negotiating with a federal agent via scrambled cell phone, I'm guessing he figured a limo would be much less likely to be pulled over. High profile, but low risk. Plus," Talon grinned, "I'm guessing he'll want a little something to ease his tension." Talon pointed towards the stocked minibar.

Dia smiled and nodded. "I wish I was going with you."

"I wish you were going *instead* of me," Talon admitted. He turned and saw Dia was staring at him, her expression curious and questioning.

"Does this have something to do with..." Dia started to ask, but Talon held up a hand.

"I'm sorry. I misspoke. I want to go. I mean, I *need* to," Talon stuttered. "I'm supposed to be there. It's my job. We need to figure out who this shooter is and what he knows."

Dia studied Talon's face, but remained silent for a few moments. She leaned forward and plucked two small liquor bottles from the glass and mahogany cabinet.

"Would you look and see if there is a Diet Coke in there?" she said, pointing to the small refrigerator next to Talon's feet.

Dia glanced at Gray who was huddled in the corner of the adjacent seat. She noticed the faint blue flashing light on the wireless headset he wore and the glow of Gray's cell phone, which sat on top of a notebook on his lap. Gray was speaking quietly, but Dia distinctly heard him say the words "Turkmenistan," "Rove," and "body."

She leaned over again and whispered to Talon, "Do you think it's such a good idea for him to be telling that agent about Rove? I mean, he's going to blame us for it."

Talon shrugged. He handed her a cold can of Diet Coke and a tall crystal glass. "We don't know who's responsible for Rove – just that it wasn't one of us." Dia cocked an eyebrow and Talon added, "At least not that we know of. If General Payte had made another...deviation, I think he would've told us. Besides, this isn't the type of thing any of our Augurs would do."

"Certainly a lot of trouble to go to for a pudgy Republican nutcase," Dia admitted.

Talon leaned back and thought a moment. He said, "That's the weird thing about it. The scene was staged – that much is obvious. But why?"

"A message? A warning?" Dia offered. "A not-so-subtle gag suggestion?"

Talon shrugged. "I'm not sure. Whatever it is, we're in no position to investigate it. Our resources are stretched thin as it is. Not to mention the fact that Gray isn't fond of deviating from our plans."

"General Payte should've known that," Dia said.

"He did," Talon said. "Payte did what he felt he had to do. And he had the resources to do it and clean it up."

"I suppose. Still wasn't one of his better ideas, though. Good thing Gray is so understanding and forgiving."

Dia emptied the contents of the small bottle of spiced rum into the glass, added the cold soft drink, and stirred the cocktail with her index finger. She took a drink and exhaled a breath of satisfaction. She looked at the small empty bottle and smiled.

"What are you grinning at?" Talon asked.

"There are times when I really despise marketing and advertising. Usually feels like I'm being teased and taunted by a clever product pimp. But, I have to admit, I sometimes really enjoy the visuals. They get me thinking."

She handed Talon the bottle. A confident, grinning buccaneer pirate stared back at him. The colorful caricature stood tall – one foot propped on a wooden barrel while balancing a sword face down. He wore a bright red coat, blue cape and pants, brown boots and had a flintlock pistol stuffed into his belt. Talon was familiar with the brand and would, from time to time, use it in a mixed drink he'd invented.

He returned the bottle to Dia and asked, "What does that make you think about?"

She looked at him as though the answer should be obvious. "Graycliff, of course. Pirate, Caribbean, rum, Nassau, freedom, libations and celebrations. Any of this registering?"

Talon thought about it, but decided daydreaming about Graycliff wasn't a good idea at the moment. He was about to take the ride of his life to the Mile High City where he and Gray would meet a man they assumed was a professional hit man. That encounter might or might not alter what remained of their mission. Beyond that, after everything was said and done, he could not see beyond the image of a beautiful woman whom he hoped would still be interested. Mission first, then the goddess, then everything else.

"We don't know how long he's been in there, Agent Tarte," Gray said impatiently. "Had we been the ones who put him there I could be much more precise. All I know is when the remains were discovered." He glanced at Talon, rolled his eyes and shook his head. This Tarte fellow must be giving Gray a hard time.

The limousine slowed down, turned, and came to a stop in front of a black iron gate and a small guard house. There were two identically dressed armed guards inside the small building. One of the guards stepped out and Talon saw the driver hand him a thin folder. The guard reviewed the information then returned inside. A few seconds later the gate retracted and the limousine drove onto the base.

Talon leaned toward Dia and whispered, "Can I have the rest of that can?"

Dia looked at him askance. He rolled his eyes and said, "I know, not my usual drink of choice. I'm thirsty and this tub doesn't have any bottled water."

Dia shrugged and handed him the can. He drained the remaining soda and sighed.

"Good shit, huh?" Dia said, sipping her drink.

"I didn't stop drinking this stuff because of the taste," Talon explained. "There's no nutritional value, it's high in sodium, contains artificial sweeteners, and really doesn't do the body much good." He looked at Dia who was grinning. He smiled sheepishly and said, "Okay, I admit – it's pretty good shit."

"Probably best that you had it now."

"Why is that?"

Dia pointed out the dark-tinted window. Talon looked in the direction she was pointing and saw what had attracted her attention. She leaned towards him and whispered, "I doubt you'll get any beverage service on those bad boys."

Talon stared at the two planes parked on the tarmac and said quietly, "Traveling well over the speed of sound – who gives a rat's ass about a drink!"

New Windsor, NY

Tarte remained silent, trying to think of what to say next. He couldn't be sure whether Gray was playing games with him or not. Instinct told him this was for real. But how could he be sure Gray and his group of marauders weren't actually the ones responsible?

"Agent Tarte?" Gray asked.

Tarte shifted the cell to the other ear and said, "I'm here."

"The body has been found and a preliminary identification has been made. Though it might be a few days before they figure out how to extract the remains."

"I assume if I were to make inquiries now, no one else would know this has happened, right?"

There was a short pause, then Gray admitted, "It's doubtful."

"And I don't suppose you'd care to elaborate on just how you got a hold of this information," Tarte said.

"We did not do this," Gray said in answer to the unspoken suggestion. "Though I can understand why you might think that. Unfortunately, I can offer you no proof of our innocence. But I can tell you that the victim was high up on our list, though for reasons I can't go into now, we decided not to pursue his...removal."

"But you just happened to learn that someone dumped his body in a lava pit in Turkmenistan," Tarte said skeptically.

"It is not a lava pit, Agent Tarte, and yes, we just heard the news. I'm sure you understand that telling you more would compromise our organization."

"Yeah," Tarte said reluctantly, "I understand."

"After your ego calms down and you've had time to think about this, Agent Tarte, you'll realize that we have nothing to gain by sharing this information with you. This information is being shared now as an act of goodwill."

"And how, may I ask, did you obtain this information?" Tarte didn't expect an answer so he was surprised when Gray provided one.

"I told you, to provide specific details would compromise our people. However, I can tell you that we have loyal informants all over the world – from Rust to Auckland to Sonoma – though most are here in the U.S."

"Rust?" Tarte said curiously.

Gray hesitated for a split second as if he'd misspoken then said, "A scenic town in Austria. One of our operatives spent some time there ten years ago."

Tarte thought he detected a sharp edge in Gray's voice. He considered pressing the point, but instead said curiously, "'Operative' sounds somewhat military."

"Some of our people are ex-military," Gray admitted, "but most hail from non-military, non-government professions."

"Recruited?" Tarte asked.

"In a manner of speaking," Gray replied, "though it has to be done very carefully. If we feel the candidate isn't ready to join *The Aenamaia* we simply tap them for information."

"So your group of merry lunatics is not static. You're always on the hunt for new talent."

Gray ignored the insult and said calmly, "Talent, or individuals with access to critical information. Both regularly seek us out."

"Average people manage to find you?" Tarte said hopefully. Perhaps nailing these guys wouldn't be so difficult after all.

"No," Gray said firmly. "Average is not the word. These are people of great intelligence and integrity who have decided not to ignore the sickness in the world. They know things are terribly wrong and that the decadence is practically ubiquitous. So when valuable information comes their way, they often quietly seek an outlet for it. From there, the process of contact and extraction is simple. Well," Gray hesitated, "usually simple."

Tarte detected frustration in the man's voice, but said nothing. Obviously something concerning an informant hadn't gone according to plan. Tarte wondered what had happened, but knew it was unlikely Gray would elaborate.

Gray continued, "We also employ sophisticated programs we call 'Sniffers' that scan internet newspapers, government sites, blogs, etc. When an informant sends news, we immediately program the Sniffers to look for related information. On top of all that....we listen."

Tarte guessed that by "listen" Gray was subtly admitting that they were illegally eavesdropping. He took a chance and asked, "Law Enforcement agencies? Military coms? Small governments?"

"Very good, Agent Tarte. But you're only scratching the surface. Through contacts, talent and technology our network is very...robust."

"And your network informed you that someone had barbecued the former President's favorite confidant. Valuable information that you've chosen to share with me out of the goodness of your heart," Tarte said skeptically.

"'Goodness' is a bit of a stretch, but yes, if you like. You may do with it what you will. However, after careful consideration, you will no doubt conclude that if you make this information known, your superiors will want to know where you learned about it. That could put a damper on our burgeoning relationship."

"Let's get something straight, Gray," Tarte said heatedly, "we don't have a relationship – burgeoning or otherwise. If there weren't two hostages I was trying to free, I'd be spending my spare time hunting you and your group of merry men. I don't give a good goddamn about your politics or your philosophy – you don't have the right to take the law into your own hands. Period."

"You're absolutely right," Gray conceded simply. This caught Tarte by surprise. He'd been expecting some kind of hostile response or threat. Or a long-winded rant about Robin Hood justice, good versus bad, or some kind of Draconian justification – anything but agreement. Tarte wasn't quite sure what to say so he remained silent.

"Our actions are unorthodox to be sure, but necessary. Some accept the axiom that the weak are always at the mercy of the strong. That may be so. But when the weak harness their intelligence, work out what's wrong with the equation and actively subtract those elements, they become imbued with a strength far greater than the mindless thugs they once feared." Gray hesitated for a moment then added, "The name of our group, *The Aenamaia*, derives from a word we created that describes all this. Aenamus."

"Well since Webster is obviously of no use to me here, perhaps you'll enlighten me," Tarte said sarcastically.

Gray sighed heavily and said, "You remind me of Kwaku Ananse, only you're a lot more pompous. Look him up some time when your ego won't let you fall asleep."

Tarte wasn't familiar with the reference so he decided not to comment.

Gray continued. "Most people feel a sense of frustration and helplessness when they see injustice. Pedophiles protected by the Catholic Church, corrupt politicians pardoning their friends, criminals suing their victims – and winning. Fire-breathing preachers in the pulpit damning homosexuality only hours before getting caught having an affair with another man. Corrupt and greedy televangelists, CEOs polluting the environment to increase profits, and the exploits of the two men about to walk out of that house. A good, intelligent person recognizes the injustice and contempt for decency right away. Aenamus is born when they decide to do something about it."

"That's a nice story, Gray. Sure, I agree that world isn't perfect. I know there are some bad seeds out there – I see some of the worst every day I go to work – but the fact that they exist and do bad things is irrelevant here. You know why? Because what you're doing is still wrong," Tarte insisted. "Don't you think most civilized societies would agree?"

"Unfortunately, I don't believe the societies of which you speak are all that civilized," Gray said heavily.

Tarte suddenly felt defensive and asked sharply, "Then just what are they?"

"Homogenized," Gray said simply.

"Come again?"

"Homogenized," Gray repeated. "Aloof. Disinterested. Lazy. Take your pick. The average citizen, in the average developed country, lives in a small world filled with a sort of fluid denial. Their brain cells are focused on maintaining the status quo of daily life. Few people have the time...or I should say *make the time* for much else. Sure there is time for a trip to Starbucks, or a few sitcoms every night, gossip, tabloids, a reality show here and there, discussions on weather and dining, gardening and interior design. Who has time to think about oppressed people dying in a foreign land, especially one very few people intend to ever visit? Who wants to experience the unpleasantness rendered by thoughts of injustice, pain, suffering, inequity, religion and complex politics? Life is much easier with a cheap lite beer, a remote control, and the instant gratification of online shopping."

Gray sighed, "No, Agent Tarte, I don't believe 'civilized' is really the appropriate term. Most people have a shrunken, homogenized and irrational ideology they cling to, and little else gets in. But when ideology and outright denial fail, all you're left with is cold, hard and inescapable reality. Those of us who choose to face reality do so head-on and without blinders. We know the patterns of history and have lost patience with ideology. So we're building a new road to the future. We're embracing Aenamus."

"And steamrolling any obstacles you don't particularly agree with," Tarte said accusingly.

"Agent Tarte," Gray said patiently, "I don't expect you to understand or condone what's being done. Legally and philosophically you're absolutely correct – no group or individual has the right to do what we're doing. But sometimes what we believe to be right and what is best for the greater good aren't always the same thing. Perhaps someday, when this is all over and you have me safely tucked away in a cell on death row, we can discuss matters of philosophy, morality, and history at great length. But right now there are more urgent matters demanding your attention."

Before Gray could continue, Tarte said, "Why are you telling me all of this, Gray? Why take the time to explain your motives and this warped sense of justice you call Aenamus? You know I'll do everything in my power to stop you and your *Aenamaia*. So why provide me with details?"

Tarte heard Gray take a deep breath. "Agent Tarte," he began, "I haven't revealed enough detail to be of any use. Nor am I trying to convince you of the merits or necessity of what we do. I've given you this information in an effort to impart the seriousness of what we're doing. To hopefully prevent unnecessary loss of innocent life. That includes your agents and yourself."

Tarte felt his jaw tighten and he said in a low voice, "Are you threatening me?"

"This is neither grade school nor a Hollywood western, Agent Tarte. We don't make threats. We're bringing a war to those who knowingly poison and slowly destroy humanity. A war, Agent Tarte. If you walk into the crossfire you might get killed. Period."

"I don't respond well to threats on my…" but Gray cut him off again.

"Time is critical, Agent Tarte. None of us have enough of it. Events are unfolding that demand attention. Karl Rove's body has been found in a flaming pit in Turkmenistan, there are rogue snipers in Denver and…" Gray paused, then said, "Excuse me for a moment." Tarte could hear muffled conversation.

Casually, Tarte used his thumb to turn up the volume on his phone. He pressed it to his ear and listened. The voices were mostly inaudible, but he thought he heard something about a flight to Denver.

Gray came back on and said, "I apologize, Agent Tarte, but I must be going. Roger Ailes and Rupert Murdoch just walked out the front door and are now safely in local police custody. The house has been completely disarmed."

Tarte was about to ask Gray to elaborate on the matter in Denver when he saw White waving. White held up his cell phone and gave a thumbs up. "You're good to your word," Tarte acknowledged.

"As I trust you will be, Agent Tarte," Gray said.

Tarte thought for a moment, then said, "I'll back off Kelley for one week. After that he's mine. That's the deal."

"What's right and what's best aren't always the same thing," Gray repeated.

"Let's hope we're both right on this one," Tarte said and hung up the phone.

En Route to Washington, D.C.

The steady hum of the jet engines did little to assuage Tarte's darkening mood. He sat staring at his cell phone, willing it to ring with a call from someone that had the answers to all his questions. The last hour had revealed so much information that his mind was having a difficult time keeping it all straight. There were patterns, that much he knew. But he couldn't quite see any structure or connections just yet. The conversation with Gray had revealed much, though the thought of having knowledge of Rove's death and not being able to report it was almost enough to drive him over the edge. The next call he'd gotten had been even more mind-boggling.

White's car and its owner were still visible outside the aircraft's windows when he'd gotten Jasmine's call. Her tone of voice told him immediately she had valuable information. Rather than delay take-off, he'd decided to risk calling her back on the jet's private line. "Doubtful anyone would be listening to this line," he'd thought. The plane began taxiing while Tarte listened to Jasmine's rapid report. As she spoke, he looked out the window and again saw White standing next to his car – watching the plane as it headed for the start of the runway. He wondered if White could see him through the small porthole. Could he see the cordless handset? White would know it was the jet's private line. Would he suspect something if they made eye contact?

White was fifty yards away from the plane. His face was partially obscured by a hand raised to shade his eyes. Tarte stared directly at the man. And though he knew it was crazy, Tarte thought he read a knowing and subtly alarming expression on White's face – as if the quiet and normally detached agent was also listening to Jessica's report. Tarte continued to watch the unmoving figure – expecting to see the man suddenly pull out his cell phone, jump in his car and race away. An amusing image of what an "Oh shit!" expression might look like on White's emotionless face flashed through his mind. He grinned and filed the image away for later.

"Roger, did you hear me?" Jasmine asked.

"I'm sorry, Jasmine, there was some static. What was that last part?"

"Bush never showed at up Fox. Apparently he had urgent business back on the ranch in Crawford."

Tarte nodded but said nothing. Jasmine continued. "Roger," she said in a hushed voice, "Floyd and White have a history."

This caught Tarte's attention and he said, "Go on."

"Agent White was recruited in October of 2001 by Steven Floyd."

"Into the FBI?" Tarte asked in disbelief.

"Yes. White was living in Nassau when they met. Floyd was on an extended assignment there, but I couldn't get any details about what he was doing. I did learn that White was quickly transferred to the FBI offices in San Juan, Puerto Rico while Floyd pushed his citizenship paperwork through immigration. His application and acceptance into the FBI went through in record time."

"What is his official hire date?"

"Hold on," Jasmine said. Tarte could hear the rapid fire of computer keys in the background. "This is strange."

Tarte waited two seconds, then said somewhat impatiently, "I'd rather not play 'prompt and ask' right now Jasmine."

"Sorry, Roger. The information I received said White started with the FBI in early 2002, but the official record doesn't show him coming on until January of 2004."

"That's not unheard of," Tarte said, "I'm guessing Floyd had him under cover well before he was officially hired. I would also guess he was working on something very secretive. Which probably meant Floyd was bending a handful of FBI rules and regulations. Inside the U.S. such operations are very tricky. But when the work is being done outside of the country, in what could still be called the third world, the gray area offers quite a lot of shade."

"Doesn't mean you won't still get burned," Jasmine muttered.

Tarte thought for a moment then asked, "How long was White in San Juan?"

"My information here is pretty sparse," Jasmine admitted reluctantly, "but it looks like the last report from San Juan that mentions his name was dated December 5, 2003. I guess he took an early break for Christmas that..."

"Hold on a second, Jasmine," Tarte interrupted. "Let me think for a second."

The line went quiet, but Tarte knew Jasmine was chomping at the bit.

"San Juan is only about four hundred miles away from Cuba," he started to explain. But before he could finish Jasmine whispered, "Guantanamo."

"What?" Tarte could hardly believe she'd said it only seconds after he'd thought it.

Jasmine's words came quickly, with barely contained excitement, "You're thinking he was spying on Guantanamo, right? I know that's it! Of course. I remember hearing rumors that the FBI, which at the time was publicly questioning the practices going on there, was also running clandestine operations at Gitmo. They were supposedly keeping a close eye on the JTF there. Though I don't know if anything ever came of it."

Tarte remembered hearing similar rumors. The Joint Task Force Guantanamo, often referred to as JTF-Gitmo, was the Navy unit responsible for running the detention camp at Guantanamo Bay. Within months of the first prisoners arriving in late 2001, rumors of torture and mistreatment began surfacing. Initial reports were largely ignored until the controversial events at the Abu Ghraib prison just outside Baghdad captured headlines all over the world in 2004. It wasn't long before the spotlight shifted to Gitmo and the JTF. Everyone from the President to the Joint Chiefs to the food preparation staff at Gitmo were under intense scrutiny.

Jasmine was now saying, "Do you suppose he and Floyd had anything to do with the uproar about torture at Gitmo?" Tarte was about to answer when Jasmine squealed and cried, "Maybe they were the ones who leaked that torture booklet! What was it called? The Camp Delta procedure book?"

"Jasmine!" Tarte exclaimed incredulously, "How in the hell do you know all this? Weren't we rather busy in 2003 fighting terrorists, defending American soil, and cramming the Patriot Act down everyone's throat? How did you have time for Gitmo gossip? Or did you fail to mention an eidetic memory on your application?"

"Roger," Jasmine said defensively, "I do have a life outside of this office. Just because I work for the United States government doesn't mean I have complete trust in it. Our government and military have a long history of doing very bad things – the majority of which is still buried deep in classified files. The American people are still mostly in the dark. We torture people, or experiment on them – like in the CIA's MK-Ultra program. We mistakenly bomb embassies, give the Bin Laden family a get-out-of-America-free card nine days after the 9/11 attacks, listen to Americans' phone calls, and Carnivore still reads our emails – though it isn't called Carnivore anymore. You know there are video and audio surveillance devices at every public…"

"Jasmine," Tarte said, cutting her off, "we don't have time to get into all of this right now. You've obviously been reading on the side, though I'm still sorry I asked. However," he said with a grin, "I do sometimes wonder if we shouldn't swap jobs."

"I'll take that as a compliment," Jasmine said, her voice calm again.

"Go right ahead."

"But when this is all over, and we find ourselves bored again, we should sneak off to a quiet little bar with dark corners and compare notes."

"It's a date," Tarte said, immediately regretting his choice of words.

"A wife's ears burn when that word is used in such a context," Jasmine warned.

"Shit!" Tarte exclaimed, "I forgot to call Jessica before I left."

"I figured you would," Jasmine said, a hint of accusation and satisfaction in her voice. "So I called her for you and said you were heading back."

Tarte wanted to breathe a sigh of relief, but first asked, "How did she take it?"

"You mean the fact that I called and you didn't?" Jasmine asked playfully.

"Yeah," Tarte admitted, "Are my balls heading for the testy guillotine?"

"Hard to predict the fate of your balls without more detailed data – which I have no interest in obtaining. However, I confided in her that what you are working on is pretty high-level. I believe I threw in just enough 'classifieds' and 'national securities' to do the trick. So I think you're golden – for the moment. I also assured her you are safe and sound." Jasmine's voice tightened and she added, "Though that was almost an outright lie since you wouldn't tell me what the hell you were doing!"

"Jasmine," Tarte said firmly, "Look, I appreciate your calling Jessica for me, but let's not forget who the agent is and who the assistant is.

Right now is not the time to go into this. Next time you can storm the castle with guns blazing and I'll stay back in the office. Okay? But for now can we get back to White and Floyd?"

"All right, all right. To be continued, though," Jasmine promised.

"No doubt about that," Tarte thought wearily.

"In answer to your original question, yes, I was also thinking White might have been involved in surveillance at Gitmo. It would explain his being stationed in San Juan and the inconsistencies in the dates. As for the Camp Delta book, who knows. But if the FBI did obtain the original copy, I wouldn't put it past them to leak it. Not only would it put more heat on the Bush administration, which might've won some favor points with the CIA at the time, but it might also keep curious eyes off other, more illicit FBI operations."

Tarte arranged the dates and timelines in his head. Seeing a few gaps, he asked, "When did White join DHS?"

"Sometime in '07," Jasmine answered immediately. "And to answer your next question, yes, we knew he came from the FBI, though I couldn't learn much about exactly why he left. The only thing I found in his file by way of an explanation was 'geographic preference.'"

"Did White and Floyd work together after San Juan?"

"White worked in the same building. Otherwise, there is nothing tying them together."

"Is there any information about their initial meeting in Nassau?"

"Not much. At the time, White was working as a manager at a place called Graycliff. When I mentioned the name to my FBI contact, she suddenly went all quiet on me. I pressed, but all she would say was 'Graycliff is where it all started.' After that she was tight as a drum and adamantly dismissed the comment as 'unimportant.'"

"Interesting," Tarte said. He paced to and fro in the tight confines of the plane's cabin. There was a connection here – he knew there was – he just couldn't see it.

"Okay. See what you can find out about this Graycliff place. Keep your eyes peeled for any info on White while he lived in Nassau. Addresses, dates, phone records, family history, the works."

"Will do," Jasmine said.

"Have Ailes and Murdoch given statements yet?" Tarte said changing the subject.

"I'm not sure. The FBI showed up without warning and pulled rank. So they have them."

"I expected that," Tarte admitted. "Something tells me Floyd will be calling soon. I'll ask him for an update."

"Banes isn't too pleased about it," Jasmine commented.

Tarte laughed, "I'll bet he isn't. But there isn't much he can do. Ailes and Murdoch are high profile witnesses to a potential domestic terrorist threat. DHS could make a case to handle the investigation, but the FBI got there first."

"But you're the one who negotiated their release," Jasmine pointed out.

"Fortunately, that isn't common knowledge. So let's keep that between us for now."

"Banes will explode if he finds out," Jessica warned. "He'll be pissed that you weren't there to make the collar and flash badge and pearlies for the cameras."

"*When* he finds out," Tarte corrected, "It's only a matter of time. I'll counter his rage by reminding him that I had to get them out as soon as I could. Were I to delay so that I or other DHS agents could be on-site to grab them just for the publicity – and that fact was discovered later – both our asses would be on the chopping block. Such information would also give the bad guys a slight up on the agency. I'm not about to do that for fifteen minutes of fame."

"A battle for another day?" Jessica asked.

"You've got it, sister."

"Ew! Don't call me sister. Goons me out."

"Duly noted," Tarte said with a grin.

The captain's disembodied, monotone voice came over the plane's intercom and announced they would be landing in D.C. in twenty minutes.

"We'll be landing soon, Jasmine."

"Are you coming here or heading home?"

Tarte looked at his watch. It would be after five o'clock when they landed. His agent brain said to go to the office and keep to the chase, but the heavy, shiny tungsten band on his finger relayed a more urgent message – one of immediate self-preservation. At that moment his stomach put in its two cents as well.

"Home, I think. I can work from there. Besides, Jess is waiting and I'm starving. I'll grab something on the way home."

"Probably a wise choice," Jasmine intoned. "Just stay away from bakeries."

Tarte pulled on his jacket and asked absently, "Why do you say that?"

"Didn't you hear?" Jasmine asked. "One of the EPA's brass was shot in a bakery today."

Tarte's mind was still elsewhere but he said, "Wasn't at Vie De France was it? That's the only place near the Capitol to get good strong coffee."

"It wasn't in D.C., Roger. It was in Denver."

"Denver?" Tarte echoed interestedly.

"Yeah, this morning. Some high-up EPA guy visiting the offices in Denver was shot through the window of a local bakery."

"Shot by whom?" Tarte asked.

"Who knows?" Jasmine said dismissively.

"Shot by whom, Jasmine?" Tarte pressed.

"They don't know," Jasmine said, sounding startled. "All they know is that someone shot him through the window. A few seconds later some nutjob claiming to be a cop or something allegedly ran after the shooter. Police showed up and tried to find the shooter and the whacko that went after him, but they came up empty-handed. The authorities are saying it was a random drive-by shooting."

"A drive-by? Are you sure that's the consensus at this point?"

"Pretty sure. Just another random shooting. The ever-colorful term 'gang-bangers' is being thrown around. But since there were no witnesses outside of the coffee shop, no one can be sure. Why do you ask?" Jasmine asked.

"Hold on a second," Tarte said as he started pacing again. He thought about his last conversation with Gray and asked, "Did the mark survive?"

"The *mark*?" Jasmine echoed, sounding surprised.

"The guy who was shot. The EPA brass."

"Oh. Yes. He's at a local hospital. Umm," again Tarte could hear the fast rapping of computer keys. "Gunshot wound to the right shoulder. The local news says he came out of surgery a few hours ago and is in recovery."

"Any mention of his room being guarded?"

"Hang on," Jasmine said. "No. Nothing specific. It just says the police are questioning the man. So far his name has not been released."

"Questioning," Tarte echoed. "I'm betting his room has a 24-hour security detail as well. Good. What about ballistics? Is there anything there about what type of gun was used?"

"Give me a second," Jasmine said, a frantic clickety-click sounding in the background. Tarte absently tapped the cell against his temple and wondered what the man was saying to the police – assuming this wasn't really a random shooting.

"I'm not seeing any details at all about ballistics or the type of gun used. In fact, there don't seem to be a whole lot of details at all. Even the speculations are vague."

"No ballistics. No name. No leads. And most importantly, no nutjob to provide critical information or take credit for trying to be a hero. No. He's long gone."

"What's going on, Roger?" Jasmine asked.

Tarte ignored her question. The connection was there. He knew it. But how did the dots connect?

"Is there any mention of the incident on the EPA's website? Any comments made by the President or VP?" Tarte began pacing again, absently rubbing his chin. He heard the clicking of keys again and the faint sound of Jasmine reading to herself. The sound reminded him of his wife talking in her sleep. Probably best not to mention that observation.

Finally Jasmine said, "Not a word. EPA.gov is clean. And if anyone high up had made a comment about the incident the local news would run with it. Roger?"

Something was tickling the back of Tarte's brain. The answer was close, he was sure of it. But how in the hell did Denver and a random shooting fit in?

"Roger?" Jasmine said more urgently.

He was about to tell her to be patient when suddenly the puzzle pieces fell into place.

"Of course!" Tarte yelled, throwing his hands in the air. "Denver, dammit. He's going to Denver. Jesus Christ! Why didn't I see this before? Informants, snipers, the process of contact and extraction is *usually* simple. Dammit! Dammit! Dammit!"

"Roger, you're ranting and scaring me. What is going on?"

"No one does a drive-by in broad daylight and shoots through a bakery window. New York maybe, but not Denver. He was giving them information. *Extraction*," Tarte smacked his forehead. "Someone found out and sent in a pro. But the pro missed." Tarte stopped in his tracks. He looked at his watch and did a few quick calculations. He was confident there was still time, but he'd have to move quickly. Then something occurred to him and he asked, "Jasmine, how many times was he shot?"

"Just once," Jasmine replied, adding, "but the police did say a second shot may have been fired."

Tarte closed his eyes and let the scene unfold in his mind. Two shots fired, only one connected. No exterior witnesses. Definitely not a drive-by. It was a pro – it had to be. A hired assassin. "Focus on the scene," he thought. The sniper would've known the hit wasn't fatal. Pride would demand he verify the kill through the scope. Professionals sometimes called it "The Blood Signature." The entry and exit point could be seen immediately – given away by the blood exiting the wound and soaking the mark's clothes. No, the wound hadn't been mortal. So why not finish the job? Witnesses? Vision obscured by cracked glass? Too early to hear sirens.

"No," he thought with a grin. Either he no longer had a clean shot or he took off because the nutjob, as Jasmine had aptly branded him, reacted and was ready to engage. An unaccounted-for variable.

"Was the guy armed?" Tarte asked eagerly.

"The EPA guy?" Jasmine asked.

"No! The guy who took off after the shooter. The nutjob."

"Oh. Umm, I don't know. Let me see."

Tarte paced impatiently. The plane began banking slightly. He glanced out the window and saw they were nearing Dulles. The runway was on the starboard side, which meant the pilot would circle and come in from the northwest.

"Yes!" Jasmine said excitedly. "I don't know how I missed it, but witnesses in the bakery all reported the second man was holding a large handgun just before he bolted from the bakery. Nearly tore the door off when he exited. Police are still claiming he might be law enforcement – retired maybe."

"Of course they are. He probably saved the guy's life by preventing the follow-up shot. They're hoping like hell he was one of them. But they won't find him," Tarte said shaking his head, "They'll never find him. Son of a bitch. Jasmine, does the article say which way the guy headed?"

"Witnesses reported seeing him heading west."

"That isn't enough," Tarte whispered aloud, tapping his chin. Think dummy, think. "Jasmine, I need you to start working Denver PD. Find out what they know. Use my name and credentials if you have to. I need to know where these guys were last seen."

"Can I assume then that you will, in fact, be coming to the office tonight?" Jasmine asked.

"No," Tarte said looking at his watch again, then out the window at the runway, "I'm going to Denver."

"You're joking, right?" Jasmine said in disbelief.

"The epicenter of this case is on his way to Denver," Tarte said, "This might be my only chance to be in the same place at the same time as my quarry."

"You're not even going to go home first?" Tarte remained silent. "Jessica is going to kill you, Roger," Jasmine warned.

"It's the best shot we have, Jasmine. I have to go."

There was a long silence, then Jasmine sighed and said, "What can I do?"

Tarte felt a pang of guilt hit him. He hated asking her to stay late, but he needed her help. No one dug up information and sweet-talked people like Jasmine. Even with his laptop and cell, it would take him a week to accomplish what she could do in a few hours.

"Thanks, Jasmine," Tarte said. "I owe you one."

"You have no idea, buster," Jasmine fired back. He smiled.

"Okay," Tarte spoke quickly. "The first thing to do is to call Floyd. Tell him we need any information they get from Ailes and Murdoch. I want a transcript of the entire debriefing. He'll expect that. Tell him my wife was upset with me for taking off today and that I'm going straight home from the airport. No mention of Denver or this conversation. Business as usual. Tell him I'll check in tomorrow morning."

"Check," Jasmine acknowledged.

"Next I need to know everything Denver PD knows about the shooting. Most importantly, I need to know where the shooter and pursuer headed – best guess. Dig deep and finesse, Jasmine. Ballistics should already be in so be sure and ask for that. Denver PD has no real leads and hasn't caught anyone yet, but chances are they know more than they're telling the media. They know people on the run can still read newspapers and watch television. If there is something important there, I need to know about it."

"Check," Jasmine replied.

"Also, I need everything you can find on this EPA guy, including what he was doing in Denver. Flash the DHS credentials and see what shakes loose. Schedule, emails and cell phone records would be great, but I'm not expecting miracles on that one."

"Good thing," Jasmine murmured. "Anything else?"

"Yes. Get into my rolodex and find the number for Casper Tournie – he's a tech with the U.S. Department of Transportation. Find him and tell him I'm calling in a Bessie."

"Bessie?" Jasmine asked.

Tarte grinned. "He'll understand. More than that, he'll know you're legitimate and that this is serious. Tell him I'm going to need access to traffic cameras around Denver. Tonight. I need a two-mile radius around the coffee shop. And tell him to keep this quiet."

"Got it. I'll also poke around more on this Graycliff thing."

Tarte said, "You're the best, Jasmine," and he meant it.

"I'll be ordering my dinner from the most expensive restaurant I can find that will deliver," Jasmine said simply. "Your treat."

Tarte laughed easily, "Yes, my treat."

The line was silent for a moment, then Jasmine reminded him, "Jess is going to have kittens, Roger."

Tarte considered that, then said, "Kittens I can deal with. It's the conniptions and blind rage that send couples to therapy and counseling."

"Or the hospital," Jasmine offered.

"True story," he admitted.

"You'll be lucky to survive this one," Jasmine quipped.

Tarte's voice grew serious. "You could be more right than you know."

Chapter 22

Bolling Air Force Base, Washington, D.C.

"Un-fucking-believable!" Gray said, his voice incredulous. Despite being awestruck himself, Talon looked at his friend and smiled broadly. It was a rare thing to see Gray in a state of stunned amazement, not to mention being present when he let the F-bomb fly. There was something in the man's expression that made him look twenty years younger. At that moment, Talon could once again see the Promised Land – the ideal future they were working towards. A time and place where amazement and fascination would once again be commonplace among all people. Where wonder would trump greed. Where curiosity and hunger for knowledge would be passionately cultivated, like the world's finest wines. A place where the desire to understand and comprehend the world and the universe would overrule the now commonplace and petty desires for wealth, prestige, and power. A world packed full of children aspiring to become teachers, scientists, researchers, engineers, doctors, and astronauts. Where greedy lawyers, cheap politicians, televangelists, and all the other parasites that preyed on humanity would go the way of the Dodo and the Bulldog Rat. Talon smiled at the thought.

Gray turned and looked at him, his face still bearing a guilty child's grin. "Sorry," he said sheepishly. "Not like me to swear without thought."

"It's not like you to swear *with* thought," Talon replied.

Gray returned his gaze to the two flat-gray airplanes sitting on the tarmac.

"'Something a little faster,'" Talon said, repeating the general's words. "Accurate, though a tad understated." He smiled and shook his head.

Taking a step towards the two planes, Gray asked, "A little faster than what – sound?"

"Quite a bit, actually," Talon said. "Sound travels at around 760 miles per hour, which is Mach 1. These metal beasts can travel up to Mach 2, which is about 1,500 miles per hour. These numbers are valid at sea level. As you gain altitude, the speed of sound goes down." Talon looked at Gray and added, "But don't worry, we won't be hitting max velocity. They'll probably keep us closer to a thousand."

"'Something a little faster' is right," Gray commented. "How in the hell did he get this cleared?"

"My understanding is he called in one of those 'I saved your life in the war' favors. You know, the kind of favor you only call in once."

Gray looked at him, his expression somber, and nodded. They both understood what General Payte had sacrificed to make their travel arrangements. The general had very few friends in Washington these days, partially due to differences in opinions regarding the treatment of military personnel and their families – namely those who died performing top-secret missions and covert operations. The general had fought hard for proper recognition of their services and benefits to their families – both of which were usually non-existent.

While this particular issue had dented the general's reputation, his outspoken opposition to the war in Iraq after the attacks of 9/11 had all but sealed his fate. Like so many others, he'd immediately been labeled as anti-American, unpatriotic, and leftist. The government and military, under intense pressure, had wasted no time throwing the general to the hungry media wolves. In the beginning the general had fought back with sound logic and reason, but the WMD pill, along with the supercilious and baseless link between Saddam Hussein and Al Qaeda, had already been swallowed by the American people.

General Payte had been prepared to launch a full scale, retaliatory attack on the U.S. government and military, including full disclosure of all the classified information stored in his head. He knew such rash action could be a death sentence, but at the time it was the only option for fighting back against the unprovoked and preemptive attack on Iraq. It was around this time that General Payte and Gray first met. Two days later, General Payte filed for an extended leave of absence from the military and disappeared from the D.C. scene, along with a cadre of skilled and loyal soldiers. To this day, Talon still didn't know how Payte had managed to convince all of his men to leave the military and work in conjunction with *The Aenamaia*. Not for the first time, he made a mental note to ask the general to furnish these details after the first round at Graycliff.

Talon's thoughts were interrupted by a young lieutenant who appeared out of nowhere and was now speaking to Gray.

"Your flights will be departing in ten minutes, sir," the young man said, his voice crisp and professional. "If you'll follow me, I'll help you get into your flight suits."

"Lieutenant Ramer, how long will we be airborne?" Gray said gesturing towards the two fighter jets.

"Both F-22 Raptors are fully fueled and cleared for high altitude flight up to Mach 1.5. The trip should take a little under two hours." The Lieutenant, seeing the look of amazement on Gray's face added, "It'll be over before you know it, sir." Lieutenant Ramer grinned, pivoted and began walking back towards the hangar. Talon and Gray turned and followed him.

"Jesus Christ," Gray said shaking his head. "That's over a thousand miles per hour."

"Nothing wrong with your math skills," Talon mused.

In a few moments they were standing next to the hangar's main door. Lieutenant Ramer gestured for them to wait and disappeared inside. Talon saw concern and anxious concentration on Gray's face. He put a hand on his friend's shoulder and said, "They were headed to Nellis anyway. They would've had to stop somewhere to refuel. We're just tagging along. Payte will cover his tracks – and ours. In fact," Talon looked to where the Lieutenant was removing two flight suits from a long black locker, "I'm guessing they think we're government spooks. Best not to ruin the image."

Gray looked at him for a few moments, then nodded.

Talon added, "It's worth it, Gray. We need to get there quickly. Commercial flights mean airports, security, video and audio surveillance devices, electronic ticket purchases, and at least a four-hour flight. The shooter is going to be conscious soon. Neil and his guys will treat his wounds, but the sooner we get there, the less time he has to figure out what's going on and whether or not he's going to talk. Besides," he said with a smile and a nod toward the planes, "this is a once-in-a-lifetime opportunity to fly to Denver with your hair on fire."

Concern melted off Gray's face, replaced by a guilty and exuberant smile.

"For the greater good?" Gray offered.

Talon nodded. "For the greater good."

Gray turned and reappraised the two F-22s sitting on the tarmac. Remarkable. In a quiet voice he said, "Can you imagine the ingenuity it took to design and build those? Hundreds of people building on the hard-earned lessons of the thousands who went before. It's been over a hundred years since Kitty Hawk. How many people have had a vital part to play in developing jet planes that can travel at twice the speed of sound? Absolutely remarkable."

"Here's one for you to gnaw on while you're awaiting your beverage service: Would we even have such planes and engineering capabilities without conflict and war?"

Talon could see his friend's gears turning hard and fast. It was a far-reaching question, and one he'd been grappling with for many years. Can a peaceful world be as technologically advanced as one fraught with violent wars? Would it really matter if the answer was "No"? It was impossible to deny the advances bred from the necessity to fight wars, but would a peaceful society have done as well? Or perhaps done better? Are the frail human mind and unstable ego even capable of maintaining a peaceful society? At times the well of questions seemed both dark and bottomless.

Gray's eyes were still fixed on the two jet planes, sitting patiently like two well-behaved twins awaiting permission to go play. After a few moments Gray said, "A peaceful world would require humans to cooperate on multiple levels. Food production, health care and medicine, infrastructure, transportation, environmental balance, energy consumption, and a level of efficiency and frugality we've never seen. And that would require the deepest commitment to the whole and the equal equity of all. Such function would necessitate a profound interpersonal concern for every human being. Even if you put aside caring, love, and respect for human life, for the machine to work well, each part must be healthy, smart and working at optimum productivity."

Gray paused and squinted, then said, "We probably wouldn't have jet planes suitable for launching missiles and dropping bombs, but it's very possible we could have something much better. An aircraft that was faster, safer, carried more people, and burned cleaner fuel. Most likely it wouldn't have the maneuvering capabilities these jets have, as such functionality would be superfluous."

"What fun would that be?" Talon joked. He knew the comment would spur Gray's already tense sense of anticipation. No doubt images of high-speed corkscrews and hard-banking turns were flashing through Gray's mind, but he only said, "This would be a good topic for Toman. We'll get him poolside at Graycliff and see what he thinks. He loves discussing theoretical history."

Poolside, indeed. Just then another image of Catherine came unbidden into his mind. Though the timing was decidedly inconvenient, he welcomed the chance to see her again. With his eyes still open, he focused on the image in his mind. Catherine was lying on an emerald green towel next to a beautiful cerulean pool, dressed in a simple black bikini that accentuated her natural curves. A pair of black sunglasses rested on her head, keeping the hair out of her eyes. She was propped up on one elbow and speaking animatedly to someone. Talon knew that pool.

It was the long, rectangular garden pool at Graycliff, surrounded by a lush, verdant landscape of tall trees, colorful flowers, sculpted bushes, and old vines. He'd know the sight anywhere – and from any angle. What he didn't know was whether or not Catherine had ever been a guest there. Doubtful the airlines would ever foot the bill for such accommodations. There were plenty of cheaper, more modern furnishings closer to the airport and the port. Regardless, Talon had no doubt Catherine's curiosity and bold personality would take her wherever she chose to go, and for whatever reason. So perhaps it was possible, even likely, that she'd once been a guest there. Though he wasn't sure why, Talon felt comforted by this idea. The idea that Catherine might have been a guest at Graycliff in the past somehow made it easier to believe she would be there again in the future.

Lurking behind the tantalizing image was a maelstrom of powerful, swirling emotions. The sense of loss and uncertainty still packed the hardest punch. But gunning for the gold medal was the feeling, the surety that she looked completely natural lying by the pool at Graycliff. She looked like she belonged there. Like she would *be* there. The thought of her being there – the mere possibility that she could *belong* there with him...with them, was overpowering. Suddenly, without warning, Talon could see Catherine everywhere. A rapid-fire onslaught of images filled his mind, each one with Catherine at the vanguard. At Graycliff. Standing next to his cabin listening to the river, her face awash in peaceful serenity. Standing at the base of the Ober Gabelhorn, hands on hips, legs spread, looking up defiantly at the giant mountain. Sitting in a meditative posture next to the silver sand at Ginkaku-ji temple in Kyoto, her eyes closed, her slender body perfectly still, her long reddish-brown hair pulled back into a smart ponytail.

Everywhere he looked, he saw her. She was a natural addition to every setting – every landscape – every moment he could imagine. And while the terrible longing to see Catherine never lost its potency, the vibrant images of her in each of his sacred places helped strengthen his resolve. It helped that he did not believe in predetermination. The future was not written. If he could just hold on to that conviction, hold on as tight as he had when hanging over the ledge of the Ober Gabelhorn, then anything was possible.

"Remarkable," he thought, "that such overwhelming power and force could be generated so quickly between two people." No emotion so foreign had ever found its way into his consciousness. It was like a powerful narcotic navigating through virgin blood, saturating everything in its path. Perhaps that explained his ineptness against the merciless elixir that continually tried to overrule his rationality – to steer him away from his chosen course. "Maybe," he thought with a subtle grin, "I'm just reaching for an answer when I've yet to formulate the question."

Motion near the plane brought Talon out of his reverie. He tucked the precious images and thoughts of Catherine into the back of his mind – silently hoping each would someday yield a delicious déjà vu. With a firm nod, he slammed the mental file cabinet shut and focused his attention on the task at hand.

Gray cocked his head slightly. Something had arrested his attention, as well. Talon followed his gaze and saw that both pilots had just climbed into the aircraft. Talon could see the spark of expectation in Gray's face. He felt it too. A tightening of the stomach muscles, short breaths, rapid pulse, and a rapt stillness throughout the body.

Members of the ground crew stood on stepladders next to each plane, holding clipboards. They appeared to be speaking and gesturing to the pilots.

"They're doing system checks." Lieutenant Ramer's voice startled both men. They turned and Ramer added, "They'll be ready to leave in ten minutes. So will you. This way, gentlemen."

Both men took a deep, thoughtful breath, gave one last expectant look at the fighter jets, then turned and followed Lieutenant Ramer into the hangar.

Washington, D.C.

Altra raised her arms above her head, locked her fingers, and emptied her lungs of air. Slowly she leaned back in the desk chair, grinning as she heard and felt the subtle, muted pops sounding off along her spine. It felt good to stretch – the taut muscles and tendons, the protest of empty lungs, the mild pressure at the base of her neck, the dormant strength of her shoulders. Acute awareness of one's body was healthy, but it required focus and concentration. She returned to a sitting posture and took a deep, deliberate breath, held it for a moment, then exhaled evenly. Closing her eyes, she reached to her right, grabbed the back of the chair with both hands and pulled. Another two pops sounded from her lower back. Turning to the left, she repeated the exercise. Facing forward, she kept her eyes closed and basked in the internal warmth the stretching had generated. "It really is amazing," she thought, "how such simple exercises can feel so good." Stretching, controlled breathing and awareness of the muscles, tendons, blood flow and temperature. This easy combination could provide so much benefit to the mind and body.

And it was built-in – no drugs or alcohol were necessary. Millions of years of evolution had endowed us with a vast internal arsenal of healing powers. It was a shame so many people chose to supplant true healing and peace with stress, pain, and longing. The world could be such a magnificent and wondrous place if all of its human occupants were more in touch with themselves. And each other.

A faint electronic beep roused her from her short meditation. Though her eyes were still closed, she knew a new email awaited her attention. Thoughts jostled and pressed at the boundary of her consciousness, each one trying to pierce her meditative bubble. She knew they were there, lurking at the fringes. They were like arrogant and petulant demonstrators demanding her attention, but she wanted to hang on to this moment of solitude – if only for a few more seconds. What good is peace and tranquility if it is only an occasional whisper? Calm the soul and sooth the mind.

From the darkness, colors began to emerge, outlining vague shapes. Next came slight shadows and depth. Within half a breath she was focusing on the memory of lush green misty mountains, a deep azure sky, and a soaring waterfall cascading down a picturesque cliff. As she savored the luxuriant landscape, a familiar voice from her past slipped into her consciousness and said, "I could spend an eternity in a single moment of peace, were it not for my addiction to the thrill of reality." Altra felt her lips melt into a warm smile. It was Kenzo's voice. He used to say that just before heading off on one of his crazy adventures. "Kenzo," she thought, silently mouthing the name. The feeling of the name as the small muscles in her lips formed each syllable felt both familiar and strange, like a long lost memory unexpectedly rediscovered.

Altra closed her eyes and conjured an image of Kenzo in her mind. He had been kind and gentle, but also energetic – even buoyant. She still remembered those warm brown eyes and his quirky smile. While most people would probably say he was Asian, a more astute observer would notice other influences at work. In fact, Kenzo's mother was of Japanese descent, while his father's family had strong roots in France and Germany. Smooth almond skin, flat face, and jet-black hair spoke to his Japanese roots, while round eyes and a six-foot frame had their origins in Europe. Thinking back now, she realized that Kenzo's unique heritage was not only responsible for his handsome good looks, but probably also contributed to his insatiable need for exploration and adventure. East meets West and creates something new, interesting and wonderful.

She still remembered the last time she saw his face – so flush with energy, vibrancy and eagerness. It had been early in the morning. The sun had barely risen above the jagged ridge and the light streaming in through the window bathed their modest bedroom in a pinkish-orange radiance. The home, known locally in Sumatra as a *rumah gadang*, had been unusually quiet that morning. It was as if the birds and beasts understood that inside this humble abode a solemn occasion dawned with the sun, and that their usual morning discord would somehow be inconsiderate. When Altra awoke, Kenzo was lying on his side wearing an odd, amused grin, accompanied by the slightest hint of tension in his brow. Judging by the light in the room, she'd known he had been awake for some time and had been patiently waiting for her to stir. The anticipation of the start of a journey always awoke Kenzo before dawn. But despite his excitement and eagerness, he always remained lying quietly by her side until she awoke on her own.

Thinking about him now brought a flurry of conflicting emotions. Regret, longing, sadness. He had been so young – so full of life. She'd never know anyone whose face could express such peace and tranquility partnered with such a wild, untamable exuberance. It was as if the very skin of his face exuded a warm, glowing serenity, while behind his dark brown eyes raged an insatiable appetite for experience. His mind craved sensory information from wherever each journey took him. "Flood the senses," he would say, "and when the flow ebbs, all will be lush and green." The verdant Shangri-La. She wondered if he ever found it. Perhaps he did, and decided never to return to his old life. No one knew for sure.

Another faint beep sounded. This time Altra opened her eyes. She waited a few seconds while the memories of Kenzo and her past receded. Once again she made herself the same promise that always followed thoughts of Kenzo, "Someday I will learn what really happened to him. I will find the truth. I have to."

Altra shook the thoughts from her head and focused her attention on the flat screen and her email. She clicked on the first message and read. The first few lines promised a revolutionary solution to the problem of aging skin along with an image of a woman wearing a towel around her head and light green paste on her cheeks. Altra stared at the email for a moment, then activated a decryption program. A few seconds passed before a thick red line appeared at the top of the email. The line began to drop. Each time it passed over a line of text the words would disappear, only to be replaced a second later by a new line of text. It took the red line about thirty seconds to decrypt the entire email.

Once done, Altra read the decoded note. It was from General Payte. The wreckage in Iraq had been quickly and quietly cleaned up and hauled away. Any unrecovered debris would soon be consumed by a dust storm that was currently pushing through the area. Payte's men had already seeded the internet and local government agencies with a story about a stray commuter plane whose navigation equipment had failed, causing them to drift into restricted airspace. The pilot maneuvered below radar, managed to call for help, and quickly got the plane back on track. The plane landed safely at a regional airstrip a few hundred miles south of Baghdad. Rumors of an explosion were erroneous. From all accounts, the story had been accepted and was quickly replaced with a story of a missing boy in Texas presumed to be floating above the state in an experimental weather balloon. For once Altra was glad for the fickle nature of the media's attention span.

After reversing the encryption, Altra filed the email, then opened the second message. This one was not encrypted and had been sent by an unregistered cell phone. She recognized the identifier. It was Talon. The message read:

> *Ready for takeoff. Fast private jet. Arriving 5280 1.5 hours. J. Bond is awake and pissed, but recovering. Dad is nervous but excited. Will call when we're down. T.*

Altra reread the message. "An hour and a half to Denver?" she muttered. "Gray nervous about flying?" It didn't take long for the answer to occur to her. "Ohhh!" she exclaimed, surprise and comprehension lacing her voice. "Fast private jet is right," she thought. "No wonder Gray is so nervous." She imagined even the cool and calm Talon was probably a little anxious himself, but must also be enjoying the sight of sweat on Gray's brow. "Two more men who love adventure," she said shaking her head. Kenzo's face flashed in her mind and her heart skipped a beat. She frowned, then quickly pushed the image aside.

"No," she muttered quietly, "No. This is different. General Payte has made the arrangements. They're with professionals. They'll be okay. Mr. Bond, on the other hand," she said with a wry grin, "now that guy should be nervous."

Denver, Colorado

Gray looked solemnly out of the passenger window as the landscape crept past. Wheat-colored fields, industrial complexes, bridges, railroad tracks, housing developments, all seemed to be moving by in slow motion, though he knew Talon's lead foot would have them doing almost eighty. But after watching half of the country streak by at over a thousand miles an hour, everything else seemed to be moving at a glacier's pace. The two fighter jets had, for most of the trip, kept to a high altitude in order to minimize the sound of their passing at ground level. Most of what Gray had seen whizzing by through his tinted helmet visor had been clouds. But every now and again the low layer of cumulus clouds would fade away, revealing a geometric patchwork passing by at high speed. At one such point during the flight Talon's staticky voice came through his helmet speaker and said, "Looks like a giant knitted a massive green and brown quilt for a geometry class project and just left it lying around. Lots of squares, circles, and grid lines."

Just then they flew over several large lakes and Gray returned, "So do those puddles indicate that the giant lacks indoor plumbing or just that he has a problem with incontinence?"

Gray heard both of the pilots laugh before Talon said, "You need professional help, you know that?"

"No doubt about it," Gray had said still staring at the passing landscape. "It's extraordinary," he'd thought. That moment, and everything about it, was absolutely remarkable.

"Certainly does help to put things into perspective, doesn't it," Talon's rusty voice remarked.

Gray nodded, but said nothing. More than once during the flight he'd found himself in awe, not only of the surreal world rushing beneath the jet, but of the preternatural byways and unexpected destinations of life. How had he gotten there? How was it he had come to be sitting in the cockpit of the most advanced military jet ever built?

Despite the incredible sights all around him, he'd found his mind wandering – contemplating each of the many critical junctions that had served to guide and define his actions for the last decade. Countless cities, plane flights, cautious and calculated conversations with potential new members in dark corners, vigilant preservation of his anonymity, multiple identities, all-night planning sessions, exhaustive target research, technology scrubbing with Osiro, training, surveillance, and so on. All leading up to the first major milestone: the night that "Aenamus" graduated from a made-up word to a plan of action. A mandate. Action coalescing out of a gut instinct – a sense of right and wrong. From intention to action – from the preface to the opening chapter. And for Tom Delay – from acquisition to execution. Delay's demise represented the point of no return – both for *The Aenamaia* and for Gray. And now look where he was.

Over ten years had passed since he'd embarked on this journey. The last day of his former life had been the first day of his new one. On an overcast day in Florida, he'd been like a soldier sailing towards a war, but still looking back towards the shore of his home and watching everything on land burn to the ground. The anger and rage of the old, coupled with the pain and burden of the new, had nearly torn him apart that day. After the explosion and ensuing chaos, he'd gone through the motions with a detached numbness, as if he were merely a spectator watching someone else's life turn to ashes. Identification and cremation. A thin wisp of white smoke was rising from the chimney when he'd walked out of the crematorium. Two hours later he found himself on the deck of a freighter bound for Marseilles. Staring blankly at the receding coastline, Gray felt an electric pain surge through his body as the thick shell of numbness suddenly fractured, broke and fell, all in the blink of an eye. He still remembered how his mind and body had reacted.

It had been a kind of shell shock crammed into several moments. There was an instant and paralyzing throb pounding inside his skull. For several agonizing moments his autonomic nervous system shut down and he could barely breathe. Clumsily, he thrust his stiff arms outward and latched onto the railing of the boat, his legs following awkwardly. Wide-eyed and filling with panic, Gray clenched his jaws and forced his mind to concentrate until finally enough adrenaline surged through his blood to force his lungs to contract. Gasping and coughing, he had inhaled the bitter, salty air and in the next moment vomited every ounce of material left in his stomach. After a few involuntary dry heaves and one deep breath, he fell hard onto his knees and cried.

That had been the beginning, not of a new chapter in the life he'd always known, but of a brand new book whose main character was now a shadow of the man he'd once been. A shadow with a purpose. And now, ten years and many adventures later, he and Talon were rocketing through the sky in two state-of-the-art military fighter jets heading to Denver to interrogate a professional sniper who had tried to murder a high-ranking official of the Environmental Protection Agency. "Both preternatural *and* surreal," he thought.

Sitting behind the pilot in the cockpit of the fighter plane, more thoughts of his former life and its fiery ending vied for his attention, but rather than get lost in the pain of the past, Gray shut them out and focused on the present. He'd asked the pilot, "Lieutenant Cohen, what kind of price tag does one of these Raptors carry?"

"Around a hundred and thirty-eight million, sir," Lt. Cohen answered. "But I hear if you buy more than six at a time you get a discount."

"Assuming there isn't a better price on eBay."

Lt. Cohen chuckled. "Yes, sir."

"Have you flown in combat Lieutenant?"

"Yes, sir. The first Gulf War, Somalia, a short stint in the Sea of Japan, a ready-alert off the coast of North Korea after one of their underground nuclear detonations, and precision night raids in Iraq and Afghanistan. Six months ago I asked to be reassigned to the States. I missed cheeseburgers, blond hair, and sarcasm."

Gray laughed, then said, "I think I understand what you mean."

"Besides, it feels more like I'm really protecting American soil when I'm able to actually stand on it once in a while."

"Lieutenant," Gray said, his voice solemn, "It's good to know men like you are up here protecting what you love."

"'The last man in the world you want to fight is one defending that which he holds in higher esteem than his own life,'" Lt. Cohen quoted.

"Who said that?" Gray asked.

"My father, sir. He's a retired military historian."

"And do you believe that Lieutenant? That there are things worth defending that are greater than ourselves?"

"Yes, sir. That's why I'm up here."

"Me too, Lieutenant," Gray said pensively. "Me too."

Blue sky and pristine white clouds above and lush green earth all around. For Gray, nature had a way of luring his mind into philosophical and metaphysical contemplation. He never sought the meaning of life, for he believed such a question was inadequate and imprecise. Instead he chose to focus on what the purpose of *his* life was. This question applied to two distinct temporal answers: life right now and life after *The Aenamaia's* activities ceased. The former was obvious, while the latter hid behind a large question mark.

When he felt doubt or fear creeping up on him, he would picture the members of *The Aenamaia* sitting around the pool at Graycliff talking, drinking and relaxing. He knew that once discussion of their accomplishments subsided, the focus would immediately shift to what came next.

Some would return to their normal lives, while others would carve out new ones. But Gray felt a certain comfort in not having a plan beyond Graycliff. He'd spent the last decade of his life researching, strategizing and planning. Should he live through this ordeal and find himself pool-side at Graycliff answering that very question, he'd be content to say he had no plan whatsoever. The prospect of that freedom, that whimsical outlook, was more enticing than anything else his mind could conjure.

"We'll be there in about ten minutes," Talon said.

Gray stirred from his reverie. Talon noticed his confusion and flashed a devious grin. "Head still in the clouds?" Talon asked.

Gray snickered. "Yeah, you could say that." He looked out the window and saw the white and brown of the Rocky Mountains rising in the distance.

Back on terra firma, the two men started their drive into Denver. The two fighter jets had landed at Buckley Air Force Base, which one of the pilot's had informed them was about twenty minutes outside of downtown Denver. The planes had pulled to a stop in front of a large hangar similar to the one they'd departed from less than two hours prior. Parked next to the hangar was a late model sedan – compliments of General Payte. After returning the flight suits and thanking their respective pilots, Gray and Talon loaded their bags in the car and got in. Talon started the car and headed north towards the base's main entrance. Five minutes later they exited the base and headed west.

A few minutes passed before Talon broke the silence.

"You look all pensive," he observed. "What are you thinking about?"

Gray took a breath, sighed, then said, "During the flight I gave a lot of thought to how I got here – or more specifically *there*. I tried to visualize and understand all of the twists and turns of the trail that left an old man like me sitting in the seat of an advanced military jet. I kept thinking, 'How in the hell did I get here?' It's something I haven't had much time to contemplate of late."

Talon nodded. He was tempted to dive deep into Gray's ruminations, but he knew there wasn't enough time to give the topic an adequate examination. Instead he suggested, "There will be time for all of that later. Maybe we'll sketch a few flow charts and timeliness in the cigar room at Graycliff."

Gray smiled, but remained silent.

"In the mean time, we have to figure out who this guy is and whether or not we've been compromised."

"That's a possibility," Gray admitted reluctantly. "Or it could be a horrendous coincidence."

"I once bet on a horse named Coincidence. Know what I learned?"

"Coincidence isn't a safe bet?" Gray guessed.

"Actually, I won three thousand dollars on that horse. What I learned was, it's okay to bet on coincidence as long as it isn't yours or someone else's life you're wagering."

"Point taken," Gray said.

Talon saw his exit a quarter of a mile ahead and signaled. The car sped down the off ramp and merged onto the frontage road. Easing off the gas, Talon slowed to the posted speed limit and watched for his next turn.

"But if we rule out coincidence we have to assume we've been compromised and targeted. Which means we should be ready to pull the plug quickly," Talon said. "Call abort on every project and tell everyone to stand clear for a week or so. Perhaps we should call Altra and have her make sure everyone is prepared to walk away. Just in case."

Talon looked at his friend, who appeared to be deep in thought. Returning his attention to the road, he saw that his turn was half a block ahead. They rounded the corner and Talon checked his rearview mirror, but no other cars made the turn.

"Gray?"

Gray's brow was furrowed, his eyes narrow. Pursing his lips, he spoke slowly, deliberately. "There's another possibility I believe we have to consider. If not coincidence, what about providence? Fate? Happenstance? What if we've just stumbled onto one variable in a much bigger, more complicated formula? One that, at the moment, has nothing to do with us."

"I'm sorry, Gray, but I don't follow."

"A chain is only as strong as its weakest link," Gray said absently.

The car pulled onto a gravel drive and came to a halt in front of a nondescript one-story brick building.

"What chain would that be?" Talon asked.

"That's what we're here to find out," Gray said, his face a mask of stern concentration.

Talon pulled the keys from the ignition, stepped out of the car and closed his door. He took a few steps towards the building, then stopped and turned towards Gray who stood perfectly still next to the car. There was a curious expression on his face, like he'd heard or smelled something out of place. Talon focused on his senses. A hint of exhaust, the pungent odor of wet dirt and sand, and the faint smell of chimney smoke floated in the cool air. Listening attentively, he could only pick up the distant sound of light traffic, the low whistle of winds picking their way through the alleys, and a commercial airliner flying high overhead.

"What is it?" Talon said quietly.

Gray's head was still slightly tilted upwards and his eyes darted back and forth.

"I'm not sure," Gray said in a low whisper, as much to himself as to Talon.

"Too quiet?" Talon suggested.

Gray's mouth opened, but he said nothing. A minute passed before he seemed to dismiss his doubts with a shake of his head. "It's nothing," he said. "Imagine doom around every corner and in every direction and you'll wind up dying where you stand. Not from fear but starvation."

"Another famous quote?" Talon asked.

Gray shook his head, "Not yet. I just made it up." He gave an uneasy smile then nodded towards the brown metal door ahead, "Let's go see what nefarious details your Mr. Bond has been persuaded to divulge."

Washington, D.C.

"Who was the first agent in the FBI to formally remove the 'brief' from 'briefing'?" he wondered. This particular briefing, characteristic of most, was pushing the three-hour mark. "There's nothing brief about it," he thought. It took less time for the terrorists to hijack Flight 11 and fly it into the North Tower. By the time the last ten minutes were up, the first hundred and seventy minutes would be lost to the coffee-saturated and thoroughly unrecoverable depths of a federal employee's disinterested mind. Absently he raised his own coffee cup to his lips, only to set it down with a muffled groan. "Saturated is right," he muttered.

He considered pulling his cell from its holster and pretending someone important was calling so he could justify a hasty retreat from the stuffy room. He was so busy mulling over the pros and cons of this convenient fiction he barely noticed the subtle tremor at his waist. The cell he used for work was in his coat pocket, which meant a message had come in on his private cell. Finally, an excuse to be excused. No one here would know it was his private cell. "Providence," he thought with amusement, "often arrives bearing the ripe fruit of irony." Liberation from this unfortunate tedium was more than welcome. As he pulled the cell phone from its holster and moved to get to his feet, a dark suspicion permeated his momentary relief. The few people who possessed this number used it sparingly, and rarely did anything trivial come through during work hours. Just like a call on the home phone at three o'clock in the morning, it was unlikely this was good news.

The flashing blue LED indicated a text message had come in. As he rose to his feet, thoughts of a phony urgent call disappeared. A few heads turned as he made his way to the side door. Pausing at the door he activated the screen and thumb-typed the six-digit pin. He scrolled to the text icon and opened the inbox. The newest message was at the top. The identifier read 13-911-411. "This can't be good," he thought. He tapped a finger on the message. The screen went blank. A second later a picture of a black bird, wings spread, materialized to the left of the screen accompanied by a second key pad to the right. He entered another six digit pin. Five rows of text appeared on the screen. "Oh shit!" he hissed. A male aide standing near the door had heard him and asked, "Everything okay, Director?"

Still reeling from the message, he managed to mumble something about his rebellious teenage daughter and hastily exited the room. Looking around, he saw that the hallway was empty in both directions. He lifted the phone and reread the text:

Attn Raven. Urgent Message.

Augurs zero and five taken off the grid in 5280. Current location: Unknown. Captor: Unknown. Condition: Unknown. All operations suspended. Op 5280 is a total blackout. Augur 1 at last known coordinates. Request immediate intel.

Please help Raven: Gray and Breckus are gone. Aenamaia is flatlined.

###

End of Book I

Look for the sequel to "Aenamus"
~ coming soon!

Disclaimer

This story is a work of fiction. Names, characters, places and incidents are either the product of the author's imagination or are used fictitiously. Any resemblance to actual persons, living or dead, events or locales is entirely coincidental.

Acknowledgments

I would like to thank my editors Nancy Hutchins and Kristin Maloney, without whom this book could never have been published. I would also like to thank Michelle Baade for her incredible work on the cover photograph – the results of which far exceeded my expectations. Thank you also to Meka Davis for the wonderful post-production graphic work on the cover image.

A special Thank You goes to Kristine Bredehoft – I really appreciate your involvement and patience!

I would also like to thank Kimberly Baltz for all of the great support, ideas and encouragement throughout the writing of this novel.

Thank you to John Latham for your invaluable expertise and instruction on firearms and various aspects of law enforcement and standard police procedures.

About the Author

T.R. Maxus lives in Denver with his wife and 3 cats. When not writing he spends time traveling, playing guitar and piano, enjoying wine, and playing sand volleyball. He is currently finishing the sequel to *Aenamus: Silent Blood.*

"Writing this book provided me with an ideal outlet for venting my frustrations through one of the most satisfying and addictive mediums I've ever known: creative fiction writing. I also wrote it to entertain myself (my wife thinks of it as cheap therapy). If readers get half as much enjoyment out of *Aenamus* as I did in writing it, I'll consider it a glowing success!"

~ T.R.

18591630R00303

Made in the USA
Charleston, SC
11 April 2013